TO CATCH THE SUN

FIONA BULLEN

St. Martin's Press
New York

Library of Congress Cataloging-in-Publication Data

Bullen, Fiona.
    To catch the sun / Fiona Bullen.
        p.   cm.
    ISBN 0-312-04438-0
    I. Title.
PS3552.U427T6   1990
813'.54—dc20   89-77977
                                              CIP

First published under the title *Painted Birds* in Great Britain by Macdonald
& Company Ltd.

First U.S. Edition
10 9 8 7 6 5 4 3 2 1

*To Patrick
with love*

TO CATCH THE SUN

Chapter One

Singapore, 1934

The girl raised dark, expressive eyes to the canopy of green above her, whistling softly at the monkey that hovered just out of her reach. It scolded her sharply, tearing leaves from the branches and showering them over her upturned face. The leaves fluttered down, black green and shiny in the swirls of steam, glinting against the shafts of sun that just entered the rooftop of trees. Ursula whistled again, her body stretching up tall and her hands reaching out to the branch overhead. The monkey leapt a few feet further from her reach and pelted her with more leaves.

With a sigh she turned away. She would have to get Yahyah to catch her a baby monkey. There was no way to tame the wild ones that came through in noisy, destructive bands, stripping the trees and screeching off into the jungle. From the edge of the garden, partially hidden still by the foliage, Ursula watched the comings and goings of the servants. Ah Jong was stooping over the herb garden and the dhoby was hanging out washing. Somewhere, Yahyah would be tending to the horses. She sighed gustily and twitched at her pinafore. It was hot here in the trees and she was bored. It was hard to live this far out; no-one came to visit anymore. She looked across at the bungalow and wondered if Billy had arrived yet. He would entertain her. She smiled at the thought and broke free of the trees. He wouldn't have forgotten. He knew that today her

7

papa had promised her a surprise. It wasn't for her seventh birthday. That had just passed. But Papa had something planned, she was sure of it. She had got up even earlier than usual and checked everywhere she could think, but she hadn't found any presents yet. Billy and Papa were teasing her, she thought. She wanted to see her surprise but she could wait. Instead she would go and find Fatimah and get changed. It was time to go riding with Papa.

Ursula's family, the Frasers, lived outside the city, beyond Bukit Timah. It was up by the MacRitchie Reservoir, in a place called Mount Pleasant, a little pocket of civilization surrounded by jungle. Their bungalow was set on a rise overlooking the black-and-white verandahed club house of the Polo Club. Every morning Ursula and her papa would ride around the padang before breakfast with the mist swirling around their horses' legs. Later it would be too hot and the sun would dry the heavy dew, baking the grass hard brown. But at that hour there was still a hint of freshness, a gentle breeze to fan cheeks warmed by the ride. It was a ritual, an expression of their place in this society, but for Ursula it was also a precious time shared with her father.

Harry Fraser was a huge man with an imposing moustache, faded blue eyes in a regulation brick-red face, and a way of cutting across whatever anyone was saying so that they realized their unimportance instantly. Many people thought him a boor. His servants lived in mingled dread and admiration of him, waiting patiently a few steps behind him for his commands. But to Ursula he was God Himself. No-one was as brave or knowledgeable, no-one as handsome or indestructible; he was the scourge of the other Tuan Bezars and the darling of the hostess trail. He was also a widower for seven years after Ursula was born.

Lillian Fraser died of fever two days after she gave birth to a baby girl. She had always been frail, the climate oppressing her to the point where long hours of each day were spent prostrate on her bed, her amah wiping her temples with gauze dipped in chilled, scented water. She was '*sakit hidup*' according to her servants, ill without apparent cause. They feared evil spirits had entered her but the real cause was not so hard to find: homesickness, a terrible, aching pain for a land where fresh air

8

blew in great gusts and the rain was cool and didn't steam as it touched the ground.

Lillian never liked the East; she never attempted to learn its ways or to master the languages. She simply existed, hating each day as the sun rose punctually at 6.30 am and went down, equally punctually, at 6.30 pm. There were no seasons like at home. No spring, no autumn, and especially no winter. Just Wet and Dry. And even the Dry was never really dry. There was always the humidity. It varied between unbearable and torrential. In the Wet the washing never dried and mould sprouted everywhere, the spores getting into even the carefully packed away lace wedding dress that she had brought out with her as a young bride.

So when her husband told her they were to make their lives out here, and the baby she bore was given immediately into the waiting arms of the amah, she really didn't feel like staying any longer. So she just gave in to the fever and died.

Ursula was brought up by her amah, Fatimah, with as much love and care as any child could know. Discipline, however, was a different matter and, since her father was at his office down in Robinson Road every day and there was no English memsahib to keep her in check, Ursula grew up self-willed. She went where she pleased and did as she wanted. By the age of five she was often to be found playing with Fatimah's son, Yahyah, down behind the paddocks of the Polo Club where the creek ran through on its way from the Chinese cemetery. There was just a small kampong down there for the families of the syces, a jumble of small wooden huts built on stilts to protect them when the creek became swollen during the Wet. It was an enticing place for a small child, full of kittens and mongrel dogs, chicks and roosters, goats, other children, and welcoming mothers who cooked wonderful smelling meals outside their huts. She spoke Malay like a native, often preferring to think in it rather than in English. Only with her father did she speak English, despite his command that she act more like a missy-sahib. To Ursula there was little distinction between the Malays and her. She simply got away with more.

At six her father introduced her to her tutor. His name was Mr Billing and he was Eurasian. His father had been Dutch, his mother Thai. The combination was a striking balance of

9

high cheekbones and delicate features stretched out over a six foot body. He smiled often with perfect white teeth against coffee-coloured skin. Ursula called him Billy and took to him immediately.

He was nearly twenty when he first started tutoring the little girl; a graduate of mission school and the subtle racial discrimination that only the Colonial expatriate knows how to dispense with any real bite. For all that, he was a pleasant young man with an open mind who took an interest in his charge. He did not allow her to get away with a thing.

Life became more ordered for Ursula. At 6.00 am she would be woken by Fatimah raising the chick blinds and opening the shutters. Her room was on the first floor, to the right of the main stairs and off from the sitting room. It was often still dark at that hour and the bullfrogs could be heard beyond the window, vying to outcall each other for their females' attention. Fatimah would pull back the mosquito netting, twirling it up expertly and knotting it above the bed while Ursula climbed out onto cool floorboards. The overhead fan swept around with a regular clunk-whisk noise that was as familiar to Ursula as her own heartbeat.

Then Fatimah would lead her into the bathroom, ignoring the child's shivering as bare feet hit cold tile. Up went her nightgown, over her head, and down came the water from the shower spout, with Fatimah singing one of her songs about little frogs and shining water. The water would run all over the floor and then down into channels edging the room. Once Ursula was as clean as her amah felt was possible, she would be towelled dry and popped into her riding clothes. They were clean every day, the result of hard work since the dhoby was always done by hand. Ursula never noticed that. It didn't occur to her that she would ever put anything on that was not freshly laundered and ironed. It was always so.

Then Ursula would go downstairs to the tack room, next to the kitchen, where one of the boys would lift down her saddle and bridle for her. Her father would generally be ahead of her, stamping to and fro outside the main house, under the entrance porch. The boy would carry her saddle for her and Fatimah's husband, Ibrahim, who was their syce, would carry Ursula's father's saddle. They didn't go down to the stables by the road but took a route that cut down the hillside at the bottom of their garden, through the rough, long grass and red mud, their boots leaving a beaten track behind them.

Ursula had a pony she had ridden since she was three. He was called Bintang, Star, because of the white blaze on his forehead. The rest of him was chestnut. He was a sturdy, gentle animal. Ursula would lean against him, smelling the warmth of his body and the dusty, animal smell of horses and straw and manure. It was so comforting just to know that Bintang would always be there, every morning, and that he would nuzzle against her for the sugar lump he knew she carried in her pocket. He was getting fat and her father had forbidden her to give him any more treats but she knew Bintang wouldn't understand if she suddenly stopped bringing them. So she hid them in her pocket and Fatimah conspired with her to steal them from the cook, Ah Jong.

Once across the drainage channel, Bintang would kick up his heels and try to gallop across the padang but Ursula would keep him on a tight rein, rising on the balls of her feet and sinking her weight down on her heels to hold him back. Her father would laugh to see her manage her pony so easily and then they would walk together a few times around the field. He would talk to her, about home in England, or about her mother. Gradually, to Ursula, Lillian Fraser became a mixture of saint and fairy princess; she became a woman of classical beauty, gentle, accomplished, uncomplaining in the face of hardship, and a pillar of moral integrity. If Ursula found it difficult at times to live up to these ideals, her father would find a way of letting her know how disappointed her mother must be in her, as she looked down on them from Heaven. It was an onorous burden but one which Ursula did try very hard to shoulder. But when she needed comfort and a warm lap to climb into, it was not her mother she thought of, but Fatimah with her round belly and smiling brown eyes.

Somehow Fraser's description of Lillian's cool blonde beauty became all mixed up with Ursula's tales of heroes and princesses. Her mother was a fairy queen up in the sky and though she couldn't visit them, she always kept a careful, loving eye out for their safety. Ursula didn't see Mary when she prayed; she saw her mother. And her mother was watching

11

over her. She didn't need a mother here on earth when she had Fatimah. So that was all right.

Had Fraser had any idea that Ursula was misinterpreting his attempts to create a mother for her that she could be proud of, he would have done his best to set things right before it became impossible for the child to accept a replacement in that role. But he thought in all honesty that what he was doing was best for Ursula. And for him there was no-one more important. He might seem rough to others but to Ursula he was always kind and caring. She was passionate about him in return.

When the horses had warmed up a little they would trot, her father's horse checking its pace to keep the pony beside it. In the morning air, their breath would steam and cloud up in front of them and, from time to time, they would ride through banks of mist so that at one moment they were hidden from each other and then suddenly they were through and the rising sun would sear into their eyes with cold pain, causing them to blink and squint away. Harry Fraser weighed seventeen stone but there was very little fat to him; just a small gut from too much Tiger beer. He would ride erect, not really looking at his daughter as she tried to keep pace, but every now and then a flicker would shoot sideways out of those pale eyes, gauging her position while he moved his knees fractionally and his horse answered his command. It was a skilled performance, effortless, seemingly without thought. Perhaps it was without thought. Because despite Fraser's emphatic opinions he really didn't seem the type who thought much about anything. He was the sort who would look alarmed when the conversation at a party turned to books or 'some high-brow, cultured foolery', and he, and half the other men there, would nod curtly and retire to the terrace to discuss horses, politics, natives, and women – with similar comments made on all of them. Not that he ever had any trouble with women. They were as available for him as the orchids that grew wild on the trees. He just had to walk into a party in his white dinner-jacket and every woman in the place would droop a little more gracefully, laugh a little louder, their voices gilding the night air like spun sugar. He knew it, of course. That was what got some of the men. But they had to admit, as far as they knew, he did not infringe on their territory. There was talk about the native women who worked for him but no-one knew anything for sure. And Fraser liked it that way.

Breakfast followed the ride. They took it outside on the verandah, the sharp angle of the morning sun screened out by the black-and-white painted rattan blinds: papaya and star-fruit, or whatever fruit was in season, lime juice, toast, butter, honey and fragrant, black tea. Their cook was Chinese and one of the old 'black-and-white' school who wed themselves into service rather than to any man. Ah Jong was a wizened old woman who, to Ursula, never seemed to get any older. She wore black baggy trousers and a white tunic top with flat black slippers on her feet. And all day long she would pad silently around the bungalow, keeping her sharp eye on the other servants and anticipating the Tuan's every wish.

Mr Billing never joined them for breakfast but would be waiting upstairs for Ursula when she returned to her room to change out of her riding clothes. A second wash was always necessary at this point but Mr Billing would wait for her out in the wicker furnished sitting room, his smooth face showing no sign of impatience. Mr Billing was a man of infinite good temper. His steadiness and composure was a relief in a household without a memsahib. Just a brief word from him could keep the servants from loud histrionics and he felt it his duty to instil some self-discipline into the child during her formative years. It was for this reason that Harry Fraser had chosen him. Not that Fraser would have phrased it that way himself. No, he would have said Mr Billing 'had light hands' and knew how to 'keep the girl in check'. But it came to the same thing. There was an air of imperturbability about the young Eurasian, a coolness that was not quite a snub but came rather close at times. Ursula never had to be told something twice, heeding his quiet tones immediately where Fatimah's shouts and scolds had previously held no sway.

The morning session started at eight with Ursula sitting up at the bamboo table beside Mr Billing, her chair piled with two extra cushions so that she could see over the edge comfortably. Rattan furniture was both the blessing and the bane of the East; its airy open work allowed a breeze to circulate around the body, but the buttocks tended to resemble corrugated sheet iron after a lifetime of such misuse. As Ursula always needed a

13

cushion to prop her up she had yet to discover this. Her hair was combed wetly back from her small, oval face and she was dressed in a light cotton frock that hung pinafore-like around her body. With the overhead fans sweeping the air around it would be quite cool in the dark verandah-shadowed room until midday. Mr Billing never seemed to feel the heat anyway and for Ursula it was a fact of life never queried or even thought about. Just like the three r's.

Reading and writing were basic to the little girl. She had been climbing onto her father's knee since the age of three to help him read the *Straits Times* and he had been patient and encouraging enough so that now she would not let him read alone but insisted on stuttering and stumbling through the long words with impatient pride. Mr Billing's initial attempts at the alphabet and such topics as Dick and Dora and Spot the dog had been greeted with scorn. They now read long tales about the unlikely habits of the people of countries where snow fell during the Wet and people had trouble getting enough rain during the Dry. Ursula found it absorbing in its sheer improbability and Mr Billing was at pains sometimes to assure the child that it really was so. But secretly Ursula was sure that if Mr Billing told her something it was right, and that was what was worrying her now. The surprise she had waited for so patiently wasn't a surprise she liked. In his quiet, gentle voice, Mr Billing had told her she was to have a new mother.

'I can't have a new mother. People only have one mother. My mother's dead and in Heaven.'

'Your papa means to marry again. His new wife will act as a mother to you. People will call her your step-mother, and she will make life much easier for your Papa and you. The servants will mind her. She will be Memsahib.' Mr Billing knew why Fraser had left it up to him to break the news. But that didn't make it any easier. He saw the child's face absorbing the news in a serious attempt to be adult. She didn't cry though her mouth puckered and twisted a few times. When she had control of herself, she said: 'But she won't tell me what to do, will she, Billy? She can't do that. Only you and Papa can do that.' There was a quiver of fear in the stubborn assertion of what her new mother could and could not do. Mr Billing sighed.

'Well, yes, Ursula. Sometimes we have to accommodate

14

new ideas, changes in our lives. Your step-mother will almost certainly tell you what to do. It will be your duty to your Papa to accept that. She will have to learn to be a memsahib with a ready-made family. That will be very strange and sudden to her. You can help to make it easier by being kind, showing her how things are done at the moment. But if she does not approve of our state of affairs then you must be calm and accept what she says must be changed. I am relying on you to show how I have taught you self-control. Your behaviour will reflect upon my teaching, and upon your Papa. And remember, I will not have you be rude to anyone.'

He noticed how she sat very still, head bowed over her hands as though she were examining them very thoroughly. When his lecture came to an end she still did not look up. He reached over and took one of her hands, the palm sweaty from gripping her lead pencil. He held it gently in his own.

'Is she pretty?'

'I hear she is very beautiful. Your Papa is a proud man to have won such a lovely lady. You should be proud also that you have such a handsome Papa who can sweep a young lady off her feet.' Mr Billing saw he had caught her interest and decided to promote it further. 'Your new mother is from Australia; from a place called Perth down on the coast of Western Australia. It is very different from here. She will not be used to being a memsahib. You must show her how to act.'

'But is she . . . why is she here, then?'

'She is visiting her aunt, Mrs Hendricks. You know Mrs Hendricks and her sons, Rodney and Stephen.' Ursula wrinkled her nose in dismissal.

'They act so big just because they go away to boarding school. They don't talk to me because I'm only a baby but they don't even know half the words I do.' Mr Billing smiled.

'Your new mother's name is Miss Hendricks. She is very anxious to meet you and be your friend.'

'Not my mother? I don't want her to be my mother. My mother's dead and lives in Heaven. I pray to her and she watches over me. I don't need anyone else except Fatimah and Papa. Oh, and you too, Billy.' She squeezed his hand in sad apology for having left him to the end. Mr Billing nodded his understanding.

15

'Your Papa would like you to meet Miss Hendricks this morning. We will go down and have drinks on the verandah and you can get to know each other. Then you will go in for tiffin and afterwards, perhaps, you will all go out for a drive. You will like that, won't you, Ursula?' There was a weary look to the little face as though she had suddenly become aware of many things; her childhood had dropped away from her in just a few moments and she had an expression as though she were indulging him, trying to make things easier for him, rather than the other way around. Mr Billing felt chastened. 'Ursula?'

'Yes, Billy. I understand.' A thought struck her. 'You will be there, won't you. You'll come down with me and stay while we have drinks?' She knew he would not be welcome at tiffin but her eyes begged for that too. For a moment Mr Billing actively disliked the unknown Miss Hendricks.

'Yes, I will come with you. You must not fear this. Your Papa would be upset. He wants you to like each other and he thinks you need female company and advice.'

'But I have Fatimah and the others. They can tell me what I need to know. If Papa is marrying this lady just because he thinks I need . . . '

'No Ursula, he is not. That is just one reason amongst many. And Fatimah is not a mem, she cannot tell you how to behave as you get older . . . '

'You could though. You've always known what's right and Papa lets me know if I don't act right.'

He took both her hands and pulled her round to face him: 'Ursula, look at me. No, look up. Now you must understand. I cannot tell you everything that a missysahib needs to know. Nor can your father. Only a memsahib can do that. But even if that were not so, you have to see that your Papa needs a wife. He likes Miss Hendricks because she is his equal and she is an adult. It is not that he likes her more than you or that he has not many friends amongst the Europeans, but he needs someone to be a companion to him after you have gone to bed in the evening and all the guests have gone home. Your Papa is lonely for this type of friendship. You would not have him continue to be lonely and unhappy just so that you can continue your life without any change. I know you better. You

16

are not so selfish.' There was no sound for a while. Then she sighed deeply, an act of release that was not despair but not, by any means, relief. It was almost a yawn.

'All right, Billy. I'll try.'

'There, that is my good girl. Now go with Fatimah and change into a pretty frock so your Papa will be proud of his beautiful daughter.' Fatimah had appeared silently, as though she had been sitting listening for her name to be called. She held out her hand for the child and smiled.

'Come, Missy. I lay out yellow frock. New one. Missy like new one. Special. Make you look *cantik*, pretty, like little princess.' Ursula rose obediently and followed her amah into her quarters.

When Mr Billing stepped out onto the cool tile of the verandah, Ursula's hand clutched tightly in his, he felt as though he were taking her to be sacrificed to the Gods. It was not such a terrible thing for a man to remarry but surely he ought to tell his own daughter himself, not leave it to the hired help? There was a tightness to Mr Billing's jawline that Fraser recognized instantly. He swallowed hastily, harrumphed a few times and then darted an uneasy look down at his little girl's face. But she was perfectly calm, perfectly poised and quite indifferent. He swallowed again.

'There you are, my pet. My, don't you look a picture. Quite the beauty, aren't you? Come and meet someone very special, darling. I want you to be good friends,' he said, repeating almost word for word what Mr Billing had told her. She smiled tightly, loathing the anxious, bluff tone her father had adopted towards her suddenly. This wasn't how he spoke to her. She almost felt as though he were a stranger for the first time in her life and she was seeing him as a stranger might. Seeing him as less than a God. It was painful.

'Papa? Can Billy stay with us for drinks?' she asked immediately, ignoring her father's outstretched arm that wanted to encircle her, draw her in closer to the red-haired creature sitting beside him. She sensed her power over her father, temporary though it might be, and wielded it with surety. She wanted Billy beside her and she would have him. Her father looked again at the tight jawline, then down at his daughter's poised determination. He glanced across at the woman, his eyes

17

seeking her permission, her approval. Ursula felt sick. Her father never asked anyone about anything. He just knew. The woman smiled, nodding her head and looking up into Mr Billing's smooth face. He didn't smile. She hesitated and looked unsure. But Fraser had swivelled his head around to face his daughter again.

'Of course Mr Billing can stay, sweetheart, if you'd like him to. Now come here.' It was a trade-off and Ursula recognized it as such, giving Mr Billing's hand a squeeze before she released it and moved over to her father's chair.

The yellow frock was crisply starched, falling below her knees in layers of cotton and broderie anglaise from a dropped waist. The bodice was pin-tucked with three buttons covered in the same material down the middle, just below the white peter-pan collar. The sleeves were puffed and gathered into white cuffs with a single button. The frock came from Harrods of London and had only arrived two weeks before. She had worn it for her birthday, revelling in the feel of it, knowing it made her look pretty. But today the collar felt too tight, the armholes were too constrictive. When her father took her into his enfolding arms and pulled her close to him she felt suffocated by his aftershave and wanted to pull at the fabric, rip it away from her neck. She looked bitterly at the woman.

'Ursula, this is Miss Hendricks, a good friend of mine. Sally, this is my little gel.' It was a proud man who made the introductions, proud and unsure, covering it up by jolly smiles that made his moustache rise at both ends and his eyes twinkle. But the twinkle was caused by excess moisture to the eyes. He blinked again, swallowed and put on the 'pukka sahib' act. 'Now I want you two gels to get along. D'you hear me?' They ignored him, intent on looking each other over. He looked to Mr Billing for support. Mr Billing was staring absently out over the verandah railing at something Fraser couldn't see.

'Hallo, Ursula. Your Papa has told me so much about you. You're such a young lady already! And only seven! I see he hasn't exaggerated your beauty. You'll be the catch of the island in a few years, if your Papa isn't careful.' The woman was trying hard. She was not used to children, especially self-possessed ones and her normal indifference left her at a dis-

18

advantage now. She had no idea what to say to the serious face studying her. She smiled instead.

'Papa has never mentioned you to me. I heard about you this morning for the first time – from Billy,' Ursula said baldly, ignoring the flattery. She sensed Miss Hendricks stiffen beside her and the sudden movement from her father as he shifted in his chair. Only Billy was motionless. Ursula felt her power surge. 'Why have you come to Singapore?' she asked in a polite tone.

'Oh, I'm over here visiting my aunt. I'm sure you know Mrs Hendricks and her boys . . .'

'Yes, but why did you come?' There was something in the careful wording that sounded both puzzled and knowing at the same time. Billy moved his arm from beside his body up to his jaw. Ursula saw the motion out of the corner of her eye. 'I just wondered what it was about Singapore that interested you, Miss Hendricks?' She smiled at the woman's embarrassment.

'Well,' Miss Hendricks laughed in the way adults do when they're flustered by a child's impertinence but don't want to seem angry. 'It seemed so exotic. Such a wonderful change after the provincialness of Perth. I don't suppose I really ever gave it much thought. Do you have some objection, Ursula?' There, it was out in the open, the gauntlet thrown down. Ursula retreated a pace against her father's knee.

'Papa? Is Miss Hendricks going to be my . . . is she going to stay here with us?' For a moment she sought to regain the intimacy she shared with her father; to exclude the beautiful woman with her perfect figure and her creamy skin. She sought to be the child again, without responsibility for her words or actions. But she knew immediately from the way he held her arm and said: 'Don't be rude, Ursula. You know better than to speak like that in front of a guest,' that she had lost. Her mouth became stubborn and her eyes stony as they examined the pattern on the tiled floor. Ah Jong broke the awkward silence that followed by entering with a tray of drinks, the glasses frosted and tinkling with piles of ice. It should have been the boy's job to bring drinks but Ah Jong gave up her power stintingly. She put the tray down on the table beside the Tuan and bobbed her head briefly before shuffling away as silently as she had appeared.

19

'Darling? A gin and tonic? Or just a lime?'

'I rather think this calls for some alcohol, Harry. Don't you?' Sally Hendricks could sound remarkably dry at times. She moved her mouth in an exaggerated grimace that should have been a smile but wasn't. Her eyes met Fraser's over Ursula's head. There were silent communications going on that Ursula knew were not conciliatory to her. She pulled away from her father and went over to Billy where he leant against the verandah pillar.

'Billy? What would you like to drink?' Mr Billing put his calm, capable hands on her shoulders and bent down before her so that he faced into the eyes of tragedy. He smiled gently to ease the hurt.

'Will you get me a nice, long, lime juice with two teaspoons of sugar? You know how I like it?' Her eyes pleaded with him again but he shook his head. Then he pushed her away.

'Papa? Mr Billing would like a lime with two sugars,' she repeated after having retraced her steps to her father's side. Fraser grunted something beneath his breath while he poured out a glass of lime juice from the pitcher and quickly added the sugar with a long silver spoon. He handed it to his daughter with a napkin, without a word. Ursula blinked hard to clear the shimmering sun from her eyes and gravely carried the drink to Mr Billing before returning for her own. Then she sat on the low stool by her father's feet, her head tilted forward so that her hair parted on the nape of her neck revealing a knobbly little backbone. Mr Billing, watching, found himself swirling his ice too fast, too loudly. He looked up from Ursula into Fraser's eyes impassively. Fraser glared at him, at the child and then at the woman before saying explosively:

'Now this is ridiculous. Didn't Mr Billing explain things to you, Ursula? I'm sure he did. Now I've invited Miss Hendricks over to meet you in the hope that you'll like each other, and I know that Sally is trying very hard.' He reached out and took one elegant, slim hand in his. 'So all you have to do is stop acting like a spoilt baby and try to get to know her. I'm not going to put up with some childish pouts or a fit of the sullens and if that's what you want my gel then you'll find yourself confined to your room with a warm backside for the rest of the afternoon. Is that what you want? Or would you rather act like a responsible adult and come out with us to do some sightseeing and then go on to the Swimming Club? It's up to you, you know.'

Ursula couldn't believe for a moment that her Papa was speaking to her. She thought he must be talking to one of the servants or, perhaps, to the mocking woman seated so casually on the cane chair in front of her. He couldn't be talking to her in that tone of voice. But, then, he had used her name. It didn't make sense. He would never scold her in front of a stranger. Then, like a huge weight rolling over her, she realized that her father did not regard Miss Hendricks as a stranger. She was now family. Like Billy. And that meant . . . Ursula shook her head in distress.

'I didn't mean to be rude,' she said faintly, the pain in her chest making it impossible to speak with any force. There was no breath in her lungs. 'I just wanted . . . I needed to know, that's all. From you, Papa. Billy told me but I wanted to hear it from you.' She turned stiffly to her right. 'I'm sorry Miss Hendricks if I seemed rude.' Then, with her throat locked tight she looked desperately around for Billy who, miracle of miracles, was standing there behind her. He put his hand on her shoulder to turn her away from the two adults and pushed her with a firm pressure towards the dark interior of the house.

Fraser didn't speak. He had had to choose sides in a battle he had hoped to avoid and he hadn't had the strength to re-assure them both at the same time. But Ursula was only a child and she would forget this very quickly. As long as Billing didn't go putting ideas into the girl's head. That man was a cold fish. No, he shook his head in disgust at the way he was taking out his rage on a perfectly decent sort of fellow. Billing wouldn't encourage her to dwell on things. He would get her to under-stand. It would all be all right; no problem. With this clear in his mind he suddenly smiled, relief beaming forth from his large face and enveloping the woman in its protective warmth. She smiled too, wryly. She said:

'I suppose this puts rather a hitch in things.'

'What? Ursula? Good Lord, no! She's just been a bit used to having things all her own way in the past. My fault, I suppose. I've indulged her, tried to make up for her having no mother. And she's become a bit spoiled. But she'll come round. No

21

doubt about that. She cares for her old Papa too much not to come round. You just wait and see Sally, she'll be eating out of your hand in no time at all. Promise you.' He looked like an overgrown boy when he leaned forward like that and put his head to one side. He was wheedling her and for a moment she felt contempt rise from the back of her throat, souring her mouth. But then, he was a good-looking man and generous. And he loved her wildly – like a schoolboy with a crush on his teacher. She raised perfectly arched brows at him.

'I think you're a hopeless optimist, Harry. But, whatever, if you say it'll be all right.'

'I know it'll be all right.' He leant forward to kiss her cheek, his wiry moustache tickling her skin and his aftershave raising pleasant memories. She stroked his cheekbone with the back of her fingers, strumming down the plane of the face to the jaw; let her deep-set eyes swallow him: 'You'll talk to her?'

'Of course, darling. Everything will be fine.' She let him kiss her again.

'Good, then let's finish our drinks and you can show me around the bungalow and grounds.' She looked out at the smooth lawns and jostling, vibrant flower beds where bougainvillaea splashed over dark green Binjai trees and poinsettia, frangipani, oleander, and palm created a scented spectacle rising up to the huge bamboo trees that swayed and creaked in the wind. Someone had told her that the bamboo lived to a hundred years and then, overnight, would die and come crashing down. It must be quite a sight, she thought. There were a lot of plants she didn't recognize and the feeling of living on land reclaimed from jungle was overpowering, the dark tangled growth outlining each border of the two-acre garden. She shivered despite the heat that would fry a snail on the pavement in moments. The back of her dress was damp, the linen crushed and sticking wetly when she sat forward in her chair. She pulled it away from her skin absently, her eyes still taking in the extent of her new domain. Harry Fraser watched her intently, his pale sunbleached eyes trying to gauge her expressions, anticipate her likes and dislikes. On the table the two glasses stood in pools of water where the condensation rolled down, leaving rivulets of beaded, blinking drops.

'Well?' he said finally. 'Think you can deal with it all? I

22

know it'll be strange at first. But you have the makings of a first-rate mem.'

She laughed, down in her throat as though she knew the sound of it was disturbing to him.

'Is that good? To be a first-rate mem?' She waved a long, thin arm around her with confidence. 'I must admit the life-style sounds attractive. Just what my schooling taught me not to indulge in.' She rolled her eyes. 'We were supposed to use our brains, you know. Frightfully blue-stocking school. How many house-servants do you have anyway?'

Harry Fraser was silent for a moment, unsure himself.

'Well, there's Ah Jong, and my boy and Fatimah, Ursula's amah, and her boy, Yahyah. Then there's Ibrahim, my syce and a couple of gardeners and the dhoby and maybe another boy. I'm not really sure. Somewhere around nine or ten, I'd say. Gets tricky when they have their relatives around and a fellow can't be sure who is and who isn't working for him. You count 'em. That's the mem's job.'

'I see. And all eating their heads off at your expense I suppose. No wonder you're ready to sweep me off my feet when you obviously have no idea who's who. And you didn't mention that tall man who came down with your daughter. What was his name? Billing?' Fraser ignored the way she referred to Ursula as 'your daughter' and instead gave her his most beguiling twinkle. God, she was a fine looking woman. Her hair shone like filaments of taut copper stretched thin and flashing fire. The sun outlined it in a halo around a thin, pale face and delicate features. There were beads of perspiration along a short upperlip, and the red hair curled about her temples in damp tendrils. Every action was languid and smooth, like the skin he loved to touch, feeling its creamy fineness beneath his fingers. She had a superb figure and knew it. But he didn't mind that. A good-looking woman had a right to be vain, and to hold herself as though she knew every man in the place were looking her over and indulging in daydreams. He didn't mind that. It just made him proud that he had her and they didn't. Let them wonder what it would be like. Only he would ever know.

'Harry? Can you wrench your mind away from my . . . away from wherever you are and back to the present for one second? The tutor? His name?' She was very assured, indulging in a private amusement that invited him to join her but which never really included him. Instead she arched her eyebrows in that favourite, rather enigmatic expression of hers and quirked her mouth to one side. Fraser wasn't really sure what she meant by it yet.

'Billing. Clive Billing. An exceptional man, especially for a Eurasian. Thinks like a white, acts like a white but puts up a stone wall like a native. Mixture of Thai and Dutch, I think. Good-looking fellow for a half-caste, don't you think?' He missed the slight pursing of her lips that was almost a wince. Or perhaps something else.

'Yes, very. Rather offish though, wasn't he? A bit uppity for a tutor?'

'Oh no, not really. That's just his manner. He's been a blessing where Ursula's concerned. Couldn't get her to mind any of the other servants. Just too much of lady muck altogether and I wasn't about to take much more of it. Billing's knocked all that right out of her.'

'Knocked? I hope not literally?' Her voice was even enough but she opened her eyes wide, as though in wonder. Fraser scowled suddenly, his eyebrows meeting across his nose in one, long, black line.

'God help anyone who ever lays a finger on my gel. If there's any disciplining to be done, I'll do it. And Mr Billing knows that very well. I'm sure there won't be any problems along those lines ever.' He was warning her now, she felt, despite the fact that he directed it at the tutor. She shrugged thin shoulders.

'I'm sure you're right. Now, how about that guided tour? I need to know my way around this barn of a place before I move in. Oh, did I tell you, Marjorie's going to give me a wedding shower?'

The next hour was spent in a detailed poking and prying into every corner of the bungalow and its outbuildings. The main house was a two-storey rectangular block in shape, surrounded by deep verandahs. There were doors and windows off from every room to catch any breath of wind and, inside, the ceilings were high with large overhead fans for air circulation. It was dark inside, a cool restful gloom created by the 'chicks', slatted bamboo blinds to keep out the tropical sun and rain. They were painted in black and white zebra stripes, giving the bungalow an almost Tudor look. The air was dank in the top floor bedroom, smelling of humidity and occasionally mould in some deeper recesses where the servants could not be bothered to clean, and the bathrooms were antiquated beyond belief. That would have to be seen to. But Sally was fascinated by the extent of the property and by the obvious inattention to cost that most of the furnishings revealed. The taste was rather outdated and the seating arrangement too geometrically formal but there was great potential she felt. Yes, great potential for making this one of the most impressive and beautiful bungalows in Singapore. She didn't bother with the servants' quarters out back too much but smiled with good humour restored at the man beside her.

'I suppose you're one of those men who think that everything is perfectly comfortable and practical just as it is and that there's no need to change a thing?'

'If I thought that, my love, I wouldn't dream of trying to get you to marry me. I know how you women like things your own way. You just go ahead, sweetheart, and order what you like from Robinson's. I'll tell them to let you sign on my account.' He grinned broadly when she slid her arm into his, the palms clinging together damply. He winked, a habit she happened to loathe. 'You didn't think I was one of those pencil-shy types did you? I mean, really, that sort of thing just isn't on.'

'Pencil-shy?'

'Mean, afraid of signing the chit. There's no worse insult out here in the East.'

'The slur on the gentleman's honour and all that? Well, considering you pay for everything by just signing your name, I can't say I'm all that surprised. Just think what a lot of fuss and bother there'd be if people couldn't be trusted to redeem their chits.'

'Fuss and bother!' Fraser laughed and his moustache laughed with him, tweaking at the corners of his lips. Women had such a quaint way of phrasing things sometimes, his tone seemed to suggest. 'There'd be all hell to pay my dear. My God, the very foundations of colonial life would shake and

25

crumble down around our ears. You'll know we're finished out here when the chinks throw our chits back in our faces and demand hard cash. When that happens I'm going to be on the first boat out.'

'Always assuming you can pay for your berth in hard cash.' She tilted her head in mockery.

'And always assuming we're not trampled in the rush to get away,' Fraser added, his smile ridiculing the idea even as he said it. Sally Hendricks shivered at the thought.

'Well,' she began in a bright voice that signalled her intention to change the subject as much as her words did, 'what are we going to do now? You know, darling, I've never even seen the older parts of Singapore. Couldn't we get one of those rickshaw things and go shopping together? I want to see, oh, all the temples and joss sticks and the buddhist monks and maybe, if we get time, a fortune teller.' She sensed a momentary hesitation and felt a surge of irritation sweep through her again. To control it she smiled tightly. This man might not be the young lord she'd chased out here, confident that given enough encouragement he would finally offer for her, but Fraser was a Tuan Bezar and out here his name counted for quite a lot. So she wouldn't be The Hon. Mrs Faulkes-Law; she would be 'the Mem' instead, and wealthy beyond her wildest hopes. There wasn't much fun in being an Hon. if you couldn't afford anyone to lord it over.

Sally swallowed her irritation very sensibly and tried to follow the workings of Fraser's mind. It was remarkably easy, all in all. Because Harry Fraser could think of few things he would less rather do than heave his huge frame into a tiny rickshaw with the slim woman beside him to balance his weight. It would be horribly hot and sticky, the smells down in the Bras Basah area were enough to choke even him at times, and the rickshaw-wallah would probably have a coronary at this time of the day. He considered explaining this to his fiancée. No, there was no need to spoil the old girl's fun. He could live with a couple of hours of heat and smell. And she would never dream of asking him again. His eyes took on a shrewd, assessing look that he fondly imagined was his normal expression and said:

'Whatever you want, my love. The day is yours, I'm

26

completely at your disposal and tiffin awaits us. Shall we eat here or just go sightseeing straight away? It's up to you, you know.' He was aware of a feeling of extreme magnanimity and self-sacrifice in the name of the weaker sex. Sally smiled.

'Well, couldn't we have lunch at Raffles and then just find a rickshaw from there? I love the Palm Court. That's where we met for the first time, you remember?' Fraser let his teeth gleam beneath his moustache. Bless the little woman, she was such a romantic. He kissed her soft, petal-pink lips with a gentlemanly reverence that suggested he was only holding himself in check with tremendous willpower. 'I'll tell Ah Jong we'll be eating out.'

'Thank you, darling.' Sally leaned against him and kissed his cheek, trying to ignore the pad of flesh beneath his skin. 'You really are too good to me. I can't think what I've done to deserve you.'

'Or I you,' he replied, his mind already on organizing things so as to best please her. He enjoyed taking charge. It gave him a sense of his worth that the humble reply he had mouthed a moment before had nothing to do with whatsoever. Sally was ruefully aware of it. She didn't mention the dark-haired child upstairs who had challenged her for this man and lost. But there was a curl to her lip that was satisfied with the way things had turned out. It would be all right, as Fraser had promised.

Ursula heard the low-toned, laughing voices when they came by her room, growing louder as the footsteps approached and then, after a muffled consultation, followed by silence except for footsteps tiptoeing away. The voices resumed at a distance again, quieter and more serious until a sudden shout of laughter from her Papa made her close her eyes hard. She squeezed the damp handkerchief in her fist into a tighter ball, squeezing it as though it were alive and she must kill it quite dead. She would kill it dead. She would. The room was cool and dark, the fan circling overhead in comforting repetitiveness, and she lay in her underclothes on the bed rubbing her cheek against the scratchy, starched sheets. The dhoby always put too much starch and too much blue in the wash. But it smelled fresh and clean and cool. Fatimah had taken off the yellow frock, putting it carefully away in the camphor-lined

27

chest against the wall and then, coming back to sit on the bed with her, had brushed her hair with long, gentle strokes that soothed. But Fatimah had gone now too, to some other part of the house, her bare feet slapping away on the floorboards and leaving Ursula to her own thoughts.

Billy had held her hand tightly when he took her upstairs. She had pressed against his side, her head averted as though she were ashamed; not just of herself, but of the way she'd been treated by her Papa. She was ashamed that Billy had seen her treated that way and maybe even scared that she wasn't worth any more than that to anyone. She was less than a servant: insignificant, and a nuisance. The castle in which she had reigned as a princess, sure of people's love and reverence for her, had collapsed around her and now, she wondered, did Billy think less of her? Oh, why had she asked for him to stay? Why had he had to see her humiliation, her shame? How could Papa have been so cold? So weak? Tears gathered in her eyes and hung suspended from her lower lashes so that the room swam in refracted colour around her.

Billy had taken her into her room, as her Papa had instructed, and he had told her that she would have to stay there for a while. His voice had been the same as always, serious with just a lilt of amusement in the back of his throat. He had picked her up and sat her on the bed, unbuttoning the top two buttons at the back of her neck where the dress was too tight. And then he had stroked her cheek with his fingers and smiled at her, and said he was proud of her. She didn't know why he had said that because she had disobeyed him and been impertinent. But his voice comforted her and she leant her head on his shoulder as he knelt down in front of her and she held him tightly, her tears running freely now. She didn't whimper but cried silently while Billy held her against him, hiccuping out the sorrow that had built so sharply in her chest. Billy didn't say anything or try to soothe her with meaningless phrases and eventually she looked up, sniffed and tried to be adult.

'I think Miss Hendricks is very beautiful, Billy,' she said with an almost steady voice. He smiled, his skin smooth and tight over the high cheekbones.

'Oh, peerless. You are very fortunate, Ursula. It would not do to have an ugly step-mother. People would say she must be unkind and treat you like Cinderella.' He laughed when he saw she was puzzled and doubtful about what to reply. 'No matter. Sleep now. I will come back later when you have rested and we will read together.'

'Billy? You won't go away for good, will you? Even if I'm bad sometimes, you won't go away, will you?' What was to keep him now that she had lost face in front of him?

'No, Ursula. I will always be here, just for you. Now go to sleep. Fatimah will help you undress.' He had turned and left before she could properly clear her eyes and see what sort of expression he had had. Then she had sighed very deeply and waited for Fatimah.

Now it was late. She had heard the car leave with Papa and Miss Hendricks. They hadn't stayed for tiffin and she had turned her head away into her pillow and feigned sleep when Fatimah had come to call her down. Now her stomach was rumbling, complaining at its emptiness. She sat up, tucking her hair behind her ears. Her head felt heavy and ached as though she had a fever but she knew it was just from lying down for so long.

She stood up, the floorboards cool under her heated skin, and walked into the bathroom. There was a large water jar and ladle that Fatimah used to pour water over her when she was hot. The shower was only to be used once a day. Now she went over to it and, pulling off her underclothes, began to ladle the water over her body. It was cold and made her flinch and catch her breath at first. But then she began to enjoy the feel of the coolness as it slid down her back and buttocks, trickling down her legs to the floor where it ran into the channels edging the room. She was absorbed in the pleasure of being clean and fresh, savouring the sensation of water flowing over her skin, the heat chilled for a second before reappearing, triumphant. She raised the ladle higher, pouring it over her head and feeling her hair slick back and her mouth wet with the deluge. She laughed aloud.

When she opened her eyes again, she saw Billy standing there smiling at her, his face indulgent. He clicked his fingers together and pointed at his watch, his words lost to her under the last torrent of water as it sluiced in her ears. After a moment or two he turned and left her alone. It could all be borne as long as Billy would be there for her, smiling the pain away, ready to protect her at all times. Maybe Papa did not want her anymore but Billy did. He would be her mother and father all rolled into one. She wanted to call out to Billy, to call him back, but she knew he would not answer. He was always pleased when he saw her coming out of the bathroom all pink and shiny from Fatimah's scrubbing, since cleanliness was very important in the East. But there were times when he thought she took too long. So he wouldn't answer her until she appeared from the bathroom.

Ursula put the ladle back in the almost empty jar and wrapped herself up in the big, white towel that Fatimah used for her. Billy was sitting on the bed, leaning forward with his head between his hands. He looked tired but Ursula knew he hadn't given her a lesson this afternoon so he couldn't be that tired. She went over to him and laid a small, cold hand on his.

'Are you sick, Billy?' She heard him make a muffled laughing sound and when he raised his head she saw that he was smiling again. The relief made tears stand out in her eyes and she smiled too. 'I thought you were cross I'd taken too long and used all the water. I didn't though. There's still some left. And I did it all myself, without Fatimah. I don't need Fatimah to wash me anymore.'

'No? Well, you are grown to be a big girl now. So why these tears again? I thought you had cried yourself out this afternoon? A big girl who can wash alone doesn't cry all the time.'

'I thought you were sick because you were holding your head in your hands. And then you weren't because you laughed. I'm not crying because of her anymore.' She was pleased when he pulled her in close to him and put his cheek against hers. His was cool and firm and smooth, not like Papa's whiskers and cologne. She snuggled closer, trying to make out what he was saying. Perhaps he was sick after all because he never normally spoke so slowly or in just a murmur. Not when he was talking to her. She listened harder. There was something about him not always being there for her and that she must learn to be stronger. But she was too little as yet, too little and too alone to be left. Left! But he had promised her only that afternoon that he would always be there for her. She felt a moment of loss and panic slice through her lungs and clung fiercely to his hand, determined not to let him go. He kissed her hair and slowly prised her hand from his. 'Don't worry, *cahayamata*. You are as my child, my soul. I will never walk from you without your being ready. And even then I will always be with you, here.' He touched his chest above his heart, his look calm and steady. Then he stood her away from him, tweaked her nose and told her to dress, as she was such a big girl. He said he would wait outside on the verandah and then they would read. Then he went out and left her, wrapped in the big towel, wondering where Fatimah kept her striped pinafore dress.

Chapter Two

She found Billy downstairs sitting on the low wall of the verandah, one knee raised and his back against the pillar. It could have seemed a pose in any other man but Billy did it with such ease, leaning back with his shadowed eyes again searching for something on the horizon. Ursula knew that far-away look that sometimes came into his eyes. It meant he was remembering. What, she wasn't so sure about. Maybe his parents, or a friend, or something important that had happened to him once. She would lose all reality for him at these times and he would almost not hear her questions, not feel her touch his arm, tugging at his sleeve to bring him back from himself. Once he had read her a sanskrit proverb, stressing the words in that quiet, contained way of his so that she felt he were talking as much to himself as to her. She had kept the proverb and read it often, particularly the bit about: 'for yesterday is but a dream, and tomorrow is only a vision.' The point, he said, was that one should live life a step at a time, enjoying and savouring it as it comes because today is what goes into memories and future visions. It was a point he liked to make clear to her often.

He was wearing a suit of pale cream linen, baggy and loose but somehow elegant as it hung on his frame. Sometimes, when her father was not there, and it was especially hot he would remove the jacket and roll back the sleeves of his white shirt, loosen the top button and tug the tie down a little so that he could breathe. Ursula always liked those days; he looked so casual and comfortable with his gilt-coloured skin, dark where his sleeves were turned back, and those long shafts of smooth arm sticking out. She had been so upset that morning that she hadn't noticed how nice he looked today. He must have dressed especially nice for that woman. Ursula couldn't help thinking of her as 'that woman' and probably never would call her anything else in her own mind. It didn't matter anyway. She clearly intended to stay, the way she hung on Papa's arm. But the woman didn't matter as long as she had Billy.

He had a tie on that Ursula hadn't seen before. It looked regimental but she didn't think Billy would wear one that he was not entitled to. Then she saw that it was pinned at the neck with a small gold bar with a horseshoe across it. She had never seen the pin before either. Maybe it had been given to him by his father. She sometimes wondered if Billy's father had been like hers. She understood about mixed marriages. Papa had explained it once, saying it wasn't the thing to do. But Billy's father and mother had done it and Billy looked all right. She didn't know why Papa had said it bred neither this, nor that, but just made everyone's life difficult. Billy didn't make her life difficult.

He looked over, eventually, to where she was sitting quietly on the front step watching him. His eyes were dreamy and, underneath, there were dark bruises as though someone had felt a ripe fruit and left their thumb imprint. When he felt her gaze he had turned away from the view over the bank down to the clubhouse and padang. It was difficult to stare for long into the distance anyway. The light made everything shimmer and little waves of heat seemed to wash about over the ground like wraiths. His eyeballs felt gritty and hot from so much staring so that when he blinked, the liquid in his eyes burned like acid. He turned his head and looked into the gloom of the verandah, unable to see but knowing Ursula was there. After a few seconds his eyes adjusted and he could make out her figure hunched over itself as it sat on the door lintel. She liked to sit hugging her knees, her chin balanced on them while her eyes were directed upwards, on him.

'Well, *kera*, you have been sitting there very quietly. Are you ready to be patient with life again?' He liked to call her pet names, like monkey, partly out of superstition. Then the Gods would not be jealous and seek revenge upon too lovely a child. Not that he believed in such foolishness. But he only had to see her to feel wonder, and a tinge of uneasiness. She was so perfect to him, so small and delicately formed, so spirited and loving. How could Fraser have treated her like that? He would have rather lost an arm than cut his own child off from him and chosen a stranger. But then the British could be like that; cold and distant to their own flesh and blood but ridiculously sentimental over animals or people they had never even met. It was odd, even so, for Fraser. He had always seemed to dote on the child. And now he doted on a different sort, Billy thought with a contempt he could not quite conceal. He had never felt anything for women like Sally Hendricks and found he had no patience with men like Fraser. 'Not deceived, but fondly overcome with female charm', the lines sprang readily to his mind. Was Fraser deceived? Or did he know very well what was going through Miss Hendricks' mind when she smiled and pouted at him. Either way it was irrelevant. It seemed that he must take Fraser's place in Ursula's heart and keep the child out of hurt's way. It never occurred to Billy to think that he might not be there to look after Ursula or that he did not have the right to take her father's place. He just knew there were limits beyond which even the new mem would not be permitted. Other children might go away to boarding school and Ursula was certainly old enough now but Fraser had always been adamant that his child would not be packed off to be reared by strangers. Not unless she provoked him. And Billy did not think he would change his mind so easily, even then.

'Come, Ursula. Ah Jong has laid out tea. You must be hungry by now. You slept through tiffin. Come and eat and then we will have a quiet afternoon reading.' He took her hand in his and pulled her to her feet. She took a deep breath.

'That's a nice tie and pin, Billy. Are they new?' She chose something at random to cut through her initial embarrassment. She still could not forget that Billy had seen her humiliation at the hands of someone who had always cherished her before. Billy hesitated.

'The tie is new. The pin belonged to my father.'

'But, isn't the tie from a regiment or something?' Ursula sensed Billy's reluctance to reply. She squeezed his hand and swung away from him so that she could look up into his face.

'Yes, Ursula. Sometimes there are regiments that are not regular army. They are . . . a sort of home defence, in case of trouble one day. I belong to one like that.'

'Really? Who do you defend against?' Ursula was surprised. She thought Singapore a very quiet sort of place. But Billy was not the sort to play at soldiers.

'It does not matter. People do not take advantage of the strong, only the weak. Now, what would you like to start with?' He beckoned her over to the table and its small pile of well-thumbed books. Ursula looked them over and shrugged: 'Oh, with ''the pied and painted birds and beans'', – why are they painted birds, Billy? You can't get a bird to stay put long enough to paint it.'

'Not a real bird, no. These are wooden birds, toys, made to look like the wild birds of the East. You cannot have such birds for real in a cold climate. They would die.'

'I don't think I'd like to live somewhere like that. Maybe I'd die and get painted to look like I was still alive?' Billy smiled at Ursula's fancy.

'Then you must remember the East is where you belong, and stay away from the cold. Now what is the next line of the poem?'

> 'The junks and bangles, beads and screens.
> The gods and sacred bells,
> And the loud-humming, twisted shells.
> And then, the level of the parlour floor,
> Was honest, homely, Scottish shore;
> But when we climbed upon a chair,
> Behold the gorgeous East was there!'

She had climbed onto a chair herself, raising one hand over her brows as though looking into the distance. She lowered it slowly and stared at Billy, almost level with his face. 'It is gorgeous, isn't it, Billy? D'you think she'll find it gorgeous?' She couldn't leave the subject alone, but kept probing to know more. The thoughts tumbled out in swift succession. Billy shrugged.

'Perhaps. Not for the reason you might find it so, but for

35

other reasons. Everyone has their own ideas about what makes something special. I don't think Miss Hendricks is going to be so unhappy here that she will leave. Not unless you make her so. And then she may not be the one to leave. You are old enough for school now, you know.' He hated the shuttered look that came down over her face, hiding her feelings from him in a way that she had never done before. Never known how to do. Miss Hendricks had begun to teach Ursula how to be a mem all too well – and far too soon. But then she had to have some protection and it was best she knew where she stood. Better to be warned and prepared than have it come crashing down on her unaware.

Ursula climbed down from the chair and sat down quietly. 'Then I shall have to do my duty, shan't I Billy?'

> A child should always say what's true,
> And speak when he is spoken to,
> And behave mannerly at table:
> At least as far as he is able.'

There was a bitterness to her voice that was new and strangely adult. Billy didn't like to hear it but had to admire the way she had turned their poetic game to serious intent. She was a bright child, sometimes too bright, too knowing; a child who had been raised to be an adult from birth. He sighed.

'That's right Ursula, "as far as you are able".'

'But if I say the truth then I may not be as dutiful as Papa would wish. What am I supposed to do, Billy? Smile and tell fibs?' Her eyebrows were straight and hard, drawn in a line across her eyes so that her face was a picture of stubborness; her father's face. Billy ignored it.

'Face facts, Ursula. Your father is marrying again with, or without, your approval. If you refuse to accept the situation as it is then you may make it worse for yourself. You know your Papa loves you but he also loves Miss Hendricks. Do not force him to make choices. Or if you do, be prepared to lose.' He spoke in an even tone that made everything he said so maddeningly logical and fair that at times Ursula wanted to scream. Now she just turned away and picked up the book of poetry, flipping to where she knew she had last left off. She ignored the tea tray, her hunger turned to sourness and her stomach aching with an unknown emotion.

'All right, Billy. Let's get on with this,' she said impatiently, cracking the spine of the book across her knee. Billy watched her bowed head as she continued to read from Robert Louis Stevenson for the next hour, his own face as tight and closed as hers. Once, long ago, he had felt this pain of rejection; he and his mother. And soon after, just he alone. But Ursula would not be abandoned like that, he thought fiercely; she would not!

For Ursula, Robert Louis Stevenson had been a favourite poet until then, just like the yellow frock had been her favourite frock. But ever after, when she thought back about that day, she turned sick at the memories of both.

They held the wedding in the garden, under an enormous tent. Sally had wanted it to be in St Andrew's cathedral down near the Cricket Club but Harry had been stubbornly against it. He said he'd been married once that way and preferred to stay out of church this time. Sally cajoled and pleaded, wept and scolded with no success. Harry turned pale eyes on her and asked how much she really loved him and how much was just the trappings. Sally gave in. It was a beautiful wedding nevertheless. The tent was made of pale yellow silk with dark green vines entwined around the poles that held it up and the tables were decked with camellias, oleander, frangipani and orchids, perfuming the air as much as the candles that blazed in the night breeze. Sally wore white and Harry smiled with the satisfaction of a deal well settled when he placed the ring on her slender finger. They both knew what they were getting in this marriage, he thought. Not like Lillian. He shrugged the thought away and led his bride out onto the parquet floor in the first waltz.

Ursula didn't attend the reception. She had been present as a flower girl for the actual wedding, her eyes fixed intently on the scene in front of her. The Hendricks boys were pages beside her, Rodney snapping a piece of twine and thorn against her legs whenever she wasn't looking. She kicked him back, earning stern looks from Mrs Hendricks and several other guests. Rodney smiled and looked straight ahead. The service took forever and Ursula could see very little, only her Papa's

37

broad back as it leaned against his bride. But when her Papa had kissed Miss Hendricks, Ursula had realized with shock that it was all over. There was no going back. As if to emphasize that fact, the new mem had leaned around Harry Fraser and given Ursula a steady smile that had far more triumph than warmth in it. Ursula had turned away, slipping between the throng of well-wishers and disappearing into the darkened gardens. Rodney watched her go with regret, turning to flick the twine at his brother instead. He wasn't surprised when Stephen burst into tears, his voice blurring in a sing-song cadence of woe that invited sympathy from anyone close enough to protect him. Stephen always cried about everything. Rodney sighed and wished Ursula would come back before the evening became totally dull. At least she had enough pluck to kick back.

Ursula went looking for Billy, as always, for comfort and cool good sense. He was sitting around the back of the house, invited to the wedding but preferring to miss it. He had turned up for Ursula's sake only. She found a seat beside him on the steps leading to the drainage channel. It was quiet and pleasant sitting there and Billy put his arm around her tiny figure, drawing her close to him in a comforting embrace. She rested an arm across his knee and muttered quietly to herself about intruders, nasty ill-mannered boys, and disloyalty in general. Billy made no reply. Finally, wondering a little at his silence, she tugged at his jacket and looked up into his face. It was shaded by the deep gloom of the back verandah, even the lights from the house not picking out his expression.

'What is it, Billy? Don't you want to talk to me?' He stirred at that, rubbing her hand beneath his, smoothing the skin over her knuckles in slow, troubled movements.

'Not now, Ursula. I must think. Just sit beside me and we will be together, but quietly.' And with that he subsided into a long, deep sigh. It wasn't like Billy to be upset about something. Perhaps he had family problems himself? But no, he had been brought up in an orphanage. And there was very little to worry about with money, Ursula was sure. Billy lived too frugally for that and her Papa paid him well. Ursula, surprised, made no sound but leaned against him. Sally might have Papa but she had Billy. She didn't doubt she had the better deal. He held her tightly against him until, finally, tired out by tension and unhappiness, she fell asleep across his knees. Her head lolled back like a doll's and Billy finally stirred from his reverie. It was dark, the night sounds clicking and whirring in the warm air, the scrape of cicadas rising against the wind that soughed through the bamboo. The child beside him seemed too small for all the emotion she had spent that day. He pulled her sleeping form into his arms and slowly rose to his feet, carrying Ursula inside and up to her bedroom. A sleepy Fatimah took the little girl from him as he entered the room, her calm face unsurprised.

'She has had a long day and a sad one. It is best the little one sleeps.' Her eyes flicked up to Billy's face. 'You must not worry so much. All will be well here.' Billy glanced once at the sleeping child, turned and left without a word. Behind him Fatimah arranged Ursula on the bed, murmuring to herself about the trance of fear before the snake strikes. And outside, in the garden, the wedding revelries continued unchecked.

It was nearly three months later before Ursula saw Sally again. The honeymoon had been in Europe and Ursula remembered her Papa had leaned over her bed in the early hours of the morning after the wedding, his moustache tickling her cheek as he kissed her goodbye. Ursula had barely acknowledged him, turning in feigned sleepiness away from him and wrapping her arms over her face. Harry Fraser had left without noticing. And now, suddenly, the reprieve was over and Sally was walking up the front porch steps, her laughter cutting through the gentle drone of late afternoon's cicadas, her fiery hair intruding abruptly into Ursula's comfortable existence. Ursula stood up and waited to be spoken to. Sally glanced in her direction but did little more than crease her cheeks briefly into a smile of greeting. Ursula tried to copy the action but it appeared as a grimace. Sally had already turned away to greet Mr Billing, stripping off gloves from pale, slim arms and hands as she did so.

'There you are, Mr Billing. The Tuan has stopped off at his offices. My God, you'd think he could at least have seen me home first, but there we are, that's men for you, I suppose. But then, you're not like that are you, Mr Billing? You're here to greet me.' She laughed and lifted a hand to briefly pat her halo of hair into place. 'Oh! It's so silly to have to keep calling you "Mr Billing" when I'm sure it'd be much more comfortable to call you by your first name. What is your first name, hmm? Come now, don't be shy of me. I shan't bite!' She had stepped closer and was half turned away from Mr Billing, her head angled around to flash dark amused eyes at him, her throat arched back in all its pale beauty. She dominated the room, lighting it with her hair and skin and swinging skirts, filling the silence with her laughter, the child forgotten in the shadowed corners of the house. What did a dark-haired little girl have that she did not? For a moment Ursula thought Billy would respond. Her stomach tensed into coils of painful anticipation. But Mr Billing remained unmoved, his face impassive, his eyes shadowed in private thought. He bowed his head in deference.

'It would not be seemly, Mrs Fraser. I do not think Mr Fraser would like it. May I call Ah Jong to you? You must be tired and in need of refreshment after your journey.' He had turned away and was gone before Sally could marshal more than an exclamation of annoyance. Her light dimmed momentarily as she glanced with irritation over to the child in the corner. Ursula smiled; just a little smile but Sally knew what it meant. That dark-eyed child had learned how to fight for her possessions.

'Aren't you supposed to be doing your lessons or something, Ursula?' Sally's annoyance tinged her words with sharp spikes of antagonism. Ursula nodded.

'We thought we'd stop to greet Papa and . . . and you. But Billy won't mind if we start again. He doesn't like wasting time anyway.' And with a small smile of satisfaction that defied the older woman to try and take Billy from her the way her Papa had been snatched, Ursula quietly went upstairs.

Weeks passed in a stifled calm that barely revealed the undeclared struggle between the two women of the house. Occasional ripples of tension washed up against Harry Fraser but he steadfastly ignored them, his pale, faded eyes seeming to see nothing before him that did not please him. And the servants became quiet and still, freezing before the occasional whiplash of Sally's tongue into dull stupidity. Ursula stayed by Billy's side at all but meal times, her normal laughter and exuberance flattened into shortened movements and nervous whispers except when Sally went to town to spend more and more of Harry Fraser's money. Then there would be stifled and furious scenes over the breakfast table as Harry Fraser opened the mail. Before the month was out Sally had taken to having late breakfast alone on the verandah, hours after Harry had left for the office or Ursula had started her lessons. Ursula was excused from joining Sally so that there were long hours in the morning when Sally found she had little to do, and that was when she developed what seemed to Ursula a strange habit of suddenly turning up in the schoolroom, draped against the doorway, smiling and pouting at Mr Billing to come and walk with her in the garden. Ursula raged silently at the woman in front of her and Billy found it increasingly difficult to think of excuses; he became still and wary, his cool indifference rising as a shield that never quite became contempt but which left Sally more piqued as every day passed. And Ursula's olive skin would warm from beneath its sudden fright, her mouth would smile in relief.

The tension couldn't go on much longer without giving in some way, Ursula thought privately and tried to devise methods of getting rid of Sally. But there was nothing that could be done that did not involve either herself or Billy and she cringed from the thought of either of them becoming mixed up in a scene between Sally and her Papa. If only there were some way to get Sally to leave them alone, then life might become bearable again. She sighed and fretted, watching Sally's movements like an old woman peeping out from behind lace curtains. And Sally finally rewarded her efforts.

It was the Fraser's first big party that cleared the air. The new furnishings had been finished only that day and Sally had nagged her way through the afternoon in an agony of worry in case the final sofa in its new glazed chintz should not arrive in time.

But by four o'clock everything was in place, flowers filled the house, the silver was polished, the new curtains fluttered brightly in the late afternoon breeze and Sally had retired to bathe and change. Ursula had been told by her Papa that she might greet the guests with Sally and stay for a little while before going up to bed. Mr Billing was asked to stay late and see to Ursula. Sally had arranged that. Sally had arranged everything. It was typical of her style that she would choose to wear colours that a red-head would normally never attempt. That night she wore a wrapped gold cocktail dress, bare from the shoulders, that flared in the warm glow of the lamps and eclipsed the other women as easily as a sun eclipses the stars. The men clustered, the women either envied or fawned, Harry Fraser beamed and Ursula kept away. The evening looked set to be a success. And then Carolyn Sunderland arrived.

'Carrie, darling! Such an age since I saw you. What on earth have you done with that divine husband of yours?' Harry Fraser heard his wife's comment and turned away abruptly, his mouth pursed tightly. He would have to talk to his dear wife, he thought. The whisky in his glass shook with the force of his grip. There had been enough of that in Europe. Darling this, and darling that, kiss on the cheek and maybe more than the cheek when she disappeared from time to time down some bloody long passageway. Too many bloody passageways for his bloody wife. Back here, he would expect her to behave herself. His face stiff with annoyance, he took a quick swig of whisky from the new crystal glass in his hand and gave Sally a hard look. Too many passageways, too many new glasses, too much expense and not enough of the things he'd expected. His eyes met hers and her lips twisted into that enigmatic smile that had charmed him only a few months ago. Then she turned away to greet the woman to whom she had called a greeting. Sally kissed the air between herself and the woman, the latter as dark and tanned as Sally was fair and light-skinned. They made a perfect foil for each other, standing together for others to admire. Carrie shrugged.

'Around. He's always around, just never right here. I swear I'm going to tie a string to a gold ring in his nose one of these days. Just to keep him in check.' She laughed and Sally laughed with her. 'Speaking of divine men, where's that tutor fellow of yours? Not confined to the schoolroom, I hope?' Carrie's eyebrows lifted as she caught a fleeting look of discomposure cross Sally's face.

'Oh, he's over there in the corner keeping an eye on the . . .

on Ursula.' Sally gave a moue. 'He doesn't care for me, I'm afraid. Thinks I disrupt his lessons too much. But Harry thinks the world of him and Ursula! My God, I think she thinks her "Billy" was put on this earth just for her. She gives me daggers if I as much as smile at the poor man. Little wretch!' She laughed again to take the bite from her words. Carrie sucked her cheeks in and turned brilliant green eyes on the far corner. She hummed gently.

'Mind if I try?'

'Try what? Oh! Well, I hardly think . . . he is Eurasian you know. Oh well, if that doesn't put you off then please, be my guest! I'd like to see him lose a little of that holier-than-thou superiority. Yes! Go on Carrie! See what you can do.' The idea caught hold and Sally was instantly in good humour. What had seemed like yet another boringly insipid colonial affair was suddenly about to prove quite amusing. Thank God everyone wasn't a provincial bore round here. She thought of Europe for a moment and the success she had enjoyed, the conquests so easily made, and her mood edged uneasily towards discontent. All those men had wanted her and some damned Eurasian tutor had the effrontery to act as though she were sullying the air he breathed. Her eyes narrowed fretfully and then cleared. What the hell! If Carrie could just break down that barrier, well then, who knew what could happen?

She watched Carrie blow her a kiss before slipping through the crowd, her body swaying effortlessly around and between people. Carolyn Sunderland was the sort of woman who wasn't actually beautiful but made people believe she was with her whip-thin body tanned from tennis and swimming, her dark head elegantly cropped, and her clothes cut to mould her figure. In her middle thirties and tied to a man who saw no reason to cut down on his affairs simply because he was married, Carrie had become one of the bored expatriate wives who constantly look for stimulation in the younger bachelor set. Carrie expected to find Mr Billing extremely stimulating. She wasn't quite sure why he appealed to her so much. It was something to do with his inner reserve, she thought, surveying him from no more than a couple of feet. He was good-looking, of course, but it was more than that. He was . . . she paused in her thoughts, unable to pinpoint it. Then, as he turned his head and caught her eye, she suddenly knew what it was. He was quietly and completely confident in himself as a man. She drew in her breath and smiled, her eyes blazing a special light that no man had ever been known to mistake. Or, for that matter, she thought, to refuse.

Mr Billing inclined his head and looked away. Beside him, sipping at a lime juice and eagerly watching the crowd, Ursula missed Carrie's approach. It was only when confronted by the folds of a dress cutting off the light of the rest of the room that Ursula glanced up. And then looked furiously at the dark-haired woman in black. Such a dress, Ursula thought! And why was she looking at Billy like that? Just standing there, less than six inches from Billy and popping her eyes at him. Ursula cleared her throat, tugging at Billy's hand.

'Let's go outside, Billy. I need some fresh air,' she said pointedly and Billy lowered his head to smile down at her.

Watching him, Carrie was astonished. He really cares about that little child, she thought. He adores her. Well! She was momentarily taken aback. But only momentarily.

'Oh Ursula, dear. Sally wants you. She's over there, by the door. Go on, I'll take care of Mr Billing while you're away. Quickly now! Sally will be cross if you're not there soon.' Carrie gave Ursula a push that was less than gentle, ignoring the stiffening in the tutor's features, the abrupt way he stepped back a pace. The child looked at the woman with eyes that were too old for her face. Too old and too knowing, Carrie thought. Nobody's fool, even at her age – what was she? Seven, for God's sake? She grimaced at Ursula and gave her another push. 'Run along and be a good little girl, do!' She saw the child reluctantly move towards Sally and turned back to face her quarry. But Mr Billing was already moving away. Out, towards the garden, where the child had wanted to go. Good, Carrie thought. That makes things simpler. She picked up two glasses from a tray circulating beside her and followed.

'You wanted me, Sally?' Ursula asked, knowing the look of confusion that would pass over her step-mother's face. 'Mrs Sunderland said you wanted me. Is that right?' she pressed. Sally recovered immediately, looking down at Ursula with lips that were folded into a secretive smile. Ursula hated her at that point.

44

'Oh yes, that's right. I did ask Carrie to fetch you. Now, why was that?' A slim finger was rested against a rouged cheek. Sally pondered. 'That was it! Would you be an angel and ask, um, Ah Jong for more, uh,' the fingers tapped impatiently, 'more ice. Yes, we're running out of ice.' That was always a safe bet, Sally thought. She glanced over at the corner where Mr Billing had been. There was no sign of him nor of Carrie. Well, well! Ursula saw her look and tried to peer over the heads but was too short. She turned away abruptly and walked into the kitchen.

'Ah Jong, more ice can? Mem want quick quick la!' She called without stopping, passing through the tiled backroom and out into the garden. Billy had whispered he would wait in the garden. She knew where. She always knew where Billy would be. But when she rounded the corner, she saw Billy was not alone. A black shadow was crushed up against him, obscuring him from Ursula's sight. Long arms twined their way around his body, the two figures locked tightly together. Ursula shrank back in fright.

The figures parted and Ursula heard a low murmur of voices, a laugh that became less amused, more peeved as the taller figure stepped back. Ursula heard Billy's voice.

'Is that what you wanted, Mrs Sunderland?' The tone was impersonal, even detached.

'Oh come on! You wanted it too. I know the difference – you don't have to pretend with me. I'm not going to tell!' Carrie's voice sounded hesitant, even to herself. She added in a stronger tone. 'Christ man, anyone would think you were doing me a favour. There are a dozen men in there who'd give their eye-teeth to change places with you right now. So, why don't you just be a good boy and . . . ' She wrapped herself across him again but this time Billy held her off.

'I think not, Mrs Sunderland. Goodnight.' And Billy had stepped away, turning to disappear around the back of the servant quarters. There was a pause of complete surprise, the events of a moment shredding themselves into unreality. It was over before Carrie knew what had happened. Ursula heard a small shriek of rage from the woman in black. She stood in the middle of the courtyard and stamped her tiny high-heeled foot like a boot, grinding it into the hard-packed earth.

45

'How dare you! Come back here you bloody nigger! I'll have you turned off so damned fast, you snotty bloody bastar . . . ' She checked when Ursula came out from behind the ginger jar. 'And what the fuck do you want?' she snarled, whirling around to face the girl. Carrie's roots tended to show when she was upset but Ursula stood her ground.

'Your husband's looking for you, Mrs Sunderland. I think he's rather angry. He said something about if he finds you with yet another man, he'll send you home on the first boat.' Ursula quoted directly the words she had heard from the gossip of a score of previous parties. She knew what was most likely to unnerve this woman. She pressed the point home. 'At least, I think it was something like that. Would you like me to tell him where you are?' The threat, though unspoken, was unmistakable. Ursula didn't flinch from the expression she saw pass over Carrie's face. This was for Billy's sake, she told herself. Then Mrs Sunderland couldn't try and make trouble. But she was shaking when the older woman swept by her without a word, the dark skirt rustling against the doorway with an angry crackle. Ursula swallowed and lifted her chin. There! That would make Mrs Sunderland think twice. Then, like the scared child defying an adult that she really was, Ursula lowered her head again and whimpered, her knuckles pushing against her lips to stifle the sound.

Billy found her there, still crying, and he lifted her into his arms, her long legs wrapping tightly around him as he held her close. 'Shh, *cahayamata*, shh. No need to cry. Billy is here for you.' He kissed her hair and she smelled a lingering fragrance from that woman caught in his clothing. It made her gag. He made no comment but held her away from his jacket and walked across the darkened back lawn to the edge of the trees. There the scent of the jungle at night overpowered everything else. He kissed her wet cheek again. 'Better now? Are you all cried out, my Ursula?'

She sniffed and nodded. 'Am I?'

'Are you what?' He smiled in the dark.

'Your Ursula? You didn't like her, did you?' She felt his hold tighten around her.

'Shh, *kera*. Do not talk of such women as this. She is nothing to me and you must never compare yourself to such as her. You are the child of my heart and will always come first with me. No, I did not like Mrs Sunderland. It is . . . ' He paused and Ursula felt him groping for the right words. 'It is sometimes difficult for you to understand. You are still only little. I forget that when we are together so much but women like Mrs Sunderland . . . they are not as I would wish you to grow up to be. They are . . . like a kind of poison. An opiate. I cannot explain it all to you. I am a man, yes, and sometimes I cannot be as, as logical as I would be, but no! She does not interest me. Not as a person and never again as a woman. Do you understand, my Ursula?' Ursula had nothing more than a vague idea of what he was trying to say to her but she nodded and laid her head against his shoulder, sighing deeply. Her tears had wet his jacket but he didn't complain. For a few moments more he rocked her in his arms, letting the stillness of the night calm her and then he carried her inside, past a startled Sally standing by the back door, and upstairs to bed.

When he returned nearly half an hour later to take his leave, he noticed Sally was distant, her head held in the attitude of a mem who is affronted and will not tolerate anything further from her servants. The Sunderlands were nowhere in sight. Billy's smile goodnight was tinged with irony.

Chapter Three

Ursula was thinking of just that on Christmas morning 1941 when she heard the car drive up under the porch and brake sharply. She had been wondering if Carrie would be turning up for lunch, her sharp looks always seeking out Ursula and passing hidden messages of spite. Ursula hoped Carrie had been left off the guest list this year. Rumour had it she was being left off most guest lists altogether. Just one too many men, so the whispers went.

The car doors slammed and there was the sound of running feet, followed by sharply raised voices and a woman's crying. Ursula was on the floor above and heard the voices float up to her, her father's tone soothing and patronizing, Sally's rising and falling in stabs of fury and, perhaps, even fear. It was about the Japs, Ursula thought, her initial complacency having long ago given way to a nagging anxiety that she had not dared to mention to her father. She was fourteen only last month and Papa treated her like an adult now. He would have mocked her fear, telling her, as he so often told Sally, that Singapore was a fortress, that it was created to withstand just such an invasion, that sixty million pounds had gone into the defences, that little yellow men were no match for European superiority. The list of reassurances were endless but they hadn't stopped the Japanese from landing at Kota Bahru, marching over the impassable mountain barrier to the West coast of Malaya and then half the way down the peninsula. And they weren't doing much for her fears. There were times when Ursula actually sympathized with Sally. Her father was impossible; he treated them like cut glass that might shatter instantly and messily all over the place under stress. And what was worse was that Ursula wasn't sure whether her father did not actually believe all the propaganda the government was putting out. He really thought there was no threat and that he could personally beat back a horde of ravaging 'slit-eyed pygmies' without drawing a breath. His confidence was sickening and she could understand Sally's anger and desperation in trying to get him to admit that Singapore really might be in trouble after all, and that she and the children should be on the first boat available down to Perth.

Ursula wondered what fresh piece of news had set Sally off this time. After breakfast with the children and the present opening, they had gone out for drinks to the Fergusons' and were supposed to be hosting a Christmas lunch themselves, for twelve people, in little over an hour. She wondered if that was all off too? But it seemed it wasn't because a few moments later Sally came rushing up the stairs shouting for Nancy, her personal maid, to lay out her green silk dress. Ursula could see from the tight way Sally was holding her mouth how much anger and disappointment was in her. She shied away from the girl when she saw her, looking irritated as usual. Ursula didn't totally blame her any more. Why should Sally be saddled with another man's child when she now had two of her own to worry about and cherish? And Sally was a good mother to them, when she was home, and when she thought about it, Ursula conceded.

Sally swept past her into her bedroom, slamming the door behind her. Ursula turned back into the sitting room, running her palms down her sides to dry them. It was hard waiting for news that only adults felt they had a right to know. It wasn't supposed to bother her that the whole island could be crawling with ferocious fighting machines who butchered babies and did something worse to women. She wasn't sure just what could be worse than being butchered, having only heard the women servants or Sally and her friends whispering about it some-times. When they saw her, they would stop abruptly and tell her to go away, that she wasn't old enough to understand. Well she was fourteen now and couldn't think what could be so terrible that she was not old enough to hear. Her imagination

49

supplied what her information lacked and she lived in cringing dread, moment by moment, that the Japanese would overrun them and she would find out the worst.

No-one else seemed aware of her pale face and strained, jerky movements as she sought to keep her fear in check. Not even Billy. He seemed too preoccupied with his own worries, and with teaching Emma to read. She was five now and still slow with her alphabet, Ursula thought. It was hard not to think the child stupid at times, but then Sally was always taking her away from her lessons to show her off to her friends and then letting Emma sit with them for hours afterwards when she should have been back with Billy learning her alphabet. Billy often grew frustrated with this behaviour but he didn't say anything. That had surprised Ursula because she had expected him to say his mind. He often had where she was concerned. But then, soon after that party, that dreadful party and that dreadful Mrs Sunderland, Billy had stopped saying anything very much at all except 'Yes, Mrs Fraser' and 'No, Mrs Fraser' and 'Whatever you say, Mrs Fraser', and Sally had given him hard, nasty looks where before she had smiled and charmed. She had tried to get Papa to dismiss him for silly, petty things that made Ursula want to scream and rage at her. But Ursula was old enough now to understand better. Sally had wanted Billy for herself. If Mrs Sunderland had succeeded . . . Ursula felt sick at the thought. She had never mentioned it to Billy, and never would; he was still her rock and he still loved her best. He didn't need to know that she still remembered.

Sometimes now she didn't see Billy for days at a time. He arrived to teach Emma after she had left for the day school she attended, and then he would be gone before she returned in the afternoon. It didn't change how they cared for each other but it left her lonely in the long evenings when she had been sent upstairs and Papa and Sally entertained their friends below. And now there were the Japanese to worry about too.

No, the only joy in her life now, apart from Billy's constancy, was baby Tom. He was two and a half almost and large with it, toddling about the rambling bungalow in Ursula's hand with a confidence that never failed to amuse people. There was nothing that frightened him; there was no-one who did not love him. He reminded her of herself before Sally came. Only nothing was going to snatch away her love from him the way Papa's had been snatched from her. She would always be there for little Tom and he knew it. But right now he and Emma were downstairs with Fatimah eating and Ursula felt at a loss to know what to do with herself. She felt churned up and sick at the thought of food.

She threw herself down in the papa san and picked up a copy of Punch to fan herself with. Outside a torrent of rain slid over the eaves and down to the ground in a sheet of water. It gouged deep holes in the flower beds around the house and deadened all sound so that people had to keep asking for things to be repeated. She hated the Wet; everything smelled of mould and felt damp to the touch. There was no end to it for weeks and weeks and the polo field was out of bounds to her because the ground was so damp and the horses' hooves churned it up and spoiled the turf. Papa was President this year and strictly enforced the rules. She sighed crossly. Emma had Bintang now, but he was old and grown fat and Emma didn't like to ride much anyway. It frightened her unless someone led her pony and walked along beside her. And Bintang would be too old by the time Tom was ready. Papa would retire the poor old thing pretty soon. Ursula had a neat bay that she had named Jambang because of the whiskers that grew wildly out of the mare's nostrils. They were both shy and skittish and Billy said he thought they suited each other well. But now there would be no more riding until the rain let up unless she wanted to plod around in circles in the covered ring.

The sound of another car arriving diverted her dreary thoughts and sent her rushing to the stairs to peer down through the banisters to see who had arrived. She recognized the voices even before she saw the bottom halves of the Wrights appear below her, liking the way Mrs Wright's skirts swirled out around her instead of hanging straight and stylishly like Sally's. Mrs Wright was nice. She wasn't worried about being fashionable or the leading light in the social rounds; she was just comfortably fat and motherly and doted on her husband in a way that Sally thought silly. Still, they were obviously a happy couple even if rumour had it that Mr Wright liked to drink a bit too much at parties and whisper into other wives'

51

ears. Or so Sally had said once when Papa had said how refreshing it was to see a husband and wife who still loved each other so much after nearly fifteen years of marriage.

'Harry, dear, are we the first? How awful of us. I am sorry but our syce always thinks he has to get us places in record times. I'm sure he's getting in practice for a career as a racing driver. Is Sally upstairs? Shall I go up and see if I can help her at all?'

'Nonsense, Joan. Don't apologize. I was dying for someone to arrive so I had an excuse to fix myself another drink. Sally'll be right down. What'll it be, Bob? Joan?'.

'A stengah I think. Might as well stick to the same poison until the rest arrive. Joan, darling, do you want a gimlet or are you abstaining like the sensible girl you always are.' Bob Wright was a tall, painfully thin man with a habitual stoop as though he were leaning down from Mount Olympus to hear your thoughts. He wore glassses and was supposed to be a ferocious polo player but looking at him it was hard to believe. He eyed his wife indulgently when she snorted and tossed too tightly curled hair around a plump face.

'Ha! A gimlet Harry and a strong one. After what we heard at the Fergusons' I, for one, need a stiff drink. My God, Harry, I can't believe it. In what, two weeks, the Japs have bombed us, landed their troops on the peninsula, captured the airfield at Kota Bahru, sunk the two best ships we had . . . '

'Yes, that was a bit of a jolt, I'm afraid, losing the Prince of Wales and the Repulse. When I heard it on the wireless . . . '

'And now they're swarming over the mountains and down the west coat of the peninsula with tanks! I mean, whoever thought tanks could go through that sort of terrain!'

Ursula felt a wave of nausea shudder through her. This was worse than she had expected. She could hear her father making noises of dismissal but, for once, someone with facts was talking him down. If the Wrights were alarmed then surely Papa ought to listen. They were sensible, level-headed sorts. He often thought Mr Wright gave good speeches at the Tanglin Club. So why was he being so obstinate now? She edged down the stairs a few steps to hear better, knowing that they had gone into her father's study. He kept the drinks there and no matter how grand and beautiful Sally made the drawing room, sooner or later all the guests ended up in Papa's study.

She could hear Mrs Wright saying something in her forthright way.

'. . . like an ostrich, Harry. Really, I think you've got to face facts. We could be bombed again at any moment and you are rather remote out here. Worse still you've got the MacRitchie Reservoir and the broadcasting station just down the road. Charbier's pulling out, you know. Taking his family back to France until it's all over. And he only lives up the road. Lord knows what could happen to Sally and the children if the Japs were to actually make it to Singapore and you were down-town in your precious godowns at the time.' Papa was laughing, ridiculing what Mrs Wright was saying in the way that most of the men did. No little yellow man was ever going to get past the might of British steel. He didn't mention the fact that all the island's defences were facing out, towards the sea, and there were none at all to protect the rear approach, from down the Malay peninsula. Perhaps he never thought about it. But Ursula had heard the excuses and hyperbole so many times that it was an effort now not to cry. Why couldn't they leave, even if it was just for a while?

'Oh well, you know the French. And Charbier's always been a bit of a fusspot. That sort of defeatist talk is a menace, Joan. You shouldn't let the women get panicked, Bob. People will think you're getting windy yourself. Good Lord, think how bad it would be for morale if the natives thought we were scared. We've got to keep the flag waving and show them what we're made of.'

'I say, Harry. I resent that remark about me being windy. I can't help it if the ladies aren't too happy about the way the war's going. It wasn't me who told them that half of the tin mines and about a sixth of the rubber plantations up country are in enemy hands. God! I'm sick of hearing about it. D'you know they're saying Kuantan's fallen?' Ursula heard a muffled shriek from behind her and realized that Sally had slid out of her room to listen. Now she ran past Ursula, down the stairs, and into the study.

'Kuantan! But that's only a hundred miles away!' Sally wailed to the three rather surprised people standing with drinks in their hands.

'Well, yes, but I say, steady on Sally girl. That's just a

53

rumour and anyway, it's nearer a hundred and forty miles away in my book. There's nothing to worry about. They'll never get past the British and Australian troops and even if they did they'd never make it through Johore or across the straits. You're fussing needlessly, my dear.' Bob's attempt at reassurance did not have the expected effect. Sally stamped her foot and contradicted him furiously.

'Oh, you men! You . . . you make me sick! Can't you get it through your dense little imperialist minds that they're going to keep coming and coming – whether you think the fleet or the RAF or your precious army can handle them or not? These aren't just little yellow men out for a Sunday picnic! They're crack troops! And they're used to jungle terrain with tanks and bombs and nothing . . . nothing! . . . is going to stop them, especially not a bunch of outdated old fools playing at Empire who can't even coordinate their own defence. Charbier's right. We should be getting out of here.'

There was a shocked silence while Sally panted for self-control. She hadn't meant to make such a scene but something had suddenly snapped inside her when she looked into Bob Wright's stupid, patronizing face. He now looked like an affronted sheep, she thought. Fraser had gone a deep brick-red and was gazing reproachfully at his wife as though she had just taken off her dress and danced naked on the table. He would probably have preferred her to have done so rather than cracked in front of friends, people to whom keeping one's back straight and one's chin up was of paramount importance. Let the Japanese come. But don't, ever, let the side down. He cleared his throat.

'I don't think Brooke-Popham or Sir Miles would appreciate that last remark my dear. Now what can I get you to drink?' He smiled a thin, tight smile that seemed to say that he could, and would, control any further hysterics if she did not get a hold of herself. Sally turned on her heel and walked past the Wrights who were standing in embarrassed silence. She continued back up the stairs, not looking at Ursula who was staring blankly at the dark wood floorboards, and went into her room, closing the door softly behind her. Downstairs Ursula heard her father apologizing for his wife's behaviour. Probably that time of the month, you know. Rather flighty at the best of times, I'm afraid, not having been brought up in England. The Aussies were good sorts but didn't always teach their women the right way to behave in trying times. Mustn't think she really means it. Ursula leaned her head against the banisters and closed her eyes tightly.

The rest of the guests began to arrive soon after that. Rodney and Stephen Hendricks were back again from school and had joined their parents for the lunch. They were seventeen and fifteen now respectively, proud of their status as sixth and fifth formers at school and determined to let Ursula know it. She nodded impatient greetings. Her mind was elsewhere. Maybe she could get her Papa alone for just a few minutes; maybe he would listen to her if she were to plead with him? She never normally spoke of anything personal to him anymore. What did it matter to him if she could do logarithms or knew who Henry V was. He would just smile absently over yet another Tiger beer. Yes dear? That's wonderful. I'm proud of you. But it didn't go in anymore. He didn't feel that old pride in her achievements. Now she was just one more minor irritation in his life, acknowledged, accepted but not . . . not the way it had been before Sally. Everything personal between them had gone on that day on the verandah when she first met Sally. But surely he would listen to her now if she were to really . . . Rodney broke across her thoughts, handing her a glass of champagne and orange juice.

'Here.' He leaned down and gave her an awkward snatched kiss on her cheek, his normally assured face losing a little confidence. He coughed. 'Special treat for Christmas. Don't tell.' He winked, watching her wrinkle her nose suspiciously as she sipped at the juice. She took another sip, larger this time and looked up at him in surprise.

'Nice! Papa won't let me have any until I'm seventeen, he says. Says I won't like it anyway until I'm older. If any of us ever last that long.' Ursula sighed, taking a gulp this time. 'He won't listen to the Wrights you know, or to Sally. Thinks we're safe as houses.'

'But we are! Don't be silly, Ursula. You're only a child so you don't understand but I'm training in military tactics and I'm telling you, no truly, don't look like that. It's ridiculous the fuss everyone's making. The bloody nips aren't going to get

55

anywhere near here. Hey, why're you looking so tense? Have you been sitting here like some old woman worrying your little head off. It's just plain silly . . . ' He smiled that old mocking smile of his that once annoyed her enough to bite his hand, hard, between the thumb and forefinger. The scar was still there. 'Oh, never mind, you wouldn't understand anyway. But I promise you . . . '

'Shut up, Rodney! I don't want to hear it. Just shut up! I get enough of that guff from Papa as it is. What do you know about it anyway!'

'I know a hell of a lot more than you do Miss High and Mighty. And we're not going to lose Singapore. That's final. It's my home and it's yours too. I'd've thought that would matter to you. What're you going to do? Just run away and hand it over to them? What about Fatimah and her family? Or Ah Jong? Or Mr Billing?' He stopped at the stricken look on her face. 'Sorry but that's how it strikes me. I won't leave here.' He shrugged and wandered off to talk to someone else. Ursula gulped down the rest of her champagne in one and took a deep breath. Maybe Rodney was right? And what would happen to Billy and the others?

She smiled automatically when Joan Wright came over to her and the conversation shifted to more mundane matters: who was taking over the Carlyle's place now that old Jonathan was dead; what Valerie was going to do now that her husband had lost his job for the third time 'and really one can't totally sympathize with her when she's always letting one know how superior her husband and lifestyle is. This should bring her down a peg or two . . . ' and where people were going for their home leave. That last topic alone had been keeping the expatriate community occupied for years, ever since it became possible to go home on yearly leaves. Home was England, of course. That was understood even by the French and the Dutch who were notorious for not understanding the simplest things. When an expatriate said 'Home' it meant the sceptred isle, red double-decker buses, Lyon's ice cream, cricket, and the King. It was traditional to sing a rousing chorus of 'There'll Always Be an England' while sitting around drinking toasts of champagne and everyone felt their eyes grow moist when they let rip with the final refrain:

56

There'll always be an England,
And England will be free,
If England means as much to you,
As England means to me.

Ursula wondered if they would ever sit around and sing 'there'll always be a Singapore . . . ' Maybe there wouldn't. And then where would they all go? This was home and they might be going to lose it. Maybe Rodney, arrogant, annoying Rodney was actually right. It was better to stay and try and keep something that meant that much to them all, even if they lost their lives doing it, than to just walk away. Walk away to where anyway? Ursula looked around the room with its familiar photographs, ornaments, furniture. This was home. And if she left, maybe she would become one of those painted birds she and Billy had once joked about. Wooden.

Sally came down again a little later and smiled her way tightly through the subsequent renditions of Auld Lang Syne and God Save The King, checking on Ah Jong's preparations for tiffin and gracefully contributing to whichever conversation addressed itself to her. She never mentioned the Japanese to her husband again, pretending instead, if he brought the subject up, to be quite deaf. Fraser preferred it that way and soon didn't mention the subject either.

Days passed, dragging out endlessly with the added free time of the holidays. And Ursula continued to fret silently, her pale face growing paler for lack of any real knowledge.

The heat was unbearably bad that year, stifling and suffocating, draining energy from even the most experienced Europeans, sapping the will to face up to facts and make a decision. If the war council chiefs couldn't do it, it was not surprising that Harry Fraser, never a man to think too hard about unpleasant facts, couldn't manage it either. He just continued to go to the office in Singapore City every day, take lunch either at the Cricket Club or Raffles, and then drive home to long, leisurely drinks on the verandah, dinner, perhaps a game of cards or billiards, and then bed. He thought his wife was sulking because she had made a fool of herself and the other wives were bound to be gossiping about it. Just a smile, a hand movement, a nod could shred a reputation out here in the East as ruthlessly as published libel. Most of the women had signed up as volunteer nurses anyway and he wished she would too. Maybe bandage rolling would take her mind off things, and show to the others she was just as plucky as they were. But then, that was the problem. Sally couldn't seem to grasp how important it was to set a good example to the natives and other Europeans at times like this. She wasn't really mem quality at all and now was the point at which that quality was put to the test. So she sulked and he took to dining alone in his study most nights. He had to hand it to his eldest daughter though. She had never said a word about the yellow peril. She knew how to behave. Never show the fear; bad for morale.

That was what was really bothering Fraser, of course. The fact that his wife, of all the wives, was not showing at all well. Other wives were refusing point blank to even think of leaving the island, knowing full well what a loss of face it would involve for the whites if they were to desert the natives and Eurasians just because of a threatened invasion. The Chinese and Malay volunteer nurses were looking to the memsahibs to stay and show them it would all be all right. And his wife wanted out on the first boat available! It galled him deeply. Fraser was capable of great personal charm socially; he embodied the gruff, genial Britisher with a heart of gold – an image the British had been selling abroad for years with considerable success. But he was also a weak man, and like all weak men he had a blind wilful streak that, once tapped, refused without any further consideration of the subject to allow his wife to desert her post. He was a man of peculiar stubbornness and so, even when reality contradicted him and some of the other wives actually did begin to leave with their children, he still resolutely demanded Sally's presence beside him. And if Sally stayed so did the children.

All through January, with the bombs from the Japanese planes raining down on the city of Singapore, the matter of evacuation was a silent battle of nerves between husband and wife. By January first the Japanese had crossed the Slim River; by the eleventh, Kuala Lumpur was taken. The middle of January brought the enemy to the borders of Johore on the west side of the peninsula and down as far as Mersing on the East.

By the last day of January the Japanese had taken Kota Tinggi and were encamped outside Johore Bahru just the other side of the causeway. The enemy was literally at the door and on the first of February the civilian community of Singapore awoke to find itself under siege.

Fraser continued to bluster, along with a great many of the remaining Tuans, that the island was secure now that the causeway had been blown up and a good sized 'moat' surrounded them. There was six months' supply of food in the big food dumps that had been created at the Capital and Pavilion cinemas and, just across Adam Road, a large dairy herd could be seen complacently grazing on what was once the golf course. There would be no shortage of milk – or water either. Why, the three reservoirs on the island were capable of supplying them with seventeen million gallons of water a day! That was far more than they would need. No, they were sitting pretty.

As if to add to the illusion, the weather suddenly took a change for the better, the rain clouds rolling away as the last of the North-East monsoon blew itself out and the humidity dropping to an almost pleasant level. People's spirits rose in spite of the new threat of shelling from the mainland, and there was a new sense of camaraderie that congratulated them on having stuck it out so far. The thing was just not to panic. The white man could show the Asian a thing or two yet! And, apart from the shelling, it was very quiet outside the city. Mount Pleasant cut between the Thomson road and Adam road on the outer side of Bukit Timah. It was an isolated place to live but Fraser preferred to have room to spread out. During the first week of February there was still almost no change in their style of living. Of course he was on a volunteer fire-fighting brigade and often was called out to deal with fires in the woodland and Bukit Timah areas, but nothing came very near them at Mount Pleasant, for all the black-out curtains they had hung and the mattresses they had piled around the dining-room table, just in case.

Sally didn't get in to the city at all during that time. She was too frightened of being bombed or strafed by the zeroes that the Japanese were now flying down Orchard Road as though it were a duck shoot. Instead she had a provisioner, who delivered food, come out to the house and she had stocked up long before with medicines, bandages, and anything else her tortured imagination could suggest. She was reminded forcibly of that first conversation she and Harry had had about chits when the provisioner refused to take anything but cash. And still Harry Fraser would not budge. Now Sally just sat listlessly, day after day, on the verandah with a glass of lime juice in her hand and a sour expression on her face. She couldn't help it. The fear of what the Japanese would do to her if they got across the causeway left her almost paralysed. She had even given up wearing make-up, or putting up her hair, letting it hang limply around her washed-out face, oblivious to Fraser's looks of contempt or the children's attempts to catch her attention. Ursula she didn't see at all.

On the night of February eighth they were woken by the sound of heavy artillery fire coming from the north-west. It sounded to Sally as though hell had broken loose and she cowered under the covers, hating the sound of the AA guns with a sudden fierce passion. She had had enough. It was more than a woman could be expected to stand, particularly a woman with small children. Tomorrow, no matter what, she would book a passage on any boat available. She didn't care what Harry said. She wouldn't even tell him. That would teach him! All she wanted to see was Rottnest Island and the approach to Fremantle again. And never would she leave Perth, for anyone, ever again. If she lived that long, she added to herself, convinced the Japanese would come pounding on the door with their bayonets at any moment. It was a long night for Sally.

Ursula also spent a sleepless night shivering and holding Tom tightly in her arms. Fatimah had taken little Emma and she had Tom. He rolled against her, his body fitting into the hollow where the bed sagged and his smooth baby cheeks were flushed with sleep. She counted the fingers on one limp hand, holding them against her lips and blowing. He didn't stir. His head lolled heavily in deep sleep and she nuzzled his soft, silky hair. How he could sleep through this barrage, she didn't know. But his eyelashes didn't as much as twitch. It didn't occur to her that Sally would want him. She knew how scared Sally was all the time now; so scared she could barely talk, or if

60

she did it was to scream at the children to leave her in peace. Ursula didn't understand how she could be so wrapped up in herself that the children didn't matter to her anymore. But then, it was hard for Ursula to realize that Sally's fear was bound up in the children as much as in herself. She was responsible for them and they were in desperate danger. The resulting anger was not directed at the children so much as at herself – and at Fraser. But to Ursula it just seemed as though Sally were rejecting the children and so she had to take over in Sally's place. That was easy where Tom was concerned. He already regarded her as his mother, turning to her with cuts that needed kissing and a nose that constantly needed blowing. He had caught a chill during the last days of the Wet and nothing seemed to be able to lift it at the moment. She touched his brow gently. It seemed warm. But he was a strong boy and Ursula wasn't worried. Not about that, anyway.

What was worrying her was where Billy had got to lately. He hadn't been by the bungalow in three days and there had been no reply from the number he had given Sally as his home. Where could he be? Surely he wouldn't desert them – her – when the Japs were coming? And they were coming, regardless of what Papa said. Lord, she could hear them just across the straits. Papa had to be crazy if he thought they weren't going to come here and murder them all in their beds. Ursula just knew that was what was going to happen. Even Fatimah had told her so. Some of the servants had left already, melting away in the night to their kampongs where they hoped they would be safer than in a Tuan's household. Ursula was sure they were right, and would have liked to have picked baby Tom up and followed the servants back to their homes. But that wasn't possible, so instead she had to pretend that nothing was happening and that she knew everything would be all right. She was a Fraser and a missysahib. She knew how she had to behave even if Sally didn't.

When they gathered around the breakfast table the next morning Ursula noticed that only Fatimah and Ibrahim and her old playmate, Yahyah, were left. Even Ah Jong was gone. Breakfast was a silent affair of discreet scrapes and chinks as silver hit china and the rustling of the newspaper as it was turned, tempered by Sally breaking into nervous sobs and

61

then, throwing down her napkin and pushing back her chair, leaving the table to run back upstairs. Fraser ignored her and carried on spooning the chilled and sugared slices of papaya into his mouth with monotonous regularity. He was still reading the paper, trying to work out what, if anything, had happened last night but there was nothing but the usual bland assurances and carefully worded communiqués put out by the military: 'offensive action is being taken to mop up the enemy.' Well that was hardly news to anyone, he thought unhappily. Maybe he should pull a few strings and try and find out how the situation really stood? He could give Bob a call perhaps? He should know. He was pretty high up now in the Army.

Ursula noticed her father's crinkled brow and the lines of worry that were biting deep into the crevices around his nose. Even his moustache seemed to be drooping. She was dismayed. If Papa was in gloom, there was no chance left at all. They would all be killed. It was what happened in wars. But she was only fourteen; she hadn't had a chance to live her life. And what about Tom and Emma? Would the Japs really kill little babies? She felt the pain of deep fear and depression working on the muscles of her stomach and throat and had to leave the table abruptly to walk outside and be sick. Her father found her kneeling in the dirt below the verandah, retching into a flower bed with arching convulsions racking her body. For the first time he noticed how thin she had become, and how pale. He put his hand on her shoulder but she didn't, couldn't, look up, continuing instead to shake and retch.

'Are you going to be all right, Ursula?' her father asked after a few moments' silence. Ironic really, she thought, that he could actually ask such a question. He saw her nod her head and then lean over the flower bed again. He left her there and went in search of Fatimah to send to the child. There was nothing he could do for her anyway.

The realization of how serious things had become hit him, like walking out of the shade into the blast of the midday sun. And for the same reason that Ursula was being sick, he became silently and deeply angry. Angry both at the Japanese for making their lives so difficult and at the government for not telling them the true story and giving them time to get out. He never once considered that he was to blame; that he should have made it his business to find out and make sure his wife and children were safely away before things even began to look nasty. No, it was the enemy and the bureaucracy that had fouled things up. They were at fault. And, by God, they were going to pay!

Chapter Four

When Ursula finally had the strength to look up from the dirt she found herself alone. Inside she could hear her Papa bellowing for Fatimah but right now she didn't want her amah. She didn't want anyone, except maybe Billy. She rocked back on her haunches and, using the verandah pillar to steady herself, stood up. Her head swam and she felt bile flood warm and bitter into her mouth. The sides of her tongue curled as the fluid rushed in and she leant forward to spit into the flower bed again. This would never do. Fatimah would be there at any moment, crooning in her soft Malay, wanting to hug her against her large, soft body. The thought was suffocating. Ursula straightened herself, blinked a couple of times as her vision blurred, and then made a determined effort to reach the far side of the bungalow where the jungle grew closest. It would be dark and cool in there and she could sit in her favourite spot and lean her head against the tree trunk.

Ursula made her way across the driveway noting, in the way one does when feeling sick, every crack and tuft of grass in the cement and earth. Her head felt balloon-sized and heavy, threatening to snap her neck with each footstep. She smelled the drains, full with the last of the rains, and her stomach quivered uneasily. But then she was over the series of cement channels, cut to let the water run away, and moving more easily across the newly-hardening lawn. The sun flashed harsh into her eyes but was soon hidden by the bamboo as she squeezed in behind it and climbed into her hiding place. This was where she came to think, to avoid Sally's sharp voice or Fatimah's gentle nagging. She had never shown anyone it, except Tom. But he would get bored and restless very easily and want to run out and play on the grass in the sun, so she didn't bring him too often. She knew Billy suspected where she went but he never mentioned it and something had always kept her from volunteering the information. This was her place, her special nook where she could be anyone and do anything. The undergrowth was beaten flat where she liked to sit, and the thickness of the tree trunk behind her made an effective barrier against the jungle. There were bird's nest ferns and orchids growing wild down the trunk and, with the bamboo in front, it was like being in a pale green cavern cut by slivers of sunlight.

Ursula knew her Papa would be angry if he thought she went into the jungle. There were snakes and poisonous insects, not to mention rats and monkeys; but this wasn't really the jungle proper, just the fringes of it. And Ursula was used to it. She knew how to take care of herself. But with the Japanese coming, things were all different now. She might have to take Tom and hide in earnest. People said the Japanese were like cats and could see in the dark. Would they be able to find her here? The thought made her shiver and then her head hurt and she felt sick again.

'Damn Papa! Damn him, damn him, damn him!' She hissed furiously into the ferns, half-awed that nothing had happened to her despite her swearing, half-afraid that her Papa actually would be damned. That was the problem with life. You never knew where you stood. Half the things they told you weren't true at all, and the rest was all distorted. Maybe there wasn't a God at all and things just happened by accident. And why they didn't think she had rights too – why she shouldn't be given a choice about where she wanted to be and what she thought might happen – it made her so angry that she could finally understand why people talked about seeing red. Her vision really did blur and her head felt ready to burst with frustration and rage . . . and fear, always that fear.

She lay her face against the bark, feeling it cool and hard under her cheekbone. With one hand she lifted her hair, twisting it up and away from her neck. There was no breeze to dry the perspiration but it felt cooler with her hair up. An ant was climbing the shaft of bamboo nearest her, a red ant, and she hummed a tune that Fatimah had taught her, adding the words as she remembered them:

> *Kerengga di-dalam buloh*
> *Serahi berisi ayer mawar*
> *Sampai hasrat di-dalam tuboh*
> *Tuan sa-orang jadi penawar.*

She knew the feeling of a red ant bite and repeated the refrain over and over, growing tuneless and finally chanting in a harsh dirge while tears gathered on her eyelashes:

> Red ants in a bamboo! the passion
> That tortures my frame is like you;
> But like the flask of rose-water in fashion
> Is the cure my dear flame can bestow.

'My dear flame . . . Oh, Billy, where are you? Don't you know how scared we all are? Why won't you come?' She was sobbing now, hearing but choosing to ignore her father's and Fatimah's calls, and instead closing her eyes and hugging her knees to her chest. Billy wouldn't desert her. He couldn't! He loved her. She knew that very well. No, he was just busy, caught up in the volunteer forces maybe. He would come if things really got serious. The step-by-step progression of her thoughts calmed her and she stopped crying. It was all all right still. Billy would come and take her and Tom away and they would be safe. Papa wouldn't come and, anyway, he would have to look after Sally and Emma. Fatimah and her family could just go back to the kampong. They'd be fine. No, she would go and live with Billy and be his wife and Tom would be their baby. It could all still work out. She leaned her head back against the tree, lifting her face to catch a shaft of light filtering through the bamboo. There was a dreamy smile on her lips.

Out on the lawn Harry Fraser was scowling furiously across the gardens, feeling the sun biting into his shoulders and back through his thin silk shirt. He was fed up with women. If it wasn't Sally having hysterics then it was Ursula bringing up her breakfast and slinking off God knew where! Bloody females! Well, he couldn't wait any longer for her to appear. He was sure she could hear him but was just being difficult. And here he was standing around in the blazing sun when he should be trying to deal with two godowns full of rubber that he had to stop falling into Japanese hands. It was enough to try the patience of a saint! It crossed Fraser's mind briefly that he should have a go at making sure his wife and children didn't fall into Japanese hands either but the effort of trying to round them up, and locate some means of transport for them was too much to think about right now. He'd give Sally a call that afternoon and tell her to start packing, maybe . . .

But by the time he got to the office and had heard the horror stories of people trying to get tickets out on the last boats, and the scenes at the docks with people fighting for a place, Fraser had changed his mind. His family was safer staying on the island than in joining the panic to get away. So he didn't call Sally after all.

Sally, on the other hand, wasn't about to give up that easily. She knew a lot of people, the useful sorts who often knew things they shouldn't know, and she decided now was the time to call in a few favours. So, while Fraser was busy in his office, Sally was even busier on the phone. It astonished her that with all the bombing and panic, the telephone lines were still open but open they were and she made good use of them. By late afternoon she had a promise of three places aboard the Vyner Brooke, leaving in three days time. It wasn't what she wanted but P&O had been flooded by calls and refused to discuss tickets on the telephone, ordering her instead to come down and queue with all the rest of the women. Since those women were regularly being strafed by enemy aircraft while they patiently and doggedly waited in line, Sally had cut short the conversation and racked her brains to think who else she might call.

Ivan had eventually sprung to mind and though it had been difficult tracking him down and even more difficult convincing him that he owed her, Sally had prevailed. Ivan Tarbuck was the sort of expatriate bachelor who always attached himself to the most attractive married women around. Sally had flirted gently with him in the past, fending off his too-pressing invitations to come waterskiing, or to take tea. In the past her reputation had mattered more than the sudden flutter in her stomach that he could provoke. There had been affairs, yes, but only with discreet married men. Ivan wasn't the sort one could be discreet with. Too many other women were watching him, wondering, hoping. Now, Sally knew from the tone of his voice that he expected payment in full for what had only been an empty promise before. For a moment she hesitated, but only for a moment. What did it matter now? Ivan was young and attractive, and he could save her life. Her voice grew husky over the telephone as she agreed to come over and pick up her tickets at his flat in Tanglin.

It was only after she hung up that it occurred to her that neither Emma nor Tom had passports. More frantic calling unearthed an embassy attaché who promised to add them to her own passport if she could get it down to him by that afternoon. The thought terrified Sally but the Japanese terrified her more and so, calling for Ibrahim, Sally drove into town.

With the children's documentation safely taken care of, Sally told Ibrahim to drive to Nassim Hill. She climbed out in front of an apartment block, Ibrahim holding the door for her with an impassive face. She didn't care what he thought. She just wanted those tickets. With a curt voice betraying her nervousness, Sally told Ibrahim to come back in an hour and wait outside until she came down. Then she walked slowly across the gardens and up to Ivan's door. Her breath was fluttering uncertainly so that she felt faint. She stopped and smoothed the dress down over her hips, feeling the firm body beneath. It gave her courage. Whatever else happened, Ivan would not be disappointed by her body. She raised her gloved hand and knocked twice, very firmly.

Ivan must have been standing by the door because he answered it immediately. His face was smooth but there was a light of triumph, almost power in his eyes. Sally tilted her head to one side and smiled.

'Hallo, Ivan. It's been a while. You're looking well.' Her voice was deep in her throat, adding resonance to her words. She saw him smile, the teeth white and gleaming beneath his dark, clipped moustache. It would all be all right. She could tell.

'Sally, darling. I'd almost decided you weren't coming. Something delay you?'

'Passports for the children.' She shrugged delicately. 'I'm sorry, these things take longer than I expected. You weren't too impatient, I hope?'

'Frantic's more like it,' he said but so languidly that it almost made a mockery of his words. He leaned down and kissed her hand, sliding his arm up along her forearm to behind her elbow. Then he steered her into his flat and closed the door.

Sally had never been there before and she was surprised by the way he had decorated his place. It wasn't just exotic, it was more like a garden of delight with ferns and plants everywhere, pillows strewn across the floor, a low ottoman, an opium bed with red and gold hangings, and a table with food set out on it beside the bed. She looked at Ivan and raised her beautifully arched eyebrows.

'For me?' He laughed and slid an arm around her waist, his hand sliding up her side to brush so gently across her breast, it could almost have seemed an accident. Sally shivered and turned her head to look at Ivan. It was a long look between two people who knew exactly what they were doing. Ivan smiled, his eyes dark and shining. He didn't say anything but kissed her lips, biting her lower lip between his teeth until he felt it swell against his own. His hands were so skilful, Sally thought, half-dazed by sensations she had begun to forget existed. Why had she resisted him so long? For Harry? For her reputation? She laughed, a soft gurgle of intaken breath as his hands moved across her stomach and around to cup her buttocks, pressing her tightly against him.

Ursula watched the car disappearing down the long drive in puzzlement. Where was Sally going? Surely if she had been too frightened to go shopping before, now was not the right time to do so? Ursula thought about going and asking Fatimah but changed her mind abruptly. She didn't care where Sally went as long as it was away from her. And Fatimah would scold her for not coming when she was called and then missing tiffin. No, it wasn't worth it. She would just nip in the back way and see what she could find to eat and then go back to her hiding-place. It was quiet and soothing there and no-one was crying or

69

screaming; there were no long silences in which Sally and Papa ignored each other; nor were there any interruptions from Emma who thought she was being cute. She would like to have little Tom with her to cuddle and make her feel better but he was lying down for his afternoon nap. No, until Billy came for her, it was best to stay out of the way.

That evening Ursula heard more arguing. She had been sent to bed early and would have been indignant if the tension in the air had not been so heavy and morose. Instead she was glad to be ordered up to her room, knowing that if she tiptoed carefully, avoiding the creaky spots, over to the far corner of the sitting room, she would be able to hear everything that was being said through the air-vents. It was an old trick of hers, more from the days when she wanted to know what Sally had in store for her than from recent years. Sally had rapidly grown indifferent and bored when Ursula had taken Billy's advice and shown no further tendencies to awkwardness. So now Ursula sat and shivered as she heard the stinging bite in Sally's voice and the rage in her father's. They were discussing the war for the first time that Ursula could remember since that dreadful Christmas day.

' . . . Don't tell me you can't! I'll find us places even if you won't!' That was Sally.

'Like hell you will!' Harry Fraser's voice was thick, almost indistinct with rage and perhaps drink. Ursula swallowed to ease the ache in the back of her throat and listened to her father's words with disbelief. 'No wife of mine is going to tell me what this family is going to do! Now I happened to be talking to some of the military wallahs this afternoon and I'll have you know that we're as safe as houses.' Ursula could almost see her father pointing his finger at Sally in that irritating way of his. 'Percival's got a plan to hold Singapore City, the airfield out at Kallang, the reservoirs out at Pierce and MacRitchie and the hill points commanding the whole Bukit Timah region. That leaves us safely inside the perimeter, in case you're not following me . . . '

'You're dead right I'm not following you. How can you possibly believe a thing they say when they've done nothing but lie and make false promises since this whole thing started. ''Percival's got a plan!'' Yes, and we all know what his plans

70

have done for us so far! You leave me speechless sometimes, Harry. Now you listen to me. We have small children here. If we're interned how do you think they're going to survive the disease, the lack of medical facilities – the lack of food, from all I've heard? I won't risk it. We have to get out while there's still time. For God's sake, Harry, you're not military, you're not in one of the crucial jobs! You could leave tomorrow if you wanted.'

'Nonsense. You're talking pure rubbish, woman. I'm needed here and that's all there is to it. Good Lord, you've got no idea of the sort of panic going on down at the docks. Why, you and the children would be crushed! No, you're much safer here.'

There was a dead tone to Sally's voice when she finally answered him: 'Is that your final word?'

'Yes, it is. Now I don't want to hear any more about it. Understood?'

'You know, Harry, the problem is I understand you far too well.' Ursula was surprised to hear Sally laugh. 'You really don't fool me at all, damn you! Well, fine, I won't mention this to you again, oh lord and master. Just don't come near me or say another word to me or I'll be sick. You can sleep down here or in the servants' quarters for all I care. You've done that often enough, God knows! Just leave me alone!'

Ursula had barely time to throw herself behind the rattan sofa before Sally came running up the stairs. She was surprisingly calm, Ursula thought. Not crying, not screaming – just a tight-lipped rage. Ursula kept her head down. The door slammed and silence followed, though downstairs the clink of glass against glass could be heard. What had Sally meant about Papa sleeping in the servants' quarters? Surely not? Ursula shivered and tried not to care. It would be all right when Billy came. She could wait. She returned to her bed, slipping in between the sheets and lying perfectly still for hours as a sort of penance for whatever she had done to keep Billy away. It must be her fault but she would make it up to him by being especially nice when he came back. With her eyes tightly closed she willed God to make Billy be there next morning. It was one of those special cases when she needed God's help and He knew she wouldn't ask if it weren't important. He had never failed her when she really asked. Billy would be there. She knew that. Her mind began to drift as sleep took over and she made a mental note to ask Papa where Sally had gone that afternoon. Eventually she fell asleep.

When Fatimah woke her the next morning, drawing back the mosquito netting and throwing it up over the hoop, Ursula was quite rested. She could tell from the angle of the sun through the chick blinds that it was later than usual. 'Did you oversleep, Fatimah?' she asked in some surprise. But her amah just muttered for Ursula to get up and wash herself, that she, Fatimah, was busy with many tasks and that Allah would see she had only one pair of hands and too many children to fill them, *la*! Ursula didn't argue, sensing Fatimah's displeasure was not directed at her personally but rather at life in general. As soon as possible she gathered some fruit and biscuits in her pockets and headed for her hiding-place. She took Tom with her for the morning. Fatimah wouldn't miss him; she would know he was with Ursula. And there was so little time left. Maybe all the time there would ever be for Ursula to hold Tom in her arms and play silly games with him, letting him wriggle when she blew against his tummy, teaching him how to count the toes on his little feet. Oh, it was so hard waiting! It seemed a long day, longer than usual with little to do once Tom had tottered off across the lawn to his lunch. Ursula had watched Fatimah come out and pick the little boy up, calling impatiently for Ursula. The woman waited briefly and then walked inside again. Ursula sighed with relief. Next time she went back to the house she must remember to pick up a couple of books to pass the time. It disturbed her that Billy had not appeared according to the agreement she had made with God last night. But perhaps she had been too specific by asking for that particular morning? Perhaps it was more a question of Billy turning up when the need arose? That seemed likely so she settled down to try and be patient.

She left the bamboo grove just as the sun was beginning to slide behind the trees, edging the gardens and casting long shadows over the lawn. She made her way carefully down the back of the servants' quarters, across the driveway and down the steps cut in the bank to the Polo ground. It was time to go see Jambang. She always tried to see her mare at least once a day, even if she couldn't exercise her. The padang was drier now and could probably have been used to put Jambang through her paces but, somehow, Ursula couldn't bring herself to go out there. It seemed so exposed, as though she were naked in front of the enemy. If they came while she was out on the field she wouldn't be able to hide in time. No, she must ask Yahyah to give the mare a few turns around the back paddocks or the poor thing would be going crazy pretty soon. She remembered once, when Papa hadn't ridden one of his horses for two days, that just as they crossed the cement bridge over the drainage channels, the horse had suddenly gone berserk and thrown Papa before charging off down Mount Pleasant Road and out onto Thomson Road – straight into the path of a lorry. The memory still made her sick.

It was a golden afternoon, the air still but vibrant with the beat of insect wings, papery whisking sounds that were drowned out by the harsh drilling noise of cicadas, and a bird as it shrilled warning. The air itself had a texture of silken warmth, a definite feel against Ursula's skin as she walked towards the stables. It was as though all her senses were especially alive, her mind telling her to make note of this moment, this hour because it would never come again. From the eaves of the tack-room a wind-bell beat lightly, its gong catching the faintest breaths, like heart pauses. Ursula hesitated, sensing something, someone, ahead of her in the shadows that barred the ground. She touched her tongue to her lips where they were dry and stepped closer, hearing the shuffling of hoofs within the stalls as the horses whisked at flies and moved restlessly. It smelled warm and close, horse-dung and straw, dust and sawdust mingling together with the sweetness of decay. Ursula peered into the first stall, surprised to see it empty. Normally Mr Wright's large gelding was there. The next one was empty too. She moved on, her sandals making no sound on the cement as she peered into one stall after another. With the exception of their own horses and two others, every stall was empty.

This was the worst blow so far; her fears confirmed by the blank walls and uneaten hay that gazed back at her. Where the other horses had gone she didn't know. Nor did it matter. What mattered was that they were gone. That other people had taken precautions, had got away in time. And they had left it too late. She felt her insides crumble away as she leaned against the post beside Jambang's stall. 'Oh God! We're done for now. It's all too late and we're still sitting around wondering what to do. Damn you, Papa!' This time she felt no fear of retribution. It didn't matter. They were all damned anyway. The sound of her voice made the mare prick up her ears and blow gently through her nostrils, waving the whiskers about wildly. Ursula stroked the velvety coat, running her fingers down Jambang's nose and under her chin where more whiskers sprouted. The mare stood quietly, sensing Ursula's bleak mood. 'We could have got away, Jambang. All of us, and you too. Now we'll either be murdered or locked away in cells and you'll be ridden by a little yellow man who'll beat you and prod you with his bayonet if you don't go fast enough. I'm sorry, Jambang, but it's all Papa's fault. Even Sally tried this time but he was just too pig-headed.' She put her arms around the mare's neck and nuzzled her face against Jambang's coat, smelling that special smell for one last time.

'Missy ride today?' The voice, coming as it did from right beside her, made Ursula jump and the mare shy away from the stall door. 'Missy ride now? Can do, *la*!' Yahyah's brown face beamed with pleasure. He had been hosing down the horses and, it seemed, himself at the same time. The water dripping from his body flashed as he shook himself, like a string of glass beads tossed in the air. Ursula swallowed with relief.

'Yahyah, you scared me. I thought it was one of the yellow peril come to get me. See, even Jambang's had a fright.' Her laugh was nervous. Yahyah smiled too, honey-eyed and straight-backed, oblivious to the imminent arrival of the enemy. He said softly: 'Jambang *seperti rusa masuk kampung*, shy like a deer entering a village, like you now, missy.' With his hand he reached over to the mare and soothed her with gentle, clicking noises. She accepted him calmly and stood still. Ursula sighed.

'Can you take her, Yahyah? Take her and Bintang and hide them from the Japanese? I don't want them to be mistreated.'

'*Can*, missy. Want I take now, *la*?'

'Yes. Right away. I don't think there's much time left for any of us.'

74

'Want I hide missy too?' His face was calm and matter-of-fact. He was her old play-mate and he cared about her still, despite the years during which they had gone different ways. Tears filled Ursula's eyes. Yahyah was offering to risk his life and the lives of all his kampong if she were found. And besides there was Tom – and Billy would come for her soon now. She touched his arm, knowing he wouldn't mind, knowing she meant it as a compliment. Most Malays didn't like to be touched, particularly never on the head. But Yahyah and she had been brother and sister long ago. He wouldn't mind. She forced a smile:

'No, Yahyah. I will be fine. Just the horses, if you can. Thank you.' She stroked Jambang again and then Bintang before nodding to the boy and leaving. She didn't look back at any of them but went quickly up the bank to the bungalow. Papa would be home by now and she wanted to talk to him.

There had been gunfire, on and off, through most of the day but for the moment everything was quiet. The bungalow stood serenely as it always had, surrounded by green lawns and colourful flower beds. For a moment Ursula wondered if she hadn't imagined everything; that it wasn't some unpleasant dream brought on by the heavy death-like sleep of the afternoon, when even the animals would lie as though felled by an axe, and only the European Tuan would make life difficult by continuing to work. She had fallen asleep in her airless little bamboo cavern and dreamed it all. And in a minute Ah Jong would shuffle out onto the verandah with drinks and she would sit and laugh about it with Billy. She looked up at the verandah, just to make sure. But it was empty.

Her father didn't come home that evening. He was out fighting fires. They could see the orange glow hanging in the night air over Thomson Village but that was all they could see. The firing resumed again, sounding closer and more continuous. Sally paced the wooden floorboards, back and forth, back and forth, her hands clenched together and working furiously as though she were literally wringing them. Every now and then she would stop abruptly and listen. Then she would continue to pace. Ursula grew tired of watching her, wishing passionately that the woman would sit down so that she could hear better the sounds of the night. To someone who had been born in the East there was nothing to fear in the noises of the jungle, the shriek of the howler monkey, the grunt of pigs, the strange clicking of insects. She could hear them, discount them, and listen only for the unusual, the footsteps that shouldn't be there, the car that had no right to be driving at night, the gunfire that seemed to be getting closer and closer. If only Sally would sit down and be still.

By midnight Ursula could no longer keep her eyes open. Sally hadn't thought to send her to bed and Fatimah was too busy with her own problems to interfere. Outside the sky was a deep purple, the waving fronds of the traveller palms etched black against it. They sighed with each breath of wind. Ursula, curled up in the papa san, closed her eyes on what was, for her, the last day of peace.

When she opened them Billy was there. She laughed. 'I suppose God got the day wrong,' she said sleepily when he sat down beside her and smiled at her.

'What day?'

'The day you were supposed to come back. I asked for you yesterday but God must have got mixed up. I expect He's rather busy right now.' She struggled into a sitting position and pushed the hair out of her face. Billy noticed how thin she had become.

'Yes, I imagine He is. Where's Mrs Fraser?' Billy was still smiling but there was something wrong in the way he was holding his head and neck. He looked tense and as though he were trying to hide it. Ursula shook her head.

'I don't know, Billy. Isn't she downstairs . . . or in the garden? Or maybe she's not up yet. We were waiting for Papa to come home and I must have fallen asleep. Sally never gets up very early anyway.' Ursula didn't like the way Billy looked so uneasy. He should be here to take care of things, not to make them worse! Her voice grew a little sharper: 'Have you checked everywhere, Billy?'

'Everywhere. And Emma and Tom are gone too. Are you sure she didn't mention anything to you?'

'No, of course not! What about Fatimah? Has the car gone? Is Ibrahim around?' Ursula had stood up and gone to the windows to look down at the driveway. She couldn't see if the car was there or not because of the covered porch.

'The car is gone, *cahayamata*.' Billy was still sitting and Ursula smiled automatically at the endearment. Light of his eyes. She felt the hard bubble building in her chest subside a little.

'Could they have gone into town? Without me?' she asked with difficulty. His eyes were soft and gentle, as always.

'Yes, I think your step-mother has left. She probably feels you are your father's responsibility, not hers. I have tried calling for Fatimah and Ibrahim but they have not come. I think they have left too.'

'Left me? Tom's gone? He can't be. I never said goodbye and anyway, Fatimah wouldn't leave me! She's my amah.' Ursula was indignant at the thought.

'Then where is she, Ursula? When I arrived there was no-one here but you, and I didn't wake you until I had looked very carefully for the others. Is your Papa at the office? Or out fire-fighting?'

'I don't know,' she hesitated, 'he didn't come home last night as far as I know. Where have you been, Billy? We haven't seen you in ages and you must have known I was worried. You could have called, or come round, or sent a message, or something! I've been scared silly!' She had come back to stand beside him and felt mean accusing him but couldn't seem to help it. All the fear was coming out in anger at him. 'You don't care about us anymore, do you? What've you been doing, Billy? Were you busy trying to find a safe place to hide. Well I've waited and waited for you. I thought you'd make everything all right. You'd take Tom and me away some-where safe. But Tom's gone, Billy. He's gone and so is everyone else and you haven't made things better. It's all worse and you don't seem to know what to do! Why don't you know what to do?' She was crying without realizing it and Billy looked so distressed that she couldn't help putting her arms around his neck and letting him hold her tight against him. He couldn't help things. It wasn't his fault. It was the Japs – and Papa, and Sally sneaking off with the children without waking her, or asking if she wanted to come too. But that was just like Sally. Selfish to the bone. Ursula hugged Billy tightly and said

77

she was sorry, several times in case he hadn't heard her or hadn't understood. He kissed her hair and let her go, standing away from her so abruptly that Ursula almost lost her balance. She tried not to mind.

'Can you call Papa's office? Maybe he's there,' she asked after a moment or two. Billy was standing by the window, seemingly lost in thought. He looked up at her voice but didn't say anything. Instead he examined her carefully, from head to toe. She was thin and delicately boned, so that would be no problem. And, thank the Lord, she had dark hair and eyes. With a little time in the sun and maybe some vegetable dye – yes, it might just be possible.

'Billy? Didn't you hear me? I said . . . ' The sound of the telephone ringing loudly in the study downstairs interrupted her and she sprang down the stairs after it. She was breathless when she picked up the phone.

'Hallo? Yes, it's me. Papa, Sally's gone and so are Tom and Em . . . ' She paused while her father cut across her angrily. Billy, who had followed Ursula downstairs, could hear Fraser's voice buzzing noisily while Ursula held the receiver a little further away from her ear. 'Yes, Papa. But Billy's here. I don't think he'll m . . . ' There was more loud buzzing and Ursula held the receiver out to Billy. She looked upset. 'He wants to talk to you.' She didn't stay to hear the rest but wandered aimlessly out onto the front verandah and sat on the door lintel. A few minutes later she heard the telephone ping as the receiver was replaced. Billy came and joined her, sitting down on the lintel with a clumsy grace that involved long arms and legs flailing wildly for a moment and then resettling into a calm order again. He sighed, lines appearing around his mouth where before there had been none. He couldn't be more than his late twenties, Ursula thought, but today he looks older.

'Papa wants me to go over to the Hendricks, Billy.' Ursula said when Billy didn't speak. 'I don't want to. Can't I wait here with you, instead?'

'Your Papa changed his mind when he discovered that I was here. He said you should wait here with me until he comes. I think he means to try and find Mrs Fraser and the children before they leave. Some friend of Mrs Fraser rang him to let him know what was being planned.'

'Carrie, I'll bet. She never did like Sally. Sweet as pie to her face and then a venomous old toad behind it. I can't think what Sally ever did to her.' That wasn't strictly true, Ursula thought. I do know what Sally did – and with Carrie's husband. But she couldn't say that, now could she?

'No, well . . . shall we try and find Fatimah? I would like to talk to her. She may be down at the kampong. The firing is getting very close, I think.' But Fatimah was not down at the kampong. She was out back trying to lock the silver into a large trunk she had dragged in from the outhouse. She started when Billy and Ursula walked in on her. Then she put her hands on her hips and frowned.

'Missy not gone! Mem gone, little missy, little tuan gone, why Missy not gone? Musoh come, very soon, *la*!'

'The enemy may be at the gate for all I know Fatimah, but Mem left without me. Billy and I wait for the Tuan,' Ursula explained, not making any comment about what her amah was about. She saw the old woman's face crumple up like a monkey's.

'No time, Missy. Must go now. I bury silver. Ibrahim go back to kampong when Mem take car. Mem say no more need – all go. Leave us here. No good.' Talking to Fatimah in English was difficult. Ursula switched into Malay. She couldn't think why Billy wasn't contributing anything to the conversation, but then, Billy seemed different somehow. As though half his mind were on something else, not their present predicament. She tried with Fatimah again:

'Where did you go this morning, Fatimah? Billy didn't find anyone here when he arrived, except me asleep upstairs. Why did you leave me?'

'The Mem said everyone would leave. We took Yahyah and all our belongings back to the kampong. I came back to hide the silver. I thought you were gone too, Missy.' This made much more sense, Ursula thought. Sally had just forgotten all about her; probably hadn't even seen her asleep and almost hidden in the papa san. Papa had forbidden Sally to leave but she had gone anyway, taking her children. Obviously she couldn't take her step-daughter without her husband's permission, and in the final panic to be away, she had forgotten to mention to Fatimah that Ursula was still here. Ursula nodded

79

and shrugged, a little embarrassed at being forgotten by every-one. But Fatimah understood and hugged her, stroking the shiny dark head and putting her cheek against the girl's. Ursula could hear Fatimah's stomach rumbling and smell the spiciness of her breath. She felt a surge of love suddenly for this woman. Fatimah wasn't even her mother but she cared more than all the rest. It was good to know someone cared. But that made her think of baby Tom and she had to swallow quickly. Beside them Billy began to stir restlessly and Ursula pulled away from her amah.

'What now, Billy?'

'Go and find something for us to eat. And maybe some lime juice if you can. I have not eaten in some time. Fatimah, come out here will you?' Clearly Billy had made up his mind about whatever was bothering him and was back to normal. Ursula turned and went into the kitchen quarters without another word.

She found a papaya and a couple of mangoes, some bread, butter, milk, and marmalade, and put it all onto a large tray with three knives and three spoons. She wasn't sure where Fatimah kept the napkins so just put a tea-towel on in case anyone got too messy. It wouldn't make any difference anyway. No-one would be coming back to clear up after them, except maybe the Japanese. There was a jug of lime juice in the ice-box and she added that and three glasses to the rest. All this took her quite a while as she had to hunt through nearly every cupboard and drawer to find what she wanted. Normally the kitchen was out-of-bounds. Of course she knew where the fruit was kept and the biscuits, but the rest had to be found the hard way. When at last the tray was ready, it was piled pre-cariously high and was far too heavy for her to carry. So she left it and went out to find Billy. He could carry it out to the verandah.

Out on the driveway Billy was talking to two men dressed in khaki uniforms. The taller of the two took off his hat and wiped his brow tiredly. They seemed rather cross but Billy was talking to them in his quiet, reasonable way. Fatimah was standing to one side looking stubborn. The men stopped talking abruptly when Ursula walked down the front steps and over to join them. They seemed nonplussed.

80

'Is this the girl?' one of them asked Billy, rather rudely Ursula thought. He nodded. The other man beckoned to Ursula and squatted down on his haunches as though he were about to talk to a child. Ursula was tall for her age and so was well above the man's head while he was in that position. He became aware of it almost immediately and straightened back up, smiling to hide his awkwardness. He clearly meant well. The other one said:

'We can't guarantee the safety of anyone this far out, let alone a child.' He sounded angry. Billy didn't say anything and the man who had smiled now put a hand on Ursula's shoulder: 'Your father's had a bit of an accident, I'm afraid. Had a nasty bump on the old head.' He laughed to take away the fear he saw spring into the child's eyes. 'I shouldn't wonder if he doesn't have a pretty beastly headache tomorrow. Probably be as grouchy as an old bear at having his nice, new car all scratched up.' He paused again, weighing up his words. 'We'll have to take you into Singapore City. Put you with some nice people until your father feels well enough to come and get you. You'd like that, wouldn't you? You don't want to stay out here all alone with the Japanese so close, do you?'

'I won't be alone. Billy and Fatimah are here. Besides, how would Papa be able to find me? Who are the people you want to put me with?' The officer was clearly surprised at how adult Ursula sounded. And how unafraid. He couldn't tell she was trembling inside, that every part of her was tense to the point of actual pain. All he saw was a very self-possessed young missysahib who wanted to know what was what before she decided anything. It threw him rather.

'Well, I say! You can't stay here with just your servants. They're good sorts but . . . ' he lowered his voice, ' . . . natives, not terribly reliable, you know. They might leave you all alone when the Japanese come.'

'I thought you were supposed to stop the Japs. Isn't it a little defeatist to talk that way?' Ursula was furious, insulted beyond belief that this tall, thin man with his pale, sweaty face could stand there and say such things about Billy and Fatimah. She was more than furious, she was sickened.

'Oh well, really, if that's your . . . '

'Simpson for God's sake stop trying to explain everything in

81

words of one syllable. The girl understands her position very well, I should think. And she has no choice in the matter anyway. She goes, now. Get on the radio and tell them to send transport. Obviously the car's gone. And you . . . ' the first officer turned to Billy, 'I'd tell this woman to get back to her kampong as fast as possible, and if I were you I'd high-tail it out of here. You're Eurasian, aren't you?' He barely waited for Billy to nod. 'Well, I'm sure you know the pleasant little tricks the Japs have in store for you if they catch you. Better get going. We're the last force between you and the enemy and I don't think we're going to last that long.'

'Who is in command of your force?'

'Brigadier Massy-Beresford. We're called "Massy Force", for all the good it'll do us. We'll try and keep the reservoir and broadcasting station for as long as we can. But that can't be much more than another twenty-four hours. Now you seem a sensible chap, so try and make the girl understand. All right?' He stopped for breath when the tall officer returned from his jeep.

'They're sending some transport over for the girl immediately. Should be here in about five minutes, I'd say. Potters want us over at the golf-course a.s.a.p. They're cut off at the end of Sime Road, he said.'

'Right. We'll be off then. You wait here.' He turned to Ursula. 'They'll be along in a minute. Cheerio.' And with that, both men climbed into their jeep, reversed over the lawn, leaving deep tyre ruts that would break the gardener's heart if he could see them, and roared off back up the drive. Ursula could have told them a short cut down the back lanes, and across up to Adam Road, but she let them drive away without a word.

In fact no-one said anything until they were completely out of sight. Then Billy held out a hand and Ursula ran hard against him, butting her head into the crook of his arm in the way she had used to as a baby. It was all too much. She couldn't cope anymore. She couldn't be expected to cope. 'I don't want to go with them, Billy. They'll put me with strangers and then, if the island falls completely, I'll be interned with the women. Or murdered. Billy, can't we go away somewhere . . . together, please?' She whispered only to

82

feel Billy stiffen. The gilded skin she loved so much was stretched taut over his cheekbones, the eyes filled with pain and tenderness.

'No, *cahayamata*. Not together. I have to go away somewhere where you will not be safe. I think . . . yes, I think you will be safer here with Fatimah. We will change you a little, make you look like a Malay girl, and you will hide when the Japanese come.'

'But what about Papa? He won't know where I am, and he may be badly injured.'

'I will go and find your Papa. Tell him where you are, that you are safe and cared for. Then I will go on to where I am needed.'

'But I need you, Billy!' Ursula wailed, desperate not to lose him, of all people. 'I won't know how Papa is . . . or even if you ever found him. We don't even know which hospital he's in!' Billy stroked her hair and wiped the tears from her face with his thumb, a gesture so gentle that it only caused Ursula to cry all the harder.

'He is at the Alexandra Military Hospital. His car was strafed going down Stevens Road, so the officer said. That is how they came for you so quickly. Your Papa had them radio your location. He cares very much for you, you see. Do not worry, Ursula, I will find him. Then I will try and come back to tell you. Now stop crying and go with Fatimah. Quick now, before the soldiers arrive to take you away. I will see you tonight.' He hugged her hurriedly and pushed her towards Fatimah who held out a hand for the child. Ursula was almost blinded by her tears and could only follow Fatimah down the track at the bottom of the garden as quickly as she could. She felt as though the enemy were catching at her heels but, at the same time, she wanted to run back and tell Billy she would be all right, not to come back to her. It wasn't safe. But Fatimah hurried her on and the house – and Billy – were soon lost to sight.

Chapter Five

The vegetable dye turned out to be quite a success. Fatimah
had pulped some odd-looking root in a mortar and then, using
her fingers, had spread the mixture over Ursula's skin. She was
now darker than she had ever been but thought it rather suited
her. Her hair and eyes looked quite natural against the brown
skin and when Fatimah pulled off her frock and put a sarong
around her body, and a little jacket on her top, she looked just
like a young Malay girl. She was thin and, at first, wary in her
movements in case the sarong should suddenly drop from her
hips but eventually she became more accustomed to it and
was able to move freely. Quite a gathering of villagers had sat
around her while the dying process went on but Fatimah had
scolded and shooed the men and boys away. This was not a
side-show! Ursula had felt self-conscious when Fatimah had
taken off her frock to dye the other parts of her body but the
women hadn't thought anything of it, looking her over as
though she were just another goat or scrawny chicken. To them
she was just a child still, and children did not need to be modest
in front of their mothers. And she had to admit the sarong was
much cooler than her own clothing. It was nice not to wear
shoes but to walk barefoot over the warm dust. Occasionally
she hit a pebble or thorn and had to hobble over to a post and
probe her sole. Her feet were still soft and tender. It would take
a while for them to harden to the horny thickness of Fatimah's
soles.

That done, Fatimah put Ursula to work minding the

younger children. This was something she knew how to do and could not have been better for keeping her mind off her father and Billy. The children adored her, hanging on to her hands and sarong and fighting for the best place beside her. She talked to them only in Malay and was soon indistinguishable from any of the other children in the village. They were a poor kampong; most of the men and boys earning their wages as syces at the Polo Club, and the women growing vegetables, rearing a few chickens and goats and weaving coconut matting. Now, without the Tuans to pay their wages, the men would have to find some other means of work. Their headman, the Lembaga, had called them together that afternoon to discuss the problem but he was old and unwilling to take on the burden of finding his men work. He wanted to step down and let another, younger man, take his place. Someone was needed who could speak with the Japanese, if necessary, and get them to leave the kampong alone.

Ursula sat a little way off from the group of men and boys, wondering what it was all about. The younger children sat around her in the dust, plaiting leaves and grass together to make her bracelets, pouncing with excited hisses on butterflies or dragonflies that ventured too close, and chattering to her so loudly that she could make nothing of what the men were saying. Every now and then she saw the Lembaga raise his hands and shake them about wildly in the air. Then the village Elder, the Buapa, would say something and things would get very heated for a while until the headman called for silence. Then he would start all over again. Ursula was puzzled and wondered, with the fear of part guilt and part vulnerability, whether the argument was about her presence in the kampong. There was no denying it put them all in danger if she were found. But what else could she do? She sat and watched them anxiously as the hours slipped away and the sun began to dip behind the jungle yet again. And still Billy did not come.

There had been gunfire all day long, with occasional shells exploding in the distance, but the villagers had been indifferent. This was not their war; maybe the Japanese would be better than the Europeans, maybe not. There was nothing they could do except wait and see. But there were still stomachs to be filled and backs to be clothed. Life must go on. At dusk the

Lembaga called the whole village to the clearing in front of his hut. He was grey-haired and thin though still wiry and erect. But his face showed his age and his eyes were yellowed and bleary. He raised an arm for silence, the skin hanging in folds where once muscles had been. He raised his voice, trembling over the words:

'The valleys have grown too deep for my going, the hills too steep for my climbing and journeys too far for my feet. Burdens have become too heavy for my back and light tasks for my fingers.' These were the ritual words of resignation. There was a low sigh from the villagers and Ursula cringed behind Fatimah, hardly noticing how Ibrahim and Yahyah stood proudly near the old headman. She knew something momentous was happening but was too self-preoccupied to really take it in. Something was happening outside her understanding and she could just watch while one man and then another spoke, the villagers swayed and sighed, and then Ibrahim stepped forward slowly. He dipped his head with dignity and said something about 'the sprinkling of the broken grain', and then took some grain and scattered it about over the ground. Ursula couldn't see what was happening but heard Ibrahim's voice in snatches, talking about 'the cocks that lay not eggs, the hens that cackle, and the chickens that chirp'. She couldn't make it out at all and thought that it was all rather a fuss about nothing. Everyone already knew that cocks didn't lay eggs. What on earth was Ibrahim pointing out the obvious for? She was tired and was tempted to interrupt and tell Ibrahim to go up to the house to see if Billy had arrived yet. But something held her back.

Ibrahim had reached the part where he was acknowledging the bond of tribal unity and everyone was silent, watching him as he pulled himself up proudly, standing tall, and said:

> 'Together we skin the elephant's liver,
> Together we dip the liver of the louse;
> What we drop is common loss;
> What we gain is common profit.'

This time the sighing became cheering. Then there was more talking, and women were rushing back and forth from their huts carrying offerings which they laid down in front of Ibrahim. The ceremony seemed to have gone on forever and the small children were fidgeting. Ursula wasn't interested in what Ibrahim had to say. She was worried that Billy still hadn't come back and that the firing was very close. Why the villagers were choosing this moment to have a feast – and that was what was going on now, she could see – she couldn't think. It was all too difficult to understand and she had the impression that Ibrahim was different, somehow, now. She didn't think he would go up to the house at all, even if she demanded it. The thought crossed her mind fleetingly, and then was angrily suppressed, that perhaps the officer had been right. She would have been better with her own kind. Then, sick at herself, she turned away from the crowd of villagers and turned hesitantly back towards the house. No-one noticed her leave.

It was quiet and dark up at the bungalow. No-one had lit the lights or lowered the blinds. No-one was singing in the kitchen, or calling for one of the boys. There was no music coming from Papa's study. The very air seemed dead and unnoticing. She slipped around the back and into the kitchen, almost falling over the trunk of silver that Fatimah had left. She must have forgotten to send anyone back to bury it. Now it would fall into Jap hands. The thought made Ursula angry. It wasn't theirs; they had no right to take it. But they would, unless she did something about it. Oh, why wasn't Billy here? The thought was automatic, the way it always sprang to mind when she needed something. Now, however, she told herself sharply to stop whining and to think, instead. Sally had tried to black out the windows in the dining room with large, brocaded shawls. Ursula took a chair and climbed up on it, tugging and pulling until she freed the shawl and it dropped heavily to the ground. It would do very well, she thought. She carried it back to the kitchen and laid it out on the tiled floor. Then, slowly and carefully, she tugged at the trunk. It was hopelessly heavy for her thin frame and the shawl just bunched up in front of it as she tried to slide the trunk forward.

She was almost crying with frustration. At any moment she expected a Japanese soldier to walk in on her and bayonet her – or do whatever that dreadful secret was, the thing that was worse than death. She stopped and listened, straining to catch sounds that might mean the enemy had arrived. Oh God, why was this happening to her? No, stop that! Panicking wouldn't help. She was in this alone and would just have to do her best. The stern talking-to gave her the strength to sit and contemplate her problem. Maybe, if she took some of the silver out first, and then put the trunk on the shawl, she could slide it along better? The lid of the trunk wasn't fastened down yet so it was an easy matter to open it and pull out some of the pieces. She tossed them carelessly onto the floor and then froze at the clatter they made. When, after a few moments of rigid panic, nothing happened she pulled out more silver and put it quietly down on the table. There were soon candlesticks, photograph frames, plates, goblets, teapots, knives and forks scattered all over the place. Ursula didn't give them another look but concentrated on lifting the trunk onto the shawl. It took all her strength but eventually she managed it. She stood back panting.

So far so good. Now where to hide it? The jungle seemed the logical place but would the trunk make tracks when it was dragged? She decided to risk it. It was heavy but the shawl made it slide better and, once she had it out onto the lawn, it slid quite well. The grass was dry still and the ground was hard. With any luck the trunk wouldn't score the lawn. It took her nearly an hour to drag the trunk over to jungle, and nearly an hour more to carry the other pieces of silver over from the house, refill the trunk, close and seal it, and then hide it under palm fronds. She couldn't be sure it wouldn't be found, but at least it wasn't sitting in the middle of the kitchen for someone else to fall over! Then she returned to the kitchen and filled a basket with food, the bottle of lime juice from the tray, a few books, and a cushion. This she wearily carried back to her hiding place behind the bamboo, pushed it in, and climbed in after.

Billy stood stiffly beside Harry Fraser, outside the Alexandra Military Hospital. The wind blew across the lawn, puffing smoke into their eyes from the main building. Fraser's head was wrapped in a bandage, the blood showing through in a brownish stain. No-one paid any attention. All eyes were fixed on the men in front of them, men holding bayonets, men who flicked cold stares over patients who toppled onto hard buffalo grass or concrete paths. Those patients were dragged away. The rest stiffened spines, knees locked tightly on buckling legs, teeth gripped hard into skin. Those who fell, died. The looting and screaming continued from the hospital and the prisoners flinched at the sounds.

It had been so sudden. One minute the doctors and nurses had been circulating calmly amongst the wounded, the next – the savagery, the screaming! Oh God, Fraser thought, such screaming! How can this be happening? He saw patients around him bayoneted to death where they lay, holding their hands out to ward off the thrusts of sharp metal, begs rising to terrorized screams. It was the screaming he couldn't take. That poor devil on the operating table, watching, knowing it was too late for him. A lunge, a trowel of steel imbedding itself in his throat, the bubbling, wheezing scream. Horror on horror! Fraser shook his head, his eyes blank. He didn't think about Billy, or about himself. Only the screams.

The wind whipped the Red Cross flag against its staunchions, the red appearing to bleed across the white. The main building was on fire now and men could be heard coughing, crying, begging for mercy. Near them young Rodney Hendricks stood uneasily, his left leg encased in plaster, his face held rigidly straight. He looked no more than a child, caught up in a madness that left no room for such excuses – too young, too weak, too ill. The cries continued from the pall of smoke and flame. Fraser bowed his head, tears stinging his eyes in the smoke and confusion.

'What'll they do to us? Are they gonna murder us all?' A small man, the sort who should be behind the counter of a tobacconists, or perhaps a civil servant, minor, low grade, chewed his lip. He didn't dare release it lest it should wobble into terrible truths. Billy shrugged instead.

'Perhaps ship us out to a camp somewhere.' The Europeans perhaps, Billy thought; not me. They won't take me anywhere. Eurasians were a breed apart, a breed despised. Billy turned to look at the man he had worked for, the tall, stern Tuan with his pale eyes and cutting tongue. He saw the bewilderment, the flinching horror in those eyes and knew he had lost his life for this man. Did Fraser even know that? Did he care? But Fraser had only one worry.

'For Christ's sake, what about Ursula!' He shuddered, leaning heavily on Billy's arm. She was too young for all this. And just old enough. Fear made channels in his cheeks, his jowls hanging deeply in folds. Billy's face was strangely calm in contrast. Perhaps it was for this day he had always known he would need such control? Perhaps there was no more than this?

'Ursula is safe. I gave her to Fatimah to look after. They will make her look like a Malay girl. She will be all right.' She will be all right. Billy closed his eyes. She will be all right. It was a prayer, a chant offered to any God or all gods.

'Jesus, how can they do this? It's a hospital, for God's sake. Flying the red cross!' Fraser's moustache drooped with fatigue, his mouth quivered. Billy did not answer. And still the screams continued.

At nightfall, the survivors were herded into a single hut on the perimeter of the grounds. It backed onto the jungle, the rotten decaying smell fogging a night air where prisoners, packed in so tightly they could not move let alone lie down, gasped for breath. Wounded were held up by doctors and staff, the dying died where they stood, unable to fall even in death.

'Are you all right? Can you breathe enough?' Billy whispered. Fraser nodded once, head tightly fitted into the neck beside him, the shoulder behind him. Don't panic. Don't think. Just be still. He swallowed over the ache in his throat, the hard knot of fear. The heat and stench within the hut was almost unbearable and it was now night. How could they stand tomorrow? There was no water, no sanitation, no air! The short cursed and stood upon others to breathe, the tall gasped at the thick, still murk above their heads. No air!

Billy was asleep, dazed into a standing stupor when the explosion went off. He wasn't sure what had happened, jerking alert to the screams again, the noise, pain, confusion, stench of burning. The side of the hut farthest from him was missing, he thought, his mind slowed in its dogged pursuit of sanity. Missing. Not there. Beside him there were tentative movements, pushing, shoving, maddening fumblings over prone bodies, objects beneath one's feet that rolled and subsided sickeningly. Billy clambered forward, desperately clinging to

Fraser's arm. Don't let him fall. I won't be able to get him back up if he falls. We'll both be trampled if he falls. The thought wound around and around the slowed mind, adding another image, another nuance on the theme. Don't let him fall or we'll never get out and we must get out, we must get out for Ursula. Don't let him fall. And then there was Rodney, boyish mouth stretched in pain, wide, staring eyes of desperation as he tried to get up, get out from under the feet, the panicked, killing feet. His leg held him pinned down.

'Rodney! Boy, give me your hand. Get up, for God's sake, get up!' And Fraser would not leave the boy and Billy could not leave Fraser. He felt again that sad, still calm. They had killed him, between them. He reached down, losing his footing, feeling the surge of bodies fighting to push him away, down, out of their way. He fell. The weight of other bodies, other men pressing him into the earth was worse than he had thought possible, more terrifying. He held tightly to Fraser's arm, inching them forward, pulling them towards that gaping hole that led to dark jungle depths. His mind began to fog, the oxygen denied in that trampling panic. Don't let go, don't let go or we're dead and then Ursula is dead. Move them forward, push, harder!

But in time there was no more resistance, the pounding feet gone, the pain dulling to bearable moments. Billy shook the arm locked in his grip, shaking it over and over. It didn't move. He pulled himself up towards Fraser's face and flinched away, the cry caught in his throat. There was no face, just a bloodied pulp. He looked away. Rodney lay not much further beyond Fraser, the leg that had pulled him to his death oddly pristine in its white plaster. His face could not be seen, the head itself flattened into the mud, suffocated beneath the weight of terror. Billy pulled away.

He found he couldn't stand at first, muscles locked into spasms of such intensity that he had to edge forward first onto his knees, rocking in that rictus of pain where death would have been a welcome alternative. From knees to feet, squatting on haunches, tensing for the final effort. And then he was up, muddied suit of cream and blood flitting like a phosphorescent insect in the dark. He lunged forward to the jungle. He could make it, he could live. If he lived, he could get to Ursula. He

91

could do it now and then she would live. And, like an insect, he was struck down, suddenly and unexpectedly, from behind. He felt himself falling forward into the mud, the blow never seen.

The morning dew woke Ursula, chill and damp. She shivered in her thin cotton clothes and opened her eyes. The sun wasn't quite up yet but hung behind a wall of mist that obscured the Polo Club and padang. She slid out of her hole, and peered about her. There didn't seem to be a soul about. Even the jungle noises were hushed. Ursula didn't like it. It was too quiet. She didn't move at first but stayed squatting beside the bamboo, looking about her intently. Finally, satisfied that there was nothing there, she stood up and ran across the lawn to the house. It was still empty. Billy hadn't come. Disconsolate, she wandered about the house, wondering what to do. She couldn't live on her own for very long. She would starve. And Fatimah and Ibrahim were different when they were in their own kampong. She wasn't sure she wanted to stay with them. Her indecision increased with every moment. There was firing again, coming from just the other side of the Chinese cemetery. That was where the broadcasting station was. But nothing came near them. Finally, after standing blankly in the hall for so long that her knees seemed to have cemented themselves into one long column of leg, Ursula left the house.

She was making her way down the garden to the clubhouse when she saw the figure. It was a man, she thought, lying in the drainage channel that passed beside the house and the main road. He was on his back and didn't move, even when Ursula crept forward to see better. The man seemed familiar, although his face was turned away. He was dressed in a cream suit that was stained from dirt, blood, water. A loose, elegant suit that she had once known. It was Billy! The realization hit her like a blow and she staggered forward, screaming in a thin, high-pitched voice that sounded to her as though it were coming from far away. Billy raised his head and turned to look at her as she threw herself down beside him. 'Billy! Oh what did they do to you, Billy?' She was still shrieking, voice no louder but pitched in hysterical cadence, breathless in her panic. He lay stiffly, half-way up the side of the channel with his feet in the

92

trickle of water that filled the bottom. There was red across his chest, a wet red that Ursula knew was blood. He parted his lips but nothing came out, no sound except a faint and hoarse breathing. Ursula touched his wet shirt. 'Billy?' This time she whispered.

He seemed to be watching her but Ursula wasn't sure if he was even conscious. His eyes moved, his mouth opened and shut, but nothing more. There were terrible marks on his face and hands, bruised, bleeding tears in the skin that made her gag. This was her fault. She had asked him to come back; she had wanted to know about Papa. Now Billy was badly hurt, perhaps dying. Her face was streaked with tears and her nose was running but she couldn't tear herself away from Billy's eyes. They seemed to be smiling at her, trying to comfort. She scooped some water up in her hands from the bottom of the channel and tried to pour it into his mouth. Most of it ran away, down his chin, but some of it went in. He swallowed, closed his eyes, and then reopened them. 'More,' it came out as an exhalation rather than a word but Ursula understood. She bent down and wet the bottom of her sarong and then lifted it above Billy's mouth and squeezed. The water trickled down his throat and after a few more minutes he said, in a voice much more like his normal tone but still weak: 'The Japanese raided the hospital. They killed doctors, patients . . . ' He paused and then continued more calmly. 'They put many of us in a hut all night. It was very crowded. So crowded some could not breathe. But then there was a bomb and a wall blew down . . . I ran with several others for the jungle. I was almost there, right at the trees when I was shot. Your father went back . . . for a friend who had fallen. It was a brave thing to do. He, Ursula, I am sorry . . . your father is dead.' He could not tell her the horror, the real death. It could not be borne. He had to stop for breath after that and Ursula wet her sarong again and squeezed more water into his mouth. She could barely take in what he was saying. She didn't want to take it in. Later she could cope, but not now; now Billy was wounded and it was her fault. She kneeled beside him, numb.

'Billy, can you get up? Can you make it up to the bungalow? I'll help you.'

She held his hand, terrified at how cold it felt in her warm

93

fingers. 'Billy? Try and get up.' She slipped her arm under his and flinched at the pain twisting his face. 'I'm sorry, Billy. I'm so sorry.'

'Hush. Help me up. I cannot stay here.' He clenched his teeth together and staggered forward against her, her arm supporting him as he swayed. There were steps further down the drainage channel for people to climb in and out, and Ursula led Billy to them. He was a terrible weight on her shoulder, her muscles burning with the strain, but Ursula supported, pushed, and pulled Billy up the stairs, across the yard, and into the kitchen. The last part, up the stairs to Papa's bedroom, was the hardest. She had to stop and let him sit on the steps on several occasions. The strain was obvious in his face but he never cried out; he held his mouth just so, as though he were angry with her. Ursula helped Billy down on to the bed. He was waxy grey under his brown skin, his face moist with sweat and blood. She put pillows under his head and helped raise his feet so that the long frame didn't dangle over the side of the bed. He was looking worse than ever, breathing in short gasps that rattled in his throat. His eyes were closed but he opened them when she wiped her wet sarong over his face.

'Good girl. Now get me some water and maybe some food. I must eat to get my strength back. Do not look so worried about me. I can do this. I must.' His lips folded into a faint smile. 'It is just the loss of blood that makes me weak. That and my bruises. It is a long walk from Mount Alexandria.' She nodded and ran to the kitchen. The water was still running because they were serviced by MacRitchie Reservoir and that was the only one not yet in Japanese hands. She filled a glass and a bowl and picked up a cloth to bathe him with. When she returned to Billy she found him with his eyes shut again. He seemed to be gathering his strength, trying to overcome the pain of his wound. But he would live. People didn't die from a bullet in the shoulder. He would be all right. He would!

'Here, Billy, drink this. Just a little.' She helped him sit up, the weight of him against her filling her with dread. He had always supported her. It shouldn't be like this. He managed to swallow a few mouthfuls and revived enough to look up at her with those dark, bruised eyes. Ursula saw he was smiling and she smiled back, some of her fear ebbing as the colour came back into his face. She offered him some rice that had been left over from a meal. It seemed years since they had all sat down to dinner at the table, with Ah Jong serving her beautiful tiffins. Ursula picked up some rice in her fingers and pressed it into a little ball. Billy was watching, his almond eyes amused, but he opened his mouth without protest when she held it to his lips. 'Oh, thank the Lord,' Ursula murmured. 'He can't be too bad if he can still eat.' She let him chew slowly and take deep breaths before pressing more rice into his mouth.

'Are you feeling any better now, Billy? D'you want me to get you anything?' she said after a few mouthfuls had been accepted. He swallowed, his throat dry from the rice, and said:

'What about some lime juice? I would like a last glass of Fatimah's specialty.' Ursula didn't like the way he phrased that 'last'. But he seemed better. She knew there was very little lime juice left but obediently returned to the kitchen. If that was what Billy wanted, she would find him some. The remains of what she had set out on the tray the night before were still there, the rest of the juice fermenting with the heat. There were small beatles making their way through the food and flies were gathering in the windows. She turned away sickened. When she searched through the ice-box again, she found the electricity was off and the contents already beginning to spoil with the heat. If only she hadn't taken a bottle to her hiding place, there would be some left now. She returned empty-handed to the bedroom, wishing things could just go back to normal. It wasn't possible to think about Papa. He couldn't really be dead. Billy had made a mistake. As she reached the doorway, she heard a gasping cry. She turned into the room.

Billy had swung his legs to the ground and was attempting to stand. He swayed uncertainly like a bamboo frond about to fall. Ursula saw the colour drain away beneath the dark skin and a tight, closed look come over his face.

'What're you doing, Billy? Lie down, please!' She tugged at his jacket until his long frame crumpled once again. He sat heavily, the bed groaning in protest. Billy didn't make a sound. Ursula pushed him back further until he was half-lying against the pillows again. 'You're not well, Billy. Why're you doing

95

this? Please, just lie still. I'll go get you some lime juice if you'll be still. Please.' She coaxed him like a child and he lay his head back against the pillows reluctantly.

'Never mind the lime juice, Ursula. There is no time. I do not know what I was thinking about. I need you to go and find Ibrahim.' He saw her open her mouth to interrupt and he hushed her impatiently.

'Be a good girl, *cahayamata*. Do this for me. Go to the kampong. Tell Ibrahim. Tell him I am wounded and must get away from here before the Japanese come. Go and tell him that, Ursula.' He paused to gather breath. 'But stay there. Do not come back to me.' He saw the denial in the shock on her face and the shake of her head. She almost recoiled at the thought. 'Please, Ursula. The Japanese are near. Please.' He was pleading but she wouldn't listen, laying her fingers across his lips to stop his words.

'No, Billy. I won't leave you. I can't. You're everything to me – all I have left. I won't go! Ibrahim won't help. It's too dangerous for them to have you there. He doesn't even want me there and, and . . . I won't leave you here to die.' The tears were making channels down her face. He stroked her hair as she knelt beside him, her face buried in the crook of his arm. He didn't move or speak again for some time, holding her tightly against him.

Outside the sun climbed high in the sky and the heat began to fill the air.

Chapter Six

Yahyah found them there, Ursula still holding Billy's hand, a little later. There was blood on her sarong and hands, and a smear of it across her cheek. She was sitting on the bed, staring out the window and across the padang, Billy's hand clasped tightly in hers. Yahyah was uncertain what to do. They hadn't known she was missing until late last night and although he had searched the bungalow and the polo grounds, he hadn't been able to find her. His father had been furious, both with Fatimah and him for not watching out for her, and with Ursula for wandering off. Now, if the Japanese found her and realized she was a European, they would all be in trouble for having dyed her skin and made her look like a native.

He had been searching for her since daybreak but in all the wrong places: the Chinese cemetery; the next kampong; the jungle. He hadn't thought to recheck the bungalow or polo grounds until now. And there she was, with Mr Billing lying there on the bed beside her. It seemed very strange to him. Then he saw the bruised and battered face, the blood on Mr Billing's shirt. It was a dull, rusty red. He saw also that Ursula had torn a strip off the bottom of her sarong and tied it over her tutor's wound. That was just as well, with the flies and sun both gathering force as the day wore on. But his mother would be cross about the sarong.

Yahyah slipped into the room and walked up to the bed until he was level with Ursula. Then he squatted down on his haunches and waited for her to notice him. He didn't like to

97

interrupt her, or to insist that she leave with him at once, even if that was what he knew he should do. Mr Billing was asleep, he thought. And he was hurt. It was dangerous for them to be sitting beside him. What if the Japanese arrived? There was nothing more either of them could do for him, except to stay with him until they were all caught. His father would never allow Mr Billing to hide in the kampong. It would be too dangerous for the village. Yahyah had seen Japanese troops that morning, just the other side of the village. They hadn't seen him crouching in the bushes and had moved on up the back track towards the top end of Mount Pleasant, but there would be more arriving soon enough. It wasn't safe to stay here, especially with a wounded person. He wondered what had happened to Mr Billing. Maybe he was a member of the resistance force that was being trained to stay on after the Japanese took over? There had been a lot of rumours about the force but no-one actually knew anyone who belonged to it. At least, no-one who would admit to it. But Mr Billing was smart: he spoke English and Dutch and Malay and Siamese. He would be very useful to a resistance force. Yahyah looked across at the man and wondered.

Ursula had seen Yahyah arrive and make his way across the room to her. She hadn't turned her head but had seen it out of the corner of her eye. When he didn't say anything, however, she decided to ignore him. He might get tired, or frightened, in a while and go away and leave them alone. That would be best. She didn't want anyone else to get hurt because of her. And if Yahyah stayed too long the Japs might come and find them all. Besides, it was a bore to speak. Unbelievably tiring. She did try, once, but the effort to dredge up a voice from somewhere down inside her was too much. So she just sat there, staring out at the white grass and the white sky, her thoughts floating aimlessly somewhere behind blank eyes. He would go away soon and leave her with Billy. Billy and she belonged together.

Yahyah was puzzled by Ursula's behaviour. He felt he ought to take command; he was the new Lembaga's son. He should be decisive, tell her what to do. He was a male and she was a female. She should obey him. But she was also Missysahib and he was frightened of offending her. He stole a look at her, and then another when she didn't seem to notice. He liked her dressed like that and, with her skin so brown and her hair hanging loose down her back, she could have been his sister – or his sweetheart. The thought was furtive, and quickly suppressed. He turned his head away and looked down at his hands in embarrassment. She was European and he was Malay. He must never think that again. But he did, almost immediately, and this time it didn't seem so terrible. She couldn't go back to her own kind until the war was over; and maybe never. She must stay with them, grow into a woman – and a woman must marry. He looked up, shyly, his dark eyelashes lowered carefully over his eyes so she would not see what he was thinking.

It was hard to remember what today was. Thursday? Friday? Ursula shook her head to clear it. It must be Friday now, she thought, and yesterday, Thursday, was when Sally and Emma and Tom . . . she mustn't think about Tom. Yesterday was when Papa had been strafed by a Jap plane and had been taken to Alexandra Military Hospital. And, for some reason, yesterday was when the Japanese had murdered every-one in the hospital, including Papa. It didn't seem possible that an army could go into a Red Cross area and butcher people. Maybe she had misunderstood Billy? After all, here they were waiting for an enemy who kept threatening to arrive at any second, and yet, still hadn't come. It was a joke – a bad joke. She almost wondered if they really existed or if everyone was being hysterical about nothing. But the cool hand that was clasped in hers reminded her otherwise.

All she knew was that Billy had seen her father killed and now Billy was lying beside her, in terrible pain. If he had fallen asleep for a while and didn't feel that pain, she wasn't going to wake him. Besides, where could they go?

'Missy, want I look after Mr Billing? You go kampong, safe there. I wait with Mr Billing. Not long now, I think. Japanese here very soon,' Yahyah said suddenly, the silence too much for him. Ursula looked at him angrily.

'No! Go away, Yahyah. I won't leave Billy. Go away. We don't need you. Billy'll be better soon and then we'll go away together. So don't bother to stay.' Her fear for Billy made her denial all the stronger. Beside her she felt Billy stir, his mouth pursing to say something. She raised the water to his lips again.

99

'Go, Ursula. Do what Yahyah says. He can help me get away. You are not strong enough to help me. So go!' His face was so dear to Ursula that she lay her cheek against his, hushing him like a child. The tears hovered on her lashes, quivering before dropping down over his face.

'It's no good, Billy. You're too weak and Yahyah has nowhere to take you. And I won't leave you.' She felt him gathering his strength again. He sat up, pushing her away from him.

'I need to talk to Yahyah. Go and find me the lime juice you promised me. Now, Ursula. Go and get it now.'

'But it's in the jungle, Billy. It's in my hiding place. Yahyah, you go and get it . . . Oh God, why did I tell you to look for Papa? I'm so sorry, Billy!'

'No, it had nothing to do with you . . . I would have gone anyway. Do you not see that, *cahayamata*? Now I need a drink. Your hiding place is not far but Yahyah does not know it. Go and get me a drink, sweetheart.' Yahyah hesitated when Ursula scowled at him. But she stood up and squeezed Billy's hand.

'All right. I won't be long. Yahyah, help Billy if he needs it. I'll be back in just a minute – you won't go anywhere while I'm gone?' Billy shook his head and pushed her towards the door.

She set off at a jog, sliding out the back way and across the lawns with all the stealth of a deer surprised by a hunter. Ursula realized, with a start, that if today was Friday, then it was Black Friday, the 13th. Somehow that seemed appropriate for the day her world had fallen apart. She couldn't quite grasp that her father was dead; she hadn't seen him die. It was just second-hand news, without the punch that Billy's wounded body, lying beside her, had added to her understanding of war. Apart from her mother, whom she had never known, this was the first time death had ever touched her. She couldn't have known how sapping, leeching, the emotional strain was; she just felt . . . nothing. She was frightened that there was something wrong with her; that she was incapable of sorrow. She laughed, a short sound that burst from her and surprised her as much as the bird skirting the bushes a few feet away from her. Then she was silent again, staring blankly ahead but moving automatically towards the bamboo. It shimmered in the heat.

Yahyah frowned and moved his mouth from left to right and then back again, as though chewing the problem over between his teeth. He saw Mr Billing sit up, his face with its cuts and bloodied bruises suddenly composed as though a difficult decision had been made. Yahyah looked at him apprehensively. What did Mr Billing want from him? It was too dangerous. He did not want to put his life in danger, not for anyone – except perhaps Ursula. Mr Billing was now standing, listening, as though he could hear something that no-one else could. Then Yahyah heard it too. The sound of lorries moving down the Thomson Road, changing gear in order to make the turn into Mount Pleasant.

'Quickly, Yahyah. Go find Missy. Stop her coming back. No matter what, stop her. They will be here in seconds. Go, go now.' Yahyah hesitated, longing to run and hide but held by something he could not understand. He looked at Mr Billing's face, so set and hard, and then he gave a cry of fear. The first lorry had drawn into the driveway. Mr Billing pushed him roughly towards the stairs and Yahyah felt the indecision leave him. He ran crouching to the stairs and bolted down them, his feet slapping hurriedly on the wood. Behind him he heard Mr Billing moving to follow him.

At the foot of the stairs he hesitated again, looking up at Mr Billing. There was no time to say goodbye. He saw movement to his left, out in front of the bungalow as the lorry pulled in and men spilled out from it. Then he ran, out through the kitchen and away, across the gardens, to the jungle. Billy watched the boy leave with an expression of pain. So, they had killed him, each with their needs and fears and, finally, with their love. He wouldn't get away now. But, for Ursula, he would do it over again without thought. He smiled sadly. Then he stepped down from the last stair as several Japanese soldiers ran forward into the room.

They fanned out in a defensive formation, bent forward over their rifles, bayonets fixed. It was dark within and their sight was slow in adjusting. Billy stood waiting patiently. Then he held up his hands and stepped forward.

Yahyah caught Ursula as she was leaving her hiding place. He knew where it was, having watched her over the years when she thought she was alone. It had amused him to know her

101

secret. Now he held her tightly against him as she struggled in his arms. It surprised him how much strength such a thin, scrawny body could possess.

'Where's Billy? Why have you left him? Yahyah, let me go, damn you, let me go!' Her voice ended with a hysterical shriek and Yahyah clamped his hand across her mouth.

'Japanese come. Mr Billing say leave. Stop you coming back. No can go back, Missy. Too late. Musoh here. Too late, *la*!' He tried to get her to understand but she just struggled harder and then bit down hard on the hand that covered her mouth. Yahyah gasped with pain and wrenched his hand away. Ursula pulled free and started to run towards the bungalow, towards Billy. He needed her. Fear made her fast and it was some yards before Yahyah caught her up. He swung her round and, without a moment's hesitation, hit her as hard as he could. She crumpled without a sound and he caught her up, slinging her over his shoulder, and ran back towards the jungle. Over at the bungalow he could hear the ruckus as the Japanese discovered Mr Billing. Yahyah sighed and then pushed Ursula's limp body into the hole behind the bamboo. He climbed in behind her. He couldn't understand the indifference Ursula had shown to her own safety. She must care about Mr Billing very much, he thought uneasily. It would be hard for her to forgive him. Now she lay sprawled awkwardly across the ground beside him. He shook her arm but she didn't move.

The soldiers seemed surprised to see Billy. They stood around him at first, uneasily threatening him with their bayonets. Then they gestured for him to walk out to the verandah. He stood stiffly, his back against a pillar, while the officer in charge came forward.

'You live here?' the officer asked in Japanese. He was a dapper little man with wary eyes. Billy nodded. 'You also understand Japanese. How is that? You are not a European.' The officer looked over the tall man with interest. Billy shrugged.

'I was a tutor. I taught many different languages,' he replied, his Japanese correct but not smooth. The officer smiled, small, almost feminine teeth glistening in the sun.

'So! A tutor?' He turned away and looked out, across the

green lawns and carefully trimmed hedges. Then he turned back and gave Billy a quizzical look, one eyebrow skewed higher than the other. 'I do not think so. I think you are a very foolish man to be still here. Where were you wounded? In your schoolroom?' The officer laughed and several men around him joined in tentatively. When he stopped, their laughter died immediately. 'I think you are somebody else, Mr Tutor. Somebody who is perhaps organizing resistance amongst the natives? That is what I think. Where are the Europeans who live here?' The sudden change of tack was, Billy imagined, intended to surprise him into blurting out the truth. Clumsy. His face became bland and expressionless, the eyes holding just that hint of contempt that had so often made Sally uneasy.

'They have gone. Many days ago. There is no-one here but me.'

'You are mistaken, Mr Tutor. We are here now. And we will find your European family. Do not think you can protect them.' The officer looked amused and then, turning abruptly on his heel, he walked into the bungalow.

Inside the bamboo it was almost like a nest, a pillow leaning up against the huge tree trunk that made the fourth wall, and a basket of food and some books completing the furnishings. Yahyah smiled. This was a good place to know: safe, hidden, and comfortable. He was happy he had found it; Ursula would never have shown him. Even now she would be frantic to get out and return to Mr Billing if he had not hit her. He was sorry about that but it had been the only way. It was the least he could do for Mr Billing. Yahyah sat down beside Ursula and held her wrist firmly in case she should wake unexpectedly. There was just space enough for them both.

Out on the lawn, more trucks arrived, Japanese soldiers spilling out to surround the house. Yahyah crept out to see Mr Billing, leaning against the pillar of the verandah, surrender himself. Mr Billing was drawing attention away from the jungle, making himself the sacrifice. Yahyah was impressed. He scrubbed at his face with the hard skin of his palm, easing the tight feeling he had across his cheeks. There was nothing he could have done for Mr Billing. They had both known that. Still he lingered, watching the scene on the porch. Finally he crawled back in. Ursula's bleached face lay still amongst the fronds. He eyed it warily. Had he hit her too hard?

'All over now. Mr Billing surrender. Too late for you to do anything, Missy,' he whispered to her limp body. Then he settled himself comfortably to wait until nightfall.

The hours passed without event and eventually Ursula stirred and sat up, holding her head between her hands. There were tear stains down her cheeks and she looked around, staring glassy-eyed at the bamboo wall surrounding her. She made no attempt to leave once Yahyah had told her he would stop her in the same way. She just leaned back against the pillow while more tears ran silently down her face. After a while, Yahyah sought to distract her.

'English come soon to look for you, Missy. You be all right.' There was silence for a while, Ursula's head pounding with the heat of the sun as it filtered through into their nest. Then she said in a tired voice:

'No more Missy, Yahyah. My name is Ursula.' She understood the look he gave her. There was pride and fear and slight sadness all mixed up together. That was how she felt too, but it was better to realize that the days of the empire were over – or at least temporarily suspended – and that they should deal with life accordingly.

'Oosalah!' Yahyah said softly. She shrugged. That was near enough. '*Can?*'

'*Can.*' It was settled; she was no longer a Missy. She sat back again, licking her dry lips with a tongue that seemed to have swollen to twice its normal size. Yahyah offered her the bottle of lime juice but she just closed her eyes, more tears seeping out from beneath her lashes.

They could see the back half of the bungalow from where they were if they craned their heads sideways and then moved quickly from side to side, like looking through a fence while going by in a car. It was a difficult procedure: Ursula's head ached from the motion and the constant fear that they might be seen made them wary. They only looked when they couldn't bear not to know, one second longer, what was happening. Very little seemed to be happening out the back of the house. For Ursula it was a frustrating means of knowing the worst. She had been surprised, at seeing her first Japanese soldiers, that they were taller than she had been led to believe. And they didn't look yellow either. She was relieved to see there were no fangs, although she had always known that was just a silly myth. Still, it was nice to be sure. In fact, they didn't look all that different to the Chinese. Perhaps a bit more stolid, but really very similar otherwise, from this distance. She understood their eyes went down, while Chinese eyes went up, but surely that didn't make such a difference? Maybe they wouldn't hurt Billy after all? Maybe the hospital killings had been a mistake? And then, when this was all over, she and Billy could go away together, like she had planned.

'What will the villagers do when the Japanese soldiers come into the kampong?' she asked Yahyah after a while. They talked in whispers, even though none of the soldiers came anywhere near the jungle edge. He hesitated in his reply, sensing that to give a good answer now would set him up well with Oosalah.

'My father, the Lembaga, often says: "When one bows to a raja's mandate, one can hug one's own interests under one's arm." I think the Japanese will let us be. There is nothing there for them.'

'But they will do whatever the Japanese tell them to do?'

'Will not the British, when they surrender? Who can defy the enemy when he holds the gun?' Yahyah leaned back against the tree, chewing a stalk he had plucked earlier. He was a pragmatist. There was no point to resistance when it meant sure death. He didn't want to die; he didn't want his family or village to die. It was better to be quiet and hope the Japanese would forget they were there. He closed his eyes against the shaft of sunlight that was blinking and flickering through the bamboo, letting it produce red flashes across the dark orbs of his closed and inturned eyes. It was warm and he felt drowsy, a sleepy stillness creeping over his mind. His lips puckered in a half-smile and then became slack while his head dropped forward on his chest. Ursula watched him fall asleep, wishing she could forget that easily, forget that Billy was dead or dying, and that the Japanese were close enough to hear them if they talked aloud. She considered leaving and trying to find Billy but she knew it was too late. There was nothing she could do.

105

They stayed there all day, eating the fruit and biscuits when they were hungry. Ursula could barely swallow the lime juice, gagging on it as though it were poison. The heat made them sweat and Yahyah plaited Ursula's hair into a long pigtail to keep her cool. It was no good trying to come out of the bamboo while the Japanese were there. They would be seen instantly and Yahyah wasn't sure enough yet of Ursula to risk it. So they rested as best they could and tried not to think how hot and cramped it was.

Ursula had become despondent again once the initial danger was over. She became listless and prone to staring blankly. Yahyah tried hard to keep her mind occupied. He told her where the horses were and how he needed to go and water them soon. They needed a lot of water, he added but she didn't respond. Then he mentioned his mother and how worried she would be when neither of them returned. Ursula shrugged indifferently. Yahyah pursed his lips in irritation. She might at least care about his mother, her amah, and how she must be frantic about them both. Yahyah looked at Ursula's taut and strained face, seeing the pain and not knowing how to relieve it. He sensed she would not be able to feel anything for anyone else until she had burned out the pain over Mr Billing and had grieved for him in peace. So he left her to her thoughts, rolled over and went back to sleep.

It was close to sundown when Yahyah was woken by a commotion down at the bungalow. He sat up abruptly and looked to Ursula, to see what she thought, but only her legs were visible sticking out of the tunnel that led out to the lawn. He caught them immediately and hauled her back into the thicket.

'What are you doing, Yahyah? Let me go! I can't see if you don't let me go,' she hissed furiously when he pulled her tight against him.

'Oosalah not go out there,' he said stubbornly, not releasing her. She struggled within his grip and said again:

'Let me go. I'm not going out there, you idiot, I'm just trying to see what's going in. They've got some whites out there. Now let me . . . ' She stopped when he released her. He looked sheepish. 'Thank you!'

'Yahyah think you leave. Think you go back to Mr Billing,'

he explained but she wasn't listening. Instead she jackknifed her body back into the tunnel. He sighed and wondered if looking after Oosalah would always be this difficult. Once at the entrance Ursula carefully edged her face around the bamboo until she could see the lawn and front porch of the house. The Japanese had four men, three Europeans – but not soldiers – and Billy, with their hands tied behind their backs, standing to one side of the rough grass area that led down to the polo grounds. They were standing perfectly still and watching a party of Malays dig trenches in the ground. The Malays must come from the next kampong, she thought, but why were they digging? Did the Japs think the silver was buried there? She tried to wriggle forward further but Yahyah had his hand tightly around her ankle and she couldn't move up any more. She cursed him instead.

There was an officer in charge and he had a large sword in his hand that looked almost more than he could manage. She wondered what he was going to do with it. The prisoners didn't look too happy. But surely he couldn't . . . ? Could he? Not to Billy. The thought brought bile to her mouth, flooding in hot and sour. She turned and called frantically into the tunnel: 'Yahyah, come up here with me.' The reply was muffled:

'No room, Oosalah.'

'Yes there is! Just slide up beside me. It's a bit tight but I need you to see this.' She knew he didn't like his body to touch hers but that was just too bad. After a moment or two she felt him struggling up beside her and then his head poked out of the tunnel next to hers. He looked across the lawn at the group and assessed the situation. Then he looked at her.

'Do not look, Oosalah. Very bad for men. Very bad for Mr Billing. Do not look,' he said.

'Oh dear God, Yahyah! Can't we do anything? I can't believe they're really going to cut their heads off! We've got to stop them! My God, they're civilians and they haven't done anything wrong. That's Billy out there! I won't let them do this!' It occurred to her that Papa hadn't done anything wrong either. She shuddered and wanted to be sick but it was impossible to drag her eyes away from the spectacle out on the lawn. She struggled to free herself from Yahyah's grip.

'No good, Oosalah. No can help.' Yahyah tugged at her

arm, trying to make her climb back into the bamboo. She refused to budge. He sighed again, loudly in her ear but she ignored him.

'No, Yahyah! Let me go! I've got to help Billy. Please! Oh no, no . . . ' The officer had waved the diggers away. Obviously he thought the trenches were deep enough. Except they weren't trenches, they were graves. My God, Ursula thought, Billy was watching his own grave being dug. The executioner was swinging about the sword that he intended to behead Billy with. Billy looked stiff and pale, the fresh blood showing like a hibiscus blossom against his lapel.

Ursula trembled when the officer shouted for the first man to stand forward. It was Billy. He stood erect despite the wound, tall beside the Japanese guards; he looked very young to die. His jacket was flapping loosely around him in the wind. The cicadas were shrilling loudly and Ursula whispered his name again and again, her thoughts frozen into immobility. After a moment's hesitation he stepped towards the first grave and kneeled there, his body held tensely as though to ward off the blow. The officer lifted the sword. Ursula opened her mouth to scream but Yahyah clamped his hand over it, holding her tightly against him so that her head was turned away.

The officer was shouting at Billy, shouting a question over and over. Billy continued to look down into the grave, his face impassive. The officer screamed at him. Billy made no sound. Then suddenly, quite unexpectedly, the sword fell. For a moment Yahyah thought the officer had missed. Billy continued to kneel, swaying in the wind for the count of five. Then he slumped forward slowly, folding at the waist, before rolling down into the shallow trench. Yahyah closed his eyes and held Ursula even more tightly. She shuddered within his arms.

Then another officer had arrived and was marching towards the execution party. He must be senior to the one with the sword, Yahyah thought, because he was shouting furiously at the first officer who had lowered his sword and was bowing his head in submission. There was more shouting and then the remaining three men were led off, away from the graves, towards a lorry parked in the driveway. Yahyah saw the dark-haired one stumble as he was led away.

Without protest Ursula slid backward into their hiding place and moved against the far wall to let Yahyah back in. He didn't say anything, just looked at her carefully, then curled up beside her again. She was stunned into silence; her terror now realized in the worst possible way. Without a glance at the boy who had saved her life, Ursula leaned her cheek against the rough bark of the tree, panting like an animal cornered after the chase. Yahyah watched her for a moment before laying his head on his arm and closing his eyes. He was tired. He hadn't slept all night. He pitied Ursula but there was nothing he could do to take away the pain. Mr Billing was dead. She had to accept that.

Ursula felt shivery, as though caterpillars were crawling up and down her throat. She kneeled in the bushes and retched dryly. Then she wrapped her arms tightly around her and let the blackness into her mind. It stilled and soothed with a numbing release. From time to time Yahyah opened his eyes and looked over at her but she was always sitting, curled up against the tree trunk. Good, he thought, maybe she had settled down to wait for the Japanese to leave. And maybe, just maybe . . . no, he shook his head. That would take time. He could be patient, but it would take time. He smiled gently and fell asleep.

Chapter Seven

In all, Ursula spent three years waiting for the Japanese to leave. When it became dark she and Yahyah slipped out from her hiding-place behind the bamboo, cutting back through the jungle until it hit the main creek. This they waded through as it wound its way back around the edge of the cemetery and down towards the kampong. It was very late by the time they crept into Ibrahim's hut but no-one was asleep yet. Fatimah alternately wept and scolded and laughed for the next few hours while Ibrahim ignored her and spoke quietly in the corner with his eldest son. He was a stern man, one whom Ursula had always been slightly in awe of, and now that he was Lembaga there was an added dignity and austerity to him. She would have to mind him as his own children did. But for the moment nothing mattered except that Billy and Papa were dead. There was nowhere else open to her. She drank from the jug they handed her, silently drawn in her pain. Fatimah spoke to her but Ursula stared blankly out at the night until Fatimah took her in her arms and rocked her gently to and fro while dry soundless sobs racked her. Later she settled down beside Fatimah, and fell asleep.

There were times over the next few weeks when she thought about leaving. Life was hard in the village, harder now than ever before, and there were never-ending jobs to be done that her clumsy and unskilled fingers could not master. She felt a burden, despite the friendliness and courtesy with which the

110

women showed her again and again how to do the task she had been allotted. Ibrahim had excused her from the mandatory prayers that took place five times a day, the villagers kneeling down in the main forecourt of the kampong and repeating the creed: 'There is no God but Allah, and Mohammed is his Prophet.' But this kindness only served to make her feel different and apart from the others. They tried very hard to make her feel one of them and accepted but everything she did seemed to be wrong, *haram*, forbidden. She let the stray dogs lick her hands; she pointed with her finger to what she wanted; she ate with both hands instead of just her right; she forgot to wash her feet with water from the jug on the porch of the hut before entering. Every action seemed to trip her up and offend. It wasn't that she had never known about Malay custom but the trick was observing them when, to her, they meant nothing. She did her best, anxious to please, but her best was slow to learn. At night she would curl herself up tightly on her pallet and try not to mind the insects or the hardness of the floor. It would all be all right she told herself; she could adapt.

Slowly she did learn, finding that it became habit for her to sit on mats on the floor with her feet tucked under her rather than in a chair. Her muscles stretched out and became more pliable, so that she could squat on the ground and tend the evening meal without constantly having to stand and relieve her aching legs and back. Fatimah taught her the proper, and modest, way in which to bathe, wrapping a sarong around the body so that it covered her chest and knees. Then water was ladled over the body from the bucket with the sarong still firmly in place. Ursula found her hair tended to get caught in the wet sarong while she tried to slip the dry one over her. It was an irritating way in which to wash but she dared not do otherwise. Modesty was all important where there was a chance a man might see you, even if he wasn't supposed to watch. She had caught Yahyah occasionally walking by the well when she was washing, knowing that he had no business being there. He had cast longing looks across at her, his eyes following the way the water made the thin cotton cling, almost transparent, to her body. It worried her. She knew he was interested in her but she still thought of him as her old playmate. His looks were not returned.

111

Yahyah was not discouraged. He had good prospects. His father was Lembaga, his family well off within the kampong, and the Japanese had done no more than briefly walk through the village, sending the women and children screaming into their huts. But they had not hurt anyone and his father had talked with their leader. There was no trouble. The crops had not been destroyed and there was food enough for all. Ursula must learn to like him, he thought. And in time she would come to see him as something more than her brother of old. In time she would see him as her lover, her husband, the father of her children. In time. He glanced across at her where she sat minding the evening meal. Such a slender, graceful girl. He felt a stirring within him that could not be eased.

Fatimah kept her busy in the vegetable garden, minding the children, helping with the cooking and housework, and weaving mats. It kept her mind occupied during the time when she had most to think about.

Finally, the tasks no longer required such strict concentration, but she still found that she could not think of Billy or Papa and Tom without pain. Something had snapped that dreadful day when her family had disintegrated around her. The voice that had tried so desperately to scream had been lost somewhere down inside her so that now she would open her mouth and say a word but no sound came.

Fatimah had been loving at first, trying to help her speak. But as time went on, and nothing happened to change her silence, the kampong learned to accept it. Malay life taught them to be accepting. The medicine man, the Pawang, tried often to explain what had happened to the girl's voice. It puzzled him as much as the villagers. He was a grizzled old man with a gap-toothed smile and a white cap on his head. He was Haji; he had made the pilgrimage to Mecca. The villagers revered him and Ursula listened to him endlessly, his gentle expression never changing when she offered no reply. And he had time to talk while she worked. He explained life with a simple wisdom that provoked thought, if not belief. He would sit, cross-legged, beside her while she weaved, her fingers growing more nimble with each passing month. The village was familiar now, its smells and gentle bustle, the children playing or trying to climb into the lap of anyone who sat down

112

for a moment, and the smiles and nods of the adults as they praised a child.

The Pawang told her that everything, living or dead, possessed a soul-substance, *semangat*, that must be conserved. It was his job to do so, to keep that vital spark alive through his magic incantations and amulets, his divinations from leaves and candle flames. Ursula was fascinated, listening with the open mind of a child to his tales of a being with a monkey's tail and a razor-edged forearm who lived in the jungle and would catch disobedient children; she learned that the rise and fall of the tides was due to a Giant Crab going in and out of his hole and that there was a fabulous mountain, Maha Meru, that existed at the navel of the earth. There was a reason for her silence, he told her. Her *semangat* had been damaged. It would take time to repair itself, with his help. She must be patient. And he would burn leaves, moving them around a candle flame until she grew tired and despondent. Nothing seemed to work.

In time the Pawang told her about the Muslim faith, explaining that God had not decreed that one man should be a Muslim and another not, but that it was the necessity of His Being that made it so. This left Ursula puzzled; she had no idea what he meant but nodded her head and smiled as though she understood. Later that night Yahyah tried to simplify things for her. He held her hand shyly within his, stroking the roughened palm, his face no longer that of a young boy but almost that of a man:

'Absolute Being is identical with the spiritual essence of man. God is like a sea, flat and calm without movement but with the potential to have waves. Those waves are man's outward body, and life is like a surge in God's infinite sea, His infinite Being. Do you understand, Oosalah?' His face glowed with pleasure at being able to teach her.

She shook her head, more defeated than ever. Why was everything a riddle? Why couldn't it be straightforward and make sense? Yahyah tried again:

'It is said in the Quran that "wheresoever you turn, there is the face of God". So you must see that man is a part of God's universe, man's backbone is the pillar of God's throne, his bile is fire, his phlegm is water, his belly the ocean, his spirit a bird.

113

For us there can be no separation and so ''only if Allah and Muhammad suffer harm, can I suffer harm!'' We are safe in His . . . '

She held up her hand, shaking her head as always. She liked the bit about his spirit being a bird. Like her own spirit, perhaps, that had turned to wood when everyone she loved had died. She wondered whether Allah believed in painted birds, like Billy. But she couldn't ask Yahyah that and the rest didn't mean a thing to her. She gave a smile that said 'Let's just drop it now and try again another time, all right?', trying to conceal the yawn that showed her inattention. His face lost some of its brightness, his smile faltered a little and Ursula felt he had lost face before her. She shook her head and smiled at him, pointing at herself and putting her hands to one side of her ear to show how tired she was. He smiled shyly, his pride restored:

'Oosalah, you work very hard for my family. We want you to understand our faith, that is all. One day perhaps it will come to you. One day, perhaps, you will become of our family.' He dipped his head before rising gracefully and leaving the hut. Fatimah sighed from her place in the corner:

'My son tries hard to teach you. He takes great pains, talks with the Pawang and with his father, so that he may explain well. It would please me if you could learn. You are like a daughter to me, Oosalah. It will be hard to part with you.' Ursula leaned over to her amah and touched her hand, signing with a touch of her fingers to her body and then out in a sweeping arc. It was a question. 'Must I leave?'

Fatimah smiled, pleased, and placed her cheek against the girl's, sniffing slightly. This was *'chium'*, and was the old Malay way to kiss.

'You will leave us one day, Oosalah. It is said that sparrows must be with sparrows, ravens with ravens. You would never fit here. My son will not accept that but in time he will see it. He must see it.' Fatimah looked uneasily across at the delicate girl who was so close to becoming a woman. Let the war end soon, she prayed, and let Oosalah return to her own kind. Before my son must be hurt. Before my husband discovers the truth: that Yahyah wishes Oosalah for his wife. She sighed and turned back to her weaving.

Ursula sighed too. Birds of a feather, flock together; that's

114

what Fatimah was telling her. And she would have to go elsewhere and make a new life with people like her. But where
would that be? She wished the war would come to an end. It
was hard to live from day to day, never knowing what the
future would bring. She liked things to be planned out, not
dependent on the whims of others. They had been lucky so far;
the Japanese had left them alone. But as time passed Ursula
became more and more impatient. One day, she would say to
herself, one day the war will end and I'll go home. Home. It
was an odd word if you said it over and over. She wasn't sure
what she meant by home even. Maybe what she really meant
was back, back in time to the old days when everyone was still
alive. Before the war, not after it. But that didn't exist anymore
and nothing could bring it back. Nothing would bring Billy
back. For the moment she was safe and cared for; the rest
would have to wait.

Yahyah, however, was tired of waiting. Ursula had been with
them for nearly a year and still showed no sign of appreciating
him. He didn't mind that she couldn't speak. That was Allah's
will. But she could show him more interest, more respect. Impatiently, he threw the stone he was rolling in his palm into the
creek. He was not bad looking, he thought. All the other girls
in the kampong of marriageable age were interested in him.
Some even from the next kampong. Why not Ursula? She
would be fifteen very soon now. Many girls were married by
fifteen. Many had children. He had noticed her body
changing, small buds of breasts forming, her hips becoming
slightly more rounded. She would never be a womanly figure
but she pleased him and he had felt the stirrings grow stronger
and more difficult to control. Yahyah breathed in sharply.
What could he do? It would not be right to force her. But he
could not master his longing for much longer. Reluctantly, he
waded into the water, feeling the chill waters swirl around his
body. He liked to bathe often but this was not to be clean. This
was to clear his head, clear his body of indecent thoughts.
Angrily, he sluiced himself down.

That night, Yahyah lay close beside Ursula in the hut. His
parents lay to one side, behind a curtain, and the children were
spread out around him. All were asleep. Ursula lay on her side,

her head pillowed on one outstretched arm, her long dark hair spread out across the straw matting. The sarong was wrapped loosely around her body, dipping in the back to reveal a smooth brown expanse of skin. Gently Yahyah reached out and traced the line of her vertebrae, running a finger along and down to where the sarong met her skin and concealed her body. She shivered in her sleep, turning to face him. The material of her sarong had slipped as she twisted her body on the rush matting, falling loose around her breasts. Yahyah held his breath. One pale pink nipple lay exposed, soft and delicate against tanned skin. He breathed out again. She did not move.

Again he reached out a finger, stroking the skin above her breasts, dipping lower, skimming the nipple. Ursula sighed in her sleep, a smile lifting the corners of her mouth. Yahyah smiled back. This time he touched her nipple, holding it between two fingers and stroking it gently in circular movements with his thumb. Like a flower that closes at night, the nipple tightened, furling into a hard bud. He moved forward. Her skin was dusty with tanaka powder, perfuming the air around her. Hesitantly he lowered his lips to her breast. She breathed with the still quiet of deep sleep. Around him, the others lay prone. Then he kissed her skin, the warmth and fragrance of it melding with his senses. Ursula moaned slightly. His other hand roved further down her body, moulding itself over her hip, dipping itself into the curves of her legs. She rolled away and he fitted himself tightly against her, kissing her shoulder, the back of her neck, breathing in her scent. He felt himself grow hard and pulled her back into him, her buttocks fitting neatly into his lap.

For some time he lay against her, scared to proceed further, too aroused to leave off. She had settled deeply into sleep again and gradually he raised the folds of her sarong, baring her thighs. He slipped a warm hand across her hip under the material. The hand moved further, across her flat belly, down to the soft fur that lay in a dark triangle between her legs. He groaned at the throbbing within his own body as his fingers brushed that fur. Easing his own clothing to one side, Yahyah pressed himself against her warm flesh, slipping his hand between her legs. She tossed her head, her hair falling in his face. He froze. But she did not wake and he pushed himself

116

tightly against her. He would not take her now, he thought. But soon. Very soon. Perhaps tomorrow. His hands roved with less caution over her breasts, her stomach, down to the area he most wanted to explore. But it was too soon and not private enough. Reluctantly he pulled away, turning and wrapping himself into a tight ball. Ursula continued to sleep undisturbed.

The next afternoon Ursula went up to the Chinese Cemetery alone. The horses were no longer there; they had been found by the Japanese almost immediately. Ursula sighed, wondering what had happened to Bintang and Jambang. It was hard to bear. But she still liked to roam over the hills, smelling the incense and charcoal burning in the braziers over the graves in a mixture of sweet and acrid smoke. It wasn't that unusual for her to go alone and although Fatimah worried in case a Japanese soldier should find her there, Ursula was not scared. She could run fast and she knew the land well. And sometimes she needed to be by herself.

There was a point where the creek grew wide and shallow, passing over pebble and scree in a clear rushing torrent. Ursula liked to go there to bathe. She had been disturbed lately by strange feelings within her, feelings that she was too shy to try and explain to Fatimah and that were yet strong enough to make her short of breath and faint at times. The way Yahyah and some of the other young men looked at her made her self-conscious. But it was pleasant, she had to admit. And that disturbed her still more. Only that night she had had a dream. She flushed and redirected her thoughts.

Squatting down beside the creek, she lowered her sarong until it skimmed her hips. She bunched up the rest of the material, tying it high on her hip. Then she knelt down and splashed water over her face and breasts, gasping at the cold. It was coming up to the Wet and the water could be quite chill. She passed her hand over her breasts, rubbing at the nipples gently at first and then harder. The strange breathlessness came over her and she felt an emptiness down in her belly as though she had not eaten in a long time. Her head felt heavy, her limbs weighted down. Around her, the land seemed to fade back, blurring. A coppersmith's single note of warning called repetitively.

When she looked up Yahyah was standing beside her.

117

She turned away and tried to fasten her sarong around her. Yahyah squatted down beside her. He reached out and touched her hair, spreading it over his hand and letting it fall down her back. She tried to form the words 'Don't, Yahyah! You should not be here. It isn't right.' But the words died in her throat and the dream came back to her; she watched him from beneath lowered eyes, wondering.

'I won't hurt you, Oosalah. You will like me. Do not be scared.' Yahyah had moved forward, anticipating her sudden attempt at flight. He caught her easily as she rose to her feet, pinning her back down against the bank. The sarong fell open around her breasts. Ursula did not try to struggle. She lay beneath him, surprised both at him and at herself, at the rush of sensation passing through her. Breathless anticipation. This should not be happening. What would Billy think; the thought intruded suddenly and she caught her breath, feeling the familiar pain shoot splinters into her.

'It is permitted when two people care for each other and intend to marry. I am permitted to take you,' Yahyah said, knowing that he lied but wanting her so much that nothing mattered anymore. She lay pinned beneath him, shivering as his hands followed the same path they had travelled the night before. She gasped when he slipped his hand between her legs. It felt strange but pleasant. But why was it permitted? She did not understand. She was shy and would not look him in the face but when he suddenly parted her legs and pressed himself up against her, she looked up at him in stunned surprise. Was this how it was supposed to be?

Fear overcame her then and she struggled harder, pushing backwards up the bank. Yahyah held her tighter, trying to soothe her building panic. She turned her face away when he tried to kiss her, burying it in the fern that lay beside her head. Her breath came in short, sharp bursts but still the scream that lodged in her throat would not come out. Instead a shout came from above them and to the left, startling them both. A guttural cry from a Japanese soldier, a long braying laugh. Yahyah dragged Ursula to her feet and together they ran, their backs flinching against an expected bullet, Ursula trailing her sarong around her hips. But no-one followed them; nothing smashed into them to leave them broken and bloody. It was as

118

though the soldier had never seen them. They reached the shelter of the jungle, panting for breath.

Ursula immediately refastened her sarong, the bold copper and purple splashes of colour exploding against the dark green of the jungle as she shook it out. Yahyah peered out, careful not to reveal himself to a sniper. There was no-one, the afternoon still and swathed in smoke from the fires. Light glinted off brass incense pots, pieces of chrome from abandoned bumpers, glass jars and tinkling windchimes. But not from a rifle, not from polished metal on a uniform. The soldier was gone. When Yahyah turned back into the jungle, he found Ursula had also gone, fading quietly back into the creepers, climbing silently over tree trunks and escaping back to the kampong. He cursed silently and wiped his upper lip across his arm.

Fatimah knew there was something wrong, something she had not yet understood about the way Ursula sat curled up on the palm-slatted porch, hugging her arms around her. She could see the girl was unhappy but did not know why. For two days she had sat like that, ignoring the children when they tugged at her hand to come and play. Only when there was work to be done did she stand and go about her tasks, but it was with tentative movements and wary looks. She kept close to Fatimah and the other women. At first Fatimah wondered if a soldier had forced himself on the girl. But there were no bruises that could be seen. And no real distress. Just that blank unhappiness that Fatimah had begun to hope had finally lifted from the girl's spirits. She had seemed so much better lately; seemed almost about to speak again. And now . . . ' Fatimah sighed sharply.

'Where is my son, Ursula? Have you seen him? He will be late for the evening meal.' That was strange, Fatimah thought. The girl had flinched at the mention of Yahyah, turning away from her amah as though she would have nothing to do with either of them. Fatimah felt her heart grow cold and heavy. May Allah in his wisdom prevent this, she prayed. May it not have happened. She stooped over beside Ursula, stroking the girl's hair back from her face.

'Tell me child. Tell me what has happened.' But Ursula had no words with which to speak and no thoughts to tell her amah.

119

Yahyah had said 'it is permitted'. They had permitted him to try and do those things to her. She shuddered, the strange feeling of shame and anger engulfing her again. She tossed her head so that her hair was snatched from Fatimah's hands. Fatimah would not help. He was her son and he had said it was permitted. His father was the Lembaga. What could she say against that?

But as it turned out, it was Ibrahim who came to her aid. An angry and shamed Ibrahim who stood before her that evening and begged her pardon for his son's behaviour. And Yahyah stood pale and tense behind his father, tears filling his eyes for all he blinked and swallowed to clear them. Ursula would not look up.

'You must understand. My son meant to be honourable. He wished you for his bride. I am shamed by him and his actions but no shame was meant to you. He truly loves you.' Ibrahim bit off the words, bitterness tinging the apology. Ursula nodded and still would not look up.

'My son would speak with you. He would beg forgiveness. Will you allow it?' Ibrahim stared at the beam above Ursula's head. Reluctantly she nodded again. Ibrahim removed himself several paces and Yahyah stood alone in front of the girl he had lost.

'Oosalah? Please. I am shamed and undone. I could not help the way I felt but . . . ' He swallowed and continued. 'I could not allow your unhappiness to continue. I confessed to my father, the Lembaga. I am sorry! So sorry! I would not have hurt you – never that! I only wished to make you love me, as I loved you.' She looked up at that, tentatively, her brow creased. Loved? Did he not love her anymore? Could they go back to brother and sister as it once had been? He saw the question in her eyes.

'I may not marry you. My father has forbidden it. I may not love you. That too is forbidden.' He gasped as though in pain but continued. 'You are Missy and I am Malay. It is not permitted. I lied. Forgive me, Oosalah. I am sorry!' He did not add what his father had told him. His father! No, the man who had reared him as his son. Not his father. That man was dead. The same man that Oosalah had called 'father'. He swallowed again to ease the dryness in his throat, knowing his sin for what it was. May Allah forgive him; may Allah forgive them all. Tears forced their way out past his clenched eyelids, spurting down his face as he fought for control. He breathed in deeply, cutting off the sob before it could leave his throat.

Ursula reached for Yahyah's hand, squeezing it tight. 'Shh' she wanted to say 'shh, don't cry. I am here and everything will be fine'. That was what Billy would have said. Her Billy. She smiled sadly at Yahyah, holding his hand still. It was all forgiven. He was her brother of old, her childhood playmate. How could she not forgive him? Gently she leaned forward and kissed a cheek wet from tears. He started, moving back to leave a space between them. Then he nodded and smiled also, his mouth twisting with pain. There must always be that space between them now. But he would learn to think of her as his sister. As she thought of him as her brother. They were brother and sister. He would try. He would do it. He sighed, a long shuddering sigh and smiled again. It would be all right.

It was sometime in early September 1945 when the soldiers walked into the kampong, slung their backpacks down on the earth and with smiling gestures, pointed to the well. They looked tired and thirsty. Ursula was sitting under a palm, playing with the babies, her body as brown as theirs now from the sun. She was startled by the soldiers' arrival and even more so by the fact that they weren't Japanese. They were Australian. Ibrahim came out of his hut when the children started shouting and the women stopped their weaving, staring with surprise and interest at these strange men. No Europeans had been by there in three years. It was very unexpected.

'Ah, goodaye. Can we drink here?' one of the men said. The flat twang to his voice brought back strange memories and Ursula couldn't help smiling. The soldier was holding both hands out to show he meant no harm. It made her giggle when he dropped into pidgin: '*Can drinkee, la?*'

Ibrahim nodded. '*Can*. Where come from?' The soldiers were relieved to see the natives were friendly and even spoke English. They gathered around Ibrahim with loud laughs, everyone talking at once. Their spokesman raised his hand for silence:

'Ah, we're from Oz – yew blokes know the war's over? We

took over the island a few days ago. Just mopping up the last of the bloody nips. Good to know ya aren't all dead – we cleaned out Changi a while back. Aw strewth, yew can count ya blessings yew aren't bloody poms!' There were good-natured laughs and some coughs from a thin, spindly-looking soldier who seemed to be upset at the mention of Changi. Ursula stood up and walked over to the group.

'I am,' she said baldly. Ibrahim and the villagers stared at her, their faces as stunned as those of the soldiers. The soldiers' laughter died abruptly. They looked uncertain, eyeing the thin brown girl wrapped in her sarong with doubt. Ibrahim sighed and nodded confirmation. The spokesman whistled:

'My very word, a bleeding pom! Aw, sorry, Miss, didn't mean to swear in front of a lady. It's just, we didn't expect to meet . . . I mean, yew look like a native, if yew don't mind my saying so.' His look compared the girl with the good-looking boy standing protectively beside her. They could have been brother and sister, the soldier thought. Ursula laughed, her quick eyes taking in the soldier's thoughts. She glanced side-ways at Yahyah and laughed again, her throat aching with the release of long unused muscles. Then she looked up at the man again, thinking how odd he looked with his flushed face and tight clothes. She turned to Fatimah and smiled, a long, sad smile.

'No, actually, I don't mind at all.'

Chapter Eight

The ship docked at Southampton in January 1946. It was a
P&O liner and Ursula had travelled third-class to save money.
She'd never known such squalid conditions, sharing the cabin
with three other women who were returning to England; going
home. They spoke of it with such longing and intensity, pining
for the cool greys and rain-misted skies after the hell of Changi.
Ursula listened with a strange feeling of being apart and different. She still longed for Singapore and the heat, the brilliant
colours, and the green jungle creeping over everything. She
couldn't feel any welcome for the cooler winds, the grey choppy
seas, and the dull leaden sky that greeted them as the ship
turned north along the coast of Africa towards Europe. It was
strange to her and alien. She was going to a country she had
never seen, to people she had never known, and she was expected to be glad. Glad, yes, to have somewhere to go but, oh, it
was so hard to leave Singapore. It was her home and now she
would never see it again. The thought brought an ache to her
throat, try as she would to appear cheerful. The other women
were sympathetic at first. But as they got closer to home, they
grew more impatient of her homesickness.

One of them, the old one called Mrs Pearson, had been out
in the East for most of her married life. Her husband was a civil
servant, a minor clerk up in Kuala Lumpur before the war. He
had died on the railway but his wife had survived internment
and was glad to be shot of the East.

'It was bad enough living there as a European with a proper

house and a proper lifestyle but when they put us in that camp! I can't understand, my dear, how you could ever have fitted in with those natives in that kampong. It really isn't a decent sort of upbringing for a girl your age. You should have turned your-self in and been interned with the rest of us. At least then you'd have been with your own sorts. Europeans. Not, well, heathens!'

She had a lot more to say on the same theme and Ursula learned to turn a deaf ear. How could anyone live in a place they hated that much, Ursula wondered. And why do so? She didn't yet understand about lack of money or husbands' wishes. Instead she looked at the women with increasing be-wilderment. These women had lived in the East and yet they still knew nothing, nothing at all about how it really was! How could she expect anyone in England, who had never known her life in the East, to understand her? Would her relatives, her aunt and uncle, feel this way about her? Surely not. They were family. They would understand. They must.

What was strange was that the other women always talked about the East before the war, or just as it was starting. They never talked about their experiences during the war, except perhaps in hushed whispers about someone else. The other two were younger: one of them silent with the grief of having lost her husband and children, the other making up for the silence with a cheery cockney chat that mentioned things Ursula could never quite fathom. They were a strange party to be travelling together and, despite the endless weeks of being cooped up in a space no more than twelve by eight, they never became friends, censuring Ursula for 'going native' without ever trying to find out more. Ursula withdrew into her bunk and pulled the curtains when she couldn't go on deck. The curtains shut out the sights even if they couldn't shut out the voices, too many of them cramped into too small a space, each of them trying to keep to themselves. The further they went north, the more Ursula felt as though her last ties to her home were being severed.

Her uncle and aunt were supposed to be coming to meet the boat: her father's sister, the one he had disliked and never spoken of except in tones of contempt, and her husband, the reason for Papa's contempt. She wondered what could be so wrong with him that Papa had never forgiven his sister for marrying him. Ursula stood anxiously in line for the immigration officer, thinking, 'Oh, she hoped they liked her!' She had a new passport, issued in Singapore by the British Embassy, and her fare had been paid by a Mr Johnson who said he was a friend of Papa's; a business friend. Ursula vaguely remembered him from one of Papa's parties and as he seemed to think it his duty to see her safely taken care of, Ursula didn't like to argue – especially when he was willing to pay for her fare and for the new clothes on her back. There was no-one else to pay for things and no money left. Mr Johnson had told her that.

People had been startled, and disapproving when she was driven into Singapore City to the embassy. They talked about the kampong, about Ursula living with Fatimah and her family with raised eyebrows, with hissed-in breath and whispers, with the effusive kindness that hid distaste. Ursula wished desperately that she hadn't spoken to the Australian soldier. That had been the beginning of the end. There had been such a fuss, with a British officer being sent for and endless questions that she had had to repeat the answers to, again and again. Then they had said she must come with them and she had hugged Fatimah and the children, trying not to see the pain in Yahyah's face or the sorrow in Ibrahim's. It had all been so beastly, she thought, so typically bureaucratic in that colonial way.

Mr Johnson had come to see her and give her money. The way he kept catching his tongue between his teeth before he spoke, almost as though he were scared of what he might really say had left her feeling an outcast amongst her own people. And then the people on the boat, people who had survived the war, had been the worst. They had been so cold, so stiffly aware that she had done things that white people should not do; that she had lived with natives. She knew they were wondering if, under her new English clothes, she wasn't really a little browner than she should be. Ursula refused to make excuses. Fatimah and her family were all she had left and she loved them more than any of the pale Europeans who criticized and whispered behind her back. Her aunt and uncle wouldn't care that she had lived in a kampong. They would only care

125

that she had lived at all. Surely they would. She turned a blank face to it all, trying to shut it out, trying to ignore the anxiety in her own mind. Ursula remembered with a cold little shudder her first encounter with such prejudice when she arrived on the boat. The interest and speculation in everyone's eyes.

'Tea, Ursula?' Such a pallid, fleshy woman Mrs Pearson was, her features blunt, her manner equally so.

'Yes, thank you. I'm so sorry to be intruding like this. It's very kind of you all to share your cabin with me like this.' Ursula thought how hard she had tried, when she had first boarded the boat and how useless it had been. The rumours had preceded her.

'We must all learn to be kind and share what we can. So many people were caught up in the war here and so few survived. Astonishing how some did, really. Take yourself for example. Many young women would rather have died than had to live like you did. Did you really not mind?' The probing, bulbous eyes avid for some real knowledge, something beyond the coffee-morning gossip circulating about this girl. What had she really done? There was talk about a young native man. Maybe some of those little brown babies that had clung to her so hard when she left weren't completely Malay? Maybe . . . the woman smiled over her teacup at Ursula.

'Fatimah was my amah. She brought me up after my mother died. There was no real difference in living with her in our bungalow or with her family in the kampong.' Ursula faced the woman squarely. 'I consider them to be my family now.'

'Really? Now that is an interesting admission.' The spectacles held up to those eyes, wavering blindly behind the thick glass; the faded lips creased into folds of cheek. Really? they said. And Ursula knew she was condemned for that admission. Gone native, maybe in more ways than we know. Ostracize the creature; God knows what example she might set the other girls. Sad, but really, really these things simply aren't done. Ursula read it all in the woman's face. She sipped her tea. Really.

And that had been all she had known on the boat. Ursula picked up her bag and moved a few steps forward in the queue.

They were waiting for her in the arrival hall, a large hand-made sign announcing her name held in the man's hand. For a moment, almost like taking a deep breath before diving into cold water, she watched them from a distance. They didn't know her; she could have these few moments to think, to see how she should approach them. She hesitated and a large woman walking too close on her heels cannoned into her with loud curses and suggestions that she watch what she was effing-well doing. The commotion caught the man's eye, and then he was tugging on his wife's sleeve and pointing the girl out. Wasn't she like Lillian? Could that be her?

Ursula felt something close to panic when the woman turned her dark eyes on her. She was exposed; they knew who she was. No chance now for a quiet look at her aunt and uncle before they all met; no chance to think over her greeting. The woman was watching her intently, addressing short asides to her husband. So this was Aunt Mary; she was as plain as her name, with a thin, bird-like quality to her and dark, wiry hair pulled back with a barette on either side of her parting. She was wearing a floral dress underneath a dark woollen coat and had a funny Robin Hood-like hat. She didn't smile once while she stared at Ursula. The man was a little more inviting; he actually forced his mouth into the semblance of a smile, nodding and ducking his head. His dark brown suit was too tight under a raincoat that looked crumpled from the journey and the rain. Ursula stepped out of the flow of people and walked slowly towards her only relatives. She wasn't sure how to behave, her eager smile wobbling at the corners from nervousness. She wondered whether they were glad to see her or if they wished her somewhere else far away; somewhere where she wasn't going to be a burden on people who didn't even know her.

'Aunt Mary? Uncle George?' Ursula stopped in front of them, uncertainly. Could these people really be the Martins; could she really be Papa's sister, so pale and small, so pinched of mouth? They sensed her indecision immediately and with-drew what little warmth they were capable of. It was difficult with a total stranger whose relationship made demands upon them that they were unable to deny. Aunt Mary nodded stiffly:

'You must be Ursula, Henry's girl.' She didn't offer to kiss the girl but held out a gloved hand and shook Ursula's fingers.

Ursula couldn't help thinking that no-one had ever called Papa 'Henry'. She smiled at the woman, her face muscles stiff from lack of use, and stepped back a pace. All around her joyful reunions were being made with arms thrown around necks and teary babbles of greeting.

'I'm sorry I took so long getting off the boat but we had to go through customs and immigration and all that. It took forever.' She sensed an apology was expected for even having survived the war but that hadn't been her fault. It was talking to that soldier that had caused all the trouble. She looked away abruptly, missing the tentative smile the man called Uncle George addressed to her. His smile faded.

'Is that all you have?' He gestured to the one small suitcase at her feet. Ursula nodded.

'But, is everything else coming later? In trunks?' That was Aunt Mary, her voice sharp with concern.

'No, this is everything. The Japanese occupied our bungalow and the godowns were burnt down in the initial shelling. At least, that's what I was told. I tried to save the silver on the last day – you know, before we were overrun – but they, the Japanese found it anyway. They found the horses too. There isn't anything left except me.' There was dead silence while her aunt and uncle assimilated the news.

'Oh, I see. Then you're totally without funds of any kind? We did hear, from the Foreign Office, you'd, well . . . been living in a native village.' Aunt Mary laughed as though she didn't believe such things were possible. 'Surely that was a mistake on their part? You couldn't have been living with natives in their huts?' The question hung in the air. Never had Ursula felt less welcome or more of a burden. She remembered Fatimah and Ibrahim's kindness with a pang of homesickness that lodged hard in her throat. It was impossible for her to speak, so she shook her head instead. No, there wasn't any money, or furnishings, or personal items, or clothes – except what that man had bought her – and there was no-one left but her. Papa and Billy. Both gone. And Sally and Emma and Tom could not be traced. They were still looking. She hung her head to hide the tears spilling over her cheeks. All gone.

'Well now, no need for tears is there? We're here to take care of you. It's a bit of a shock that you've no . . . no money to help out with things. We're not rich, you know. And things are very difficult nowadays, what with people being laid off work and things costing so much. But we'll manage I daresay. So stop crying, there's a good girl.' Uncle George was clearly trying to be kind in his brusque way and Ursula sniffed and hunted for a handkerchief in her sleeve. She was wearing her warmest clothes, a heavy cotton dress and long white socks, and a woollen cardigan buttoned up over the dress. Clothes had been hard to get hold of in Singapore and winter clothes impossible. Her sarong had been taken away almost immediately she arrived at the embassy. One couldn't have her going around like that, could one? She shivered in the bitter, damp air, wondering if England were always this cold.

Her aunt and uncle looked at each other, sending silent messages over Ursula's bowed head. What were they to do with her? She was painfully thin and tall, her brown skin turned sallow with the lack of sun and warmth. Her hair hung limply down her back, a dull brown that did nothing for her, Aunt Mary decided. Like Lillian indeed! George must have rocks in place of brains. There was little chance of getting the girl married off in the near future, not when she looked no more than fifteen and had absolutely no figure.

'What about your step-mother and the children? Were they in Singapore too?'

'They can't trace what happened to them. They're still trying to find out,' Ursula managed to say after a few moments. Aunt Mary's face became more pinched still. She sighed heavily.

'Well, come along then. Let Uncle George take your suitcase. We're going to have to hurry if we want to catch the next train.'

They missed the train by just a few minutes and had to wait on the platform for another half-hour until the next one came through. The chill from the cement platform penetrated Ursula's light shoes and her toes became numb, her feet frozen to the ground. All around her people in dark colours huddled in their coats, their breath steaming out in front of them. There was a funny smell to the air, a smell that she couldn't quite define but that was clearly England: ashes on damp earth, smoke, wet greenery, something sharp and fresh like mint. The other passengers were used to all this, the waiting, the cold, the smoke-laden air. It didn't bother them; they didn't even see it. They had never known heat that engulfed the bones, sending them limp, nor sun that seared through the clothes on one's back; they had never seen the brilliant purples and reds, the savage green of the jungle or the blinding white of the sun on whitewashed walls. These people had known a different war to Ursula; one she couldn't comprehend. She shivered between her aunt and uncle, wishing the train would arrive.

It took them three and a half hours to get home. The train was badly-heated, scorching the back of their legs from the vent underneath their seats, but never managing to lift the chill from the air. Every few minutes they stopped at a small station and people got on, or off, the open doors blowing gusts of cold air into their compartment that eddied around them, nipping at their faces and hands. Then they lurched on to the next station, the train never managing to get up any speed. They were travelling second-class and Ursula wondered, through the cracks of a sheltered and privileged childhood that had disintegrated around her, if this was how the world really was. Second- and third-class. She almost couldn't believe in the days before the war. It was like another century; another world even. And she wasn't sure if she could fit into this world; not when it looked as though her aunt and uncle really didn't want her. Why, why had she survived when everyone else had died? The question haunted her.

From time to time, she would open her eyes and stare out through the windows. Papa and Billy had painted pictures of an England of green patchwork-like fields and stone cottages with roses tumbling over the doorways, of heather like purple mist on the moors and streams meandering through green banks. Instead she saw bare trees lining the sides of the track, rows of terraced houses with tiny windows and dull red bricks, and a darkening, rain-clouded afternoon. The trees looked stark and dead, the branches wetly black under a lowering sky. She had never seen anything but evergreens. It filled her with a sense of desolation to see the wood bare like twigs of firewood.

She closed her eyes and kept them tightly shut, holding the memories of the kampong and the bungalow in her mind, trying to feel the heat and smell the flowers, frangipani and oleander, bougainvillaea and zinnias, orchids and camellias, trying to hear the wild monkeys chattering in the trees or the birds shrieking raucously to each other with the joy of being alive. She tried not to think about anything except getting home to a nice, warm house and a hot bath.

The Martins lived in a Victorian terraced house in a suburb of London called Pimlico. It wasn't very fashionable but it was comfortably middle-class and they owned their house's free-hold which was unusual in that area. It was dark by the time they arrived and there was a light shining through the frosted glass in the front door. It looked welcoming and cosy from the pavement and Ursula tried to look pleased when Aunt Mary said:

'Well, this is it. We're home.' A young man opened the door while Uncle George was fiddling in his pockets for the latch-key.

'Hallo! We thought you'd have been back earlier than this. You must be frozen. I'll tell Christopher to put the kettle on, shall I?' The man sounded younger than he looked and anxious that they were finally home. He stepped back, holding the door wide for them to come in and Ursula looked at him curiously as she passed him. Was this a cousin of hers? He looked pink-faced and embarrassed as he glanced at her from dark eyes under heavy eyebrows. She smiled and he disappeared back down the hall.

The house smelled of food, a stuffy gagging smell that made Ursula swallow hard. The others didn't seem to notice it and she followed them up the stairs trying to adjust her breathing. After a few moments the nausea receded. She was just tired. It would be better tomorrow. They led her into a small sitting-room with comfortable slip-covered chairs and sofa, and a blazing fire.

'Sit down by the fire, Ursula. That'll get you warm in no time. Rodney, come and meet your cousin from Singapore.' Uncle George didn't notice Ursula's start. Rodney. She compared the boy to Rodney Hendricks, her cousin in Singapore who had been willing to give his life for his home. Her dead cousin. 'You're both nearly the same age so it'll be nice if you can be friends,' Uncle George said, and both Ursula and

131

Rodney retreated into their shells like snails poked by a stick. They glanced nervously at each other and then looked away. 'Now come on, don't be shy. Rodney go and shake hands with your cousin. Where's Christopher?' The man-boy shuffled over towards Ursula and held out a large hand. She shook hands briefly and let go at once. Uncle George laughed. 'Well, I expect it's a bit strange for you both. You'll get used to each other soon enough. Now how about some tea, my lad? I'm fair frozen to death.' Rodney nodded and escaped with relief, his heavy footsteps echoing down the hall and stairs. Ursula sighed and relaxed back into the chair.

'We'll have to move the boys into a bedroom together if Ursula is to stay with us,' Aunt Mary remarked from the sofa where she had settled herself. She didn't seem to be aware of Ursula's guilty face or tentative disclaimer. 'What d'you think, George? Rodney moves in with Christopher and gives his room to Ursula?' When she was sitting down, her neck seemed even longer than normal, and the angle of her chin struck a determined note that George clearly never disobeyed. He smiled and nodded.

'Whatever you feel is best, my dear.' She lowered her chin and picked up a tapestry she was working on.

'Good. I'll tell them both when they come upstairs.' She glanced at Ursula. 'We're rather crowded as it is, you see. We didn't expect to have another person staying with us for any length of time. It's all been rather a shock, what with poor Henry and now you tell us about his wife and the babies. Of course we don't know they're dead for sure but it's certainly beginning to look like that. Otherwise, I expect you'd have gone to live with them in Australia. They're more used to the East anyway, down there I expect. So you'd have fitted in better. Considering, I mean . . . ' She carried on with her tapestry while she spoke and Ursula felt her eyes filming over, while a spot of red flushed her cheek. What were they to this woman? What did she know? She turned away sharply in her chair and stared into the fire, her lips clenched together firmly between her teeth.

After a while the sound of a tea tray being carried up the stairs warned Ursula that both her cousins were arriving. She sniffed hastily and blinked to clear her eyes. Rodney came in first carrying one tray. He put it down on a table beside his mother, the teacups rattling nervously in their saucers. The second tray was carried by another young man who looked a little older than his brother. This must be Christopher, Ursula thought with surprise. He didn't really look like he belonged to this family at all. He was dark and thin, with a pleasantly assured smile that made Ursula smile in response. He laid the tray down on another table and immediately walked over to her and held out his hand, his mouth quirking a little while he took her in.

'Hallo, Ursula. I'm your cousin, Christopher. Welcome home.' When she smiled shyly and held out her hand, he grasped it firmly and then leant forward to kiss her on the cheek. It was the first real sign of warmth that any of her family had shown her and it completely undid the tired and miserable girl. She felt tears spilling over her lashes and before she could choke it back, she was sobbing loudly and noisily. The Martins froze with embarrassment, Uncle George coughing and saying: 'Dear me!' several times while he rattled the evening paper, and Rodney going red while he stuffed bread and butter into his mouth. Aunt Mary continued with her tapestry, her chin tilted higher than ever while her needle stabbed in and out of the canvas. Only Christopher seemed to understand and he patted Ursula's hand and said: 'There, there,' in a soothing voice. After a few minutes Ursula regained control of herself and sniffed loudly into her handkerchief a few times.

'I'm sorry. I'm just a bit tired, that's all,' she said. Christopher gave her another handkerchief to wipe her face with and Aunt Mary said:

'Yes, I see you must be. Well perhaps it would be best if you went to bed right now? You must be used to early nights anyway. I mean, there was no electricity was there in your native village. Not much to do in the evenings.' She paused in confusion. 'Anyway, Christopher, Rodney is to move in with you. Why don't you show Ursula her room and where we keep the fresh sheets? I think she's really too tired to sit up with us any longer.' There was no warmth in her aunt's voice and Ursula stood up awkwardly, not sure what she should do. Christopher held out his hand and gestured to the door.

'Come on. I'll show you where everything is and get you

133

settled in. Then I'll bring you up a cup of tea and cake. You probably don't feel hungry right now but you will be soon.' He continued to talk to her in the same soothing voice about trivial things while he took her upstairs, changed the bed, took Rodney's belongings next door, and showed her the bathroom. He ran her a bath while she unpacked the few items she possessed and then left her to herself.

It was much colder up on the third floor and there were no fires in any of the bedrooms. She shivered while she undressed and tiptoed over the cold tile floor to the bath. At least the water was hot. She stepped into it with relief. The water lapped over her chilled limbs as she slid down into it and then right under the water. She looked down at her body, at the way she looked so pink and white with her hair floating out around her. That body had been brown and fit only a few months ago. Now she looked like a pale rag doll. She sighed, telling herself it did no good to pine for things that were gone. People who were gone. She was alive. That was something to be grateful for.

She splashed the water between the palms of her hands and thought how much of a luxury this was compared to the boat. It felt good to be clean again.

Ursula stayed in the bath until the water cooled. Then she stepped out and wrapped herself in a towel, rubbing her body hard to keep the heat in. Her nightgown was thin cotton and she didn't have a dressing-gown or slippers so she opened the bathroom door and made a dash for her bedroom and the bed. Somehow Christopher must have known when she was finished in the bathroom because a few minutes later he brought her up the promised tea and cake and put it down on the bedside cabinet beside her bed. Then he smiled and tucked the covers around her as though she were a child.

'All right now? Are you warm enough?' he asked.

'Oh yes, I'm fine now,' Ursula lied, trying to still the shivering of her body. He shook his head at her and went into his own bedroom. A few moments later he appeared with a down quilt which he put over her.

'If you want to be comfortable here, Ursula, you're going to have to say when you're cold. You're not acclimatized yet and it's a pretty bad winter this year anyway. Don't just sit there and shiver when we can do something about it. Tell us,' he lectured her gently, shaking her arm and smiling so that Ursula couldn't help smiling back.

'Sorry. I just feel like I'm putting everyone out enough as it is. I'm not exactly the most welcome visitor your parents ever had, I gather.'

'Don't mind them. That's just the way they are. And Rodney's a good fellow, just a little shy. You'll like him if you give him half a chance. Now, drink your tea and go to sleep. It'll all seem much better in the morning.' Ursula obeyed him, her head already beginning to reel with fatigue. She couldn't manage more than a bite of cake but snuggled back down into the bed's warmth.

'Christopher? Am I an embarrassment to your family? I mean, they haven't once asked about how Papa died or . . . or any of that. And they haven't mentioned how I survived. Is there something I don't know?' Her face was pink from the bath and her hair hung wet down her back making her look more like a child than the eighteen-year-old girl she was. He looked perplexed at first and then shrugged.

'They're just not that interested, I think. It happened somewhere else to people they either didn't know or hadn't seen in years. My parents aren't really very good at visualizing what it must be like for you; they just want to see you fit into their life. They're only capable of seeing it from their angle I suppose. So don't fuss if they don't seem interested. It's a little hard for them to deal with your family's death and the lack of any funds to support you. They're probably just a little anxious about money at the moment. Just don't worry about things. They'll relax soon and I think it's lovely to have a new and pretty cousin.' He leant over and kissed her again. 'Now get some sleep and I'll see you at breakfast.' He left the room walking with light steps and turned off the light before closing the door. In the dark Ursula curled herself into a ball and let the tiredness wash over her, pulling her down into sleep.

135

Chapter Nine

Ursula passed her first winter in a daze of homesickness. Aunt Mary had little sympathy to spare. She couldn't understand how it was that Ursula was not everlastingly grateful for having been taken away from a dreadful, heathen place like Singapore – a place that had seen the murder of her father and family! Why would the girl persist in talking about it as though it were her home? It was really too provoking! Aunt Mary tended instead to ignore Ursula as much as possible. When it wasn't possible it was because Ursula needed to be lectured on her shortcomings – for her own good. Who would want to marry her otherwise? This was a recurring theme with Aunt Mary and Ursula listened with dull, inattentive ears that seemed always to be listening to another conversation that no-one else could hear. It was a trick that irritated her aunt.

There was also the problem of her fitting into society. They had had to get ration books for her which involved long hours queuing in draughty, neon-lit rooms full of furniture but no chairs. Each official had passed them on to another, like parcels, and Aunt Mary had seemed to be as confused by the process as Ursula. Could there really be something called the Ministry of Food? She grew thin-lipped with frustration, and Ursula stood quietly beside her trying not to breathe too loudly.

Then there had been the matter of schooling. Ursula was eighteen. That was old enough for it not to matter anymore, she thought. The Martins thought so too. The problem was, what qualifications did she have? What could she do? Could she type or take shorthand? Could she speak French, or German, or Italian? When Ursula confessed that no, she couldn't do any of these things very well, and some not at all, the family threw up their hands in disgust. Well, what could she do? Ursula was tentative in her reply. She could speak Malay and some Chinese, she could ride and look after horses, and weave coconut mats, and grow vegetables, and cook. They grudgingly conceded that cooking was useful and when she offered to make dinner that night, the offer was accepted. But Ursula's cooking was Malay. And the Martins weren't particularly impressed, stirring the food around with their forks and then going out in the kitchen for big slices of bread and butter. After that, Aunt Mary cooked and Ursula was put in charge of keeping the house clean.

It wasn't that the Martins were trying to be unkind. In fact, they thought they were being remarkably tolerant. Financially, Ursula was a burden on them that they had never expected to have to shoulder and had made no provision for. Relations also became strained when Ursula mentioned something about her past. Strained and resentful. If her family were trying to put her existence in the kampong behind them, the least she could do, they felt, was the same.

They were united in the knowledge that the war had been something that had happened to them there, in Europe. What took place thousands of miles away on a tiny island in an uncivilized part of the world was of no consequence to anyone. It was a minor wrangle between the natives – the Japanese counted as 'natives' to the Martins – and a few Europeans who should have known better than to be there in the first place. That was all. And the sooner Ursula learned that, and stopped talking about things that bore no relevance to life here, where it mattered, the sooner everyone could get on with their lives. Ursula would catch herself up guiltily in mid-speech, see pinched expressions of distaste on her aunt and uncle's faces, and let her words falter. After a while she didn't initiate conversation at all, having little to say when her entire previous life was considered irrelevant or, worse, actually indecent. So she just replied, briefly, to questions and tried not to irritate her aunt any more than she already did by simply existing.

Things would have been a lot better for her if Christopher had stayed on, but two weeks after she arrived he had returned to University and left her to his parents' care. He was up at Cambridge, a feat his parents were inordinately proud of, he being the first one in their family to ever make it to those 'hallowed halls', as Uncle George liked to refer to them. Ursula had been devastated to hear that Christopher would not be there for her; he was the only one who seemed to really understand, or who wanted her to be there. He was kind and funny, his thin face lighting up with the most beguiling smile when something amused him. And a lot of things amused him. That was what Ursula liked about him. Life wasn't a long drudge or a burdensome duty – it was fun. He liked life and he liked his little cousin. Ursula began to feel loved again. And then he went away and left her with his parents and Rodney. It was fitting somehow. After all, nothing good was ever going to happen to her again so why should Christopher stay there for her. She took to laughing, with an odd bitter quality, at life. And her aunt thought her even more peculiar.

Rodney was still in school and trying hard to pass his exams, and Ursula saw little of him except at dinner. Then he spoke to her only by necessity and would flush a deep and blotchy red if she happened to look up at him. As she sat opposite him at the table, dinners were a painful ordeal for both of them.

Mr Martin worked at a bank in the City. Ursula didn't know what he did exactly, but it involved his getting up at six every morning, dressing in a dark suit, eating a heavy breakfast, and leaving with a bowler hat on his head, a tatty looking satchel that he called his briefcase in his hand, and a black umbrella over his arm. Aunt Mary considered it her wifely duty to get up with her husband and to cook his breakfast personally while he splashed water around in the bathroom and left his toothpaste spattered on the mirror. This last habit particularly annoyed Ursula, who had the job of cleaning the bathroom. Rodney tended to leave his rugger boots, grass, mud, and small pieces of gravel in a pile underneath the washbasin where he could tread the dirt into the tile grouting more successfully. He flushed red, a tidal flood rising up his ears aggressively, whenever Ursula reminded him that boots were for outside, on the field, and that cleats were not a good substitute for scouring pads on the bathroom floor. Aunt Mary considered Ursula to be rather difficult on this point and sympathetically told Rodney not to mind his cousin's nagging.

When the house was clean, and Aunt Mary had left for the shops with her basket firmly clenched in one hand, her umbrella in the other – the Martins didn't believe in going anywhere without their umbrellas – Ursula was free to go out and look for a job. The problem with that was that, now the men were home from war, there were less jobs to go around. There were particularly less jobs for eighteen-year-olds with no qualifications – since she had been tutored at home by Billy, no useful skills for a modern age, and no figure to attract a husband. Ursula felt she had been born too late; a century earlier her weaving or living-off-the-land skills would have been useful but, in this 'brave new world' everyone kept talking about, there didn't seem to be a place for her. She went from agency to agency, from newspaper ad to newspaper ad, and heard the same things said different ways. It was depressing.

On this particular day, her pace got slower as the afternoon wore on and around four-thirty she stopped in a Lyon's corner-house for tea and a biscuit. The tea was horrible, she thought, with milk and sugar. At home they had taken tea black, some-times with a slice of lemon in it. And it had been different tea: fragrant and golden in colour in thin bone-china cups that she would hold up to the light so she could see the liquid dark against the pattern. Ah Jong used to make coconut slices, and almond cake for tea and they would have it out on the verandah so as to catch the first stirrings of the evening breeze. She closed her eyes and drifted into a daydream where everyone was still alive and they were all waiting for her at the bungalow, pacing the verandahs and looking down the hill for her to arrive. She smiled at the thought.

It was while she was sitting, sharing a small table in the corner with two other women, that Ursula finally heard some-thing useful and constructive. The women were discussing a friend who was about to leave her job as a nanny and general help. She sipped her tea cautiously, flicking her eyes up as she raised her cup to take a look at the women. The one on the left, with the dark green coat was saying she knew the Pattersons

139

were going to be looking for someone to care for their two children since her friend Emmy would be having to give up work soon, she was that big. The one on the right, in the blue coat, remarked that Emmy didn't seem to have been married long enough. The lady in the green coat thought not either. They both tittered. Ursula wondered whether she dared ask them who Emmy was, and who she worked for? Suppose they were cross at her listening in on their conversation. Though what could they expect at such a small table and with such loud voices? And what did she have to lose anyway? She cleared her throat.

'Uh, excuse me. I hope you don't mind but I couldn't help overhearing you talking about a job. As a nanny - your friend, won't she be giving it up? I mean, would her employers be looking for someone else? I know I shouldn't have been listening but I couldn't help it. I need a job, you see and . . . not one person's been willing to . . . '

'You're a little young, aren't you?' the woman in the blue coat said, cutting across her confused explanations. Ursula shook her head.

'Oh no, I'm a lot older than I look. I'm actually eighteen. And I've looked after a lot of children before. Really.' Neither of them were smiling. Ursula's spirits sank a little further.

'Well, I don't know. Mrs Patterson's awfully picky and I know Emmy won't let just anyone look after the children. I could take your name and telephone number if you like and pass it on. Then it would be up to them to decide.'

'Oh would you? Please! It would mean so much to me.'

'I'm not guaranteeing anything mind, just passing your name on. That's all.' The woman in the green coat wasn't the sort who took anything lightly. She had responsibilities in life. Ursula bit her lip and smiled.

'I understand. It's very kind of you.' She opened up her bag and pulled out a small notepad, ripping a page out of it without compunction. 'Here you are. I do appreciate this.' She passed her name and number across to the woman who took it reluctantly.

'Well, I'll do my best. I don't know that you're the sort they'll be looking for though. You don't look like Help, if you know what I mean.' She looked disapprovingly at Ursula who felt a great tiredness wash over her. She needed work as much as the next man, maybe more, but few people seemed willing to believe it. She tried to keep her voice light.

'My family lost everything in the war. I have to work to support myself. I'm good with children, and experienced.'

'Well, deary, we all lost a lot in the war. As I said, I can't promise but I will give them your name. I can't do more.' Ursula nodded and stood up.

'Thank you. That's very kind of you. It really would mean a lot to me. I, uh, I have to go now. Goodbye.' And with that small hope in her chest she walked out and into the gathering dusk.

When she got home it was already dark and there were snow flurries biting into the exposed parts of her face and neck, her hands numb and useless. She opened the door after a few moments of fumbling with her key and impatient stomping on the doorstep. It was bitterly cold and she could have wept with the aching, bone-chilling fatigue that only comes to those who have reached the end of their resources. The door swung open and she stumbled in, closing it behind her and gasping for warm air to fill her lungs.

'Is that you, Ursula?' Aunt Mary's voice called from upstairs. Ursula leaned against the door, letting the last shudders of cold work their way through her. Then she un-buttoned her coat with stiff fingers and hung it up. It was an old one of Aunt Mary's and not long enough.

'Yes. It's me.' She went through to the back of the house and picked up the kettle, filling it with water. She could smell fish. Did that mean fish pie again or was it just last night's she could smell? The stove was gas and made her jump when she put a match to it, blowing back a blue flame at her. She put the kettle on to boil and sat down wearily at the table. After a few moments she heard her aunt coming down the stairs.

'You're home early. No luck with the job hunting?' Ursula shook her head, her teeth clenched together from the cold. 'I must say I'd have thought you'd have kept going until five-thirty at least. Or was the weather too bad?' The weather was always too bad and Aunt Mary knew it. But she felt it was up to Ursula to get used to it, and how was she to do that when she sat home in the warmth all day? It wasn't as though George didn't have enough problem with money without having this young lady muck sitting around eating her head off.

'I tried everywhere. I don't think anyone wants to employ me in the whole of London,' Ursula said.

'Oh, it can't be as bad as all that. You're just not looking in the right places, or maybe you're being too choosy? We all have to do unpleasant or boring jobs at times, you know.' Ursula wondered if Aunt Mary really knew just how bloody she was being? Looking down at her hands, mottled white and purple, the nails a deep blue, Ursula also wondered whether it was possible to get frostbite in London.

'I'm trying, Aunt Mary. I really am.'

'All right. All right. You mustn't be so sensitive. No-one said you weren't. I just wondered whether you couldn't try a little harder. But I won't say another word. I'm sure you would do your best when you know how difficult it is for us to keep you here.' Aunt Mary sniffed, went over to the kettle, lifted it, and poured out half the water. 'There's no point in heating more water than you need. It's a waste of gas and we have to pay the bill.' Ursula closed her eyes.

Three days later Ursula received a telephone call. It came after dinner, about eight o'clock, and Uncle George picked up the receiver. He seemed quite puzzled when he came back into the sitting-room and looked at his wife.

'It's for Ursula,' he said. 'Shall I say she's in?' He waited for his wife to answer while Ursula sat up and looked from one to the other.

'Who is it, George?'

'I don't know, m'dear. A woman called Patterson. Wants to talk to Ursula.' Ursula stood up immediately and walked past her aunt and uncle without a word. How dare they? Deciding right in front of her if she could, or couldn't, take the call. She was raging silently within herself when she picked up the receiver.

'Hallo? Yes, Mrs Patterson, this is Ursula Fraser speaking. I'm so sorry I kept you waiting but my uncle is a little hard of hearing.' She heard a gasp behind her that told her she would be in trouble when she got off the telephone. 'Well, yes, that would be no problem at all . . . Eighteen, yes.' There was a pause while the woman at the other end went into a long monologue. 'Oh, I see. Yes, all right. Two then. Fine, thank you, Mrs Patterson. Goodbye.' Ursula hung up, her heart swelling with hope and triumph. She turned and looked at her uncle and aunt. 'That was about a possible job. I'll know tomorrow.' Then she walked away from them and their disapproving faces, up the stairs, to her own room.

Rodney was studying in his bedroom, the door partially ajar. Ursula was tempted to go in and talk to him; she needed someone to talk to. But she knew he would freeze into rigid embarrassment and she couldn't help but pity that sort of self-consciousness. His parents were responsible for it, she thought. They never entertained, never introduced him to anyone. How could he be expected to have any poise when he never met any females? She wondered if Christopher had ever been like that? But it seemed too unlikely. She wished he were there to tell her news to. The woman had sounded so nice; so normal! 'Oh, please let it work out, let her like me,' Ursula whispered to herself. 'Let me get out of here.'

She lay down on her bed, closing her eyes. If only Christopher could come up to town more often it would be bearable. She smiled at the memory of his last day before he returned to Cambridge. She had been dragging around the house, totally depressed at the thought of him leaving when he had suddenly rushed into the room and pulled her after him, down the stairs and out into the street.

'What is it, Christopher? Where are we going?' She had laughed, running breathlessly after him as he tugged her this way and that through the crowded streets. But he just winked and said he had a surprise for her, his eyes dark and intensely alive in that thin face. She grinned back and followed where he led her. She was totally lost in the maze of alleys, squares, and sidestreets and had no idea where they were when he finally stopped. A square full of people, stalls, rides, noise, bustle, fun! It was a fête. She laughed with pleasure. He was standing close beside her, his arm slipped around her waist to protect her against the tide of people surging around them. And when she turned to look at him, she found him smiling at her in a way that made her heart knock hard in its thin cage and her face flush. She looked back to the fête again very quickly.

'D'you want to go inside?' he asked and she nodded without

looking back at him. 'Come on then. I think I can spare you a couple of hours, just this once. Maybe you're worth it.' He was teasing her and she smiled, kissing him suddenly on the cheek in an awkward, swooping motion.

'You are a dear, Christopher. I don't know what I'm going to do without you. You won't forget me while you're away, will you?' Her tone became anxious. Christopher squeezed her waist even tighter.

'Forget my favourite cousin? Never!'

'I'm your only cousin!' she pointed out doubtfully. He smiled, his face growing tender in that way of his whenever she needed cheering up. Lately that had been rather often.

'I won't forget you and I'll write to you every week and when I come back at Easter . . . ' he paused, thinking of something special to say to her, ' . . . I'll take you for a trip somewhere – maybe to Windsor, to see the castle, or . . . I don't know! Wherever you like. You say.'

'Will you? Really? Anywhere will do. It would just be so nice!' Her face was alive with pleasure. He felt guilty suddenly, leaving her with his parents. It would be hard for her.

'Easter isn't very long. And then soon after that I have the long hols. I'll have to get a job, of course, but I'll be back up here and we can go out a lot. You'll see. It won't seem so bad and the time will fly by when you're busy working.' He had been almost as anxious as her at that point, she remembered. And then he had kissed her cheek. Except that he must have missed slightly because he seemed to kiss part of her mouth, the corner part, as well as her cheek. And his lips had lingered there for a moment, his aftershave pleasantly light and fresh. When he pulled away she was flushed and even he seemed confused. He shook his head and muttered something about having to remember they were first cousins. And then they had gone into the fête.

Lying on the bed, her smile faded; she brushed her cheek and lips with her fingers. First cousins, he had said. So that was that. She closed her eyes tightly. Let her get the job. Please!

Chapter Ten

Mrs Patterson lived in a tall Edwardian, or was it Georgian? house in a street that led off from Smith Square called Lord North Street. Ursula thought it the most beautiful street she had ever seen. Every window had plants, now mostly ivy, in a box outside it, and the street was lined with expensive cars that glinted in the sun. And it was really sunny, as though the bad weather were reserved for the uglier parts of London and this area only lived in a wash of yellow and cream. Even the way the light shook down through the leaves of the trees seemed like tinsel glinting in the sun. Ursula stood on the corner and breathed in deeply, feeling her spirits lift. On days like this, when the clouds were puffy and tinged with gold haloes, blowing across a washed blue sky, she could really believe in God. Billy would have loved all this; he had an eye for beauty in even the most mundane things. She smiled at a woman walking by and was welcomed by an answering smile. This was so nice, so ordinary and real after everything that happened lately. Oh, please God let her get the job!

She was too early by an hour but it was warm in the sun so she retraced her steps back to the square and found a bench. The wood was weathered an ash grey and it was comfortably smooth and warm where it had soaked up the sun's rays. She sat down, admiring the ordered buildings and clipped hedges, the well-kept gardens and the tidy footpaths. It wasn't anything remotely like Singapore but there was an answering chord in her that said the same sort of people lived in both places. The sort who wouldn't think her life irrelevant; or the East a heathen, foreign place where no God-fearing man would venture. Ravens with ravens, sparrows with sparrows as Fatimah had once told her. She sighed and tilted her face up to catch the sun. Papa must have lived somewhere like this before he went out to Asia. Ursula could hardly comprehend that her father and Aunt Mary had been brother and sister; they were so different. He had appreciated beauty, whether in surroundings or, more often, in the women around him. That was why he was contemptuous of Aunt Mary. Of her tight, constricted soul. She didn't understand about nice things, or beautiful places. She would never have known why Sally put lemon verbena balls in amongst the linen, or why she wore various shades of cream and white and lace together. Aunt Mary would have thought they were mismatched. And the little individual vases of flowers, sometimes just a blossom, that Sally put beside each person's plate at the table; that would have been a waste. Uncle George would never have grasped the need to change two, sometimes three times a day and to wear loose clothes so they didn't chafe, or make your face look pink and strangled. He would have smeared his ash down his front and then worn the same waistcoat again the next day. They were different and they didn't understand her life before the war. Staying with them just made all their lives a misery. Besides, being a constant financial irritation was upsetting for her too; it made her feel uncomfortable to eat more than the absolute minimum or to bathe in more than two inches of water. She sighed again.

Ursula could see the spires of Westminster Cathedral at the other end of Lord North Street and, behind some of the houses, she could get glimpses of the Palace. It was nice sitting in the sun, drowsy and quiet, the wind blowing the odd gust or two just as she began to think she was really warm. It was funny to think that she once would have died of heat just looking at the thick material of the clothing she had on: the clothing that now wasn't quite able to keep the chill away. She had bought the suit at a secondhand stall especially for today and she still felt slightly guilty about it. Not that the Martins would mind the few shillings she had spent on it – money Christopher had lent her – but she worried Aunt Mary would find her own dresses pushed untidily into the bottom drawer. Ursula fingered the wool and sighed. She missed that sun-warmed glow on her body, where the perspiration dried and left white, salty tears on her arms. She even missed the prickly-heat itchiness when cotton rubbed against flushed skin. Oh, to be hot, really hot with the sweat trickling down the small of her back and the wind a warm breath on her cheek. She sat with eyes half-closed seeing a tangle of green sparked by reds and yellows and blues, vibrant, vulgar colours that were hot and passionate and alive.

The front door was black and heavy with iron studs banding it. It opened while Ursula was still knocking, swinging back easily on solid hinges. The maid looked almost as young as Ursula, her hair neatly pulled back under a frilly white cap and her front covered with a white pinafore. Ursula cleared her throat nervously:

'I've come to see Mrs Patterson. I have an appointment.' It was exactly two, Big Ben striking the hour as though to emphasize how punctual Ursula was. The maid nodded and stepped back to let Ursula in.

'If you wouldn't mind waiting a moment, I'll tell Madam you're here. Uh, what name shall I say?' She seemed as inexperienced and nervous as Ursula. They both smiled with relief at finding each other so accommodating.

'I'm Ursula Fraser. I've come about the position as nanny.'

'Oh, yes, I see. I won't be just a tick . . . uh, a moment.' The maid turned and hurried up the stairs, her face flushed at having forgotten her careful instructions. It was only her second day, Ursula discovered later, and it was hard to remember everything Madam had had to say. She returned almost immediately and told Ursula to follow her upstairs, that Madam would see her in the drawing-room. Ursula wondered briefly if Fatimah had felt like this once, when she was about to be interviewed by the Mem. Then she walked into the drawing-room and came to a startled halt. Mrs Patterson was beautiful and quite young, no more than twenty-five certainly. Her hair was almost white it was so fair and it was waved in wings about a wide forehead. Her features were tiny and perfect, set in a composed, perhaps even complacent face, and when she smiled she kept her mouth at exactly the right angle

147

to show a glint of pearly teeth. Ursula stood staring at her until she realized how rude she was being. Mrs Patterson's smile inched a fraction wider, her eyes serious and laughing at the same time. Ursula was enchanted.

'So, you're Ursula. I must say I thought you'd be a little older looking. But come,' she patted the sofa beside her, 'come and sit down and we can talk. Ruth, would you bring some tea up please? I know it isn't tea time, Ursula, but I'm sure you'd like something and I don't dare offer you a real drink. Or perhaps you'd rather some lemonade?'

'Oh no, tea would be fine, thank you Mrs Patterson. It's too cold for lemonade.' She didn't know why she'd said that but Mrs Patterson seemed to find it very funny and trilled a reedy little laugh that was as beautiful as all the rest of her. Ursula felt suddenly very plain.

'You're quite right. It is too cold for lemonade. I've been telling my husband for years that England isn't habitable in the winter but he insists we stay. His work, you know.'

Ursula didn't know and couldn't imagine this beautiful creature married to anyone who did anything so mundane as work. She ought to be married to a lord, who had inherited wealth and a family seat and scores of servants; not to someone who worked, like Uncle George. Ursula had read her fair share of romances; she knew how things ought to be. But Mrs Patterson continued to smile and gesture with her long, delicate hands and Ursula thought her absolutely wonderful. Much more beautiful than Sally and even, perhaps, as beautiful as her own mother had been. She smiled back, forgetting her nervousness.

'I haven't been warm since I got here, to tell you the truth. And it's so heavy wearing all these clothes!'

'Got here? But where did you spend the war then? In America?' Mrs Patterson was interested, her whole attention centred on the girl before her. Ursula sighed, sensing that this woman understood her better already than Aunt Mary ever would.

'No, in Singapore. I was born there and only came to England for the first time in January. Papa never came home on leave. He didn't like England very much, I think.'

'And what does he think of it now?'

148

'He doesn't. I mean he's . . . he was killed when the Japanese invaded. So was my tutor too. And my step-mother and the children . . . Emma and Tom, they're missing. They think they may have gone down on one of the ships that were sunk when they tried to get away from Singapore. That's why I came back here to live with my aunt. She's the only family left.' Ursula found it harder to keep her voice steady and factual in the face of this stranger's obvious sympathy. Blue-grey eyes surveyed her calmly, the face never changing its expression, but Ursula felt it showed a curious note of concern for her. She took a deep breath and looked around the room.

'Oh you poor child! I'm so terribly sorry. It must have been such an ordeal for you. But how did you . . . that is, I don't mean to probe, but . . . '

'How was it I lived when everyone else was killed?' Ursula could feel the tension leaving her. These were the sort of questions her family should have asked. And she had to tell someone. Why not a stranger who cared? Ursula folded her fingers into her skirt's pleats and nodded when Ruth brought the tea tray in and poured out two cups. It wasn't this woman's problem but she seemed so kind. Ursula blinked hard and stared at her tea, rocking slightly. Then she started to speak. For the next half-hour she told it all; the horror, the pain, the good times in the kampong, the boat trip home. She paused when she got to the part about her aunt and uncle. How could she tell this woman, sympathetic as she was, how awful her own family was? How they badgered her about money and froze her about the past, about the kampong. She faltered and took another sip of tea. Fragrant tea in bone china cups with almond slices. And cloves on rounds of lemon.

'And your aunt and uncle met you at Southampton? Where do they live in London?' The woman meant it well, sensed there was something more Ursula needed to say. But Ursula couldn't tell her. She just nodded and said:

'Near here.' It was near there but worlds apart. Mrs Patterson didn't ask again.

'Well, and so you really are awfully used to looking after children, aren't you? I have two: Benjie, or Benjamin is three and Lucy is five. They're having a nap at the moment but Nanny will be getting them up again at three-thirty and you

149

can meet them then. I normally hire my nannies from an agency, you see, but when Nanny said there was someone who was interested in the job; someone who seemed quite a "lady", I just thought I might sound things out. It would be such a relief to have someone I could actually talk with, have tea with, without feeling I have to keep my distance or my authority will be questioned. I'm sure you know how that is, Ursula? You obviously had quite a few house servants yourself.' Ursula sipped her tea and wondered if she could explain that she had never kept her distance; the servants had been her friends, her family. Downstairs the sound of the front door being opened made Mrs Patterson look around in surprise. She glanced at the watch on her wrist, frowned, and then smiled again:

'That must be Simon.'

Ursula walked home in a daze of happiness, building a new and brilliant life for herself out of the snippets of real information she had and the fantasy she invented. She and Mrs Patterson would be best friends; she would learn to look and dress and laugh like her. And sometimes they would invite her down for a dinner party – just to make up the numbers – and she would meet a wonderful young man who would fall madly in love with her. It would all be so right, she could see it now. Perhaps it might even be Simon. Ursula almost skipped she was so happy. Simon with his sandy blond hair so ruffled and careless and his pale, pale eyes that watched everything with such interest, especially her. Mrs Patterson had said she would need her in a fortnight, when Nanny left. Did that mean she would be called 'Nanny' too? But no, Mrs Patterson had called her Ursula all afternoon, and the children were adorable. They would all call her 'Ursula' and she would live in their house until, well until the right young man came along and claimed her. She wondered why Simon had looked at her so warmly? As though he already knew her very well. Mrs Patterson hadn't noticed, introducing him off-handedly as her husband's son. That had puzzled Ursula until she realized that, of course, Mrs Patterson must be the second wife, just like Sally. Did Simon like his step-mother, or was she difficult with him, like Sally had been with her? But no, they seemed to be good friends. And he had stared at Ursula and laughed when Mrs

150

Patterson had asked him what he was doing home at that hour. His answer had been amusing:

'It's simple really, Julia, dearest. My grandfather was one of the best politicians in this land, my father is renowned in the political field, and I don't see why I should work either.' He grinned and popped an almond slice into his mouth while Julia pouted at him.

'That's so terribly clever of you Simon but I've heard someone tell it before. Try to be original next time.' She laughed to take the sting out of her words and Simon brushed the crumbs from his neat, clipped moustache, seemingly unfazed.

'You never let me get away with anything, darling. How am I going to keep my reputation as a wit if you keep revealing my tawdry, plagiaristic nature? It's simply impossible – and just when I think everything's going along tickety boo!' He laughed, short sucked-in breaths like coughs. 'Uh, uh, uh, uh'. Ursula watched him closely and then was confused when he returned her look, checking first to see that his step-mother was leaning forward to pour out more tea. It was strange, but Ursula could have sworn his eyes changed colour as he looked at her, from pale blue to almost white. She blushed and looked at her hands.

He had sat with them while they finished tea, laughing and teasing his step-mother with an intimacy that Ursula found charming. Then he had left them to go and meet friends and Mrs Patterson had taken her upstairs to see the children. Such sweet children with fair hair and pink cheeks! Would she have to call Mrs Patterson 'Madam' like the other servants, or 'Julia' like Simon did, or perhaps she would just stick to 'Mrs Patterson' until they all got to know each other very well? Until Simon showed he was in love with her and his parents gave him their blessing. And then, after she married him, they would all be best of friends, entertaining together and going out together. Oh, it was too good to be true! The traffic let her cross without any trouble and she walked over the railway bridge to Ebury Street with an expression of beatitude on her face. People smiled but she didn't see them, her eyes watching a different road and different people. Then she turned into her own street and opened the front door.

151

Aunt Mary heard the door open and was there before Ursula could take off her coat, or run upstairs and change. There were two spots of anger in Aunt Mary's normally pale face, just over the cheekbones, and her eyes were darker than usual. Ursula knew she'd been sitting in the kitchen, stoking her indignation into rage, over successive cups of tea. She ignored her aunt while she unbuttoned her coat and hung it up, keeping herself aloof. She didn't want to argue with Aunt Mary or cause a permanent rift; all she had to do was hang on another two weeks. Just two more weeks.

'Ursula, I won't ask where you've been all day, when you should have been helping me here. It's little enough to ask of you when we provide you with everything else, but I wouldn't dream of making you feel you owe us anything. But what I do want to know is where you got the money to buy yourself an expensive suit like that, and how you could be so ungrateful as to bundle up the dress that I gave you – off my own back – and stuff it into a drawer. Now answer me that, if you please, young lady!' Aunt Mary had drawn herself very erect and was standing barring Ursula's path down the hall. She sounded righteous and martyred and Ursula knew she'd been rehearsing her words for an hour or more. It was daunting to be confronted with anger after such a wonderful afternoon, the ill-will seeping into the memories and spoiling them already, before they had had time to mature. Ursula swallowed and answered her aunt politely:

'I'm sorry Aunt Mary but I had to go for that interview with Mrs Patterson – about the job as a nanny?' she prompted her Aunt's memory.

'And I'm sure you didn't hear me calling after you down the street?'

'No, I didn't. I expect there was too much noise from the traffic, or that I had my mind on other things.'

'You always have your mind on other things! It would help if you kept your mind on what you owe your uncle and me for taking you in! But then, I would never want you to feel guilty on that score . . . And where were you going at that hour? I thought your appointment wasn't until two? And you haven't answered me yet about where you got that suit. You might think I've forgotten or can be talked around it, but what I want

152

to know is where a girl who's absolutely penniless, or so she says, gets the money for a suit like that? Answer me that if you can, Miss!' Aunt Mary's neck was strained rigid, her nose pinched with distaste. She seemed to be more angry about the money than anything else.

'I bought it at a secondhand stall at the market with a few shillings Christopher gave me. I don't have any money of my own and if I did I would give it to you. But I didn't think you'd mind a few shillings. After all, Christopher gave them to me for an emergency. And if I hadn't bought the suit, I wouldn't have got the job. That's just in case you're interested, by the way. I know what a store you set by me getting a job and not being a burden on your family anymore. So you'll be happy to know I'll only be with you for another two weeks, and then you can say goodbye. I'm sure you won't mind taking on the cleaning again as long as you know I'm well placed.' Ursula smiled sourly and brushed by her aunt. She climbed the stairs slowly, feeling the euphoria fade like the fizz going out of lemonade. Only two more weeks. Behind her she heard her aunt shouting that she wouldn't take any more cheek. Ursula went into her room and closed the door.

The next few days were difficult. Uncle George hadn't wanted to be involved in what he saw to be a domestic dispute, and no-one ever knew what Rodney was thinking anyway. Rodney lived in a world of homework, rugger, and self-conscious mortification that had no room for anyone else's problems. Ursula thought it was probably best that way; the less he came into contact with his parents, the more chance he had to eventually turn out normal.

The first night Uncle George had come up to her bedroom and knocked on the door. He had been sent by Aunt Mary and, as he was an habitually silent man with no real dislike for his niece, he was at a loss to know what to say. Ursula thought him weak but she didn't want to make his life impossible. She tried to look penitent instead. He began by blowing out his cheeks, and making a long, sighing noise:

'You're not making life very easy for any of us lately, Ursula. Your aunt's very cross about, about you being so careless with the dresses she's loaned you. She's a bit picky about her personal things, if you know what I mean. So be a good girl

153

and tell her you're sorry, and it won't happen again. All right?'
A finger brushed across his moustache, feeling for the hard
bristle. Ursula blinked. He really thought that was all there
was to it. Two women fighting about some clothes. She
wondered if he couldn't help himself, if he'd been brought up
with such a low opinion of women that it was inconceivable for
him to see their clash of temperaments as anything more than a
domestic squabble. She could see him flushing under her gaze,
small beads of perspiration popping up on his forehead and
chin; she could smell stale cigarette smoke in his clothing. He
couldn't grasp the wider picture, nor the detail work – like
Aunt Mary's nagging her to get a job but not being at all
pleased when she did, or telling her to polish the silver,
knowing full well that she didn't know how and would have to
be taught; little things, pinpricks really, that Aunt Mary used
to get at her, like calling her 'my girl', or 'young lady'. Uncle
George never saw them, never heard them. And he thought
this was about clothes. She shook her head.

'I'll try hard to keep out of Aunt Mary's way over the next
fortnight. Then I'll be gone. I don't expect any of you will be
terribly upset to see the back of me, but I think you ought to
know I've tried as hard as I could. I've already apologized
about the dresses. I'm also sorry we haven't really got on as
family should. I wanted us to and I'd been looking forward to
becoming a part of your family all the way from Singapore. I
thought you'd accept me and let me fit in. I did truly want us to
all get on and it hasn't just been my fault that we haven't.' Her
tone was flat, trying not to show any emotion but a shake in her
voice warned Uncle George not to push her any further. He
didn't really care anyway; it was enough that he had been seen
to come up and talk to Ursula. His wife would be content with
that, he thought and, nodding to himself, he left Ursula alone.
He had his own problems anyway, the way they were laying
people off in his section. His forehead puckered with worry and
Ursula was forgotten.

Ursula went about her own business over the next few days,
cleaning the house as always and making snacks for herself so
she could avoid meals. Aunt Mary would have seemed more
distant if she had behaved as she always did, but instead she
found it necessary to walk into a room that she knew contained

154

Ursula and then, pointedly, walk back out. Ursula found it hurtful at first, wondering why she should be excluded and made to feel an intruder. Life could be so sad sometimes. But it was people who made it that way, people like Aunt Mary who only ever saw their own side of things and who could find the world wrong, and still be sure they were right. Ursula left the house as much as possible and then, finally, it was time to leave for good.

She'd been there nearly two months. It seemed like two years. There was nothing she wanted to take with her. She left the lavender scented dresses neatly hung up in her wardrobe and used the last of her money to buy herself some stockings. The dress she had arrived in, and the rest of the clothing she had brought with her from Singapore fitted into her bag with room to spare. She wore her suit, promising herself that she would buy herself another with her first week's pay. Then, leaving a thank-you note to Uncle George for having taken her in and another note with her address in an envelope addressed to Christopher lying on Rodney's chest of drawers, she went down the stairs for the last time. Boiled cabbage from the night before scented the hallway and she carefully stepped over Rodney's rugger boots which he had taken to leaving by the front door rather than in the bathroom. Ursula barely saw them, her mind set in rigid tracers that had one goal before her: the door. She left without saying goodbye to Aunt Mary.

Chapter Eleven

Mr Patterson was a quiet man in his sixties, nice looking but preoccupied by much of what he sought to achieve in Parliament in the limited time he felt he had left. Ursula didn't know why he thought he had so little time but wondered whether he might be ill. He looked strained and undernourished, his thinning hair grey and swept across a polished head to hide the bald patches and his skin flaky and raw. He looked like he washed too much in hard water and had scrubbed all the colour out of himself. But he had a sweet smile and a witty tongue that made him one of the more popular MPs with the public. Ursula thought it a terrible shame that Julia – she thought of her as 'Julia' now – should have married a man so much older than herself. Especially a man in ill health. But Julia was like that; totally self-effacing and capable of acts of the greatest sacrifice. Why, only the day before, Julia had insisted that Ursula accompany Mr Patterson on his evening nature ramble just because it was a lovely evening and Ursula hadn't been out all day. And Mr Patterson really was very interesting and kind, and he did have such a sweet smile. And when they had returned home, Simon was already there and in a merry mood. No, perhaps it wasn't such a sacrifice for Julia after all. It must be nice to be married to a man who doted on you like that, Ursula thought.

Ursula was happier than she had been in the longest time; not since before the war, or even before Sally. There was a cordon of security and warmth and love around the house in

Lord North Street and she was inside it, enveloped by Julia's kindnesses and the children's adoration and Mr Patterson's sweetness. And Simon was enveloping her too. It made her giddy to think of him, a thrill of crossed glances and secret smiles. He was there at the oddest times; she never knew when to expect him but would turn around from putting the children down for the afternoon and find him lounging against the door of the nursery. He had a way of smiling that made her stomach drop and his eyes did that colour change whenever he got close to her. She didn't know whether to be flattered or frightened. Julia went out quite often in the afternoons and there was nothing for Ursula to do while the children were sleeping so she spent the time with Simon, shy and unsure of herself at first so that she spoke in a low voice and quickly, half hoping that he wouldn't hear what she said. Only after she was sure that he found her interesting and amusing did she find the confidence to laugh or tease him in the way he teased her.

Simon was twenty-four and knew a lot about the world. Compared to his wit and sophistication she often felt like a pea-hen who had never done anything of interest. But he seemed intrigued by something in her that she couldn't understand. He tried to explain it to her, saying she wasn't innocent – he was tired of girls acting as though they didn't know the facts of life, or worse still, of girls who weren't acting – but that she was pure. There didn't seem to be any difference to Ursula but Simon discerned it and put great store by it, so much so that Ursula became frightened of losing it, just because she didn't know what it was. Occasionally Julia would return early and find him talking to Ursula, a guilty smile on both their faces when they looked up and saw her at the door. But Julia would simply ask how the children were and then warn Simon that Ursula was too young to be losing her heart to him. It became a standard saying and they always laughed about it but Ursula couldn't quite stop the embarrassment showing in her eyes. Nor could she stop the twinge of pain that came from their amusement.

The news about Sally and the children came only days after Ursula had begun her duties, her uncle coming to see her with an official-looking envelope. She had prepared herself for the moment again and again, knowing in her heart that there could be no hope. She could cope now. She knew she could. Now that she wasn't alone anymore; now that there was hope in her life again. It would be all right. Quite bearable. But still, Ursula took the envelope from her uncle with trembling fingers, almost unable to slit through the flap and extract the letter inside. She read the official words of sympathy without expression. Drowned, after the ship had been shelled in the China Sea. It was what she had secretly known all along. They were all dead. For a moment she visualized baby Tom as she had last seen him, asleep in her bed with his pink flushed cheeks and soft hair. And suddenly she couldn't bear after all to think of where he was now. She nodded her thanks abruptly to her uncle and retreated to her room to grieve and mourn their loss. There was no one else to do it.

Simon brought her tea and gentle cheer; the Pattersons brought her understanding and sympathy. She clung to them all and slowly the pain dulled, the anger that accompanied it stored away carefully, like precious linen in tissue paper, for future times, fading and growing threadbare in places.

About five weeks after she had moved in to the Lord North house Christopher came to see her. He was down for Easter and had come to check on her as soon as he found she had gone. Ursula felt cherished that two such handsome young men seemed to care so much for her. She grew breathless and a little pink when Ruth came into the nursery to tell her her cousin had come. Julia was talking with Christopher in the drawing room when Ursula came downstairs, her face bright with the news. Christopher stood up immediately and went over to kiss her on the cheek, his eyes worried.

'Hallo, Ursula. How are you? Rodney gave me your message.'

'Christopher! I didn't think you'd come down until the summer. Aunt Mary said not to expect you. Oh, it's good to see you!' She hugged him tightly. He was so kind and so handsome. It was nice that Julia could meet the only decent member of her family.

'Christopher's been telling me he's up at Cambridge reading Geography and History. Why didn't you tell me you had a cousin there, Ursula? Simon was at Trinity, you know. And you're at Gonville and Caius, aren't you, Christopher? They

158

might even know each other.' Julia seemed thrilled at the
thought and Ursula smiled with relief. Now they knew some of
her family, there would be no problem getting their blessing. If
only Simon would get around to proposing! He was taking
simply ages about it. She turned to Christopher and was taken
aback by the sullenness of his expression. Now what was the
matter with him? Could he be jealous? But he had said they
were first cousins in such a discouraging way! She looked at
him uncertainly.

'Christopher? Do you know Simon?' she prompted him
when he didn't seem inclined to answer.

'Simon Patterson? I don't know him personally. I know of
him, though.' His voice gave nothing away. Ursula grew
impatient.

'And? Surely you're not going to tell us you've heard bad
things!' She was laughing, trying to cajole him into his
normally sunny temper. Julia put down her drink on the table
and stood up.

'I really must be running along, Ursula. I have to meet some
friends at two-thirty and it's nearly two now. Feel free to stay
here and talk with your cousin. Christopher, it was nice to meet
you. I hope you'll come again some time. Goodbye.' Her voice
had become clipped all of a sudden and Ursula felt she had
meant the reverse. Oh, why was Christopher acting so difficult? They both waited politely for Julia to leave the room
before turning to look at each other again.

'What's the matter, Christopher? Why are you acting like a
bear with a sore head? Don't you like Julia? Or Simon?' She
couldn't keep the hurt out of her eyes, or the reproval from her
tone. Christopher continued to look sullen.

'No, I don't! I don't like any of this. Why would you take
work as a nanny when you had a perfectly good home with us?
And why did you have to choose this household, if you absolutely couldn't take ours any longer? Oh, I've been filled in on
the way you acted in the last few weeks at home.'

'How I acted! How about how your mother acted – and not
just during the last two weeks but throughout the whole two
months! I didn't do anything but try and then try again to
please her but there was no way I could do it. So don't go
throwing it in my face that I was difficult and couldn't get on

159

with anyone, or that I left a loving household to take on menial work in a stranger's house. They're kinder to me here than your family ever was. So I don't need that sort of rubbish being thrown at me, Christopher!'

'What are you doing here, of all places? I don't understand, Ursula!' He turned away from her and sat himself down in the wingchair by the fireplace. Ursula could see he was upset. But what was the matter with him? Why was he so changed?

'Christopher?' She knelt down beside the chair and took his hand in hers. He was cold and she chafed his fingers absently. 'I know you're probably hurt that Aunt Mary and I fell out. But I couldn't help that. Really I couldn't. We're just like chalk and cheese, never saying anything that the other approves of. Besides which your father really couldn't afford to keep me much longer. I felt like such a burden. I just couldn't take it anymore. And they don't treat me like a servant here. They act like I'm almost one of the family. You'll like Julia when you get to know her better . . . '

'And how well do you know her? I'll bet you have no idea whatsoever of what's going on around here, do you?' He stared at her so hard that she thought he might be a little touched; perhaps he'd been studying too much? She gave a quizzical smile, patting his hand with hers.

'Everything's fine, Christopher. I've never been happier. I don't understand what you're getting at.'

'Do you know what the rumours going around Cambridge were?'

'About what? Simon? I can't believe you'd listen to gossip about someone you don't even know and then presume to judge him by it. Simon's the sweetest, nicest person! After all, look what people were saying about me in Singapore. All that nonsense about the kampong! That's how much rumours resemble the truth.' She was angry now, angry and indignant. How could Christopher be so beastly? She pulled her hand away but he held it fast.

'Well then, if you're so sure of his character after your five weeks' acquaintance with him, you won't mind listening to the gossip. After all, it won't change the way you feel about him, will it?' So, he was jealous. She laughed.

'No, it won't. But if you really must . . . '

'Yes, I really must. He was there before me, of course, about four years ago but he never finished his degree. He was sent down. Do you know what for?' Ursula shook her head. She didn't want to hear this.

'He was sent down because he was involved with a married woman. Rumour has it he got her pregnant. The university authorities took a dim view of that and he was asked to leave. Any idea who the lady involved was?' She struggled to pull her hand free of Christopher's grip but he wouldn't let her go. 'Well, do you want to know?'

'I don't think she does actually. And I really think you ought to let go of her; you're bruising her.' Simon was standing in the doorway, his face very pale. Christopher started up in surprise. 'That's right. Now, Ursula, do you want to hear the rest of this sordid tale or shall we ask your, cousin is it, to leave? He's certainly not welcome here as far as I'm concerned. But,' he smiled sensing Ursula's confusion, 'perhaps you believe in your cousin more than you do me? Perhaps you'd like him to go on with his accusations?'

'No! No, I don't believe any of it. It's just gossip. Christopher, I know you mean well and you're just trying to protect me, but I don't need protecting. I'm very glad you came to see me, really. But, I think it would be better if you left now.' She could barely meet Christopher's eyes, knowing how badly she was hurting him. But couldn't he see he was making her choose, and she had to choose Simon? He took her hand one last time.

'Ursula, listen to me! You don't know this fellow and I'm family. I wouldn't lie to you. Why should I? I don't have anything to gain from it. Can't you see what he's trying . . . '

'Please, please, Christopher, stop it. I can't take any more. I'm sorry but you don't know Simon like I do. He wouldn't do something like that. And this is his father's house. I don't think you have the right to come in here and say things like that about him under his own roof. Please try to understand.' Her words were little more than a whisper and she touched his arm in an effort to console him. But Christopher shrugged her off and walked past her, pausing in front of Simon.

'Don't think she doesn't have anyone to look after her, Mister, because she does. And I'll be here the minute you put a foot wrong. Do you understand me?'

'I can't think how the whole household can help but understand you. Now, if it really isn't too much trouble to ask you to leave, I'd appreciate having my own house to myself.' Simon hadn't lost his poise but he was as dangerously angry as Christopher. They squared up against each other while Ursula watched anxiously. She couldn't think how women enjoyed being fought over; this was too awful, too embarrassing. A muscle throbbed in her cousin's throat revealing the effort he was making to keep control of himself.

'It's not your house I mind leaving; it's my cousin, I mind.' Christopher said softly and then he turned and went down the stairs without looking back. Ursula felt as though her last friend in the world had abandoned her and she collapsed into the chair, her face between her hands. Was it too late; could she run after him? But then what? Was she supposed to go back with him and plead with Aunt Mary to be let back in, while he waltzed off back up to Cambridge? And Christopher could never marry her anyway; he was too close in blood. He could never be anything more than a friend. Oh God! Why did everything have to be so difficult all the time? Why couldn't they have liked each other or at least tolerated one another? She felt tears prickling behind her eyelids and waited, her head bowed, for Simon to come and comfort her, to tell her the true story. But when, after a few minutes, he hadn't approached her she looked up. The room was empty and Simon was gone.

She stood up in sudden fright. Had he gone out? Did he think she believed all that vicious nonsense? She ran to the door and looked down the stairs into the hall. His coat was still on the rack. She breathed in deeply. All right, then he must be upstairs. Perhaps he was too upset to face her right now; perhaps he thought she was angry at him? She ran up the next flight of stairs, peeping into the nursery to check the children were still asleep. Ruth was sitting there with them while they slept and she didn't look up from the magazine she was reading. Ursula tiptoed past the doorway and up the stairs again. She knew where Simon's bedroom was, even though he hardly ever stayed there. He had a bachelor's flat in Chelsea somewhere and spent most of his time there. But the door of his old bedroom was shut and Ursula sensed he was in there. She walked over to it, her breath quivering in her lungs so that she had to

162

keep taking one deep breath after another. Finally she stilled it enough to knock quietly on the door.

'Simon? Simon are you in there? . . . Please Simon, let me in.' She couldn't hear anything from the room and she hesitated with her hand on the doorknob. 'Simon?' The door opened abruptly, the doorknob snatched away from her hand. She took a step backwards, embarrassed at having been caught so close to it. He looked distrait, his hair standing up as though he'd been running his fingers through it and his tie was pulled loose. Ursula could see his eyes were bloodshot and there was a glint to them that hinted he was close to breaking down. She felt a terrible aching pain for him and, almost before she knew it, he'd pulled her into his arms and was burying his face in her shoulder. He told her he was sorry over and over so that she felt fiercely protective suddenly, stroking his hair and murmuring consolations into his ear. No-one was going to hurt him anymore; it would be all right.

It was difficult being held that close for so long and after the initial impact wore off Ursula began to feel stifled and a little off balance. Simon seemed to realize it at the same moment because he released her and turned back into his bedroom, throwing himself down on the bed.

'It's not all true, you know. All right, yes, I became involved with an older woman. She, I cared about her a lot. It wasn't like they make out, just one affair after another. God, those sanctimonious bastards! As if they never made a mistake in their lives. I . . . she was married and she couldn't leave her husband and I couldn't leave her. They found out and I got kicked out. But I never made her, I mean, there was no child or anything. That's all made up. I guess I thought they'd have forgotten about it all by now but I don't think anyone's ever going to forget. They're certainly not going to let me forget.' He laughed. 'You want to hear the best bit? Well, no-one knew who she was, my . . . no-one knew who, so they had to invent someone to fit the bill. And you know who they found? God,' he ran his fingers through his hair again. 'I've blamed myself a thousand times for letting this happen but I don't know what I could've done about it. And she's been such an angel – never saying a word against me, or throwing my stupidity up in my face. Julia, they say it was Julia. Can you believe that? My

163

own father's wife! And Lucy, she's supposed to be mine, not my father's. Do you think for one instant that my father would let me in the door if there were a word of truth in any of it? Do you?' His look agonized over the question; he held out his hand for Ursula. She took it and sat on the bed beside him, stroking his face and crying at the sight of his tears.

'No, I don't believe a word they say against you. People are hateful, they just want to bring you down to their level. Don't cry, Simon. I believe you, sweetheart. Don't cry.' He was holding her round the waist, his face averted from hers, but she could feel the shivers running through him. 'They did it to me too, you know. After I came out of the kampong, there were all these rumours, people whispering and pointing fingers, suggesting . . . well, you know. It was all lies but they were so sure there must have been something like that just because I adapted and learned to live like a Malay. People are so awful Simon. I know what you're going through.'

He squeezed her hand in thanks, his voice muffled:

'My poor love. Why does it always happen to the innocent? Julia's the best, the kindest step-mother anyone could ever have. Just because she's young and beautiful doesn't mean that she doesn't love my father, or that I would ever do such a thing. She's been so good about it but I know it's getting her down. I don't know what to do to stop the rumours. How does one ever kill a rumour like that? Even your cousin believed it and he's never met me, until now.' He held her tightly, his face against the smooth, cool skin of her neck. Ursula shivered.

'Maybe if you . . . if you were to get married. And if your wife and Julia were friends . . . that might help, don't you think? Are you still seeing your . . . the woman you were mixed up with before?' Simon pulled away from her, his face remarkably handsome despite the tears on his cheeks and the sadness in his eyes, Ursula thought. When she cried, her face turned red and blotchy but his was still pale and smooth. Too pale. He twisted his mouth bitterly.

'No. I gave her up when I left Cambridge. I was infatuated and young and stupid. That's all there was to that. And I haven't had a serious friendship with another woman since then. Lots of flirts and going out to parties together, of course. But nothing serious. I'd begun to think I'd never feel that way

164

again until, until recently.' He looked at her with a gentle, wry expression. Ursula felt her mouth trembling and she bit her lower lip to steady herself. He did care! She knew he was in love with her but wouldn't speak for some reason. And now she knew why. Oh, he was so noble and generous, and so handsome.

'Simon? I don't, I mean . . . ?' She smiled and turned pink, waiting for him to tell her. Why wouldn't he get on with it? He continued to look at her, and then abruptly he let her go and turned away.

'It doesn't matter. Please just leave me alone. I need some time to think things through. And whatever you do, don't tell Julia or my father what happened with your cousin. Would you do that for me? They've been through enough hell, God knows. Maybe I should join the Foreign Legion?' he said with a sudden laugh. 'That'll scotch the rumour. There's not much fun in talking about someone who's no longer around.'

'Simon, you can't deal with this alone. I'm here to help you, don't push me away.' She didn't know how to handle this. It was beyond her limited experience of life. But somehow she had to make him realize that he wouldn't be ruining her, or dragging her down into the mud with him. Did he know how she felt about him? Maybe if she told him? Her mind sheered away like a colt avoiding a halter. No, that wasn't possible. He ought to know.

'You're so sweet, sweet and pure. You don't want to get involved in this, Ursula. You've been through enough already. And I'm all right, really.' He smiled at her again. 'It's happened often enough over the last four years. I just, I'm just so tired of it. If only it would stop, or people would get bored with it and forget!' He stroked her hair back out of her face and she smiled sadly up at him, seeing the pain barely held in check. Simon hugged her to him.

'I care about you, Simon. You're everything to me. I could make you happy.' She was barely aware she'd said it before he tightened his grip on her, pulling her tight against him.

'Oh sweetheart. I love you. Don't you know that? But I can't . . . ' He broke off to kiss her, his lips gentle and soft and very experienced as they brushed hers. She clung to him, shivering with excitement. At last he released her. 'You're the sort of girl I've always dreamed of falling in love with and marrying,' he said, 'and now I've ruined my chances of that forever. Your family would never agree, and besides, I couldn't do that to you.'

'Yes you could. I love you, Simon. We'll put a stop to the rumours and my family, well they don't care anyway. They'd be glad to get rid of me, glad to put my rumours to rest.'

'Your cousin certainly seemed to care. If I didn't know better I'd have thought there was something going on between you two.' He tightened his grip on her, almost painfully.

'No, Christopher was just trying to be kind and protective. But he'll come round eventually. And even if he doesn't, my aunt and uncle won't put up any objections. They'll be glad to see me taken care of.' She was terrified he might say no, that he might be too noble. But eventually, after a lot more discussion, they decided to ask permission from both families. Ursula kept poking her finger into her skin to see if she could feel it, just to be sure. She was going to be Mrs Simon Patterson. Oh, if only Billy could see her now and know how happy she was. He'd have liked Simon and believed in him. Billy never listened to gossip. The thought made her calm. That was her measure for life: would Billy have approved? She smiled and kissed Simon gently on the cheek before going down to the nursery again.

Ruth was still with the children but she was looking cross. 'There you are! I thought you'd run off and eloped with your cousin, the time you were. I've got other things to do, Miss, than sit around minding the children for you.'

'I know, Ruth. I'm terribly sorry but something very important came up.' She was bursting with the joy of her news and wanted desperately to share it with someone. Ruth's face brightened, sensing something momentous was about to be disclosed. 'Don't tell anyone, Ruth, because we haven't got permission yet, but Simon's asked me to marry him!' Ruth's mouth opened in a silent 'Oh!' and she sat staring at the excited young girl in front of her. 'Well, aren't you going to congratulate me?' Ursula demanded, smiling at the maid.

'Oh, yes, Miss, to be sure. Congratulations. I must say, it's rather a sh . . . I mean, surprise an' all. You and Mister Simon. Well!' Ruth didn't seem to be as enthusiastic as she ought. Ursula's smile became uncertain.

166

'Um, you better go and have your tea now, Ruth. I'll look after the children. And don't tell anyone yet, remember?'

'Yes, Miss. My memory's very good. I shan't say a word.'

She left the nursery and went downstairs, her shoes making clunking noises as she hit each step. Ursula looked across at the sleeping children. They looked like little angels with their baby-soft skin and blonde hair. Her children would look like this. Hers and Simon's. And of course Lucy looked like Simon; they were half-brother and sister. What people would say! Poor Julia! No wonder she had left so abruptly when Christopher said he knew all about Simon. Ursula put her hand to her face, feeling the warm flush. It must have been so terrible for Julia with people whispering and pointing fingers, and she couldn't help but be loyal to Simon. How could anyone who knew him, really knew him, help but love him? And as though the other young men up at Cambridge were plaster saints! She clicked her tongue angrily against the roof of her mouth. People!

The Pattersons were having a dinner party that night for some of Mr Patterson's political friends. Ursula had urged Simon to leave telling them until later, perhaps after dinner if they were in a mellow mood, and he had reluctantly agreed, seeing the nervousness in her face. He had told her to leave it to him to sort things out and she had been happy to do so. It was nice and quiet in the nursery, quiet and secure. There was no need for her to leave it once the children had had their tea. So she settled down with a book in her favourite armchair and stared into the fire, her thoughts painting her lifestory in rosy hues. Everything she had dreamed was coming to pass; fidelity had its rewards. She smiled to herself as she heard laughing voices and a babble of conversation, glasses and silver chinking together. Soon she would be a part of all that again. She could hear Simon telling a joke, her ear sensitive only to his voice and the rest a blur of sound. He sounded happy and she went to the door, opening it to listen:

' . . . swear it's so! No, really, I asked my tailor just today why he never sends me a bill. And he said that he never asked a gentleman for money. So I said, well, what would happen if someone didn't pay him - just hypothetically, you understand - and he thought about that and said: ''After a certain period

167

of time I would conclude that he was not a gentleman and ask him for the money.'' Uh, uh, uh, uh!' Everyone laughed with him and Ursula beamed with pride. He was so witty, always the centre of attention at a party. She couldn't think what he saw to love in her, but she was so thankful that he did anyway. She closed the door softly as Julia was saying something. She didn't need to hear any more to know that Simon was happy. That was all she wanted. She returned to the fire and sat passively waiting for the guests to leave.

It was late when Simon knocked on the door and came in to see her. She had fallen asleep for a while and was woolly headed, wondering what he wanted. Then it came back to her all of a sudden and she looked up at him anxiously.

'Did you tell them?'

'Yes. They're very pleased, darling. Don't look so worried. You know how fond of you they are. I've explained everything to them and they said to bring you down now, if you're still awake. Do you want to? Or would you rather leave it till tomorrow?'

'Um, no. But I need a few minutes, I'm not quite awake yet. Sorry, I didn't mean to fall asleep.'

'It's late, sweetheart. You couldn't help it.' He squatted down beside her chair and leaned over to kiss her. 'Can you get ready now? I'll go down and tell them you're coming.'

'Oh, couldn't you wait for me? I'd rather we went in together.' Simon laughed at her fears.

'Don't be silly, my love. You know Julia and father already. And I think I better go tell them one way or the other. They'll be wondering.'

'Yes, of course. I'll just brush my hair and fix myself up a little. I won't be long.'

'That's my girl.' He kissed her on the forehead. 'I'll see you in a few minutes.' Then he left the room quickly and went down the stairs. Ursula stood up, feeling suddenly weak and tearful. She wished Simon had waited for her, but he was probably right. His father and Julia would want to know one way or the other. She smoothed down her skirt and tucked her blouse in more neatly before slipping across the landing into the bathroom. She brushed her hair neatly behind her ears and twisted it up into a knot again and splashed water quickly over her face. The water was cold and brought colour to her skin. Now she looked better. With a deep breath she went out and down the stairs to the drawing room. She could hear Julia whispering something but couldn't catch the words, just the sibilant hissing. She hesitated and heard Simon laugh. It was all right. She was imagining things. Julia was probably whispering so as to not wake the children. It was very late. Slowly she walked forward into the light.

'Ursula, darling. There you are. I thought I was going to have to come and get you.' Simon stood up and went to her, taking her hand and pulling her forward. 'Ursula seems to think you're not going to be happy about this. I keep telling her what a goose she is. Everything's just tickety boo!' He grinned into her face, teasing her as always and she smiled hesitantly back. Then she looked at Julia and Mr Patterson. Julia looked amused, as though there were a particularly entertaining joke that they were all sharing – except Ursula. She didn't say anything, just took a long sip from the wine glass she was dangling in her hand. Mr Patterson stood up and smiled at Ursula, taking her hand and patting it in his kind way. He seemed terribly happy, or perhaps relieved.

'We're delighted, Ursula. Simon couldn't have found a nicer or more welcome bride if he'd brought home one of the princesses. Now don't you fret, we'll talk to your aunt and uncle and sort things out there. What about some champagne, Simon? I think this calls for it, don't you.' Ursula sighed deeply and murmured her thanks. It was going to be all right. Simon had managed everything, as always. She smiled shyly at Julia who raised her glass to her.

'To the bride, all dressed in white.' Then Julia laughed and raised her eyebrows at Simon. 'That is going to be appropriate, isn't it, darling?' Simon frowned her down and took Ursula's fingers between his, leading her over to the sofa. He whispered:

'Julia's had a skinful tonight. Don't mind her.'

'What are you two love-birds whispering about? Come on, share your light with us poor old married things,' Julia called, her voice the tiniest bit slurred. Mr Patterson looked embarrassed.

'It is late, isn't it? Perhaps we ought to leave the toasting until the morning? What d'you say, Simon?'

169

'Nonsense, Father. We must toast while the iron's hot! Mixing my metaphors but you know what I mean, of course. You'd like some champagne wouldn't you, darling?' he asked Ursula who stuttered uncertainly. If Mr Patterson wanted to leave it . . .

But Julia spoke up as though Simon had addressed her.

'Of course we want champagne. Right now and plenty of it. I think we have an awful lot to celebrate, don't we, my loves?' She beamed at her husband and Simon, and then balanced her wine glass precariously on a corner of the side table. 'I'll go drum some up, shall I? Let's wake the house and get them to celebrate with us.' She levered herself up on the arm of the sofa and walked perfectly erectly and without the slightest wobble out of the room. Simon looked at his father and then patted Ursula's hand again.

'Won't be a second, sweetheart. Just better check on Julia. She's awfully merry and we don't want her falling down the stairs, tonight of all nights!' He grinned and followed Julia out. Ursula looked across at Mr Patterson and smiled, her mind frantically hunting for something to say.

'Uh, I gather you had a fun party tonight?' Mr Patterson smiled rather painfully.

'Quite fun, yes. I think Julia was rather worried about it going off well and ended up drinking more than she normally does. She doesn't have a terribly good head for the stuff, you know.'

'Oh no, I suppose not. I mean, I certainly don't. Mr Patterson? Are you sure you're both in favour of this marriage? I mean, Simon explained, that is, we . . . talked about things. The rumours, I mean. And I think it'll be good if we marry because it's bound to squash things, isn't it? Don't you think?' She saw him flinch as though she had struck him physically and suddenly she understood why he looked so ill all the time. It wasn't just Julia and Simon who were suffering; it was Mr Patterson as well. She felt desperately sorry for him. He was such a nice man! He cleared his throat and spoke to the carpet.

'Yes. But we're not just happy for that reason, even though my wife's been through hell. We really do like you, Ursula, and we're thrilled that Simon's fallen in love with a suitable and very sweet girl.' He looked up and smiled. 'You're going

170

to be awfully good for him. You'll stabilize him. Get rid of that wild streak. And he seems to be terribly fond of you. I think that's nice.'

Ursula found herself going pink. 'I'm so glad you feel like that. We really do care a lot about each other and I think it's the best thing for everyone. I really do. I just hope my aunt and uncle think so too. They're legally my guardians, you know. I can't marry without their permission.'

'Yes, I know. Don't you worry your head off about that. I'll talk to them. Everything will be fine.' From downstairs a smothered burst of laughter exploded out and Ursula could hear Simon murmuring something. She smiled at Mr Patterson and he smiled back. Then there were footsteps approaching and Simon walked back in clutching two glasses and a bottle of champagne. Julia had slung her arm around his shoulders and was carrying two more glasses in her free hand. She was giggling and Simon raised his eyebrows at Ursula in mock horror. Ursula giggled too.

'Here we are, here we are. Now, everyone take a glass. Quick, before I drop them or Simon lets the bottle drop. But then he's already done that, hasn't he, darling?' Julia was clearly not sobering up fast and Simon led her over to the sofa where she peeled herself off him and fell back in a slump. Ursula stood up and took the glasses from Julia's hand, passing one to Mr Patterson and keeping the other one for herself. Simon smiled and kissed her cheek while he poured her out a glass. They were wide, shallow champagne glasses rather than flutes and Ursula laughed when the bubbles fizzed up her nose. She hadn't had champagne since her cousin Rodney had given her a glass that last Christmas in Singapore before it fell. The memory was quickly quashed. Mr Patterson's glass was filled next and then Simon filled the last two and handed one to Julia. She raised it to him with a smile and winked.

'To the happiest couple in England. May they never be parted!'

'Hear, hear!' seconded Mr Patterson and everyone laughed.

'You're spending too much time over at the House dear. The next thing we'll be hearing is you want a three-line whip at the wedding!' Julia seemed in a terribly good mood and everyone took turns in toasting everyone else. Ursula got quite tiddly herself and had to lean against Simon, which he didn't mind at all. Then, when the bottle was dead, everyone blinked sleepily and happily and went to bed.

It was very late, somewhere in the middle of the night, when Ursula heard the voices. Coming from just outside her door, at first, and then fading down the stairs to be cut off by a door shutting quietly. She lay back against the pillows, wondering what it was all about. Because it had been Simon's voice she had heard. And Julia's.

Chapter Twelve

Light streamed into the bedroom, cutting diagonal patterns across the counterpane, and picking out the colours in the patchwork. Dust motes swirled in the light shaft. It was only a tiny room with space enough for a bed, chest of drawers and hat stand in the corner. Ursula hung her few dresses and skirts from that. She didn't need much more. Not out here in the country where she was lucky to see another person once a day. Sometimes not even then. The bed was old and sagged in the middle so that she rolled into the depression every time Simon turned over. Then she would have to claw her way back out, holding on to the side of the mattress and hauling herself up to perch uncertainly on the edge. It wasn't like the bed at the Savoy where they had spent their first night of marriage. That had been firm and springy with starched white sheets and soft blankets. She would have enjoyed it if only she hadn't been so scared. And if it hadn't hurt so much. That had surprised her. She thought she would feel all quivery in her stomach, the way she had that once with Yahyah. Not that she had ever told a soul about that, but still, she thought it would be like that. But maybe, if Yahyah had actually made love to her then it would've stopped being nice and become painful. Simon said it was always painful the first time and if it hadn't been he'd have known she wasn't a nice girl and he wouldn't have wanted to marry her. She wondered if Sally had been a nice girl when Papa had married her?

Simon had been as gentle as he could but she had been rigid

with embarrassment when he insisted on keeping the lights on, and then when he walked around the room naked, swinging that bottle of champagne around in his hand and laughing! That had been difficult for her to get used to. Only at first, of course, because she'd never seen a man naked before. She was used to it now – almost. And he had told her she was only inexperienced, that soon she would want him as much as he wanted her. She hoped so. Because he didn't always seem to spend enough time trying to arouse her before he just plunged into her. She was small, he said. And he needed to make love to her. She excited him to the point where he couldn't control it anymore and he couldn't wait for her to catch up all the time. Sooner or later she'd get better at it. When she learned to relax. If she tried harder, he said. And Ursula began to feel dreadfully inadequate.

It wasn't just the physical side of their marriage that left her feeling inadequate. Simon had started to criticize almost everything she did. The first day they had arrived at the cottage down a rutted, overgrown driveway to splintered paintwork, holes in the thatch, and general neglect, some of her dismay must have shown on her face because he became angry, slamming the front door open when it caught in the catch and throwing his newspaper down on the hall table. She had followed timidly.

'Simon? Is something wrong?' She could just clear the doorway without stooping. He had disappeared into the dark hallway and she stepped over the lintel, smelling dank mould, dust, cold. She stopped and looked around. A room opened off to the right and the stairs were on the left. The hallway itself went towards the back of the house and another doorway. That was open and she assumed Simon must have gone through there.

'Simon? Simon!' He didn't answer and she felt a moment's irritation. He surely could hear her. The place was so small there was nowhere he could go where he couldn't hear her. So he was ignoring her. Well, to hell with him! She turned to her right and opened the door there. A small sitting room swathed in sheets and gloom appeared before her. Immediately she walked over to the shuttered windows, tugging at the catches so that the shutters swung open. She folded them neatly back and opened the windows. Sunlight streamed in and at once the place looked better. She pulled off the dust sheets, bunching them up under her arm. It was really very attractive. Someone had once put a lot of care and love into this room, she thought with approval. The covers on the sofa and chairs were worn but a lovely pale yellow and peach chintz on a cream background and the curtains at the four windows matched. The floor was polished boards, faded and scuffed now but still showing how they had once been looked after. A threadbare oriental rug covered most of the centre of the room, and there was a walnut writing desk against the window with a chair covered in the same chintz. Two small occasional tables and a chest of drawers finished the room and a mirror hung above a carved oak mantelpiece. Ursula thought it charming. And it was hers! A place of her own. Her spirits soared and she ran to find Simon.

He was standing in the kitchen by the back door.

'Oh, Simon! It's lovely! The little sitting room is just beautiful and by the time I've cleaned it all and put flowers around the place, you'll just love . . . ' She faltered, her words running down to a standstill. He was staring out at the garden, seeing it perhaps as a stranger might for the first time. And it was a mess. Overgrown, neglected, dried-up, a mess.

'You think you can take it then? It'll do for you?' His tone was hard, as though he were steeling himself to be indifferent. He didn't look at her but continued to stare straight ahead. His shoes, polished brown brogues, were covered in dust and scuffed where he had kicked the door. She swallowed hard.

'Yes! Of course. We'll turn it into the prettiest cottage around here. It just needs some work and I'm used to that.' She laughed tentatively. 'You should've seen how I lived in the kampong. But it was a wonderful way to live, really, and everyone helped everyone else. No-one ever went hungry. You'll see. This'll be fun getting it back in shape.' She went over to him and put her arm around his waist. He didn't respond.

'I may have to go away sometimes. Up to London - on business. I can't be here to hold your hand all the time. You shouldn't cling so much, Ursula! You need to stand on your own two feet sometimes. You're a married woman now, not a

175

child anymore!' He stepped away from her abruptly, walking out into the sunlight of the back garden. The sun shone on his hair; his body was tall and broad shouldered in its white shirt and faded jacket. He was so very handsome, Ursula thought with a pang. And I can please him. I'll try harder, I won't cling, I'll learn to like making love even if it hurts sometimes. I can do it, I know I can.

'I'm going down to the shops . . . get in some food, cleaning things. You have a look around the place. Get things sorted out here. I won't be long.' He had turned around and walked into the kitchen again, talking to her almost over his shoulder as he left. Ursula swallowed to ease the ache in her throat, blinked away the silly, childish tears that Simon hated to see, and set about putting things straight.

Simon didn't return until nearly three hours later. He came bursting in with a large bag of shopping, his good humour restored, and his breath smelling of beer. He'd just stopped off for a quick one at the pub when he saw an acquaintance of his. She didn't mind, did she? Ursula smiled and said of course she didn't. What did he think, he'd married one of those nagging sorts? He laughed and pulled her into his arms, his moustache wet and ticklish as he kissed her.

'God, I love you,' he said and held her so tightly that the breath was quite squeezed from her. She held him tightly back, kissing him, savouring the way he slipped his tongue into her mouth. Oh, he did love her! She knew he did! He didn't notice how the floors shone from being freshly scrubbed or how the place had been dusted and swept. He didn't notice the bunches of wild flowers arranged in pots. He only noticed that the bed was freshly made up. And how lovely his young wife looked with her hair falling down around her face and fresh colour in her cheeks. And so he took her to bed for the afternoon and was pleased by how hard she tried. A little more practice, he said. Maybe she'd learn to like it yet. And then he'd rolled over and gone to sleep and Ursula had cuddled in beside him, thinking it would all be all right.

Later, they had taken a bath together, screaming with laughter when the soap kept slipping down between them or the water overflowed. Simon had brought some wine up to drink while they were in the bath and the gentle dusk, the

176

candles he had lit, the wine and hot, soothing water all combined to seem like some fantasy dreamworld to Ursula. She had lain back languorously against his chest, murmuring her love to him as he soaped her skin. And he had held her tightly, telling her over and over how much he loved her. And then they had gone back to bed and that time it had almost been good for Ursula. She stretched, arching her back at the memory.

But mostly Simon wasn't there and she had the bed to herself. Lately, that was a relief. She felt so ill and he couldn't, or wouldn't understand that she didn't want to be touched. It made her feel like gagging when he rolled over on top of her and she would have to push him away. Then he would be irritated and slam out of the bedroom, yelling that he was her husband, damn it, and she should act more like a wife! That had reduced her to tears and then he would hold her to him, saying he was sorry, that he couldn't help it when she pushed him away like that. Why couldn't she just be more responsive? Didn't she love him?

He hadn't been that way until after he went up to London the first few times. Before then he had been gentler, not wanting to scare her any more than he did by simply being there in bed beside her. The first few weeks had been nice. He really seemed to want her body, and that made her feel proud. She thought she probably was underdeveloped compared to most of the women Simon had known before. In fact he had said something rather like that. But she knew she could arouse him. If only he could just be a little slower, a little more tender, a little more . . . what? She wasn't sure. But soon after the first trip up to London, he had begun to change, and she caught him looking at her with a frown between his eyebrows that would clear when he saw her but reappear again when he turned away. He looked . . . guilty, she thought. And unhappy. There was a clouded look in his eyes that sparked fear within her and she would try twice as hard to please. But still she was not experienced enough and he had grown impatient for her to respond with the same passion that he clearly felt. The kissing bit was nice and so was the cuddling. And sometimes he would make her feel like she was floating and shivering in his arms. But then he would get excited and careless of her feelings, pinching and kneading her body as though she were dough, and entering her roughly. She had tried hard to smother the nausea but it had been getting worse lately and she was sick for most of the morning. She knew what that meant. She wasn't stupid.

The thought frightened her. It was at least half a mile to their nearest neighbours: a farmhouse with a family of hearty children, a silent and morose farm manager and his sharp-tongued wife who substituted for the local telegraph. There was nothing that missed that woman's eyes and Ursula felt exposed and bereft every time Simon disappeared back up to London without her. Mrs Clow knew about it, of course, and dropped by at least once a week to let Ursula know she knew. But with a baby on the way it seemed Mrs Clow might be needed and Ursula bit her tongue to keep from saying what she might have. It was silly to alienate the woman just now. Ursula smiled tightly and nodded agreement to comments such as:

'Your husband's not here again, I see. What with you being newly-weds and all, I can't think what he's doing up in London all the time. Can you?' Jane Clow's fat cheeks would brighten and her body would sway to and fro with amusement, supported by legs without ankles and sturdy, sensible shoes. Ursula would answer bravely:

'He has to earn a living. That's what takes him away. His father can't support him forever and we both agreed it was best this way.' And Mrs Clow would laugh, her eyes buried in layers of fat but still not missing a thing. She enjoyed her round of the neighbours, tushing her horse and telling him to 'Get along now, Jack, get along!' as she skilfully turned her little pony trap around in the rutted lanes and whisked off to spread more good cheer. And she might be right, of course, Ursula thought. Maybe Simon shouldn't be leaving all the time? The doubt appeared and, much as Ursula tried to deny it, the heavi-ness that doubt brought with it filled her chest with pain and made sleep an impossibility. Ursula began to hide when she heard the trap rattling down the lane to the cottage.

It wasn't that life was unpleasant out here in the wilds of Essex. She thought it a beautiful area, full of gently undulating fields and wide, washed skies. But it was lonely and very cold. It was supposed to be high summer – August – but the wind never let up for a moment even when the sun shone, and there was a nip to the air that made her keep the windows closed at night and the fire lit. Simon thought it ridiculous and had told her so often, arguing that he couldn't afford to keep a fire going through the middle of the summer and anyway, she would never acclimatize like this. And she just smiled agreement and went out looking for more wood. At least there was plenty of that.

The cottage had belonged to Simon's maternal grandmother and he had been using it as a hunting lodge the last few years. It had two bedrooms, a bathroom of sorts, a kitchen and a sitting room. Out back there were a couple of sheds, a small barn, and a glass potting-shed but several of the panes were broken and there were no plants anyway. Simon had tried to fix them one day when he was feeling enthusiastic about life in the country. But the new pane had fallen out almost immediately and he had managed to embed a long splinter under his thumb nail that left him cursing for hours. The garden had been allowed to run wild, all half an acre of it, and the lane that led down from the main road was full of pot holes and tyre-ruts. Simon told Ursula he thought it charmingly rustic. Then he left for London – on business. And Ursula dealt with things.

It had taken her a while to realize that this was not just an odd occurrence but would continue. After all, she was in love with him and wanted desperately for them to be happy together. Perhaps she had been overly optimistic that they would live in London. It was, as Simon had said, very expensive to live in town. But she could learn in time to please him in the way that other wives pleased their husbands if he stayed down there with her more often. It was just that she'd never had any practice before; she'd never even really kissed anyone. It would get better once she learned how to relax and he grew less impatient. Maybe she would even get to really like it. Some women did, she believed. She sighed and closed her eyes.

The wedding had been small and quiet, only immediate family, and they had had it mid-week at St Margaret's, just around the corner in London. Christopher hadn't come. She had written to him, asking him to be there, but he hadn't answered her letter. Rodney had said he was studying very hard. Ursula had nodded. Her aunt and uncle had been pleased and bewildered that she should have managed such a good marriage in su :h a short time. Especially, as Aunt Mary had whispered to Uncle George, without a figure of any sort! And especially, Uncle George had whispered back to her, when another mouth to feed would have just about broken them right now. Quite a relief things had worked out this way, now he was out of work. It was good to know the girl was taken care of. Aunt Mary had snorted her agreement.

Simon had made a dashingly handsome bridegroom and Ursula an elegant, even beautiful, bride. That had surprised her aunt even more. Love had brought back the delicate glow to Ursula's skin and given her an exotic beauty that while not in the usual style was still quite attractive, Aunt Mary had grudgingly admitted. And they had looked to be very happy.

Julia had been equally taken aback at how Ursula had blossomed into such an elegant young woman. That wide, pouting mouth in golden skin, those taut cheekbones and dark eyes had an allure that not many men could miss. Certainly not Simon. Julia eyed them both with an expression that even Uncle George had commented on, despite the fact that he found Julia's looks by far the more attractive. And Aunt Mary hadn't replied to that either.

The honeymoon had been there at the cottage, Simon asking tenderly if she minded; money was so tight. And of course she hadn't. This was the sort of cottage Papa and Billy had talked about: the stone one with the thatched roof and roses rambling over the door, and the brook running by at the foot of the garden. Of course, it needed work, but that was half the fun. Simon and she would get it back in shape in no time. That was what she had thought.

Three weeks after they arrived, Simon had had to return to London. Urgent business; and money was so tight. Did she mind terribly? She did but hid it from him, thinking herself difficult and ungrateful. And she didn't want to cling. He returned four days later full of apologies and a dozen red roses. Ursula wondered how he could have afforded the roses when money was so tight but he told her that she was worth it. And she had held him close, kissing him passionately so that he would know how much she loved him. She had tried so hard to

180

give him what he seemed to need. And she felt she was getting better, relaxing more with him. Maybe if he were to stay longer this time . . . Two days later, he left again.

'Where's Mr Patterson then, Mrs Patterson? Not gone back to town again, has he?' That was the man who had been sent to check on the meter. Ursula didn't even know him. She glared at him.

'My husband has to work. Just like you. I don't expect you're home with your wife much during the day either.'

'No, Mrs Patterson, you're right there. Just in the evenings. But my wife would probably be happy to trade places with you, just to get me out of her hair once in a while.' He had gone off whistling through his teeth with a smiling face that had no idea what harm his words had done. And Ursula had tried to pretend it wasn't a problem. Simon loved her. He told her that every time they went to bed. He held her in his arms and said 'I love you' as clearly as anything. She sniffed and picked up her tea-towel, resisting the impulse to use it as a handkerchief.

'Hallo, Ursula, Jane Clow here. Where's that devil husband of yours?' bellowed from beneath the kitchen window. 'I need him to pay my bill. He didn't leave any money with you, did he? It's not much, God knows, but I do need it or I won't be able to let you have any more eggs or milk.'

'Oh! Jane, I'm terribly sorry! It must've slipped Simon's mind. I rather thought he'd paid you already. I gave him the bill. I'll tell him to come over the minute he gets back.'

'And when might that be? No, never mind. I don't expect you know any better than I do. That's Simon. Known that boy all his life and he never grows up. Well, mustn't say things like that to you, must I dear? After all, you're still on your honeymoon practically, aren't you?'

'Well, no, not really. We have been married nearly two months now, so I'd say the honeymoon side of things is over by now. That's why Simon goes away, of course, to earn some money. We're a bit tight really and I know he works quite hard at making sure all the bills are paid. I'm very sorry, Jane. It won't happen again.'

'No, not till next time.' Jane laughed, not really minding about the bill as long as she could have a good gossip. 'Well, give him my love and tell him he's a lousy husband. Just like he was always a lousy son. He'll know what I mean. Must go, love, bye, bye.' And off Jane went, merrily calling to her horse as she negotiated the narrow entrance to the road. That time Ursula did use the tea-towel. And so it went on.

It had been difficult for her to recognize the truth but, when the pattern continued throughout the first three months of their marriage, and his visits grew shorter and less frequent with every discussion they had about it, Ursula slowly tried to swallow the unpalatable. She was just a cover; the wife in the wings who lent respectability to Simon's philandering. Maybe he had cared about her briefly, the way he might be taken with a different recipe, or a new type of aftershave, but the novelty had worn off. Now she was just a wife. A pregnant wife.

The only fight they had had, funnily enough, had nothing to do with Simon's absences. It had been to do with an invasion of Ursula's privacy. At least, she considered it as such. Simon had told her she was being ridiculous and why shouldn't he open her mail, when he was her husband? The letter itself had been from a firm of solicitors in Perth, Australia. A Mr Waters had written to tell her she had inherited Sally's property up in Gidgeeganup but that he had organized for a farm manager to run things for her. There wasn't likely to be any money from the property since it was barely making ends meet as it was. Simon had been cross about that. He had thought something might be coming through, now that it was confirmed all her family were dead. Even a little might have helped, he added with a look at Ursula that made her feel she had not kept to her side of the bargain.

Ursula had protested angrily when she came downstairs to find Simon reading the letter. It wasn't addressed to him. It wasn't anything to do with him. How would he like it if she opened his personal mail? And Simon had tossed the letter in Ursula's face and slammed out of the house, leaving her thinking fiercely that if the worst came to the worst she could always go and live on that property. It was a daydream of course, but it made her feel better to know it was there.

She rolled over in bed, her hands spread over her stomach to stop it joggling. But it was no good. She threw back the covers hurriedly and, shivering as her feet hit the cold floor, she staggered into the bathroom and was sick. That was the third time that morning. Slowly she let herself down onto the floor, her back against the bath and her head close to the lavatory bowl in case she should have to throw up again. There was chill sweat across her face and streaking her nightgown and she alternately shivered and gagged. She had always had a weak stomach. But if this was what pregnancy was like, she never wanted Simon to touch her again. She didn't even want the baby that much; not when its father didn't seem to care. She had been pleased at first, thinking how close it would bring Simon and her to be parents. And it would be wonderful to have a baby like little Tom. She knew she could be a good mother. But not alone! And she was so young herself. Not even eighteen yet. How was she going to manage the baby and the cottage and the garden all alone? Simon wasn't giving her enough money. It always seemed enough when he handed it to her, telling her he'd only be two days, or three days at most. But then it became a week, ten days, and the money was gone. He didn't seem to understand, telling her he wasn't made of money. And then he would make everything up with a huge bunch of flowers or some chocolates from a West End confectioner and she couldn't help thinking that they had probably cost more than it took for her to live for a week down here.

The bath was tin with one end much higher than the other. It was white, mostly, but years of use had put scratches in the enamel and it needed constant scrubbing to look decent. But at least it was plumbed in. Mrs Clow had told her how spoiled she was by that little luxury. Luxuries weren't quite nice, Ursula gathered. And the floor was waxed boards that spotted whenever water got on them. Ursula was very careful to dry herself off in the bath but Simon thought nothing of splashing soap and water half-way up the wallpaper and out across the boards in pools. She didn't say anything. The last thing she wanted to be was a nag, and that's what Aunt Mary had told Rodney she was. She sighed and leant her head back against the cold metal, wishing she could get her strength back. There was so much to do! There had been a rather nice pencil sketch framed and hung above the bath at first. It was a cartoon-style characterization of a woman taking a bath and Ursula had liked it a lot. But that had been drowned in one of Simon's waterworks, and now it hung in the hall, a little spotted and brown at the edges. She sighed.

When it became clear that her stomach had settled down for the while, Ursula levered herself up and plodded back to the bedroom, collapsing limply across the bed. She knew it was past ten but there was nothing she could do about it so she rolled under the covers and pulled them tightly around her body. Let the neighbours talk! They should all be condemned to morning sickness for at least a year! So far there had been no change in her body's size. Except perhaps for her breasts. They were larger and tender to touch. Simon liked to touch them a lot, even though she had told him they were sore. But her belly was as flat and tautly stretched across her hipbones as ever. The baby didn't seem quite real. She could almost think it was all in her mind but the morning sickness was real. And, by her reckoning, she was about three months gone. She had heard the sickness stopped after three months and that it was a good sign to be sick; it meant the baby was lying right. At least, that's what Fatimah and the women in the kampong had used to say. Oh, what she wouldn't have given to have Fatimah's warm body holding her tight and crooning lullabies to her, as she had when Ursula was a child. Or baby Tom who had loved to nestle in against her, his soft cheek lying against hers. Or Billy smiling at her and calling her *cahayamata* again. She closed her eyes and felt tears burn against her lids, seeping out through her lashes and down her cheeks. Billy! Oh, Billy! Everyone who had ever cared about her was dead or on the other side of the world. Except Christopher. But he hadn't replied to any of her letters and what could he do anyway? She was married and going to have a baby. He couldn't help her. She buried her head further into the warmth of the pillow.

Simon had been gone five days this time. He had said he'd be back in three but she hadn't believed him even when he grinned at her and chukked her under the chin, his eyes sliding away with that almost pained look. He suspected she was pregnant but he hadn't asked and she had been too shy to tell him. But this time when he returned she would. She'd lay it on the line; either he started staying home more and helping her until the baby was born, or she was going back to her aunt and uncle's. It was a bluff, of course. With her uncle out of work

184

there was no hope of that. But with any luck Simon wouldn't recognize it as such. It wouldn't be so bad if she knew more about what to expect. But she was scared, and alone, and she needed someone. Even her husband. He had to stay with her until after the baby came. Then he could spend all his time in London if he wanted. She felt a twist of anguish, the pain of loss, and resolutely steeled herself against it. He could stay in London, with women who liked what he wanted to do to them, who thought it sexy when he pinched and kneaded. She would be better by then and strong enough to work in the garden. She knew how to grow vegetables and weave mats. If nothing else, life in the kampong had taught her how to live off the land. But she had to be strong to do the work. This baby was going to be first and last. She'd see to that.

Ursula lay on her back staring out the dormer window at the bright sky. The bedclothes were warm again and soft, and she felt better. The nausea had gone for the day. In her mind she catalogued the things that needed to be done. First, she needed to find out what vegetables should be planted and when. Then she should make a plan, a yearly plan with each season's crop marked out, and the planting, fertilizing, and harvesting times noted. This could be fun. She enjoyed working with her hands and seeing things grow. Simon couldn't be relied upon for money, though he might be better when the baby arrived. He could hardly have it starve, or go without warm clothes. And she'd want a herb garden too. And some chickens, perhaps even a cow. Oh, perhaps they could manage a horse! It would be so wonderful to ride again. She was sure she could look after one herself. And Simon might want to ride when he was down for the shooting. He'd buy one if he wanted to use it. She'd already begun to realize there was plenty of money for the things he wanted. Probably his father's money. He was only a miser to her, and then only when he was tired of her. The problem was, that seemed to be all the time lately. Maybe if she hadn't got pregnant so soon things would have been different? A tear slid down the side of her face, trickling unpleasantly into her ear. She brushed it away angrily.

With a horse, she could go to market and buy the rest of the food. And maybe, just maybe, she could start a small business. A sort of cottage industry, weaving and arranging dried

185

flowers? And maybe cooking cakes, or drying herbs, or making vinegar and jams? She'd show Simon she could cope, all alone. And then he'd be bound to respect her more, maybe even want to spend more time with her. It was all possible. Just as long as she was healthy and strong. She spread her hands over her stomach again and felt a twinge of impatience. Six more months! It was such a nuisance that it should happen right now when the cottage needed a new coat of paint and the garden had to be weeded. Bother babies and being pregnant!

She gave a long, gusty sigh and then climbed out of bed. Enough was enough. It was late and she had things to do. She'd never even been into the next village, in all the time she'd lived here. Simon had gone and stocked up on things for the cottage and arranged for the milk and eggs from Jane Clow and for the grocer to drop by on a regular basis. But now she felt it was time to go and have a look.

Elsing seemed large and prosperous in the noon-time bustle of shoppers and clerks hurrying out for lunch. She walked down the main street with a pleased expression on her face, noting the chemist, the greengrocer, and a small brass plate against the front door of a Georgian terrace house that said: 'R.B. Cullens, MD.' That was good. A doctor only two miles away. She dropped in and made an appointment to see him the following week.

Further down the street there was a secondhand shop and she walked in, hearing a bell tinkle somewhere above her. It was musty and dark in the shop with chairs and tables, boxes, jugs, tennis racquets, suitcases, and kitchen implements all stacked haphazardly on top of each other. Ursula looked at the prices casually and was astonished at how little things cost. Why, at this rate she could finish off the cottage in no time. She didn't have the money at the moment but whoever heard of a whole pile of kitchen implements costing threepence? The discovery elated her and she began to look in earnest. That chair would be perfect in the bathroom to put clothes or towels on while she was bathing. And that stool would be useful in the kitchen. There was only an oak dresser and table at the moment and no chairs. Perhaps a settle might be more useful though? The one against the back wall was nice and only a little scuffed. It just needed some linseed oil and a rub-down. She climbed over two trunks to reach the settle. Yes, it was really in very good condition and only one and six. She wondered if the owner might let her put a payment down on it and come back for it later, with Simon.

The owner was nowhere to be seen, despite the bell that had gone off to warn him a shopper was browsing amongst his treasures. Ursula backed up into the hall and walked towards the back of the shop. It went on quite a way further than she had expected and suddenly she found herself in a tiny room lined with books. A sign announced that this was Elsing's lending library. Ursula smiled. How were people supposed to find it, hidden away as it was behind a secondhand furniture shop? There were a couple of other people in there, a woman with her shopping basket full of books and her face almost hidden under an unruly mop of hair, and an old man in tweeds and elbow patches. They both smiled politely at Ursula.

'Can I help you?' the man asked and Ursula started. She hadn't expected him to be the librarian. He looked more like, well, the gardener maybe?

'Yes, I was looking at the secondhand furniture and liked a settle. The one up the back by the two trunks. But I didn't realize there was a library too. How do I join?' She kept her voice hushed, not wanting to disturb the woman, but the librarian seemed to be unaware of such delicacies. He spoke up loudly and briskly: 'Two and six to join, and you'll have to fill out this form. Then you may take out six books at a time for a fortnight. The fine for overdue books is a halfpenny a week per book. If you have books of your own you may bring them in and, if they're of equivalent value and quality, you may exchange them for a book here. Any questions?' She noticed the other woman watching her and nodded her head in greeting. It might be a small library and have rather strange rules but Ursula was familiar with this sort of thing. It reminded her of the Tanglin Club Library, on a minor scale. Still, it was a start.

'Yes. Could I join now, and could I put a deposit on the settle and then pay the rest when my husband comes back from London? It would just be a few days and then he could fetch it in the car, you see.'

'Quite all right, Madam.' Ursula filled in the library card and turned to look round the room. It was cramped and overflowing with books and she wondered if there was any order to their arrangement. She browsed idly, enjoying the thrill of so many unread books to choose from. The woman with the shopping basket paused beside her.

'Hallo. You must be Mrs Patterson. Jane Clow told me you'd moved into "Cotters". I've been meaning to drop by and introduce myself. I'm Lettice Dunham.' Ursula smiled and held out her hand. Lettice Dunham? Was she the one who lived in the Old Rectory, or did she live in Elsing House just near the common? Mrs Clow had told her so much about so many people it was hard to keep it all straight.

'How d'you do? I can't think how you knew who I was! Or did Mrs Clow describe me?'

'In excruciating detail,' Lettice Dunham laughed, her voice gravelly as though she had a sore throat. 'You probably realize by now that there isn't anyone Jane doesn't know about, or tell about. We all rely on her for our information. How would anyone know the gossip otherwise?' She laughed again and Ursula laughed too. It was such a relief that her throat muscles seemed stiff from lack of use.

'Please call me Ursula. I'm not quite used to the Patterson bit yet anyway.'

'Good, then I'm Lettice. I'd have guessed you were a newlywed even if Jane hadn't told me. You look awfully young and inexperienced to be married. I hope you don't mind me saying things like that. I'm a bit blunt but at least people know where they stand with me. No beating around the bushes! What was your maiden name by the way? I used to know some people out in Singapore.'

'Fraser. My father was Harry Fraser, of Gooch & Fraser, Singapore. Except there wasn't really any Mr Gooch anymore.'

'Really? You didn't know the Howards did you?' When Ursula shook her head, Lettice shrugged. 'Worth a try. But how exciting to have grown up there. I've always wanted to go somewhere exotic like that. You must tell me all about the Far East. I'm dying to hear everything. Why don't you drop by my place on the way home and have tea? We can talk and get to

188

know each other, and I can tell you where the best shops are.'
She was enthusiastic, her long nose and pink cheeks poking out
of her blonde fluffy hair so that she looked like a sheep. A very
nice sheep, Ursula thought a little guiltily.

'Oh, that's terribly kind of you. I'd love to! But, where do
you live?' Lettice laughed again. She seemed to be a happy
sort.

'It's a little Georgian house overlooking the common and the
pond. Called "Elsing House". You can't miss it, and if you do,
ask someone. Everyone knows it.' How nice. To be known by
everyone. Just like they were in old Sing. Ursula smiled as
Lettice gathered up her basket and turned for the door. Things
were looking better already. She had a doctor and a friend.
Now all she needed was a husband!

That last thought reminded her that she needed to find out
about gardening in England. It was bound to be totally different to Singapore. Different climate, soil, terrain – everything!
She'd have to learn it all from scratch. Hunting for anything in
the library was time-consuming. Eventually she found a book
on vegetable growing, called *War Gardens*. It was old and
tattered and well-thumbed, most of the thumbs seemingly
mud-stained rather than green. But that was a good sign.
People really used this book and got results. At least, she hoped
they got results. She picked up two more that didn't seem as
helpful but which had pictures that inspired. A little inspiration
could be worth a lot of knowledge, she thought. *Good House-
keeping* might be useful too. She pulled it from the shelf. Then,
almost as an afterthought, she picked up a book on babies.
Why not? She had to learn sometime.

'Elsing House' was impossibly perfect, set back from the road
with a low wall separating it from the common. It was built of
mellow red brick in an absolutely ordered Georgian style and
there were two full storeys and then a third up in the roof with
dormer windows. Ursula felt a terrible pang of longing grind
into her as she looked at its tidy garden and beautiful gravel
drive sweeping in an arc up to the white painted front door.
This was what she had been expecting when Simon had said he
had a small place in the country. This was what she had
thought would be her lifestyle, with a gardener and maid and

cook, just like before the war. She knew she was being silly but oh! it would've been so nice to have been wealthy again. She swallowed painfully and walked up the drive, noting the rhodo-dendrons underneath the copper-beech and the splash of colour against the wall where a whole bank of flowers and plants were massed. It was warm and sunny with the wind blocked by the wall and she could hear the hum of bees as they searched for nectar in the flowers. Against the front of the house dusty-pink roses edged with gold were climbing around the windows and there was a nest of mud stuck to the door lintel. Ursula paused in front of the door, wondering if her knocking would disturb the birds.

'Ursula! Come on round this way,' Lettice was calling from the side of the house, a large and sleepy tabby cradled over one shoulder. She disappeared from view and Ursula followed after her, wondering if she'd accidentally escaped into *The Secret Garden*. At any moment Dickon would walk up and tell her 'tha art a strange lass'. She shook her head and laughed at herself. Everything was too perfect.

Lettice had set the tea things out on an old marble table in the garden and there were two wicker chairs pulled up beside it with a comfortable pile of pillows in each. The cat raised his massive head, showing the battle scars of countless past engage-ments with the other cats of the neighbourhood. He blinked yellow eyes and then lowered his head back on to Lettice's shoulder, his chin up against her neck. Lettice held him in the crook of one arm and gestured to Ursula to sit with the other.

'We're not using the front door at the moment,' she said, 'because the first nest dried out too much and then fell down when Hugh let the door slam. This is their second batch and we're hoping they're going to be ready to fly before winter comes. Mudlarks are such stupid birds. They always build in the same place, even when the first nest doesn't work. So now the door's off-limits to everyone until they fly away.'

'That's so nice. Most people wouldn't do that. They'd just let the second nest fall down. Or pull it down. I mean, the birds must make rather a mess, don't they?'

'Bird shit all over the place, not to mention feathers, twigs, eggshells. Messy little devils!' Ursula blinked and smiled. She liked Lettice and her blunt way of putting things. The table was laid with a white embroidered cloth anchored by plates and teacups. There was a sponge cake with sugar sprinkled over it and jam inside and a tiered plate with digestives on the top, little sandwiches on the next tier down, and almond slices on the bottom. Ursula smiled, a warm, happy feeling flooding through her. She sat down on the pillows, pushing one into the small of her back and breathed in deeply. There was a smell of grass and roses, lavender and hydrangeas all mixed up together with the dry, mustiness of the wicker chairs. Lettice sat down awkwardly, transferring the cat to her lap where he curled tightly into a ball and tucked his face behind his tail.

'What's his name?'

'Toby. He's a fool for the ladies and getting too old for that sort of roaming. I'm trying to encourage him to stay home for a while. Silly old bugger. He won't learn. In a few days he'll be off again.' Just like Simon, Ursula thought bitterly. Except Simon was still young and handsome. Lettice seemed to read her thoughts.

'Where's that handsome devil of yours then? Up in London roaming?' She didn't seem bothered by the sudden rush of colour to Ursula's face, just picking up the teapot and pouring out the tea. 'Milk?'

'No, thank you. I like it black. Without anything.'

'Right. I'll add some water then. If I'd known that's how you drank it I'd have made you a separate pot. Lemon?'

'Oh no, no, just black. And this is fine; I don't need another pot.'

'Good. Now I've got Toby settled I don't want to get up again for a while. So, where is Simon? He hasn't been to see me in the longest while. Probably scared what I'll say to him. You love him?' She had the oddest habit of darting terribly personal questions at someone after she'd made a lot of trivial comments. Ursula found it disconcerting.

'Yes! Of course I do! Uh, why? I'd hardly have married him otherwise, would I?' She laughed nervously. Lettice shrugged.

'I don't know. You might have had your reasons. He's supposed to be a good catch, though God knows why, and then again, you may have had to marry him. I'm not saying it was either of those reasons or any others, I'm just asking. Do you love him?'

191

'Yes, and that was the only reason I married him!' Ursula snapped, putting her teacup down on the table with a rattle. She found her hands were shaking and her face grew red under Lettice's unabashed stare. 'Simon's just . . . well, we're not very rich, you know. And he has to work in London. There's nothing for him down here. We've talked about it and agreed that's how it'll have to be for a while.' How dare Lettice ask questions like that, as though the thought of position or wealth had ever entered into things. Well, only to the point where a marriage to someone who could look after her . . . And she had loved Simon, still loved him, no matter what. A picture of Simon's face floated in front of her eyes, his lips full under that natty little military moustache, the eyes bright and full of light. The familiar pang of longing and loss ground into her so that she had to focus her memory on something else. Just look at the face and don't think about the rest. Look at his moustache. She didn't like moustaches anyway. And particularly not military ones.

She pressed her knuckles into her temples, trying to re-capture that certainty she had felt when Lettice first asked her if she loved him. Did she? Had she ever? She didn't even really know him. Was it simply that he had been right for what she had been looking for, and she had thought she could depend on him to give it to her? And now she knew better. Ursula looked across at Lettice, her defences faltering.

'I don't know. I thought I did. I thought I could trust him and that he'd make everything wonderful again, like before the war. I don't really know anymore, not now. I still miss him. How long have you known Simon?' Lettice hadn't changed expression. She just quietly sipped her tea and scratched Toby's ears. He gave a loud rumble and twitched his tail.

'Since he was born. Before that even. Old Hilda, his grand-mother, used to live in your cottage then and, when he was little, Simon and his mother came to visit her quite often. Sometimes he'd stay with her in the long hols. I suppose I've known him on and off for most of his life. His mother and I were friends before she married. We went to school together and we spent most of our time together until she met Humphrey. Nice man! And then Simon was born and I got to see more of Clare again until the accident. Car crash, you know, late at night on a wet road. She was killed instantly. After that Simon came and stayed with Hilda for quite a long while. I think Humphrey couldn't bear to see him running around so happy and carefree when Clare was dead. It was very hard on both of them, I think.

'Then, about seven years ago or so, Humphrey met and married Julia. I've only met her once, up in London. At the wedding actually. I don't think she likes the country very much and, besides, she's such a ravishing creature I'd think she'd look quite out of place here. London's her natural setting. Humphrey was something quite important during the war I gather; something in Military Intelligence. He's frightfully bright you know, all brain and no brawn. I can't think why he didn't have more sense where Julia was concerned, but then, that's all water under the bridge. I wouldn't want to go pointing fingers.'

'You just have, I'd say,' Ursula said drily. 'I thought you were the blunt, no beating around the bushes type? Please, don't hold anything back on my account. I don't think it'll hurt me too much anymore. I suppose I've heard most of it anyway.' She leaned back in her chair, the wicker creaking under her. It was hard not to look at Lettice; the woman seemed to draw her gaze. Their eyes met.

'All right. You know Simon was in the war as a pilot? Quite the fly-boy, decorated and everything. He joined up after they threw him out of Cambridge, but I daresay he'd have joined anyway. He's the sort to enjoy a good war, all the excitement, all the glamour. And really, he's quite brave under the right sort of conditions. On that count you can be really rather proud of him, I'd say. Can't adapt to life in the slow lane though. That's why he gets into so many scrapes. He had so much leeway when he was a brave, daring fighter pilot. Now he's just one of the crowd. That doesn't appeal. Don't expect him to settle down, he won't.'

'You're very sure of that?'

'As sure as I am that he and Julia are having an affair.' Ursula had expected to feel shattered, or to deny it hotly and argue in Simon's defence. Yes, there was that sharp, breathtaking pain for a moment, and then the heaviness. But as Lettice said it half her mind agreed, and the rest was almost

193

indifferent. Lucy was Simon's child; maybe Benjie was too. Who was to know the difference? She blinked and looked at her hands, white and thin in the sun's glare. They looked like putty that had been moulded too finely. When she was a child she used to play with her fingers for hours, imagining they were living creatures, each with its own character, likes and dislikes. She had had a puppet show at the end of each wrist. Now they were silent and didn't tell her a thing.

'How do you know? I mean, really know?'

'Simon told me. He used to confide in me a lot; treated me like his own mother at times. I suppose he needed to tell someone. Humphrey just closes his eyes to it. He's hopelessly in love with Julia and I think he feels that as long as he doesn't know for sure, he can keep denying it. The last thing he wants is for someone to prove it to him. Then he'd lose Julia for good. It's been going on since the first year of marriage. I don't know if anyone knows who the children's father really is.' Lettice laughed, a really amused laugh that shocked Ursula. How could she be so callous? This was awful! Poor Mr Patterson! She didn't really think, 'poor me!' because she couldn't quite feel a part of all this. It was as though someone else's family skeletons were being revealed; not her own. 'And Simon used to come and visit me when he was on leave and wanted to get a breath of fresh air. He feels sorry about it all but he doesn't feel sorry enough to change any of it. I didn't know about you at all until Jane told me Simon had brought his bride down to ''Cotters'' and dumped her there while he high-tailed it back up to London. But then, Simon hasn't been to see me in quite a while now; not since I told him he was driving his father into an early grave. Simon's not good at dealing with guilt. He prefers sympathy. That's why I asked if you loved him. It would be a pity if you did. Jane says you're going to have a baby?'

There, she'd done it again! Slid up on Ursula and stuck the question in before Ursula could see it coming.

'What makes her say that?'

'Oh come on, Ursula. Jane says you've been sick every morning that she's been to see you and my cleaning woman says she saw you going into Dr Cullens's surgery. It doesn't take a lot of brain-power to figure that one out. How far are you along?' The wind was blowing Lettice's hair around her face and Ursula recalled how she had thought Lettice looked like a nice sheep. She laughed to herself.

'Three months, give or take a week. I'm going for a check-up next week. I guess I might as well just tell everyone everything quite frankly as they're all going to know soon enough anyway. Or will Jane Clow do that for me, do you think?' Her voice was bitter.

'Don't think people are saying bad things about you behind your back, Ursula. Everyone's very sympathetic. They think it's very wrong of Simon, especially when you're so young. How old are you, anyway?'

'Eighteen. I'll be nineteen in November. And I don't want to be the object of the whole district's pity!' Her cup was empty and Lettice leaned forward to pour her another. She seemed to be thinking.

'What are you going to do? Stay until the baby's born and then go back home?' For a brief, reeling second Ursula wanted to do just that. Desperately. And then she remembered.

'Home? Where's that? Singapore? My mother died having me, my father was killed by the Japanese. I just heard a few weeks ago that my step-mother and Emma and Tom were . . .' she paused and only continued with difficulty ' . . . were drowned when their ship was sunk. They were trying to get out in time before the Japanese overran Singapore. I suppose I could go back and live in a Malay kampong for the rest of my life but I don't think that's really the answer. My aunt and uncle weren't at all happy when I lived with them and there's not much chance they'd take me back now that my uncle's lost his job, and especially with me having a baby. I inherited a worthless piece of land in the Australian outback that the solicitors tell me I haven't a hope of selling. So what choice do I have? The cottage is home now and I'm going to make it comfortable. Simon can do what he wants.'

'Bravo! You sound like you've got some spunk in you after all. I was a little worried at first.'

'If I could live through the Japanese occupation of Singapore, I can live through a baby and a broken-down cottage.' She laughed suddenly and looked puzzled. 'You know the really odd thing – apart from the fact that I've told all my problems to a total stranger – is that Simon never told me he was a pilot, or decorated or anything. Why is that, do you think? I'd have thought that would be the first thing he would have told a girl to impress her.'

'Not really. Simon can be odd. He takes the easy way generally but sometimes he just digs in his heels. He lost quite a few of his best buddies in the war. I haven't actually heard him talk about it at all. Not even when he came down here on leave. He'd talk about Julia, or about the latest plays or gossip or anything really, as long as it wasn't about his own role in the war. I can't tell you the reasons behind it. He's deeper than he seems.'

'Hmm. The women who'd lived through Changi were like that. They'd talk about anything, except that. I guess Simon does have feelings then. Just deeper than I can dig for them. Did he fly fighters or bombers, or what?'

'Bombers I gather. They were all so ridiculously young to be in charge of so much destruction and Simon was one of the best. Got his plane over the target, got the bombs away, and brought his crew home safely. Again and again and again. That's why he thinks he's special and doesn't have to pay attention to the rules. Because he broke them all in the war and everyone loved him for it. He hasn't woken up to the fact that the war's over and now he has to find something else to do where the rules mean something and if he breaks them, he's finished. Can't keep a job down, you know. One after the other. Bored within a week and no-one looking up to him. You have to pity him. And, of course, Humphrey bales him out all the time with that private income and the trust fund Simon inherited from his mother. It won't last much longer, the rate he's going through it,' Lettice said.

Ursula shrugged. 'Well, here's to being a permanent addition to Elsing.' She raised her teacup and Lettice followed suit, the delicate china chinking musically as they toasted. Toby raised his head, gazed impassively at his mistress and then jumped clumsily to the ground. He limped off down the path.

'Oh dear. There he goes again. That bite on his leg's given me more trouble than I care to remember, and does he think about that? Hell no, he just waltzes off looking for another lady of the night, and another street brawl.' Lettice shook her skirt

196

to rid it of fur. 'How are you managing for money? Does Simon leave you with enough?'

'No, not really. I have to keep asking and asking and I know he thinks I'm being unreasonable. I hate being dependent. I thought I might start growing my own vegetables. I got a book on it.' She pointed to the pile of books she had laid on the grass beside her chair. Lettice nodded.

'It's a start, I suppose. Have you done much gardening before?'

'Only in Singapore. But I'm strong and used to hard work. When I lived in the kampong I often worked all day long tending the vegetable plots and weaving straw mats. I can do it, if I put my mind to it.'

'All right. But you'll need a little advice to begin with. Why don't I send Old Bill down to you for a few hours each week. Just to begin with. He doesn't really have enough to do around here and I think he'd enjoy it.'

'Your gardener? Oh, that's awfully kind of you Lettice but I don't have enough to pay for him and buy seeds and fertilizer and all the rest.'

'Don't be silly. Bill works for me, all day every day. He doesn't have nearly enough work for all those hours and I'd be happy to send him to you, if it will get you started. There's no question of money. And I won't hear a word against it. I think it's a good idea and so it's settled. I'll send him out to you tomorrow, around three probably. He's got a bicycle and the exercise will do him good. Lose some of that pot he's got.' Lettice rode roughshod over Ursula's protest, her imagination fired with the project in hand. Before she knew it, Ursula had been dragged through the outbuildings in search of old gardening tools that Lettice swore she had no use for, and had a list of shops drawn up that could provide her with provisions of a superior quality for a minimal price. Ursula was out of breath by the time Lettice had finished organizing her life for her. She finished up at the garden gate, her books in her hand, and the tools set aside for Old Bill to bring with him the next day.

'Lettice, I'm embarrassed at what a moocher I'm being. How can I take all this from you. It isn't right.'

'Simon's mother was my best friend, almost my sister. I've often regarded Simon as my son since I've no children of my

197

own. So that makes you my daughter-in-law. You're not mooching at all. You're being brave and sensible. I like a girl with some spunk. Now trot off home before it starts to rain and I may drop around tomorrow. Or certainly the next day. In the afternoon, don't worry. I may never have had a baby but I know all about it. Now off you go.' She kissed Ursula on the cheek and gave her a push in the small of her back and Ursula smiled and obeyed. It was a relief to know there was someone she could turn to. The next few months didn't seem nearly as frightening all of a sudden.

Chapter Thirteen

Old Bill was a gnarled, uncommunicative sort. It was impossible to guess at his age. His face had that weathered, contented look of a man who has spent most of his life out of doors. Ursula saw him bicycling down the lane from the kitchen window and she opened the front door to greet him. The tools, a spading fork, an iron rake, a scuffle hoe and some hand tools were tied with twine to the back of his bicycle so that he took up as much room as a car. He seemed oblivious to the fact, cycling steadily over and around the pitted driveway, his trousers fastened with clips and his jacket patched in several places. He came to a halt outside the front door and tipped his cap at Ursula.

'Arfterrnoon mum. I'm Old Bill.' Ursula smiled a welcome.

'I'm Mrs Patterson. It's very kind of Mrs Dunham to let me have you, and it's very kind of you to come all this way. I hope the tools weren't a bother?' He had climbed off his bicycle and was untying the tools and the only answer he offered was a grunt. Ursula's smile faded a little. Overhead the clouds that had been gathering all day, rumbled ominously. Ursula looked up.

'I'm afraid we're in for a storm. You're going to get terribly wet going home.'

'Doann you worry, mum, it's no'ing but an Essex show,' Old Bill muttered, not looking up from the task in hand. Ursula frowned.

'An "Essex show?" Is that a storm?'

'All but. Everythin' but the rain. No rain. I recall a time when it din rain for near five year. Back around the turn of the century. Harsh, that were. Ver' harsh. Plenty of shows tho'.'

'Have you been a gardener all that time?'

'Happen so. None but us old uns left now. The young uns go to the towns. My own son, young Bill. He's goan too.' He looked at the cottage critically and twisted his mouth. 'It's a fair average place for such as these parts. Some of them are right tumbled down.' Ursula followed him anxiously while he wandered around the cottage and grounds, trying not to mind the way he sucked his teeth and made smacking sounds with his lips.

'Will it grow a good crop, do you think? Enough to feed us and perhaps some to sell?'

'Well now.' He paused and tilted his cap back on his head, scratching his crown. His eyes were small and perky, almost buried under the ridges and furrows of his skin. 'This is a nice enough spot and it's a funny season when we doan get a crop.' Then he continued pacing over the land, his boots crushing the grass and weed alike. Where Old Bill went, he was master. Ursula trailed after him, wondering if she would ever get him to be more specific. How large a crop did he mean?

She learned, over the next two months, that Old Bill knew his business. He sat with her in the kitchen and made a plan of the garden, having previously paced out the dimensions. He told her the soil was good, with plenty of humus and that it would be easy to work with and would retain moisture. It was a little clayey but he told her she could slake it with lime as this caused 'the flocculation' of the clay particles. Ursula had no idea what flocculation was but she soon gathered that it meant opening up the soil and making it more permeable to air and water. He told her to put her ashes from the fires in the cottage on the soil too. That, it seemed was almost as good as lime. The plots were to be 100 by 23½ feet with boards running between them to walk on, and the site should be open to the south and sheltered from the north and east winds. It was too late to plant most of the vegetables since the land hadn't been cleared or turned over yet. But he told her she could seed cabbages indoors in February and then transplant them outside in March or April. Cauliflowers too. And radishes and spinach could be planted until September. The rest would have to wait until April or so, some not until June. Four plots would be rotated on a yearly basis, he told her, with grass followed by potatoes, then something of the pea-and-bean family followed by brassica (cabbage family, he explained patiently), roots, and then grass again. Ursula listened attentively and took endless notes.

Old Bill's recipe for an all-round fungicide spray called for four ounces of lump lime, four ounces of bluestone and three gallons of water. Ursula wrote that down too with instructions for how to mix it. She didn't know what lump lime or bluestone were but she would find out. The best fertilizer was horse manure and Bill told her of a stable down Barwenton way. She smiled wanly. Manure. How was she going to get that home? But he told her they would deliver for a small fee. If only she had her own horse; she made a note to talk to Simon about it. The chickens were to be penned in the back, but allowed to free-range over the freshly turned earth to eat as many grubs as they could find, and the goslings could be bought from Jane Clow. A goose was as good as a guard-dog, produced eggs, and needed a lot less care. Ursula nodded her head and scratched furiously with her pen. A cow wasn't a good idea. It needed too much land to graze and she would need most of it for cultivation. Besides which, he added with a dark look, she might not be up to milking twice a day every day come rain or shine. He didn't suggest that Simon might be interested in helping. Instead he said Jane Clow could continue to provide her with milk. She sighed, hating to be dependent on the woman. Old Bill ignored her and carried on, reeling off his instructions as though he had previously written a book on the subject. Ursula listened to it all.

When Simon came home, bursting in the door with a loud ringing of the doorbell and long, skinny legs bent to let him under the lintel, his face split in a grin of such charm that Ursula had no choice but to smile, the gardening came to a halt. Ursula rang Lettice and told her not to send Old Bill. She didn't want him knowing she'd accepted help from Lettice because she knew he'd be furious. It would make him look bad. So it became Lettice's and her secret and though Simon asked why she was digging up the garden, Ursula could tell he wasn't

201

really interested. She mentioned something about a vegetable garden but he hardly listened, and there were, after all, other more important things to discuss. Like the baby.

Simon had been genuinely happy when she told him she was pregnant, something that had surprised her. He thought it romantic and hugged her to him, lifting her up and surveying her stomach intently. He liked the idea of being a father and Ursula had tactfully refrained from mentioning his other possible offspring. For a long, glorious afternoon she had thought the baby would do what she alone could not: bring Simon home for good. He had sat with her in the sun, drinking champagne that he had rustled out of the cellar, kissing her hands, her hair, her cheeks, finally her mouth. He was so terribly good-looking, she thought, loving the way his hair curled off his brow and the slight bronzed colour his skin had taken on. He nuzzled against her neck and she laughed at the way it made her shiver.

'Can it get any better than this?' he had asked her and she had readily admitted that, no, it probably couldn't. She hadn't thought about the long absences, or the lack of money. She had just wanted him there beside her looking into her eyes with that proud, tender look.

'I do love you, Simon. I do,' she had said and he had caught her up in his arms and taken her to bed, the sun blocking out rectangles of dark and light where it filtered through the shutters. He had lain beside her and counted her fingers, running his hand down her body, leaning his face lightly against her belly. And she had stroked his hair, loving him desperately.

The next day he had even made breakfast, padding around barefoot in his robe, long skinny feet pacing between stove and table, singing an aria from an opera at the top of his voice. He beckoned her to the table, seating her with a flourish of tea-towel over arm. On the plate were bacon and eggs. She was sick. And that had taken the shine, the joy from the day. He became distracted, wanting to be there for her but also wanting to be gone. The guilty look appeared in his eyes again. Lovely to have a baby but don't ask for too much, will you? She saw it but ignored it, pointing out that she needed help around the house until the baby was born and for a while afterwards, and she needed more money for baby clothes, linens, a cot, fresh paint to decorate the other bedroom and turn it into a nursery, and new maternity clothes for herself. And a horse for transport. Simon had been gracious and charming, agreeing instantly to it all. Whatever made her happy. He gave her a little, arranged for the roof to be mended and for painters to come and redo the woodwork and interior of the house. And he told her he would bring her more but money was tight right now. And then he left for London again. Ursula cried grimly to herself and called him all the names she knew, and some more Lettice had been teaching her. And then she carried on.

Lettice had been a godsend, coming round regularly with advice, gossip, consolation, and newly-knitted baby clothes. She taught Ursula how to knit and the two would often sit comfortably through cold, rainy afternoons, knitting booties and jackets. Some evenings Ursula would go to dinner at Lettice's place, Hugh fetching her in the car and telling her the history of the area for the length of the car ride. He knew when he had a captive audience and made full use of it. Ursula thought him a dear. He was short with curly, greying hair and red cheeks. He smoked a pipe and wore old, comfortable clothes and had a tendency to repeat stories several times. And he was kind and attentive, especially so when Ursula grew so large that she could only waddle with difficulty out to the car, and lowering herself into the passenger seat became almost more than she could manage. Ursula wished Simon was a little less handsome and a little more present.

Jane Clow became a frequent visitor, her initial spite mellowing into the occasional crass remark scattered amongst a lot of useful and good advice. She promised Ursula chickens and goslings in the spring. Whenever the spring arrived. It was bitterly cold, sweeping gales spreading across the fields and battering at the windows and doors, seeping through cracks and chilling the wood floors and stone walls. Ursula spent more and more time in bed, hot water bottles piled around her distended belly, and bedsocks knitted by Lettice on her feet. The kitchen had a solid fuel burning Aga stove that helped to keep the downstairs warm and the water hot. Tim Clow's farmhand came and stocked that up for her on a regular basis. But upstairs there was no heating except for an open fireplace

203

and she couldn't bend down to clean it out or stack it, and carrying wood up the stairs was impossible. Lettice loaned her a portable butane heater and Ursula began to wonder, as December showed what Essex weather could really produce, whether she could stand much more. She had chilblains on her knuckles and heels and her back ached with the weight of the baby.

Simon hardly ever showed up at all. The guilt was too much for him to handle, every time he looked at her. If he stayed away, he didn't have to think about how uncomfortable and lonely she was out there in the country. And Julia was there to comfort him, ease the guilt, tell him not to worry, sweetheart, I'll take care of everything for you and make your life worry-free. Just stay with me. And he did. Not that Ursula wanted him there at the cottage after a while. He was more of a nuisance than a help. He still expected her to cook for him while he sat in front of the fire and read the paper. And he still thought she was spending too much money. Ursula looked pointedly at the new cashmere cardigan he was wearing. He didn't notice.

It was two days before Christmas when Christopher called. Ursula picked up the telephone, expecting to hear Lettice's gravelly voice or perhaps Simon telling her he was taking her to London for the next few days. Instead she heard Christopher, awkward and excited, asking her if he could come and see her? Would she be there? Would Simon mind? He had something terribly important to tell her, well, show her really. Ursula couldn't help but laugh, her mind racing over the possibilities. He sounded so close as though she could touch him through the telephone. She had a vision of him as she had seen him last and suddenly she wanted to cry, wishing she'd believed him. She remembered that serious face and those dreadfully unhappy eyes as he'd left. And all she'd been thinking about was Simon and how he must feel. Christopher was the one who cared for her. And he was family. She told him to come immediately, that Simon wouldn't mind. It was too difficult to tell Christopher the truth but they could have a long talk when he arrived. Maybe she wouldn't have to stay here in this cold, lonely cottage much longer? She felt hopeful, and correspondingly impatient and intolerant of her situation. As soon as the baby was born, and the summer came, things would be different. All the careful acceptance she had built up, first through disillusion and then through painful endurance, crumbled at the first touch. She paced the floor anxiously wondering how long it would take for him to drive from Cambridge. Oh, it would be so good to see him!

When the car's headbeams finally lit up the drive, and came to a halt outside the cottage, it was well past five, dark, and sleeting in fitful blasts. Ursula was sitting in a straight-backed chair in the kitchen, her feet against the Aga and a blanket wound around her body. She stood up with difficulty and, wrapping the blanket tightly around her, went over to the front door. Christopher was already there, darkly handsome in that elfin way of his, his smile creasing deeply into his cheeks as he stood stamping his feet and blowing on his hands. When Ursula opened the door he gave a gasping laugh and stepped forward over the lintel. A second person followed: a girl. Ursula was hardly aware of the extra company, Christopher having thrown his arms around her and hugged her soundly. He realized immediately that the blanket was not distorting her figure but merely draping it, and, as he stepped back in embarrassed surprise, the other girl closed the door against the wind. In the lull all three looked at each other. Christopher spoke first.

'Ursula, I didn't . . . I mean, no-one told me. Congratulations! When's it due?' He seemed to be out of breath. Ursula smiled and looked at the girl, her mouth stretched tautly in greeting. Was this his surprise?

'February. It's lovely to see you, Christopher. Is your friend from Cambridge too?' She didn't look at her cousin, her attention fixed on his friend. Christopher hesitated.

'Yes. This is Tiffany. I told you I had someone special for you to meet. Tiff, this is my cousin, Ursula. Where's Simon?' He was tense, waiting for Ursula's husband to appear at any moment. Ursula winced.

'Come on into the sitting room. There's a fire lit and it's much warmer than standing around here. Simon's up in London on business but I'm expecting him at any time. Tiffany? It is Tiffany, isn't it? Would you like something hot to drink? Tea, hot chocolate?' Tiffany! Whoever heard of such a name? Ursula looked her over critically. Blonde and fluffy with a beautiful face, no neck, and a short, podgy figure. She looked at Christopher, and then back at Tiffany. Was it the face? Or did she have a wonderful personality? So far Tiffany hadn't said a word but now she dimpled and told Ursula that she'd prefer brandy if there was any going. There was: Simon's own private hoard. Ursula, with fierce enjoyment, told Tiffany to help herself and to get Christopher one too.

The girl was from London, Ursula thought. And she looked . . . well, as though she'd been around a bit. She was about the same age as Christopher, perhaps older. Ursula looked at Christopher again. He had a long scarf wound around his neck and a heavy overcoat with its collar up around his ears. His face was thinner and more finely etched than she remembered, the mouth not as firm. The eyes were as darkly alive as ever but now they seemed only relieved to find Simon absent. He was still having difficulty in looking at Ursula. Or rather at her stomach. Ursula felt a sour taste well up in her mouth. What was the matter? Couldn't he take the fact that she was pregnant? Or was he embarrassed about something else? She told him to sit down, suddenly tired herself.

He took off his coat and laid it over the back of the sofa. All the furniture was old and scrunched-up from too many years of heavy bodies dropping into it. The slip-covers were hard to pull back into place when one couldn't bend properly anymore. And Simon never did anything that he considered to be women's work. Christopher settled himself into Simon's chair without thought and smiled proudly when Tiffany came and perched on the arm. Ursula lowered herself slowly into the other wing-chair and pushed pillows into her back. Christopher looked at the pattern in the rug.

'Can you stay long? It's such a beastly night and I can put you up for the night without any problem if Tiffany doesn't mind sharing a room with me,' Ursula said into the quiet. She was trying to act as though there were nothing the matter but Christopher was making it difficult. Couldn't he just relax? Why were men so bloody?

'We don't want to put you out, Ursula. I just wanted you to meet Tiffany, and I suppose I wanted to see how you were. I'm sorry I blew up last time.' He winced and shifted his view from that of the rug to that of the fire. Ursula wished he'd look her in the face. 'Just sounding-off I guess. I had no right. Sorry about not coming to the wedding either. That was childish and . . . well, I guess I didn't really want to see it happen. Not with him. As I said, it wasn't anything I had any right to get huffy about.'

'Yes you did. But it doesn't matter anymore now. That's all water under the bridge. How're Aunt Mary and Uncle George and Rodney. Did Rodney pass his exams all right?'

'Oh they're all fine. Yes, Rodney scraped through. He's not going on, you know. Says he'll never make it. Father's trying to get him a job in the City. It's probably the best thing for him. He never did like the books. No, there's no problem with any of them. Father likes his new job; the money's pretty awful but at least he's not on the dole anymore. The only problem around is with us.' Christopher looked depressed. He'd always been so sure of things before and now . . . Ursula looked at Tiffany and then back at him. They were waiting for her to comment.

'Am I being too inquisitive if I ask how things stand between you two? I think you're more than just friends.' The minute she said it, she regretted it. It was as though she were confirming things, even rushing them along. But some irritating impulse kept pushing at her to have it out, to have the worst said. And they were expecting it, prompting her almost. She smiled brightly, wishing the blanket was more concealing.

Tiffany was blushing prettily and Ursula had the strangest feeling that she could do so at will. The girl was no innocent, despite her young, missish airs. Ursula tried hard to pretend she believed them and Christopher took a sip from his brandy balloon. He winked.

'We wanted you to be the first to know. Tiffany and I are getting married. We're probably going to need your support because I don't think my parents are going to be too thrilled and we already know Tiff's parents are dead against it. They think I'm some sort of latter-day Lothario intent on doing Tiff harm. Will you stand by us, Ursula?' He seemed so young all of a sudden, not the wise, kind, older cousin upon whom Ursula had relied for support. And now he wanted to lean on her for strength. Something was all wrong here. She had thought he would be coming to rescue her from Simon and the cold and everything else. Or at least that he would be here for her while she went through the next two months. She was terrified about having the baby. And no-one even thought about that. They both just wanted something from her – Simon and Christopher – the two men in her life. Ursula closed her eyes for a moment, weariness aching through her bones. She was younger than both Tiffany and Christopher and yet they looked to her for advice. Did a wedding ring automatically confer years of experience? Or was it being pregnant? She opened her eyes to Christopher's worried face.

'Of course I will, Christopher. What did you think? I know what it's like to get married in the face of family disapproval.' He smiled wryly at her, aware that he was the only one who had disapproved. Then he nodded his head.

'I guess you owed me that one.'

'No. I wanted to thank you for caring enough to disapprove. That showed a lot of courage and concern. Anyway, um, how did you two meet? Tiffany, are you a student too?' Ursula smothered a yawn in the back of her mouth. Being pregnant was such a nuisance. She got so tired and crotchety all the time. Now all she wanted was to go to bed and lie flat for a while. Tiffany giggled.

'Oh no. I'm not brainy at all. I'm a secretary at Knight and Fallows. Simon an' I met quite by accident, didn't we love?' Accident, my foot, Ursula thought indignantly. The girl didn't look like the type who left anything to accident. No, that wasn't fair. Just because she had expected Christopher to be the answer to all her problems and instead he'd brought a little strumpet home with him . . . well, maybe not a strumpet, but not a nice girl either! Where were his brains? But then, she hadn't done too well herself, so who was she to criticize? Christopher was clearly infatuated. Ursula raised her eyebrows in an interested smile.

'Accident?'

'Yes. I walked right out in front of Chris's bicycle – without even looking. Could've knocked myself silly! And Chris brought me home to his place and bound up my ankle, and that's about it. We've been together ever since. Maybe it's fate.' Tiffany looked amused at the thought. Ursula had another name for it but refrained from telling Tiffany. And there was Christopher smiling like the cat who'd swallowed the canary. Really, men are either fools or worse! Ursula closed her eyes again. This was too much! Wasn't she going to be allowed a break sometime, just for a change?

'Well, wasn't that a coincidence! I'll bet you're just made for each other too?' She hadn't meant her tone to sound so sarcastic. It had just slipped out and immediately she regretted it. It wasn't up to her to decide and she didn't want to go alienating Christopher. There was no-one else left that she cared about. She saw Christopher freeze, the hands cradling the brandy balloon stilling as he took in her tone. Tiffany looked at Ursula.

'Yes,' she said firmly. 'We are. Chris said you'd approve. Don't you?' So, the silly little girl had a mind of her own. And a thin veneer. Ursula shifted her weight so that she leant more comfortably against the cushions.

'I really don't know. I hardly know you at all. But it's not my marriage, it's yours. Do what you want. You're both old enough, I'd say.' She was tired of the subject. Tired of everything, come to that. What good would come from discussing it? Christopher wasn't going to be her knight errant and she wasn't going to be taken away from this place anywhere in the near future. The only thing that was going to happen soon, whether she liked it or not, was the baby. And Christopher wasn't going to be able to help her with that. After what she'd just said, he wasn't even going to be particularly friendly. Her fault. But it was too late now. She wished they would just leave.

'You're right. It isn't any of your business. But Christopher wanted someone from his family on his side. And he thought you'd do that for him.' Tiffany took Christopher's hand in hers, her face even more beautiful now that it had lost its vacant innocence. Ursula began to understand what Simon had meant about her being pure. This girl turned her innocence on and off like a switch. Ursula wondered what Christopher thought about that.

'I'm sorry then. I guess it isn't my place to judge. I'll tell you quite frankly, Tiffany, I'd have had a lot less qualms about this if you'd not put on that phoney little girl act when you first

209

arrived. I don't think you need it, and it doesn't work very well. If you both love each other, then fine. Say so, openly and without any act. I'm not Christopher's mother, you know! I might be your friend if you're a little more honest.' She didn't give a damn what they made of that. Her back ached and the baby was kicking hard enough to make her want to gasp and put her hand on her stomach. But Christopher was too squeamish for that. She'd embarrass him even more. She leaned her head back against the pillows. She heard Christopher shift his weight in the chair, an irritated, sudden movement.

'Ursula, don't you think you're being too hard on us both? Especially on Tiff. You seem to think you've got all the answers and that you did so well for yourself, despite my disapproval. Well, where's your husband now? I've heard he's been in London for most of the last three months. Don't you think that's odd?' He was angry and lashing out to hurt. He couldn't know how hard he was being. Ursula breathed deeply and evenly to still the pain.

'Don't you ever, ever suggest something like that again Christopher or I'll never speak to you again. What's the matter? It was perfectly all right for you to try and ruin things with Simon and me - that was just caring advice - but the minute I say something you don't like, you lash out like, like . . . ' But Ursula couldn't finish because suddenly there was no point. Nothing had any point any more. Not when Simon didn't love her; and Christopher just wanted support for some-one else. Oh, God damn you, Simon!

Tiffany tugged at Christopher's hand to stop him from saying anything more. She seemed less offended by what Ursula had said than Christopher was.

'Let it go, love. I don't mind. Ursula's got a right to say what she thinks. Besides, she's right. I was trying to be the sort of girl I thought your family would want me to be. Young and missish, and a simpleton. So Ursula saw straight through that. I'm glad. I couldn't have kept it up for long and I wouldn't want to have her think that I'm acting all the time. So let it be, okay?' She shook his hand lightly and he sighed.

'Right. Why don't we start this all over again? And I'm sorry if I hurt you, Ursula. I guess I wasn't being very fair myself. I wish I hadn't said what I did.' He put the glass down by the fire and leaned forward so that he could touch Ursula's knee. His face was wistful, the dark eyes that used to smile so mischievously at her holding only a glimmer of that memory. She smiled a tired, sad smile that was more despondent than tears. What did it matter if everyone knew Simon was cheating on her? What did anything really matter? The thought of living the rest of her life in this desolate cottage with no company but a baby, or child, and no money to get away, and nowhere to go to even if she had the money, left her with a gaping blackness inside her chest. She didn't care anymore. There was no point. Nothing good was ever going to happen to her. And Billy couldn't help her. She remembered how she had thought he would, like Simon. That was a laugh. It was a couple of seconds before she realized she had laughed out loud. Christopher was looking at her strangely.

'Never mind.' She laughed again. 'I think I'll make that my personal motto! "Never mind".' She struggled to get to her feet and Christopher took her under the arm and steadied her against him. He seemed to be over his squeamishness. 'I'm tired. I have to have a nap. You'll understand about all this soon enough. Don't think I'm against your marriage. I'm not. You'll probably work out quite well. At least you really know each other. That helps.' She pulled away from Christopher and smiled at them both. 'Feel free to stay the night. The bedroom on the right of the stairs is empty. There are blankets in the chest under the window. Goodnight.' She turned her back and walked over to the stairs, resting her weight on the banisters. Then she began the climb. She didn't expect them to stay.

When she woke in the morning it was chill and quiet. She lay back in bed thinking about them both, trying to sort out what they saw in each other. She was rather relieved that she'd seen Christopher last night. Otherwise she might have gone on building fantasies about him being strong and reliable. Well, maybe he was reliable. But Tiffany was definitely the strength in their relationship. Ursula couldn't have stood another man without fibre. What had happened to all the real men? The ones who were supposed to be rocks for you to lean against, and who would cherish you in their arms at night, and be right there beside you in the morning? The ones who didn't ask you what you thought was the best thing to do all the time, or wait for you to make things better. Someone like Billy had been. Was that so unlikely? It wasn't that she wanted someone like her father who wouldn't let a female think for herself, but did she have to always end up with weak men? It occurred to her then that her father had been weak in his own way. That depressed her and she turned her head abruptly to still the thought.

It was a still, sunny morning, the sky pale blue in the square of window. Things didn't seem so impossible now that it was light. It was only at night that she wondered if she could make it through the next twenty-four hours without slashing her wrists. In the morning that seemed melodramatic and, besides, she didn't really want to die. What good would that do? It would only make Simon's life easier. And she had no intention of doing that! The baby was being quiet and good this morning, not kicking viciously the way it liked to most mornings. She was getting to seriously dislike the unborn child inside her. It seemed to enjoy hurting her, and was fretful in its kicking as though it were in a permanent bad mood. She wished it would hurry up and get itself born. A boy would be useful in a few years for the heavy gardening work. She hoped it was a boy. Maybe even like Tom. If it was a boy, she'd name it Tom.

It was nice lying there quietly, knowing it was too cold to work in the garden and that she was too large to do so anyway. The cottage was clean and she wasn't expecting visitors until late afternoon. Then Lettice had said she would pop over to see her. She could just lie there and drowse with the sun shining in on her. It felt good. A soft scraping at the door warned her she was not alone. Then the door opened and Tiffany walked in with a tray balanced on one hand. She did it with surprising skill. Ursula wondered if she was a waitress normally, rather than a secretary.

'I thought you'd probably left last night. Was the bedroom warm enough?' Ursula said calmly. It was too nice a morning to spoil with bickering.

'Yes. Besides I had Christopher to keep me warm.' Tiffany smiled, a broad, mature smile that made Ursula want to laugh, it was so different from the simpering of last night. She thought she could actually learn to like this girl. 'Are you hungry?' Tiffany asked.

'Not much. People are always telling me I have to eat for two but I can't see how anyone ever has much appetite when they're bloated up like this. I feel like a sea-cow most of the time. There's simply no room for the food.' She wrinkled her nose in disgust when Tiffany burst out laughing. 'Just you wait! Your turn will come.'

'Maybe. But not for a while. Chris and I . . . we think we should wait a few years before we start a family. Here, at least drink the orange juice.' Tiffany laid the tray down beside Ursula on the bed and handed her the glass, totally unaware of the turmoil going on inside Ursula. Wait before starting a family? But didn't it just happen when you made love together? Was there something she didn't know? Ursula took the glass without argument, even though she loathed orange juice at the moment. Too much acid. She looked at Tiffany, wondering if she could possibly bring herself to ask. Well, why not? They were both girls and they were going to be related. She had to ask someone.

'Uh, how, exactly, do you intend to wait?' She could feel her face burning with embarrassment and was cross at herself. It was a totally reasonable question and shouldn't have her twittering with alarm as though she were some sheltered child. Tiffany widened her eyes and looked amused.

'How old are you, Ursula?'

'Nineteen, last month. Why?' Tiffany shrugged.

'I guess that explains it. Haven't you ever heard of rubbers?' She looked a fraction self-conscious herself. Ursula was puzzled.

'You mean the things you rub out pencil marks with?' Tiffany gave a hoot of laughter, shaking so much that she fell onto the bed, the tray tilting awkwardly and tea splashing over the bedcovers. She straightened up immediately and begged Ursula's pardon. Ursula didn't even notice the stain.

'But tell me what I said that was so funny? If it isn't that kind of rubber, what kind is it? For Heaven's sake, I ought to know this sort of thing. I am married, you know!'

'And very pregnant! Yes, you're right, you should know. I suppose your husband never suggested he use a rubber. All right, it's well, it's like the finger of a rubber glove, and it fits, well, over it, if you see what I'm getting at?' She demonstrated with her fingers and Ursula's cheeks burned brighter.

'Uh, yes, I think I understand. But . . . oh, never mind.'

'No, go on, ask. Who else can tell you?' Tiffany seemed remarkably matter-of-fact now that she had the worst of it over with. She smiled encouragingly at Ursula.

'Well, is it something the husband has to deal with? Is there no way the wife can, well, do it without her husband knowing?' There, she'd done it now. What must Tiffany be thinking? Tiffany, it seemed, wasn't thinking anything bad. Rather she was contemplating the problem very seriously.

'Not using a rubber, no. That's the husband's prerogative altogether. I don't honestly know of another way except for those terrible lead pills they used to take. And you don't want to do that!'

'Lead pills? But what did they do?'

'Women took them in the last century and the early part of this one. They were supposed to stop you getting pregnant but most of them got lead poisoning. You don't want to try it, believe me.'

'No. That doesn't sound too useful. Oh well, I guess I'll think of something.' She sighed so heavily that Tiffany was touched. What wretch of a husband had got an eighteen-year-old girl pregnant and left her on her own for the first seven months of their marriage? He sounded a right bastard. She leaned over and squeezed Ursula's arm.

'Tell him the doctor says you can't have any more. It's too dangerous. Are you narrow-hipped?'

'Uh, yes, I think so. I know my amah used to say I would have problems with childbirth.'

'There you are then! Tell him you're too small to have babies safely. Then, if you change your mind later on, when this one's grown up a bit, you can always say you're prepared to risk it. Nothing simpler!' They both laughed. Nothing simpler. 'That'll fix you, Simon, my darling,' Ursula thought with satisfaction. Then another thought occurred to her. Was she too narrow-hipped? The doctor hadn't said anything about it. She looked down at her stomach with a worried expression. Too late now.

214

Tiffany had clearly decided that Ursula needed her advice and was determined to give it to her. It was such a change from their roles of last night that Ursula wondered how she could have felt so bereft and put upon. She must have been tired. Being pregnant made everything difficult. Tiffany sat down comfortably on the foot of the bed and drank the orange juice that Ursula had given her back. She was enjoying herself.

'I suppose there is one major flaw in my reasoning,' she admitted. 'If you want to have sex with your husband. Do you?'

'Not much.' Ursula was shocked that she could actually mention the subject, let alone reveal her feelings: indifference, distaste. Sex without love wasn't much of a turn on to her. And while Simon might have once loved her, he didn't any longer. Tiffany shrugged again.

'Then it's no problem. And if you want to fool around with someone else, just make sure they've got some rubbers handy.' Ursula's mouth opened in surprise. It had never occurred to her that she would ever sleep with anyone but her husband. And here Tiffany was, telling her how to 'fool around'. She laughed.

'No. That's not likely, I'd say. It's not my favourite pastime.'

'Then you haven't done it with the right person. Now Chris, umm!' Tiffany took a bite of toast quite unself-consciously. She didn't notice Ursula's embarrassment.

'You didn't want to wait until you got married?'

'No. We love each other, and I always knew I could get Chris to marry me whenever I wanted. He's a dear and he's crazy about me. I guess we couldn't see the point in waiting. Besides, how could we be sure we were going to be good together? In bed, I mean.' Ursula was startled by the idea that marriage could be based on how good people were in bed together. She didn't think it was an idea in great circulation just at the moment. But it made sense. After all, Simon seemed to want it all the time before she became too large. And Tiffany wasn't bothered, and seemed so fresh and lovely that Ursula wondered if she weren't missing out on something.

'Is it, I mean, do you actually enjoy making love? I know the man seems to, but I can't see how the woman might.' Tiffany

215

paused with a piece of toast half-way to her mouth while she stared at Ursula with pity.

'There'll be someone, someday, who'll make you feel good about it. Don't mind this bastard you're married to. He sounds like a right prize.' She ignored Ursula's stammered disclaimer, the wave of her hands that said, no, really, he's not. Tiffany knew better. 'But all men aren't like that. You'll see, if you don't bury yourself down here for the rest of your life. Come and visit us in London as soon as we're set up. I'll introduce you to some fun sorts.' Fun sorts, Ursula thought. No, she didn't think so. But it was kind of Tiffany to offer. She smiled her thanks.

'Darling? Can I come in?' Christopher called from the passageway, and Tiffany and Ursula smiled conspiratorially.

'Of course you can, Christopher. I'm quite awake,' Ursula called. Her cousin walked in, looking uncertainly from one to the other.

'Everything all right?' he asked.

'Tiffany and I have been having a lovely chat. We've decided to be friends after all, so you can stop looking so worried.' She held out her hand and he took it and squeezed her fingers.

'Well, thank God for that! I was brooding down in the kitchen thinking you'd carved each other up for breakfast. I'm so glad you like each other. It'll make my life a damned sight easier I can tell you!' They grinned happily at each other and Christopher sat down on the bed to help Tiffany finish the breakfast that Ursula had refused. It was amazing how different things could seem with the sun shining. They discussed plans for the wedding and Ursula promised to stand up for Tiffany if her parents couldn't be brought round. That started Christopher thinking again and it wasn't long before he ventured, tentatively:

'Can you manage on your own, sweetheart, or do you need someone here with you?' He wanted to take Tiffany to London and get things over with his parents. Ursula understood completely.

'I'm fine, Christopher. A friend is coming by this afternoon and if Simon doesn't call, or come by, I'm going to be spending Christmas with her. She's a dear. I'll introduce you both next time you're down. Now, don't worry about me. I know you're anxious to tell Aunt Mary and Uncle George. Give them my . . . regards, and Christopher? Don't tell them about Simon not being here. I couldn't stand to have your mother thinking, well, you know, the worst about him.' She winced, trying to get him to see it from her side. He nodded.

'All right. I won't say a word. Now we really must be off, sweetheart. It's nearly ten and it's Christmas Eve. The traffic's going to be murder. I'll call you tomorrow and check how you are.' He leaned down and hugged her, kissing her forehead in the same way that he had when she first came to his house. That was over a year ago now. She felt she'd aged ten years. Tiffany hugged her too and then they both left, the front door slamming a few minutes later and the sound of the car receding down the lane. Ursula rolled over and went back to sleep.

'Thinking of waking up in time for Christmas?' Simon asked. Ursula turned in her sleep, angling her head out of the sheets to peer up at the face suspended above hers. She blinked sleepily.

'Hallo. Thought you'd decided not to make an appearance. What time is it?'

'Late. Nearly three. If we're going to make it up to town, we need to be on our way pretty soon. I'm assuming you want to spend Christmas with everyone? The family?'

'Your family. Thanks for the warning. I didn't really know what was going on, not having heard from you in, how long is it? Ten, no eleven days now. Silly me. I should've known your conscience would eventually get the better of you.' She heard Simon sigh.

'Don't start that for God's sake, Ursula. I've taken nearly three hours to drive down here and now all I get is abuse. I thought you'd be glad to see me.'

'Ohh, Simon! Yes, I'm glad to see you. Do I get a kiss?' She tried so hard to stay mad at him but she just had to look at that face, those cajoling eyes and that grin and she was lost. Maybe in time it would die: that spark she still felt for him. Maybe he'd start to really look like the bastard Tiffany had called him. Dorian Gray style. Ursula didn't think she'd hold her breath for it though. He kissed her instead and she felt that immediate rush of longing for him to hold her as tightly as he once had

217

done, to tell her he loved her. God, it was good to see him. He nuzzled her ear.

'Come on then, sleepyhead. Up we get. I'll run you a bath, if you like. But we must be quick. You can't imagine what the roads are going to be like.'

'That's what Christopher said,' Ursula commented mildly. She knew it would provoke a reaction.

'What? Christopher who?' She almost laughed at that. He could be so transparent sometimes.

'Christopher, my cousin, that's who. He came by last night and spent the night here. He's only been gone a few hours now I'd say. Pity you missed him.'

'What brought him here then?'

'Me, obviously. Is that so unusual?'

'Well, yes, quite frankly it is. He hasn't been to see you since that time at my father's house and he missed the wedding too. I'd've thought he'd decided to cut you dead forever for marrying me. Or maybe just for marrying?' Simon had always had that jealous streak. Ursula dimpled to herself beneath the sheets. So, let him have a few bad minutes. It would do him good.

'Yes, I expect you're right. At least he said something like that last night. But he's decided to make things up with me. Not you, just me.'

'Kind of him. Is that what brought him here then? The desire to make up? He must have been disappointed to find you rather more of an armful than when he last saw you.' Simon's face was pleasantly amused but his eyes had a still expression that Ursula knew. She shrugged.

'I don't know really. He wants me to come and stay with him in London once the baby's born. Have some fun. I don't suppose we can afford a nanny, can we?'

'No, not a chance. Besides, you're trained for that role already, aren't you?' The smile had left his face and he was in his wounding mood now. Ursula felt she had probably teased as far as she should.

'Well, I expect Lettice will help out if I occasionally need to get away. The country can get rather dull sometimes. Anyway, Tiffany said I could bring the baby too if I wanted.' She smiled up at Simon. 'Tiffany and Christopher are getting married.

They want my support at the wedding. I said I would.' It was satisfying to know the thought of another man being interested in her could still provoke a territorial impulse with Simon, if nothing else. And Simon, like the pheasant with the biggest tail who could end up getting shot instead of attracting all the females, looked suitably divided in his desires. Get even for the sheer satisfaction and risk Ursula making life difficult over Christmas, or sensibly swallow his gall and let her get away with it. He compromised with a casual wave of his hand.

'Really? Why? Is she totally unsuitable?' He hadn't forgiven her yet. The clock on the bedside stand ticked in a hasty, snickering sort of way. Ursula shrugged again.

'Yes, I suppose she is rather. But then, our family seems to have a habit of making rather unsuitable marriages.' She pushed back the covers. 'Bath?'

The drive to London was accomplished in near silence. Simon didn't ask how Ursula had managed to afford the presents he had loaded into the car and she didn't offer an explanation. The fact that, for the last two months, Lettice and she had been scouring the junk shops of the nearby area was not something Ursula wanted Simon to know. It smacked too much of still caring. And that was the last thing she wanted to seem. That made her vulnerable. Simon always sensed weakness in people and made a point of exploiting it. Besides, she didn't want her offerings mocked by Julia if she knew their source.

Lettice and Hugh's presents were dropped off along the way, Simon's grumbles that it wasn't the right direction for London and they would lose yet more time ignored. Ursula insisted and that was that. And Lettice hadn't provoked Simon with any sharp remarks or guilt-inducing lectures. She hadn't looked him in the eye and delivered those 'home-truths' he so dreaded. Why was it considered so wonderful to be blunt and honest, Simon wondered? That way people got hurt. He got hurt. But no-one cared about that as long as they were protecting the weak and defenceless. He wondered sometimes if the weak weren't so well defended that they totally got one over on the strong. Lettice was obviously championing Ursula now. And that could be awkward for him. He'd have to charm Lettice or she might just write to his father. He smiled and

219

kissed her cheek, commented on how well Toby was looking, shook Hugh's hand and asked after the mudlark family. Lettice didn't fight it. Instead they had had a civilized chat over a glass of sherry and parted on renewed friendly terms.

'What time d'you think we'll get there?' Ursula asked after nearly an hour of darkness rushing through the windscreen at her, scraps of hedge shredding beneath the glare of headlights, and the cold seeping in around the blanket tucked around her legs. Simon didn't seem to feel the cold. She envied him.

'Ages yet. We'll be late for dinner and I promised we'd be back for it. Father will worry about the roads and Julia will worry we're not coming. I wish you hadn't taken so long getting ready.'

'I wish you'd warned me you were coming. Then I could've been ready when you arrived. But I expect it was a bit of a burden to pick up the telephone and give me a ring,' Ursula said coldly and Simon relapsed into silence. He didn't speak again until they were actually in London.

'I . . . ' he hesitated and Ursula suddenly knew what was coming. They were rounding the sharp bend past the College of Arms that led down to the Embankment and she could see the uncertainty in his face, almost feel it in the way the car responded. 'I'd like this to be a nice Christmas for everyone, especially my father. He's looking forward to it a lot. So I'd like you to . . . ' He broke off, unsure how to phrase it. Ursula filled in the blank.

'Behave myself? Don't go mentioning the fact that you're never with me or that the cottage is cold and falling to pieces? Try not to upset anyone with the minor annoyance of me being seven month's pregnant and alone, without enough money? That what you're trying to say Simon? Or was it something more personal still?' She almost pitied him then. He looked so upset.

'For God's sake, Ursula! I told you I'd start putting more money in your account and I will. You don't need it until the baby's born anyway, do you? I'm sorry I'm not down there more often but if you want that money – and that seems to be all you're interested in quite frankly, not me being there with you . . . ' He scrubbed at his moustache and Ursula wondered if that was something Julia had said to him. It didn't sound like

Simon somehow. Maybe Julia was saying, she doesn't love you, she just wants security, money, a place in society. You've kept your side of the bargain so why are you feeling guilty? Yes, that was probably it. Simon had convinced himself. It was obvious.

'No, actually, that's not it at all.' I'd rather we were both living off the land, only just surviving but together, she wanted to say. I still care about you, Simon. God knows why but I do. But she didn't say any of it. She just shrugged and said.

'Don't worry. I don't want to upset your father either. He's too nice for that. But don't provoke me, Simon, or I might just forget my good intentions, all right?' He didn't answer.

Julia was the same as always, perfectly poised, gently amused, confident, gracious. Ursula hated her for it. They came crowding to the door to greet Simon and Ursula, hurrying them in to the warmth of the fire and lamps lit against the faint sleet flurries outside. Ursula was given the wing-chair nearest the fire and a glass of mulled wine, Lucy coming to sit at her feet and burble about nursery school, Benjie rushing back and forth with his latest toy. Simon had smiled indulgently and stood beside Ursula, leaning down to ask if she was warm enough. And Ursula had wanted to scream, the hypocrisy of it all! But then she looked at Humphrey Patterson and the anger died before it could work its way clear of her throat. How could she put this man through anything else? He was looking so eagerly, pathetically happy at the pretence, putting an arm through his wife's, patting Benjie on the head. It was every-thing he had always wanted. How could she tell him it was a farce?

The Christmas tree stood in the bay window, presents piling out from beneath it and across the side tables, flanking the room. Tied to the dark, spindly branches of the tree were red silk ribbons, glass baubles that reflected the lights of the candles' flames, creamy bunches of dried flowers, tin ornaments, small embroidered toys, wooden soldiers. It was a beautiful tree. Ursula stared at it.

'Dinner, Ursula? We've been keeping it until you both got home. The children have had theirs some time ago but we thought we'd let them stay up until you got here. They've been so looking forward to seeing you,' Humphrey broke in on her thoughts and Ursula smiled. Home. He really thought it was. Such a dear. And Lettice had said he was one of the foremost brains in the country. It seemed inevitable really. The intelligent were fooled and used by the savvy, the honourable were compromised by their very integrity. Pity the Humphreys of this world. She brushed the hair from Lucy's face and kissed her cheek.

'Goodnight, sweetheart. Don't let the bugs bite.'

'Night, night, Ursie. Will you come and tuck me in?' Lucy clung to Ursula's neck until Simon lifted her away.

'Not tonight, Luce. Ursula's tired and needs to eat. But we'll come and see you both later on. And don't forget, the sooner you go to sleep, the sooner Father Christmas will come. Come on, Benjie, up we go.' And he hoisted Benjie up on one shoulder, Lucy tucked under his arm. They chorused their goodnights all the way up the stairs. Ursula had to turn away sharply when Julia's smiling gaze followed them.

'Well, having a baby obviously agrees with you, Ursula. You're quite blooming. Or is that the country air? I do so envy you out there in that quaint cottage with no dreadful responsibilities, no servants to constantly chase, or dinners to arrange. So totally carefree. It must be bliss!' Julia smiled directly into Ursula's eyes. Testing.

'It is rather. I'm more used to the country than town-living. And the cottage is coming along so well. Simon's been a godsend with all the workmen he's organized to get it back in shape, and then Lettice and Hugh have been wonderful too. They pop round all the time. And my cousin – you remember Christopher, I'm sure? He came over last night and stayed until this morning. It's quite a change to London and funnily enough, Simon seems quite different when he's down there with me. Much more mellow and relaxed. You'd hardly recognize him, I expect.' Ursula smiled and sipped her wine. Julia's mouth tightened.

'Really? I must ask Simon about this. I really can't imagine it at all. And he's there so seldom.' Julia knew she'd made a mistake the minute the words had left her mouth. Humphrey straightened and looked at her.

'What's this? Hardly ever there? But surely not, Julia.

222

Simon's been away most of the time. Hasn't he?' He looked between Julia and Ursula, gauging the expressions, the truths being filtered past him.

'Oh, well!' Julia laughed, flustered. 'Perhaps it just seems that way. You're probably right, Humphrey. I'm just so used to having him around, I suppose I assume he's still here. And he's so good with the children. That'll be nice for you, Ursula, to have a husband already so experienced with babies.'

'Yes, it will. Simon's so thrilled about finally having an heir Even if it's a girl, at least she'll carry on Simon's name. He's mentioned, just in passing and I'm not sure he'll remember when it comes to it, getting Lord and Lady Deming to be god-parents, did you know? Simon's terribly excited about the baby.' Ursula smiled at them both shyly. 'Our baby.'

Humphrey beamed. Julia beamed. Simon, coming in the door, beamed. All for different reasons. It made Ursula want to laugh. Or maybe cry.

'Well, let's go into dinner shall we? Cook will be getting worried if we delay much more and I expect you're rather hungry, Ursula. Eating for two and all that extra bulk to take care of.' Julia shooed them through, Ursula leaning on Simon's arm. She felt him stiffen at the taunt.

'Not at all, Julia. I seem to eat much more normally, when I'm not pregnant. Then I was always eating my head off, if you remember, but nothing could make me put weight on,' Ursula chatted brightly. 'You remember you were always wishing you were the same, not having to worry about your weight. Though really, now that you're in your late twenties and have had both your children, I don't know why you get so anxious. You can afford to relax and not worry about those few extra inches.' Ursula heard Simon hiss with amusement beside her. 'Right now I seem to be quite without any appetite at all. Once the baby's born I expect I shall disappear if I don't get hungry again. My arms are really quite skinny already, aren't they, Simon?'

'Quite.' Simon shifted uncomfortably under Julia's wide open stare. 'Uh, Father, how about some more wine? If you'll take Ursula and help her get settled, I'll go have a word with John. I know there's some more of that Nuit St Georges some-where. I thought that would be rather nice, don't you?' And

223

Simon was gone again before Humphrey had time to collect himself. He muttered beneath his breath about John being perfectly capable of taking care of the wine and what did Simon think he was about, interfering with the running of the house? But Julia understood and so did Ursula. Don't put any strain on Simon. Or he'll be gone. They smiled sourly at each other.

Chapter Fourteen

The baby was born on the nineteenth of February while a snowstorm raged outside and the whole of East Anglia ground to a standstill. Ursula didn't have an easy time of it, the baby that had kicked and fretted to be born for so long, now stubbornly refusing to appear. After eighteen hours in labour, a solid, seven-pound girl emerged and Ursula quietly wept tears of relief.

She had been staying with Lettice and Hugh for the last week just to be on the safe side, Hugh insisting that it was too dangerous for her to be alone out at the cottage that near her due date. Ursula hadn't protested too much, feeling secretly relieved that someone else was taking charge. She didn't want to go through this alone. Simon hadn't bothered to remember when she was expected to give birth and so hadn't returned from London in time. Or perhaps he just couldn't deal with the responsibility. Ursula wondered if he'd been present for Lucy and Benjie. Probably not.

Lettice and Ursula had been watching the news on television when Ursula had suddenly gasped and looked frantic. Lettice had called Hugh down from his study and they had half-carried, half-supported Ursula to the car and Hugh had driven furiously through the whirling snow to the hospital. None of them had ever had a baby before. It was all rather frightening.

Ursula had thought the baby was never going to come out, but would tear her to pieces inside. She had never felt pain like it, real physical agony, but once it was all over, she could barely recall the terror and misery. It faded under a calm, almost floating feeling of release that left her senses dulled. She hadn't seen the baby except for a few moments and then they'd taken her away and Ursula had been wheeled back to her room. Some time later, the nurse had brought the baby back to be fed. It was such a tiny, red, wrinkled – ugly! – thing that Ursula was quite taken aback. She cradled it in her arms, examining it all over. The babies she had seen in the kampong hadn't looked like this. Or had they? And they hadn't cried all the time either. Ursula wrapped her daughter back up in her blanket and cuddled her in the crook of her arm. The baby continued to scream. Ursula wondered what Simon would think of his daughter.

Simon didn't turn up until the third day, the snow-drifts conveniently blocking the roads and making Nurse click her tongue reprovingly every time Ursula asked if her husband had arrived yet. Didn't she know what conditions were like on the roads? Couldn't she be patient? Nurse was equally critical of Ursula's complaints that the baby tugged too hard on her breasts when she was feeding. In those three days, the baby had become pale and smooth with blonde wisps of hair and watery blue eyes. There was no mistaking the fact that she was Simon's child. Her character seemed equally self-willed. Breast-feeding was supposed to be a pleasant experience but to Ursula it became an ordeal, her breasts tender and swollen under the infant's determined grasp. Nurse told her not to be so difficult, and then discussed Mrs Patterson's shortcomings with the rest of the nurses over strong cups of tea. Ursula told Lettice to get her out of there as soon as possible.

When Simon did arrive, he went first to see his new daughter. Nurse thought him terribly handsome and dashing, the way he rushed in from the snow outside, his face glowing with colour and his eyes alight at the thought of seeing his child. He was allowed to hold his daughter for a few minutes, admiring her colouring and perfect form, tiny hands and feet. He carefully counted all her fingers and toes, and then he christened her Rhea Clare Louise Patterson before handing her back to Nurse. The baby didn't cry once but beamed up at her father with total acceptance. Nurse smiled approvingly and thought what a good father Simon was going to be. Unlike the mother.

Then Simon called in to see Ursula. She shared a room with three other women and Simon poked his head around the door with such a sweet, enticing smile and such a large bouquet of roses that the women were charmed immediately. They sat up and fluffed their hair surreptitiously and smiled back. Ursula tried hard not to laugh.

'Hallo, Simon. Nice of you to drop by. I'm sure your daughter will appreciate the effort in years to come. You do know you have a daughter, don't you?'

'A beautiful, bouncing seven-pounder. I'm proud of you, darling.' He leaned forward to kiss her mouth, his aftershave heady and expensive. Ursula shifted her face away so that he kissed her cheek instead. Once she had been desperate to be kissed by him, for him to show any sign of caring. Now she almost hated the smell of him and the tickling of his moustache on her skin. If only . . . but what was the point? There was no question of 'if only'. Not unless the baby made that much difference. And, she didn't really think it would.

The birth had been her weakest point in all the long months they'd been married, the time when she'd needed him most. And he hadn't been there for her. He hesitated and then presented her with the flowers.

'Here you are, sweetheart, white roses for a winter baby. I think Rhea's the most beautiful child I've ever seen. Did you notice that she's got almost a whole head of hair already? Blonde hair and blue eyes! No guessing who her daddy is, hmm?' He was in a gay mood. Ursula looked at him in disbelief.

'Rhea? You want to call our daughter "Rhea"?'

'That's right. Rhea Clare Louise Patterson. It's got quite a ring to it, don't you think? Rhea was my paternal grandmother and I always said I'd name my first girl after her . . . '

'What about Lucy?' Ursula interrupted harshly and Simon's face blenched white, the skin growing tight over his cheekbones.

'What? I don't follow you . . . I thought we agreed that that was just a vicious rumour. I can't believe you're going to start throwing that at me now, of all times!'

'Oh? Is there a better time, do you think? Perhaps at the christening? Then Julia and your father will be there too. Yes, you're probably right, Simon, that's the time to sort things out. I sort of left things at Christmas because it seemed inappropriate, but the christening will work out much better.' It was pure spite, Ursula admitted to herself, but she felt Simon had deserved it. He didn't know she was only bluffing, his eyes pale with anger and thwarted violence. She knew if he could have got her alone for a few moments, that he'd have hit her. Somehow now, after the agony of the birth and the loneliness of the last three days, that didn't bother her. She just felt glad that she'd scored where it hurt. And would continue to hurt. It was time Simon learned what it was like to be on the receiving end.

'I really think I should have some say in naming our baby. Or doesn't it count that I carried her for nine months and then spent eighteen hours in labour?' She looked up at his struggle to regain self-control, a small smile on her lips.

'You . . . bitch!' he hissed it under his breath, before swallowing and sitting down on the chair beside her bed. He ran his fingers through his fair hair in the way that had wrenched her heart with pity only a year ago. Now it didn't move her. 'You can name the next baby, Ursula. We'll take it in turns. But I want this one to be called Rhea. Do you understand me?' He was in control again, determined to get his way. Ursula couldn't quite believe that he really thought she would let him touch her again, even now, after what had passed between them. But he did, it was astounding. She felt some of the tight lump in her chest subside. He wasn't worth getting upset over. He couldn't help it. He was just born with something lacking. She smiled suddenly, her good humour restored.

'All right, Simon, Rhea it is. But I hope you'll explain to her when she's older and getting teased by the other girls at school.' He relaxed and smiled too, and Ursula couldn't help admiring his sheer physical beauty. What a waste that there was nothing within! The mention of school had obviously triggered something in his mind because he suddenly took out his notepad and jotted something down.

'St Mary's. My mother went there. I'll put Rhea down on their list first thing on Monday.'

'She's only three days old, Simon! Don't you think you're

rushing things a little?' But Simon didn't agree at all and Ursula didn't really care enough to argue. She wondered if her indifference was due to fatigue or something more disturbing. Did she really care that much about her daughter? Of course she did. It was just a little disconcerting to find the child took after her father so much in looks – and attitude. But she would get over that. It wasn't Rhea's fault that her father was as he was. She couldn't be held responsible. If only she didn't remind Ursula so much of Simon, every time she looked up at her mother with those pale, almost opaque eyes, and that tilt to her head, and that wispy, silver hair. Ursula shook herself and smiled at Simon.

'When would you like to have the christening?'

He stiffened warily, wondering if she meant to renew her attack, but something in her amusement seemed to reassure him.

'You frighten me sometimes, Ursula. Promise you don't intend to make a scene?' She nodded, her amusement deepening. Oh, this was where he came up short. She sensed her power but was careful not to show it. She would need it later, when the subject of money came up, tight or no.

'I rather thought we might have it in April and down here, at St Luke's.' He said after a moment's thought, 'Would that suit you?' So no going to London and no big fanfare about him being a father for real. Ursula shrugged.

'That'll be fine. Then Lettice and Hugh can be godparents. Have you anyone else in mind?'

'Well, there's Lord Deming and Lady Mary. I mentioned them to you before, didn't I? We had a chat about it last time I was down here for church and Lady Mary said she'd be delighted. A child needs some heavyweights behind it for the future. That'll be a good combination, don't you think?' He was actually interested in the subject in hand and Ursula blinked with pleased surprise. Did this mean his attitude would change towards them now? She gave his hand a gentle squeeze.

'I think that would be wonderful. Would you arrange all that? I don't know them very well and would feel awkward asking. I can book the church if we decide on a date. I'd rather like the 17th April if that's all right with you.' The 17th was

229

Billy's birthday. How old would he be now, she wondered. If he had lived. Twenty-nine? Thirty? For a moment the aching emptiness in her chest reappeared and she had to breathe in sharply. Simon was talking and she tried to listen.

'. . . some time to arrange. I'll check with Julia. She should know.' The mention of Julia did nothing to Ursula. She didn't believe Simon would ever change, and she knew now that her love for him was finished, if it had ever been love to begin with. Perhaps it had just been a need to be loved, to be taken care of, to be wanted? She had admired Simon, been infatuated by his good looks and sophistication, yes. But loved him? Probably not. That sort of love, between a man and a woman, was an entirely different emotion, and it had to be shared. She thought she had probably never loved anyone in that way. It was a sad thought.

Ursula smiled dutifully and held her mouth up to be kissed when Simon decided to leave. She was relieved to see him go, the matter of money finally settled and the baby's christening sorted out. He had been reluctant at first to give her the amount she had demanded – a hundred pounds a month straight to the bank in Elsing – but when she had tactfully suggested that she talk to his father instead, if he couldn't afford to support his wife and child, Simon had become more accommodating. Ursula smiled sleepily and said goodbye without a pang.

It was high summer when Tiffany and Christopher were married. Ursula left Rhea with Lettice for the day and took the train to Cambridge. It was a simple affair, neither set of parents attending, and the bride merely wearing a cream-coloured dress with a small lace veil. Christopher looked blissfully happy and Ursula remembered, with a touch of bitterness, how happy Simon had looked at their wedding. Happy to be married so that he could have a perfect cover for his affair with Julia. And Julia had looked as though she were torn between happiness and envy. Ursula remembered that look suddenly, and the puzzlement she had felt at the time. But Julia had won anyway. She had him and she had her beautiful London town-house and her witty, sophisticated friends, and her reputation restored. God, what a coup she must have thought she'd made! Ursula shook her head irritatedly. What did it matter? She didn't need a man she didn't love, so never mind. She looked across at the bride standing beside her new husband and smiled. Tiffany was such an uncomplicated character: strong, resourceful and good-humoured. She knew they'd be happy.

Then it was time to throw the rice and hug goodbye, the newly-weds anxious to be off on the four o'clock train to London and, from there, to Paris for a week. Tiffany threw her arms around Ursula and laughed, promising she'd call as soon as they got back. They meant to live in London, Christopher having landed a job with a merchant bank in the City. As soon as they were settled, Tiffany repeated firmly, she was to come and stay with them and have some fun. Ursula laughed, knowing what Tiffany meant. Then she kissed Christopher and the two climbed aboard the train as it was pulling out of the station. Ursula stood waving until the train was out of sight.

She got back to the cottage around six-thirty. Lettice was to keep Rhea for the night, in case she were held up or wanted to stay on in Cambridge. So many people kept urging her to have fun. But what was she supposed to do? Sleeping around with other men certainly didn't appeal, and she had been to several county dances with the Dunhams. She knew quite a few families in the area and, while it was difficult to entertain without a husband, she often had the wives over for tea. What else did they expect her to do to have fun? The minute there was a whiff of scandal, she knew she would be condemned on all sides. Well, most sides. And Rhea was quite a handful all on her own, not counting the garden, and the cottage. There wasn't time for anything else. And, quite frankly, she hadn't met anyone who even tempted her. Was there something wrong with her? Was she cold? Simon had flung that at her once, after she had pushed him away. Maybe she was? At least he hadn't tried to sleep with her again since the baby. She hadn't even had to use the excuse of narrow hips. He just wasn't interested.

She walked into her bedroom and pulled off her dress, looking critically at herself in the mirror. She was tall and still very slim, but her breasts were a little larger than before the baby. Her hair was long and thick, her face oval, the dark eyes still fringed by long, black lashes, and her skin was a warm, golden colour from her hours in the garden. She liked the way her eyebrows grew straight and then winged upwards at the outer edges. Perhaps she wasn't classically beautiful but she felt she was attractive. And her body was firm and lean. What more did Simon want? An image of Julia's face flitted unwelcome into her mind and she twisted her mouth. That was what Simon wanted. And what he had. She turned away from the mirror abruptly and slipped her dressing-gown on. Maybe it was time to face up to things. The East was over for her, and life in England wasn't going to change. She was just going to congeal into the perfect little country wife, the perfect little mother, a poor wooden painted bird. She hit her hand against the windowsill. No! Damn it! She wouldn't!

Chapter Fifteen

Essex, 1956

'Mother? Mo . . . ther!' Rhea's voice echoed around the stone walls of the cottage and Ursula, caught in the middle of sorting out fresh linen for the bed, looked up in surprise. It couldn't be two already, could it? She glanced at her watch and saw it was half-past twelve. Then she climbed quickly to her feet and ran out onto the landing.

'Rhea, darling? Is that you?' She started down the stairs as Rhea came up. 'But you're so early! I wasn't expecting you until two and then I was going to run down to the station to pick you up. How on earth did you get here?' She hugged her daughter while she talked, noting how tall and leggy the child was getting. She had turned nine in February and now it was July and she was home again for the long holidays. Ursula swept a wisp of hair out of her eyes and smiled with delight. It would be so good to have some company again.

'I met Hugh at the station and he offered to give me a lift. He's unloading my trunk now.'

'Oh, good Lord! All on his own? He'll get a hernia. Quick, Rhea, out of my way. I must go and help him. How could you let him do it alone?' She pushed past her daughter and ran down the rest of the stairs. How like Rhea! And why had she caught the earlier train? Ursula came to an abrupt halt just outside the front door at the sight of a total stranger lifting

233

Rhea's trunk down from Hugh's roofrack. Hugh was supervising from a safe distance.

'That's it, Tim. Just put it down there until we ask Ursula where she wants it. Oh, there you are, m'dear. We've brought Rhea home.' Hugh beamed with pleasure, his face a pale pink from the heat. It was a hot, still day. Hugh mopped his neck and brow with his handkerchief and gestured to the stranger.

'D'you know Tim, Ursula?' Ursula looked uncertainly at the young man. He was about average height and sturdily-built with dark blond hair and a clean, square jaw. His eyes were narrowed as though he were used to looking into the sun. He was somewhere in his late twenties. She smiled.

'No, I don't think so.' She held out her hand and the stranger grasped it in his in a brief, firm shake. 'I'm Ursula Patterson. Have you come to live around here?'

'Tim Nowlton. I'm over on a visit to see my grandmother actually, Mrs Patterson, so I'm not sure how long I'll be there. Hugh here came to pick me up at the station. And that's when we met your daughter, Rhea.' He smiled and the lines around his eyes wrinkled deeper. Ursula stood staring, her face a shade paler under her tan. He was Australian, his accent slight but unmistakable. She hadn't heard that accent since Singapore. He was looking at her closely now, and suddenly he put out a hand and took her elbow in support.

'Here, are you all right, Mrs Patterson? You look a bit crook to me. I guess this is considered hot weather at the moment. Maybe you've overdone it?' He had her firmly against him now and was leading her into the house while her mind reeled with sudden flashbacks. Hugh hovered uncertainly behind her and Rhea, with her usual presence of mind, rushed upstairs for a wet flannel. Ursula sat down on the sofa with Tim's arm still round her, her face ashen. Oh God, poor Sally and Tom, my Tom, and Emma! How awful to drown like that, and Papa – she couldn't think of his death, and Billy . . . Billy! She felt her head spin as though she were about to pass out but she knew she wouldn't. It was just the shock and the sudden memories Tim's voice had provoked. He pressed her back against the pillows on the sofa.

'There you are now, Mrs Patterson. You'll be fine. It's just the heat maybe.' Ursula heard him asking Hugh if she were prone to heat exhaustion and she shook her head and tried to smile, to reassure. They both ignored her protests.

'Lord no! I've never seen Ursula take a turn like this before. Not even when she was about to have Rhea. Maybe I should call a doctor?' Ursula felt something cool and wet being wiped across her wrists, and then the man, Tim, was saying she'd be all right. Hugh muttered worriedly to himself but Ursula was feeling better by now, the shock fading. She leant back against the sofa and smiled again.

'Really, I'm fine. Sorry if I went a bit pale then but I promise you I'm not going to faint or anything silly like that. I never faint.' She swallowed awkwardly, her mouth dry and bitter.

'Rhea, go and get a glass of water for your mum. And be careful coming back. Don't trip!' That was Tim again and Ursula relaxed, taking deep breaths to still the fluttering within her chest. 'That's right, Mrs Patterson. Your colour's coming back now. My word, you did look bad for a minute!' She raised her eyes and looked into his face as it hovered above her. 'Feeling better?' he asked her.

'Oh, yes, I'm fine. I'm so sorry. It . . . just for a minute there . . . ' she hesitated, wondering how to explain without sounding melodramatic. Rhea appeared behind Tim, the glass of water in her hand and Ursula took a sip gratefully.

Rhea was looking shocked, as though she had never realized until now that her mother was fallible. Ursula smiled reassuringly at the child.

'It's all right, darling. Not to worry. I just overdid things a bit, and I wasn't expecting you back quite so soon. I'm fine now, really.' She held out her hand for the child and Rhea knelt down beside the sofa and held her mother's hand tightly.

Ursula looked up at Hugh and Tim. 'I'm awfully sorry. That wasn't much of a welcome for you, was it, Tim? Hugh dear, don't look so anxious. I'm absolutely fine, I promise you.'

'What was it you were going to say Ursula? For a minute there . . . ?' Hugh's pink cheeks were cooling down inside the cottage and he pulled up a stool to sit on. Tim was perched on the end of the sofa. He looked interested.

'Oh, it was silly.' She laughed self-consciously but, when

neither man laughed, she shrugged and said: 'It was Tim's accent. I haven't heard an Australian since Singapore. It brought back some bad memories in a rush. I'm terribly sorry. I'm not normally so stupid.'

'You lost some family out there? During the war?' Tim asked. Hugh shook his head but Ursula smiled.

'No, it's all right, Hugh. Yes, I lost everyone when the Japanese invaded. I survived and then, after the war, I came back here. I haven't thought about it in years. But my stepmother was Australian, like you. It just triggered a lot of memories, hearing your voice.'

'Look, I'm really sorry. If I'd had any idea I'd've kept my big mouth shut. Are you sure you're all right now?' Tim was frowning and Ursula thought how nice it was to be fussed over for a change. She nodded.

'Not your fault at all, Tim. Just one of those things. Now, who's your grandmother? Not Mrs Chadwick, is it?'

'Yeah, that's right. She's my mum's mum. I haven't seen her in nearly fifteen years and I reckoned if I didn't get around to seeing her soon, she wouldn't be here for me to see.' He grinned, shooting a quick, sideways glance at her. Ursula smiled in answer.

'Come on now, sweetheart, help me up,' she said to Rhea and struggled to stand up. Tim put a hand beneath her arm and helped her to straighten up. 'Oh, thanks, Tim. I don't expect you thought you'd be playing nursemaid to me when you decided to come see your grandmother. I do hope you won't mention my little scene to anyone? I hate being the centre of village gossip.' Ursula felt more in control once she was standing upright again, and both Hugh and Tim were on eye-level. They both shook their heads and promised not to say a word. 'Good, then how about some tea?' But Hugh said he couldn't stay and Tim smiled and shook his head again.

'I don't think you're up to entertaining right now, Mrs Patterson. Why don't you just tell me where you want Rhea's trunk and then we'll be off. I'm kinda anxious to see Nan anyway.' He looked at Rhea. 'Come on, tigger, why don't you show me where your room is?' Rhea stood up immediately, her actions more consciously feminine than Ursula had ever seen. Ursula suppressed a smile. Well, why not? Tim was a very attractive man even if Rhea was too young for him. It didn't hurt for her to learn how to flirt.

'Thank you, Tim, and by-the-way, my name's Ursula.' She wasn't sure she appreciated the way he gave her an assessing look before he nodded and followed Rhea outside. He called his answer over his shoulder.

'Right. Ursula it is.' She turned back to Hugh who was examining a pulled thread on his trousers.

'He seems a nice chap, doesn't he?' Hugh said mildly. Ursula laughed. She could read his mind.

'Very nice. Perhaps we can have you all over to dinner one night soon. D'you think Mrs Chadwick would come?'

'Not very likely. She's eighty-six and not too steady on her legs anymore. I think the journey would probably upset her. But I'm sure Tim would like to come. That would make up a nice foursome. Shall I ask him?' He had a twinkle in his eye that made Ursula blush in spite of herself. Now what was he thinking!

'No thank you, Hugh. I'm quite capable of doing my own asking, if and when I decide to do something. Now it sounds like Tim's coming back. Why don't you just trot along and I'll see you tomorrow at church. And . . . ' she held up her hand to still any further enquiries about her health, 'I'm absolutely fine. Just "tickety-boo" as Simon would say. So don't worry.' She kissed him fondly on the cheek and showed him outside. Tim was standing by the car talking to Rhea but he looked up when she came out.

'All done. If you need the trunk stowed away somewhere after you've emptied it, just give me a call and I'll come and take care of it for you.' Ursula felt herself flushing. Had he heard about Simon?

'Thank you Tim but I'm sure my husband can deal with it. Give my regards to Mrs Chadwick.' She smiled breezily and stood waving until the car turned out of the lane and onto the road. Rhea ran after the car, calling goodbye. Then she turned and walked slowly back towards her mother.

'Mother? How old d'you think Tim is?' Ursula was always amused by the fact that Rhea had elected to call her 'Mother' ever since she had gone away to school. Now she tried not to smile and considered the question carefully.

'Oh, I'd say about twenty-seven or -eight. Perhaps more. He has that sort of boyish look that's hard to be sure of.'

'He is not boyish! I think he looks very manly!'

'Well yes, you're right. He is quite manly. That's not what I meant when I said he looked boyish. I just meant he's got good features and his skin's drawn tightly over his facial bones so that he could be anywhere between twenty-five and thirty-five for all I know. It's hard to tell with some people. Why? Do you think he's nice?' She smiled and Rhea turned away abruptly. Oh dear, she was offended. Ursula tried to make amends.

'Your father called yesterday. He said he was going to try and make it down here to see you over the next few days. Now won't that be fun?' Rhea brightened immediately and gave a couple of quick skips.

'Will he bring me a present? I asked him for some perfume last time and he said he'd bring it. Did you ask him if he was bringing me a present?'

'No-o, I didn't. Rhea dear, I don't think you should always ask your father for things. It isn't very nice. If he wants to bring you something, he should do so without being asked. Besides, you're too young for perfume.' It only took a few minutes in Rhea's company for Ursula to sense her self-absorption. She was just like her father. Rhea scowled and kicked at a stone with her shoe.

'Daddy doesn't mind. He says I'm his little princess and that I can have my heart's desire. It's only you who minds! Just because Daddy doesn't bring you things.'

'That's quite enough, young lady. It isn't polite to ask for gifts every time your father comes down here. It sounds mercenary. Do you understand mercenary?'

'Yes. Then how come all you ever do is have fights with him about money? Isn't that mercenary?' Ursula breathed in deeply to control a surge of irritation at the child's wilfulness.

'No, that's called survival. If you want your pretty clothes and your nice horse and your good school, then I have to get the money out of your father. Otherwise he forgets.'

'That's not true! Daddy always remembers me. Just because he's busy earning a living up in London and you just nag, nag, nag at him when he does come to see us! You keep him away from us, not me!' Rhea stamped her foot in rage, her voice growing shrill, and then she suddenly ran off behind the cottage.

Ursula sighed and tucked a piece of hair back behind her ear. If only she got on better with her daughter; if only Simon didn't bribe Rhea's affection away from her and make it seem as though she were the awkward one in their marriage. Ursula walked into the cool of the sitting-room and sat down on the sofa again. She could still see the mark where Tim had perched on the arm. He seemed so bright and sane and attractive after the in-breeding of the county set. She wished he had stayed longer.

Chapter Sixteen

Simon walked in the door late that night, after Rhea had gone to bed. He was carrying a small leather suitcase, as usual, and a candy-striped package tied up with a pink bow. Ursula didn't ask what it contained. She knew it was the perfume. He kissed her on the cheek, picked Sheba up from the stairs where the cat had been rumbling to itself between the banisters, and settled himself down in his wing-chair as easily as if he had just gone out that morning, instead of a morning nearly three months earlier. It was warm within the cottage, the heat from the last few days building between the stone walls like a kiln. Every window was open, a soft night breeze blowing the curtains in furtive, snapping sounds that had made Ursula nervous while alone. And now her husband was here, she didn't feel any more at ease. There was a different fear in her mind. She decided to precipitate the argument that had been fermenting inside her for most of the day. She looked across at him, calculating his mood. He seemed comfortably unconcerned, scratching Sheba at the base of her tail so that she growled appreciation and tried to hide her head under his arm. No doubt about it, Simon knew all the right moves where women were concerned.

Ursula carried on with her dried-flower arranging while he rustled the paper and made casual comments about life in London. He made it sound gay and sophisticated, one amusing party after another, one scandal after another. She made no response. The curtains flipped in the wind again and she jumped at the sound. He didn't ask about Rhea and she didn't offer any information. Finally he sighed and said:

'Now what have I done, for God's sake? I said I'd be here for Rhea and I'm here. I said I'd bring her a present, and I brought it. I said I'd put the money in the bank and I did. What else do you want, Ursula?' He sounded so reasonable, so disappointed in her attitude that she laughed, unable to contain the bitterness within her. She could feel it corroding her every time he turned up, self-satisfied and indifferent to her fate. She wanted a husband, that's all! Not so terribly much, was it? She worked hard, managed all of Rhea's school bills and her own household on the pittance Simon paid her. That pair of shoes would've cost about a third of what she lived on for a month. And he thought she was difficult. God, was it really possible to hate one man so much? No, not hate, despise. She despised him. Just comparing that handsome, thin-nosed effeteness with the sturdy masculinity Tim had shown her that afternoon made her insides coil tightly as though in pain. She examined the new brogues he was wearing: very natty with those argyll socks. She glanced at him coldly.

'Your daughter seems to think I'm the reason you don't come to see her more often. Perhaps you'd care to enlighten her? Or shall I? I'm not going to take the rap all the time, Simon. You better start letting Rhea know what's going on, or I will.' She saw him slowly open his eyes, raising his smooth eyebrows, sucking in his cheeks and frowning slightly.

'You'd tell a nine-year-old child that her father has a mistress? Come off it, Ursula! And besides, she'll only assume I have one because you're inadequate, won't she?' He held her gaze for a moment to make sure she understood him, rustled the paper again and carried on reading unconcernedly. God, what she wouldn't give to pick up the knife on the table in front of her and stick him, like a pig, while he squealed! She breathed deeply, hands flattened against her hips to control her rage.

'I think you're going to have to do something, Simon. Rhea's getting impossible to handle, and you condone it by bringing her gifts every time, and telling her that her mother doesn't deserve gifts.'

'Now when did I ever tell her that?' he demanded in exasperation, the paper flung to the ground. Sheba jumped off his lap and strolled to the door, her tail held tightly up in an exclamation of annoyance.

'Every time you bring her a gift and not me. I'm not saying I want one. I don't. But that's what you're telling her, whether you realize it or not. You're saying that you don't care about me, and that that's the reason you don't come to see us more often. Now she's blaming me. I can't take much more of this, Simon, so you better do something. I don't care what, but do something!' Her voice grew shaky and she dropped the flowers suddenly onto the table and left the room. Simon continued to look surprised, as though a particularly difficult problem had suddenly been dumped in his lap while he wasn't watching – which it had. Then he picked up the paper again.

Ursula didn't return to the sitting room and when Simon eventually decided to go to bed, he found the bedroom door locked against him. He rattled the doorknob ineffectually before retreating downstairs and making himself comfortable on the sofa. He punched the cushions into shape. Damn Ursula. Why did she have to be so difficult all the time?

Church was at eleven and Ursula had Rhea and herself ready by quarter past ten, breakfast eaten and the plates washed up. She sent her daughter out to pick some sunflowers for the table, pacing the flagstones impatiently while the minutes ticked away. Simon emerged from the bathroom at quarter to eleven, looking perfect and smelling wonderful as always. Rhea loved the smell of his cologne and she ran up to him as he came down the stairs to give him a kiss.

'Hallo, Daddy. I found the perfume! It smells so nice! Don't I smell nice? Just like you.' She glanced disdainfully at her mother who wasn't wearing any perfume at all. Mother didn't smell nice, like Daddy. She just smelled of soap and water. Only sometimes, on special occasions, would she put any perfume on. And then so little that you had to stand right next to her and lean in to smell it. Rhea thought she was mean. And now she wasn't even paying attention to Daddy and how wonderful he looked. She was just putting on her gloves and telling Daddy they'd be late. She always chivvied Daddy so!

They arrived just as the last bells were ringing and took their place in the pews without a word. Up ahead and to the right,

Ursula could see Mrs Chadwick's hat and next to it, Tim's fair head. She glanced away immediately, searching for Lettice and Hugh in the throng. There they were, two pews ahead. Mr Bailey, the rector, appeared out of a side door, sliding past the large flower arrangement on its stand like a rabbit appearing from a hat. He took his place. The first hymn was beginning and Ursula noticed Tim pass his hymn book across to his grandmother before picking up hers and finding his place. She liked that. It showed consideration for the old lady's failing eyesight. Not that she probably needed the book at all; she knew most of the hymns off by heart. But it was a nice gesture. Ursula smiled approvingly before her attention was distracted by Rhea kicking the pew in front of her. Rhea gave her a sullen look when told to stop. Simon smiled sympathetically at his daughter. They were both scamps and always in the dog-house with Ursula, his look seemed to say. Ursula swallowed over the hard lump in her throat while the organ thumped away under Jane Clow's energetic playing and Lady Mary's voice soared quaveringly into the refrain.

After church and the long filing out to exchange words with Mr Bailey that seemed interminable that day, the parishioners gathered on the side lawn of the church, milling about and calling subdued greetings to each other. Children darted between legs and dashed around graves, playing tag. Mr Bailey's robes streamed out whitely in the wind and women held onto their hats with one hand and their skirts with the other. Rhea ignored the curious glances from the village children, standing close beside her father, her hand swinging in his. She barely knew them except from sight. Ursula had tried to get Rhea to play with them but Simon had objected. What did her daughter want to play with them for, he'd demanded? They weren't the right sorts for his family to know. He'd take care of introducing Rhea to the suitable playmates when she was older. What was Ursula thinking about, encouraging such things! And Ursula had given way, knowing Rhea was not interested in making friends anyway. She had her friends at school, she said. She didn't need any others.

Simon greeted Lettice with a hug and Hugh with a hand-shake, inviting them both over to dinner the next night. His head shone a polished, smooth blond as he chatted easily. So charming; Ursula could see the village people thinking. So handsome. Such a good father. Lettice grimaced at Ursula, fully aware that Simon had just thought of having them over to dinner, without consulting the cook.

'Well, Ursula? Is that convenient for you? Or shall we make it another night?'

'No Lettice, tomorrow will be fine. I'll go to the shops in the morning. I always love to see Hugh and you. Don't worry about it. He can't help it.'

'Won't help it, you mean. I don't think that boy's ever had a thought for someone else in his life! Unless it's Julia. Well, I'm sorry, I shouldn't have said that but sometimes he gets my goat.' Lettice and Ursula were standing slightly to one side of the group, while Simon was engrossed in conversation with Hugh about the forthcoming hunting season. The scene imprinted itself in Ursula's mind: splashes of colour where the flowers edging the stone walls of the church, clashing red, yellow, and pink, twirled in the breeze, and the dun-coloured hues of the parishioners fading into the sort of respectability that was as jealously guarded as Simon's own snobbery. Ursula felt a small pulse of nervousness throb down in her stomach. Her own suit was pale grey, quietly self-effacing as she had learned to be in the face of such implicit strictures as the village laid down. Only Simon got away with being stylish. She was a nobody, simply married to a somebody. She couldn't try too hard. And she could seldom be bothered anyway. Until now. Lettice noticed Ursula's distracted air and winked. 'I hear you did a very becoming swoon yesterday. And such a handsome young man to catch you! My, if I didn't know you better, my dear, I'd think you were a designing female! Not that I blame you one bit. I think Tim's quite a dish, and I'm old enough to be his mother!'

'And I'm married, in case you've forgotten!' She hadn't meant to snap like that. She looked at her watch.

'Twaddle! You're no more married than Sally Jenkins, and she's the village sweetheart! Just because you've got a ring on your finger, and a ten-year-old daughter is no reason to think your life's over. Simon's having fun, why don't you? Hugh said Tim seemed quite taken with you,' Lettice added, smiling as she saw Ursula look up and flush.

'Really? Oh, don't start on about this again, Lettice! I'm just not the philandering sort, gorgeous though Tim may be. And he doesn't strike me as the type who plays around with other men's wives. He's too - wholesome, I suppose - for that.'

'Oh-ho. Wholesome is it? Well, whatever you want to call it, I wish they'd bottle some so we could distribute it to the other pseudo-men around.' She laughed, her hearty, frank laugh that always made Ursula feel glad to be alive. 'And besides, you're both about the same age I'd say. How old are you now, Ursula? Twenty-eight?'

'Twenty-nine in November. I'm an old crock practically, and certainly not about to start acting like a . . . Oh Lord, here he comes. Now don't go saying anything to embarrass me, Lettice. Don't forget Simon and Rhea are here.'

Rhea had already attached herself to Tim's hand and she was drawing him, and his grandmother, steadily over to her parents and the Dunhams. Lettice took command.

'Hallo, Mrs Chadwick, Tim. How are you? We were just wondering if you were going to come and say hallo but I gather Rhea cornered you and dragged you over. You both know Ursula, don't you? And have you met her husband, Simon? Simon? Simon! Come and be sociable and stop talking about butchering poor, defenceless birds. You don't shoot, do you, Tim?'

'Not birds, if I can help it, Lettice. But dingos, and sometimes boomers, yeah, I'm afraid so. I'm a bush-bunny you see, and sometimes you have to do it to save the sheep.' He grinned good-naturedly at Lettice and then glanced over at Ursula. She smiled and nodded her head.

'I know what a dingo is, but what on earth is a boomer?'

'Big male red kangaroo. They knock down the fences and eat all the feed that the sheep need. Sometimes their herds get too big so we go out and cull a few.'

'You shoot kangaroos!' Lettice was horrified but distracted from the few choice words she was about to deliver by the arrival of Simon and Hugh. Simon eyed Tim with a superior smile.

'Well! What on earth is an Aussie doing on this side of the world?' he laughed good-humouredly. 'I thought you'd all forsaken civilization and decided to go bush. Isn't that the phrase?' Tim smiled easily, his eyes sizing up the man in front of him and dismissing him as easily. So this was the beautiful Ursula's husband? Good-looking bloke but no stuffing. He wouldn't last five minutes out in the bush. Tim held out his hand, his fingers squared and solid as they took Simon's long, shapely hand. He was blunt against Simon's sharpness and Ursula watched them together with interest. There was no doubt in her mind who was the better man.

'That's the phrase all right. Have you been down under, Mr Patterson?'

'Never. And I don't intend to either. No offence, but talking to sheep isn't my favourite pastime. The name's Simon.'

'Tim, then. Well that's a real shame. There's some beaut country down there, and some pretty great cities. I'd be sorry to think you thought so badly of us.' Tim didn't look sorry. He looked indifferent. Ursula smiled and took Tim's arm.

'We're having a small dinner party tomorrow night, Tim. Perhaps you and your grandmother might like to come?' She was leading him to one side while Simon talked to Mrs Chadwick, and she had the advantage of Simon having to battle Mrs Chadwick's deafness. She glanced across at the man beside her and was startled to see him looking at her as though he were indulging her. 'Unless, of course, you have other plans?'

'No, none that I wouldn't break to come and have dinner with you. But I don't think Nan can make it. She's not up to much entertaining anymore. It's about all she can do to make it to church. In fact, I better be getting her home soon.'

'Oh, but . . . that's no reason for you not to come. I can easily make up the numbers, if that's what you're worried about?' She felt ridiculous she was so anxious for him to come. But perhaps he didn't see it? It was hard to tell what Tim was thinking, his face a perfect barrier between her and his thoughts. But he gave the arm she had slipped through his a friendly squeeze and said:

'That'd be nice. Thank you, Ursula. What time shall I come?'

'Oh, about sevenish, I suppose. And come casual. I'm not giving any black-tie affair!'

'Casual? With your husband, does that mean a suit?' He

was teasing her and she smiled, her liking for him showing in her eyes. He smiled back, equally happy.

'No, not even a tie I promise you. Simon might wear a cravat but I don't think that's your style, somehow.'

'Acute of you, Ursula. And I thought you had me pegged as a man-milliner.' He was teasing her again. 'Simon just come down from London this morning?'

'No, last night. Quite late. Why?'

'No reason.' He shrugged. 'Just wondered. The offer still stands about the trunk if Simon forgets or, something . . . ' He trailed off, noticing the pink stain in her cheeks.

'Simon can handle it, but thanks.' What was he trying to say? She didn't know.

'You ever been to Australia?'

'No, uh no, I haven't. We were going to once, when I was quite young but . . . anyway, I never did get down there. Pity really. I'd've liked to see it.'

'Um. You'd fit in well down there. You're open-minded. Your husband - well, he's already condemned before he's even seen. That the way he always is? Makes up his mind about something before he's got any idea what it's all about?' She could sense his antagonism through his words. And she hadn't thought he'd cared what Simon said about Australia.

'Not generally. I guess he just thinks the way most European people do. Australia's a long way away and it's pretty rough compared to London or Paris, say. He didn't mean to offend you.'

'It's not me he's offended. And I wasn't just talking about Australia.' He hesitated and then said, 'Look, I better be going. Nan looks tired. She can't stand up for too long.'

'Oh yes. I'm sorry. I shouldn't have kept you.' Ursula was bewildered by his words, by the look he gave her. When they turned back towards the group it was to find that only Rhea had missed them; her dark looks directed at her mother as though she thought of her as an adversary. Tim flicked his finger across Rhea's cheek and brought her smile out again.

'What's up, tigger? You were looking pretty glum just then.' Rhea looked across at her mother, who was talking to Hugh, and then back at Tim.

'Nothing. Mother's just been sort of down on Daddy and me

this morning. She's always nagging us about something. You don't know how difficult she can be!' She slipped her hand into his and he ruffled her hair.

'Oh, all mums seem like that when you're young. Later on you get to see what they were on about and have a bit more sympathy for them. Your mum seems pretty special to me.'

'But Daddy thinks Mother's difficult too. And he's not young,' Rhea said obstinately. She was kicking a stone again and Tim wondered what exactly did go on at the Patterson's house. His grandmother had told him about Simon, but he couldn't understand why Rhea wasn't on her mother's side.

'How often does your daddy come down to see you both Rhea? I hear he's often away in London.'

'Only because of her!' Her voice became passionate and several people looked over to see what young Rhea was saying to the Australian fellow. She became aware of it immediately and lowered her voice. 'Daddy loves me; he never forgets me and he always brings me presents. It's just Mother he can't stand for too long, and that's why he goes back to London all the time. Besides, he told me he has to work very hard to earn money for us, and all Mother does is spend it all the time. And then she always tells me that she doesn't have any, and that she can't buy me presents like Daddy does. She's mean!' Rhea scowled furiously at the ground. Tim ruffled her hair again.

'Life isn't always that cut and dried, Rhea. You're old enough to know that. Maybe there are things you don't know, that you can't know. I think you should give your mum more credit than you do. She cares a lot about you.'

'No she doesn't. She just puts up with me because I'm her daughter and she can't do anything about it.' She looked up at Tim's face, seeking his opinion. He shook his head, grey eyes clear and even.

'You're wrong, tigger. But come on, we better be off.' He'd said that so many times and yet he kept delaying, spinning out the few minutes so that he could see how these people fit together. It was a puzzle. And young Rhea was going to be trouble unless someone sorted her out. He sighed as she swung her hand to and fro in his.

It was still light at seven in the evening, the long summer nights drawing out until nine. Ursula had set up a table outside under the wisteria vine, and brought two long wooden benches from the garden to line both sides of the table. A white, embroidered cloth was spread diagonally across the table, anchored by three miniature potted bay trees cut like poodle dogs, Rhea said. It was going to be a simple, rustic meal with salads and cheeses, bread, rack of lamb marinaded in herbs and roasted in the Aga until it was pink in the centre and pale beige around the edges, baby onions, and carrots from her own garden. Simon was in charge of the wine and he had set off that morning to deal with things, not returning until gone five. Ursula had been glad to have him out of her way and she had arranged her menu so that she need spend only the minimum of time in the kitchen. She liked to entertain and saw no reason why she shouldn't enjoy her guests while they were there.

Rhea had been difficult, asking constantly what she should wear until Ursula had sat down and explained that this was a grown-up's dinner and that she would be eating beforehand. Rhea had bitterly denounced her mother and demanded that they ask Daddy. But Daddy was already gone for the day and Ursula had smoothed Rhea's ruffled feelings by telling her she could come and sit with everyone before dinner and have a drink.

It was six before everything was ready and Ursula could take herself off for a bath. She closed the bathroom door firmly on Simon's requests that she iron another shirt for him because he'd decided to wear a different cravat: the next hour was hers. The bath was filled with lukewarm water, all the hot having been taken by Simon and Rhea, and, on impulse, she poured some perfume under the running tap, its light, citrus scent filling the air. Oh, she hadn't felt this way in years, full of expectation and delight, fluttering nerves only just under control. It was a wonderful feeling and she realized, for the first time, just what she had been missing. It took her only ten minutes to bathe and wash her hair and she stepped out of the bath feeling cleansed both outside and in.

Her mind was calm and indulgent where Simon and Rhea were concerned. Everyone had problems; hers were just a little more difficult than most. She had selected her dress carefully and carried it into the bathroom with her so that she could dress without interruption. It was a pale cream linen with a lace collar that made her skin seem warm and vibrant and her hair darker than ever. It was her one purchase that year that had nothing to do with pure survival. And looking at it she decided it had been worth every penny. She dried her hair in a towel and combed it back into a heavy chignon, then slipped an ivory silk petticoat over her head and smoothed it over her body. She has worn this petticoat for her wedding. The dress followed and then Ursula pulled out the few cosmetics she owned. She never normally wore any, not even lipstick, but tonight she intended to be beautiful.

Hugh and Lettice arrived, bringing Sally Jenkins with them. It was Lettice's mention of her the day before that had made Ursula invite the girl. She was a pretty girl with medium brown hair that curled around a plump, pouting face. Most of the unmarried men of the area, and quite a few of the married ones, were trying to fix their interest with Sally but she wasn't about to rush things. She was having too much fun being the village belle, and she was only twenty-one. She had a little time in hand before eyebrows were raised, and gentle whispers suggested that she was flighty. Ursula knew that Sally would balance her time out to the second, and then marry the most eligible man possible at the apex of her career. It was nice to see a woman getting the upper hand for a change, and Ursula had decided that Sally would be a good companion for Tim while he was there. Someone whose heart wouldn't be broken when Tim waltzed off back to that beaut country he liked to talk about. Ursula envied them.

Tim arrived a few minutes later, driving Mrs Chadwick's vintage jaguar. He had taken Ursula at her word and wore an open-necked shirt and comfortable-looking moleskins. Ursula forced herself to look up calmly when he came through the back door out onto the flagstones. Simon was telling him a joke and she listened attentively while smiling at Hugh's third recital of his trip to Leicester.

'So the first man said to his friend: "I'm very happy, I have a wonderful home, a great job, and the finest wife in the country." And his friend replied: "Who wouldn't be happy with his wife in the country?" Uh, uh, uh, uh!' Ursula felt some of the happiness ebb out of her, as though she were a tyre and had lost some air. She looked up to see Tim watching her.

'Don't mind Simon, he's always stealing jokes from other people. Come and sit down, Tim, I want you to meet Sally Jenkins. Sally, this is Tim Nowlton from Australia – where in Australia Tim?' He sat on the bench beside her and smiled a greeting at Sally and the others.

'Well, I live in Melbourne now but I come from a property near Gisburne. Back of beyond but there's good land for sheep up there. My parents still live there.'

'Really, and what d'you do in Melbourne? That's Victoria, isn't it?'

'Yeah, I'm a lawyer for a prospecting company. Nothing too glamorous, I'm afraid. I'd like to get into politics one day, but who knows?'

'Well, Simon's the one to ask about that. His father's Member of Parliament for West Dorset and . . . Simon, are you going to enter politics or not? You've been talking about it for years.' That was Lettice, gently needling. Simon laughed and clapped Tim on the shoulder.

'It's a mean business to get involved with, Tim. You want to have some friends in high places before you try it. Believe me, I know.' Simon poured another glass of wine for himself and raised his glass to Tim. 'To politics! May it never have anything to do with the people!' He laughed that coughing, uh, uh, uh, that had once delighted Ursula. Now she shrugged and said:

'As you can see, Simon's not thinking of sitting in Labour's benches. And as he must know every single person of importance in "high places", I can't think why he isn't Prime Minister already, if that's what it's all about. How about you, Tim? Know anyone useful to get you going? Or are you going to do it the honourable way and actually convince the people you can do something for them. Now think what a lesson in humility that would be for my dear old husband.' But she laughed as she said it and everyone laughed with her, even Simon.

'Aw, a mixture of both I guess, Ursula. I know where I can pull in some support . . . ' He looked unhappy with that and broke off, taking a look around the garden. The others didn't notice. Only Ursula. And when Tim looked back at her, he

251

had a strange expression on his face. Almost defiant. Ursula turned away.

'Then you're not about to join Evatt and his bunch of communists in the ALP?' said Simon, showing off his knowledge of Australian politics. Tim looked amused.

'Not in the immediate future, no. I'm a Country party bloke myself. Not much into the sort of muck-raking that's been going on for the last couple of years in the Labour party.'

'What, not even over the Communist Party Dissolution Act? Wasn't that what it was called. I thought Menzies was a bit over the top on that. Bloody unconstitutional, wasn't it?' Simon grinned, dismissing these colonials with all the liberality of an enlightened and ancient civilization at his back. Tim sipped his wine.

'Menzies is Liberal Party, actually. And he did try and take it to the country. The referendum only just failed so I'd say quite a few Aussies were behind the idea of outlawing the Communist Party.' He sighed. 'I didn't actually approve of it myself, but then I guess I had my suspicions over the Petrov affair too.' He smiled at the expression of bewilderment that crossed Simon's face. 'You must know about that, surely? Being so up on Aussie politics and all?'

'Can't say I do. We don't always hear about some provincial case from downunder.' Simon was languidly bored, ready to change the conversation.

'Nonsense, Simon. The Petrov affair was big news. Even we heard about it out here in the country. You must remember? That Russian third secretary to the embassy in Canberra who defected and then his wife was nearly kidnapped back by the Russians? I don't know how that affected the politics of the Labour Party but I do know we were all agog about the way Petrov's wife was rescued at the last second from some airfield up in Darwin. Good thriller stuff!' Hugh was enthusiastically drawn into the conversation.

'What were your suspicions about it, Tim?' Ursula was intrigued. There was a lot more to this rough Australian than even she had divined. A shrewd mind, for one thing.

'Aw, well, the backlash really broke up the Labour Party's revival, especially the right wing lot they were trying to attract, and it sent Evatt over to the left in the Labour Party and then

252

they lost the '54 elections mostly because of it. Menzies went into a coalition government with the Country party who, I might add, came out against Evatt and said he'd been indulging the Communists and cosying up with the left. Anyway a lot of us think Menzies knew about the whole affair long before it was disclosed. He used it for maximum effect at a point in the elections when it looked like Labour might just win. I dunno, he's since denied any sort of domestic political motivation but it makes me wonder a bit. Kind've leaves a sour taste there.'

Tim drank some wine and seemed to relax. Simon had decided to retire gracefully from any further polemical discussions and was trying, instead, to tickle Sally Jenkins with a feather. Sheba was chirruping around his legs but he had found a more interesting female to entertain this time. Tim watched him, his expression revealing very little. The candles flickered in the evening breeze and the talk became general, about the state of the economy, and unemployment. Ursula excused herself to check on the lamb just as Rhea appeared wearing a dress Ursula had never seen before. It was pale blue and she pirouetted in front of her mother, her silver hair flying out around her face. In that moment Ursula realized Rhea was the image of her father, in feminine form. And Ursula's mouth seemed to fill with the acrid taste of ashes.

'New dress?'

'Daddy bought it for me, at The White House in London. He said it was blue for my eyes. Don't I look pretty? Tim, Tim, d'you like my new dress?' She ran past her mother to show Tim and Ursula looked up at Simon.

'Is that your way of handling the problem, Simon?' Simon smiled sheepishly.

'I'm trying to sort things out, Ursula. It's just going to take time. She needed a new dress anyway.'

'Just like she needed perfume, at nine years old. So help me Simon . . uhh!' She pushed past him into the kitchen, feeling the rage sweep through her, searing the moisture in her eyes so that it stung as she blinked her way to the table. Why did she let him get to her? Why? Thank God she'd had the sense to put aside a few pounds every month from the standing order Simon paid into their bank. It meant they were always running short and Rhea's bills at school were just appalling, but there was

253

always that little nest-egg that no-one knew about except her. Sometimes she thought she'd just walk out the door and never seen any of them again. But of course she wouldn't, couldn't really. It wasn't Rhea's fault; it was Simon's. And he was going to be around for a long, long time. She leant over the sink for a few minutes, regaining her composure, and then she moved over to the Aga. The rack of lamb was nearly done and Ursula moved it down into the lower oven where it would cook more slowly. Then she straightened up and wiped her hands on the tea-towel, flushed with the heat of the oven.

'Can I help? I'm pretty handy in a kitchen. Just say the word and I'm yours.' Tim was holding two wine glasses in his hands and leaning against the door. Ursula faltered. Did he have any idea how that could be construed? No, she didn't think so.

'Uh, no, that's all right, Tim. I've just about done everything, and now the lamb's just got to finish cooking. I was coming right back outside actually. Oh, thanks.' She took the glass from his hand and let the wine run over her tongue and down the back of her throat. Maybe she should just get drunk tonight and embarrass the hell out of Simon? She sighed. No, that wasn't her style, and he knew it.

'I was hoping you and Sally would like each other. It'll be fun for you while you're here to go out with a younger bunch. I'm afraid we're mostly old fogeys around here.' She swept a strand of hair back, a gesture that was becoming a habit when she was nervous. She wished he wasn't standing so close to her. It made her clumsy. Tim didn't smile.

'I wouldn't've said you're any older than I am, Ursula. You seem to be the one who's out of place in the older crowd.'

'Oh no, I'm nearly twenty-nine. And apart from Lettice and Hugh there aren't many people that I'm fond of, to tell you the truth. I wouldn't give up their company for anything.'

'There you go then. I'm twenty-seven and not really looking for a "younger bunch" to spend my time with. I'd rather be where I like the company, just like you. And I like your company.' He paused, looking down at his glass as though thinking something through. 'Your husband kinda spoils Rhea, I guess. The kid's got some dumb idea you don't love her. I know it's none of my business but I thought you might like to know. Sometimes it's hard to see things straight when you're too

254

closely involved. Couldn't you tell Simon to lay off with the pressies?' He gave a tentative grin and Ursula's face lost some of its rigidity.

'Pressies? Yes, I have already. It's no good. Simon's hopeless where Rhea's concerned. It undercuts all my discipline the minute he walks in the door with another "pressie". And I don't know what to say to Rhea.' She gave a long, gusty sigh. 'I'm sorry that Rhea's been talking to you about it. It must've put you in a very awkward situation.'

'No problem. I've got a thick skin when I want. Can I do anything to help?' he repeated, but Ursula knew he wasn't talking about kitchen help. She smiled and touched his arm lightly.

'You already have. You can't think how nice it is to have some fresh blood in the village. Sometimes I think I'll scream if I see the same old faces yet again, at every party, and in every shop.'

'And every Sunday at church? Yeah, I know. It's like that where I come from. That's why I moved to the city. I needed to get away, where people didn't know everything I was doing and wouldn't be interested, even if they did know.' He swallowed some wine and Ursula couldn't help watching his throat, the way the adam's apple bobbed up and down, the light hairs glinting at the top of his shirt where he had left the first two buttons undone. She looked away, striving for something trivial to say.

'I can't imagine you ever doing anything that would cause too much gossip, Tim. You don't seem the type.'

'Oh? And who would be the type?' He was indulging her again and she stiffened.

'More Simon's sort, I suppose.'

'Yeah? How come you don't give him a dose of his own medicine then?'

'Me? I . . . uh, no, I don't think so. Come on, the others will be wondering where we've got to.' She walked past him and out of the kitchen into the cool of the evening. Tim followed after a few moments.

Simon was refilling everyone's glasses and he came over to Ursula with the bottle in his hand. The candlelight gleamed on his fair hair, and his face was shiny with heat and too much drink. He poured her out another glass and then kissed her cheek, newly amorous with the wine, the garden and the candles, and the way Ursula looked that night. God, there were times when he wondered why he stayed away so much. She was stunning when she got herself up like that. If only she could be as passionate as when he first married her; then she had been trying to please, and he had wanted her every time he looked at her. Like tonight. And tonight she wasn't going to lock the bedroom door. He giggled to himself as he patted his pocket. Ursula pulled away, her face blankly impersonal.

'What about you, Tim? More wine?' He started to fill Tim's glass before Tim could answer. Tonight everyone must have fun – even this boor from Aussie – and then he'd show them out the door and take his beautiful wife who smelled so nice – where did that perfume come from? It wasn't any that he'd given her. 'That's it, my boy, drink up. Tonight's a celebration.'

'A celebration of what, Simon?' Lettice called from the table where she was retying Rhea's bow. Simon giggled and put his finger to his lips.

'Sshh! Can't tell! That wouldn't be gentlemanly, now would it?' Simon grinned his perfect smile and Sally giggled back. Ursula felt her face grow red. She wasn't sure what he really meant, but she knew that giggle and the pale colour of his eyes. The thought made her sick.

'Is everyone ready to eat? Or would you rather drink some more first? I've a nasty feeling you're all drinking on an empty stomach as it is,' she said brightly and fended off another too personal hug from her husband. Lettice stood up immediately.

'I, for one, am starving. Let's eat whether they want to, or not. I'll help you carry out, Ursula. Tim, you and Sally help clear the table of glasses, and Hugh – you keep Simon out from under foot. Rhea, sweetheart, come and help us in the kitchen, will you?'

'Daddy says I can eat with you. Can't I, Daddy?' Rhea said firmly and Ursula glanced at Simon.

'Of course you can, princess. That's what your new dress is for. Showing off at dinner. Just don't get it dirty in the kitchen.' Ursula turned away before Simon had finished speaking. Rhea smiled triumphantly.

*　　*　　*

256

The dinner was a success, the lamb done to perfection and the salad, bread and cheese filling in any holes in the men's appetites. It was dark by the time they finished and Ursula left the men drinking coffee outside while she took Rhea up to bed. Lettice accompanied her but Sally stayed with the men. She was more comfortable with men anyway.

'Insipid creature,' Lettice muttered under her breath as she climbed the stairs. 'One more lisp and bat of the eyelids . . . '

'Or one more pout and "That's so amazing. You must be so clever!" and we'll all be sick. Yes, I know, Lettice, but it was your fault. You mentioned her yesterday and I had to make up the numbers. Though, why I bothered when Rhea here ended up staying anyway! Don't you think you can get away with anything you like, Rhea, by just appealing to Daddy. I let it go this once because I didn't want a scene in the middle of my dinner party but, if I say you can't do something, I mean it. D'you understand?' She was pushing Rhea down the hall in front of her, her tone more in mock-anger than real and Rhea laughed.

'Oh Mother! You're so stiff all the time. Why can't you be more fun, like Daddy?'

'Because there has to be at least one adult in every family. I guess I'm it. Now into bed fast before I decide to make you do the washing-up.' Rhea took the threat seriously and slipped out of her new dress and into bed. She held up her face for Lettice to kiss, and then kissed her mother quickly and perfunctorily. Ursula turned off the light and closed the door softly.

'What am I going to do with her, Lettice?' she said after they had moved down the hall to the stairs. 'She gets more difficult to handle every day. Even Tim's noticed.'

'I don't know why you say, "even Tim". Tim's been noticing just about everything all night long. My, I wish he'd turn those eyes on me the way he watches you. Don't let this one get away girl. I'm serious.' Lettice's face lost its humour just for a moment and she looked at Ursula hard. 'I don't think they come along like Tim very often. Have you ever considered just jumping ship?'

'Don't be silly, Lettice. You're overreacting totally. Tim's very nice, and maybe he does find me attractive but he's not going to do anything about it - and neither am I! Have you noticed Simon looking at all worried? Hmm? No, so I don't think things are quite as marked as you seem . . . '

'Oh, Simon! He wouldn't notice if you took off your clothes in public! He's only concerned with himself, number one, and you know, I think he thinks so well of himself, I don't think he even considers Tim a rival? Now that's funny!' She laughed her gravelly laugh and the two went downstairs to join the rest.

Out under the kitchen window, Simon was setting up some music, Sally hovering beside him making small intimate remarks that made Simon part his lips in silent appreciation. Lettice pushed Ursula past the two, towards Tim.

'Lettice! For God's sake behave yourself!' Ursula hissed.

'Nonsense. Are we going to have some dancing then? How nice! I haven't danced in ages. Hugh my dear, you may lead me gently around in a sedate waltz. I don't want any fast, new music, Simon! Totally beyond me and besides I don't really like it. We need something slow and mellow. What have you got?'

'Don't get bossy, Lettice. I know exactly what we need. There! How's that?' He lifted the needle into place and Lettice applauded.

'Excellent! Hugh, darling?' She lifted her arms and Hugh stood obediently and stepped into her embrace. They danced gently around the table, moving in the lamplight like shadow puppets, to the lyrics 'I'll be loving you, eternally . . . '

'Ursula?' Tim smiled, knowing Lettice's tactics had embarrassed Ursula and that she would not approach him. Simon and Sally were laughing in the corner, Sally leaning up against Simon heavily. Ursula turned away from them and looked at Tim.

'If you'd rather not, it's perfectly all right . . . '

'But I rather would. I like dancing and I like you. Will you?' He held out his hand and she took it uncertainly, feeling herself become rigid and ungraceful. Tim pulled her in tighter than she wanted until his warmth and the music slowly eased some of the stiffness from her. He made no comment when she gave a deep sigh and finally relaxed.

'That's what I like about you, Tim,' she said softly so the others would not hear.

'What?'

258

'Your patience.' She saw him smile.

'I'm not all that patient, you know. Only when it really matters.'

'Waiting for me to stop being such a stiff marionette? That matters?'

'Waiting for you to relax with me, to trust me. Yes, that does matter. You matter to me.'

A burst of giggles from Sally intruded. Ursula shook her head.

'You shouldn't say that, you know.'

'Why not? You think he cares? Anyway, I can't help it, so I might as well be honest.' He laid his cheek against hers and she felt his fingers digging harder into her back. She sighed.

'I'd almost forgotten how it felt.'

'Dancing?'

'No, caring.' He shifted his hold so that she fitted into him, his mouth almost against her skin.

'I . . . When's Simon going back? Tomorrow?'

'Yes, perhaps. I never really know. It's no good anyway. I shouldn't've said that.'

'No?' He was silent, moving languidly to the music. 'Well, we'll have to see. Maybe I'll drop round tomorrow anyway.' She didn't reply but followed his lead further out beyond the table where the shadows cast by the lamps were longest. No-one paid any attention and Tim held Ursula against him as though he were the one leaving the next day. And Ursula let him.

Chapter Seventeen

The key was missing. It was the first thing Ursula noticed when she entered the room. Simon was still downstairs, closing up, putting out the candles. She had come ahead, thinking about that giggle and those pale eyes, wanting to be in and the door shut before he could appear. And now the key was gone. She felt a moment's blind panic. She couldn't make love with him. Not after the way Tim had held her out there in the garden. The thought of Simon disgusted her. She shivered as she stepped out of her dress, hanging it from the hat-rack. He must have taken the key earlier, so she couldn't lock him out. She pulled her nightgown on hurriedly and climbed into bed. Maybe he would be too drunk?

But he wasn't. When Simon appeared at last, edging the door open and peering through it at her, Ursula tried to pretend she was asleep. He tiptoed in, closing the door firmly, replacing the key, turning it. Ursula felt her breath catch in her chest, tightening. She would just bluff him that she was asleep. He could hardly force her, after all. Could he?

He was breathing heavily, through his nose, in that way he had when he'd drunk quite a lot and was tired. It wasn't a snore, just a heavy breathy sound with a little wheeze at the end. She shivered again.

'Ah, you are awake. I thought you must be. I haven't taken that long to close up.' He giggled, pouncing suddenly from across the room onto the bed, his knees drawn up beneath him, his arms scooping her up and in towards him. She struggled, some of her fear coming out as a nervous laugh, a disclaimer.

'Don't, Simon. I don't want to. It's late and I'm tired. For God's sake, why don't you go back to Julia if that's what you want.' She pushed him away so that he toppled backwards, falling across the end of the bed. A spurt of irritation went through him.

'Don't bloody push me away, Ursula. You know how much that gets to me. I'm not just some fellow you can use for money or social purposes. I'm your damned husband and I have a right to make love to my wife if I want. So, don't . . . bloody . . . push . . . me . . . away.' He was holding her down again now, each word punctuated by a shake from the hands gripping her upper arms. She could see perspiration on his top lip, and smell the sour wine on his breath. Oh God, don't let him do this! I can't take it if he does this.

She felt him pulling back the covers now with one hand, the other still holding her down. He was smiling, falling forward on top of her while she made stifled and increasingly panicked motions to hold him off. Her breath was flattened out of her, leaving a whisper that said 'No, no, please don't', over and over. He ripped her nightgown, pushing her back against the pillows, running his hands over her breasts, down her body. She brought her knee up, hard, trying to free it from the tangle of sheet around her legs. He anticipated the move and caught her knee, pushing it back, opening her legs to him. The lamp on the bedside cabinet fell suddenly, knocking against the wall before crashing to the floor. Simon giggled.

'Relax, Ursula. It's not as though we've never made love before for Christ's sake. We're married.' He pulled her nightgown away from her lower body, fitting himself between her legs. She squirmed violently away from him.

'No, Simon! No! Get your damn . . . ' But her words were cut off by the pain of his sudden thrust, upwards, inwards – dry, rasping, thrusting pain. She groaned, feeling him rise up higher on her, stabbing deeper, again and again. It hurt! God, it hurt!

She rolled sideways and he overbalanced, pulling them both over the edge of the bed, slamming down onto the floorboards,

261

his weight crushing her into the floor. He slapped her then. A hard, clean blow to the side of her face. She whimpered in fear but he was enjoying the feeling of total power now and pushed her back, scrabbling at her breasts, thrusting himself at her again. He could do anything to her, she belonged to him. The wine lurched up in his throat and he swallowed it back, giggling again, stabbing. She lay quite still. That took the fun out of things. He tried to make her squirm away again, tried to make her fight him. He'd liked it best that way. But she wouldn't respond. He slapped her. She moaned and lay still. He lay on top of her, gasping, wondering what to do next.

Rhea was asleep when the sound of something heavy being thrown against her wall woke her. She sat up and listened, freezing with the fear that only a child who still believes in ghosts can know. But there were no more heavy thumps, just whisperings, harsh and sibilant from behind the wall. That was her parents' room. She unbent slightly, her heart still beating fast within her ribcage but the aching stillness in her muscles relaxing as she realized it was nothing unnatural making that noise. It was her parents. The whispering stopped and she lay silent, wondering whether to get out of bed and see what was the matter. No, better to stay out of it. Mother was probably arguing with Daddy about money again. She couldn't think what it was that had hit her wall but maybe Daddy had knocked over the hatstand? He tended to forget it was there and often tripped over it in the dark. She wasn't sure what time it was but the night had the feel of total stillness that only comes in the dead hours. She hated being awake at that hour, if she were awake, something could get her. Only if she were sleeping would they leave her alone. And now she was awake and it would be hours before morning.

The whispering had started again. Rhea heard her mother's voice suddenly clearly, through the wood and plaster.

'No, Simon! No! Get your damn . . . ' She stopped abruptly, in mid-speech, and Rhea heard the bed squeaking the way it did when she jumped up and down on it. Mother wouldn't let her do that anymore. Something heavy fell on the floor and then there was a strange sound, almost a clap. Rhea got out of bed and stood, trembling, on the cold floor. She heard her

262

father giggling, high-pitched and staccato, but it didn't reassure her. It sounded too wild. Mother hadn't made another sound and Rhea hesitated between the door and her bed. She wanted to get back into bed and pull the covers over her head; she didn't want to hear her parents fighting. But if they were fighting, why was Daddy laughing? It was strange, and scary. Something was wrong and she should go and make sure, but what if Mother was cross with her for getting out of bed? Rhea whimpered, a thin, reedy breath of sound, torn between anxiety and not wanting to know. There was a groan, and then another clapping sound from next door. Rhea opened her door, walked silently down the hall, avoiding the board that creaked, and paused with her hand raised to knock on her parents' door. There was nothing to be heard now. She knocked softly.

'Daddy? Daddy? Can I come in?' A sudden scrambling noise, like rats on wooden boards, came from inside the door, and then the bed squeaked heavily. Rhea hesitated, her hand on the knob. 'Daddy? Please, Daddy! I'm scared!' She was almost crying, her voice rising in a whine that had nothing to do with bad temper. It was the whine of a child standing in the dark, frightened and unable to get her parents to reply. She knocked again, harder. 'Daddy? Mother?' Then the door opened and her father was standing there, still fully-dressed though his shirt was hanging out and his cravat was missing. Rhea looked at him uncertainly, not liking the way he was breathing so hard or the stillness from within the room. Where was Mother? Daddy's face was all shiny and wet. He wiped his face on his sleeve and then smiled at her.

'Go back to bed, Rhea. Everything's all right. Mummy just had a nightmare. Go to bed, sweetheart, and I'll come and tuck you in, in just a minute. Don't worry, princess, Daddy's here.'

'Is Mother all right? Can I see her?' She didn't know why but she suddenly wanted to see her mother desperately. Just to be sure. Daddy shook his head, a note of anger creeping into his voice.

'Mother's not feeling well right now. She hit her head against the table when she had her nightmare. Now be a big girl Rhea and . . . '

263

'It's all right, Simon. Let Rhea in. I'm better now.' Ursula's voice called from behind Simon and Rhea slipped under her father's arm. The bedclothes were piled up awkwardly on the bed and Rhea couldn't see her mother at first. Then she saw her face, the covers pulled up right to her chin.

'Mother? Did you hurt yourself? You've got a great big red mark on your cheek. Does it hurt?' Rhea climbed onto the bed beside her mother and stared with horror at the blotch disfiguring her mother's face.

'Don't jog the bed, Rhea! Mummy's not well.' That was Simon, hovering over them both, his figure dark against the window. Ursula smiled at Rhea.

'I'm fine, darling. I'm sorry if we . . . I woke you up. It was just a silly nightmare and I jumped out of bed and knocked myself. Don't worry. I'm perfectly fine. Now why don't you let Daddy take you back to bed. He'll read you a story if you want.' Mother's voice was gentle and affectionate, trying to soothe. Rhea nodded, her fears gone.

'All right. If you're sure I can't help. But Daddy doesn't have to read to me. I'm too big for that now, Mother, you know that!' She slid backward off the bed and Simon picked her up around the middle and carried her, squealing and laughing, back to bed.

Ursula closed her eyes, the tears sliding between her lashes and then sideways, down to the hollow of her ear. She raised one arm from beneath the covers and probed the side of her cheekbone with her fingers where the bruise was already forming. It felt soft and painful. The shoulder that was showing from under the covers was bare, the nightgown she had been wearing, ripped and lying in tatters around her body. She shivered, ripples of nausea vibrating up and down her throat and chest. Then she put her hand to her mouth to smother the sounds that kept coming out, try as she would to still them: small, panicked, breathy sounds that rose with each shudder of her chest. Her mind was bleak, not even Billy's memory able to comfort. Then Simon came back.

He stood in the doorway for a long time. Ursula didn't turn to look at him. She kept her eyes shut and her fingers clutched at the covers with white-knuckled fear. She could hear him breathing. Then he turned away and went downstairs. Ursula heard him plumping pillows on the sofa, and then he stretched himself out. The house grew quiet again and she lay staring up at the ceiling. She didn't move for hours. Only when the first light of morning had turned the sky a pale violet and the birds were starting their dawn chorus, did she push back the covers and climb, stiffly, out of bed. Her head ached and her lower-back felt as though it had been crushed. She picked up her dressing-gown and wrapped it tightly around her and then made her way down to the bathroom. She thought she was going to be sick at first but the nausea went away while she sat on the side of the bath and watched the sun rise over the trees in the distance. It was going to be another warm day. Then she ran herself a bath and scrubbed every part of her until her skin was red and angry-looking.

Ursula was dressed and cooking breakfast when Rhea came downstairs. The table was laid for three people and there was toast and marmalade, butter, milk, HP sauce, and coffee in a pot all set out. Simon was sitting at the table reading the paper and Rhea sat down too, smiling with relief. There was nothing the matter. It had just been a nightmare, like Daddy said. Everything else was just her imagination. Daddy and Mother weren't angry at each other. And Daddy would never have hit Mother. He just wouldn't.

'Hallo, sleepyhead. We didn't think we'd wake you since you had such an interrupted night. Do you want some milk?' Simon asked Rhea and she nodded, her attention centred on her mother's back. Ursula didn't turn around.

'Mother? How's your face this morning? D'you have a big bruise?'

'Yes, a bit. I'll have to avoid people for a few days, I suppose.' Ursula laughed self-consciously, her back still to the child as she turned sausages in the frying pan. There was a pause. 'Your Daddy's thinking of taking you up to London with him for a week or two. Would you like that?' Rhea turned large, excited eyes on her father and he nodded.

'Time you saw the bit city again, hmm, sweetheart? Mummy thought it would be nice for you and I think she could do with a little rest herself. So, how about seeing Grandpapa and Julia again. Benjie and Lucy will be up for their hols too and we may all go to the seaside one day. What d'you think?'

He was smiling, his lips pink and wet under his moustache as he took another sip of coffee. Rhea looked up.

'Is Mummy coming too, then?'

'No, princess, Mummy's staying here – she doesn't want to go anywhere with a big, black bruise on her face. Now does she?' He spread marmalade on his toast with concentration.

'But, don't you need someone here to help you, Mother? Won't you be lonely?' Rhea badly wanted to go to London but something was nagging at her. She wished her mother would turn around.

'Oh no, Rhea! Of course I won't be lonely. You're normally away most of the time anyway. I'll miss you but I'll be fine. I think you should go to London. Daddy hasn't taken you anywhere for a long time. It'll be nice for you to be together, just the two of you.' And Julia, and Simon's other children, she added to herself under her breath. Then she picked up the frying pan and rolled the sausages out onto a plate, dabbing at them with greaseproof paper. 'Who wants sausages?' She turned to face the table and Rhea gasped. The bruise spread over the cheekbone and up to the eye-socket so that it looked as though she were a harlequin. Rhea shook her head.

'How did you do that, Mother? I thought you just hit your head on the table? It looks awful! All black and brown and yucky. Like Nessie.' Nessie was Rhea's piebald pony. Ursula laughed, a thin, shaky sound and then put her hand to her cheek.

'It hurts when I laugh, and besides, remember that poem I read you? "Glory be to God for dappled things"? Well, this week I'm dappled.'

'Pied Beauty. Not too beautiful to me!' Rhea said with a laugh. Simon looked blank and vaguely irritated. What were they on about? They were always spouting bits of poetry at each other when all he wanted was a straight answer. Was Rhea coming, or not? It made him uncomfortable to look at Ursula. She'd brought it on herself by being so damned cold and pushing him away. But he didn't like to think he'd done that. Not even when he was drunk. Was Rhea coming? He wanted to be away by eleven. She'd better make her mind up fast.

'That's right. Good girl, I didn't think you'd remember it all

266

that time. When you come back we'll read some more, if you like.' Ursula put two sausages down on Rhea's plate. Then she put the rest on a plate in the middle of the table. Simon helped himself.

'You could call it your "rose-mole", couldn't you?' Rhea said suddenly with a laugh. Ursula smiled and leaned down to kiss her daughter's cheek. There was hope for Rhea yet. Simon hadn't got all of her.

The last two sausages should have been hers but she couldn't face the thought of food. Instead, once the others were finished, she chopped the sausages into small pieces and put the plate down beside her chair. Sheba jumped down from the window-sill and sniffed carefully. Then she turned away and walked out the back door. Simon smiled.

Ursula saw them off an hour later, having spent most of the time with Rhea deciding what she should take. Lucy was quite a fashionable young lady of sixteen and Benjie, at fourteen, was old enough to appreciate how a girl looked. Rhea prattled happily about how much fun it would be to see them again and Ursula kept packing steadily. She didn't direct a word towards Simon, just spoke round him, or through him, to Rhea: 'Daddy thinks', or 'Daddy will be getting impatient.' Rhea was too happy to notice. Then, at last, they were off and Ursula waved goodbye, her bruised face uncomfortably warm in the sun. She retreated to the kitchen to put her old sunhat on and tie it comfortably under her chin. It folded down over the side of her face and made her feel easier. Then she went to work in the garden. The asparagus were growing wild. She picked up her secateurs and advanced on them with deter-mination.

Intent on cutting a particularly stubborn stalk, Ursula didn't hear the sound of footsteps on gravel. A shadow fell over her and she looked up quickly, alarmed. It was Tim.

'Strewth! What the hell happened to you?' He knelt down beside her in a quick, abrupt way that made Ursula jerk away from him. She pulled the hat further around her face.

'I bumped into a table in the night.'

'Bull! No table did that to you unless it came at you through the air. Did Simon do this? The bastard!' He was white under his tan. Ursula felt his anger coming across in waves, each one stronger than the last. She straightened and turned so that her face was away from him.

'I hit it on a table. Now please just leave. I don't want to talk to anyone right now.' Her voice trembled. Why did Tim have to see this? Why had he come over, without even a phone call to say he was on his way? Damn him!

'Where's Rhea?'

'Uh, she went to London with Simon for a little while. To see her grandparents and the rest of the family.' There, now let him go. But he didn't seem to have any intention of going. Ursula bit her lip. 'I . . . I don't need your help, thank you Tim. I know you're always offering it, but I really don't need it. So, if you wouldn't mind excusing me . . . '

'I would mind. I do mind. Look, who d'yer think you're fooling? Damn it, Ursula, I'm not blind. I know what's going on. Why d'you stay?' He had taken her elbow, pulling her over towards him so that he could see her face more clearly. She didn't resist. Instead she felt tired and weak, her belly empty and shaken, as though her insides had been pulled out of her. Gentle fingers pushed back her hat so that it hung, by its strings, from her neck and he ran his thumb down her cheekbone. She could see a glimpse of white teeth between his lips and sweat beaded over the top lip. Her face lost colour and he slipped an arm around her.

'You shouldn't be out here working in the sun. With a bruise like that you could have concussion, for Christ's sake. Come on. Let's get you sitting down in the cool.' He was leading her down the path and she laughed.

'You're always picking me up and looking after me like I was some sort of invalid. I'm sorry, Tim, really. I hardly ever get . . . well, sick, I suppose, you could say. I'm normally as healthy and fit as you could hope for.'

'And if your damned husband stayed away completely, I guess you'd stay that way. I suppose being happy doesn't count?' He was angry. Ursula shook her head.

'Don't . . . please. I can manage if you leave it alone. But if you start poking and probing into things, I don't know. It's just easier to leave it be. Please.' He was sitting her down in a wicker chair just outside the kitchen door. The sun was behind the cottage and created a small ledge of shade. He sat down on the doorstep beside her.

'Sorry. I don't have the right to tell you how to live your life. I just hate to see you throwing it away. You're too . . . ' He stopped abruptly and took a breath. 'Well, sorry. I'll keep my nose out of it.'

'You'll have to. You're going away again soon and if I start getting dependent on you, and then you're gone, it won't be good – worse than now. So don't, all right?' Ursula wasn't looking at him but out, across the sun-bleached garden and the dry, caked soil of the beds. She needed to water, she thought. Tim shifted beside her, but she didn't turn. She couldn't bear to look at him and not touch. He said, after a pause:

'I've got some things to take care of at home. A problem that needs sorting out. That's partly why I came away. It's easier to see things from a distance.'

'That's what you said to me about Rhea. Have you come up with any solutions for either problem?'

'Yeah. But I can't . . . I need some time to deal with things. Ursula?'

'Yes?'

'I'm not like this normally. I want you to know I don't interfere with married people. It's their life to lead and their problems to sort out. But it's not like you're even really married. Simon doesn't live with you. He just turns up when he feels like it. Does a bit of shooting, or riding, sees his daughter if she's here, and then heads back to London. I know all about it.'

'Who told you?'

'Nan told me some. And Hugh and Lettice told me the rest. They weren't gossiping for the sake of gossiping; they care, and they're worried. Looking at your face today I can see why. Simon was pretty drunk last night. I should've stayed to help.'

'There! You're doing it again. Tim I don't want and I don't need your help! Who appointed you saviour this week? Because that's what you're doing. And you know the really scary thing is that I'm getting to like being fussed over and having someone take care of things. And what's going to happen when you go? Hmm? Think about that and don't damned well tell me you should've been there to help. What exactly d'you think you could've done anyway? Besides, he's never hit me before.'

'Oh, and that makes everything all right then? I'll just sit back and watch him bash you black and blue and then you can tell me he's only done it once before, or twice before, or whatever! And what else did he do to you, while he was giving you a taste of his fist? Huh?' His voice was bitter. Ursula didn't reply. A chicken was scratching its way over the newly-turned celery bed and, watching it, Ursula suddenly knew what it felt like. Scratching away for the odd worm all day long, its eggs taken away before they can hatch, knowing it was destined eventually for the soup pot. Some life. Her mouth quirked.

He sighed. 'Okay, okay . . . ' He held up a hand and then let it drop, the action as defeated as his words. Then he added, in an attempt to keep some conversation going. 'How many chooks you got?' Tim was watching the bird too.

'Ten. I prefer to let them free-range. I get more for the eggs and it's less bother feeding, or coping with grubs.'

'So who finds the eggs?'

She shrugged. 'I do, or Rhea when she's here. Rhea still thinks it's a game and she's pretty good at second-guessing the chickens for hiding places. I just watch them all day long, so I know where they go.'

'Sounds like an exciting sort of life.'

Ursula shifted impatiently. 'Get off my back, Tim! What gives you the right to judge?' She turned around, her eyes dark and angry. He was staring at the ground, his arms across his knees and his hands clasped together. He looked up when she said that, and stared at her in silence. After a few minutes he looked down at the ground again and sighed.

'Nothing. I . . . Nothing.' The silence stretched out between them and Ursula turned back to stare across the garden again. Why didn't he say something if he loved her? Love! How could it be love in only three days? The whole thing was ridiculous. So, why did he continue sitting there, not saying a word? And why was he so ready to get involved, to help her out, if she would just let him? It could only be because he cared about her. He hadn't said anything about when he would return to Australia. He just kept offering his help. It wasn't his help she needed! She needed him to turn around and say that he loved her, and she needed him to ask her to come with him. That's what she needed. He wasn't listening to her thoughts.

'Where did your step-mum, was it, come from in Australia? You said she was from there, didn't you?'

'Perth, or rather, just outside. A place called Gidgeeganup. I inherited the property when she died. I've never even seen it. It's just sitting there, as far as I know. Have you ever been to Perth?'

'No. It's too far. I hear it's a beaut place though. Nice beaches and set right on a big river, kinda like Melbourne but different. I hear it's more modern and more American in style. Less of the Victoriana Melbourne's famous for.' He seemed anxious to talk about anything that didn't involve them too closely. Ursula smiled wearily.

'Simon left two bottles of white wine, believe it or not, last night. Would you like some?'

'Oh look, why not? We might as well get blotto. There's not much else we're allowed to do.' He laughed and she joined him. God, why was life so difficult sometimes. The one man she'd ever wanted, really wanted, as a woman and he turned out to have as many scruples as she did. If not more. But that was probably why she wanted him. She laughed again and stood up.

'Come on. Let's raid the cellar. At least it'll be cool down there.'

It was almost dark by the time Ursula held up her glass and announced she was successfully drunk. Tim smiled from the sofa where he had sprawled himself after they had finished the second bottle. Now they were working their way through Simon's special reserve wine, enjoying it all the more for the anguish it would cause Simon when he found out. Tim offered to fill Ursula's glass again but she shook her head, the room swimming for a moment as she did so.

'Oh no, I've definitely overdone it. My God, the wonder of it is - I don't care! We've posh . . . polished off nearly four bottles this afternoon and I just feel - floaty, not bad, or anything, but not totally right either. You know?' She had been carefully wending her way across the room to pull the curtains but on the return journey her legs suddenly gave out, bending under her like rubber. She sank to her knees in

271

surprise and burst out laughing. Tim laughed too and stood up. He had drunk the lion's share of the four bottles but he was far less bothered by it than Ursula. But then, as he pointed out to Ursula as he picked her up and slung her across his shoulder, he'd been brought up in the land of booze.

'Boozing Aussies! I've heard about you,' Ursula said from over his shoulder, as he carried her up the stairs. He laughed again and agreed with her.

'Too right, my love. We're just a land of crude barbarians with thick heads. But at this point you should be glad I've got a thick head 'cos who else is going to see you to bed? Hmm?'

'No-one. I don't want anyone else to see me to bed. Only you.' She laughed again and Tim put her down carefully across her bed, cradling her head and neck in his hand as she fell backward. He wasn't going to stay, he said, but she pulled him down beside her. 'To hell with scruples, Tim. No-one else bothers. Why should we?' He smiled and kissed her gently.

'I don't know, Ursula. I really don't know. But,' he pitched his voice higher and gave her a wink. 'Will you still respect me in the morning?' She laughed and snuggled in closer, kissing his neck and then his ear. Tim's smile became tender and then faded altogether when he looked at her. 'You know I'm in love with you, don't you?' he said and she nodded, her face as serious as his. With one finger he traced the bruise down her eyebrow, across her cheekbone and then he moved it along her jaw and tilted her chin towards him. 'Don't be sorry, love, promise me that?'

'The only thing I'm sorry about is that I didn't meet you before I met Simon. I wish . . . ' He kissed her before she could tell him what she wished and then she couldn't remember, her thoughts filled with the wonder of his hard body, the smoothness of his back under the shirt, the feel of him tight against her, the smell of his skin. She rubbed her hand across his shoulderblades, fitting her fingers under the bone, down his back, moving her hands in circles while he held her pinned against him. He wasn't like Simon, he wasn't rough or impatient, he didn't pinch at her breasts but cupped them gently and kissed them so that she lost her sense of the present and was wholly lost in him and his caresses. Later he cradled her in his arms, murmuring endearments, letting his hand

272

sweep down the curve of her hip, fitting her in tight against him. She went to sleep with her face pressed against his shoulder and his breath on her cheek.

When Ursula woke in the morning she expected Tim to be beside her, his naked body twisted up in the sheets as he had been last night. Instead the bed was empty and she was alone. She sat up and looked around but his clothes were gone from the floor. Even his shoes were missing. Her dressing-gown was hanging on the hat-rack and she got up and put it on, wandering to the door in vague disquiet. He must still be here. Maybe he was having a bath? The bathroom was as neat as she had left it, although a towel was folded up on the hamper as though it had been used. She walked back down the passage-way and paused at the top of the stairs.

'Tim? Tim? Are you down there?' There was no reply. 'Tim?' She went down the stairs, expecting at any moment that he would appear from the kitchen, but he didn't. He wasn't anywhere to be seen. Ursula swallowed back the pain that was trying to rise in her throat, and went quickly to the front door. His car was gone. She felt like she ought to sink to the ground, or burst into loud, hysterical sobs. Instead she just closed the door and went back into the kitchen. Her head was pounding dully and she felt sick. She sat down at the table and stared blankly at the kitchen wall. He was out shopping. He'd gone to check on his grandmother. He . . . but she had run out of ideas. He would be back; she knew it. A man didn't tell you he loved you, and then make love to you, and walk out of your life before you woke up. Not a man like Tim. He'd be back.

She went back upstairs and bathed and dressed, pulling the sheets from the bed and carrying them down to the laundry-room. Then she made the bed up afresh and tidied up the bottles and glasses from the sitting room. With the windows open and a fresh breeze blowing the curtains into billows, she sat down again and looked at her watch. It was nearly ten. Where could he be? She stared at the telephone, hesitating. Then she picked it up and rang Mrs Chadwick's number. Tim answered the phone; his voice sounded guarded.

'Tim? It's me, Ursula. What happened? Why did you leave? I've been half out of my mind worrying what happened to you.'

'Oh . . . look. I was coming over to see you in a while. You

273

were fast asleep when I left you and I didn't think you'd be awake yet. I called Nan's early this morning – just to check she was all right and so she wouldn't worry. She doesn't sleep much anymore. She . . . there was a telegram for me. I have to go home. I, I need to talk to you. I'll be over in a few minutes, all right?'

'It's not bad news, is it? None of your family's ill?'

'No, it's to do with that problem I was talking about. Look, I'll see you soon. I've got to go, love.'

'All right. Bye Tim.' She hung up, the momentary surge that his calling her 'love' had given her dying away to a dull anxiety. He had sounded strange. And why had the telegram come just then to call him home. It was very convenient. Maybe he was just like all the rest? But even as she thought it, she knew it wasn't so. And she paced the floor, waiting for the sound of the car.

It was nearly half an hour before his car came to a halt outside the front door. Ursula willed herself to sit down and wait for him to come to her. She mustn't seem too anxious, too frightened. The car door slammed and she heard his footsteps on the stone of the front hall and then he walked into the kitchen. For a moment, the sight of him shook her. He was so beautiful and dear, every part of him pleasing her. She wanted to go to him and put her arms around his neck, kiss his mouth, feel him against her. But she continued to sit at the table, while he stood there, trying to find the words to explain. Ursula could see the struggle and felt herself withering again. He hadn't made any promises, she reminded herself. Was he trying to tell her that it had been wonderful but that was all there was to it? No, a part of her whispered, it hadn't been like that; he loved her. She watched, dumb with pain, wanting to hear him speak, to say anything, just as long as he spoke. Tim put his hand to his forehead as though it hurt him.

'Hangover?' The word forced itself past Ursula's lips, as involuntary as her breathing. He shook his head and sat down opposite her at the table.

'I've got to go home. Things . . . oh shit! I'm sorry, love. I just . . . have to go home for a while. Sort this out.' She took a deep breath. He did love her. Everything would be all right. It would! Whatever this problem was, he would sort it out. He

274

was staring at her with such concern, that she had to glance away, her voice blurred with tears.

'I don't understand. What problem is this? Are you married, for God's sake? What?' He gave a snorting bitter laugh, and took her hand in his.

'No, love. Look, I can't . . . don't want to explain it all to you right now. I need to get back as soon as I can, and then I'll deal with it. I'll sort it out somehow. You know I love you. Don't make this any harder than it is. Please.' He squeezed her hand tightly in his. She shrugged.

'If that's the way you want it. I know you're not the type . . . I trust you. Will you write to me when you get there? Or . . . ' She realized suddenly that he had never mentioned her coming out to Australia, never mentioned a future for them both, together. But he was smiling so tenderly, and gripping her hand so tightly, that she couldn't believe he didn't love her or want her beside him. He nodded.

'I'll write. As soon as I can, love. Will you hold on a little longer? Can you do that, for me?'

'Yes. But, what . . . ?' She took a deep breath. 'I need to get a few things clear here, Tim. What's going to happen once you sort out your problem? Is there any future for us? I need to know.' He was silent for a moment.

'Yes! Yes! We're going to work this out. I'm not leaving you. I can't. God!' He seemed to be arguing with himself. Ursula felt cold. He looked at her, holding her gaze firmly. 'I'll send you the fare for the passage. Don't worry, love. It'll be all right.'

'And Rhea? We need to talk about that. Are you prepared to take on another man's daughter?' She saw him start, as though the thought had never occurred to him. His mind was turning over the possibilities while he sat there.

'Bring Rhea. She'll be better with us than Simon. I like her, and without Simon putting a spanner in the works all the time, she'll be all right. She's a good kid.' Ursula smiled. Her lips felt cracked and dry as she licked them.

'All right then, darling. I'll wait for you to write.' She leaned forward and kissed the hand holding hers.

After he had left, she put on her sunhat and returned to her work in the garden. It was almost as though the twenty-four

275

hours in between had never happened. She wondered if it weren't her imagination, or perhaps brought on by the blow. Her cheek today was at the peak of its colour. It would take another week for it to disappear completely. Then she might, just for the hell of it, go up to London and surprise everyone. Yes, that might be well worth it. She hoped Julia would be as broad-minded about it as she was.

She smiled at the thought and rocked back on her heels, looking over the garden. It was beautiful, she thought with a pang. The vegetables were arranged in patterns of colour and shape, cabbages, broccoli, kale, brussels sprouts, cauliflowers – all as lovingly arranged as a herbaceous border – edged by low hedges to protect them from the wind, patches of lawn, lavender, mint, and bricked paths entwined between them. Arcs of water shook out from the two sprinklers, scenting the air with wet greenery. She had made it beautiful herself – all alone. And it was hers. Could she bear to go back to being dependent on a man again? What if it didn't work out? What if she suddenly had to support herself and Rhea with no husband, no home, no money? Was Tim worth that risk?

Ursula passed the rest of the week in an agony of indecision. Tim called to say he was leaving but had not come round to see her. He had asked her to wait. And that's all she could do. Gradually her cheek became smoothly tanned again, the bruise just a memory. Like Tim; just a memory.

On the following Monday, Ursula dressed herself in her cream dress, put a large straw hat on her head, gloves on her hands, and calmly walked to the station. Time to go to London. It would only be for the day but she wanted to see how Rhea got on with Julia and the other children. Maybe it would be best to leave her with them for a while, not take a risk with her life, until things were sorted out with Tim. The thought had grown in conviction until Ursula felt it necessary to go to town and surprise them all; see how their relationship really was. She wasn't thinking of leaving Rhea for good, just until she was settled with Tim and could offer a stable home. Simon would kick up a fuss of course. She'd have to work a way round that.

But when she got to town, she found things weren't quite as she had expected. There was an atmosphere of tension that had little to do with her presence. It was entirely to do with Rhea.

Julia had pretended pleasure, inviting Ursula into the drawing room and sending Ruth to call the girls down from their rooms. It was after lunch already and Julia said she couldn't spare Ursula very much time because she had to go out in an hour.

'That's perfectly all right, Julia. I didn't give you much warning, after all. I just thought I'd spend the day with Rhea – and Lucy if she would like. I haven't seen Lucy in such a long time. I hardly recognize her each time I see her.' Ursula sat herself in the same wing-chair she had occupied the night Simon's and her engagement had been announced. She looked across at Julia. Time was being kind to her, Ursula thought with slight resentment. Still a little overweight but that seemed to keep the skin smooth, the wrinkles at bay.

'Actually, that's what Lucy says about you each time she sees you. What do you do with yourself in the country? I'd be bored stiff. Ah, here are the girls. Rhea, dear, here's your mother come to see you.' Julia's voice had an edge to it that Ursula couldn't mistake.

'Mother! What brings you here? Is your cheek all right now?' said Rhea, in her artless way, prattling out the information that Ursula had sought to keep private. But Julia didn't seem interested. Instead, she began to suggest in a halting, delicate way, that Rhea might want to return to the country with Ursula.

'Not perhaps immediately but we are rather full up right at the moment and you only have the school holidays with Rhea, don't you? Not very long, after all.'

'But Rhea's only been up here a week. Simon intended her to stay at least a fortnight. Is there some problem then, Julia? Or has my unexpected presence just put this into your mind. I don't think Simon would be very pleased, you know.' Ursula reminded Julia that it was not her idea that Rhea come up to town. Quite the reverse.

Julia laughed, the musical sound giving way to a more brittle one. 'Not at all, Ursula. In fact, I'm almost relieved to see you.' She looked across at the girls. 'Why don't you two go and see if cook's got any of her lemon cake left. I'd like a quick word with Ursula in private, if you don't mind.' Lucy looked fully aware of what that quiet word would entail; Rhea looked embarrassed. They got up immediately and left the room. When Julia turned back to face Ursula, she found her looking rather grim. Julia lifted her hands in a helpless gesture and gave a half-laugh that hinted emotion, of any sort, was quite beyond what she wanted to deal with. She began haltingly.

'Rhea's being rather trying, you know. Rather difficult altogether,' Julia clasped her elegant hands together, admiring her rings. 'She won't sleep in with Lucy and she won't even talk to Benjie. Goodness knows what's the matter with her. Simon doesn't seem to notice tension within the house – just like a man! But it's beginning to disrupt my life and I am rather tired of it. I wouldn't mind if I thought Rhea had a good reason but both Lucy and Benjie have done their best to make Rhea feel at home. Would you please have a word with your child? After all, you must teach her some manners sometime and she is a guest in this house. I'm very surprised at her behaviour.' Julia glanced crossly at the door through which Rhea had exited. Ursula, sitting with a stiff back in the wing-chair raised her eyebrows slowly. 'Really?'

Lucy halted in the corridor, glancing back over her shoulder at the girl who trailed so hesitantly after her. Rhea's face had a pinched-in look and Lucy thought how annoyingly similar she was to Simon. Much more so than herself. That was so unfair when it was her mother Simon had always loved, not Rhea's. Lucy felt a stab of irritation.

'Mother's going to tell Ursula how badly you've been behaving. She's quite tired of it, you know. I can't think why you aren't more polite, considering we're putting you up and all. But then, your mother was just my nanny so how can you be expected to behave properly. Mother's quite shocked and Benjie thinks you're an awful bore to be with. I agree.' Lucy paused in the still room, sampling a macaroon that cook had put aside for her own tea. Rhea glared at her. What she wouldn't like to say to this wretched girl, she thought. This girl who always hung on Simon as though she had more claim to him than his own daughter. And Benjie! He was altogether impossible, rude, arrogant, constantly needling with veiled jibes that Rhea couldn't quite fathom but which left her anxious and short of breath.

'What would you know about it, Miss Snooty? My mother was much richer before the war than your mother could even imagine. She had dozens of servants and a huge house and horses and . . . and she only became a nanny here because your mother knew she was special and wanted to be friends with her. Daddy's told me all about it and in front of your mother too, so if it weren't true Julia would've said. But she didn't. She just agreed with everything Daddy said. So there!' Rhea pushed past Lucy into the kitchen. Cook wasn't there. Lucy followed her, her face tight with annoyance.

'You're always going on and on about what "Daddy" said. You hardly even know Simon compared to us and I know a lot better what Simon says about your mother. And it isn't complimentary. So don't try and get superior with me! Simon's my family too and he's much happier up here with us than down in that boring, tedious little cottage with you two yokels.'

Rhea's chin came up stubbornly. But, unlike Lucy, she was determined to keep from saying anything that might then be used against her. She wasn't going to be the one to start the fight.

'You keep saying things like that, Lucy, all the time! I don't mind when Daddy's up here. He has to work, after all. You're the one who seems to mind. You mind him coming down to us!'

'That's not so! He's hardly ever there anyway. It's just you clinging to him all the time. "Daddy, can we do this? Daddy can we do that?" He isn't just yours. He's ours too!' Lucy dipped a long finger through the bowl of cream. She knew she'd unnerved the girl in front of her. She smiled.

Rhea hated that smile. It was so cruelly knowing, some dark secret that she meant to lay on you where it most hurt.

'What d'you mean "yours"? He's my father!' Rhea demanded, the vague hints and taunts from Lucy, and Benjie too, frightening her. Lucy smiled. She was tempted to ignore her mother's warnings of the past. She was tired of this pretence, and tired of this child who made such obvious claims on Simon's loyalty. Why weren't her own claims equally valid? She narrowed her eyes.

'Don't push it, Rhea, or you'll hear things you don't want to. Things I'm not supposed to tell you but I will . . . if you're not careful.'

'You're a liar.' The scorn in Rhea's voice was like a whip.

279

'You don't know anything. You're just trying to frighten me into believing you do, like a witch. You'll be the one who'll be sorry when Daddy hears what you've been saying. He's my Daddy and he'll listen to me.'

And then it was too late, the words were blurted out in anger and jealousy before Lucy could stop them.

'He's mine too! He was my father long before he was yours! And he lives with us because he loves us. He loves my mother, not yours! He only married Ursula to put people off about how much he loves my mother. We're his family, not you!' She picked up a spoon and threw it at Rhea. Rhea ducked.

'That's not true! You're a bloody liar! You bitch, you lying bitch! Daddy isn't, he isn't! I'll make you pay for that! I'll make you eat your lying, filthy words. It isn't true!' Rhea was screaming, her face streaking with tears as she launched herself on the taunting, beautiful face across the room. Lucy fell backwards under the onslaught, her hand reaching for Rhea's hair. She tugged it hard.

'Tis so! He's mine and he hates you both. He hates having to see you. He hates everything about you. It's us he loves. You hear me? Simon loves us!' She picked up the cream bowl, raising it above her head.

'No he doesn't! You're a liar, a filthy rotten liar!' Rhea saw the bowl coming towards her but, with her hair held tightly in Lucy's other hand, she was unable to avoid it. It smashed sickeningly against her head, dollops of cream mixing with blood. She screamed.

'Mummy! Mummee!'

Lucy was frightened now and tried to quieten Rhea, holding her hand over her mouth, pushing her down to the floor.

'Shut up, Rhea! Shut up. You're not badly hurt. It's just a cut. Shut up, for God's sake . . . or I'll really hurt you!' Rhea continued to scream.

Then there was the sound of running feet and Ursula burst through the door, Julia a few paces behind her. They stopped, appalled at the scene before them.

'Let her go, you little animal!' Ursula stepped forward two paces and knocked Lucy away from Rhea, bending over the blood-streaked head and cradling it in her arms. Lucy fell back against the table.

'It wasn't my fault. She suddenly started hitting me, throwing things at me. I was just defending myself. Mother?'

'Be quiet, Lucy! We'll sort out the blame later. How is she, Ursula? Is it a bad cut?'

Julia raised her hand to stop any further outbursts. Ursula's hold tightened on Rhea's waist and she sat on the floor, hugging her daughter, trying to stem the anguished tears. She could see already that the cut wasn't serious; it was the emotional injuries she was more worried about. She looked across at Lucy who, at sixteen, had become a younger and more delicate version of her mother. Lucy, in control again now, looked back coolly. Ursula would learn nothing there.

'Rhea, darling. It's all right. I'm here now. I won't let Lucy touch you again. Shh, sweetheart, don't cry like that. You'll make yourself sick. Can't you tell me what it's all about?'

Julia laughed, a small still sound. 'Oh dear, girls will be girls. Still, Lucy was only defending herself. I think you'll have to agree Ursula that this is exactly what I've been talking about. Rhea's becoming impossible.' She smiled and brushed back the hair from her daughter's face. 'Of course, Rhea's just a child still. I tend to forget. Lucy and Benjamin were always mature for their age. I suppose it's to do with the way Rhea's brought up in the country. No sophistication. One really can't blame her at all.'

'Blame her for what? Being a nine-year-old child who's been attacked by one almost twice her age? Blame her for bleeding all over your kitchen while Lucy there, who says she had to defend herself, hasn't a mark on her?' Ursula's voice became as cool as Julia's. Her arm tightened around her daughter and she turned and smiled at her. 'What happened, sweetheart? What made Lucy hit you like that?' But Rhea wasn't in a fit state to answer. Ursula hugged her. 'Would you rather come home with me tonight?' Rhea nodded, gripping tightly onto Ursula.

'Rhea was just peeved because Simon spends more time up here with us. But, as I pointed out, we're family too, aren't we, Mother?' Lucy's voice was mocking, her tone stressing the word 'family'. 'I was only trying to calm her down but she went crazy, picking things up and throwing them at me, hitting

281

me. I didn't mean to hit her so hard. I was just trying to shock her into behaving herself. She's got a ferocious temper.'

'Yes, I can see that. Lots of things thrown round the room aren't there Lucy? And such a good way of getting a child to calm down. Smashing a cream bowl over her head. Full marks, my dear. And I don't suppose you'd like to tell us what set Rhea off? Did you happen to say something to her that you, perhaps, shouldn't have?' Ursula held Rhea tightly, soothing her with any words that came to mind. Rhea knelt beside her mother, laying her head in her lap. She hiccuped through her misery, burying her head in Ursula's dress while her mother held her gently, stroking her hair, murmuring endearments.

'I couldn't help it. Rhea kept demanding to know and she was being such a little witch about it all. Anyway, don't my rights come into it at all? Simon is my father and was long before Rhea ever existed. I shouldn't have to put up with her telling me he's "her Daddy" all the time! Should I, Mother?' And now Lucy was squeezing out a few tears, claiming her share of the sympathy. Julia dabbed a handkerchief against her daughter's face.

Well, it had had to come out eventually, Ursula thought. But Rhea was still so young. And it shouldn't have been like this. 'Shh, my love, shh, Mummy's here, shh.' There was a long pause while everyone gathered strength, only the sound of Rhea's sobbing breaking the stillness. Then Julia sighed.

'Oh dear! That's rather put the cat amongst the pigeons, hasn't it? Simon will be cross. You really are naughty, Lucy.' But her smile was satisfied with her daughter's performance. Ursula looked at them both and then down at the little girl crying in her arms. She turned back to Julia, her smile equally cold.

'Well done, Julia! What a sophisticated young lady you've got there! Happy now? You've just ruined a child's life between the two of you. Well, just one little thing before we go. Do tell Simon I've taken his legitimate child home because his bastard doesn't have any manners! And tell him not to bother coming down. I'm sure he fits here with all of you much better.' And with that Ursula led the still sobbing Rhea out of Julia's house for good.

'So now what? It's your decision.'

'I won't see him! I don't want to ever see him again! He's not my father anymore. I . . . disown him!'

'Even though he cares about you? What happened with Lucy and Benjie, well, that was long before you were born. Long before Daddy met me even. He loves you a lot, you know. I've had him on the telephone most of last night and all this morning.' Yes, she thought, ranting on about how Lucy was provoked into attacking Rhea by my presence in the house. Oh, Julia had really been working on him.

'He wants to come down and see you, to explain. He's very angry with Julia and Lucy.' And me. Ursula sat at the long table in the cottage's kitchen, drinking coffee. A puffy-faced and still weepy Rhea sat opposite her, the cut nothing more than a red line across the left temple. There didn't seem to be much to say.

'He has no right to . . . to anything anymore! Not to me, not to you. Why didn't you tell me, Mummy? Why did you let me think you were being so difficult when all the time it was Daddy!' More tears seeped out beneath Rhea's tightly closed eyes. She looked ill.

'Just because of how badly you feel now, sweetheart. How was I supposed to tell you? I wish you didn't know still. Lucy's a little . . . well, she takes after her mother, that's all. But you know what Lucy said isn't true – not the bit about Daddy not caring about you. Of course he does! You're the most important thing in the world to him.' She hesitated. 'But right now he's angry and not thinking very clearly. I'm afraid there's more bad news, Rhea. Your Daddy says,' she sighed and took her daughter's hand. 'Daddy says if you won't see him, then he won't pay your school fees anymore. He won't pay anything anymore. I don't think he means it, he's just upset. And anyway, I can go to your grandpapa and ask him for some money. We won't starve, darling. I promise you that! Everything will be all right.'

'Tim said it was Daddy's fault and that I'd see that after a while. He said you put up with a lot. I'm so sorry, Mother. I've made things very difficult for you, haven't I? And it was Daddy being selfish and mean all along.' Rhea squeezed her mother's hand back, not seeing the tentative hope in Ursula's eyes. Maybe this was the chance to sound Rhea out about going to Australia. Maybe it had all happened for the best.

'Umm, did you like Tim very much, sweetheart? I mean . . . ' she brushed back her hair and took another deep breath. 'How would you like it if we were to go and live with him in Australia? He wouldn't be your Daddy exactly but he'd be your friend and . . . and, maybe, in time, my husband. If you like, that is . . . ' Her cheeks were flushed red and she could barely look her daughter in the eye. When she did, she was surprised by the expression she read there. It was a mixture of elation, hope, and just a little bitterness. Rhea had thought Tim perfect in every way, Ursula realized, and perhaps she now thought less of him? Or perhaps she thought less of her mother?

'Really? All the way to Australia? For good?' Rhea asked and Ursula nodded. She saw her daughter mulling the thought around.

'Would I have to see Daddy again?'

'No, darling. Not if you don't want to. No court in the land would grant him the right if you didn't want it. And anyway, it's so far away I doubt your Daddy would get much time to come down . . . unless you want him to.'

'I don't! Not ever! Would I go to a nice school and have my own horse like here? Could I take Nessie with me? And Sheba?'

'No, darling. Nessie and Sheba will have to stay here. Lettice will take Sheba, I'm sure, and Mr Clow said he would buy Nessie when you got too big for her. They'll be looked after, don't worry. And of course you can go to a nice school down in Australia. And I expect Tim will let you have a horse. Everyone rides in Australia. It's such a big place and there's so much land down there. And it's much warmer than here. They hardly ever get any snow, you know. And Christmas time is hot. It's summer down there then. Everything's topsy-turvy. Can you cope with that, sweetheart? Because if you can't, well, we won't go. That's all. I'll get grandpapa to pay for things and we'll just go on living here – the two of us.' But even as Ursula said it, she knew it sounded hollow and depressing. Rhea looked at her.

'Are you and Tim having an affair like Daddy and Julia?'

284

She was far too young to know of such things, Ursula thought, going red with embarrassment.

'No, darling. Not like . . . them. But Tim loves me and I love him. And he wants us both to come down and live with him in Australia. He likes you very much and says you'll be better off living with us. But I won't go if you don't like the idea. You needn't think I'll leave you or that I'll make you come down. I won't. It's entirely up to you.'

Rhea stood up from the table and carried the cups and saucers over to the sink. She placed them in it carefully and then stared out the back window at the garden and fields beyond. Sheba was outside, rolling in the dust. Rhea stood there for several minutes.

'And I never have to see Daddy again? We can leave right now and he won't know where we've gone?'

'I'll have to ring and find out how soon we could get tickets, Rhea. I don't know at this stage. I'm supposed to wait until I hear from Tim. And I think you should see Daddy one more time before you make a decision. You may find he's very sorry and that you forgive him. Just, please, don't tell him anything about Tim.' Ursula had come up behind her daughter and placed her hands on Rhea's shoulders. The two of them stared out the window.

'No. I don't want to see him. Ring now, Mother. Find out about the tickets. I want to get out of here. Please!' She was crying again. Ursula kissed the top of her head.

'All right, darling. I'll do my best.'

Chapter Eighteen

Melbourne, November 1956

South Yarra lay along Toorak Road, a sleepy suburb basking in early summer sun. Bougainvillaea spilled over walls, splashing red, orange, yellow against the brighter green lawns. Striped shadows from the wrought-iron verandah overhead laced the ground and the smell of sun on hot earth reminded Ursula of the East. Some of the tension eased around her eyes. She sat on the low stone wall, near the corner shop, and peered at the money in her hand.

'Here, darling. You go and get us a couple of drinks and I'll try phoning again. Once we know what we're doing, I'll have a better idea what to do with the trunks.'

They had only arrived that morning, the Northern Star docking against the stone pier with a lumbering grace. And their trunks were now sitting in the Left Luggage office, waiting, like themselves, for a place to go. Ursula hadn't wanted to turn up in a taxi with trunks spilling out, as though they were taking over Tim's life without a word of consent. It seemed so presumptuous. Rhea thought she was being silly. So now they were in the middle of suburban Melbourne, near the Botanical Gardens, and Rhea was buying them drinks.

Ursula turned her face up to the sun, squinting into it. There was a strength to the rays that England never achieved, like golden spears of heat. She basked in it, thinking everything could be managed as long as it was sunny; even the potential embarrassment of turning up at Tim's door unannounced.

She hadn't known how to find him at first but had relied on the telephone directory. There weren't that many T. Nowltons around. Only three. And she'd hit the right one on only her second try. Tim had answered, his voice flowering over her like a warm blanket, enveloping and protecting. She loved that voice so much! And suddenly she hadn't been able to answer, the questioning hallos ignored. She'd rung off, flustered. She'd never been good on the telephone, saying sharp words when she meant to be gentle, running out of anything to say when an answer was the most important thing. No, she wouldn't call back. That would make things worse. She'd go see him in person. That was much the best way. In person.

Rhea came back with two lemonades, straws bobbing out of the bottles.

'Did you get hold of him yet?' She was totally sure Tim would want to see them. Much surer than Ursula herself. Oh, if only they'd waited for his letter. But Rhea had been so desperate to get away, to never see Simon again. And then when Shaw Savil had said there were two berths available due to a cancellation and that if they turned them down, it could be months before another came up, well . . . it had seemed so stupid just to wait for a confirming letter. Tim had said he wanted them. There was no real reason to wait, after all.

Sitting on that wall, Ursula wished she had waited. The sound of his voice had unnerved her and she felt quite light-headed. Rhea tugged her arm.

'Mother? Did you get hold of Tim yet?' Ursula started.

'No, still not. But it doesn't matter really. We know which one must be him.'

'Didn't he answer the telephone the first time you tried him? I thought you'd spoken with him.'

'Uh, no. It was just a process of elimination. The other two definitely aren't Tim, so the one in South Yarra must be. Right?' She sipped on her straw, avoiding Rhea's eyes.

'But, if he's out, how are we going to get in touch with him?' Rhea was so very logical, Ursula thought. Where did she get it from. Not from either of her parents, surely?

'We'll just leave a letter under his door, explaining we're

here. Then he can come and get us at the hotel. It may not be convenient for him to have us move in with him immediately. We may have to stay at the hotel for a while.' She faltered under Rhea's accusing stare. 'Just for a while. And maybe not even that long.' She wished she could leave Rhea somewhere while this first meeting took place. But Rhea had refused to stay in the hotel, and where else could you leave a nine-year-old child?

'I want to go see the Gardens. The man in the shop said they've got lakes and fountains and swans and every flower in the world. Can we go there, Mother? We can try Tim again in an hour. I think it'd be better if we saw him. Then it's surer. You know?' Rhea sucked hard on the straw, bending it in the middle. Ursula did know. Surer.

'Um, how would it be if we go there now for a while? I'll write Tim a note and then, if we still can't get him on the telephone, I'll just pop over and put it in his letter box and you can stay on in the Gardens. How does that sound?'

'Oh, all right. If you want.' Rhea shrugged her shoulders. Why was Mother acting so strange, so tentative. Didn't she want to see Tim? Sometimes mothers were very difficult. Rhea sighed. And then they wandered over the road, criss-crossed with the tram-lines that had brought them this far, over dusty paths with crab-grass running over them, through tall iron palings and into the Botanical Gardens.

'Now you're sure you'll be all right here? You won't talk to any strange men and you won't wander off?' Ursula still felt uneasy. Rhea didn't know anyone here or even where the hotel was. Maybe she shouldn't leave her?

'I'll be fine, Mother! Go off and find Tim. I'll be right here when you get back. See, there's a nice lady over there and if anyone bothers me, I'll go and sit with her. Okay?' Rhea was exasperated with her mother. Never had she seemed so ridiculously over-protective, so anxious. She hoped Tim didn't see her mother like this. It would put him right off!

Ursula laughed. 'Yes, I know you'll be fine. Just don't lose that piece of paper with the hotel's address on it, will you? I won't be long.' She held up a hand to quell Rhea's threatened outburst. 'See you soon.' She walked quickly away, leaving the child sitting on the grass by the lake.

Tim lived in Marne Street. It was only a few blocks from the east gate of the Botanical Gardens and Ursula didn't think it would take more than a few minutes. She had decided to push the letter into the box and not try the door at all. She was in too much of a state right now to see Tim. It would ruin everything. Better to let him come to her. That would be better. Not this way. She walked quicker still.

That was it, the red-brick one with the black shutters. Oh, it was beautiful! A laurel hedge concealed a small front garden that led up to a black-painted door flanked with tubs of tulips and ivy, a brass knocker and letter drop set into the door itself. The ground was covered with flagstones and edged along the sides with red bricks stacked half on top of each other on their sides so that they made a series of steps, like jagged teeth. Ursula stood staring at them blankly, trying to force her mind to think beyond the sudden fear that had engulfed it. She hesitated, seeing a flash of motion against one of the windows. Tim? Could that have been him? And had he seen her standing there, like a lost relative unsure of her reception. The thought unnerved her and she quickly leaned forward to thrust the letter through the door. She was startled when it swung open, pulling the letter through her fingers so that it stuck in the door like a fish-tail hanging out of a cat's mouth.

'Yes? Can I help you?' A young woman, blunt features crossed with freckles, wide hazel eyes, fair hair framing her face, and an apron not concealing her belly stood there. Such a very large belly. Ursula swallowed, unable to tear her eyes away from it.

'I, uh, I came to see Tim.' She couldn't think of anything to say.

'My husband's out back. I'll just get him for . . . oh, there you are, darling. I was just coming to get you. This lady wants to see you.' But by then even Tim's wife had noticed the bleached white face, the bones standing out starkly beneath the skin. Ursula stared at Tim. He didn't say a word, just stood one step behind his wife, his pregnant wife, and looked at Ursula.

For a moment Ursula thought no, this can't be happening, it's just a silly dream and I'll come to in a second and Tim will be there welcoming me into his arms. But they both still stood

289

there, the wife beginning to look sullen, angry, Tim looking sick, wretched, like death. Like Ursula. She cleared her throat.

'Uh, I was just bringing round a letter for Tim. But it doesn't matter anymore. Nice to see you again.' And then she turned and walked out of the garden, turning into the street, quicker now, almost running. She had to get away. Oh God! Oh sweet Mary, how could it have happened? He had said he loved her! He had promised her he wasn't married! Why? Why? What was the point in lying. Where did it get him? But then she remembered that night they had spent together and her mouth twisted bitterly. Tim, how could you? All that honesty and integrity shining out of his eyes like some sort of trap for the unwary. And she had certainly been unwary. Oh God!

She had reached the corner, her breath coming in spurting sobs, almost retches, when Tim caught her up. He ran up behind her, pulling her full tilt around the corner, out of sight of his wife. Ursula pushed him away.

'Don't! Just don't touch me!'

'Aw Jesus, Ursula! What happened? Didn't you get my letter?' He saw the denial in her eyes. 'Oh God sweetheart. I am so sorry.' He scrubbed his fingers through his hair, massaging the pain as though he could fix everything that way. Finally he sighed. 'I can't believe you had to just go through that. I thought by now you'd know the worst. I never suspected for a moment you'd miss the letter! What in Christ's name am I gonna do now? You saw Joanna? I had to marry her.' He leant against the wall and was silent for a long time. Ursula didn't speak either. She thought if she did she might say words that could never be unsaid. Or worse, that her words wouldn't come at all and that the bile in her throat would pour out along with the sickness in her heart. He was swinging around her now, pacing backward and forward, the same look of betrayal and anger in his eyes. 'I wrote and told you all about it. I never thought, not for an instant, you wouldn't wait . . . ' He reached over and turned Ursula's face towards him. 'I am so bloody sorry, love. What a way for you to find out! I really loused things up this time.' He was surprised when she laughed.

'We both did. You're right. I should've waited for your

letter. I knew this would happen! I just knew! Nothing could be that good or that easy! My fault for thinking it would, for thinking you were any different.' She laughed again, the sound defeated and quite without joy. 'Rhea found out about Simon and Julia and life just became unbearable. She wouldn't see her father and he wouldn't pay any of our bills and oh, well, it just seemed like the solution to everything I suppose. That was your problem, I gather? A pregnant wife?' He flinched at that.

'No. I, uh, I wasn't married then. I was going out with Joanna before I came to England. We'd been seeing each other for about a year, and, well, she was pressuring me to marry her. I wasn't sure about that – even though, I'll be honest, her family's political influence was tempting me a lot – but anyway, I decided to get away for a while and see how I really felt. Then I met you. And I fell in love for the first and probably only time in my life. And I was determined to have you. So I sent a telegram to Joanna, saying it was all over between us. She sent one back saying she was pregnant. I didn't believe her. That's why I told you I'd work it out. I really thought Joanna was just pulling one of her tricks. She does it all the time. And I thought, if I told you about it, you'd never agree to see me again. But, by the time I got back here, Joanna was very clearly pregnant and her family were insisting I do the right thing.' He ran a hand over his face, scrubbing at his eyes. 'I still don't think that baby's mine, to be honest. I was just too careful. But she says it is and I can't prove other-wise. So I married her and sent you that bloody letter. End of story.' He stopped his pacing and leant back against the wall, closing his eyes. Ursula looked at him. She couldn't bring herself to not believe him. She still loved him too much for that.

'Tim?' He opened his eyes, feeling Ursula's hand on his arm. He started to kiss the palm of her hand but she snatched it away.

'I'm so sorry, Ursula. I love you more than anything or any-one in this world. And I've done you more harm . . . ' His voice broke in a cough and Ursula saw there were tears in his eyes. He still looked as honest and open and trustworthy as when she had first met him, squinting into the sun outside the cottage. She felt angry that he could still look like that.

'Tim, what am I supposed to do? I've brought Rhea with

me. Where will we go?' She was not going to cry, she told herself. Not this time. But when he tried to hold her again, his cheek warm against hers, the clean smell of his skin and hair, his arms trying to comfort her, it took all her strength to pull away. She stood with her arms folded, warding off his approach. Tim's face became grim.

'I'll sort it out, Ursula. Don't worry. I got you out here and generally messed up your life. I owe it to you to sort things out now.' He saw her shift her stance, the irritation in the movement obvious even without her expression. Anger and resentment had returned to her eyes.

'I don't want to be some damned obligation in your life, Tim. I deserve a hell of a lot better than that!'

'You deserve a hell of a lot better than me,' he said drearily. Ursula had no sympathy.

'Oh? Is that your way of saying that you're not going to be a part of my life, obligation or not? Well, thanks a lot. I guess it really pays to be noble sometimes.'

'Don't Ursula! For God's sake, don't get bitter. I promise you we'll work things out. I don't know what else to say. It's all taken me so much by surprise, I just can't seem to get my brain to work properly. Look, let's just . . . ' But Tim wasn't allowed to finish, another thought occurring to Ursula.

'Does your wife know about me? Did you tell her when you came back from England?'

'Yeah. That caused one hell of a fuss, her dad yelling at me, calling me a bastard and a cad. God!' He sighed again. 'I told Joanna everything but then, when I couldn't get her to say the baby wasn't mine, then I guess I just lost heart. My courage folded up and I wrote to you telling you what was going on and that I would have to marry Joanna. She must've realized who you were just then, because, after you'd started to walk away, she started yelling at me that I'd brought you out from England anyway and that I was the biggest shit on earth. She's probably right.' He looked older than Ursula had ever seen him; no longer the light-hearted golden lad that Hugh had winked about with such pleasure. She felt sorry for him.

'Oh, I suppose it's not entirely your fault. Things've just gotten away from us. I didn't mean to sound so hard. It's just, I'm scared! What am I going to do in a strange country with no money, no skills, and a nine-year-old daughter to support? I can't go home. Simon wouldn't have me back and anyway, Rhea just won't go. She won't see Simon at all. So what do I do?'

He put his arm around her again, trying not to mind the stiffness in her shoulders, the way she leant away from him. 'Well, I was going to offer you your fares home but if Rhea feels like that, then, I'll find somewhere for you to live. It may not be what you're used to. I won't have that much money with a baby on the way. But you won't go hungry or . . . '

'Tim, I could've stayed in England to have a life like that. In fact, I had a much better one. The cottage was beautiful and I had friends in the village. I can't believe I've given that up, taken away Rhea's schooling and pony, her whole identity, to end up being put in a rotten little flat somewhere in Melbourne, existing on sufferance. I don't suppose your high morals could include your being a part of our lives, could they?' She couldn't help the way her emotions were see-sawing up and down. She just wanted to lash out and hurt. It was so unbelievably awful. 'Could they?' He didn't answer.

'No, somehow I didn't think so. God forbid that someone should find out and ruin your budding political career. Well thanks, Tim, but no thanks. I don't need your charity.' She pulled away and started walking back to the Botanical Gardens. Tim cursed and then caught her up.

'Don't be bloody silly, Ursula. Where're you gonna go? What'll you do? For God's sake, it isn't charity I'm offering you. It's because I love you and I want to help you. I'm responsible!' He caught her elbow and pulled her to a stop. She lifted her chin and gave him a tight-mouthed stare.

'No. I'm responsible . . . for myself and for Rhea. I just remembered – I've got somewhere to go and I've got enough money to get us there. So don't worry yourself any further. I won't be around to mess up your happy little family life. Now let me go.' She wrenched her arm free and walked on. And this time he did let her go.

Chapter Nineteen

Gidgeeganup. November, 1956

The place was a disappointment. But then, she had expected
that. Nothing she had ever heard about this place had ever
given her reason to think otherwise. And, lately, everything
was a disappointment, knowing Tim wouldn't be there to share
it with her. Beside her, Ursula heard Rhea sigh.

'Is this it?' she asked, her voice hard and bitter. Ursula
didn't trust her own voice. She nodded instead. 'Mother.
Can't we go home? I don't want to stay here. It's a dump. And
it's so hot!' Rhea swatted another fly away from her face,
disgusted by the way it clung to her lips as though drugged. She
spat, hard. Ursula looked across the dry, grey, brown fields
filled with stunted gum trees and flat rocks. The heat made the
homestead, with its corrugated iron roof and whitewashed
walls shimmer like melted steel in the distance. Home. She had
wondered that herself, a long time ago when she was living in
the kampong in Singapore. Couldn't she go home? She spat a
fly away from her own lips where it was trying to drink the
moisture at the corners of her mouth.

'No, Rhea. This is it. Our property. At least, it is for me. If
you really can't stand it, we'll find a way for you to go back to
your father. But I think you should give it a chance. After all,
this is our own place!' Ursula didn't look at Rhea while she
spoke. She continued to stare across the fields at the farm her

294

step-mother had left her. No, not 'farm'. They called it 'station'.

'No! I won't go back to him! Or any of them! They're all such a happy family. They don't need us. And Julia doesn't want me. It's not fair. He's my father too!'

Ursula could hear the anguish still fresh and very real in her daughter's voice, brought to the surface again by Tim. Poor Rhea. She was too young to have been told the truth. Lucy shouldn't have done it. But then, children could be cruel creatures.

Ursula breathed in deeply, looking around at the land she now owned. It was an odd feeling, to know it was hers. Nothing else had ever really belonged to her ever before, not the cottage, not the bungalow. But this was hers! And it came, of all things, from Sally. She wondered what Sally would have thought of that.

Rhea was silent and finally Ursula turned and looked at her daughter. Rhea was crying, the tears sliding down her cheeks without a sound.

'Oh, Rhea, darling. Don't cry. We'll sort it out. I promise you. Don't cry, darling. You'll make me cry.' Ursula pulled her daughter into her arms and held her, rocking backward and forward, while the sun stabbed harshly into her eyes and a few crows planed across the fields. Nothing else moved.

'Mother, why did we come? Tim . . . ' But Rhea couldn't talk about Tim without crying harder, her sobs becoming loud and angry.

'Shh, sweetheart. Don't. Tim couldn't . . . he couldn't help the way things turned out. Don't cry. We'll be all right. I promise.'

'He could've! He made you think he was in love with you and then he married someone else! Why did he do that? I hate him!' She tried to pull away from her mother's arms. Ursula fought down her own tears.

'It wasn't his fault, Rhea. He had to marry her. You don't understand. She . . . Oh God!' Ursula stopped to try and control her emotions, to try and still the aching, tearing feeling inside. She pressed her hand to her mouth. 'You don't understand.' The two stood silently by the car, both crying bitterly for something they couldn't have. A kookaburra cawed

295

harshly, its cry building to a pitch of mocking laughter. Ursula shook her head.

'Rhea. Take a deep breath and look around. All right, so it's a bit rough. You should've seen the cottage when I first moved into it. The garden was a mix of wilderness and rubbish dump, the cottage itself needed paint and extra furniture. It was a mess. And yet, we made it comfortable, even beautiful by the time we left. We can do the same here. The countryside is really quite lovely. Look, look over there at that bush with the red flowers. It's gorgeous. And so is that lake. It's ours, you know. Our very own lake! And the homestead, well, we can do things with it. Those wide verandahs are lovely and cool-looking, and we can paint the roof. I don't see why it has to be red. This'll be fun, darling. You'll see.' She coaxed her daughter to look up and around at the property. 'Well?'

'It's ugly and you know it, Mother. But,' Rhea smiled sadly, 'for you I'll try. Really, I will.'

'Good girl! I knew you were brave enough, if you just gave yourself a chance. We'll make it beautiful, I promise.' Ursula kissed the top of her daughter's head.

'With what? We don't have any money left, do we?'

'Uh, well, not much, no. But the property must have some way of supporting itself. We'll sort it out. Come on, let's get on down there.' They had stopped at the entrance to the property, the road sweeping down below them in a wide snaking curve to the homestead. It was more land than they had ever seen belonging to one person but by Australian standards it was a small property, only five hundred acres. Ursula wondered how they would cope with it all. But there was a couple who looked after things, she understood. A Jack Winby and his wife Ellen. Or so the lawyer in Perth had said. Things would work out. She opened the door of the Holden stationwagon. Rhea scooted across the bench seat and Ursula climbed in after her.

When they pulled up outside the homestead, Ursula realized that it was not just one house, but a series of buildings; the main one, sprawling haphazardly in several directions at once as though it had been added on to without any formal plan in mind. It was perched on stilts about four feet high. Ursula parked the car to one side of the drive and approached the house on foot. She climbed three wooden steps that creaked

under her weight and walked across the verandah, her footsteps drumming hollowly on the wooden boards. The front
door had a fly-screen door across it and she opened it
awkwardly, the catch stiff and rusted. The door itself had glass
panels in the top half. Ursula knocked loudly.

'Hallo? Is anyone there? Hallo?' She knocked again, and
rattled the doorknob. But the door was locked fast. She tried to
peer in through the window-panes but they were coated with
dust and the interior was dark. She gave up and walked around
the verandah to the back of the house. There was another fly-
screened door there. Ursula noticed that at the back of the
house even the verandah was fly-screened. In the gathering
dusk she could understand why. There were mosquitoes everywhere, droning around her in a cloud so that she felt if she
breathed too deeply she would suck some into her mouth. She
swatted at them and began to retreat around the side.

'Mother? Mo-ther!' Rhea sounded impatient and frightened
at the same time. Ursula walked faster. As she turned the last
corner of the house, she saw her daughter standing rigidly
beside the car, a boy beside her with an air-rifle in his hands.
He wasn't pointing it at Rhea but he didn't seem to be happy
at her presence. They seemed like two halves of a folded ink
blot, each straining away from the centre. Ursula called out
sharply.

'Who are you?'

The boy seemed surprised at the question, his dark head
turning up at Ursula with a gaping mouth. Ursula could see his
tongue flicking along his lips as though searching for an
answer. She walked over to him and repeated her question, a
little more calmly.

'Who are you? D'you work here?'

The boy nodded warily. 'My dad runs this place. Who're
you?'

'I'm Mrs Patterson. I own this place. At least, I assume this
is the old Hendricks place?' He nodded again, even more
slowly, as though any admission of his might be held against
him. He was about fifteen, Ursula thought, with darkly
tanned, dusty skin and brown, shaggy hair falling over one
eye. His clothes – loose, khaki workpants, scuffed, brown boots
and thick, cotton shirt, his hair, everything was covered in a

297

fine silt so that his eyes stood out sharply blue in contrast. Ursula wondered if he were a little slow.

'Is your father Jack Winby?'

'Aw, yeah. Look Mrs Patterson. We weren't expecting you. Does Dad know you're here?' No, Ursula thought, not slow at all. Just very cautious. She smiled.

'Not yet. We've only just arrived. This is my daughter, Rhea. And what's your name?'

'Will.' It was a grudging admission directed at Ursula but his eyes were flicking sideways at the young girl standing beside the car. He frowned, a small crease appearing between his eyebrows. 'You're not coming out here to live, are you?'

'Yes, that's right. I would've called your father, or sent a telegram, but our decision was rather sudden. Still, we're here now. Can you go find your father for us, please, Will? It's getting dark and the mosquitoes are biting us to death. We'd like to get into the house as soon as possible.' Will appeared dumbfounded. He licked his lips again and stared at Ursula and then at Rhea. He looked back at Ursula.

'It's mossie time. You'll be sorry later. I'll call Dad.' He hesitated and suddenly volunteered. 'It's a bit of a mess in there. I dunno if you wanna stay there tonight. I guess maybe Mum can put you up in my room. I'll sleep on the verandah, if you like.' He scuffed his boot through the dirt and looked up awkwardly from under the hair that was falling over his face. He needed a good haircut, Ursula thought.

'That's very kind of you, Will. Perhaps, after we've talked with your parents and looked around a bit we'll accept your offer. But I don't want to put you out of your bed.'

'Aw, look Mrs Patterson. It's cooler on the verandah anyway. Mum 'n' Dad'll sort it out. The verandah'll do for me. I'll be back in a sec.' He turned and ran off towards the other buildings behind the main house. Ursula watched him leave, his clothes flapping loosely around his body, the rifle clutched in one hand. Then she looked at her daughter. Rhea looked sullen, her chin held forward stiffly as though she might repel unwelcome events that way. Ursula smiled.

'Why don't you get back in the car, darling? There's no point in both of us getting bitten, is there?' She opened the door for Rhea. Rhea shook her head.

298

'I'm fine. I'll wait out here with you.' She paused, looking across at where Will had disappeared behind a water tank held high on stilts. 'So, that's the company round here? What about school? D'you think they have such a thing here?'

'Of course they do, Rhea! You mustn't be too harsh in your judgements. Give it a little time. Will must go to school somewhere around here. You can ask him.'

'What makes you think he goes to school at all? I think he's thick!'

'Nonsense. He was just surprised, that's all. Please, Rhea, don't go getting all awkward about this until we've looked into things. By the way, before they turn up, let's decide on our story, shall we? I rather thought we'd say your father's just died. I know that sounds terrible but it might make life a lot easier if we just pretend and then there's little or no chance of Daddy finding us. Especially if we also take one of the ''t's'' out of our name. Paterson with one ''t''. All right?' She saw Rhea shrug, her most difficult look on her face. 'Oh look, here come the Winbys. My, Mrs Winby looks rather fierce, doesn't she?'

'She looks like a man. I don't think I want . . . '

'Shh, Rhea! Don't be rude.' The Winbys, with Will leading the way, came towards Ursula at a fast pace. They looked like they were going to walk right over them and just keep on going. Ursula stepped back a pace involuntarily. But the Winbys came to an abrupt halt in front of her, the three staring hard from between narrowed eyes. Will broke the silence.

'Mrs Paterson, this is my Mum'n'Dad.' He stepped away as though his task were done with and the Patersons could now be forgotten. Jack Winby held out a thick forearm coated with dark hair and dust. His sleeves were rolled up above the elbow and his hand was rough from work. Ursula shook hands with him and smiled into the man's blank face.

'Mr Winby, it's nice to meet you. And Mrs Winby?' Ursula held out her hand to the heavy-set woman with steel-rimmed spectacles perched on her nose, the sun glinting in the glass. She was standing a pace behind her husband. She ignored the hand but nodded in agreement. She was Mrs Winby. Neither of them smiled.

'And this is my daughter Rhea. I'm sorry we didn't let you

299

know we were coming. As I told your son, the decision was made rather suddenly. We were in Melbourne just a couple of weeks ago and decided at the last moment to continue on with the ship that had brought us from England. We barely had time to make the boat before it left. I hope it isn't too inconvenient for you?'

'Aw, I'd've liked to know you were coming Mrs Paterson. But you're here now. You better come'n have tea with us tonight. Will can move 'n you an' yer daughter can have his room. That okay with you, Mum?' Mr Winby called his wife 'Mum'. Ursula found it odd. She nodded and smiled, but Mrs Winby still didn't smile, her arms crossed firmly across her body. Ursula's smile slipped a little.

'Shall I drive the car over?' The Winbys stared.

'What for?'

'Well, to get things out. We've got suitcases in the back.'

'You're not staying with us forever, Mrs Paterson. Just for tonight. You don't need to unload your suitcases.'

'Mr Winby, I may only be staying in your house for tonight but both my daughter and I will need a change of clothing, not to mention our wash things. And tomorrow we're moving into this house, here. We're staying, Mr Winby, do you understand? This is my property and I intend to live here. Now is there anything else you would like to discuss?' Ursula had seldom felt so coldly in control of herself. If these sullen bumpkins thought they could frighten her away, they were sadly mistaken. She glared at the two adults and they gave way before her.

'All right, Mrs Paterson. Take a damper; there's no need to get angry. Drive your car over. It'll do for now. There're too many damned mossies to argue about it out here anyway. Will, run ahead and show Mrs Paterson where to park, and then unload her suitcases. We'll be there in a sec.'

As Ursula lay in bed that night, Rhea curled up beside her, she knew it had all been a terrible mistake. She should have accepted Tim's offer of a return fare and brazened things out with Simon. What had possessed her to leave England without contacting Tim first? She should have sent a telegram at least. What a fool she was! Almost all her savings were gone on the berths on the Northern Star and getting them to this property in the middle of nowhere. And now a hostile farm manager who wanted her anywhere but here! She couldn't believe the way her luck seemed to be running.

In bed, the night sounds alien and unwelcoming, Ursula closed her eyes and tried to block the pain, the shame, from her mind. Even now her body was swept with the heat of extreme embarrassment when she saw the look on his wife's face, and the white, strained face Tim had shown her.

It had all gone by so quickly, those few moments while they stood in the road and tried to sort their lives out. Ursula regretted, with the ache of final parting, that she had been too bitter and hurt, too awkward to really look at him and save up those precious last moments of time together. She had left him without touching, without anything but words of anger. It hurt to think about it.

Ursula snuggled in tighter against her daughter, wishing she had never met Tim, never come to Australia. God, she hated the place!

With the first light of dawn, Ursula was up and dressing, and in a far more cheerful frame of mind. If they had to stay here, then they would make a good showing and let these people here know what determination was all about. She fastened the last button on her dress and picked up her shoe. They had been shown the bathroom last night, a tin shed out back with a chain-operated shower that brought ice-cold water down in a sudden deluge, a mirror that had lost most of its silvering, and a bucket that served as a washbasin. The 'dunny' was further away still from the house, a small shack that was reached down an over-grown path with a green painted door and a half-moon cut out of the top of it. It smelt strongly of sheep-dip and the door was warped. Inside, Mrs Winby had warned them about 'red-backs' lurking under the lavatory seat.

'Red-backs? What are they?'

'My word, you are new out here, aren't you?' Mrs Winby had laughed, not altogether kindly. 'Spiders. They've got a red splotch on their back and they're kind of browny in colour. Not that big, but that's a serious bite if you get one. Unpleasant on the backside, let me tell you! And it might be fatal for your little girl. Nasty, anyway. So check before you sit down. If you have

301

to come out here at night, there's a torch by the back door.'
Ursula and Rhea had been horrified, nodding dumbly as Mrs
Winby showed them how to pour sheep-dip down the bowl
after they had used it. 'We only flush once a day, and my
husband does that last thing at night. Water's a problem sometimes. No point in wasting it.'

'But, what about the water tanks we saw? Aren't they ample
for the house?'

'Nah. Not in January and February. It's still cool now, so
there's no real problem. When summer starts you'll have to be
careful.'

'But, it was so hot today, Mrs Winby!' Rhea broke in, her
face flushed with the rank smell of the dunny and the mosquito
bites that were swelling into raised lumps. 'Hot? Today?' Mrs
Winby laughed again. 'Nah. That's not hot. I'll tell you
when we get hot!' She turned her back, the checked dress
showing wet crescents under each arm, and walked back up the
path towards the house. Rhea looked at her mother in silence
and then followed Mrs Winby in to tea.

Tea had been another surprise. Out here it meant dinner
and dinner was steak, boiled potatoes, green beans, and gravy.
Ursula shook her head and wondered how they could afford to
eat meat every day. Especially steak. You just couldn't buy it
in England. Rhea was suspiciously turning the slab of meat
around and around on her plate. Will watched her.

'Why don't you eat it? Don't you like it?' he asked. Rhea
started, unaware he had been watching her. She looked uneasy
when Mr and Mrs Winby put down their own knives and forks
to look at her too.

'Yes. I just never had it before. I'll eat it.' She was growing
red and Ursula leaned over and whispered that she could leave
it, if she were too tired to eat. The Winbys were staring, all
their mouths open.

'Never had steak before? What d'yer eat then?' Mr Winby
asked. Ursula smiled.

'Oh, a lot of fish, or maybe lamb. It's hard to get steak in
England since the war.' She felt like she had been caught,
remiss in her duties as a mother. Will stared at Rhea and then
picked his steak up with his fork and offered it to her. His face
was quite serious, washed paler in a circle that had missed the

dust at his temples, ears and chin. Rhea shook her head.

'No! I mean, no thank you. I'm having trouble with this one as it is,' she said. The Winbys looked affronted and settled back into silence. Ursula tried another tack.

'What d'you grow out here, Mr Winby? The property is self-sufficient, isn't it?'

'Olives, citrus fruit. We keep our own cow and chooks, horses, that sort of thing. But we're not self-sufficient. The crop pays for our clothes and the food we don't grow: sugar, tea, flour. Then there's the kerosene and diesel, farm tools, stuff like that. There's not much left after that.'

Ursula digested that in silence while Mrs Winby collected the plates and stacked them in the sink. Rhea offered to help but was brusquely told to sit still.

'Do you have any other help? It seems a lot of land for just you to handle.'

'Most of it's no good. Too rocky, or too dry. We have Stoney to help with fence mending and odd-jobs, and we get pickers in at harvest time. It's a small crop.'

'Stoney? Is that . . . I mean, who is that?'

'Palmerston Jones, Stoney. He's a boong. Lives up the back in a shack he built himself. Good bloke for an Abo but needs someone to give him a kick up the pants from time to time. They're mostly lazy buggers, excusing my French.'

'Boong? Abo? I'm sorry, Mr Winby, I'm afraid I'm not up on Australian terms yet.' Ursula had the feeling that not understanding Mr Winby put her lower down in the points scale. She also had the feeling he was using particularly obscure slang for that very reason. She smiled calmly.

'Same thing. Means Aborigine. Blackfella. You get it?'

'Perfectly, Mr Winby. I'm sure you'll find I catch on fast.'

That had been last night and now it was time to go out and face that frightening world of spiders and snakes. Will had been serious when he had told them both to check their boots before putting them on in the morning, and to stamp their feet through long grass. Ursula shivered with distaste. She finished tying her shoelace and stood up. Rhea was still asleep and Ursula was reluctant to wake her. Lying there like that, with her silver hair spread across the pillow and her pink cheek flushed by sleep, Ursula couldn't help thinking her a beautiful child. But then, Simon was nothing if not good looking and Rhea took after Simon in looks. Just not in attitude anymore. Ursula smiled to herself and closed the door softly behind her.

Chapter Twenty

'Goodaye. You're an early riser. You'll need to be round here. The main house has a wood-burning stove like this one and my word, it gets hot in the middle of the day. You'll need to do your cooking early, mostly. Wha' d'yer wont for brekkie?' Mrs Winby was standing by the table with a frying pan in one hand and a fork in the other. On the table in front of Mr Winby and Will were two plates, two steaks and four fried eggs. Ursula swallowed.

'Steak again? For breakfast?'

'You'll need it when you put in a long day's work. Mum can't be cooking all day long and it's a fair way between six in the morning and dinner at one.' Mr Winby's mouth was full of steak and he talked around it as though it were just a part of his tongue. Ursula shook her head.

'No, nothing. Just coffee, thank you.' She sat down at the table. Will was glancing at her from beneath lowered eyelashes. She couldn't guess what he made of her, sitting there in a linen dress that was as out of place as her pale skin. She thought again how much he needed a haircut. It looked like they just let the boy run wild. 'Are you going to school today, Will?' Will's fork faltered on its steady route between plate and mouth.

'Nah, Mrs Paterson. I'm finished. I'm fifteen now and Dad needs me here.' He took another bite of steak covered with egg yolk. Then he mopped his plate with a piece of bread. Ursula had to look away sharply. What was the matter with her? She wasn't normally this bad, her nerves frayed, her stomach heaving uneasily at the sight of food. She stared at the formica table, noting the edge where it chipped back to brown wood. Damn Tim!

'But,' she took a breath and looked at Will again. 'There is a school around here, isn't there? Rhea's only a child still – she must go to school.' The Winbys looked at each other, consulting.

'Not really, no,' Mrs Winby offered, her face brightening at the thought of being rid of these unwelcome visitors. 'There's the correspondence school, of course – yew know, "school of the air?" But the real school burned down in a bush-fire about two years ago, wasn't it Will?' He nodded his head. 'There's a kindy for the liddlies; the mums take it in turn to run that. But mostly the rich kids go down to Perth, to one of the private boarding schools, and the other kids, well they learn by radio or they don't learn at all. They'll build another school one of these days but I don't think the government can keep up with all of it. So much needed doing after the war and schools . . . well, they'll get to them when they can. There aren't many kids left round here anyways.' Mrs Winby put a mug of coffee down in front of Ursula and turned back to the stove.

'More eggs, Dad?'

'Naw. I'm right. Best be off.' He took a deep slurp of his tea and stood up. 'C'mon, Will. You've eaten enough. Let's go. Goodaye, Mrs Paterson. If you're still here at tea, I'll go over things with you. Mum'll show you the house.' He put on a battered felt hat and walked out onto the verandah. Will followed him, unconsciously mimicking the older man's walk: bowed knees, heave to the left, bowed knees, heave to the right, arms hanging loosely beside him. It was the walk of a man more used to a horse than his own two feet. Ursula drank her coffee in silence.

'Your liddle girl? She getting up today, d'yer think?' The older woman had finished the washing up in silence and now stood near the table with her arms folded across her apron. Ursula wasn't sure if Mrs Winby had eaten herself or whether she just fed the men in the mornings. There was perspiration showing in a ring around her armpits already and small droplets clinging to her top lip.

'Rhea's tired. We've been travelling for quite a while and . . . she's been rather upset lately. I want her to sleep as long as possible. I'm sorry if that doesn't agree with your plans.' The two women were silent in their appraisal of each other. Abruptly, Mrs Winby sniffed and turned away. Ursula ignored her and continued drinking her coffee.

'The key to the main house's over there, hanging by the door. Yew can move over there today. We haven't got enough room for you here. Either Will or Stoney'll bring your things over later. We're not very grand round here, Mrs Paterson. No bellboys to hop around you.' She wrung out her tea-towel and hung it over the front of the Aga. 'Your husband coming across too? Just so's we know where we stand, you know?' Mrs Winby looked up, her broad features merciless.

'No, he won't. My husband just died. That's why I'm here and that's why I'm staying. Mrs Winby,' Ursula hesitated for a moment, feeling her way. 'I don't quite understand the problem you seem to be having about me being here. After all, this is my property, I'm sure you'll agree?' Again she paused but the woman wasn't about to be outfaced and simply stared back at her. Ursula felt her anger surface from somewhere deep down inside her, somewhere that had been hiding it, carefully, ever since she left Tim. 'I'm afraid from now on it's what I want that's important around here Mrs Winby – not what suits you. I'm sure if you find the situation intolerable, you can find yourself a job somewhere else. Do I make myself clear?' Ursula held Mrs Winby's gaze again for one long, frozen second before the woman shrugged. 'Good. Then in that case I think I'll look at the main house now. Thank you so much for everything.' She got up and took the key from the hook with a steady hand, swinging the screen door behind her with a flat bang that echoed some of the rage within her.

She had always heard how open-handed, generous, friendly, and out-going the Australian people were. 'Good on yer mate! How yer goin' cobber?' and all that rubbish. The Winbys were a prime example of Australian hospitality all right! She marched on fiercely, each movement and swing of her arm building her indignation. She'd show them. They weren't getting rid of her, by God!

Intent on her fuming, Ursula didn't see the black man until

she was almost on him. Then she stopped abruptly and looked up, her mouth opening to cry out almost before she realized this must be Stoney, the Aboriginal fellow Mr Winby had talked about. She closed her mouth and smiled, nodding her head. Did he speak English? He was leaning against the verandah, a pair of workpants even baggier and more tattered than Will's drooping about his hips and his feet bare in the dust. They were broad, the toes curling as though to grip the ground. His brow was heavy and overhung warm, moist, brown eyes in deep sockets, a splayed nose so broad at the nostrils that Ursula wondered if someone had broken it in a fight, and lips that were drawn back over strong, white teeth. His hair was wiry brown with orange highlights and worn almost down to his shoulders; a checked shirt was hanging open and loose around his chest. Ursula found him immediately likeable. He knew how to smile.

'Stoney? I'm Mrs Paterson. I understand you work here . . . for the Winbys.'

'Yeah. Mr Winby . . . he said I should help you with your stuff. Yew wan' me go ahead and open the place up? Might be snakes. Saw a dugai near there the other day. An' goannas'n' spiders too. They like warm, dry places. The missus doan go in there much, no more.' His voice was flat and broad, like his nose. Ursula nodded, the heat gathering beneath her linen dress, making it feel like warm sacking against her skin. She pulled it away from her throat. She didn't know what a dugai was but it sounded poisonous. Everything was poisonous.

'Is it always so quiet around here, Stoney? You might think there was no-one else around for miles!'

'There ain't.' He grinned again and she fanned herself with her handkerchief and walked behind him across the verandah.

The door opened reluctantly, yielding only when Stoney put his shoulder to it and shoved hard. It scraped across the boards, warped with the last of the winter's rain. Stoney stepped warily across the threshold. It might be normal for there to be snakes, but he was still careful. Ursula watched him while the lesson sank in. He was stamping his feet on the floor as he walked, the soles slapping down hard on the wood. Dust flew up in choking clouds. There were slithering, rustling sounds from the corners

308

of the room. Ursula waited breathless, afraid to move in case she stepped on something. Thank God Stoney was there.

'Just goannas. They hiss a bit, and bite if they can. But not too bad. They're only littluns.' Ursula followed Stoney's pointing finger to where a huge lizard was backed into the corner, its mouth open and a silent, wheezing coming out as it shook its head slowly back and forth. It was actually hissing, just like a snake! And if that was a little one . . . Dear God!

'Can you get rid of it for me, Stoney? I don't think it cares for me a whole lot. And I don't care for it.' She stepped away from the door, treading more easily, her eyes taking in the room. It was large, bordered on three sides by louvred windows and on the fourth by a wall with two doors. Both doors were shut. There was no furniture and the floor was covered in dust and newspapers, yellowed with age and the sun. Ursula stood still, the goanna briefly forgotten. So, this was to be home. The sun beat strongly through the louvred windows on the east side of the room where the sun was still low enough not to be obscured by the verandahs. It lit the room with a spare and harsh light, showing every crack in the dun-coloured plaster, every splinter in the wooden floor. Already it was breathless with heat. She turned and walked out onto the verandah again, leaning against the post and staring out across the road as it snaked its way back up to the main highway. It wobbled in the rising heat.

Stoney appeared beside her after a few minutes, his face shining a bright chocolate brown where he had sweated catching the goanna. 'He's all gone now, missus. Yew can move in now.'

'Thank you, Stoney. What about the other rooms? Did you check them too?' She didn't look at him but continued to stare back up the road. There were strings of barbed wire, rusted and wrapped around the occasional wood post, skirting the road and the light was a flat glare, so bright it was almost hazy; ragged gums, creepers, ugly grey-green trees with brown wattles, so stunted and dry that they appeared to shiver in the wind. There was a monotony of colour, like army fatigues bleached by the sun until they achieved just that nothing shade of khaki. This was the bush she had heard so much about. Tim had grown up on a station, maybe something like this but on a

309

bigger, sheep-raising scale. She breathed in the air, dry and acrid with a scent of gum. How were they going to live here? On what? Was there no money?

Her eye picked out the two windmills, dark against the white glare of the sky, starkly functional. And yet, there was a strange beauty to it all; calmness, deliberateness that either purged or withered the soul. She knew now what they meant by the fatalism of bush people. Who else could live here and take it? It was so unyielding, so primitive; a vast human wasteland that had no time for weakness and no need for refinement. She felt strange leaning against the post, feeling the 'heat in her guts, the light in her bones'. The line floated back to her and she finally understood it.

'Missus? Yew feeling all right? Yew look kinda pale. It ain't too hot just yet but yews being from England an' all, maybe yew should sit down or something?' He seemed relieved when she nodded and sat on the front step. She did feel a bit strange. He stood beside her, anxious to find out more but shy of intruding. Finally he asked, 'Yew and your liddle girl staying for good? Yew come all the way from England to live 'ere?' Stoney was puzzled. He smiled a lot to hide his nervousness with this new lady with her funny accent and her white, soft skin. He wasn't used to women; only Mrs Winby and she didn't count.

Stoney was nearly seventeen and had grown up on the property ever since he was left there by his mother. She had drifted in to do odd-jobs, piece-work that would give her enough to buy another bottle of beer and to put something in her belly. She hadn't wanted the kid anyway; he'd been a nuisance. So when she moved on, she left him behind. Stoney hadn't been sorry. He liked the property and he liked Will. They played together when Will came home from school and, when they were older, they worked together for Will's dad and rode the stock horses out along the boundary, racing each other in a desperate, sweaty gallop that inevitably ended in Stoney reaching the kerosene drum nailed to the fencepost first. That was always the starting and finishing line; the letter-box.

But now things were going to be different. There was going to be a lady and her little girl living with them and Mr Winby was in a towering rage about it all. Will and he had stood warily to one side while Mr Winby had thrown sacks of feed and fertilizer into the back of the utility and driven off down the road spewing gravel out in an arc. Then Will had got on with the milking and he had come to give the lady a hand. But she didn't seem very interested in the house. He couldn't understand that. It was a beaut place. He wished he could live there, instead of his rusty shack. What did the lady want?

Ursula became aware that Stoney was still standing there behind her and that he had asked her something.

'What? I didn't hear you. I was thinking . . . '

'I dunno. I just figured yew might need some things. If yews stayin'. I shouldn'a thought yew'd wanna stay 'ere. Not when yews from England.' Stoney became shy again, staring down at his feet and digging his fists into his pockets. Ursula looked at him.

'I'm staying here, Stoney. My husband's . . . dead and I don't have any other source of money. I don't have a choice. My daughter may stay, or she may go home . . . back to England. I'm not sure. But for me, this is it. So . . . let's have a look at this place, shall we? And then I better have a chat with Mr Winby. D'you know where he is right now?' She shooed Stoney back into the living room, her mind suddenly made up. She would manage this, just like everything else. At least this time, when she made the place habitable, it would really be for her. It was her property, her house, her land. The thought was immensely comforting.

Stoney was looking unhappy. 'Mr Winby's gone out to the far paddock. He won't be back till dinner.'

'Oh, I see. Well then, let's see what we can do until then. The kitchen's all right, is it? No dugais or red-backs or goannas?' She was leaning forward from the waist, peering through the doorway. Stoney smiled broadly and stepped into the kitchen.

'Nothin' here, missus. I look'd already. Yew can cook an' everythin' if yew like. I can get yew some wood.' Ursula followed him into the kitchen. Heavy porcelain sinks stained brown, brown cupboards, brown floor, beige walls. Her spirits sank, just a little.

'No, never mind the wood just now. I think we'll have to stay with the Winbys a while longer. In fact, we may have to

311

stay with them permanently unless something rather major is done in here. Oh well, perhaps I'm just hungry . . . ' She meant that she was probably despondent because she hadn't had breakfast. But Stoney was a literal man. He grinned.

'Yew wanna vegemite semwidge? Mrs Winby makes um fer Will 'n' me sometimes. I can get yew some. Ow meny jew wan'?' Ursula noticed that when Stoney became excited his accent broadened perceptibly. She wasn't sure what a vegemite sandwich was, but it sounded better than steak. She smiled in amusement and nodded.

'Um, would you do that, Stoney? I'll have a couple if Mrs Winby doesn't mind. I'm going to go through the other rooms. They're all okay, aren't they?' Her stomach twisted suddenly and she had to grip the countertop firmly. Her vision blurred and then slid back into focus. She knew that feeling. It had been a long time but she still remembered. Oh Lord! It couldn't be, could it? She tried to think back to her last period. Nothing came to mind. Her mind gave a frightened lurch and Stoney looked across at her. She tried to look as though nothing were the matter.

'Yeah, missus. They're fine. It's a beaut place. Just needs a bit of a pain'n'stuff. Will'n'me'll help. Where's your kid then?' Ursula looked across at the young man.

'Coming.' She smiled again, but this time her eyes remained worried, her thoughts turned inwards. 'Her kid,' Stoney had said. Maybe he ought to have said 'her kids'.

Tim called on Christmas Day. Ursula didn't know how he had known where she was, nor how he got the number. But there he was, sounding awkward and hesitant. She nearly hung up. Something stopped her. It wasn't that she felt it was wrong of her to love him, or that it was wrong that she had followed him out to Australia. A mistake, yes. But not wrong. What was wrong was that he was now married, and his wife about to have their first child and he was calling her, on Christmas Day too, to tell her . . . what? That was why she didn't hang up. She wanted to know what.

'Are you there, Ursula. It's me, Tim . . . can you hear me? Ursula?'

'Yes. I can hear you. What is it?'

312

'I, uh, I wanted to say Happy Christmas. Are you all right there? It was hard to find you. I thought you'd gone home . . . Is Rhea okay?'

'Yes, she's fine. No, I didn't go home. How could I? Who. told you I was here?' Lettice of course. Ursula knew the answer before even Tim told her.

'Lettice did. She nearly snapped my head off in her letter back to me. I guess I'm not their favourite person right now. That's understandable. I should never . . . Are you really okay? Lettice seemed to think money might be a problem.' He was asking questions haphazardly, unsure what to say, what not to say. Ursula didn't answer for a few moments. What was she meant to say?

'The property's a bit run-down. I understand farming's in a depressed state right now . . . '

'What? Are you kidding me? Farming's booming. Who told you that?'

'Uh, the manager, Mr Winby. He grows olives and citrus fruits and he says the land's poor and there, there's not much market for it right now, and, and . . . ' Ursula had to stop and breathe deeply, the quiver in her voice threatening to shake into tears.

'Sweetheart? Hey, take a deep breath and then tell me about this Mr Winby. I don't know much about orchard farming, I'll admit, but I can find out. He sounds like he's giving you a hard time. Is he?'

'Uh, yes, a bit. It's just that I don't know anything, and everything's so strange and they don't like having us here. It's rather difficult, I'm afraid. But we have to stay. Rhea won't go home to Simon. She says she won't ever see him again and I, I don't want to really go home either. If only the Winbys were a little more friendly. And there's no school either. What am I going to do about Rhea's schooling?' Ursula hadn't meant to tell Tim her problems, certainly not in the first few minutes of the telephone call. But there was something about him that always invited her to lean on him and share her troubles. He cared so much, even now, she could tell. She wiped the outer edge of her eyes with the back of her hand.

'Well love, couldn't you put her into school in Perth. They've got some good girls' schools there and she's used to

313

boarding anyway. That might give you more time to get things fixed up at your end.'

'But those schools cost money, Tim! And the property doesn't make enough for that. Oh Lord, I'm sorry, I didn't mean to start on all this. Why are you calling, Tim. After what I said to you last time, I never thought I'd hear from you again. Why aren't you with your wife and family today, of all days.' She could hear her voice getting bitter. And she hadn't even told him the worst of it yet. But then, maybe it wasn't his. Maybe it had been that night with Simon. God no! Please don't let it be Simon's! She turned away from the living room to stare out of the window. Rhea was outside playing with a kelpie pup Will had given her. She'd named it 'Mannie' for some reason.

'I'm, hell, I'm calling because I miss you. I was worried about you and then I couldn't help thinking about you all the time, wondering if you really meant those things you said and if you were really okay. Oh, I'm sorry, love, I know I have no right to be doing this. I just had to hear your voice. Just because I'm married now doesn't mean I can stop loving you. Maybe that's stupid and futile but I can't change it. I can't help it. Anyway, Joanna's gone home to her parents for Christmas and I'm supposed to be turning up there today. She's due in January, you know.'

'January? But, I mean. Isn't that cutting it a bit fine for the baby to be yours? Oh damn, I shouldn't have said that but really . . .'

'She's due at the beginning of January. I left Australia near the beginning of April. It's possible all right. I wish to God it weren't and I still don't really believe it seeing how careful I always was. But, that's just the way it is.'

'Just the way it is. Yes, I guess you're right.' Ursula spread a hand over her own belly. She wondered why he hadn't bothered to be careful with her. 'It's Rhea's birthday in February. She'll be ten! And you're just having your first.' She laughed uncertainly, so close to breaking down that she didn't dare speak for a few moments. It would be so nice to be able to demand his presence beside her, the way Joanna clearly did. To have him there to take care of things for her. Just to have him kiss her and say, 'there there, I'll make it better'. But it wasn't going to get better and he wasn't for her. The only person who had ever been just for her was dead. 'I'm sorry too, Tim. I haven't changed either. We just got dealt a bad hand, that's all. How are things between you and Joanna?'

'Barely speaking, to tell the truth. She got what she wanted, a husband with a good future. But she hasn't got me, not the me inside all that proper front we face the world with, and I guess that's cutting in deep. I should feel sorry for her but I can't. I'm too busy feeling sorry for you love, and for me. Besides, now we're together so much, Joanna and I find we don't really even like each other that much. I dunno . . . maybe the baby'll set things right.'

'I'm sorry, Tim. I guess you're in the mess I once was, only on the other side of things. It's almost funny. And I'm stuck out here in the outback . . . '

'No, that's not outback, darling, just the bush. Outback's different altogether. There's nothing there.'

'Well, there's nothing here either! Oh, hell! Can't you come over for . . . no. Never mind. Forget I said that. It's no good and the sooner we come to realize that, the better for us both. I hear in the cities people take turkey sandwiches down to the beach. Is that right?'

'Some do. Not Jo's family. We have to do things properly. Hot or not. Listen, Ursula, can you tell me how big your property is, and where it's located exactly. I'll try and get hold of someone to sort out what you should be growing and how much. I think this Winby fellow's giving you a run-around.'

'All right. But I'll have to write it to you. Rhea's coming in and I don't want her to know . . . '

'Write to my office then, not home.' He quickly gave her the address. 'Goodbye love and Merry Christmas.'

'Merry Christmas to you too Tim . . . Bye.' She put the phone down and moved carefully away from the table to the door. Should she tell him? Was it even his? She was five months gone by her reckoning but very little was showing yet. No-one had even noticed with the loose-fitting dresses she'd been wearing to keep cool. Rhea came in carrying the pup in her arms.

'Mother? Can I bring Mannie inside for a while? It's so hot out there! Neither of us can breathe.'

315

'Yes, of course you can. There's nothing in here she can ruin anyway. It was kind of Will to give you Mannie, wasn't it? He and Stoney are nice boys.' Rhea ignored her mother's words. She was looking at her with a frown.

'What's the matter?' she asked baldly. Ursula flinched and covered it by bending down to stroke the pup's ears.

'Nothing, darling. I'm fine. Shall we have lunch now or would you prefer to wait a while? It's cold anyway. I couldn't stand the thought of lighting the stove in this heat.'

'Let's leave it a while then. I want to teach Mannie to sit. Sit Mannie! Sit!' Ursula watched while her daughter tried again and again to get the puppy to comply. Nothing was going to order that day, she decided.

'I'm going to lie down for a while, dear. Call me in an hour, would you?' She turned and left the room before Rhea could ask again what was the matter. She couldn't say what.

The bed was iron-framed with springs and a thin mattress. The boys had helped them paint all the walls inside the house a light cream with white gloss on the woodwork. The kitchen now seemed a different place. And the floors had been washed and varnished so that they gleamed brightly against the pale walls. But there was still almost no furniture. Mr Winby had bought two beds at the market along with some other pieces: a table, two frayed armchairs, a sofa that should have been retired years ago, and a chest of drawers. He said that was all he could find or afford. He was just like Simon. Often Ursula wondered if she owned the property or if Mr Winby did. Sometimes she wondered aloud, but he didn't listen to her. She was only a woman. And this was a man's country.

She had bought some unbleached canvas and was slowly making slip covers for all the chairs and sofa. Rhea was painting the table and chest of drawers a silvery green and grey. The place looked quite nice, really. And soon they would paint the outside, especially that ugly red roof, all white, to reflect the sun. She lay down, the sheets cool and scratchy beneath her skin. It was well over the hundred mark, even in the shade. She fanned herself slowly, her hand limp in the heat. Some Christmas.

Rhea knocked on the door about an hour later, peering into the warm gloom.

316

'You awake? I'm getting hungry. Shall I start lunch?'
Ursula opened her eyes, feeling the heat of the sheets beneath
her back and face, drowsy and unwilling to move. She flipped
her hand at Rhea, a white movement in the darkened room.

'You start. I'll be there soon.'

'D'you want some lemonade. Stoney brought some that Mrs
Winby made. It's cold.' Ursula tasted the stickiness in her
mouth, her tongue dry against her teeth.

'Yes please. I'll get up in a minute.'

'Mother? . . . Are you all right? You seem . . . funny. Did
something happen?' Did something happen? Ursula laughed
and sat up, propped up on one elbow.

'Now what could possibly happen out here? I'm fine,
darling. Just get me the lemonade while I wash, there's a good
girl.' There was a galvanized iron bucket in the corner of the
room. Ursula sat up slowly, her head pounding from the air-
lessness and drugged sleep of hot afternoons. Then she went
over to the bucket and lifted it on to the windowsill, splashing
the water over her face and arms, not caring that it ran down
her neck and wet her dress. It was cool and smelt strongly of
sulphur: bore-hole water from the pumps; no good for
drinking, but not too bad to wash with. It was brown in the
bucket, slopping wetly up the sides. Ursula lowered it to the
ground and opened the louvres, trying to catch a breeze. There
wasn't one. The sea breeze was blocked by the hills, and the
easterly, that came across the Nullabor plain – 300 miles of
treeless, waterless desert – scorching as it touched skin. Ursula
hated that wind. She spread her hands across the small bulge in
her stomach, flattening the material across while she looked
down at it. She would have to tell Rhea soon. She would say it
was Simon's, of course. Maybe it was.

'Here you are, Mother. I put the rest of it out on the verandah at the back with a wet tea-towel over the bucket. It was the
coolest place I could think of.' If Rhea noticed her mother drop
her hands abruptly and turn away, she didn't say so. She just
held out the glass until her mother took it.

'Good girl. We have to get a refrigerator. I don't care what
Mr Winby says. After all, he's got one! Umm, I'll have to give
it to Mrs Winby, she knows how to make lemonade. Of course,
they're our lemons anyway.' She winked at Rhea. 'And we

317

need a proper bathroom. I'm just not going out to some "dunny" in the middle of the night with a torch anymore! God knows what's out there. We need a shower and a lavatory. That wretched solicitor didn't care a snap of his fingers about getting us properly sorted out; not his problem, he said. Mr Winby's the man to talk to, he'll sort it all out. God knows why there's still a solicitor handling the property when everything, including payment from the crop goes to Mr Winby. He's just been using our land rent-free for years. Profit? What's that? If there is any it just goes into the Winby's pockets. Oh, thank you dear.' She took a wet handkerchief from her daughter's outstretched hand and wiped it over her neck and face. It dried within a few seconds but felt good anyway. Ursula looked at her daughter and smiled again. She'd been so brave about everything. All Ursula had to do was mention going home and Rhea would stop complaining and manage whatever new problem had to be faced. But it was hard on the girl, no school, no friends – except Will and Stoney who ignored her most of the time.

The only things to be enjoyed were the horses and the lagoon. Mr Winby had corrected her when she called it 'lake'. Here, it seemed they only had lagoons. And creeks – not brooks or streams. Up the back of the lagoon there was a creek running through a gully, a tiny trickle of water threading through deep, dry-erosion walls of red clay streaked with yellow. The boys took Rhea to play sometimes, sliding through the clay and water until they were plastered red and then running across the break and diving into the lagoon. There were water-ticks in the lagoon and it was too dark to see the bottom, a muddy green and brown, like everything else. Ursula hadn't been in.

'Come on, let's see what we can put together for lunch. Sorry it's not very Christmassy, darling, and that I didn't have a present for you. I'll make it up to you, I promise.' She hugged Rhea to her side and kissed the top of the girl's head. Rhea put her arm around her mother's waist.

'It's okay. I didn't have one for you either or for your birthday. Anyway, I know you're not very well at the moment. Mother? I also know about . . . well, you know. You're going to have a baby, aren't you? Does Daddy know?' Rhea felt her mother stiffen beside her. 'It's okay. I mean, why didn't you

318

tell me sooner? I could've helped more with things instead of running off with the boys. You should've told me.'

'Oh Rhea! I'm so glad you know. I haven't known what to say. I didn't even know myself until we got here and then, I kept hoping something would happen to explain it to you. I don't know why I've been so silly about it. You don't mind having a baby brother or sister, do you?' Ursula squeezed her daughter tightly to her.

'No! Of course not! I just didn't think you and Daddy liked each other enough to want any more children.' Tentatively, Rhea reached out and placed her hand on her mother's stomach. She drew back immediately.

'Well, it wasn't on purpose. Sometimes these things just happen. And anyway, he's got no idea. I'd rather not tell him either, if that's all right with you?'

'Fine. I don't want him to know where we are anyway. Mother?' Rhea hesitated and Ursula tilted her daughter's chin up so she could see her face. It was embarrassed.

'What?'

'It is Daddy's baby, isn't it? I mean, you and Tim didn't have an affair, did you?' There was dead silence for several seconds. Ursula looked at Rhea, astonished by the calm, adult tone. The child had gone, replaced by a woman with a woman's knowledge peering out of too-young eyes. Ursula wondered how it had happened.

'No Rhea. It's your father's baby. Don't worry about that. Of course, how we're going to afford another mouth to feed, clothes, school . . . Well, we'll just have to manage somehow. I better go see a doctor sometime soon.'

'That's kind've what I've been wondering about. Couldn't we, maybe, take a trip down to the city one day soon. You could go see a doctor and anyway, we never got to see Perth on the way in. I'd really like to go and look at it. Will says there're some beaut beaches.'

'Beautiful beaches. Don't turn stryne on me, for God's sake Rhea! . . . Sorry, I didn't mean to snap like that.' Ursula breathed in deeply. 'All right. Why not? We can go next week if you like. No, not next week, that's difficult. The material I ordered for the curtains is coming in then. But the one after. It'll have to be a quick trip. Just to see the doctor and maybe that solicitor fellow, and then a look around. We don't have much money to go staying in hotels and things. But it would be fun, wouldn't it? Maybe we could have a look at schools too – just to check them out. Would you like that?'

'Oh Mother! Could we? Just a look. I know we can't afford them. But just to see real people again.' Ursula laughed and squeezed Rhea against her again.

'Yes, now wouldn't that be nice!'

Mr Winby thought it a good idea that they went to Perth. Ursula knew he was hoping they'd stay there. She smiled tightly at him and asked if there was anything she should pick up for the property while she was there. He took off his hat and put it back on again, more firmly, before saying.

'Naw. We don't need anything from the city. Too bloody expensive. You ladies go and enjoy yourselves.' His tone suggested they would be indulging themselves with expensive fripperies from morning to night. Then he turned on his heel and walked away, his broad back as arrogant and uncompromising as ever. Ursula clamped her lips together rather more tightly and walked back into the house. She'd had no reply to her letter to Tim yet and wondered if one would come while they were away. But she couldn't help it. Once the idea of leaving the property and going into the city had taken hold, it was impossible to abandon. The sickness and nausea had come back steadily in the last two days and at times she wondered if she should attempt such a journey. But she and Rhea had taken to counting the days. It would be too disappointing not to go. She would manage somehow.

The Holden was packed and ready to go, one suitcase with a few days' worth of clothing and wash-things already in the back and the map spread out across the dash-board to keep it from overheating. Will was taking Mannie while they were away. He stood around sheepishly, smiling and offering advice, then remembering that he was a boy and that girls were not to be paid attention to. Ursula knew he wanted to come with them but she also knew better than to offer. Mrs Winby had not come out of her kitchen at all. She thought they were daft going to Perth in the heat, especially when money was a problem and they now had more mouths to feed. Ursula ignored her.

'Bye, Will. We won't be away long. Tell Stoney we said goodbye too.' She climbed into the driver's seat, wincing as the hot vinyl burned through her dress. Rhea climbed in beside her, calling excitedly to Will through the window so that half her body was once more outside the car.

'Look after Mannie and don't feed her kangaroo meat. She's too young still; it'll give her worms. Oh, and she likes to sleep at the foot of the bed with a blanket that I left in the house. It's a little grey one and I gave it to her so you can let her chew it . . . ' The last of her instructions were cut off as Ursula pulled her back inside the car and drove towards the first gate. There were only three altogether because this wasn't really a livestock property and so fences didn't matter as much. Rhea climbed out, hoisted them clumsily onto her hip and pulled them back as Ursula drove through. Then she repeated the process and closed them fast. It took them nearly twenty minutes to reach the main highway and then they sat back happily singing 'Ten Green Bottles', and 'The Gypsy Rover', all the way through the hills and down to Perth.

Perth was a beautiful city, Ursula thought as she drove along the side of the river, staring out at the shimmering water and the white sails that dotted the bay. There was a single bridge spanning the Swan River, gracefully arched and shining in the sunlight. Rhea was kneeling on the seat so that she could swivel around in all directions at once to see everything. Just before the bridge two ferries were moored alongside a jetty with a sign saying 'Barrack Street Jetty' and then further down 'South Perth' on it in faded lettering. Ursula drove by slowly, wondering if she were going the right way. The city seemed to be more to the right but her road was leading her along the river again, hugging in against a green, fern-covered cliff on the right and the water on the left, past a red-bricked building that smelled of hops and beer, curving around in a wide sweep and then opening out into a highway. She pulled over and consulted her map again as soon as she could.

'I don't know, Rhea, but I think we missed the city proper. This looks like suburbs to me. We're here, right now, I think. Where d'you want to go? On towards the ocean? Or back into town?'

'Let's go see the ocean. It sounds so exotic. ''The Indian

Ocean''. I feel like it'll have palm-trees and dates and maharajahs wandering around. Can we stay somewhere near the sea? Please, Mother?' Rhea was hard to refuse when she pleaded and Ursula laughed.

'Well, why not. There'll be plenty of time to see the city tomorrow. I could do with a long glass of lemonade and a fresh sea breeze.' She tried not to think of the pain that had been building in her lower back for the last few hours. 'Let's try this place. Cottesloe. It's not too far from here, I think. We must be in Claremont right now I'd say, so Cottesloe's only just down the road.'

They drove on for a couple of miles, wondering if they were going the right way. There was another intersection ahead. Ursula slowed down and turned right, pulling in to the kerb. They were in a shopping street bustling with women in floral dresses, hats and gloves. Ursula opened her door and went around to Rhea's side.

'All right, darling? Would you like to get out and have a walk around for a while? We can get something to drink if you like?' Rhea climbed out and the two stood, leaning against the car, wondering where to go. There was a corner delicatessen selling ices and lemonade and they walked along the street, admiring the first shops they had seen since arriving in Western Australia. A girl about the same age as Rhea, dark-haired and pretty in her sundress, walked past licking at an ice-cream. Rhea's head followed the girl's figure for some distance. She looked at her mother.

'D'you think there are any schools around here maybe? It seems a nice sort of place.'

'Could be. We'll ask in the delicatessen. They'd know if anybody. I'll bet all the children go in there after school for drinks or ices. Are you feeling all right, darling? Not too hot for you?' Ursula was worried at how pale her daughter looked; pale and sweaty, her fair hair plastered wetly across her forehead and her eyes red-rimmed. She stroked the hair back behind Rhea's ear.

'Yes, I'm fine. Really. What's this street called anyway?' Rhea would never admit to feeling anything less than fighting fit.

'Bourke Street. We'll ask directions to the sea. It'll be easier than map-reading. What d'you want? Lemonade?' Ursula pulled open the fly-screen door and walked into a dark, musty-smelling shop. Groceries were piled from floor to ceiling along every wall and along three centre aisles. There were two counters and she walked over to the one that a man in white apron and rolled-up sleeves was standing behind.

'Hallo. Could we have two lemonades and an ice please?' She smiled when the man looked over at Rhea and winked.

'Wha' typa ice d'jer wan'? Ducky-double? Drink-on-a-stick? Wha'?' Rhea was looking in the big freezer, trying to get as cool as possible while seemingly looking for the right ice.

'Uh, I'll have this one please.' She handed one out to the man. Ursula picked up a packet of biscuits and added them to the pile.

'We were wondering, while we were here, if you knew of any good girl schools around here? Ones that take boarders?' She smiled again. The man leaned forward on the counter.

'Lady, every girl school's round here. There's MLC, Methodist Ladies College just back aways, down the Stirling Highway, and then there's Loretto, the Catholic one, and PLC, Presbyterian Ladies College over there on View and St Hilda's over in Mosmans and right near it is Iona, but that's only a little school. There are some more scattered around someplace, like St Mary's but you'll find mostly what yew want right round here. Is it for this little lady here?' He grinned when Rhea grew shy and sidled closer to her mother.

'Yes, that's right. We live up near Gidgeeganup but there's no school of any sort there, so we thought we'd look at some down here in Perth. Which d'you think is the best?' Ursula couldn't quite believe that she was asking a shopkeeper which school he would recommend, but then again, these people probably did know the schools very well. He'd certainly know how the girls behaved. The man was considering the question seriously.

'Well, you know, they're all pretty good, I s'pose. We see mostly PLC and St Hilda's girls in here I reckon, comin' for lollies after school, and they're both nice-mannered, polite girls I'd say. You couldn't go wrong with either as long as you're Protestant. If you're Catholic there's not much choice – Loretto it is. Not that they're not nice girls too,' he added

323

judiciously. Rhea was looking interested and Ursula pulled out her map and asked the man to mark the two Protestant schools. While he was at it, she asked the best way down to the beach.

'Take a left at the end of the street, run along the tracks to the next intersection, turn right and bob's your uncle. Just go straight. It's about a mile, mile'n'a half. Something like that. Got somewhere to stay?' She shook her head and he wrote the names of several places down on the side of the map. 'There are lots of boarding houses too, y'know, guest houses where yew can stay for the night. Pretty cheap too.' Ursula thanked him and paid for their purchases. They wandered out into the sunshine again, and looked down the street. It was a lazy, hot afternoon and people were slow in their movements as they walked along, or stopped to peer at something in the windows.

'Beach first? Or would you like to look at the schools now we're so close?'

'St Hilda's. I want to look there first. Can we?'

Ursula smiled, ignoring the pain that made her want to gag. Rhea needed something to go her way. She shrugged.

'Why not? It's all academic anyway.'

'Oh, Mother!'

Chapter Twenty One

The school was set back from the road with a wide, sweeping drive that circled around the gardens with their dark cypress trees and back down to the road again. Ursula drove up to the stone building, its windows blank and reflecting light as if to show how empty they were, framed by Virginia creeper that shook in a huge, rippling mass. Ursula parked to one side of the drive and Rhea climbed out, her head craned back to see to the top of the building. Her skirt spread out, flipping lightly in the wind and, looking at her, Ursula was still amazed at how indomitable such a fragile-seeming girl could be. Rhea stood surveying the building, arms folded across her chest, her pale hair pulled neatly back behind her ears. She was contemplating the buildings, lips firmly held together as though her decision now would be final. This was a school to last, she pronounced solemnly.

The gardens with their well-tended beds, their immaculate lawns and their swept paths all spoke of endurance. It was important to know where one came from; Rhea knew that now with a relentless grind in some back part of her mind. She wished she could belong here; become part of this place and this time. Abruptly she turned away and leaned against the car again, still unused to the feeling of loss that had become part of her since that day with Lucy. Lucy had robbed her of her father, her home, her identity. She would never forget that. Ursula held out her hand.

'Shall we see if anyone's in?' She walked up the front steps under a shield with the inscription '*Domine Dirige Nos*', and knocked on the doors. The sound was absorbed in the thickness of the wood. No-one came to answer it. Ursula glanced back at Rhea, at the firm expression on her young face. Sometimes Ursula felt as though she were the child and Rhea had grown beyond her, into an old woman with her jaded knowledge of life held tightly inside. It was in the droop of her eyelids, in the pursing of her mouth. Ursula tried to rally them both.

'Well, let's take a walk around while we're here, shall we? I expect there may be some offices or schoolrooms round the back, and maybe someone'll be there.' They walked back down the steps and around the side of the building, their footsteps echoing sharply on the driveway. At the back there were more gardens flanked by pre-fabricated houses with corrugated iron-roofs. Sprinklers shook arcs of water out in jerky shivers of light and the paths were spotted with brown blemishes from the bore water. Ursula muttered to herself about 'Queen Anne in front, Sally-Anne behind', while she tried the doors of the classrooms. They were all locked up tightly. They wandered around the grounds, which were strangely quiet in the way that any school seems when term-time is over and the holidays have begun; quiet and a little dejected, as though left without anyone to care. The pain in the small of Ursula's back spread cold tentacles around to clasp at her belly. She breathed in sharply. Rhea slid a hand into hers.

'It seems rather nice, doesn't it?' Ursula said after a few moments, the pain retreating back into its lair just below her navel. It sat there quietly, dully. 'A bit like your old school. Maybe they even have riding here? And piano? I'd like you to keep that up.'

'But we can't afford it, can we? Even if it is nice. And the other schools, the state ones, I can't board at. So that's that,' Rhea said firmly, her hair pulled back behind her ears, revealing the determination in her face. Ursula shrugged.

'You have to go to school, Rhea. Maybe we can sort it out somehow. Maybe Daddy would pay?'

'No! I don't want him to know where we are. I won't ever see him again. You know we decided that, Mother! You promised! Just like I did about the baby.' Her mouth was pink and cracked, like old enamel, where she'd been licking her lips against the drying sun. Now her tongue flicked out to wet them again. Ursula looked across at the main buildings again.

'We'll work it out somehow. I won't tell Daddy. Promise.' In the silence of the afternoon a single cicada was shrilling, its sound exploding against the walls and throwing itself, magnified, back into the quadrangle. The sun beat with a flattening force on their heads. Ursula looked around aimlessly. It was hard to keep a fixed purpose under such relentlessness.

She let her eyes wander again past the gym, across the lawns to the main building. And then she started suddenly, her gaze narrowing against the glare. There was a woman walking by the far building, her arms filled with large rolls of paper and her face turned away. She walked quickly, impatiently, with little, forceful steps that should have left dents in the pavement. Ursula pushed herself away from the wall she had been leaning against, out into the vacancy of the quadrangle after the woman, calling 'Excuse me, excuse me!' She felt self-conscious but there was no-one to pay any attention. The wind, fitful in its timing, snatched her voice away. Finally, just as the woman was about to disappear into the building through a side-door that Ursula had missed, hidden away under an overhanging roof, Ursula caught up. 'Excuse me,' she said, breathless and feeling flushed from having walked so fast in the dead heat of the afternoon. The pain had reappeared triumphant and Ursula caught at her side with tensed claws of fingers. The woman jumped and then laughed, one hand pressed to her heart.

'I didn't see you there. Did you want something? I'm afraid the school's closed for holidays, you know.' She relaxed a little when she saw Ursula properly. A reluctant Rhea trailed along the path towards them. The woman looked from one to the other, her pale hair streaked with wings of blue that Ursula thought odd, and her face squashed and wrinkled into round cheeks and small, dark eyes that shone wetly. She rustled the papers over to her other arm, still watching Ursula.

'I realize you're closed but my daughter and I are on a short trip to Perth and we wanted to look around for schools for her while we were here. I don't suppose there's anyone I could talk to, is there?'

'You're English. Have you just arrived in Australia? I must say, you look rather hot. Why don't you come in with me to my office? You can sit down for a minute and, my dear, I do think you ought to sit down. It's lovely and cool in the main building – all those thick stones! They knew how to build back then. Not like those pre-fabs. So ugly! But then, they're only temporary. I'm Mrs Murton, the assistant head. I'd shake hands but all these papers would fall everywhere. Class schedules for next term, I'm afraid. No-one else seems to be able to work them out, and I'm supposed to be retired but they keep calling me back. Things get in such a muddle!' She talked distractedly while she led them in through the door and across a wide hall with polished boards and portraits hanging around the panelled walls. A clock hanging over the main entrance chimed the half-hour, its sound dying immediately in the silence of the hall. Mrs Murton's office was round to the right of the stage and she walked in and dumped the papers gratefully onto her desk before turning around.

'Now then, how-do-you-do Mrs . . . ?'

'Paterson. Ursula Paterson and this is my daughter, Rhea. Rhea, this is Mrs Murton, the Assistant Headmistress.' The young face smiled obediently, old eyes looking out and assessing.

'Rhea? My, that's an unusual name. Nice to hear something so old-fashioned when everyone seems to be trying to be so modern and trend-setting these days. Do please sit down and tell me how I can help you.' Mrs Murton gestured with limp, faded hands to the chairs. Now that she could be seen clearly, Ursula realized Mrs Murton was even older than she had first thought.

'I was wondering actually about scholarships, Mrs Murton. We're newly arrived as you guessed, and there doesn't seem to be a school anywhere near where we live. Rhea's used to boarding in England but since her father . . . died . . . we can't afford to send her to a private school anymore. I was rather hoping there might be some scholarships that would cover our situation? Rhea's very bright.' She had seated herself on a chair by Mrs Murton's desk and was beginning to feel better, the pain back in its place. Rhea sat still and wary on her chair. Her normally pale cheeks were flushed an ugly, blotched pink, a line of white circling her mouth. She breathed deeply to cool herself, knowing she could manage this heat. She could manage anything now; it was as though her childhood had seeped out of her in the last few months just like the enveloping cloud of surety and happiness had cleared to let her see the world as it really was. Only tenderness for her mother remained. Mrs Murton was looking at her.

'Well, yes. We do have two for girls about to enter the senior school. That's Lower Four through Upper Six. How old are you, Rhea?'

'Ten in February.'

'Oh, I see. Well, that's a little young but then, the English system is rather more advanced I've often found. We've had a few girls here from England and they've nearly always been a year ahead. Do you have any records of Rhea's schooling with you, Mrs Paterson? The scholarships are, of course, open to fierce competition.' She smiled and a thousand tiny wrinkles networked across her face, like crushed tissue-paper. Ursula nodded her understanding.

'I haven't brought them with me. That was rather stupid of me, I'm afraid. But I could, of course, send them to you as soon as we get back to the property. Rhea has always been top, or near top of her class.'

'Oh well, that sounds promising. Perhaps you would send them to me then, and if you wouldn't mind filling out this form? Just so we can have some details. How are you finding Australia? Rather hot for you at this time of the year?' She glanced at the child's face, at the stoic acceptance that should not have been there. But then, the girl had just lost her father. That would explain a lot. She noticed the mother grimace, as though in pain, as she reached forward for the form. So young looking to be the girl's mother. Nothing more than a child herself.

'Very hot for Rhea. She's only ever known England and the cool. But I was born and brought up in Singapore and my step-mother was actually from Perth. I inherited her property up near Gidgeeganup after her death.' Intent on filling in the form, Ursula didn't see the suddenly alert look in the old woman's eyes.

'What was your step-mother's name, Mrs Paterson?'

329

'Hendricks. Sally Hendricks.' She looked up in surprise when she heard Mrs Murton make a sound almost like an apple being bitten crisply in half, teeth clicking shut with unexpected force. 'Mrs Murton? Are you all right?' The woman was sitting back in her chair, one blue-veined arm crossed over her chest, the hand clutched at her collar. Ursula began to stand. But then Mrs Murton shook her head.

'Yes, yes, so silly of me. I was just taken aback. I knew Sally for years, of course, while she was at school here. You should have told me you had a relative who had been here. She was always a favourite of mine. Such a beauty! I heard she'd gone out to Singapore and married a man named Fraser but that was the last I think any of us ever knew. Not many people come from Gidgeeganup you see, and those that can get out. Or so I gather. She's dead then?' It was difficult for the old woman to speak calmly. Her students were her children; the 'Mrs' merely a courtesy title. Ursula looked upset.

'Oh, I'm so sorry, Mrs Murton. I had no idea Sally went to school here. I wouldn't have told you so bluntly if I'd realized you knew her.' She sat forward as though she would take the woman's frail hands and chafe some life into them. But there was too much distance between them and she felt too old herself: as though she were watching the scene from a different angle, not inside her own body. Her belly felt very warm and then very cold, in turns.

'How did she die? Was it the war? We were so worried for all our girls during the war. So many of them were abroad, in Europe or Asia. Some of them were killed. Even here we were worried for the girls, made them dig trenches in the grounds and sent the boarders who were left off to Bencubbin. And such a loss of life for our young fighting men. It's a terrible shame.'

'Yes . . . I know. Sally and my father had two children, Emma who was about five, I think, at the time and baby Tom. He was only two and my favourite.' She smiled painfully. 'Singapore was on the point of falling and Sally decided to get out on one of the last boats with the children rather than risk internment.' She lifted her arms and shrugged, all the despair of that knowledge still with her. 'The ship was sunk and everyone drowned.'

'Oh how awful! The poor things! Oh poor, poor girl! She

was always so lively and determined. Had to have her own way but not a bad bone in her. That hair was so beautiful, now wasn't it? Such a lovely girl.' Mrs Murton dabbed at her face with a square of lace, her powdered skin dewed with perspiration. She looked up slowly and smiled.

'I am being silly, I know, but she was very dear to me. All my girls are dear to me, but Sally was special. So many years I wondered, hoping to get a letter, to hear some news and I didn't even know!' She shook her head, the blue hair waving about her face tiredly. 'And so you're her step-daughter, Mrs Paterson. And that would make Rhea a sort of step-grand-daughter. My goodness, it sounds as though Sally was so old and she wasn't! Connections do get rather puzzling nowadays, don't they? Well, that certainly helps things for you. There's an Old Girl's scholarship for children of previous students. I'm sure we could qualify Rhea as such. Sally's step-daughter's daughter.' She laughed, like dry rustling leaves crunched up in a hand, and carried on moving things around her desk, placing the ink-stand to one side and then moving it back.

Ursula glanced across at Rhea. The girl was frowning as she watched the old woman's erratic movements. How could an old woman who seemed, well, a bit dotty still have it in her power to grant scholarship, Rhea wondered? Ursula could feel some of her puzzlement, some of her expectation. But nothing showed on her face and her hands remained clasped together in her lap. She would make no overture until invited.

'When would Rhea have to take the exam? I could bring her down again with her reports from her school in England if we know the date.'

'Oh my, yes. I'm not sure of the exact date but I know it's soon after the girls arrive for their first term. February eighth for boarders. Why don't we just enrol Rhea anyway – if you could send me her school records and I've got all the information on this form – and then we'll sort it out after the exam. I'm sure we can do something to help an Old Girl's family. Miss Mitchell, the Headmistress, likes to keep our own sorts returning here. Well, isn't this exciting, Rhea? Are you liking Australia?' She held her head to one side, the shiny eyes bright with pleasure. Rhea looked down at her hands.

'It's fine. I'm sure I'll like it here very much, Mrs Murton.'

331

Rhea's face was still composed, her elation contained. She was keeping her distance. And then Ursula was smiling and holding out her hand to the woman, prompting Rhea to stand and do the same. Rhea's hand was soft and sweaty in the woman's. She bobbed her head a little as she said goodbye.

They were walking out again, across the empty hall with its small-paned windows high in the air shedding squares of light on to the boards with their smell of old wax and dust. The light shafts glittered with dust motes, circling lazily in the air. It almost looked like gold-dust against the dark of the hall. Rhea smiled with her furled, secretive smile, holding the feeling in tightly until they were outside. Then she turned and hugged her mother, her arms tight around her waist. Ursula held her daughter against her thigh, trying to ignore the sudden scalding pain, feeling the lightness tip up and over the quadrangle of sun, folding in on itself as she rose and fell with it. She heard Rhea calling her from a long distance, the voice circling with herself up again and down again, up and down, until the firm, hardness of stone scorched her cheek and her mouth filled with bile.

When she came to, she was lying in a bed with a curtain all around her. There was no-one there, even the light was dimmer and cooler as it filtered through the curtain fabric. Sounds of other people were curiously absent. Where was she? She felt tired – she wasn't used to such weariness that she couldn't even lift her hand. It seemed anchored to the bed, set in the folds of the sheets. Her mouth was dry and she licked her lips carefully. There was no pain anymore. Not yet. Perhaps it had given up on her, decided she wasn't worth the effort. Why was she here? She tried to remember and some of the day drifted back in snatches of ten green bottles and Barrack Street jetty, blue hair – Rhea! Where was Rhea? But the hum of silence continued and she couldn't find the force to call out and break it. A lassitude that climbed heavily over her, twitching as new thoughts occurred and tried to shrug it off, drew her down deeply into the pillow again. She drifted with it.

The metallic hiss of the curtain being drawn back on steel rings disturbed her and she turned her head lazily to one side. Was there someone there? A nurse with a tray of instruments stood back at the foot of the bed. A doctor pushed past her impatiently, lifting Ursula's wrist between two fingers, checking his watch. He returned her wrist and then lifted her eyelids. A light gleamed for a moment. The doctor stood back.

'Mrs Paterson? Can you hear me all right?' She nodded slowly, up, down. 'Good. Are you feeling better? No pain?' One nod, one shake. 'Good.' He smiled and gestured to the nurse for the tray. 'We're keeping you here for just a little while. This'll help.' She nodded again. There didn't seem to be much else to do. Her head only worked in two directions at the moment. She barely felt the needle as it slid into her arm. 'Then, when you're a bit better, we'll have a talk. How does that sound?' She fumbled to get her tongue set right.

'Rhea? Where . . . ?'

'Your daughter's just fine, Mrs Paterson. Mrs Murton is looking after her for the next day or so. And then, when you're better, you can go back to your property.'

'Wha' . . . Wha' happened?' Strange the way her tongue seemed twice its normal size.

'You were very sick for a while, Mrs Paterson. You haven't been looking after yourself, now have you? A woman in your condition should've been taking it much easier, eating more. When you collapsed at St Hilda's and an ambulance brought you here, that's when we found you were pregnant. We'll need you to take much more care of yourself from now on. You nearly lost the baby, you know. I know how you must feel about this child with your husband having just died . . . That's why I want you to stay here for a day or two. Just take it easy and we'll look after everything for you. And your daughter's just fine. She's quite a competent young lady. We'll let her see you when you wake up again.' He patted her hand between his, cool and professional. She felt numb and already the room was receding, dipping away. She closed her eyes and slept.

Ursula wasn't sure how much later she woke up, but Rhea was sitting by her bedside and the curtains had been partially pulled back. She could now see another bed opposite, empty, and the corner of the room. She tried to smile at Rhea, her mouth wobbling at the corners. Rhea sat very still.

'Are you feeling better now, Mother? The doctor said you would be.'

'Yes. Yes, just tired really. Are you all right with Mrs

333

Murton?' Ursula saw Rhea's face with all its responsibility carried carefully as though it were fragile and might break if dropped. Her tone was soothing.

'Everything's fine, Mother. Mrs Murton's going to let me stay with her until you get out of here and then Mr Winby's going to come down and drive us back to the property. He said he can catch the bus down. They're very sorry you got sick. So am I. I should've taken more care of you, what with the baby, I mean. Mrs Winby sounded quite excited at the thought of a baby on the property.' She looked wary. Could her mother discuss such things yet? But Ursula just nodded and smiled again, more firmly this time.

'That's good of them. I'm sorry Mr Winby's being bothered like this but it's just one of these things. Perhaps it'll be for the best. Maybe they'll finally thaw out and learn to like us?' Was keeping this baby for the best? Perhaps it was Simon's baby, conceived in pain and fear. Maybe that's why she was having such problems? She shrank from the thought. But how much worse to think it was Tim's and she had nearly lost it. Hers and Tim's. And now she could keep a part of Tim with her always. Yes, it must be his. She couldn't believe it was Simon's child. She blinked quickly and cleared her throat.

'I'm going to need to see the solicitor while I'm down here, darling. Could you ask Mrs Murton to ring him? You know his number, don't you? It's in my black address book. Mr Waters. Ask him to come and see me, would you? I must sort some things out before Mr Winby comes to collect us.'

'I'll take care of it, Mother. Don't worry. Everything's going to be just fine,' Rhea said. She put her hand in her pocket and brought out a piece of paper. She laid it by the bedside. 'Mrs Murton's number. In case you need to talk to me. But I'll be back here in the morning anyway.' She reached down and kissed her mother's cheek before getting up and disappearing through the gap in the curtains. Ursula continued to stare after her.

Mr Waters was a short, compact man dressed in a suit that seemed too tight over his thighs and too long in the seat. It made him appear to waddle, his jacket thrown over one shoulder and his short-sleeved shirt curiously out of place with a tie. But that was a style Ursula knew she would have to get used to. For a moment she remembered Billy in his cream suit, his jacket off and shirt sleeves rolled up. So elegant. She smiled at the figure Mr Waters made in comparison.

'Please sit down, Mr Waters. I hope it wasn't too much of an inconvenience for you to come down here.' She waved to the chair beside the bed. Mr Waters sat down. He was a pleasant-looking man with short mouse-brown hair, premature lines around his mouth and eyes from the sun, and ordinary bluish eyes. The sort of man you passed in the street every day without noticing. His manner was equally bland.

'Sorry to hear you're ill, Mrs Paterson. It was no trouble at all to come down here but I can't imagine there's much more I can tell you than last time. Mr Winby handles all the property accounts. You need to talk to him about those.'

'And what exactly do you do, Mr Waters?' Ursula sounded friendly, interested.

'I, or rather my father, originally found Mr Winby to manage the property. We make sure taxes and rates are paid, and we keep the title deeds in your name. That's about it.' He was relieved she was being so sensible about this. The last thing he wanted was to get between her and her manager about money issues.

'I see. And who pays your fees?'

'Well, you do. Or rather, Mr Winby does from the property accounts.'

'So, you will admit that both you and Mr Winby do, in effect, work for me?' Ursula saw the solicitor tense.

'Well, yes, in effect. But I'm sure Mr Winby knows what the prop . . .'

'I'm not interested in what you are sure about, Mr Waters. I'm interested in you doing what I pay you to do. And that means sorting things out with Mr Winby so that I get some profit out of the property. At the moment, and for the last thirteen years or so, every penny earned by that property – my property, Mr Waters – has gone into Mr Winby's pocket or yours. I don't think that's good enough. It's time you started earning your fee and it's time Mr Winby started making me a profit. Is that clear? Otherwise I will find myself another farm manager. And another solicitor.'

'And what exactly do you want me to do, Mrs Paterson? Take a drive out to your property and talk to Mr Winby in person? Tell him he's not working hard enough? Is that it?' He had become aggressive, unused to a woman taking the assertive role and not liking it.

'Mr Winby will be here in Perth tomorrow, Mr Waters. I will set up an appointment for him to see you and then you will explain that while I feel Mr Winby works very hard on the property, I do not feel it appropriate that he should be in charge of the accounts with the power to say who will get what, nor do I find it acceptable that, at the end of the day, any profit is clearly going into his family's pocket rather than mine. I don't even have a refrigerator, Mr Waters, but you can be sure Mr Winby has one! I will take over the accounts once Mr Winby has shown me how they are kept. I want you to tell him that. I know you think I should talk to him myself but as I'm sure you're aware, since you hired him, Mr Winby doesn't believe in listening to women about anything. So, you chose the man; you sort it out. Or you find someone else.'

'Well, I hardly think he'll stand for this sort . . . '

'I won't stand for any more, Mr Waters. And I'm the one you better start paying attention to. I own the property. I employ Mr Winby. I employ you. And if you don't sort things out to my satisfaction tomorrow, I will fire Mr Winby and I will fire you. Understood?'

Mr Waters wiped his handkerchief over the sudden sweat that covered his face. He had been getting a steady and very comfortable fee for doing nothing for several years. He couldn't imagine his father or the other partners would be too happy if Mrs Paterson took her business away. Bloody autocratic bitch! And he had thought her so gentle and timid, so pretty. He glanced at her in dislike.

'As you say, Mrs Paterson. I will see Mr Winby at one o'clock tomorrow in my office. Is that all?'

'For the moment. Thank you, Mr Waters. I'm sure you'll sort everything out very comfortably. Goodbye.' He left without shaking hands to Ursula's relief. Otherwise he would have seen how much hers were trembling. She smiled in sudden elation. God, she'd show them!

* * *

336

The letter was waiting for her when she walked into the living room, tied up in a packet with two from Lettice and Tiffany. Ursula saw it immediately. She kicked off her shoes, laid her purse down on the chair and walked, barefoot, over to the table where Will had left their mail. The floorboards were cool beneath the soles of her feet, cool and smoothly varnished. Rhea was busy with Mannie, rolling her over on her back and rubbing her tummy, exclaiming at how much she had grown while Rhea was away, and spilling some of her delight about the school over Will who was carrying their suitcase in from the car. He tried hard to be nonchalant but Ursula noticed the scowl beginning to form; like Mr Winby's scowl all the way back to the property – and his heavy silence. But he'd held his tongue and he was going to show her the accounts. That was one battle won. Ursula picked up the letters and carried them into her bedroom. She shut the door quietly behind her.

'Darling,' it began, 'I got your letter a week ago and would have replied sooner but the baby decided, unexpectedly, to arrive three weeks early which sent us all into a panic. He's fine, a bouncing seven and a half pounder with little or no hair and pink gums. When he smiles, he looks like Buddah. Maybe all babies do. I would have thought he'd be smaller, being premature. Joanna says this proves he's mine. I'm trying not to think of that. Joanna had an easy birth and is now spending some time at her parent's place. I've pleaded work – truthfully enough – to stay here in town. I miss you so much when I'm here alone in the evenings. If only things hadn't messed up like this. My own fault. What can I say?'

'I spoke with a friend about your problems and he has promised to take a look in on you while he's over in Perth – sometime around the end of February, I expect. His name is John Balham. He'll have a much better idea about things than I will. All I know is sheep. About Rhea's schooling: I know you'll refuse but I'm insisting anyway. I got you out here and I owe you something, so please let me pay the fees. I can afford it without any problems and Joanna will never know. Please, darling, don't argue. Just go and find a good school.

'I'm not much of a letter-writer. I prefer to see a person, face-to-face, to say what I feel. But that may not happen anywhere in the near future, and maybe it's better if it doesn't.

337

I'll always regret things couldn't work out the way they should have. You should have been my wife, not Joanna. And we should have had a baby between us. I'll try hard to love this son of Joanna's but it would help so much more if I really thought he was mine. He doesn't even look anything like me. Dark hair from two blonde parents? I could bear it better if his conception hadn't been responsible for ruining our lives. Sorry, darling, I know this is hurting you too. I'll always love you . . . and only you. Don't hesitate to write when you find a school for Rhea or if I can ever help you, with anything.

All my love,

Tim.'

Ursula lowered the letter to her lap and closed her eyes.

Rhea came to find her some twenty minutes later with the news that Mr Winby had gone into town to buy a refrigerator for them. Her eyes were full of amused awe.

'Will says his dad's fit to split a gut over what Mr Waters had to say. Says he's never seen his dad so angry. But he's doing it. And we'll have a refrigerator! Oh, can you believe it?'

'What about the inside bathroom? Did he say anything about that?'

'Oh, Mother! One step at a time or you'll give Mr Winby a stroke. Besides, Will says he can turn the shed on the verandah into a sort of shower room, if we like. I said we liked.' She smiled, glad to be back on the property.

'And when did poor Will take all this on?' Ursula asked. Rhea waved her hand airily.

'A few minutes ago, when I mentioned it.' Her smile slipped and she became serious. 'He's very sorry about you getting sick with the baby. Said would I tell you. He's too shy himself. And he says he and Stoney will carry anything heavy for you, so you're not to go overdoing things again. We're all going to help, okay?'

Ursula sighed heavily. Everyone was being so helpful, so sorry they'd let her get sick. Everyone except, perhaps, herself. Was she really sorry? If she knew, for sure, that it was Simon's child, would she still want it? Perhaps, like Tim, she would only tolerate this baby; like the happy buddah he and Joanna had at home. An easy birth and three weeks early. It must be his then, dark hair or not. But what if her baby was Simon's?

Of course Rhea was Simon's too but she had been conceived when Simon had cared about Ursula. There was a big difference. One child conceived in love, the second in . . . what? Rape? Or anger? Not pretty either way she looked at it. Yes, of course she would love this baby – not matter what. But not knowing who the father was, that made things quite different. Perhaps it would've been better for them all if she had lost it. She looked up at Rhea.

'How d'you feel about it?'

'The baby?' Rhea shrugged, her lids drooping lower over her eyes. 'I'm happy if you are.'

'And am I?'

'I don't . . . I don't think so. Is that because you and Daddy were finished anyway after he hit you? Or because there isn't enough money?' When her mother didn't answer, Rhea sighed. 'Besides, it doesn't matter that Daddy and you were over by then. He'll still be your son and my brother. I can't wait!' She looked surprised at what she'd admitted.

'Really? Well, that's lovely, darling. I guess I'm not too sure about things yet, but no, I wouldn't have wanted to lose it. Oh, I don't really know. Funny, I keep thinking it's a boy too. Anyway, you're all I need right now, sweetheart. Come here and give me a kiss.' And for a moment Rhea forgot how adult she was now and hugged her mother like any ten-year-old child.

'Can you reach?' Will was impatient. Any minute now Stoney would come back and catch him in this stupid position. 'Push off from my shoulder and then swing yourself up,' he instructed Rhea. She wobbled in his arms as he pushed her up the tree.

'I, I can't! It's too far. Don't let me go, will you?' She wobbled again and kicked back with her leg in panic. Will stifled an oath and pushed harder.

'Try and catch hold of something in the bark. Find a toe-hold or something? Christ Rhea, you're getting heavy.'

'I'm not a good climber. I've never done this before. Can't you hold me a little steadier?' She found a foothold on his shoulder and stood up warily, clinging with her face against the trunk. Slowly she raised her arm and grabbed the branch he

339

had initially told her to climb onto. That had been some time ago and she was tired already, the thrill of swinging from the rope attached to the branch out into the lagoon having lost some of its appeal. But the boys did it all the time and she wasn't going to stand and watch them forever. She was going to learn to do it too.

'That's it! Now pull yourself up and on to it.' Will couldn't understand how anyone could be so uncoordinated. He took his own agility for granted. Rhea was obviously something entirely different. She had grazed her leg in climbing and her bathing suit was torn slightly from a snag further down, but finally she was in position. Will swarmed up the tree to join her.

'Go on then, move out further, pull the rope up to you and then jump. When you fall, the rope will swing you out into the deeper water.' He glanced at her face, feeling sudden mis-givings. Maybe he shouldn't have brought her up here. What if she made a mess of things and got hurt? With her hair tied back in a plait, her expression was one of grim determination. That worried him more than panic.

'Okay! Just give me a sec'. I'll do it!' Down below her she noticed Stoney had returned and was staring up at them. She didn't like the way he looked so far down. Carefully she pulled up the rope, her legs dangling either side of the trunk into space.

'Remember. You've got to hold very tightly and jump in an arc, so the rope swings you forward. Don't let go of it until the last second. Okay?' Will's tanned face seemed pale as his mind's eye saw Rhea plummet down onto the hard-packed ground. He shook his head, clearing the image. His hair was shorter now, cut by Rhea's mother, and he could see more easily. Now he wished he couldn't see. He glanced down at Stoney. The Aborigine boy stood with both arms folded, staring up. His face was expressionless.

'All right. Here I go. Oh God. Ohhhh . . . !' Rhea let go in a long wail of fright as she rushed towards the ground and then flew outwards, towards the shining water. The rope snapped taut in her hands and she let go, tumbling head over heels into the water. She emerged a few seconds later, laughing and waving to the boys.

340

Stoney grinned. 'Good goin, Rhea. Nice goin'.' He pulled off his trousers and took a long, flat racing dive into the water, splashing messily out to join the girl. Up the tree Will was still recovering from his fright. He had seen how close she had come to losing her grip. For a second there . . . He felt his heart slowly return to a normal pulse and waved to Rhea.

'Well done! That was just right.' Then he stood up himself, balancing easily as he pulled the rope back up. 'Watch out, here I come.' He ran along the branch, whooping with delight as he swung down and out, landing gracefully in the water with a final splashing plop. From under the water he grabbed the other two's legs, pulling them under with a fierce tug. That, it seemed, was the signal for a noisy water fight to begin and it was some time before anyone noticed the time. It was Will's father who reminded them, their faces stricken with guilt as they realized they had been gone nearly an hour.

'You lazy buggers gonna play around all day? Pardon my language, Miss Paterson, but if you want your crop picked . . . I need workers not loafers. Get your trousers on and your asses over to the barn before I come in after yews. Now!' Mr Winby emerged from behind the tree where he'd been watching them. He was leading his horse, knowing full well where to find the kids when they were missing. And he wasn't really angry. Just fed up with having to round them up all the time. It was that bloody little Rhea that made them skive off all the time. They never used to be this bad, he told himself. Her and her mum were a right pain. He gave Will a cuff as the boy walked out of the water past him. Not hard, just his palm across the boy's head in a quick blow. Will turned his head away without a word. Behind him he heard Rhea protest.

'Five minutes or I'll come lookin' for yews and then yews'll be really sorry.' Mr Winby swung onto his horse and left at a fast trot. Rhea grimaced after him.

'I'm sorry, Will. I asked you to show me how to jump.'

'Doesn't matter. Don't you go trying it again without Stoney or me here.'

'I couldn't. I can't reach without you to push me up,' Rhea said. She didn't notice the grin Stoney gave Will. Will scowled.

'Well just don't. C'mon Stoney or Dad'll belt us both,' Will added and Stoney's smile disappeared. He swore.

341

'Not really! He wouldn't really use his belt on you, would he?' Rhea ran along beside the boys as they climbed the bank to where they'd left their own horses. Rhea was riding behind Will.

'You seen the marks on our backs? Where you think they come from Rhea?' Stoney snorted. 'Mr Winby's got one hell of a temper when you don't do exactly as he says. Even, sometimes, if he's fed up or your mum's been on at him for something.'

'But that's terrible! Does Mother know that?'

'None of her business and none of yours, Rhea, so just shut up, all right? C'mon.' Will pulled Rhea up behind him and the boys broke into a canter, suddenly unnerved at the thought of Mr Winby's anger. Rhea clung to Will's bare stomach, feeling the muscles tensing beneath her hands.

'But I'm going away to school tomorrow. Couldn't your father let you have just an hour off with me? I could ask him,' Rhea said. Will shook his head.

'Not at late summer harvest. We need as many hands as we can get. I shouldn't have taken the time off as it is. You aren't much help so you might as well go to school.' She knew he was angry with her about going away. But he had Stoney left. And she'd be back for holidays. She leaned her cheek against his back.

'Don't be mad, Will. I have to go to school.'

'No you don't! You could do correspondence school like I did. Like Stoney did.'

'And how good was that? You can read and write but that's about it. I want to know things,' she said stubbornly and was rewarded by total silence. She stared at his back with the welt marks now obvious against the hard, brown skin. Why hadn't she realized before what they were?

'I'll write,' she offered when the silence became too much for her. They were nearly at the barn, Stoney a few yards ahead of them.

'Well I won't. I won't have anything smart to say to you, will I?' Will swung her to the ground and jumped off himself, pulling the horse past her to the barn. Mr Winby stood by the door, looking at his watch.

'Your collecting bags are over there. Gloves, clippers. You

342

helping, Miss Paterson? Your Mum's out there.' He made it impossible to refuse. Rhea nodded.

'I wish you'd call me "Rhea", Mr Winby. I feel silly being called "Miss Paterson" all the time.'

'Wouldn't want your Mum thinking I'd forgotten who owns this place, now would I?' Mr Winby said. Rhea drooped under the sarcasm. 'Come on then! What're yew boys waiting for? The ladders are over in the paddock already. We've got a lot to do.'

The harvest at this time of the year was mostly summer greens: Valencia oranges that had turned green again when the summer temperatures returned the chlorophyll to the rind. They looked ugly compared to the earlier crops of Valencias and Navels but the fruit inside the skin was as juicy and ripe as ever. Rhea hefted the cloth bag, climbing through the canvas straps so that it hung from her like a bib. The bottom of it could be opened to let a full bag be emptied easily into the loading bins. On her hands she wore a pair of soft gloves to prevent her damaging the fruit and she carried a pair of clippers to snip the fruit from the tree. It was backbreaking work in the heat, climbing up ladders perched against the white-painted sides of trees and reaching out again and again to pick the fruit.

After two hours Rhea had had enough and returned with her mother to the house. Ursula had been picking fruit for several hours. Her shoulders ached and her head swam from the blinding sun. The pain in her back, more than anything, warned her to take a rest. She didn't understand how Mr Winby and the boys could continue the way they did. There were just the three of them because the late summer harvest was smaller and they didn't bring anyone else in. Mrs Winby did all the other chores, like milking the cows and feeding the chooks, and the men picked the fruit. Watching them, stripped to the waist and shining with sweat, Ursula felt a twinge of guilt. Mr Winby did work hard. She knew that. If only they could get off on a better foot, share some sort of working relationship. She decided to make them some lemonade and have Rhea take it out to them. They looked exhausted.

'Not much fun, is it? You should be careful you don't overdo it. Mr Winby doesn't expect you to work when you're pregnant,' Rhea said. She had soaked a towel in cold water and was wiping herself down with it. She watched Will's distant figure, climbing down another ladder, another bag of fruit hanging heavily from his shoulders. 'Mother? Did you know Mr Winby whips the boys with his belt? They've got marks all over their backs from it. Will told me to shut up about it but I don't think it's right, do you?'

'Oh dear. No, of course it's not right, darling, but there's not much I can do about it, is there? Mr Winby dislikes me quite enough as it is for interfering. I can't tell him how to treat his own son.' Ursula washed her face and hands in the sink and then towelled herself dry. She didn't want to hear what Rhea was telling her and she disliked herself even more for that. 'I thought we'd make them some lemonade. They must be dying of thirst. Give me a hand will you, darling?'

'Okay.' They worked in silence, cutting and squeezing the lemons in tandem. Then Rhea added sugar and ice cubes from the freezer tray, stirring it up in a metal pail. She lifted it down from the counter and walked to the back door.

'Just a minute, Rhea. You forgot the mugs.' Ursula tossed three tin mugs into the pail, letting them sink into the liquid. 'There! Off you go with it before they collapse with heat exhaustion. It must be about 110 out there in the sun. Tell them I'll be back in about half an hour. I just need a bit of a rest.'

'Well, all right. But you're really not supposed to be overdoing it, you know. The doctor said to take it easy and you're getting too big to climb ladders now.'

'I'm just fine, Rhea. And I'm not dying, just pregnant, so I don't see why I need to take everything easy. Those men out there aren't! And it's our crop. Tell them I'll be there soon.' Ursula pushed Rhea out the door before she could protest any further.

Ursula wished John Balham would turn up soon. It was frustrating not knowing anything about growing oranges and having to depend on Mr Winby's remarks, let drop like spikes of steel. He resented her terribly; her presence, her interference, even her help. He just wanted her to go away. And she had nowhere to go. She could almost sympathize with the man until Rhea told her something else about how Mr Winby treated the dogs, the boys, Mrs Winby, or the horses, and then she wanted to take the spade and rap some sense into that thick authoritarian skull of his. He was pushing his luck too far with

Will. The boy was fifteen and large with it. Soon he'd start standing up for himself, rebellion already showing in his eyes. There'd definitely be trouble there. She sighed. This year would be a long one.

'Mr Winby? Will, Stoney? Mother made you some lemonade. It's cold.' Rhea put the pail down in the shade of one of the trees, reaching down into the lemonade for the mugs. She pulled them out and passed them to each of the men as they shrugged off their cloth bags and stooped wearily for the drink.

'Aw God that's good!' Mr Winby said, draining his mug immediately and filling it again. 'Thank yer mum,' he added stiffly once his thirst had lost some of its edge. Will and Stoney leaned or squatted against tree trunks, their eyes shut against the glare. The ground had hardened to granules of powdered earth, coating their skin. The leaves shivered above them, their glossy exterior almost sweating in the heat. All around a heady scent of oranges filled the air.

'Mother says she'll be out again in about half an hour. She said she's sorry but she needs a bit of a rest first. But then she'll come back and help again. So'll I,' Rhea said firmly. She expected protest or worst still, sarcasm. But none came. The men were glad for any help. A trickle of sweat was running down the inside of her bathing suit under shorts and shirt. She rubbed her hand over it. From behind the fence a butcher bird could be heard arguing fiercely with another, smaller bird. There was no breeze at all today, the sun ringed in haloes of heat. Rhea looked up at it, wincing as it stung her eyes.

'Any more?' Stoney held out his mug and Rhea filled it again.

'Will? You want some more?' Rhea squinted over at Will slumped in the shade. He shook his head. There was something about the way he was keeping his face turned away from his father that worried Rhea. She looked at Stoney. His eyes were guarded and he shook his head slightly, pursing his lips in a silent 'no'.

Reluctantly Rhea gathered up the mugs and the nearly empty pail. Mr Winby had turned away to begin work again and Stoney was putting his bag on. Rhea walked over to Will.

'You sure you don't want any more, Will? You only had

345

one. There's just a little left.' But Will stood and handed over his mug with just a shake of his head again. Rhea could see his lips were white as though they had been tightly compressed together. Or as though he were going to pass out from heat exhaustion. He didn't look at her but walked past her to pick up his own bag. It was when he passed her that she saw his back. There were two red weals, different from the marks made by the canvas straps. These were made by a belt. She turned away without a word.

It was late that night when Will rapped softly against Rhea's window and then climbed through it, his body dark in the shadows. Rhea sat up.

'Will? Is that you? What's the matter?'

'Shh! I don't want yer mum to wake up an' find me here. She'd be mad.' He groped his way over to her bed and sat on the end of it. Rhea saw he'd been crying, the tear marks scrubbed from his face with the back of his hand. She reached out and took his hand.

'Did your dad belt you again? Why? What did you do wrong?' She could feel him shaking.

'He said I was cheeking him. Told him I was tired and wanted a rest earlier. He belted me then. And then later, after tea, he was yellin' at Mum for something. Hell, I don't even remember what now. I told him to lay off. Well, he didn't belt me. He knocked me flat. Jeez, he's never punched me before.' Rhea saw now the swollen jaw, the darker colouring against the skin. She touched it carefully with her fingers, sucking in her breath when he flinched. 'I tell you, Rhea. I've about had it. Sometimes I think I'll hit him back, I get so mad. Maybe I'll just take a runner. Head off for some place where they'll pay me for the hours I work and where I'm my own boss . . . But Mum can't handle everything alone and then Stoney'd have to take on my share of the work. It wouldn't be fair on them.'

'Don't go, Will! Please don't. I mean . . . just don't please!' Rhea had started to cry, the despair in Will's voice and the trembling in his hand shocking her more than his words. It would be terrible if he left. How would she bear it? She had come to rely on him to fill the place her father had once held in her heart. Mother was always there for her, she never

346

doubted that, but she needed someone else who was all important in her life. And Will had shown himself willing to be that person. If he left now . . . He pulled her against him, his tears running freely now, her hair spilling against his cheek.

'It's okay, Rhea. It's okay. I'm not going anywhere right now. I'm too young. They'd catch me and send me home and then Dad'd really lay into me. Don't cry,' he told her, his own tears making wet channels down his face. After a long silence, he added. 'As long as you'll come back on holidays I guess things won't be that bad. Stoney's kinda busy right now. He met some girl down at Gidgeeganup. She works in the hotel. I think he's gone soft on her and so he takes off every chance he can. I'm supposed to just sit around and twiddle my thumbs, I guess.'

'Can't you go into town with him sometimes?' Rhea asked, trying to think of something to cheer him up.

'With no money? Dad banks my wages straight into his account. Says I don't need any, he provides all my food and clothing. A place for me to sleep. I guess that's all I'm supposed to need. Like one of the bloody horses! God, sometimes I hate him so much!' Rhea hugged him tighter, scared as much by his anger as by his earlier misery.

'Can't you ask Mother to pay your wages straight to you? You mustn't hit your dad, Will. He'd murder you. He's much bigger and, anyway, he's mean. Please don't hit him back. I'll ask Mother about the money.' But Will shook his head.

'She'd never agree. I'm under age, remember? Anyway, it doesn't matter. I'm just sounding off, I guess. I'm angry right now. Don't worry so much, Rhea, everything'll be fine.' He flopped back on the bed, his arms above his head.

'I'll be back for Easter. That's only two months. And there won't be so much work then. Maybe you can take a few days off and go camping or something?'

'Camping?' Will sat up and stared at Rhea. Then he laughed. 'I do enough camping just living here. But, I guess you're right. Two months isn't very long. And then there are the breaks in between. I was just, you know, fed up, I guess.' He lay back again and Rhea lay down beside him, his arm around her. He pulled her in tightly and Rhea breathed in the scent of him: a mixture of warm skin, sweat, and oranges. It

347

was odd, she thought, snuggling against him; odd but nice. They lay in companionable silence for so long that Will eventually dropped off, his breath becoming slow and heavy. Rhea slipped a pillow under his head and went to sleep beside him.

Ursula found them still asleep when she went to wake Rhea at daybreak. Will's face, crushed heavily into the pillow, showed signs of the beating he had taken from his father and there were tear tracks still on his cheeks. He looked very young, she thought, her heart twisting at the thought. Maybe she should say something to Mr Winby? Rhea was curled up beside Will, her hair flopping across his face. Ursula closed the door on them, letting them sleep on undisturbed.

Ursula was in the kitchen making up sandwiches for the cool box when Rhea came in. She was dressed in her new school uniform, tugging at its unfamiliar fit. Ursula smiled.

'Sleep well?' she asked. Rhea pulled a face. Her eyes were heavy this morning, Ursula thought. She hoped Rhea would sleep a little on the drive down to Perth.

'Mother, Will stayed the night with me last night. His Dad beat him up. It isn't right! Can't you do something? I said I wouldn't tell you 'cos he was so worried you'd be mad . . . about him coming in the window, I mean. So if you could maybe pretend you don't know about that, though why . . . anyway, anyone can see he's been beaten up! He looks like you did, except it's down here, on the jaw.' Rhea showed her mother on her own jaw. Ursula sighed.

'Oh, no! Perhaps you better tell me about it,' she said reluctantly. Rhea hugged her and then launched into a recital of the tale Will had told her last night, Ursula stroking her daughter's hair absently as she listened. Now what? She couldn't let that boy be whipped or beaten for no good reason except that Mr Winby was taking his bad mood out on a child rather than the person he'd really like to hit. Her.

'I'll talk to Mr Winby. This can't go on,' she said finally, her tone quietly determined. Rhea hugged her again.

'Oh thank you, Mother. I know he'll listen to you. And you know what else? Will doesn't get any pay. His dad banks all Will's wages into his own account and doesn't give Will anything. I think he ought to get some pocket money at least, don't you?'

'Well that I really can't do much about. Mr Winby's just a miser at heart. He doesn't spend the money, just hoards it in the bank. I don't have to sit back and watch a child being beaten but I have no say about what his parents do with his wages. Will is under age still, you know. Never mind, darling, I'll think of something. After all, I hold the purse-strings now.'

Rhea had been at school nearly two weeks when John Balham turned up. He was a tall, rangy looking fellow with dark hair, a large aggressive nose and two sharp creases running down between his eyebrows. He was dressed in moleskins, white shirt, elastic-sided riding boots and felt hat; the quintessential Australian bushman. Ursula saw him as he climbed out of his utility and wondered briefly if Eastern States men took more care in how they dressed or whether she had just struck unlucky with her district. And heavens, who kept all those pale colours clean? Mrs Winby looked up and snorted her opinion. The women were setting up a new chicken run between them, stretching out the wire on the frame that Stoney had made for them and hammering it into place. The utility had pulled up beside the main house and the stranger was now walking towards them. Ursula looked down at her faded sundress and sighed.

'Goodaye! Yew Mrs Paterson?' When Ursula nodded, her hand going up to push back the strand of hair that never really needed rearranging, John Balham smiled. The change was remarkable. Instead of impatient good looks, his face was transformed to easy charm. Even Mrs Winby smiled in return. 'And you must be Mrs Winby? How d'you do, ladies? Warm weather for that isn't it? Let me give you a hand. I'm John Balham. Work for the CSIRO.' He gave Ursula a slow wink. 'We're looking in on properties in the area, trying to improve output. You look pretty well organized here.'

'Oh. Well, yes, I suppose. I'm fairly new to all this but if you'd like to talk with my manager, Mr Winby, I'm sure we could find him. He's out with Will and Stoney on the far water tank, isn't he, Mrs Winby? It sprang a leak, and anyway, it's getting rather gungy inside.'

'Gungy?' John Balham seemed to smile without turning his mouth up. He twisted the last of the chicken wire into place

349

with professional ease and hammered it down. 'There! That's that. Well, if it wouldn't be too much trouble, I'd appreciate any time Mr Winby could spare. We're very keen on improving productivity, especially amongst citrus crops. Would you consider telling your husband I'm here, Mrs Winby?' He smiled at her again and Ursula bit her lip. Staid, dour Mrs Winby was almost smiling. Ursula turned away.

'You just go into the house and have a cup of tea with Mrs Paterson and I'll go find my husband, Mr Balham. I won't be long.' And with that Mrs Winby took herself off to her bungalow for the keys to the utility.

'Uh, please do come in Mr Balh . . . '

'John. Yew know, of course, Mrs Paterson that I'm a mate of Tim's. I do actually work for the CSIRO but I'm here as a personal favour to Tim.' He took her arm and led her towards the house. 'He said you were beautiful and I've never known Tim to talk like that before. I see he wasn't exaggerating. Tim'n'I grew up together. We're pretty close, best mates I'd say. So he told me everything. Damned shame, I say. Never did like that Joanna much. Nose too bloody high in the air for an Aussie. D'yer know her grandfather came from Italy and opened a deli in Melbourne? On the father's side anyway. They keep it fairly quiet.' He grinned. 'Mother's side's pretty toffee nosed. Tim's leading a dog's life. Serves the stupid bugger right in some ways.' He gave her another appreciative look as they paused on the verandah. Ursula looked even more flustered.

'Oh, not really. It wasn't all Tim's fault what happened. He'd have done anything to make things right but Joanna out-witted us really. Anyway, it's over and done with. It was very good of you to come all this way. And I appreciate your subtle approach. The Winbys can be rather difficult and they're not happy to have me here. Well, that's not true entirely. Mrs Winby can be fine when she's in the mood. I suppose I haven't made life easy for them. But then, they haven't made it easy for me. I'm in charge of the property accounts now but Mr Winby's still in charge of everything else. If you could some-how see that the property is doing everything it can to produce as much income as possible without Mr Winby thinking I'm interfering, well, I'd be everlastingly grateful!' She smiled as they went inside. The sofa looked cool and inviting in its new slip cover. She seated herself opposite him. 'Oh, dear, I'm afraid I'm rattling on but my daughter went off to school two weeks ago and I haven't really had anyone to talk to. Mrs Winby said more to you than she's said to me since I arrived. Would you like a drink, by the way?'

'Love one. Got a beer?'

'Yes, of course. Just a minute.' Ursula got up and went into the kitchen, unaware of the turmoil she had just left behind in John Balham's mind. My God, Tim had really blown it this time. What a little beauty! And a charmer with it. He wished he weren't such good mates with old Tim. Still, the least he could do for her was sort out this bastard manager she'd been saddled with. He noticed when she returned how thin she was, even with her figure disguised by the sundress. And, if he wasn't mistaken, that was a bulge that meant only one thing. Maybe that explained why she looked so tired under that seemingly healthy tan. He wondered idly who the father was. Tim? Well, if he couldn't console her, at least he could take some of the burden off her. He stood and let her sit down again, the glass of beer held idly in his hand while he looked the place over.

'Nice place. You've done most of it yourself, I guess? I like the pale colours and that's smart with the blinds.'

'Well, I found I didn't have enough for curtains so I just made blinds. We can't afford any rugs, so the boards have to make do. It's cooler that way anyway. And Will, that's Mr Winby's son, potted a couple of the smaller orange trees for me and brought them in here. They look rather nice, I think. He's a very nice boy and so's Stoney. They're very helpful. I'm afraid I put my oar in there too. Mr Winby was taking out his rage at my being here on his son, beating both boys actually but especially Will. I told him it had to stop or I'd make a formal complaint to the authorities. Mr Winby hasn't spoken to me since and that's been a fortnight now.' She sighed, the worry showing in the taut lines of her throat. John Balham winced.

'Pretty much of a bastard, this fellow then? I asked after him a bit in Gidgeeganup. Just to get a feel for things. Opinion's pretty much on your side, I gather. In fact, there are quite a

351

few people in town who think you're having a rough time of it. If you need any help, you can always call on Ron Carstairs. He runs the hotel and he thinks Jack Winby's a right bugger, s'cuse my French. He'd do anything to give some grief. Course he's not gonna say that right out; you'll have to become friends first. But people are ready to get to know you. Take a run into town from time to time, even if it's just for a lemonade or something. Make yourself known. And as far as Winby goes, well I'll do my best. Show my official badge sort of thing. His type always listen to that. Yew considered just getting a new manager altogether?'

'Well yes, of course I have. And I would've done if I'd realized how awkward Mr Winby was earlier on. I was hoping he'd get used to me and we'd become friends but I guess that's a pipe dream. And now it's really too late. If I asked him to leave that would mean Will would have to leave here too and God knows how he'll be treated if I'm not there to keep an eye on things. I'd rather put up with the Winby seniors if I can keep Will and Stoney. Besides, I was thinking I could teach Will while he does some odd jobs around the house for me. Give him pocket money that way and get some sort of schooling into him at the same time. My daughter and he are very good friends already. I'd hate to separate them.' She trailed off, aware of sounding weak. But John Balham was smiling in a wry sort of way and didn't seem at all critical. He just nodded.

'Yeah. That sounds like a tough decision. Okay, well I'll do my best with what I have to work with. Um, I don't like to be too much of a nosey parker but when are you due? I don't think you'll really want to have it out here on the property. There's only the one doc round here. He could be anywhere when junior decides to appear.' He laughed awkwardly and Ursula felt her face grow stiff. She didn't want John to know and was hoping he hadn't noticed.

'Um, near the end of April, I'd say.' She didn't elaborate, her very stillness holding out an invisible bubble of remoteness that kept John Balham from saying more. It was with relief that they heard the sound of the utility as it rounded the bend toward the house. 'Tim sent his love by the way. He asked me to give you this.' He dug in his pocket for a small package and tossed it across to Ursula. 'I reckon I'll be around here about three or four days if everything works out all right. I'll stay in town. Looks more official that way. I'll talk to you later, okay Mrs Paterson?'

'Ursula. And yes, John, that's more than okay.' With her hands clutched over the package, Ursula looked like a young girl asked to her first dance, the ice thawed quite away. John Balham grinned and picked up his hat.

'I hear Attila's footsteps. Best be off.' He winked and walked outside to shake hands with Mr Winby. Ursula followed him, the package slipped into her pocket.

After Mr Winby had taken John Balham off to view the rest of the property, Ursula retreated to her own bedroom and, with trembling fingers, unwrapped the small package. Inside was a letter and a small box.

'Darling, by now John will have arrived and hopefully things will get better. He's a great bloke and I know you'll like him. If anyone can get your property sorted out, he can. I took the chance of sending this with him since I didn't want to risk it through the mail and I don't know exactly when I can get across to Perth. But I will get across sometime. I've thought about it all some more and maybe you won't want to see me but the way we left it last time in the street was no good for either of us. I need to see you again.

'The package is something I'd like you to have. It was given to me by my nan - that's grandmother to you - for my bride. Well, maybe I should've given it to Joanna but I don't really feel married to her. Funny really because I've known her a couple of years now and you only a few days but I feel more as though I'm married to you than to anyone. Anyway, I'd like you to have it and wear it, if you will.

'I'm dashing this off because John has to catch his flight. I envy him terribly. Don't forget I love you.

Tim.'

Inside the box was a strand of seed pearls with an intricate clasp of diamante set in silver. The clasp was in the shape of a ribbon bow holding up a swallow. It wasn't terribly valuable; Ursula knew that. But it was delicately beautiful and it was sent with Tim's love. She held it against her throat in the mirror, tears stinging her eyes. Then she put it on. The bow fit perfectly into the hollow of her neck and the swallow lay flat across her chest. She stood, fingering it for a long time.

John Balham was as good as his word. By the time he left, Mr Winby had become as enthused as a young man setting out on his first farming venture. They had discussed crops, new varieties, hybrids, fertilizers, irrigation, a grant from the Government, and a great deal more. The property itself, John Balham told Ursula, was quite capable of doubling its present production levels, perhaps more. It wasn't harder work that was needed, just more intelligent work. And he was there to help them with that.

Mr Winby agreed to the property becoming a test centre, with someone from the CSIRO turning up on a monthly basis to record results, suggest innovations, and generally keep an eye on things. Ursula smiled ironically when Mr Winby told her, his tone arrogantly asserting himself yet again, that he'd been chosen because he was such a hard worker and could be relied upon to follow through with their suggestions. She drily congratulated him and told him she would agree to whatever he said on the farming side of things. And she would continue to keep the accounts. They struck an uneasy truce.

By the end of March, Ursula could do very little work. She was eight months pregnant now and needed assistance to even clean the house. Will and Stoney hovered around her like watchdogs, ready to fetch and carry before she even knew she needed something. Mrs Winby had taken over the cooking and washing, and even Mr Winby would put a helping hand beneath Ursula's elbow when she climbed in and out of the car, or tried to climb the verandah steps. Her doctor had advised her, like John Balham, to come down to Perth for the birth, her earlier illness making everyone uneasy. And she had agreed.

'Just don't let Mannie get under my feet, will you, Stoney?' Ursula asked as she turned sideways in the doorway to the verandah. It was late evening and much cooler out on the back verandah, screened against mosquitos and lit with a candle. This was her favourite time of the day. It would have been lovely to have Rhea there to talk to or even a radio programme to listen to. The BBC World News perhaps. But the house didn't have such luxuries yet. She smiled at Stoney. He was a good boy.

'There yew are, Mrs Paterson. I put some pillows in the chair an' Mannie's right out of the way. Yew won't fall down now, will yew?' He watched her anxiously.

'Good heavens, no! I'm not an invalid, Stoney. It's very sweet of you to fuss so but really I'm perfectly fine. See? I've got the bell.' She lifted a handbell from the table beside her chair; her version of an alarm signal. 'And if I need you at all, I won't hesitate to use it. Now run along and eat your dinner. You must be starving by now.' She shooed him away.

She settled more comfortably into the chair and opened her book, *August Folly* by Angela Thirkell. Mrs Winby had picked it up in a jumble sale in Gidge for her. She really wasn't too bad, Ursula thought with a smile, as long as Mr Winby wasn't along. That's when she went all hard and aloof. When he wasn't there, Mrs Winby could be quite companionable, especially with the baby on the way. She was looking forward to it almost more than Ursula. In fact, a lot more than Ursula. Ursula stroked her belly, wondering as always whose offspring it held. Please, she wished hard with her eyes tightly shut, let it be Tim's.

The screen door banged and Ursula wondered whether Stoney had forgotten something. Perhaps Mrs Winby had sent him across with some more biscuits. She liked the shortbread ones. She twisted her body around carefully, waiting to see Stoney appear through the back door. Instead Tim walked through.

He stood there, staring at her, hair gleaming a dull blonde, face shadowed by the overhanging beams. The candle sent strange ripples of light over his figure as it stood quite motionless, only the sound of his breathing, quick and jumpy, breaking the stillness.

'Tim?' She couldn't think of anything else to say.

'John told me. About the baby.' He moved forward then and came to a halt by her chair, squatting down beside her. His eyes, those light grey eyes that had delighted her on first acquaintance with their habit of squinting as though into the sun, were the colour of mercury now as it spills out of the bottle, gleaming, curved, almost metallic, but shot through

355

with a red spiderwork of fatigue. They alternated between her face and her stomach. He tried to smile. 'Why didn't you tell me, love? I mean, is it mine? Or Simon's?' He put a hand out and rested it briefly on her belly before dropping it back to his side. She hesitated, unsure how to react. His hand had been warm as it touched her skin and the sudden coolness that followed was like him leaving her all over again. She felt the same pain.

'I didn't really think you'd want to know. Not when you've got your own family now. And anyway, as far as who the father is . . . I truly don't know, Tim. I know that sounds awful but that night, after the dinner, well Simon forced me – that's how I got that bruise. And then, with you the very next day . . . I can't believe we didn't think to take precautions but I guess we were too drunk . . . '

He sighed. 'Too something . . . infatuated, in love? Too much passion and not enough sense.' He shrugged. 'It doesn't really matter that much anyway, does it? I mean, it may well be mine so we might as well just treat it that way. Trust you not to tell me it is mine just to put pressure on me like bloody Joanna. In fact, trust you not to tell me anything about it at all! Just going to manage on your own, were you? As always?' He leaned over to kiss her on the lips. He smelled, tasted, of cigarette smoke. She gripped the arm of the chair tightly, feeling that familiar longing. She forced it down and turned her head away.

'Everyone, including Rhea, thinks it's Simon's. I've told them Simon's dead, so they all think this is a posthumous baby and that it's terribly sad and all that. I feel like such a fraud sometimes, but I have to watch my reputation or I'll be shunned. You know what small communities are like.'

'Too right. Yeah, well, don't worry about it. I'll still know better. I really think it is mine too, don't you?' She was staring intently into his face, that tight skin over the cheekbones, the light eyes seen almost as though for the first time. She looked away. Odd, really, to be having this conversation with someone she'd only met three, perhaps four times in her life. So embarrassingly intimate for almost strangers.

'Perhaps. I don't know. Maybe when he's born . . . '

'He? You know that much, do you?' He was teasing her and

356

she frowned, jerking her face away when he tried to cup her cheek in his hand. If it had once been presumptuous of her to turn up at his door unannounced it was now, equally presumptuous of him to assume he could just walk back into her life.

'I don't know why I think it's a boy but I do. Rhea does too . . . Look Tim, you seem to be expecting something from all this. I can manage quite well without you. You've made your choice and you've got your life. I've got mine. Here.' She stared out into the night.

'I was hoping you might have forgiven me. You sounded so . . . pleased to hear from me at Christmas and John said you'd defended me when he said I'd been a bloody idiot – which I was! Damn! If I had to marry someone who was having my baby, why didn't I choose you?' Tim said.

'I suppose because you didn't know. Rather an embarrassment of children around, isn't there?' Ursula couldn't keep the bitterness from her voice. 'I'm booked into a hospital in Perth. My doctor thinks there may be problems.'

'Problems? What sort of problems?' His face had gone taut again, the self-pity wiped instantly from his eyes. And so, reluctantly, she told him about the time she had collapsed and how worried the doctor had been. Tim sat back in the chair beside her, his hands steepled together so the tips of his fingers rested against his chin. He looked as though he were praying. Ursula finished and shrugged her shoulders again.

'Nothing you can do. Nothing really to do with you. Don't look so worried.'

'Oh, and is that supposed to make me feel better? What's the scenario? I seduce you, get you pregnant, get you to leave your husband and your home, and then marry someone else leaving you to handle things on your own? And now you tell me you're likely to have problems with the birth. And I'm expected to just have a nice visit and toddle off back to Melbourne without another thought. Is that what you think of me now? Is that how you'd expect me to react? I must have really made an impression. Nice going, Tim!' He had swung out of his chair half way through and was now pacing up and down the verandah, his footfalls loud in the night.

'Isn't that the way it happened? Or have I missed something?' Ursula said angrily, the words souring in her mouth even as she bit them off.

'Yes! Yes, you have! You've missed the fact that I love you. No-one else. You! God help us both!'

The night rang out in its stillness as they both stared at each other. The moments ticked away. She must say something now, Ursula thought, now before the moment is gone and there's no chance to ever get it back. She could feel the seconds shredding, the moment passing and still she felt frozen in that stare, not taking him in so much as gazing blankly at him. Tim broke it, finally, himself.

'Ursula?'

'Yes?'

'I can't undo things. I can't make time go backwards. I wish to God I could. That we could go back to that day in the garden at your cottage. Then . . . then I'd do things differently. But that's like a child to keep hoping, wishing for something that's over and done with. We can't go back. But we can go on and I'll make things better this time, I promise. If you'll let me.'

'How odd. I was thinking along those lines myself.' Her voice quivered. 'Ohhh, why can't we ever go back! What makes things so set in stone all the time! I'm sick of it! I'm sick of dreadful things happening and never being able to get the good times back because they're over and finished and it's no good anymore! Nothing's any good anymore without . . . ' She stopped abruptly, and stared at him again.

'Without?' Tim asked gently.

'Without . . . ' she sighed deeply, 'oh, without you. It's no good without you.'

She didn't flinch away this time when he ran his hand across her cheek, fitting it into his palm. She didn't pull away when he kissed her. It was too much to fight anymore and besides, it felt too right. Like coming home. He cradled her in his arms and whispered.

'I'll make it right this time. I promise.'

It was such a lovely change, she reflected with a contented sigh, to be cossetted and worried about by someone like Tim. She wished she could keep him forever. Well, maybe . . .

'How long will you stay?' She stroked his hair, running her fingers through it to his neck.

358

'A few days or so. I've told Joanna about you. Told her I wouldn't divorce her, that I wasn't leaving her or the baby, but that I love you and want to see you on a regular basis. You know, she didn't even care that much? As long as we keep up appearances, she's quite happy to do her own thing. I think there's someone else for her too. And I'm more and more convinced Josh isn't mine.'

'Josh? That what you named him? It's nice. I like it. Your choice or hers?' Ursula tried to deflect some of Tim's bitterness.

'Hers. I didn't really care that much what he was called. Then Jo's mum put up a shriek 'cos Joshua is a Jewish name and Jo said she didn't care, she thought it was great, so I added my bit just to annoy Jo's mum, snotty bitch that she is. So now the poor little blighter's called Josh. Not that it's too bad a name.' He was amused again now and Ursula felt a sharp but sweet pang at the way the humour made his eyes crinkle up and his gums show when he opened his mouth; silly, insignificant things that meant so much to her. She leaned forward and kissed his nose.

'Wretch!'

'Yeah, well, I don't get much to humour me these days. I've gotta have some fun! I'll enjoy naming ours a lot more. Got any ideas yet?' For a moment Ursula thought, guiltily, that Tim wasn't being very fair to his family. It clouded her joy before being blown away again like a tendril wisp of cloud over the sun. Why should Tim be fair to a woman who had manipulated him into a marriage that had ruined his life? Or to a son he didn't believe was his? He didn't owe them anything and yet he wasn't deserting them or letting them starve. He would always be there for them. More than she could expect, quite frankly. That small nagging voice was quietened and she ran her finger down his arm.

'Um, some. I used to have a little brother, once, before the war. His name was Tom.' She paused. 'You didn't tell me if you could be here for the birth.'

He bit his lip. 'In a month or so, right?' She nodded. 'Yeah, should be okay. Anyway, if there's any chance you'll have problems, well, of course I'll be with you. I can live without all that hoopla of political wheeling and dealing anyway.'

359

'What d'you mean?'

He saw her alarm and shrugged it away. 'Just that I'll be trying for a seat later on in the winter. The encumbent for the area around Gisburne's retiring and it's a pretty safe seat for the Country party anyway so I'm being backed to take it over. Everyone knows me round there. If they hear about you, or junior here,' he patted her stomach, 'I might as well take up permanent residence with you, because I won't be welcome over there.' He shrugged again as though it didn't matter that much to him. Maybe it didn't.

'Well don't take any chances, Tim. I don't want you ruining all your dreams just to be here and hold my hand.' She didn't say, 'just to hold my hand while I risk everything, even possibly death to have what may well be your baby.' But she thought it. And then she thought she was being melodramatic, which she was. But it didn't help. She studied his face intently, the lines around his eyes and mouth that bit in when he smiled, the skin that was acquiring a slight pallor, a sallowness that only perennially tanned skin achieves when deprived of sun. Ursula thought of it as an internally lit office look. He was still the wholesome looking man with the serious smile who had made her realize that she was young and attractive herself – the caring, sturdy, dependable Tim she had fallen in love with – but now there was a part of him that didn't ever quite relax. That must be what Joanna had done to him. Or maybe it was natural and she had never noticed it before – the politician's part, she thought. He sensed her detachment and tried to snap her out of it.

'You are my dream. One of my two. The other, yes, is politics. I'd like to have both but I guess that may never be totally possible. We'll have to make do with a compromise between them. But you're worth the risk of discovery to me – and anyway, sometimes lately I've wondered whether it wouldn't be better if we were found out. I'm not important enough to cause much fuss with the papers but I'd still have to leave, at least for a few years. Then we could be together permanently. It's quite a thought.' He kissed her. 'If you get any flak from your bloody Winbys over who I am – you know, trying to push you into leaving – well tell 'em to go right ahead. Then I'll take over as farm manager and they can go live on the

360

dole. That'll shut 'em up.' He smiled at the thought but Ursula had the strange feeling he'd already considered this possibility in his mind and come up with an answer. Quite likely he had. Politicians had to think twenty steps in front of everyone else and Tim had never struck her as a fool, quite the reverse. There were depths to him that she might never understand. She sighed.

'You'll meet them tomorrow. Who d'you want to be? My brother? My long-lost cousin? A friend of the family?'

'Kissing cousins? No, best not. Too many chances it could get checked out if I ever come to power. Lots of poms have Aussie family friends. You can say we had a yen for each other when we were sweet young things and now I'm gonna be coming across a lot to check you're okay. No problem then with the school fees either.'

'Oh, Rhea won an Old Girl's Scholarship, didn't I tell you? But thanks anyway, Tim. I really needed that back-up in case she didn't make it.' She was glad, in some small hidden away part of her, that she didn't have to be beholden to Tim for anything. Let him come and see her, like a husband who has to travel most of the time, but returns eventually every month or so. But don't let him start becoming a mainstay of her life. Don't let him start becoming so important her every thought was directed towards him, what he was doing, or how she would manage if he didn't turn up. No, she wanted to stay independent this time.

'You know, you only ever call me "Tim" when you're saying something serious or unpleasant. The rest of the time you say "sweetheart" or "darling" but I always know something's up if you say "Tim". What is it? You don't want me to intrude or impose on your life? Turn up and be nice but don't try and be too important? Is that it?' Tim was quick to catch the flow of her thoughts. And quick to take offence. She looked at him slowly, her face betraying no emotion. That was something she had been accused of too often by Simon. She was too sentimental, too emotional. Now she had learned some distance. She smiled.

'You won't impose. You'll never be here long enough for that.' She wondered at first if he really felt the pain she saw cross his face. And then she shook herself clear of that paralysing coldness and put out her hand. 'Oh Tim! I'm sorry, I really didn't mean to say that. I don't know why I did. I'm just glad you're here at all, even for a little while.' She was stricken by the way she had hurt him; not in anger, but in cold detachment. He held her fiercely.

'I don't have to be here if you don't want me. I can just support you and stay out of your life. There's nothing I can do to make up for what you've been through except to make sure you don't go through any more hell. You just tell me what you want and I'll do it.' He paused, as though gathering strength. 'I love you, Ursula. I can't keep saying that. It loses its meaning if I mumble it in your ear every five minutes. But it's the truth. And I'll have to assume you know it, because I'll feel stupid saying it too often, and I won't. But I want you to know I do.'

She stroked his hair, trying to make sense of the tangle of words that had come out so violently.

'Yes, I know. I do too.' And she did.

Mrs Winby came over just before bedtime to check on Ursula. It was odd how, no matter how well they knew each other, they still continued to address each other as 'Mrs Winby' or 'Mrs Paterson'. It would always be like that, Ursula thought, as she nodded in greeting.

'Come in, Mrs Winby. Come and meet an old family friend, Tim Nowlton. Tim, this is Mrs Winby, the farm manager's wife.' She was amused by the way Tim stood up to shake hands, his innate good manners triumphing over less worthy feelings.

'Nice to meet yew, Mr Nowlton.' Mrs Winby was surprised at the addition of a friend to an already rapidly increasing household. Surprised and a little dismayed. 'Yews gonna be staying here?' she asked, expecting the worst. Not that he wasn't a good-looking fellow but still. It was one thing to have liddluns running around, livening things up, or even Mrs Paterson who wasn't such a bad sort once you got to know her, but another bloke? Dad wouldn't like that one bit.

'No. No. I live in Melbourne. I'm just over to see Ursula, check she's okay with the baby. I'll be back on a two-monthly basis probably, to see everything's all right and to make sure

Ursula has what she needs. It's been a bit tough with Simon dying, no money, and now the baby,' he added in a confidential tone that Mrs Winby responded to immediately. He saw her lean in towards him, anxious to be one of the team, the ones who were in charge of making things better. People always wanted to be on the team.

'Yeah, it's a real shame about that. But we'll look after Mrs Paterson for you. See, I brought some shortbread biscuits over. She does like my shortbread, if I say so myself.' Mrs Winby offered the plate to Ursula who smiled, more at Tim's performance than the biscuits. Mrs Winby was pleased.

Beside Mrs Winby, Ursula, even eight months' pregnant, looked elfin thin, long muscles taut in her arms with no flesh to cover them. Perhaps she hadn't been eating as many biscuits as Mrs Winby thought. Tim noticed the black shadows beneath Ursula's eyes, hollows beneath her cheekbones that hadn't been there in England. He was conscious that their presence was a direct result of his carelessness, his inability to manage their lives, and he made a silent vow never to let that happen again. Mrs Winby didn't notice his abstraction, Ursula noticed but couldn't fathom it.

'Well, yew're obviously gonna be fine with Mr Nowlton here with yew. How long did yew say yew'd stay? 'Till the baby's born or will yew go home before then?' The two things that had reconciled Mrs Winby to Ursula's presence were the baby and her defence of Will. Nothing Mrs Winby had said had stopped her husband beating Will. And then Ursula had stepped in and miraculously, it seemed, the beatings had stopped. For the time being. That alone would have brought her to check on Ursula; the thought of another baby was an even bigger attraction. Mrs Winby didn't have many things to think about. There was no fashion in the bush, no tea parties, no ladies' luncheons. Nothing but hard work and now a baby. She loved babies! She beamed at Tim and Ursula.

'A few days this time, I think. Then I'll come back for the birth. I have business over here anyway.'

'Aw yeah, we'll all be looking forward to the baby coming, won't we, Mrs Paterson. And Rhea's real excited. You know Rhea, of course Mr Nowlton? Yew'll be here when she comes home for the long weekend. I expect yew'd planned it that way.

Will can't wait to see Rhea. He's been counting the days, as much as that boy can count. But he seems to be getting better with your help, Mrs Paterson. We just mustn't let Dad know about it or there'll be hell to pay. Well, mustn't stop here nattering all night. I'll come over and cook breakfast nice and early tomorrow. How would that be, Mrs Paterson?'

'Oh no! I wouldn't dream of it, Mrs Winby.' Ursula was horrified at the thought she would have to share Tim with a newly garrulous Mrs Winby. She wasn't sure she didn't prefer the silently morose Mrs Winby of old. She shook her head. 'Absolutely not. You have far too much to do as it is. Besides, I must do something for myself. And Tim can help me, can't you, darling?' That 'darling' had slipped out before she could correct herself. But Mrs Winby didn't seem to notice. Ursula realized suddenly that keeping Tim's true identity, not as family friend but as lover, from the rest of the community would be a lot harder than she had ever imagined. But Tim was already filling in for her, smoothing over the gaffe.

'Don't "darling" me, Ursula. I get invited for a visit and end up having to cook for myself. Some greeting that is!' But he laughed to deride his words and promised Mrs Winby that they could manage. With obvious reluctance, she was at last edged towards the door and the night.

'Is she gone?' Ursula whispered, when Tim returned to her side. Tim nodded, leaning down to envelop her in his arms, his mouth searching for hers.

'Gone and good riddance,' he muttered. She giggled.

'I've never known her like that before. You see what an effect you have on women? They go all soft and gushy.' She whispered into his ear, exhaling the words so her hot breath filled the shell of his ear. He shivered.

'Like you? As soft and gushy as marble?' He hadn't totally forgiven her for trying to manage her life without him. She kissed his neck.

'Molten marble.' He laughed at that.

'Not bad for starters. How about the main course?'

'The main course wallows like a sea cow, so I wouldn't be too hopeful if I were you.' She twitched her eyebrows together, giving a wry, regretful look. Tim grinned.

'You have no imagination my girl. In every relationship at

least one person has to have lots of imagination. Luckily I do.'

'Oh? And just what sort of wild imaginings have you been indulging in?' Ursula wasn't sure why she always felt so comfortable with Tim, so sure that whatever happened it would be good between them. She had never felt that sort of confidence or trust with Simon. Not even when she was more experienced. With Tim it didn't even matter that she was this size; it was their baby together and he still found her desirable. She even found herself flirting, fluttering her eyelashes, dimpling her cheek. For a moment she felt silly. But then Tim kissed her and it wasn't silly at all.

'Nothing to worry the baby. I'm not stupid. Just, ooh a little cuddling, caressing. Maybe a little . . . well you can wait and find out. I quite like all that extra bounty on offer.' He flipped a finger across her breasts and she gave a startled laugh.

'I see. And what about that dinner you promised me?'

'Later.'

Chapter Twenty Two

Rhea was sulking. That was the only word Ursula could use to describe the heavy silence; the tight, closed face. Such a limited word when Ursula knew Rhea was also hurting, a not yet healed wound peeled open. Tim was bound up with their reason for leaving England, with Rhea's rejection of Simon and his other children. It was all too new and fresh still to bear peering into. Ursula understood Rhea's sulks.

'Won't you even try a sausage, Rhea? You'll be hungry later.' Ursula brought a plate over to where Rhea sat beside Will. They had all taken the day off for a picnic, even the Winby seniors, and had climbed the hill at the back of the property to where the black, granite slabs made a natural barbecue with no risk of the fire getting out of control. They always had to consider that. Tim looked over to where the three were grouped together, his brow tight with worry. If Rhea didn't accept him, Ursula wouldn't let him keep coming back. It was that simple.

'I'm not hungry now,' Rhea snapped. Will, beside her, shifted uncomfortably. He didn't know why Rhea was acting so badly. Something to do with that Nowlton bloke who'd showed up a few days ago. Some family friend. He glanced up at Ursula, seeing the pain and frustration in her eyes. Rhea didn't look up.

'All right, Rhea. Have it your own way. Will, would you like some more?' Ursula offered the plate to Will who accepted gladly, more to please Ursula than from any real hunger. He'd already eaten too much for that.

'Thanks, Mrs Paterson. But you should go sit down now. You don't want to go slipping on the rocks.' No, and you don't want to go trying to charm Rhea anymore when she's acting like a prime little whatsit, he thought, as Ursula nodded and left them alone. He waited for a moment.

'You enjoy upsetting your mum then? Is it good fun?' he asked, his voice free from any hint of criticism, revealing simple curiosity. He continued eating the sausage. Rhea swung around in surprise.

'Don't be stupid, Will! Of course I don't!'

'Oh? Then how come you're doing it then? She's looked so happy in the last few days since Mr Nowlton turned up and she was so looking forward to you coming home too. So was I. But you're being a right pain. Hurting her, and him too come to think of it. And not much fun for me. I guess I'll go hang round Stoney and his girl. They don't talk to me much but at least they're not rude or mean. If that's what your new school's doing for you, I, for one, can live without it.' He started to get up, his rough trousers scraping across the gravel and stone. Rhea pulled him back down beside her.

'Don't, Will! I'm not being mean. He's the one who hurt Mother before. And now he thinks he can just wander back into her life again and upset her all over again. And just when the baby's due. I could kill him!' She shook with the force of her anger. Will sat and looked at her.

'So? What happened? You tell me your version. Then I'll tell you what I think.' He lay back, his head cradled by his arms and his eyes closed against the sun. Somehow, his relaxed attitude took a lot of the steam out of Rhea's recital. She tried not to exaggerate, not to get worked up by her wrongs simply because Will had borne much worse and could still laugh about it. When she finished, he was silent.

'Well? Now what d'you think?'

He pursed his lips, his eyes still shut. 'I think the baby's his.' There was a long silence. Rhea didn't respond. And then Will continued. 'And he's doing everything he can to make your mum feel loved and happy. He even wanted to pay your school fees. Did you know that? I heard him saying something about it

367

to your mum and she said they'd discussed all that already and that you didn't need anything 'cos you've got a scholarship. Then he said, for other things, like piano and your uniform and stuff. I don't know what they agreed but it seems like he wants to do everything for your mum. He even said he'd fly over specially for the birth. Must cost him a bomb! I dunno, but seems to me he's in love with your mum and she is with him. Don't you go spoiling it for them. They both deserve a break. And your dad now, you're well off without him. Jeez I thought mine was bad. But I'd rather get a clout every now and then than see my mum made a fool of like that. What a shit.' He still didn't open his eyes but, when Rhea gave a single, plaintive sniff, he took her hand in his and squeezed it. Rhea didn't want to be comforted and she tried to ease her hand away. He held it tightly until she stopped resisting. Then he let it go.

'It's up to you, chook. You're the deciding factor round here. You don't like Tim and your mum'll send him away. And then she'll be lonely and miserable. And so will he. Just 'cos you were too selfish and too much of a baby to accept him and forgive him for a mistake that wasn't even really his fault. Jesus, Rhea!' He stood up and walked away from her then, and she sat on the rock alone for some time.

From where she sat she could see her mother in her large straw hat perched on a comfortable slab with another making a natural rest for her back. Tim had arranged cushions behind her mother so that her back wouldn't be strained. She was resting, her hat tilted forward over her face. Tim was looking off into the distance, the wind riffling through his hair, his knees scrunched up beneath his chin. He looked unhappy.

The Winby seniors were further away, near the barbecue, Mr Winby stretched out in the sun, his hat covering his face and his arms flopped by his side. From the occasional snores that floated through the afternoon silence, Rhea knew he was asleep. Mrs Winby was knitting. Stoney and his girl Kim were sitting together, her floral dress bright against the dark rock, her legs drawn up beneath her. They were playing with a goanna, twitching a stick at it to make it hiss. Will was with them but lying down flat, his face turned into his arm. He didn't look round when Rhea walked past.

368

'Tim?' Rhea squatted down beside him, catching her arms around long, bony legs. He looked at her.

'Yeah, Rhea?' She could see the unhappiness lining his mouth, putting creases into the skin where before it had stretched taut. She swallowed awkwardly.

'I had a think about things. About you and Mother. And I guess Will's right. It wasn't your fault you had to marry that woman. So, as long as you don't forget Mother and you don't . . . hurt her, and I know you wouldn't want to but sometimes things happen. Look at last time. You didn't mean to hurt her then but you did. So, you mustn't let that happen again, okay? 'Cos she got sick and nearly lost the baby.' She hesitated. 'Tim? Is it Daddy's baby or yours? I mean . . . ' She flushed hotly, her eyes seeming to flinch away from his. 'Will said, he thought it was probably yours. I told him all about you and Mother, but he won't tell anyone. He'll keep quiet, don't worry.'

Tim didn't attempt to slip a hand into hers, or give her a false hug. She was glad about that. He had dignity and could be relied upon not to embarrass her. He did smile but it wasn't much of one, just a sad creasing of his mouth. Rhea suddenly felt petty. She disliked herself for what she'd been thinking about him, what she'd thought of saying.

'Would it upset you if you thought it might be my baby?' he asked. Rhea felt her stomach give an odd lurch.

'Is it?'

'Maybe. No matter what, he'll be treated like my son by me. He's your mother's son, that's what counts.' He looked at her then, and she thought suddenly how lucky her mother was, being able to inspire that kind of love. She hoped she could do it someday. The wind flicked Tim's hair over his brow, making him seem very young and he looked into Rhea, right into her mind, with his clear eyes so that she knew he was being honest with her. And that pleased her more than anything. She nodded.

'Good. Then that's all that matters, isn't it? You'll come and see us a lot? Not just every now and then?' And when he nodded she smiled tentatively and held out her hand. 'Then we'll be friends again. All right?' She looked around to where her mother had lifted her hat and was watching them both. Tim held out his hand.

'All right,' he said and shook hers.

Tim took them to a dance in Gidge that night, at the hotel on the corner of the main street. There was really only the one road in Gidgeeganup anyway, the houses straggling back from it in a haphazard sort of way, bales of barbed wire, tin cans, and rubbish stacked in ugly piles along the side. Tim winced.

'Not the most prepossessing place I've ever seen. But at least there's a pub. Where would we be without that?' He was driving the utility, neither of the Winby seniors wanting to join them. They were past dancing, Mr Winby said and Mrs Winby had done her best not to look too wistful. She had waved them off long after they had disappeared up the road. Will, Rhea, Stoney and Kim were in the back, bouncing over the potholes and swapping tall stories with little success. No-one believed anything.

'Bunch of cynics we've brought with us,' Tim commented while he helped Ursula out of the cab. She smiled.

'National pastime, being a cynic. Or so I gather?'

'Nah, only when we're trying to impress. The rest of the time we're as gullible as lambs,' Tim said and Ursula shook her head.

'Gullible, my foot! Lot of Turkish rug salesmen if you ask me. Come on then you lot. Will, careful! Kim's got her skirt caught.' But Kim had freed it and jumped out, as graceful as a young springbok, before Ursula's warning had registered. Will looked pained.

'How am I supposed to help you if you go leaping about like that?' he demanded and Kim grinned.

'You're too slow, boy. Gotta be a lot quicker to catch me.' She liked calling him 'boy', knowing it annoyed him. He flushed and looked at her crossly.

'I don't want to catch you, Kim, so don't get so high and uppity. Stoney's the only one trying to fish round here.' He then walked off, his back very straight while Kim's laughter echoed in his ears.

Rhea was already at the entrance to the hotel, trying to peer in round the doors. Will called her away.

'Not that side stupid. That's the public bar. You can't go in there. C'mon, the saloon's round this side.' He pushed her away from the door, one hand firmly on her shoulder. Tim lifted an eyebrow at Ursula. She shook her head.

'They've both got a lot of growing up to do before anything of that sort starts to occur to them. That's rather why I thought I'd try and get some learning into Will before Rhea starts to make him feel stupid or left behind.'

'Um, not that much growing up. You might want to keep an eye on them. Will's fifteen, isn't he?'

'Yes, but Rhea's only eleven. Just a child still. You're fussing. Besides, I'd trust Rhea with Will under any circumstances, no matter what their age.' She didn't like the way Tim laughed at her then.

'My little novice. Come on, let's go find this dance.'

The back room of the hotel, where they normally had the lunch room set up, had been cleared leaving a long empty space in the middle while both sides of the room were lined with chairs. The room was brightly lit from every possible corner. Ursula was daunted to find women were sitting on one side, men on the other. Only the children seemed to be mingling sexes and that simply because they were too young to know the difference. Rhea had stopped by the door and Will had dropped his arm from her shoulder with a guilty glance at the other young men in the room. They hooted at him, calling rude names before being cuffed by their mothers who had crossed the room to restore order. Will flushed hotly and disappeared in search of Stoney.

Ursula paused, looking at Tim.

'Aw, yew must be Mrs Paterson.' Ron Carstairs, if in fact it was him, was beckoning them from behind a hastily set-up bar. Tim led them over.

'Nice ter meet yew. And your friend.' He didn't introduce himself, his steel-wool hair capping a large, weathered face, a surprisingly small, neat nose, and eyes like a siamese cat's. He was an odd mixture, none of the parts seeming to belong to the whole. Even his teeth looked like they belonged elsewhere: to a ferret perhaps, but not to such a large man. He stood well over six foot three, dwarfing everyone around him. Ursula held out her hand.

'Mr Carstairs?' When he nodded, taking his identity for granted, Ursula introduced the rest of her brood.

'Mr Nowlton. Nice ter meet yew. And yew young lady. We haven't seen yew in here before, have we?' Rhea shook her head. Then he caught sight of Stoney and Kim, hovering uncertainly behind Will. He shook his head, one hand pointing to the door.

'Now then you two. Yew know a damned sight better than this. Out yer get, right now. We're not having your sorts in here.' They turned immediately and left. Tim put his hand on Ursula's wrist. She ignored it.

'What sort is that, Mr Carstairs?' Her high English voice carried over the music, catching people's attention. They stopped and looked.

'Bloody abos. They know they can't come in here. Kim works for me in the hotel as a maid but I won't have none of them in here. They're a dirty bunch and can't hold their drink, none of 'em,' he said firmly. Ursula stood looking at him quietly. Then she motioned to Rhea and Will.

'I see. Well, thank you, Mr Carstairs. Goodnight.' And with no hint of anything but polite thoughtfulness, she led her party outside. Tim grinned ruefully.

'Now what the hell did I say wrong?' Ron Carstairs asked in an aggrieved tone. Tim looked at him.

'I don't think Ursula liked the company after all. Too monotone,' he said evenly enough. Carstairs looked even more puzzled.

'Monotone? What's that?'

'Round here I guess that's synonymous with "bigot". Hell, you haven't even got a television set to mix the blacks and the whites.' He grinned, but there was no humour in his eyes. 'Oh, and just for the record, neither Kim nor Stoney drink. Goodnight, Carstairs.' And with that, Tim followed Ursula from the room.

Stoney and Kim were leaning against the fence, Stoney's feet brushing through the dirt aimlessly. They looked up in surprise when Ursula called to them.

'Come on kids. We're going home. We'll have our dance there, where we all belong.' She held out a hand and they stood up uncertainly.

'It's okay, Mrs Paterson. We didn't really think he'd let us in anyway. You don't have to leave on our account.' Kim was

372

a bright girl and didn't like to be patronized by anyone. Ursula shook her head.

'No, it is most certainly not all right. I really don't think I could enjoy myself in there anyway. There seemed to be as much segregation between the sexes as there was between the colours. Come on, let's go home where we can enjoy ourselves properly. Will, would you go buy a case of lemonade?'

And so, to Tim's amusement and complete admiration, Ursula hosted her first impromptu dance at the homestead, pulling Mr and Mrs Winby in from their self-imposed evening chores and setting up their radio in the large sitting room. They pushed the furniture back against the walls and, with gentle encouragement, showed Will and Stoney how to lead their partners in a waltz.

Mrs Winby admitted to Tim, after a beer or two, that she'd never liked that Carstairs fellow ever since she'd caught him beating Stoney's mother.

'Not much of a mother, I s'pose, but Ron had no cause to do that. The woman wasn't doing anything, just sitting on his verandah. But he's like that. Heard a rumour he used to be a station manager for some property up North but got kicked off for brutality to the abos. I don't like to think of Kim goin' back there after what you had to say to him. He'll take it out on her.' Her gaze followed Kim's bright dress across the room. Tim watched too.

The waltz soon degenerated into a hop but at least, Ursula thought, the children were enjoying themselves and not frightened to talk to each other the way the other young people had been at the dance. So silly! Mr Winby surprised everyone, particularly Will who gaped, his mouth hanging down to his chin, at the sight of his father expertly whisking his mother up and down the room. And then Tim took Ursula for a careful and rather distant twirl, her expression quite calm and content for all the pink flush on her cheeks.

The long-awaited birth took place on the 26th of April and Tim was there for it. Not actually in the delivery room but leaning against the wall not far from the swing doors through which a herd of nurses and doctors seemed to sweep from one moment to the next. Rhea sat patiently waiting next to the water fountain, half amused at the look on Tim's face, half impatient to be introduced to her brother. No-one even dreamt it might be a girl. They hadn't considered the possibility when thinking of names. It was all firmly fixed in advance. He was to be Thomas Henry Timothy Paterson. Tom.

'Rhea? Come here. I think your mother's given birth,' Tim called. He was standing now by the doors, one foot forward as though to jam it between the next opening and force an entry. A nurse pushed him back, politely but firmly.

'You can see him in a few minutes in the viewing room, just down there. Your baby, down there.' She pointed down the corridor. Tim looked at her steadily.

'And Ursula? When can I see her?'

'Your wife will be taken back to her room shortly, Mr Paterson. Do please stay away from these doors. You're not allowed in there.' The nurse was engulfed once more by the swinging doors but Tim stood his ground, waiting with a determined look in his eye to catch the next nurse who appeared.

'Come on, Mr Paterson,' Rhea giggled. 'Let's go see Tom.' Tim shook his head; he wanted to know about Ursula. He stopped another nurse as she exited under his chin.

'Mrs Paterson. She just gave birth to a boy. Is she all right? The doctor thought there might be complications. I just want to know everything went well and that she's all right. And the baby.' The nurse smiled professionally, taking in Tim's obviously worried state and the glint in his eye that said he was not moving for anyone until he knew the facts.

'Fine. She's really fine now. We had a bit of bother with her blood pressure dropping suddenly on us but we took care of it so you needn't worry. Mrs Paterson will be taken back to her room and you'll be allowed to see her as soon as the doctor's checked on her again. In the meantime, you can see your son down there . . . ' She started to point the way, yet again, but stopped when Tim cut across her.

'Blood pressure? That won't have harmed her in any way, will it? Or the baby?' He was frowning, a small crease in his forehead etching in deeply. Rhea looked up in alarm.

'No, no. They're both perfectly well. It was just a momentary drop and we noticed it immediately. Just as well she was in hospital though and not out on that property of yours.' She

374

turned away as Tim thanked her and pushed Rhea gently toward the corridor.

'Well thank God for that. C'mon, Rhea. Let's go see your baby brother.'

Rhea knew what was on his mind. Would Tom look like him – or like Simon? Rhea hoped they'd be able to tell.

It took some time before the nurse behind the glass held up a bundle of blanket and brought it close for them to see. A pink crumpled face, no hair, no teeth and pale blue eyes greeted them. They stared at the baby carefully, absorbed in trying to see some hint of paternity. The nurse bounced Tom gently and he yawned, one small fist clenched tightly and waving in the air.

'I can't tell, can you?' Rhea said at last. Tim hesitated.

'Not really, no. We probably won't know until he's a lot older, if ever. Maybe if he turns into a long, thin beanpole we'll have an idea.' He sounded despondent.

'What about his blood type? Mother's A-type, I know because I saw it on her medical card. And Daddy's O. He's very proud of that because he says he gave blood in the war to some fellow who was dying and he was the only one with the right type blood. It's called the universal donor or something. What're you?' Rhea was looking at Tim as though she were sizing up a prize bull. Tim looked blank.

'No idea. Never thought about it before. Why, what're you?' But the nurse was getting tired of holding up baby Tom and she took him away again, distracting their train of thought. Reluctantly they returned to the waiting room.

'A, I think.' Rhea said after a few moments.

'What?'

'I'm type A, I think. Mother should know. Maybe we can ask the nurse what blood type Tom is?' Rhea was taken with the idea of playing medical detective and Tim told her to trot off and find out. He didn't want to disillusion her. But it seemed pretty obvious. If she was type A, so, in all likelihood would Tom be. And then there would be no way of knowing. He wished he had paid attention to what blood type he was. Surely he must have been told at some point in his life?

Rhea returned a few moments later.

'A. Not much help, is it?' She seemed discouraged and he ruffled her hair.

375

'Never mind. It doesn't much matter either way. He's ours and Simon knows nothing about him,' Tim said. That cheered Rhea up and she began to plan when the christening should be. Tim tried to take an interest. But all he really wanted was to see Ursula.

She was tired when they were at last permitted to visit her. Tired and lethargic as though she had been sick for some time and was only now convalescing. Tim sat beside her, holding her hand and Rhea waited anxiously for her mother to look up and smile. When she did, it was with an obvious effort.

'Hallo you two. Been waiting long?' Ursula said. Tim was peering into her eyes with an expression of such tender caring, trying to winkle out her moods and thoughts, that Rhea felt she should look away. She examined the flowers beside the bed instead. Ursula touched Tim's cheek with her fingers and smiled at him.

'Have you seen Tom yet?' He nodded.

'Yeah. He's a pink crumpled little scrap of a thing with a big yawn and no teeth. Totally uninterested in us, wasn't he, Rhea?' He smiled proudly. 'You feeling better now?'

'Oh I guess. Tired though.' Tim leaned forward and kissed her hair, taking care not to lean too heavily on the bed. He smelled of Cusson's soap and tobacco as always. She thought with a contented sigh how nice it was to have Tim here with her, holding her hand. Not like Simon at Rhea's birth when it had taken three days for him to appear.

'What about you two? You going to be okay for tonight?'

'Fine. All sorted out, isn't it, Rhea? We'll be here first thing in the morning with the car all set up, blankets, pillows, you name it. It'll be like riding in a bed,' Tim reassured Ursula. They were to stay in a hotel for the night and take Ursula and Tom home tomorrow if there were no complications.

The Winbys had stayed on the property, even Mrs Winby admitting there was no point in them going all the way to Perth just to hang around in hospital corridors. Rhea now seemed to be in charge of sleeping arrangements, Tim was simply concerned about Ursula and how she was holding up. Rhea slid her hand into his as she saw her mother's eyelids droop.

'C'mon, Tim. Mother's tired and needs her sleep. We'll come back in the morning. Tom's great by the way, Mother.

Looks a bit ugly at the moment but he'll be lovely by tomorrow, I'll bet.' She led Tim away from Ursula, leading him by the hand as though she were the adult and he the child. Tim looked amused and Ursula smiled her goodbyes before drifting off to sleep again.

Kim stayed on at the property once Tom was brought home. Stoney wanted her to stay permanently anyway, and Mrs Winby, Tim and Ursula all thought it a good idea to get Kim away from the hotel in Gidgeeganup. She could help keep the homestead clean, cook meals, and do the laundry – all the jobs she was used to doing in town. And Ursula could look after Tom herself – when she could get him away from Mrs Winby. It suited them all very well.

Tim had returned to Melbourne a few days after the birth. He had to start preparing for the by-election, he said, his expression one of resignation. He always wanted to be where he wasn't, Ursula realized with a pang. Too many different directions demanded his presence, too many different people made claims on his time. Mostly he wanted to be with her and the baby, she knew that. But even when he was, he was feeling guilty about wherever else he wasn't. Ursula could almost have been irritated, if she weren't so much in love with him and if she didn't realize he had no choice in his perpetual sense of responsibility. It was just the way he was made.

Ursula's own sense of responsibility was much more localized and focused. It centred around her children, her home, and Tim. Everything and everyone else could go to hell, she thought fiercely, holding Tom close to her at night as she sat feeding him in bed. She liked the way he clung to her, little pink mouth pursed up to her breast. He was a much easier baby than Rhea had ever been, sleeping most of the night away without waking, and smiling whenever she went to pick him up. On nights like these, with the wind moaning around the house and the rain falling steadily, she liked to have Tom with her in bed. Rhea was away and Tim was away and the house seemed curiously lonely without them, she realized. She held Tom against her breast and crooned to him, 'Bye baby bunting, Daddy's gone a-hunting, to try and catch a rabbit skin, to wrap poor baby bunting in.' Except it wasn't a rabbit skin this time, Ursula worried to herself; it was a Parliamentary seat. And it wouldn't keep them warm at all.

A screen door was flapping somewhere, banging desultorily in the wind without any real consistency so that she couldn't relax until the next bang came. Ursula called out to Kim. She didn't expect an answer. Kim was often with Stoney in the evenings. Perhaps it was time they thought of getting married. The door banged again and Ursula sighed.

'Well, we're going to have to go shut it ourselves, aren't we, Tom?' She wrapped a blanket around them both, and slid out of bed. It wasn't that late. Probably no more than ten o'clock. But when you got up early and had nothing to do in the evenings, it made more sense to go to bed early. She wished she could afford to stay in Perth sometimes. If only for a few nights.

'Damn, Kim. She's left the back door unlocked again. I wish she wouldn't do that.' It was silly, really, to worry about locking up. There was nothing to steal and no-one around anyway for several miles. But still, it made her uneasy to think of the house being left open and with her alone with a baby. She shifted Tom to her left hip and reached through to fasten the screen door. It latched on a single hook. Then she closed the inner door more firmly and turned the key. Something slid past the corner of her eye, out beyond the verandahed porch, making her swivel quickly, her heart suddenly pounding in her ribcage. Surely not . . . no, it was all right. It was just the flapping edge of a sheet that Kim had forgotten to bring in before the rain started that evening. No point in bringing it in now; it would be soaked. Funny though, the way the mind played tricks, building hobgoblins out of trees, murderers out of shadows . . . husbands out of flapping washing. Because that's what, for a split second, she had thought she had seen. Simon, out there somewhere, in the dark, the way he always was in the shadows of her mind, lurking, ready to pounce.

She shook herself and laughed. Simon was out of her life and she would do anything necessary to make sure he stayed that way.

'Yew mind your tongue, Stoney, or I'll mind it for yers.' Kim was indignant in the way that only very strong young women can be. She held her fist up and waved it in Stoney's face. The

378

sun was blazing down on them both as they stood before the vicar, Stoney's face running rivulets of sweat down into his tight collar, and Kim's white dress growing damp in the space between her shoulder blades. The vicar was trying, half-heartedly it seemed to Ursula, to calm them both down, saying 'Oh, now really, there's no call for that.' But Kim wasn't having any of it. She jabbed a finger at Stoney's chest.

'I won't, yew hear me? Obey! That's out. Flat out!'

'It's just part of the preaching bit, Kim. I don't expect yews to obey. Yew never have anyways!' Stoney said bitterly. He intended to sound plaintive. His wife to be wasn't impressed.

'If it don't matter then we're skippin' that bit. Okay, vicar, yews can go on now.' The vicar wasn't too sure. He was only a visiting, bush cleric and he hadn't liked the fact that Kim was already large in the belly when he arrived. Ursula had tried to hide that under a peplum of sorts but no-one had been fooled. Quite frankly, apart from the vicar, no-one really cared. Kim and Stoney were living together like man and wife anyway, only waiting for the next vicar to pass through and make things official. The vicar felt almost superfluous. And now there was squabbling over the words of the ceremony. No-one had ever squabbled about that before. He breathed deeply and wiped one hand over his face.

'Are we quite sure we are ready for this holy state to be visited upon us? Marriage is a serious matter, my children.' He tried to think of every cliché he had ever uttered on the subject. Kim cut him short.

'Yeah, and so is a baby. Yews go right ahead, just cut the bit out about obeying. I'm not obeyin', Stoney, no how.' She thrust out her lower lip and stood there firmly, both legs sturdily apart. The wedding dress looked inappropriate with its white frills. Stoney and the vicar sighed, yet again.

'What d'yer want, vicar? Jus' get on with it, will yer?' Mr Winby added under his breath and shuffled his feet awkwardly through the dust. They weren't getting married in the church anyway. Neither one of them had wanted that. Under the sky, was how Stoney expressed it. He liked the sky. It made him feel like he could tip himself into it sometimes if he just fell forward, like rolling into a big blue bowl.

The vicar was repeating his question to Kim, being careful

to omit anything this time that he thought might give offence. She glared at him for a moment before nodding. 'Yeah, okay.' He winced.

Ursula and Rhea were smiling from the sidelines, trying to urge the two along with good thoughts and encouraging nods of the head. Mrs Winby was swatting at flies and Mr Winby had started coughing now. He wiped the sweat off his brow and put his hat on before hastily doffing it under the vicar's beady stare. Only Will stood still and seemed to be paying attention. He was the best man.

'Right then, that's it,' Stoney muttered as the vicar told him he might kiss his bride. He didn't feel like kissing her. She would only nag him about something and embarrass him in front of Mrs Paterson. He compromised by kissing Kim chastely on the cheek. She laughed.

'That's it, Stoney. Better be a good boy now we're married!' And then she'd flashed him one of her dark, sassy grins, her eyes shining and he couldn't help but grin back. She was a good-looking woman.

The others were pressing forward to congratulate them and for a moment Stoney was tempted to actually roll forward and try his theory out with the sky. It was so blue, so tipped over today. He hung his head back and stared up at it, feeling his feet become light and giddy, his chest filling with air. But Kim grabbed his arm and started shaking him about something and he felt the heaviness return to his body, anchoring it to the ground and preventing him falling away. He shook his head and looked around. Will was punching him in the arm.

'It's all over now, Stoney. Your wandering days are done.' Will knew about his secret dream to tip himself into the sky. They'd talked about it when they were kids. Now he was watching Stoney with a sad, regretful look that meant he knew what Stoney had been thinking. He was too late for that now. Kim would keep him heavily planted on the ground.

'Yew better run free while yews can, Will. I won't be there with you so much now.' Stoney punched Will back. 'No way Kim's gonna let me run out on this lot.' He grinned but there was a hint of panic in his flashing teeth, his wide smile. Will nodded.

'Yeah, I know. I'm in no hurry to tie any knots around

myself.' But that was a lie, he thought. He glanced over at Rhea.
No good there. Way too young still. But he'd been so restless
lately, watching Stoney and Kim when they thought they were
alone, feeling out of place with everything and everyone. He
wished he knew what he was supposed to do. He looked at his
hands. They were brown and dirt-stained, his nails broken
from hard work. Ugly hands, the girl in Gidge had said, in her
mocking voice. Ugly hands and ugly face to match. He felt
himself flush. She wasn't so great herself. And she smelt stale,
when she'd let him kiss her that time. Stale cigarettes, cheap
perfume, sweat, her body fleshy where he hadn't expected it
and squeezed too tightly into her clothes. He shuddered at the
thought, and at her taunting voice still echoing in his mind.
Not man enough to get it up. He flushed again, wondering why
at that moment of all moments, his body had failed him.
Normally he had no thoughts except how to control those
awkward tents in his trousers. He had to walk away from Kim
all the time, so she wouldn't see. And that stupid, fat girl had
said . . . He ground his teeth.

'What's the matter, Will? You look good and mad about
something.' Rhea was squinting into the sun, her fair hair
flying loose around her face. She wasn't aware of how much
she bothered him. She didn't even know she was pretty. Her
mother never encouraged her to dwell on any personal
vanities, and Rhea herself never really thought about it. She
looked in the mirror to wash her face, or tie her hair back, or
sometimes, to see if she could see her father's face in hers. But
not for vanity's sake. Will wished she were older, or if not that,
then at least less attractive. It seemed so unfair that she should
be both young and lovely when he was old and ugly. Sixteen
and brutishly dark, full of scars and callouses, big feet . . . She
slipped her hand into his when he looked at her with eyes full of
unshed tears.

'What is it, Will? Why're you so sad? Stoney and Kim
aren't going anywhere. It won't change anything round here.
And I'm here for three long, glorious months now. Oh! It's so
good to be back! We'll have a great time!' She swung his hand
back and forth with hers.

'Yeah, I guess. Where's Tom? Your mum leave him alone?'
he asked suddenly, to change the subject.

'He's only on the verandah in his cot. We can see it from here. Besides, Mannie's there. She wouldn't let anyone touch Tom.' And that was true. Mannie had adopted Tom as though he were her own pup and was fiercely protective of him. Rhea encouraged her mother to leave Tom with Mannie for short times, so the dog could get used to being in sole charge of the infant. That way, Ursula could spend a little more of the precious time she had with Tim simply being alone with him. Rhea knew that was seldom enough.

'Tim's becoming quite a celebrity, being so young for an MP and so handsome with it. It really shook everyone up when he took Gisburne so easily, and what with all his speeches about the importance of rural communities, he's become the darling of the Country Party voters. Even some of the girls at school have fallen for him. They're so impressed he's a family friend! God, if they really knew. They'd have a fit! Half of Australia would have a fit.'

'Yeah, he'll have to be careful. Too many nosey parker's round here who'd like to pretend they know more than they do.' Will worried about that sometimes. People like Ron up at the hotel. Who knew what was being said? He liked Mrs Paterson. She was really nice. He hoped nothing went wrong for her.

Rhea was thinking along the same lines.

'That's why Tim's not coming over so much now. He said every two months to begin with. Now it's more like every three to four. I know he wants to be with mother but he's too worried about the scandal if they get caught. You know, sometimes I wish they would be!' she said fiercely. 'Then they could stop all this skulking around and living their lives for everyone else. Tim'd be perfectly happy here. He grew up on a property anyway.'

'Yeah, and left it. I dunno. He might feel like he'd had to give up too much if he came and lived here with your mum. Tim's one of those sorts you can't tie down. Or if you do, then they start to die, like a wild animal that's been stuck in the zoo.' Will knew he wasn't original in his thoughts but he also felt he was right. Rhea nodded.

'Like Mother's "painted birds" ', she murmured. Will looked at her. 'Oh, nothing. Just something Mother mentioned to me once. Come on, let's go toast Stoney and Kim.'

*　　*　　*

382

Tim wasn't there for Christmas; their second Christmas, Ursula thought ruefully. But things were better. The property was in shape, the Winbys were talking and even friendly, Kim was a godsend with her chatter and noise, her bossiness, and both Tom and Rhea were healthy and happy. There wasn't much more she had a right to ask for. Her own happiness was something so ephemeral anyway, soaring up when Tim called or walked in the door, sinking back into aching misery when he started packing his bags to leave yet again. It was like Rhea packing hers for school, but almost worse. Rhea would always come back but who knew with Tim? She thought she would get used to it, in time. But she didn't.

If only she could climb on top of her feelings for a while, and learn not to care so much. Then she would see things in perspective. Tim wasn't the most important person in her life. Rhea and Tom took first place and always would. She had to remember that. And maybe, if he showed her he loved her more, perhaps took her in his arms and said 'I love you', more than once or twice a year, then perhaps she could relax and accept that he did really cherish her more than his wife or his life away from her. If he would just reassure her that he didn't still act like a husband to Joanna at night, when everyone had left . . . But he didn't and there was no point in wishing. He had told her he wasn't demonstrative and couldn't say the things he felt. That ought to be good enough.

The silly thing was she found herself drawing back from him, scared to touch that skin that she so wanted to run her hand along, to kiss, worried that he would think she was clinging. Those old, wounding words of Simon's came back to haunt her and she became aloof, almost cold at times. And she felt Tim respond to that distance with a chill of his own. Each one compounded the other's errors until there came a point where they must either fight to clear the air or solidify into pure ice where nothing warm could ever stir them again. So far they had always fought, and then made up, the joy made more exquisite for the fear that they had almost left it too late that time. And each time that fear grew greater so that Ursula wondered if she could take Tim turning up anymore. Their relationship never stabilized in the way in which she imagined other couple's doing. There was never any steady plateau of 'hallo, darling, had a nice day? Dinner's on the table.' Maybe if there were, the spice, the frisson they both felt would also melt away? She didn't know.

Tom stirred in her arms and she tucked him more neatly away beneath her left shoulder, letting him ride on her hip. He smiled painfully. Gas. She eased him over her shoulder, hoping the others wouldn't mind. But they were all intent on their Christmas lunch anyway. Kim and Mrs Winby had been up since before dawn, making sure the lunch would feed everyone and be a real celebration. And there was a lot to celebrate, after all. Tom belched obligingly and she wiped his mouth with a flannel.

'That's my good boy.' She planted a kiss on his fair head. His eyes were grey now, flecked with green and even amber. Tim said they were like his father's. Maybe that was so. Certainly Simon's were perfectly blue and so were his father's. Rhea had inherited them but with a spark that had been missing from Simon's cool good looks. But that was all they could see. Tom would have to grow a little more before they could guess at his other features.

He was a sturdy and obliging little boy, none of Rhea's fretfulness as a baby showing up. Could that mean he wasn't Simon's? Oh! She wished she knew! Rhea caught sight of her mother's look, questing out the truth yet again. She sighed. Did it really matter that much? Did her mother maybe resent the fact that she was Simon's daughter? The thought flashed into her mind for a brief instant before being angrily dismissed. Of course not! Things had been quite different then.

'Can I hold Tom for a while, Mother?' Rhea tried to compensate immediately.

'Yes do. I'd like a break anyway.' And that was true, Ursula thought. I'd like a break from all of this. A good holiday away from all this worrying, all this uncertainty. Just lying on a beach somewhere, thinking about nothing more strenuous than where the next cool drink was coming from. Maybe, some-time, the idea tickled at the corners of her mind, Tim and she could take a holiday up to Singapore. It wasn't so very far away from Perth – nearer than Melbourne anyway. And she could go see Fatimah and Yahyah. Go see the bungalow. Her mind sheered away from that. Billy was buried up at the bungalow, in the garden. She wondered if anyone ever put flowers on his grave.

'Mother? Did you like my present? I made it in sewing class.' It was an apron, carefully embroidered along the top of the pinafore with daisy-chain flowers. Rhea had worked pains-takingly on it for several weeks.

'It's beautiful, darling. And I needed an apron too. I'll just be too scared to wear it in case I get anything on it. Maybe I'll keep it for special occasions, like Christmas or your birthday.' Ursula hadn't the heart to tell Rhea the bib string wouldn't reach over her head. She would quietly alter it when Rhea had gone to bed one night.

'What did Tim send you, Mrs Paterson?' Will asked sud-denly, his thoughts blurted out into words before he could consider their effect. Ursula flushed.

'Oh, a book. On flowers. He knows I want to try and grow a bit of a garden around the house.' She didn't mention the other present, the rectangular cut diamond ring. To wear instead of Simon's. Only Rhea knew about that. And she hadn't said anything when Ursula had swapped the rings over. Will nodded, his curiosity satisfied. Tim had remembered Mrs Paterson. That was all that mattered to him.

With the meal over, everyone sat around in easy chairs, either listening to the radio or pretending to read the papers. Ursula dozed off for a while. It was hot and airless and there was nothing much better to do. Stoney and Kim disappeared off to their little house, newly built with Will's and Mr Winby's help, and Rhea put Tom back in his cot before sliding out the back door with Will. They were too restless to sit and snooze the afternoon away.

Will gave a skipping jump as they rounded the back of the barns and headed for the flat rocks. He always felt that rush, that sudden intake of breath leaving him quivering with delight, when he got away from the others with Rhea. He jumped and grabbed for a handful of leaves from the ghost gum. He missed by several feet.

'Your dad's not going to make you work tomorrow, is he?' Rhea asked. Will shrugged.

'Dunno. Probably. Why?' They had come out on the side by the gully, the creek slipping down from the flat rocks and down

385

to the red mud gulch. Rhea hesitated before sliding down it. Normally it didn't matter but today she had on a dress.

'I was hoping we could have another picnic, like last time. Say, Will. I'm going to get this dress ruined if we go down this way. Can't we back up and go round the rocks?' Will looked impatient.

'Just take it off, Rhea. If we go round the long way, it'll take us forever to get to the lagoon. You're the one who didn't want to take the horses anyway, 'cos you had that stupid dress on. Why couldn't you've got changed before we left?'

'Oh, all right. But I can't get the top buttons. You'll have to do them.' She was matter-of-fact as she slid it off and wrapped it around her neck. Will looked sharply away. There had been a change in her body in the last few months. No longer were her hips straight and childishly bony. Now there was a shape to them that, while still painfully immature, caught Will's attention. Her nipples seemed to be tipping outwards, in a way they hadn't before. She hadn't noticed. She started clambering down the mud rocks and sliding between the boulders, her underpants coated in clay. Will followed her cautiously.

When they reached the bottom, where the creek ran deeper and over a jumble of pebbles and scree, the dress was flung aside as both automatically ran whooping into the water, splashing it up over themselves and at each other. It had been a hot walk and climb down and they felt in desperate need of a cooling off. Rhea sat in the water, hanging her head back so that her hair washed wetly down beside her.

Will flopped back against the side of the creek and squeezed the water out of his shirt before throwing it up onto a boulder to dry. His trousers followed. He had only stopped to kick off his boots before running into the water but it didn't matter. The sun would dry everything before long.

Rhea giggled when the cold water made Will suddenly turn over on his front. He frowned into the water.

'Shut up, Rhea. Just shut up.'

'What makes it do that. Sit up like that?' she asked. Will ignored her. 'Will? Really, why does it do that?'

'Same reason you get all pointy chested I guess. I don't know.' Rhea looked down at herself then, noting in surprise the tightened nipples. She poked one with her finger. Will watched, absorbed. Then he reached out a hand and poked the other nipple. Rhea didn't react.

'It seems kind've stupid really.' She shivered. 'C'mon, I'm getting cold. I'm going to lie out on the rocks and sunbake for a while.' She stood up and waded out of the creek, totally unaware of Will's confusion. She lay flat, stretched out on a hot rock and wincing as the stone burnt her skin. Eventually Will joined her.

'Has it gone down now?' she asked, after a few moment's strained silence. Will sighed.

'Yeah. Don't keep going on about it, will yer, Rhea? I don't know much more about it than yew do.'

'Oh, all right! If you're going to be all huffy about it. I don't know what all the fuss is about anyway. It's just another part of you, isn't it? I mean, it could just as easily be another hand, or a foot. Why does everyone get all het up about things like that?' She lay back again, offended. Will was silent. He'd never thought about it like that before. Maybe Rhea was right and it was just some other part of his body. Why his Dad called it naughty and dirty, he really didn't know. He'd just accepted that it was so.

'Rhea? Doesn't your mum tell you parts of you are dirty and shouldn't be shown to anyone?' he asked haltingly. Rhea sat up in surprise.

'No. Of course not. Why, does your mum?'

'No. She doesn't even talk about it. It was my Dad said that. Said you're not supposed to think about it or touch it and never, never show it to anyone. But that gets really difficult sometimes.'

'That's stupid. Why would you have it if it weren't useful for something. And why can't I look at it if I want to? What's going to happen anyway? You get to see my breasts when I go swimming. Nothing happens then.'

'No . . . but it's different when you're older and have bigger, well, you know.'

'Breasts, Will. They're called breasts.' Rhea was impatient with Will's obvious embarrassment. 'And I'll still swim without a top when I'm older. You and Stoney've seen me so what difference does it make? It's much more comfortable without a top. They make us wear a one-piece at school and that's nowhere near as nice.'

'You can't. It isn't considered, well, right. And anyway, your husband will get mad at you when you don't wear a top and all the other men look at you,' Will pointed out crossly. Rhea considered his words carefully.

'Well that's silly. I'll just marry you and then I can do whatever I like. You won't care and Stoney's married so it doesn't matter. Doesn't Kim swim without a top?' Will was silent for a long time.

'She doesn't when I'm around.' He didn't elaborate, still thinking hard about what Rhea had said. It would be good if she married him. Then he wouldn't have to leave the property, and all his work would be for himself, not for his father. The thought pleased him immensely.

'Well I'm going to do what I want, not what Kim does or your Dad says. And if I want to swim without my bottoms then I'll do that too. See.' And with a neat movement, Rhea slipped her pants off and continued to sit unabashed as Will stared at her. His face grew blotchy red.

'Don't, Rhea!' he said but she laughed and stood up, wading unconcernedly into the stream, her buttocks hollowed as she clenched them against the cold. She lay down in the water and splashed it over herself before returning to Will's side. He looked away.

'That feels even nicer. I don't know why we wear clothes to go swimming anyway. It doesn't make much sense. Why don't you try it?' She couldn't understand his embarrassment. Why was he acting so silly? Will flinched when she squeezed the water out of her hair over his chest.

'Leave me alone, Rhea. You're too young to know what you're talking about but you can bet your mum'd be real upset if she knew you'd just done that. You're not supposed to go about naked. It's not polite, for a start.'

'Not polite? Why? Am I ugly, or offensive?' She lay back beside him, liking the strange feeling of power she had over him, liking also the way he was looking at her now.

'No-o. It's just unfair on me, that's all. You make me feel things that I'm not supposed to feel, not with you or, at least, not until we get married. I dunno. But it isn't right.' And with that idea firmly set in his mind, he stood up, pulled on his clothes and started climbing the walls of the gulch back up the way they had come. Rhea stared after him.

'Wait, Will. I'm coming too.' She pulled on her pants and caught up her dress and shoes quickly, scrambling after Will's rapidly receding back.

He was waiting for her at the top and helped her back into her dress. She didn't tease him further and seemed subdued so that he finally nodded at her as he buttoned the last hole.

'That's better,' he said. 'And next time bring a top.' He walked away before she could answer.

When Tim arrived next, it was nearly March and the weather had begun to change, thin cloud hazing the sunshine and an occasional cooler breeze marking the beginning of autumn. Ursula was out back, digging in the newly turned earth that she intended to plant with vegetables and Kim was in the kitchen. Both babies, Tom in one cot and Kim's new arrival, Percival, in the other, were on the verandah with Mannie keeping guard. They made a curious contrast, one so fair and the other so dark. But Kim and Ursula looked after them both indiscriminately and Mrs Winby spent far too much time away from her chores making goo-goo eyes at them, according to Mr Winby, for them to ever feel neglected. The babies didn't seem to be sure who they belonged to.

Ursula first heard the commotion when Kim came bursting out onto the verandah, singing loudly. 'He's come, Mrs Paterson. Mr Nowlton's here.' Tim followed the black girl out onto the verandah and stood shading his eyes as he peered across the yard. Ursula straightened up, cursing. Why, oh why couldn't he give her some warning? Why did he always have to turn up when she looked like some slattern, her old dress sweat-stained, her face brown and freckled without a shred of make-up, her hair tied back severely to keep it out of her eyes. She waved one work-stained hand briefly.

'Ursula! What on earth are you doing?' He stepped down from the porch, his moleskins gleaming whitely in the sun and Ursula felt as though someone had given her a hard jab just below the ribs. The air left her lungs and that familiar bitter-sweet pain lodged hard in her chest.

'Digging, what else? Why don't you put some work pants on and come and give me a hand?' She kept her tone casual, for Kim. He grinned.

'Okay. I guess I can do with some good physical work. I've been stuck behind a desk far too much lately. I never guessed being an MP meant so much paperwork!' He came over to where she stood, leaning on her hoe, and kissed her on the cheek. Kim waved wildly from the verandah and disappeared inside.

'Have you met Percy?' Ursula smiled into Tim's eyes, at the look of longing and frustration there.

'Yeah. Kim showed him off proudly. Nice little thing too. Be good for Tom to have someone to play with. He's looking great. More and more like me,' he added with emphasis, and Ursula thought it was true that Tom did look more like Tim than Simon. Maybe it was just mannerisms, or maybe something more. She shook her head.

'Your imagination, darling. He's just a baby still. You can't tell.' She wasn't sure why she wanted to deny him that hold on Tom. But something inside her urged her to make noncommittal remarks whenever the question of paternity was raised. She took a letter out of her pocket and flapped it in front of Tim.

'From Lettice. Go ahead and read it.' He frowned and slid it out of its envelope.

'Dear Ursula,' it began conventionally enough. 'Just had the most amazing news. All of London is talking about it and we poor things down here in Essex naturally took our time to hear such things. Still, everything filters through in time. Simon has been thrown out of the house by Humphrey! Julia was given the option of leaving with Simon but, sensible girl that she always was and always will be, she recognized on which side her bread is buttered and elected to stay along with the children. Humphrey evidently has resigned his seat and intends to settle down and write his memoirs! Can't begin to think what they'll be like!' Lettice was fond of exclamation marks. 'Humphrey's repudiating all Simon's debts, letting it be known far and wide that Simon's been cut out of his will and generally acting like he should have done more years ago than I can say. Maybe if Humphrey had acted like more of a man back then, you and Rhea would still be with us here in Elsing and not out in the middle of nowhere. How is Tim, by the way? Do give him my worst.

'Well, Simon is of course in serious debt and has gone into hiding to avoid all the collectors suddenly dunning him left and right. He's been living off the expectation of Humphrey's will for years now and will, I fear, have a great deal of trouble in clearing even a fraction of what he owes. I rather suspect he may be down at Cotters and I intend to take a drive over this afternoon to find out. That is, if Hugh doesn't take another turn for the worse. We really don't know what's the matter with him lately but he's just not himself, flagging out in the garden and having to sit down suddenly. He gets rather an unpleasant pain in his tummy too, and if I'm not mistaken it's been getting worse just lately. I can't imagine what I'll do if he's actually seriously ill. I've been trying without success to get him to pop in and see someone about it. Cullen's no good, too old, but there's a new chap now who might just know something. Wish you'd write and tell Hugh that. He won't listen to me.' Tim looked up at Ursula.

'She doesn't believe in paragraphs too often, does she? And I guess her worst is now conveyed. Did you read this about Hugh?' When she nodded, he shrugged and continued reading.

'Rhea sent me a poem she wrote about the bush. I do think it shows talent, don't you? So graphic in its descriptive detail. Sounds God Awful to me! How you can bear to live there, I really don't know and with Tim only showing up when it suits him, well! I won't go on about that because I know it only upsets you but sometimes I wonder about all men – except Hugh, of course, who's an absolute dear and not like the rest of them at all. Speaking of men in general and the devil in particular, look who's just walked in the gate. I'm writing this in the drawing room and who should be walking up the drive at this very moment but your errant husband. Whoops, he's just arrived at the front door. Better go and let the poor, bedraggled thing in and clean up on all the gossip. Mind you, his version will be something to hear! I'll finish this later.

'The wonderful thing about letters is, you never have to wait when someone writes that sort of thing to you. Several hours have gone by and Simon has come and gone. He's looking

quite appalling my dear, and I'm not about to tell you otherwise. Quite run down and seedy looking. Not himself at all! No
money, of course and no woman to look after him. Worse still,
no expectation of ever having any money again. He's talking
about going out to India or the Far East. I told him one place is
much the same as another; if he can't make it here, he's not
going to make it anywhere else either. He never did like my
home truths. I gave him tea anyway which perked him up a bit
and he tells me the cottage is terribly small and quite impossible. No-one should expect him to live there! When I pointed
out he expected you to live there, he turned quite sour and took
his leave. I don't expect he'll come visiting again soon. The
only thing that worries me, Ursula dear, is that I caught him
going through my desk when I came back in with the tea. He
said he was looking for a piece of writing paper to make a list of
errands he has to run. I don't believe it for an instant and am
quite sure he was looking for a letter from you with your
address.

'Anyway, my love, must go. Please write soon. Your letters
are such a joy to receive. Love Lettice.

'P.S. Nearly a month has gone by since I wrote all that. I
know I should've sent it sooner but I've somehow put off
letting you know, in case he did actually find a letter. I am
sorry but who could have thought he would be such a
snoop!'

Tim folded the letter up and replaced it in the envelope. He
returned it to Ursula.

'Still quite acid about me, is she? I was hoping I'd been
forgiven by now. Poor old Hugh. I don't know but it sounds
like a tumour to me. You written back yet?' Ursula nodded
briefly. 'And now this, with Simon. You don't really think
he'd come out here after you, do you?'

'Possibly. He needs somewhere to live and he has to get
away from all those debts. I think it's something we have to
consider. After all, he might think the property's quite big by
English standards and you know what a snob he is; being a
gentleman farmer probably appeals to him.' She smiled
ruefully, holding up her filthy calloused hands. Tim took one
between his own and kissed it.

'Maybe you should think about divorcing him?'

392

'How can I, Tim? For a start, I left him so he'd have to be the one to sue for divorce and I don't think he will. And then, of course, he'd know where I am – and where Rhea is. You know she refuses to see her father. It would be dreadful if he just turned up and said he was moving in with us. I don't know what I'd do, particularly having told everyone round here he's dead! And what about Tom? God knows I don't want him finding out about him – or you.'

'You think he's vindictive enough to try and do something to Tom or me?' Tim sounded unconvinced.

'Not physically, no. Not Simon's style unless you're smaller than him. But he'd wreck your career without a thought. We just can't take the risk. It's not worth a piece of paper saying I'm not his wife any more. And anyway, why do I need it? You can't marry me.' She looked away at that. Tim sighed.

'Yeah, you're right. Look, I'll get changed and come and give you a hand.'

They worked solidly throughout the afternoon and by evening were satisfied with their results. Kim was calling them into the house and the lights were lit and the mosquito coils sending up snaking tendrils of smoke over the porch by the time they responded. Ursula showered first, leaving Tim nursing a beer out in the rocking chair by the back steps with Tom lying in the crook of his arm. He looked content.

Kim left them soon after, disappearing off to the Winbys' where everyone else had dinner. She took Percy with her. Ursula sat in her big bathrobe on the porch, her wet hair tied up in a towel and Tom lying against her shoulder. While Tim cleaned himself up, she fed Tom and crooned a lullaby to him. He was then put to bed in the cot in Rhea's room.

'Is Rhea getting on all right at school?' Tim asked when they turned the light off and partially closed the door on the sleeping child. Ursula smiled.

'Loving it. She always liked boarding school. Can't imagine why, myself, but Rhea's very independent. Will's lost without her.' She reached up and put her arms around his neck. 'Uumh! You don't know how much I've missed you and how much I've wished Kim in Timbuctoo this afternoon.' He held her so tightly she thought she might crack in two.

'Along with the Winbys and anyone else within a hundred

miles. Yeah, I know!' He kissed her. 'I'm not hungry yet, are you? Come to bed.'

Later, when the night noises had died down to a gentle murmur and the bedroom had become cool again after the heat of the day, Ursula lay awake across Tim's chest, her eyes staring out the window at the shadows. She remembered that flapping sheet and she shivered. Maybe Simon really would be there soon, hiding in the dark, waiting to make his move.

Tim breathed slowly and evenly in his sleep. Ursula kissed his chest. He didn't stir.

Chapter Twenty Three

It began very simply. Just a letter, written in an illiterate hand, saying 'I know who you are'. There was nothing more. No threats, no demands. Not even a signature. Ursula received three in one month, folding them away silently in her bureau desk with a tightened mouth that betrayed little of the fear inside. Tim had been in Parliament a year. Long enough for everyone to know him. She knew the letters wouldn't stop at just that.

By the time her birthday arrived in November, the letters were becoming more specific. 'I know who you are and I know who he is. If you don't want the world to know, you better start thinking.' Thinking! She'd done nothing but think ever since the first letter arrived. Ursula at 31 was unwilling to be pushed around in life any further. She knew Simon was behind the letters. Somehow he had found her and found out about Tim. And now he thought he could blackmail them into supporting him for the rest of his life. She scrunched the latest letter in her hand.

Well let him go ahead! Let him tell everyone that wonderful, young, caring Mr Nowlton had a mistress and an illegitimate child whom he kept on a property in the back of beyond so that his constituents and his proper young socialite wife and son wouldn't find out. The scandal would kill Tim's political career. And ruin him socially. He'd have nowhere to go but Gidgeeganup Ursula smiled grimly at the thought of what Simon would say to that!

She hadn't shown the letters to Tim yet. There was no point in upsetting him if she could handle it herself. He had too many people pulling him in too many different directions as it was. She didn't want to add to that load. Who was it Simon had asked to write the letters? It wasn't his handwriting, certainly, and anyway, the postal stamp showed the letter had been posted in Subiaco, a suburb of Perth. Did that mean Simon was in Perth too? Living off yet another poor woman who wouldn't wake up to what he was until it was too late. Or was he still back at the cottage and just using someone in Perth to throw her off?

'Not this time, Simon my boy,' she muttered to herself as she straightened the letter out again and placed it with the others in her bureau desk. 'This time I don't give a damn what you do. I'm not having you back in my life either as a husband or a blackmailer.'

By New Year 1959, Simon had come to the point: money, of course. What else had ever mattered to him, Ursula thought bitterly. But so much! He must be crazy to think she could afford such a sum, every month, for the rest of her life. He would be bleeding them dry! She sat, composing her reply, at her desk. Tom and Percy were crawling around on the floor, tugging at Mannie's tail and generally enjoying themselves. Ursula wondered what Simon would think if he knew about Tom. For a moment she went quite cold. Maybe he already knew. Maybe he . . . but no, even if he did know about Tom, he would assume he was Tim's child. As in all likelihood he was. There would be no trouble there.

'Dear Simon,' she wrote. 'Who do you think you're kidding? I don't have money like that and even if I did, I wouldn't let you have a penny of it. Blackmail only works if what is threatened is considered worth the money to prevent it happening – a small point I feel you ought to know before you take up this line of business as a career. I don't mind in the slightest if you let the world know, since it will only give me my heart's desire. Feel free.

Your disillusioned ex, U.'

She had been deliberately cryptic in case he tried to use the letter against her in some way later. She sealed it in an envelope and posted it to the box office as specified, feeling eminently satisfied with herself. And she wasn't all that surprised when the letters stopped arriving, and no word leaked about her to the press. Really, she thought, Simon was too easy to deal with.

Tom was two in April, a sunny-tempered, attractive child with pale hair and large grey eyes. He looked too much like Tim for it to be a coincidence. Everyone commented on it, asking whether Tim was connected to Ursula's family in some way? Ursula said she thought he might be on her mother's side, airily dismissing the question, and wishing Tom would suddenly shoot up into a different looking child altogether. Tim quietly beamed.

They held the birthday party at the lagoon, picnicking on a blanket laid over the rough grass by the side of the water. Everyone had taken a couple of hours off for the event and Tim had flown over especially. He had missed Tom's first birthday.

Tom sat, in pride of place, in the middle of the blanket and Ursula put a paper hat on his head and helped him blow out the two candles on his cake. He was excited, burbling disconnected words to himself before making loud explosions by blowing his cheeks out and slapping them together with his hands. He had only just learned how to do this and was pleased with the results. There was chocolate cake smeared around his mouth and tomato sauce on his chin from the sausages they had barbecued. He looked enormously happy.

A dragonfly hovered, dipping over the water, skimming across the blanket and landing on Tom's head for a fleeting moment. He started, 'mouth puckering up to cry, but Rhea laughed. 'Look Tom, a dragonfly.' She pointed up at it with her finger. 'It's very lucky to have a dragonfly choose you to land on. Isn't it pretty?' Tom held out his hand and the dragonfly flitted closer before taking off in a warm air current and soaring up into the trees. He stared after it, muttering 'dagfy' with concentration. Then he turned back to the presents lying around him.

Tim had given his son a bucket and spade, amongst other toys, and Tom was determined to try them out, banging the spade noisily against the bucket again and again until everyone was tired of the noise. Will and Rhea offered to take him up to the clay-filled gully while everyone else lay out in the milder autumn sun and slept off their lunch. Ursula handed Tom over with a grateful smile.

It was hot between the walls of the gulch, the wind blocked and the rains of the last week causing the clay to suck like mud at their feet. Tom laughed uneasily, lifting his feet clear slowly and then sinking them back into the ochre-coloured mix. Will dipped his finger in the clay and painted two red stripes on each of Tom's cheeks.

'There yer are mate, a good little injun. Where's yer bow an' arrow then?' Rhea picked up a stick and handed it to Tom.

'That's your arrow, Tom. We'll have to go find your bow. You sit here while we go look for one. See? You can dig in the mud while we're looking.' She patted him on the head and moved away, further up the gully, looking for a piece of twine to tie to a stick. Beneath lowered eyelashes, she kept a steady gaze on Will. He was shooting up now into a tall young man, sun-streaked brown hair still shaggy across his brow and dusty tanned skin. She couldn't help herself watching him lately. The other girls at school talked about boys incessantly but few of them knew any, and those they did know all seemed prone to acne and greasy hair. She liked Will's indifference to his appearance and his strong sense of right and wrong. He would make a nice husband, one day.

Will had crossed the creek and was checking along the further bank. He didn't look across at Rhea at all, although he knew she was watching him.

'Here! This one'll do,' Rhea called and Will crossed the creek to examine the long strip of sapling Rhea had found. He flexed it in his hand and whipped it in the air.

'Yeah, this'll do fine. Good goin', Rhea. Now all we need is some string.' He glanced up at her, catching her watching him intently. 'What's up? Why're you staring at me all the time?' he asked, his face flushing with annoyance. Rhea turned away and shrugged.

'No reason. Just looking. C'mon, let's get back to Tom.' She started back down the gully.

They had only been gone a few minutes. It barely seemed that. But Tom's scream, a single, high-pitched, terrified scream, brought them racing back, their faces anxious, their hearts beating nervously. What they saw, an empty creekbed and shore, made their hearts beat even faster. They stopped, looking around helplessly for the child. And then Will realized where he was.

'Aw Jesus, no! Please no!' Will said softly.

Tom had somehow found a crevice in the walls of the gully and climbed into it. His movements had dislodged the already weakened sides of the crevice, where the rain had ploughed a channel all week, and it had collapsed inwards, on top of him, giving him time for no more than that single shriek of terror. He was being smothered to death by mud.

'Tom! Rhea, run and get help. I'll try and get him out.' Will reacted faster than Rhea, throwing himself at the pile of mud and scooping it out desperately with his hands. Rhea hesitated and then ran for her mother and Tim.

'Oh God no, don't let this happen God, please!' Will pleaded as he shovelled even faster. He could see a space behind the pile of mud where the clay had lodged against a boulder and not yet slipped back. He squirmed himself into the space and dug faster. Almost immediately he uncovered Tom's face, lying close to the end near him. The rest of Tom's body was lying, like a hot-dog in a bun, under several feet of mud. The weight of it was crushing the air out of the child almost as quickly as he could be smothered. Will cleared the boy's nose and mouth and dug again, forcing himself against the boulder and the mud wall.

He had got Tom's head and chest clear by the time Tim and Stoney reached them. They hovered above him, unable to help. The space was too tight and the chances of another cave-in too likely. Will pulled Tom again, and succeeded in edging him a few more inches clear of the crushing weight above him. Tim braced himself against the crevice further up and reached down for the little boy's hands. Tom was conscious still, small pale face sheened with sweat and mud and his mouth emitting tiny whimpers like a hurt animal, as Will passed him up to Tim. He came clear of the mud with a deep sucking plop. Tim passed him across to Stoney and then leaned back against the walls, wiping an arm across his damp brow.

'Well thank God for that! I thought we'd lost him then,' he said. He grimaced and squatted down to look at Will. 'You gonna stay there all day? Looks kinda unhealthy in that space to me.' The entire face of the gully was poised against the boulder that had saved Tom's life. And Will was between it and the only logical place it could roll to. Tim leaned over, reaching out a hand. He saw Will was pale with the fright and the sudden exertion of digging Tom out. 'C'mon mate. Gimme yer hand,' he said. And then the boulder began to give.

'Will! Give me your hand, for God's sake!' Tom reached down again for Will, feeling the sides of the gully giving, his own foothold slipping as the boulder rolled backwards under the weight of the mud slide. Will's face showed pure terror. He would never live through this, if the boulder went. He reached up and grasped Tim's hand, smacking palm against palm and flinging himself clear of the space. They tumbled backwards down the outside of the crevice as the walls caved in, rolling in front and on top of pounding, ripping clumps of mud and stone. Stoney, poised at the side, yanked them clear of the main slide, moments before it came down. It slid to a sullen, lethal stop against the far wall.

Ursula was bent over Tom, cradling him in her arms, checking his body for broken bones, when she heard the walls begin to collapse. She screamed, gathering Tom to her as she saw Tim and Will throw themselves down the outer wall, rolling over and over before Stoney pulled them to one side. It was over before she could think, the mud packed across the creek, the men lying panting at its side. She saw Will's face was torn open, blood oozing down a gash in his cheek. Tim was bruised and cut. Both of them lay there shaking, staring at the flow of red clay that had become a dam blocking the gulch. Red clay that would have made a certain grave if they had lingered a moment longer.

Then they grinned. All three of them, Stoney too, suddenly giving a whooping wail of joy, of fright, of thanks. And then Rhea picked herself up from beside her mother and threw herself at Will, gripping her thin arms around his body like a limpet that refuses to be dislodged. He patted her uncomfortably on the back, making soothing noises. Stoney made his way down to Kim. She gave him a mock slap across his cheek and slid her arm around his waist. He grinned. And Tim stumbled forward to clasp his arms around both Ursula and Tom, laying his face against theirs. The Winby seniors stood at the edge of the near disaster, surveying it with blank faces. For a few minutes there was total silence, even the birds in the trees stilled in their song. Mr Winby shifted on one foot and then another, trying to express how he felt. Finally he said:

'That's it then,' his arms crossed over his body. 'No more playing in the gully.'

He couldn't understand why everyone began to laugh. And continued laughing all the way back to the homestead. He didn't hear the high note of hysteria threading through the laughter or see the panic lurking still in their eyes. Instead, he sulked. He thought it had been a sensible remark to make under the circumstances. His wife didn't comment. She never did.

Will was ordered into the bathroom with Tim, to get the mud off themselves so their cuts could be treated. Ursula carried Tom into the kitchen and filled the large porcelain sink with warm water. He was still sobbing, the fright making his eyes large and circled with black shadows. He clung to his mother with desperate strength. His body was bruised under the layers of red mud, but there were no crushed ribs, no broken bones. Ursula kissed him again and let him play with the soap. She didn't care if he wasted a ton of it. Just as long as he was all right. Rhea stood nearby with towels for everyone.

They built a fire in the fireplace and everyone sat around it drinking hot coffee laced with brandy. It tasted awful to Rhea but she couldn't stop shivering any other way. Neither could Will. His face was bandaged across the cheek by his mother and they all sat in front of the fire, laughing nervously and hugging Tom. Despite his fright, he seemed to have come to no harm and was now intent on playing with his other toys, one hand entwined in Ursula's cardigan for safety's sake. Rhea kept a firm grip on Will's hand, remembering with little shudders of horror how nearly he had been entombed behind that boulder. Eventually she fell asleep against him, his arm holding her crooked into his shoulder.

The fire hissed and spat small flames of gum resin, its bright gaze becoming hypnotic as the aftermath of the adrenalin surge set in. Eyelids fluttered, mouth drooped lower, and Mr Winby began to wheeze deeply.

'Time for bed everyone,' Tim said with an effort, levering himself out of the depths of the sofa. He leaned over Rhea, plucked her out of Will's hold, and carried her in to her bedroom. Tom was to sleep with his mother that night. Ursula passed Tom to Mrs Winby for a moment while she said goodnight to Will, noting the way the boy swayed in his exhaustion. She hugged him tightly to her.

'Thank you, Will. I can't tell you . . . ' She halted, tears rushing into her eyes. 'You saved something so precious in my life that I don't think I'll ever be able to repay you and you did it at the risk of your own. I won't forget that. I promise you.' She then kissed him on his good cheek and let his mother lead him away. Baby Tom she gathered against her shoulder and carried off to bed. Tim waited a few discreet moments, locking up the house and turning out the lights, before he followed them into the bedroom and climbed in beside them. They lay tightly together all night.

In the morning, Tim seemed subdued. He sat at Ursula's desk, eyes turned in, lost in thought. Ursula and Rhea walked around him, tidying up after the night before, glancing at each other questioningly. Each shook her head. No, they didn't know what was wrong with him. Ursula brought him a cup of coffee and he thanked her absent-mindedly, tapping his pen against a blank sheet of paper. Ursula laid a hand on his shoulder and reached down to kiss his cheek. He smiled, and patted her hand. Then he slipped back into his reverie.

Tom was out back on the porch wrangling with Percy over whose turn it was with the drum. He seemed to have no bad memories of the day before, smiling sunnily at his mother when she came to pick him up. Percy was tucked under Ursula's other arm and the two brought in for lunch. They sat, like mismatched peas in a pod, in the double swing chair that Mr Winby had found in Gidge. It saved time for everyone and convinced Tom, who could be a picky eater, to loudly demand his share when he saw Percy open his mouth obligingly to choo-choo trains and toot-toot buses. Rhea grinned and popped another spoonful of peas in each mouth. Ursula left them to it and wandered back into the sitting room to where Tim still sat at the desk.

He was staring out through the louvred windows at the

orchards, his expression painfully drawn. Ursula sat down beside him.

'Want to talk about it?' she asked gently. He didn't respond at first. Then, slowly, he turned and looked at her.

'I found these, when I was looking for writing paper. I recognized them straight away.' He held out the bundle of threatening notes from Simon that Ursula had tucked away in the drawer. He winced. 'You've been paying too?'

Ursula felt her heart contract, the pain was so intense. She stared at him in horror. 'Too? You've let Simon blackmail you all this time?' He lifted his chin sharply.

'And what would you have had me do? Let the scandal ruin your name and Tom's? Rhea would've been asked to leave school. Everyone round here would've turned their backs on you, including the Winbys. Jesus Christ, what was I supposed to do? I just thought you'd been doing the same when I saw these.'

'How . . . how much?' Her voice cracked.

'The same as he asked you for. It's been crippling me. I just thought it best if you didn't know; I didn't want to add to your worries.' He rubbed a hand over his forehead, kneading at the line that was puckering between his eyebrows. Ursula loved him at that moment more than she had ever done. She reached out and smoothed the line with her finger.

'Oh Tim! You mustn't pay it any more, darling. He's just a bully, frightening you with horror stories. He won't do it. I already wrote and told him he couldn't do me more of a favour. Then I'd get you to myself for good.' She laughed bitterly. 'The last thing Simon wants is to please me. He won't do a thing. I promise you.' He leaned in against her, laying his cheek on her cool neck.

'Oh God, I'm a fool! I should've told you about it all. But I couldn't bear the thought . . . ' He broke off, sighing. Ursula stroked the back of his head, running her fingers through his hair.

'I know, sweetheart, I know.'

'How could you be so sure at the time? Didn't it worry you that you might read him wrong. That he might actually do it?' Tim asked eventually. Ursula felt a tinge of nervousness slice through her mind. Tim thought she had bluffed. Would he be

403

devastated if he knew she actually had wanted the scandal, had wanted his career ruined? She hesitated only briefly.

'I know Simon. And I know how he thinks. He's just a bully in the schoolyard and if anyone stands up to him, he caves in immediately. He preys on other people's worst fears. I wasn't going to let him do that to me anymore. Besides,' she shrugged. 'I didn't have that sort of money anyway. I didn't have any choice.' She felt Tim relax against her. So, he had wondered at her motives. She gave a shiver.

'Come on, let's write something really filthy back to Simon. He'll be furious but he won't do anything he thinks will make me happy. He hates me too much for that.'

'Why should he hate you?' Tim asked. Ursula gave a twisted smile.

'Because I'm a survivor – and he isn't.'

Chapter Twenty Four

Rhea was to meet Ursula on the front lawn as arranged. It was the third of December 1963, Speech Night, and Rhea's last few hours of school stretched out before her as no more than an instant's breath. All the long years that she had spent aching to be home, hating the day-girls who left at three-thirty in the afternoon to see their mothers, wishing she had a room to herself instead of the crowded dormitory of Margaret House, loathing the intricacies of algebra. All that was suddenly very dear to her. Even the gym, with its smell of dust and its flaking, splintery wooden rungs had become a place of retreat, a haunt that she had visited with her close friends Jennie and Libby again and again in the last few days. It had once been a stable and still smelt of horses when they climbed on the foam-filled gunny sacks and drowsed in the late afternoon quiet.

She hated leaving St Hilda's, hated leaving all her friends, her teachers, the warm, enclosing atmosphere of the school where the girls knew what it was to belong and take pride in their school. Now in a few short hours she would be an Old Girl. It was so hard to leave, knowing she would see very few of them again. She looked around the spreading shadows of the gardens, smelling the pepper trees and oleander mixed together in the warm, still evening. Her dress shone whitely in the night like a glow-worm beckoning for a mate. But she didn't have a mate, or even a boyfriend; not like the other girls who produced eligible fellows at the Upper Six Dance and laughed and whispered into the night about who was going with whom. Only Will sent her flowers on St Valentine's day and wrote her letters when he remembered. Only Will really cared. She smiled suddenly, feeling the inrush of breath as she thought how soon she would see him. Tomorrow.

Her mother was late. All around her on the lawn, families walked together, the girls floating like cabbage butterflies across the paths, admiring the grounds and the buildings, showing where music lessons were held and sports classes assembled, where Assembly was held every morning with hymns and prayers, where long hours of detention had been patiently endured. It was a nostalgic pilgrimage, a last visiting of favourite places, some of the girls crying through their farewells, everyone crying through the school hymn that afternoon. Rhea just had to hear 'Thy Hand O God', to feel a lump lodge hard in her throat and tears prickle beneath her eyelids. She stared across the lawns and wondered where her mother could be.

Near her, Jennie linked arms with her brother, Charles, and led him proudly by the gaggle of girls on the front steps. He was tall and long-legged, his face beginning to show the lines of manhood in the hollowed cheeks, the chin with blue shadow. He had finished University last year and was working for his father now in the family bank. Jennie smiled and waved at some hopeful cries of greeting but steered her brother away. Rhea watched, amused.

'Rhea! There you are! I thought we were going to meet on the south lawn. I'm so sorry, darling. I've been wandering around frantically trying to find you. Did you think I wasn't coming?' Ursula kissed her daughter and held her arm awkwardly, gesturing to Tim beside her. She was nervous, looking around at people, wondering what they were wondering. Tim stepped forward and took Rhea's arm. He smiled and kissed her on the cheek.

'Hallo, gorgeous. How did I know you'd end up such a beauty? We'll be beating back the men pretty soon. You don't mind me turning up for this little affair, do you? Your mum's been having kittens about it but I wanted to come.'

'Don't be silly. I was hoping you'd come. I just didn't think you'd be able to,' Rhea said, kissing him in return.

Ursula wondered if Rhea felt the way she had when Sally had said that to her, nearly thirty years ago. 'You're going to be quite a beauty.' But the difference was Tim cared for Rhea like a father. He was proud of her. And Rhea was beautiful: tall and slim, with a grace that was a mixture of child and young woman, fair hair bound tightly up in a knot on her neck, wide, high forehead and clear, pale blue eyes. She was Simon and yet not Simon. She was better than Simon could ever have been.

Around her, families were whispering, young men circling to get a closer look. Ursula felt a tight feeling within her chest as she watched two of the people most dear to her in the world eye each other. They were sharing a joke of some sort that Ursula clearly did not know. And that pleased her almost more than being included. They loved each other through her. What more could anyone ask? Oh, if only she could keep them both with her for always. She was torn between the pain of always saying goodbye to Tim and the fear of what a scandal would do to them all, even now starting at loud laughter, smiles that were transparently innocent. She found herself praying, under her breath, and thought immediately what a stupid thing it was to be pleading to some omnipotent power up there in the sky. Tim wasn't hers anyway; he was only on loan. The way she'd always had him.

'Are you going to come and stay with us for a few days after this, Tim? It's very hot already but, then, summer's always the best. It's a shame Joanna couldn't make it across,' Rhea said solemnly. Tim's eyes showed his amusement at her careful chit-chat. Just in case anyone overheard. Rhea saw her mother's face grow taut as someone commented within hearing distance on Tim. Oh yes, he was quite the celebrity. For a moment Rhea was angry, thinking it unfair that Tim always got things his way, and that her mother only existed for him in snippets of time. He wanted it all, didn't he? The power and adulation, the publicity – and he wanted her mother too. No, that wasn't fair. He wanted Mother more than all the rest put together, she decided suddenly. Mother and Tom, and, even, herself. Our little family, living on borrowed time until someone finds out. No, Tim was risking a great deal just to be here for her, on her day.

Rhea felt churlish, as though she were degraded a little by what she had thought of saying, even if she hadn't said it. She felt contrite. Her mother was saying something about feeling like an old crock with a grown-up daughter and Rhea cut across her words.

'Well you're not!' Rhea kissed her mother's cheek. 'You're just as gorgeous as always and you must know that or you wouldn't have anyone like Tim around.' She had lowered her voice to a whisper. 'And he's attracting quite enough attention all on his own.' She laughed suddenly, the sound joyous even amongst the excited chatters of the girls around. 'You really are a devil, Mother, letting Tim talk you into allowing him to show up here. You constantly surprise me. Just when I think you're staid and conservative you prove to me you're the most outrageous woman I know!' She didn't notice Ursula's rueful look. Outrageous? What was Rhea thinking about? All Ursula could do was worry about who thought what. But Rhea was ignoring her thoughts. 'Come on, I want you to get good seats. Tim? Are you staying for the weekend, then? Will promised to take me down to Cape Leeuwin. It'd be fun if you and Mother came too. Can you?'

Tim smiled. 'Why not?' He really was gorgeous, Rhea thought. And why shouldn't her mother have some fun, showing him off to all the other dowdies. She'd earned the right to enjoy herself, surely?

'Good, then it'll be even better. Otherwise Will might keep proposing and that gets tiresome. Almost.' Rhea had a funny way of sounding world-weary and then flashing out a hard, sardonic remark that gave the lie to everything she had said before. It took time to get used to it, springing up just when everyone had relaxed. She enjoyed its effect. Beside her, she felt her mother tense again. She was worrying what was going on between Will and Rhea. Rhea smiled mysteriously.

'Here are the best seats. You can really see everything and besides, you're special this year because I'm an Upper Six. The other parents will just have to wait their turn. Oh, hallo, Mrs Peel, you know my mother don't you? And this is Tim Nowlton, an old friend from Melbourne. Has Jennie gone to line up already?' A dark-haired woman with a stylish dress and large hat was already seated near the end of the row Rhea had selected. She smiled when Rhea introduced her mother and shook hands with both Ursula and Tim.

408

'No dear, she'll be along in just a moment. She's busy showing Charles off to everyone. She's hoping to make them all green I think.' Mrs Peel laughed and Ursula laughed too. 'Pity he's too old for you though. Jennie's mentioned you to him a few times. I know he's interested.' She was a frank woman with a loud laugh that seemed at odds with her appearance. But Ursula thought it refreshing after the silence of the Winbys. Rhea blushed and looked around as unobtrusively as she could.

'Well, I better be getting along. I'll meet you back here afterwards, all right?' Rhea squeezed her mother's hand and left, her skirt flipping smartly in the night breeze. Ursula sat next to Mrs Peel, Tim on her left.

'Nice girl, Rhea. You must be very proud of her. Winning the M.F. Parnell Prize! That's quite a feat. My Jennie'd never make it. She's too much of a scatterbrain and her writing . . . really, I sometimes wonder how her teachers cope. I can't read anything of hers! It's just as well she's not trying for Uni. Is Rhea going on then?'

'Oh, well, we hadn't really decided. I know she wants to stay down in Perth and I can understand that. The property gets to be quite dull for a young girl. It gets to be dull for an old girl too! But she's so young. Only sixteen at the moment. I couldn't possibly allow her to live here alone.'

'Really? And what were you doing at sixteen, Mrs Paterson?' Mrs Peel raised one eyebrow, the thin, black pencil-line arching with amusement. Ursula laughed.

'Well yes, you rather have me there. I expect Rhea's told you – at sixteen I was living like a native in a kampong in Singapore and trying to avoid the Japanese. It's surprising how well you can cope when you have to, isn't it? But I still had my amah looking after me. And it wasn't a big city like Perth. Lord knows what could happen.'

'You mean, sin and decadence and wild goings on? Can you really see Rhea doing all that? Hallo you two! We thought you were never coming back. Jennie cut along quick and get in line. Charlie, do you know Rhea's mother? Mrs Paterson and Mr . . . Nowlton was it?'

'Yes, Tim Nowlton. Hallo, Charles. Shall I move along one? There, that's better. I hear you've been the centre of female attention for the last hour or so. Had enough?' Tim let Charles squeeze past him to sit on the inside so that Ursula and Mrs Peel could continue their conversation. He liked the look of the boy and his rueful grin.

'I never want to come to one of these things again, and I've got three more sisters to go! God, Jennie might as well've put a ring through my nose and led me around by that. It's downright indecent. Sometimes I wonder about these segregated schools. I don't think state schools have the same problems but you can't really blame these girls. After all, they only ever see the gardener who's an old crock of sixty or more and the mailman who rides through at breakneck speed with his face glowing red like a beacon. Jennie says half the girls are in love with him anyway. Too much of the hot-house round here for me!' He winced and straightened his tie. Tim laughed.

'Yeah. I went to Melbourne Grammar. Same thing. Just in reverse. We were all in love with matron and the kitchen maids. Kinda stupid really. You went where? Christchurch?'

'Yeah, look, Mr Nowlton. If any of Jennie's friends come round afterwards, how about saying I took a walk down to the river or something? They'll be nattering for hours anyway about how Libby messed up her curtsey and what the Bishop had to say to them and Lord knows what else. There's a moonlight race on tonight and I'm supposed to be crewing. D'you think I could maybe slip away during the awards?' He was still young enough to prefer male company to female. Tim shook his head.

'Oh no you don't! Your mother would skin you alive and your sister would be hurt. I'll bet she was there on your Speech Night wasn't she?' The young man sighed and sat back in his chair.

'Yeah, she was. All right. I'll stay put. But it's pretty hard when I was supposed to be bowman on *Starfire*. First time too. They'll probably never ask me again.'

'I expect they'll understand. They probably have sisters too. Besides, I hear you haven't met young Rhea yet. It'd be a shame to miss her, wouldn't it, when she'll be leaving Perth tomorrow for Gidgeeganup?' Tim saw a flicker of interest in the boy's eyes.

'The blonde, skinny one I saw standing with you earlier.

410

Yeah, she's a good friend of Jennie's, I hear. But, what with me being away at Uni in Sydney and her being up on her property during the holidays, I never met her. She's a year younger I guess. Pretty good going getting the Parnell Prize. You a relation or something?'

'Friend of the family. I live in Melbourne normally. Just flew over for the weekend.' Tim heard the boy shift beside him as the headmistress came on stage.

'You must be doing pretty all right flying all that way for a weekend.' Tim didn't answer because the headmistress was twitching her white, pompadoured hair for silence, the tassle of her mortarboard swishing from side to side. She smiled imperiously and began the ceremony.

Two and a half hours of speeches, presentations, choir renditions and a short play followed, the girls throwing themselves into the most important evening of their year with surprising professionalism. Ursula was moved by the singing by a small group of girls of a poem by Dorothea Mackellar, the girls' voices high and reedy as their emotion won through. The second verse most people in the audience knew by heart and, as the girls sang about the wide brown land of Australia, Tim caught Ursula's eye, knowing what was going through her mind. It was a hard country, and it was lonely and frightening and uncivilized sometimes. But it was his country, and now it was hers. She smiled at him before turning back to the ceremony. Rhea was onstage now, curtseying before the Bishop and the Governor, talking with the headmistress. She moved quietly and surely, shaking hands as though she had known these people all her life. Charles was watching her intently and Mrs Peel leaned over to Ursula and said, loud enough for her son to hear.

'Jennie's been clamouring to go spend some time with Rhea at your property. Why don't we do a swap? Rhea can stay with us for a fortnight or so and then Jennie can go to you next.' Ursula nodded, her eyes on the stage.

'Why not? And if Charles would like to come, I'm sure he'd be more than welcome.' She smiled as Rhea successfully negotiated the steps down from the stage with her book and leaving certificate in her hand. They all clapped, Mrs Peel more loudly than most.

'That's a good idea! Now why didn't I think of that? And you know, it might do the girls good to get a flat together here in Perth next year. Rhea could go to Uni, and Jennie can work. At least that way Rhea wouldn't be buried forever in the bush. It'd be a shame to waste all those looks.' The two women looked at each other and laughed. Beside him, Tim saw Charles lean forward to watch Rhea walk down the side aisles and back to her place. His face had an absorbed look.

'Still want to be out there sailing?' Tim asked. Charles didn't notice.

Ursula leaned back and relaxed. The ceremony had gone well and now that Rhea's turn was over, she could ignore the rest. She let her mind drift, touching on memories over the last few years. There had been times when she thought she'd never make it here, never fit in or learn to enjoy what Australia had to offer. If Tim hadn't come back into her life, she didn't think she could have survived. Or if she had, it would have been as one of Billy's painted birds. Tim had made up for everything she had given up, everything she had ever lost. He had told her he would. And he had, she thought, leaning back to watch him beside Charles. He had made everything worthwhile again. She smiled when he sensed her watching him and turned to look at her. Maybe he was only hers on loan and maybe it was only a few times a year that he managed to get away to her. But when he was with her, she knew she was the only woman in his life. And that made up for the rest.

Chapter Twenty Five

Rhea dangled her legs in the water. It was cool and felt good sliding over her skin. Beside her Will lay on his back, his own legs disappearing into the green water and appearing to break and start again at a different angle. The distortion fascinated Rhea and she kept lifting her legs clear and then plunging them back into the lagoon with a plonking sound. They dried as fast as she lifted them into the hot air, the brief, dry wind scorching across the wooden deck and rustling the tall grass near the edge of the lagoon. They were both quiet. Will had his eyes shut against the sun, his body brown and salty except where a pair of old, faded shorts hung at his hips. When he moved, a thin line of white skin appeared above the shorts. Rhea wore shorts too and a shirt that was tied up around her middle, revealing a flat, brown stomach where she lay back on the decking. The pontoon wasn't tied to the dock but floated aimlessly around the lagoon, moving with the faint current where the creek emptied itself into the pool, bumping up against the dead tree in the middle until Will kicked against it and sent them back the way they had come. It was a lazy sort of day. Mr Winby had gone into town so Will had taken a few hours off to be with Rhea. But she was being difficult, he thought. She kept talking about Perth and how she was going to go and stay with her friend down there. He didn't like to hear her talk about going away again - not when she'd only just come home. So now they'd run out of things to say to each other.

Rhea turned over on her stomach and leaned her head over

the side of the pontoon, watching a water-beetle greeny-brown and warm in the sunlight, swim through the water for a few feet before becoming dark and cold as it disappeared below. There was a flat glare over the surface of the water that struck like a blow into her eyes. She wished she'd worn her bathers. It would be lovely in the water right now, all green and cool with the world shimmering above the surface like a mirror. She moved further to the edge of the pontoon, feeling it dip beneath her weight like a see-saw. Will, perched in the middle, suddenly slid down beside her and the raft tipped completely, shucking them off into the water before shooting up and away from them like a dolphin suddenly freed of its captor. Rhea went under and surfaced a few feet away from Will. It felt wonderful after the heat of the sun. She laughed when Will rolled over on his front and floated, arms and legs out, on the surface, playing dead. The water was almost hot in the first inch or two. Will's hair floated out around his face and Rhea pulled at his leg. He sat up, flicking his hair back wetly.

'You did that on purpose, I suppose,' he said.

'Sort of. I didn't think it'd roll like that. It was your weight that sent it over. It didn't hit you, did it?'

'No. I just wasn't expecting it. You might've given me some warning. I was nearly asleep.'

'That's why I did it. You were getting boring.'

'So sorry. Maybe I need my sleep more than you and anyway it's your fault. If you want to talk about Perth all the time, then I don't have anything much to say, do I? I've only been a couple of times. Your friend sounds like a right snob to me. Parties, and yacht races and tennis clubs. What the hell do I know about any of that?' His voice was gruff and churlish. Rhea trod water near him and laughed again.

'Poor Will. Stuck out here with no-one but the cows and horses to talk to. Maybe you should get married like Stoney. He seems happy enough.' She was teasing him, her voice mocking his self-pity. Will put out a hand and ducked her. She came to the surface laughing so hard she nearly choked. 'Feeling less sorry for yourself?'

'No. You go ahead and enjoy yourself down there. Just remember I'm up here slogging my guts out for you and getting paid damn all. I hope you have a beaut time of it.' He flipped over on his stomach and started a fast but messy crawl towards the pontoon. Rhea swam after him, her own strokes neat and well-trained. She caught up just as they both reached the raft.

'Will? You're not really mad are you? You'll like Jennie, really you will. She's not a bit stuck-up. She can't help it if her family's rich.' She paused for breath as they both clung to the raft, the water slapping gently at the drums beneath the deck. Will wasn't looking at her, but down into the water. She touched his arm tentatively. 'Will? What is it? Have I hurt you in some way?' She didn't know what to think, he was so silent. Finally he looked up.

'Aw look, Rhea. Give it a miss, would you?' He saw her puzzlement and was suddenly angry. 'I'm twenty years old and what have I ever done? Looked after this bloody place, taken Dad's orders, been paid damn all for twelve hours work a day and now you tell me you're going down to Perth to live. Well that's just bloody wonderful. I really needed that. Your mum's about the only one I can talk to up here. You know what my parents are like. And Tim's a good bloke all right but he only comes a few times a year. What the hell d'you think I'm gonna do? Just sit around and rot away my life. You and I've been talking since we were kids about, well, getting married and now you say it was all just a lark and we didn't know what we were saying. Well, you go off to Perth then and see how great it is. I'll be right here, after all, so you know you can change your mind as many times as you want. God, I can't even spend my evenings with Stoney anymore since Kim stopped him going to the pub with me. Shit!' He spat out the last word with such force that Rhea flinched.

'Why didn't you tell me how you felt? I thought you liked it up here. I know it's pretty boring and all, but I thought you wanted to stay and work the place. If you don't, what's to stop you going down to Perth yourself?'

'And do what? I don't have any formal schooling or diplomas. I'm not trained in anything. All I know is the bush. Anyway, I don't like cities. I like being out here – but not alone! You used to like it too until just this last year. I don't know who's been filling your head with a lot of bull, but you'll find out you're only really happy here some day and by then

415

it'll be too late. And then I hope you remember what I told you.' He turned his back to the raft, lifting his body so that his elbows were on the deck and his legs kicked out at the water in front of him. He thought once again of how much he had looked forward to Rhea's homecoming. That was a right laugh, all right.

The sky was full of the heat and brilliance of an Australian summer, almost white as it bleached the colour from the landscape and sent the odd crow wheeling across its blankness. Rhea climbed up onto the pontoon and lay back, her legs dangling over the side once more. There was a pool of water trapped in the middle of her stomach over the navel, blinking and quivering in the heat. Will reached over and stuck his finger in it, an old, familiar game they had played as children. He was unprepared for the way Rhea jumped and pulled away from him.

'Don't.'

'What'd I do, for God's sakes? Don't be so damned jumpy, Rhea. I can't stand jumpy girls.' He rolled over, offended, and Rhea closed her eyes, wishing things could just go back to the way they always had been. She didn't know why she felt so irritable and unhappy. Maybe because Will was unhappy and she didn't know what she could do about it. Why did he have to tell her? If only she hadn't known she could have gone away without another thought, knowing he would always be there for her when she got back. But now he had made her feel guilty and she couldn't quite control the thin stab of irritation that cut through her mind like a wire. Why was it her fault? And why did she feel so awful?

'Will, d'you ever wonder sometimes if we're all really living the same life? I mean, are you just a kind of prop in my life, or am I just a prop in yours? Or maybe this isn't really life at all. Maybe I just went to sleep a few years ago and I'm dreaming all this. All my life from Australia on is nothing more than a dream, and so are you. D'you ever wonder that?' She was puzzled and a little embarrassed that she'd voiced her thoughts aloud. But who else could she talk to if not to Will?

'No. I don't.' There was silence again.

'Well, what about at night when you really are dreaming. D'you ever have dreams that are so real, and so wonderful, that when you wake up you look around for the book you thought you were reading, but there isn't one?'

'You're weird, Rhea. Why would you think you're reading something? Why not watching a film? That'd be more believable to me. But then, I don't see many films around here anyway. And I don't have any money to go see them with.' He was bitter and determined not to understand her. Rhea stared up at the sky, her eyes watering in the light.

'You could go to another station where they'd pay you. And there'd be more company too.'

'Is that what you want? You want me to go away?'

'No! But if you're unhappy here, and you won't go to Perth, what are you going to do?'

'There's no chance of you staying here then?'

'No, Will, there isn't. Look, it took Mrs Peel and Jennie and I hours to talk Mother into it as it was. Even Tim thought it was a good idea for a while. I just don't like the bush. Sorry.'

'Yeah? Since when? This is where you belong, you're a part of all this! Well, anyway, it's up to you.' Will had an arm across his face to shield it from the bite of the sun. Rhea sighed heavily and sat up.

'When I come back with Jennie, her brother Charles is supposed to be coming too. He's about your age, maybe a little older, and that'll be someone for you to talk to about getting a job somewhere else. He's very intelligent and knows a lot about those sorts of things. You'll like him.'

'Says who?' Will sat up too. 'You like him?'

'Well, yes, I s'pose so. I don't know him very well. He seems nice.' Rhea didn't know why she felt so defensive talking about her friends to Will. Why wouldn't he want to know them? It wasn't just Charles. She could have understood that, maybe. But Will didn't like the sound of Jennie either. What was the matter with him? Was he jealous of anyone she knew who might take her away from the property? He had refused to come down for her Speech Night, saying he wouldn't fit in. Was he always going to feel inferior and be abrasive about it? She remembered Charles's calm assurance and couldn't help contrasting it favourably with Will's behaviour. The irritation came back twice as strongly as before and she turned, shielding her eyes, to look at Will.

'I'm not staying here, Will. You better get that clear. You may be taken by "the vision splendid of the sunlit plains extended" and all that crap but I'm not! I like Perth, I like going out in the evenings, not once a month to dance in a shed in Gidge! What d'you want from me anyway?' They stared angrily at each other.

Rhea didn't know what she wanted Will to do. There was a breathless expectancy about the way he leaned back on one arm, the muscles tensed and rigid in his chest. She could feel an ache in the back of her throat that wanted something to happen to make things better. But she didn't expect him to do what he did. He reached around and pinned her under him, trying to kiss her as she struggled to keep her balance. The raft tipped as before and they both slid deep down into the water, Rhea laughing so hard that she had trouble keeping herself above water. Will didn't think it funny. It had taken all his frustration and anger to actually make a move and now she was laughing at him. He had had it firmly in his mind that all he had to do was kiss Rhea and she would realize how much she wanted to stay here on the property with him. He pushed her up against the raft, his arms either side of her face, and tried again. His body pressed her against the drums and his mouth was inexperienced as he forced hers open. For a moment she squirmed angrily in his hold. Then his kiss became less an assault and more a tender exploration. Rhea tasted the warm, saltiness of his mouth, the gentleness of skin against skin. It was a disturbing, oddly enjoyable feeling. He smelled so good. She lifted her arms to put them around him, forgetting the depth of the water. Her body slipped through his arms, dropping down into the water underneath him. The coolness of the water on her face came as a shock.

Rhea swam away to the other side of the drums. She surfaced with the raft between them and hung to it, gasping for breath. Her body shook from within, from somewhere down in her belly.

'Don't, Will! I don't like being kissed.'

'You could've fooled me! And who the hell ever kissed you before?' Will was angry with the shame of rejection and jealousy. Why had she started to respond? And what exactly had he been intending to do? He didn't attempt to go near her again.

'Some guy at Guildford. It was one of those socials and he slobbered all over me. I don't like kissing. I don't know what all the fuss is about.' Rhea was wary, unwilling to offend Will further, but not sure enough of either of them to come back around to his side. Will didn't say anything for a few minutes. The afternoon wind had sprung up, ruffling the surface of the lagoon and turning it dark. Rhea shivered.

'Yeah, well, you said that once about wearing a bathing suit. You changed your mind about that, I guess. I gotta go, Rhea. I've got work to do. You do what you want. You always did anyway.' He struck out for the dock and Rhea watched him go, the heaviness in her chest growing with each stroke. It's your damned fault, Will, she thought angrily but something inside wouldn't quite let it go at that. She felt responsible somehow. Damn it all, she thought, and climbed back onto the pontoon. When Will looked back, she was spread out to dry in the sun, her eyes closed. She didn't wave goodbye as he left.

She saw him only in the distance for the rest of the day, tending the trees up by the bore-head. He was silhouetted blackly against the skyline, working tirelessly in the afternoon heat. She sat on the back verandah and swirled the ice in her drink angrily, willing him to turn around and look down at the homestead. But he didn't.

Ursula and Tim spent most of the weekend together. They had invited Rhea to join them for a barbecue lunch and then a lazy afternoon ride down to Gidgeeganup but she had declined. It would be wonderful if she had someone like Tim, Rhea thought. Someone who shielded and protected, humoured and loved her, like Tim loved her mother. And someone who didn't make unreasonable demands or think anything involving the rest of the world was stuck-up or snobbish. Rhea thought about how her mother had looked that morning in her moleskins and big man's shirt, dark hair pulled back in a low knot behind her head. That was what was so wonderful about her mother; in her quiet way, she totally flaunted all the rules. If she wanted to wear men's clothing, she did – and made it look better than any dress could have. If she wanted to have a married man as a lover, she did – and made every other woman green. They looked so good together, young and beautiful and totally happy. That's why she had decided not to spend any of their

419

short time together with them. She had wanted to leave them to themselves and, besides, she had wanted to spend time with Will. They had been supposed to go to Cape Leeuwin. Only now Will didn't seem to want that. He said he had to work.

Percy and Tom were playing in the shade of the barn, fixing a hoop to a piece of wood. Rhea wondered if she should go and check on them. But it was too much effort. She continued to stare out through the haze of the fly-screen.

The shadows were stretching out across the stony ground now, long fingers of black in rows, like sentinels. And still Will worked on.

'Well, if the mountain won't come to Mahommet . . . ' she muttered to herself, 'then I'll just have to go to him.' She stood up and left the verandah, the screen door snapping back in place behind her. Will didn't notice her approach until she was standing almost beside him. And then he just glanced at her and looked away.

'What's so thrilling about the bucket, Will? And why're you slogging away in this heat? Your dad's still in town and you know he probably won't be back till the pub closes.' She couldn't help the taunt, something inside her prodding at her to spark a reaction. She did.

'Lay off my dad! You think you're so smart with your stylish friends and your university entrance. Well that doesn't count for much out here, Rhea, so why don't you just go back where you belong?'

'Oh great! Now you're acting like your dad's the greatest thing since the electric light and I'm the heavy for saying you don't have to work while he's away. Well, so sorry. I'll just get out of your life. Is that what you want?'

'I don't need you Rhea and I don't need your sarcasm.' He turned to look at her, squatting on the balls of his feet where he'd been painting the boles of the trees. She knelt down beside him. The ground was warm and gritty beneath her skin. The anger and frustration died within her.

'Well maybe I need you, Will. Have you ever thought of that? You're like, oh, a brother to me, only better. Because you're not my brother. Oh hell! I don't know why everything's gone wrong. What's the matter with us, Will? We never normally argue – not seriously.' She reached out and touched his face where he'd grazed it. The sun had browned the cut, drying the blood. It was like everything else out here: brown, in varying shades. He closed his eyes, feeling her fingers strum his cheek, catching her hand against his face and holding it there.

'I want you to stay with me. That's all. I know it seems boring to you but it's my life. Somehow I thought when you'd finished school you'd want to return here, to be with your mum and Tom - and me. It's not much fun on your own but it could be good together.' She had to lean in to hear his words, his eyes shut fiercely against everything that was wrong in his life. Against hearing Rhea say no.

'Oh Will. I'm so sorry for what I said earlier. Of course the property's important to me. It's home. You're home. But I just want to get away for a while, be really free.'

'You've been away.' He opened his eyes, brown like the rest of the place.

'Not on my own. School's different. There's no freedom. I never got to see much of Perth. But if I were at Uni, I'd be my own person. Don't you see that?'

'No. You're your own person here too. And what am I supposed to do for the next three years? Things won't change. After Uni you'll be so used to all that freedom, you won't want to give it up and come back here. I might as well just say goodbye now, 'cos you're not ever coming back.' He stood up and walked away, toward the utility. Rhea trailed after him.

'I will come back. You'll see! Please, can't you wait just a little longer?' She caught him up, tugging at his arm.

'You know, you said something like that to me once before. A long time ago now. We were just kids and you were going off to school. I wanted to get the hell out of here and you begged me not to go. Well, I didn't. Okay, maybe it was because I was only a kid, but mostly it was because you said you'd be back. I won't wait this time. I'm not a kid anymore and I'm tired of waiting.' He leant against the side of the truck. Maybe he was just sounding off again, gauging her reaction but Rhea felt suddenly as though a dark pit had opened in front of her. She put out her arm and steadied herself against the hot metal door.

'Will?' All the air in her lungs had collapsed, leaving her breathless and frightened. 'Don't talk like that. Will, please.'

421

She touched his arm and he saw the stricken look on her face, the panic in her eyes.

'Aw Rhea! God, can't you see what you're doing to me? Jesus!' But it wasn't said in anger and he swung around, pulling her in tightly against him, her arms wrapping themselves around his neck. She clung to him fiercely, kissing his cheek, his mouth, letting him ease himself against her so that they fit into each other like moulds. He kissed her back and she opened her lips eagerly this time, wanting desperately to hold him tightly against her so that he could never leave. He groaned. 'Don't go, Rhea. I can't be here alone anymore. Oh God, don't go.' He buried his mouth in her hair, kissing her neck, her mouth, pressing her hard against the side of the truck.

'Only for a little while. I'll come back to you. I promise.' But Will wouldn't let her go. He held her angrily, his fingers digging into her arms.

'No, not for a while, not for a minute. I want you now. Can't you see that? Can't you feel it?' He held her tightly, his body hard against hers. She felt strangely light-headed, running her mouth over his.

'Please, Will. It won't be long. Maybe I'll be bored with it all in just a few months. But I need those months. And I am going.'

'Is that it, then? That's your answer?' He stood away and looked out, across the property. Behind her he saw two riders approaching from the east. They were lit in the last glow of the sun's rays, which were bathing the landscape, the riders, the sky, a scalding red. He let Rhea go. 'I won't wait,' he said. Then he opened the door of the pick-up and climbed in. 'You staying here or coming with me?' Rhea shrugged.

'I don't know. Oh, go without me! I don't care.' She turned away and started walking toward the riders, her back very straight. She heard the engine start and the truck spurt away down the track but she didn't turn round.

That night, as Tim lay beside Ursula reading, she commented. 'Will's not going to stay, you know. He'll be off the minute Rhea goes to university. He told me so.'

'When?'

'When what? When did he tell me?' Tim nodded, his book laid flat on the sheets. Ursula sighed. 'Before we went for Speech Night. I tried to get him to come with us, and I know Rhea wrote asking him to come. But he wouldn't. Said he wouldn't fit in. He asked then if I thought Rhea would be coming back here permanently. I said I didn't know. And that's when he said if she didn't he'd be leaving. Oh Tim! D'you think I have any right to interfere? They're so young and Rhea doesn't know anyone else but I can't help thinking Will's the best man she'll ever know. I'm sure she loves him. But is she in love with him?'

'She's too young to know about how she feels yet. Maybe Will thinks he knows but he hasn't been anywhere else, met anyone else, had a bit of a roll in the hay with some other girl. That's what he needs, sweetheart, not a full-grown love affair or marriage with a child. It'd do him good to get off the property. If he really loves Rhea, he'll wait for her. I'm sure of that.' He smiled and kissed her, leaning over to switch off the bedside light. Ursula curled into him.

'Oh I hope so. I hope you're right, Tim. I'd hate Will to lose the girl he loves just because the world thinks she's not right for him.' She felt him start in her arms.

'You sound like you're speaking from experience.' Ursula was silent for a moment.

'Perhaps. It's been a bit like that for us. I haven't thought . . . ' She broke off as the sound of several metal pails being knocked over rocked the still night air. Tim slid from the bed and walked over to the window, peering out through the side of the blind. The full moon lit the scene as though it were day.

'Jesus Christ! Get dressed love, it's Will and his dad. They're slugging it out. I'll go out and try and stop them.' He pulled his trousers on and was half-way to the door when Rhea flung herself into the room, her face sharp with fear.

'Oh thank God, hurry up! They'll kill each other.' She ran from the room and out of the house, her feet bare and her nightgown catching around her legs. Ursula slid into her dressing gown and anxiously followed Tim.

The two men were pinned together, grappling each other as they fought silently in the dirt, teeth bared in fury, panting for something that neither of them could have. Tim could almost

423

see the words written over their heads: obedience versus freedom. It was all so inevitable really. He edged closer, trying to
get between them. Mr Winby pulled his arm free from Will's
hold and backhanded his son, sending Will rolling back against
the chicken pen. He stood swaying uneasily, his chest heaving
with exertion. Rhea ran past him to where Will was crouched
ready to spring forward once more. They had been at this for
some time now, silent until Will had toppled the milking pails
over in a clatter. He wiped the blood away from his mouth.
Rhea knelt at his side.

'Stop it! For God's sake, Will! He's drunk, can't you see
that?' Rhea cried, pulling Will away from Mr Winby, trying to
hold his arms. He pushed her away roughly as his father came
at him again, holding out his hands to ward off the heavy,
sledging blows. It didn't work and another fierce jab sent him
spinning into the verandah post. His father leant over him,
punching indiscriminately while Will kicked at his legs, trying
to topple him backwards. Tim grabbed Mr Winby from behind
in a bear hug, the two of them rolling around in circles, shaking
each other until Mr Winby suddenly crumpled in Tim's arms.
He fell to the ground and Tim leant over him, feeling for a
pulse. A sour smell of beer came from the manager's breath.

'He's okay. Out cold. How's Will?'

'Oh God! I think he's hurt pretty badly. What happened,
Will? Mother, come look!' Rhea was crying, holding Will
against her where he had fallen backwards against the porch.
His face was covered in blood and he hadn't said a word,
panting out his pain and frustration in great ragged gasps. Mrs
Winby appeared in her robe, walking steadily over to where
her husband lay. She looked at him and then turned away,
walking over to Will.

'Yew all right?' she asked, her voice flat and emotionless.
Will nodded. 'Get yerself cleaned up then and give me a hand
with yer dad. No need for yews to concern yerselves, Mrs
Paterson. Will'n'I'll see to things. Goodnight.' She stood,
implacable, over her son. Ursula knelt down beside Will.

'Are you all right? What happened, Will? You've taken an
awful beating.' It was Mrs Winby who answered for him.

'Provoked his dad with wild talk about leaving. Yew knew
Dad was drunk, yew stupid chooky. And you paid for it didn't

yer?' Mrs Winby looked at Will's face. 'Yew took a good old lot there.'

'But I don't understand, Will. You're stronger than your father. And he hasn't beaten you in years. Why did you let him hurt you like this?' Ursula was worried and upset at the bruises. Will leaned over and spat blood into the dirt. He didn't answer.

'Didn't want to hurt his dad. Knew he was drunk so he kept pulling the punches, tryin' to quieten his dad down. Got hurt a lot worse that way, didn'ya, Will? Yer should'a given him one good belt. Yer'll know next time.' Mrs Winby shook her head.

'There won't be a next time,' Will said finally, his mouth so swollen he could barely speak and a cut above his eye still oozing blood. Ursula reached down and helped Rhea to stand Will on his feet. He leaned against Rhea's slight frame, feeling her body through her thin nightgown. Her skin was cool and smelt of talcum powder. With an effort he straightened and touched his face.

'Sorry, Mrs Paterson. I'm all right. Yews go back to bed now.' He tried to free himself from Rhea's hold.

'No you're not all right. Mother, make him see sense. He needs his cuts washed and . . . '

'I'll do that. He's my son.' Mrs Winby held out her arm and Will took it, pulling himself free from Rhea. He moved like an old man.

'I'll bring your husband in for you, Mrs Winby. Will's got enough on just standing up,' Tim said, leaning down and slinging Mr Winby's dead weight over his shoulders in a fireman's hold. He steadied himself and then carried the limp figure up and into the house. Mrs Winby and Will followed, the door slamming shut behind them.

Out in the yard, Ursula and Rhea stood suddenly alone, the night cicadas picking up their song and shrilling almost painfully in their ears. A firefly lit its globe on, off, on in front of them, dancing along in the warm night air. Ursula gave her daughter a grimace.

'There's nothing more we can do, darling. C'mon, let's go back inside. I could do with a cup of tea. How about you?'

'No. I just want . . . '

'What . . . Will?' Ursula asked when Rhea paused. Her

425

daughter didn't answer, turning and running into the house instead. Ursula sighed and waited for Tim to come out.

'He's all right. Don't worry, love. Just a bit of blood and a few bruises. He'll be fine tomorrow.'

'No, Will took that beating on purpose. It's almost like . . . I don't know, maybe he wanted to be hurt or maybe he just wanted to provoke things to the point where he has an excuse to leave. Oh Tim, do you think that's it?'

'Yeah, maybe. Or maybe he just hoped Rhea would be more sympathetic if he got hurt. The old Tom Sawyer ploy.' For a moment he smiled and Ursula relaxed. He put his arm around her and led her back to bed.

Rhea tapped on Will's window when the lights had all gone out and everyone had gone back to sleep. Everyone except her. She couldn't bear to lie in bed, staring at the ceiling, wondering how he was. Not for one minute more. So she gathered up her nightgown around her legs and climbed carefully out of her window, taking care not to disturb a sleeping Tom. His steady breathing reassured her.

It was hard on her feet between the two houses but she didn't dare pull on shoes. She had to be quiet. She wasn't sure why she felt such a need for secrecy. Will and she had been sneaking across to each other's bedrooms for midnight consultations for as many years as they had known each other. She knew her mother heard them but had never said anything. But tonight everything was different. It had all become terribly serious and she felt frightened in a way she had never suspected possible. She had to talk to Will.

He heard her tap. When she repeated it, he sighed and carefully eased himself over. He hurt.

'Yeah, Rhea? What is it?'

'Can I come in?' Her voice sounded small and upset. He was silent for a long time. 'Will?'

'Yeah. The flyscreen's unfastened anyway. Come on in.' He was breathing the words out to her from the darkness of his room and she almost missed them. He sounded funny, she thought. Depressed. Cold. She slid through the window, easing the screen back into place.

'Will? Are you okay now?' She couldn't see his face in the dark. Just the outline of his body lying on the bed. She sat

426

down beside him and put out her hand. She felt him wince.

'Jesus, Rhea. Watch what you're doing. It bloody hurts right there.' She drew back her hand.

'I'm sorry. I can't see you so I don't know where it hurts.'

'Then don't touch me at all. Okay?' he snapped. There was no sound at all for a while and he wondered what she was doing; she sat so quietly on the bed, not moving at all. He reached out a hand to her face but she turned it away, the moonlight catching the reflection of her tears. He pulled her down against him then, feeling the jerks her body made as she tried to muffle her sobs.

'Oh, for God's sake don't cry, Rhea. What am I supposed to do? Apologize? Okay, okay,' he held her tightly. 'I'm sorry. Does that make it all better now? As long as I say everything's okay, you can go off to Perth and forget all about me. Good old Will, he'll still be there when I get back. If I want to go back.' He held her tighter still when she struggled against the bitterness of his words. He could feel the wetness of her tears sliding against his cheeks. She pushed at his arms uselessly and then went limp. They lay in silence.

'I don't want to lose you, Will,' she said eventually, in a voice so tired that it almost didn't make sense. He let her go.

'No, well, you know your options. At least you've got options.' He turned away from her, catching his breath at the pain in his ribs. Rhea stretched out a hand and laid it on his back.

'Please, Will. Why does everything have to be so black and white? Either I stay now or I lose you forever? Why can't we compromise a little? I'll go for six months. That's all. And then I'll come back to you.' She ran her fingers under his shirt where it hung loose over his workpants. She felt him shiver at the touch of her skin against his. He turned abruptly towards her again.

'What are you trying to do, Rhea? Sweet talk me into doing what you want, as always? "Please Will".' He mimicked her. ' "Just a little compromise". Except I've already compromised for some time now. Why don't you try giving in occasionally? See how you like that?' He held her wrist in his hand and pulled it into his chest, laying it against his skin. She shivered this time.

She knew what she wanted now. She wasn't experienced but then neither was he. It didn't really matter all that much anyway. They just had to touch each other to feel that flutter, that strange urge. Will would be a good lover. He had already proven that to her. And if he made love to her, he would stay. It was that simple. A taste of what was to come later, when she came back. She strained forward and kissed his mouth, his full, ridged lips. They were bruised but he didn't notice, caught up in the feel of her, the sudden willingness in her eyes and in her clinging arms, in the legs that twined around his and the soft pointed breasts beneath her cotton shift that pressed themselves to him. He felt a rushing in his ears and groaned, before pushing her away.

'I don't want you like this, Rhea. I want you for good, not on a temporary offer that you're going to withdraw when someone better comes along. You go offer yourself to your precious Charles. Maybe he won't be so choosy.' He almost didn't feel the slap, or the sudden pummelling of fists against his already bruised ribs. He was hurting too much inside to feel anything more. And then she was gone, climbing out the window with the ease of many years' practice. He lay back and stared sightlessly ahead, tears blurring his eyes and running unheeded down his cheeks. She wouldn't be back; he knew that.

When Rhea woke up, Will was gone. No-one knew where. He'd just packed up his few belongings in the night and left. Rhea suspected Stoney had had something to do with it; had probably driven him into Gidge or somewhere where he could get a lift further inland. But Stoney just shook his head and said he didn't know. Rhea was distraught. She felt cheated and angry beyond anything she could ever remember. The pain of loss ground at her, appearing just when she thought she had recovered, making her feel like a film of dirt had obscured everything, the shine of promise gone from life. But there was nothing she could do about it, nowhere she could go looking for him. He was gone, and that was that.

Charles and Jennie had done their best to make her forget and she had enjoyed having them to stay. But when they were swimming in the lagoon, or riding around the boundary, or

428

taking picnic lunches out on the flat rocks near the top, Will was there in her mind, the way he had been so many times in the flesh. She couldn't believe he was gone and that she would never see him again. Charles said she would forget when she got back to Perth and got into university, but that seemed flat somehow too. It was as though it were only fun if she could tell Will about it. Now it was just something she had to do. Ursula promised to come down to town with them to get them settled into their new flat. And Charles promised to buy her another dog. Will had taken Mannie with him. Rhea agreed to it all. She didn't really care anymore.

Once she and Jennie were set up in their flat in Cottesloe, things were better. They took weeks to paint the walls and wax the wooden floors, to fix up bookcases for Rhea's books and fill the shelves with food that Jennie said she couldn't eat because she was on a diet and then ate late at night after Rhea had gone to bed. Jennie took a job in a boutique down the Stirling Highway called 'Ma Casita' which sold ridiculously priced European clothes to overweight women who should have known better. She tried hard to lose weight by staring at her reflection in the mirrors lining the walls.

Rhea started at university reading English Literature and Charles became a regular visitor. He took them sailing on the weekends or to watch the Head of the River rowing race between the boys' schools. Aquinas won as always. There were parties and dinners, afternoon teas or drinks at 'Steve's', tennis games down at the Peppermint Grove club where Jennie had spent so many Saturdays and Sundays over the years practising at the hit-up wall, moonlight races from Freshwater Bay yacht club and barbecues afterwards up on the lawn outside the clubhouse. Rhea settled in well, enjoying her new life even more than St Hilda's. She had a scholarship to cover her tuition and her mother had told her the property was earning enough to cover her rent and living expenses. Not that she ever had to pay for very much. Charles liked to see to that. He was a dear, she thought nearly once every day. And then she thought about Will. And everything seemed flat yet again.

Ursula began to come down and spend some time with Rhea on a more regular basis. Tom was six now and more than happy to be left with Kim and Percy or with Mrs Winby. The latter was pining for Will and Tom was as good a replacement as any. Ursula didn't try to interfere. Besides, she needed to get away at the moment from the monotony of the property as much as Rhea needed her company. They were both lonely, trying to put up a front of enjoying themselves when what they really wanted was to be with the men they loved. Rhea sensed that far more acutely in her mother now that she, herself, knew the pain of loss. But Tim was very busy trying for the deputy leadership in the Country Party. He couldn't afford any scandals right now. So he hadn't been seen in WA for some months. Ursula saw pictures of him every now and then in the papers or some magazine, Joanna often by his side. She looked very good. And she was younger than Ursula by several years.

That was when Ursula went down to Perth and stayed with Rhea, spending time shopping or just sitting in their pretty back garden with long drinks talking. Rhea wasn't just her daughter anymore, Ursula thought with satisfaction, she was also her closest friend. And then Charles would sweep in after work and take them out to dinner and they would try hard to forget why they were both sad.

'Tim sent his love, by the way,' Ursula said, sitting outside on the garden bench while Rhea sat on the stone flagstones and tanned her legs. They were very long and thin, an annoyance to Jennie and her endless diets.

'How is he? And his wonderful Joanna?' Rhea didn't mean to be sarcastic. She just couldn't help it sometimes, seeing her mother's unhappy eyes, the slight droop to her shoulders. She should be seeing other men, Rhea thought. She wasn't old. Only thirty-six this year. And she didn't even look that old. Ursula turned cool eyes on her daughter.

'Don't say it in that tone, Rhea. You know Tim can't help it. Joanna is his wife and a politician needs a wife by his side. Besides, she's born and bred for all that. She's very useful to him.'

'Yes, I know.' Rhea sighed. 'How's his son now? Is he over the flu? It must be a terrible worry the way that boy catches everything going. And then asthma on top of it. Just compare Josh to Tom – he never catches anything.' Tim had sent a photograph of Josh on his seventh birthday, a bony, serious-looking dark-haired child with the thin, veined skin of someone who was constantly ill. He had been holding tightly to someone's hand in the picture, the person cut off and only the hand visible with its carefully manicured red nails. Ursula had put it away without comment. But Rhea had noticed her mother taking more care with her own hands, soaking them in soapy water to get the earth out of them and even using a pale pink nail polish occasionally. She grimaced at the pain her mother must be feeling.

Odd the way her mother never talked about Tim as though he were the love of her life; it would be so tempting to do so, to invent a larger-than-life tragedy out of what had happened to them. But her mother didn't do that at all. She just accepted what they could have together and got on with the rest of her life accordingly. Once, she had said something about having stumbled into love. Rhea wondered whether that was true of Will and herself. They had stumbled in and then, for lack of knowledge, out of sheer stupidity, they had let that all slip away from them. Rhea stared at a picture of herself beside Will, the two laughing as Tim took the shot. At least she didn't have to be jealous of anyone with Will. She didn't even know where he was.

It was during the second winter, 1964, that the letter from Will came. Ursula forwarded it to her from the property and Rhea opened it with trembling fingers, so anxious to read it that she almost didn't take in the sense of the first sentence before her eyes had rushed on to the next. She stopped herself with an effort and went to sit down at the table, holding the letter away from her while she took several deep breaths. Then she started it again:

'Dear Rhea, It has really been very difficult to be apart from you all this time but I know it has been for the best. I don't want you to think I am still angry or hurt. I know now that you must do what you think is right with your life and no amount of pressure from me can change that. So, with that in mind, and knowing how you feel about living in the country, I have decided to forget about any ideas of us getting together. I am marrying a girl called Susan, who is the daughter of the manager of the station where I'm working now, on the 10th of August. She's a real country girl and she cares a lot about me.

431

It won't be the same as it would have been if you'd cared about me and married me but I don't think I'll be unhappy. Susan tries too hard for that. I hope you and Charles (?) will be happy too and that you will write to me sometimes and tell me what you are doing. I miss you, as always. Love, Will.'

Rhea stopped and stared blankly at the floor, Jennie anxiously coming to stand beside her. That was it then. The date today was the 17th. He really was gone forever. To a country girl. She felt like her stomach had turned to water.

Jennie put a hand on her arm.

'What is it Rhea? You look like . . . '

'Will got married.' She pushed Jennie away and stood up, swaying for a moment so that she had to clutch the table for support. Then she stood straight and breathed in again. She folded the letter firmly and put it back in its envelope, turned and smiled at Jennie, and walked out of the sitting room, her heels making careful clicking sounds on the wooden floor. They halted at her bedroom. She closed the door quietly but firmly behind her, inviting no-one to share her sorrow. Jennie left her alone.

Chapter Twenty Six

Ursula was worried. She had read the letter from Lettice several times but nothing more came through to her. She wished sometimes that Lettice would be a little more vulgar and tell her everything. But what else could she have said? Simon's father had died a few weeks ago and the funeral had been in the Abbey. The real shock was not that he was dead, but that he had left all his money to charity and not a penny to Julia or the children. People were wagging their tongues about it all over the place. And Simon was furious, of course. He had always hoped against hope that the money would still come in sometime soon, if not to him then at least to Julia and the children. Poor old Humphrey; not to be lamented even in death, just squabbled over for his money.

Ursula wondered if Simon would stick by Julia now and finally marry her. But first he had to get divorced. Lettice said he'd been cooling towards Julia for some time now, particularly since she had elected to stay with Humphrey when Simon had been thrown out. Lettice thought he would leave Julia and the children to their own devices and skip the country before the debt-collectors really had him locked up. Ursula pursed her lips. That sounded like Simon.

It was the second letter that had her really worried. It was dated a week later, November 9th 1964, and had obviously been sent with haste. Julia wouldn't see Simon anymore! She had found someone new to fund her lifestyle and wanted nothing whatsoever to do with Simon. She had closed her doors to him and wouldn't lift a finger to help him with his creditors. She had finally had enough. Simon was desperate, Lettice wrote, and had come down to live in the cottage again to escape London and his debts.

Ursula had no doubt that he would try and put out more feelers in the blackmail stakes if he could, despite his lack of success with her before. He was no fool. If he really put his mind to it, he would find a way of getting money out of her. Maybe he didn't like Australia but, sooner or later, he would get desperate enough to decide that the property she had inherited was, by virtue of his status as her husband, his for the taking.

Ursula crumpled the letter between her fingers and paced the verandah in the half-light of dusk. There were huge moths batting against the lights and she sat down in the rocking chair to avoid them flying into her. Damn! Just when things were going so well, just when the property was looking so beautiful with its orange trees in orderly lines and the whitewashed houses surrounded by the last of winter's grass. It was paying for itself now and making a profit besides. Damn, damn! She was thirty-six years old and still worried about a man who had barely touched her, either emotionally or physically in ten years of marriage. Would he never be out of her life? She rocked harder in her chair, staring out at the herb garden with bitter eyes.

Should she call Tim? But then, he couldn't really help. And it might be a sensitive time politically. It was, if she admitted it, just an excuse to talk to him and she had to be stronger than that. Last time he had sounded so impatient and cross. Though how she was expected to know there had been a reporter in with him at that point, and she had thought he would want to know Tom had won a scholarship to Christchurch, just like his sister before him at St Hilda's. But Tim still hadn't recovered from his scare with that woman estate agent and didn't want to take any chances. Funny how much that had meant to her then – the thought of having a place in town. She remembered taking Tim to see the house and exclaiming excitedly over everything until the estate agent had turned up and recognized Tim instantly, her sandy blonde eyebrows shooting up into the air. Tim had left immediately, the disappointment souring his entire visit. And that was before he even thought of the deputy leadership. Or before Simon had become such a threat.

No, Ursula realized with a grim smile, the house in Perth was definitely out. No parties for her – not with Tim at the head of the table anyway. No parties at all if Simon got his way. But he wouldn't. She'd make sure of that. She shook her head and looked at the letter again. No, she'd have to sort this one out alone, if and when the time came.

Charles and Rhea were married in March the following year. They held the wedding at St George's Cathedral in town and the reception was at Freshwater Bay yacht club. Rhea had wanted it outside and with the cooler weather of March, the gardens were green and fragrant again on the promontory that hung over the Swan River like the head of a whale. The breeze lifted any mugginess from the air. Tiffany, Christopher, Lettice, and Hugh all came over for the ceremony, the latter complaining that if he didn't come this once, he'd never see his goddaughter again. And he was looking old, Ursula thought uneasily. Old before his time.

Lettice had been hopeful for a while that it had been nothing more than a temporary indisposition of some sort or another. Hugh hadn't been ill for nearly a year, she had written in her last letter. But, looking at him now, Ursula thought it was only a matter of time. His skin was like flyscreen wire, grey and pitted. She had tried not to let him see how shocked she was when she first saw him. But he knew; the knowledge was there in his resigned expression, even the gentle self-mocking humour that she loved about him becoming more tentative, less amused.

They came to spend a few days at the property before the wedding. Lettice wanted to see if it measured up to the rigours of Rhea's poetry. Hugh wanted to rest. Tiffany and Christopher wanted to look around, see if they could make the move. England, they said, was getting to be a dismal sort of place. Ursula greeted them at the door to the house, having sent John Dempsey, the extra hand she had hired to replace Will, to pick them up at the airport. She would have gone herself, she explained to them as she threw her arms around them, but Tom had started a funny-looking rash and she was praying it

435

wasn't chicken pox. Not just before the wedding. The four of them stood there, each a subtly different person to the one she had last known.

'Oh! It's been too long, darling. We should never have let you go away. You can't imagine how boring Elsing's become without you and Rhea. And now Simon's taken up residence at Cotters, drinking himself into an early grave! God! How Julia could do that to him!' Lettice threw herself into Ursula's arms. They had just arrived from the long flight from Singapore, sensibly breaking their journey from England in manageable stages. Still, they looked worn out. Ursula hugged Lettice back.

'Simon deserves everything he gets. I've no sympathy to spare for him. Besides, if Julia's put up with him for nearly twenty years, she deserves a break.' They laughed and trooped up the stairs of the verandah to the house, exclaiming over the heat, the dryness of the air, the amount of land they could see with no-one else around. Ursula shooed them into the extra two bedrooms she had added on to the house a year ago, angling them out so they caught as much breeze as possible. Tom normally had one and the other was a guest bedroom. But Tom had moved into Rhea's and she was still down in Perth preparing for the big day. Once they were settled in, they gathered again in the sitting room.

Kim brought out a tray of glasses and a bottle of champagne.

'Here yer are, Mrs Paterson. Chilled'n'all. Stoney said to tell yer he'll pick Percy and the others up from school today so don't go worryin' about that.' She smiled brightly at the four strange faces and Ursula tried to see them through her eyes as they lifted their glasses, toasting Rhea and Charles.

Tiffany and Christopher looked well, the former putting on the weight that the latter had lost. But they were clearly happy and still in love. And Tiffany was as outrageous as ever, shocking poor John Dempsey on the ride from the airport when she told him what she thought about outside loos. Christopher related the tale with glee and Ursula tried not to splutter her champagne down her dress. But outside loos weren't a problem anymore, she reassured Tiffany. They had long since had a plumbed-in bathroom inside the house.

Tiffany was wearing a tightly-fitting suit of black wool that was as appropriate to Gidgeeganup as Ursula's own lightweight cotton dress would be to a London winter. Her hair was a brighter shade of blonde than Ursula remembered and was clearly helped along with the aid of a bottle. But her face was as arrestingly beautiful, with its Botticelli pouting lips and limpid blue eyes as it had ever been, with the added fillip of a mature expression that found life and people all too fallible. Kim eyed her wistfully.

Christopher was greying prematurely but his face and body had that sort of leanness that would keep him young for life. He looked relaxed and at peace with the world. Ursula tried to remember how she could have been attracted to him. His smile was still wonderful, and the humour, yes that was all still there. But real physical attraction? Ursula thought about Tim who was arriving in a day or two. And she looked at Christopher again. No, there was nothing there for her. She smiled.

Lettice was anxious even though she smiled brightly and threw her arms around in loud, theatrical gestures. It looked incongruous in a woman of her age, pale grey hair waved elegantly around her head – the sheep look had been abandoned – and a pale green and cream checked dress with pearls at the throat. She looked as though she should speak quietly, in discreetly genteel tones, of the theatre, her grandchildren, the Royals; not about adultery and debtors, following each remark with a wild shout of laughter. Hugh smiled obediently, pink cheeks paled to lead.

Kim refilled the glasses and took one for herself at Ursula's urging. They sat around happily swapping stories and life histories for some time until Tom wandered out from his bedroom, his blond hair disarrayed from sleep and his face flushed and spotted. Ursula went over and picked him up.

'Were we making too much noise, darling? How're you feeling?' She kissed his forehead and sat him on her knee, checking his temperature automatically. He yawned and leaned back in her arms, looking curiously around at the room full of strangers. They, in turn, were looking at him.

'My, he looks like his father, doesn't he?' Lettice remarked. Her eyes were twinkling. 'Hallo, Tom. You don't know me but I'm your Aunt Lettice. I've just come all the way out from England with your Uncle Hugh for Rhea's wedding. We're her godparents, did you know that?' She held out her arms to take him and Ursula passed him across.

'I hope you've all had chicken pox? Kim? You better keep away. I don't want you passing it on to Percy.'

'Don't you worry, Mrs Paterson. That ain't chicken pox. That's jus' some rash. Tom'll be fine for the wedding, won't yer boy?' She grinned when Tom nodded emphatically. He was blinking and yawning as he tried to make some sense of what a godparent was.

'People don't say I look like my dad. They say I look like Uncle Tim. He's Mummy's friend,' Tom said finally. Lettice controlled herself admirably, the others looking away.

'Really? Well, I expect you do at that. I haven't seen Tim in a long time,' Lettice said.

'He's coming tomorrow, isn't he Mummy?' Tom said, suddenly excited at the thought. His grey eyes grew large, and his blonde hair flopped over one eye. Hugh looked thoughtful.

'Must cause problems that,' he remarked to Ursula. She knew he meant the likeness to Tim. She shrugged.

'Not so far. People have accepted our explanation. But who knows. We'll cross that bridge when we get to it.'

'He doesn't know then?' Hugh indicated Tom. Ursula shook her head and sighed.

'No. We're not sure how to handle it, or if to at all. Maybe we'll just let things go as is.'

'Um, tricky. I'd tell him when he's older. It's always for the best. Nothing worse than it coming out when he's already full grown. Makes for awkward situations. Hallo, Tom. Are you going to come and say hallo to your Uncle Hugh?' He leaned down and held out his arms. Tom obligingly slipped from Lettice's lap and wandered over to Hugh.

'Like father, like son,' Lettice said softly to Ursula. 'Tim always was a friendly sort.' Her tone was ironic.

Later, when Hugh had gone to have a rest and Tiffany and Christopher were walking around the homestead, admiring the sentinel rows of fruit trees and well-kept barns, Lettice sat back heavily on the verandah chair and sighed.

'Hugh's got cancer. He's dying,' she said. Ursula nodded.

'I knew something was terribly wrong. He looks so much older, so . . . ill. Is there anything I can do?' Lettice shook her head.

'No. He knows, of course. But he doesn't want a fuss made. I was hoping the trip would help but he's too far gone. I'm going to lose him, but at least he'll have seen Rhea and you again. That's so important to him.' There was a long painful silence between them, Ursula holding Lettice's hand tightly in her own.

'And what about you when he's gone? Will you stay in Elsing? Or would you like to come out here. There's plenty of room and now Rhea's getting married, and Tom will be off to boarding school soon and Tim's away so much with his politics, well . . . ' But Lettice shook her head again.

'That's terribly kind of you darling but I just couldn't bear to leave the house and the village. I may talk about it being boring but it's home to me. And Hugh will be there, in the churchyard. I want to be buried next to him not somewhere out here, in brown dust. I know you're happy here, Ursula, but I couldn't be. It's too raw.' That was the thing with Lettice. She always told you how things were with her, straight out. Ursula smiled ruefully.

'Yes, it is raw, isn't it? Beautiful and spare but I grew up with tropical greenery. It takes time to adapt.'

She was thinking that again when they arrived at the reception, and looked around at the gardens of the yacht club: neat and orderly but not luxuriant, not wildly, overwhelmingly green and vibrant, full of colour, like the gardens she remembered in Singapore. For a moment she wondered if she would ever see them again. Then Bettina Peel came over and handed Ursula a glass of champagne. The Peels had organized everything, from the flowers and the food down to the car the bride and groom would leave in. Ursula was vastly relieved. She couldn't have coped alone and, quite frankly, didn't have the money this called for. The Peels liked a bit of a splash.

It worried her that Rhea had been so silent when she was being dressed this morning. There had been none of the excitement Ursula had expected. None of the confidings, jokes, fears even about what would happen tonight. Instead Rhea had stood like a doll while she was dressed, her speech confined to polite, distant answers to questions posed by Jennie and her sisters. She hadn't even talked much to her own mother. There was a tightness about her that Ursula didn't like. Bettina had put it down to pre-wedding nerves and not thought much more about it. But Ursula knew better. And she was worried. Maybe this wedding had been too hurried, too close on the heels of that dreadful letter from Will? Ursula tried to talk to Rhea, to bring up the subject but Rhea cut her off abruptly, hurrying out of the room to search for a brooch that had suddenly disappeared. And Ursula had let her be.

The Peels were a large, noisy family of five children, myriad cousins, and countless other relations. Ursula lost track of their various connections, constantly watching her tongue in case she said something about someone who turned out to be a third cousin once removed. Most of Perth seemed to be connected to the Peels.

By the time the reception had begun, the party was in full swing and when Charles and Rhea cut the cake, there were loud cheers and explosions from champagne bottles in all directions. Rhea was coolly beautiful in an ivory silk wedding dress that hung off her shoulders in large knots of roses. Her hair shone in the sun and her veil was suspended from a row of delicate rose buds across her forehead. She was everything Charles could conceive of wanting in a bride. The look on his face told everyone that. Bettina Peel and Ursula sat on the stone bench just by the steps that led down through the gardens to the fuelling docks and toasted each other quietly. Tim had offered to give Rhea away but it had been decided that Hugh ought to do the duties, both because he was her godfather and because it would cause less talk. Now Hugh was giving a speech that no-one was listening to and Tim was trying to coax him away with some more champagne. Mr Peel came to help and between the two of them Hugh was subdued.

Bettina laughed. 'Can't stop an old fool, no matter what. But I'm glad things've gone so well. I was worried the Greens would cause a fuss – or rather, Lucinda would. She and Jeff are still at war and when he decided to bring Julie it was nearly all over!' She caught Ursula's blank expression. 'Oh, then you don't know. My God, Peppermint Grove and Mosmans have been buzzing with this for the last couple of months. It seems Jeff Green started having an affair with Julie Sumner. Lucinda moved out to stay with Jack and Libby and ended up stealing

Jack, so now Libby's left holding the baby, or rather all three of them. Charming little village we live in isn't it? Are you sure you're so deprived living out there in the bush?' They both laughed.

'Yes, I'm sure. I had no idea divorce and scandal were becoming such acceptable things nowadays. No-one seems to be giving any of the Greens or Sumners or whoever the cold shoulder about it, do they?' She said it musingly. Bettina shrugged.

'No, don't see why we should. They're all old friends and let's face it, every marriage has its problems. You're lucky off where you are. Comfortably and respectably widowed and with two lovely children and enough money to be quite your own woman. I envy you sometimes, Ursula.'

'Well you shouldn't. Not that I'm not very happy and the property's doing well but I miss my children, let me tell you. Tom's out all day at school – they built a new one, did I tell you? – and he's off to Christchurch next year, so I'll never see him and now Rhea . . . ' Ursula looked across at her children. Tom was playing with one of the Peel boys, racing round and round the legs of the tables set up for the lunch. As Kim had prophesied, his rash had disappeared the next day and he was in full spirits again now. Rhea was smiling by her husband. 'Oh well, things are going better now as far as money. We've got a good crop this year. I was thinking about moving down here and getting a little house round the back of St Hilda's. There are some nice weatherboard ones going for a song.' She didn't mention the fact that Tim had told her, after this one appearance at Rhea's wedding, he could only see her on the property from now on. She pulled a strand of hair back into place, the wind whipping at her hat as though determined to wrench it off and send it flying, like several others, over the parapet and down to the boats below. Bettina Peel looked at her and thought again how young she was to have such a grown-up daughter. She wondered if there were any truth to the rumours about Tim Nowlton. Such a good-looking pair they made.

Over on the dance-floor Tiffany had cornered Charles and was doing a tango that took no notice of other dancers in their way, the black fringe of her scarf tangling over his arms. Ursula smiled. Actually things were going too well. This was

441

home now, her daughter was beautiful and married to a wonderful young man, Tom was bright and athletic and a joy to even look at, since she could see so much of his father in him. And Tim, well, Tim was there when she needed him – mostly – and all her best friends were here around her. She kept waiting for someone to snatch it all away again. It was dangerous to be this happy. She waved to the dancers who were beckoning her to join in and then Tim came to get her. They waltzed sedately, dodging around Tiffany whenever she came flying down on them.

'Happy?' Tim asked.

'Very. I keep looking for the dark side in things, just so I can be prepared. Like Lettice with Hugh.'

'You've had your share already.'

'Oh, do people only get so much good, or bad luck per lifetime? And I've used up all the bad so from now on it's only good luck all the way?'

'That's it. My pet theory.' He felt Ursula stiffen in his arms and turned to see what she was looking at.

'Your theory's a little premature I think. Will's here.' Ursula glanced across at her daughter who was dancing with Hugh, oblivious to Will's presence. 'She hasn't seen him yet. Lord, why did he have to come? If it wasn't bad enough of him going off like that and breaking her heart the first time, now he has to turn up at her wedding and spoil that,' Ursula said. Tim led her to the edge of the floor, his hand tight and reassuring on her arm.

'Don't worry, love. Will isn't here for spite. He's too nice a kid for that. Whu-up, Rhea's spotted him. Here we go. Want to go intervene?'

'No-o. They're better off sorting it out themselves. There's nothing we can do anyway. Come on, sweetheart. How often do I get to dance with the man of my dreams?'

'How often?' he asked, pulling her in tight against him, her scent light and elusive. Like Ursula herself, he thought. He liked the dress she was wearing, pale yellow silk with a loose dropped neckline so that he could see down it to her smooth brown skin. She wore his necklace nestled in the hollows of her throat. Everyone was getting drunk and he considered just abandoning good sense and kissing her there, in front of the

442

whole lot of them. But Ursula anticipated the move and turned her head away in time.

'Steady. We've got hours ahead of us before we can go home. So let's just dance, all right? You don't want that gossip columnist to have a field day, do you?'

'Yeah, you're right. But one day love, one day soon.' He was dreamy-eyed as he watched her, a slight curve to his mouth. She laughed.

'Promises, promises.'

Rhea stood quite still, her back so straight and rigid she looked like she might snap if someone touched her. Will gave her a lop-sided smile.

'Congratulations, Rhea. Thought I'd come and kiss the bride good luck. You don't mind, do you?' He was casually dressed and looked out of place amongst the morning-suits and tea-gowns. He looked at her in her roses and silk, hair gleaming back in a knot and the veil pushed back from her face. He could never have given her any of that. The thought pained him. Rhea nodded stiffly and he leaned over to brush her cheek. She smelt his skin, warm and wholesome like fresh bread, and abruptly pulled away.

'Thanks. Congratulations yourself. How did you know?'

'Not from you that's for sure.' Some of Will's old truculence surfaced. He did his best to keep calm. 'So, old Charles it is, huh? Thought that might be the way of things. You still liking Perth? Is it that beaut a place?' He had his hands in his pockets, digging deeply down with clenched fists as he looked around and moved from foot to foot. He didn't like what he saw. 'That him – the one standing by your mum?' Rhea looked to see who he meant.

'No, that's mother's cousin, Christopher. He's a little old for me, don't you think? Or were you joking?' She didn't like the way he was standing there, eyeing her friends. 'Charlie's over there, by the cake. He's drinking right now.'

'Very suave and debonair, I must say,' Will mocked. That had been a joke between them, calling anyone who looked just too perfect 'suave and debonair'. Rhea resented the comment and let it show.

'What'd you come for, Will? So you could be all bitter and

twisted? I don't need that, thanks all the same. This is supposed to be my happiest day ever and you're doing your best to spoil it. I didn't ask you to come, you know.'

'Yeah, I do know. And now I'm here I could just about chunder. Is this you, Rhea? All this social snobbery bit? All this vulgar show? I never guessed it. I thought we were the same, out of the same mould and then you go and choose all of this.' He had turned away and walked down the drive to a point where he could look out over the lawns and jetties lined with yachts, the metal stays humming and thunking against the aluminium masts in the wind. The salt air filled his lungs, ruffled his hair. Rhea came up beside him. Her eyes widened, as though to take in as much as possible of him, to imprint him on her mind before it was too late.

'Why did you just cut out on us – on me – like that? I didn't know where the hell you'd gone. I, I loved you Will and you said you loved me!' Her voice became high and cracked. 'You just had to wait a few months! Will! No word for two years and then a letter to say you're married? Well, thanks a bunch.' She didn't look at him but stared hard out at the river, her eyes slitted against the glare. Will shrugged.

'I needed to get away. You didn't really care anyway. Love's just a word you use to get your own way. Sue's a nice girl. She likes the bush and she likes me. I wasn't even going to come today but I thought I'd just . . . check, you know. That you were happy with your life here in Perth. You've got every-thing you want here, haven't you?' He turned to look at her when she didn't reply. 'Haven't you?'

'Yes.' Rhea looked at him for a moment, her young face suddenly tired and a little disillusioned around the set of her mouth. 'Yes, I suppose I have – now. You think you can tell me what I mean by "love" but you're wrong. I'm not so heart-less . . . so manipulative, no matter what you think. And I know what we had. If you'd waited for me Will . . . I'd've come back to you. But you didn't trust me, you had to go off and get married to the first girl who showed willing, just so you could turn around and say, "see, she wants me!" Well, believe it or not, that's not much of a surprise to me, Will. I always knew you were worth ten of every other man I ever met. I'm not even completing my degree now. That should make

444

you happy.' She turned away. 'So, anyway, once I got that letter from you, that's when I decided to stay here. There's not much point in going back to the property when you're not there anymore, is there?' She straightened her back and walked back up the slope to the reception. Will saw Charles come over to her and put his arm round her, laughing at the way Tiffany was spraying champagne out over the dancers. When Rhea looked back, Will was gone.

Chapter Twenty Seven

The phone rang twice, shrilly, by Ursula's head. She put out her hand and picked it up, knocking the clock as she did so and swearing. 'Hallo? Hallo? Tim? What time is it? . . . Five? What's wrong?' She sat up abruptly, pushing back the covers of her bed and groping for the light. 'Then why're you ringing me in the middle of the night for God's sakes? You scared me! . . . Who? Western Mining? Never heard of them . . . Oh, I will, will I? . . . Nickel shares? Look Tim, couldn't you just call me back later when I'm more awake? I don't know anything about playing the stock-market, or mineral deposits or nickel finds . . . You're sure about it? Well, about fifteen thousand at a pinch, I guess . . . All of it? You must be kidding! . . . Well, I don't know. That's all I've got to put down on a house in Perth and I need one with Tom about to start school. I really think he's too young to board . . . Oh, I am listening to you Tim but there are all sorts of things we have to do here on the prop . . . of, course I trust your judgement . . . Oh, all right if you're absolutely one hundred percent certain . . . Who gave you the tip? . . . Oh, I see, well, ye-es, it sounds good. All right. First thing in the morning. I hope to God this is for real . . . Yes, I trust you. Okay, sweetheart. I'll call you at the office as soon as I've bought them . . . Four dollars a share now? Okay . . . Yes, I love you too. Bye, sweetheart.' She replaced the receiver in its cradle and stood up, walking like a sleep-walker to the bathroom, bare-foot. It was still hot, even in the early hours of the morning. But then January was always a beast. She pulled the cord for the light and stared at herself in the mirror.

It was ten months since Rhea had married. Since Lettice and Hugh, Tiffany and Christopher had left. And she'd barely seen Tim in that time – just once, for a long weekend. She listened to the telephone conversation replaying itself in her mind; listening to his voice. Damn, she was sick of being alone. She splashed water on her face and dried it.

Charles's father would know who to call and buy the shares from. Maybe she ought to pass on the tip? No, Tim had said not to tell a soul, and what if it went wrong? Fifteen thousand down the drain. She didn't dare tell someone else to risk their money. Still, it sounded like a sure bet. 'Massive nickel sulphides averaging 8.3% over a length of 3 metres,' Tim had said. Impressive, whatever it meant.

She yawned and wandered into the kitchen, hunted for some milk in the refrigerator, and put the kettle on to boil. Outside the sky was streaked with the first paler washes of dawn. She liked it at this time of day and wondered why she didn't get up more often to see it. Just as well she hadn't bought that house she'd looked at. Then there'd be no money to spare at all. Mr Winby didn't think there was anyway. He'd be furious if he knew what she was going to do with it. As furious as he was capable of getting now, since Will had left. But, what the hell, it was her money. And Tim had sounded so sure! Oh, what if he were right and it was really a major find and the shares went through the roof! She'd be rich! And able to do whatever she wanted. She laughed to herself, sitting alone in the kitchen with the kettle screaming out a thin wisp that turned almost immediately to a cloud. She got up and poured it into the teapot, put a cup on a tray with the tea and carried it outside to the verandah. Fragrant, clear tea in a bone-china cup; her answer to any problems.

In the next few weeks, Ursula watched, astounded, as her shares rose to ninety dollars a share, split, and rose to sixty again. She wasn't sure what to do with herself, ringing Rhea in town every few days to exclaim over another jump in the price. Mr Peel was offended that she hadn't let him in on the tip but relented when she pointed out that Charlie and Rhea would get it all in the end anyway. Her broker advised selling when the price slipped back to fifty-eight and she told him to go ahead, so happy with what she had made that she didn't dare risk it a second longer. Tim was an even bigger winner than she, his initial stake nearly five times hers.

Together they celebrated their new-found fortune in a trip to the barrier reef, each of them wearing dark glasses and ridiculous straw hats in the hope that no-one would recognize them. It was staggering to realize how wealthy they were. Nearly four hundred and fifty thousand dollars for Ursula; Tim wealthy beyond even his dreams. They didn't really have the expertise to invest it, Tim never having paid much attention to the stock market and Ursula never having had any reason to do so. But Charlie's father knew exactly where to put the money to make it work for them both. And that way it was all in the family. Ursula had the feeling 1966 was going to be good to her.

Tim met her at Brisbane with a rental car and they drove north along the coastline past Deception Bay, and Nambour to a place called Coolum Beach. It was a quiet place to spend the first night, north of the Gold Coast and Surfer's Paradise but not yet as far as the reef. They booked themselves into a motel on the road that ran along the beach, Tim registering them as Mr and Mrs Paterson. He wasn't too worried that they would be recognized up here in some provincial town but he didn't want to take chances with his name.

Ursula had brought very little clothing with her; just a couple of pairs of shorts, a few shirts, and her bathing suit. She was tanned and fit from hard work around the station and hours of riding, something other women paid a fortune for at health resorts. Joanna could do with a little of Ursula's trimness, Tim thought, but with the indifference of someone who was not physically or emotionally involved. Joanna did her own thing and maybe her men liked her with flesh on her. He didn't care.

He admired the view he had of Ursula's body while he lay stretched out, arms beneath his head, on the bed watching her change. She really was beautiful, he thought with an ache that he refused to acknowledge. Beautiful and intelligent and loving . . . His thoughts were interrupted by Ursula climbing on to the bed beside him, her dark hair dangling over her shoulder to tickle his chest.

'Are you going to just lie there and stare blankly into space?' She kissed his throat. 'Or have you got something else in mind?' The look he gave her made her laugh, back in her throat. He smiled.

'Later, hussy. Right now I thought we'd go out and spend some of that hard-earned money of ours.'

'Oh really? On what? I take it you did look around when we drove into town?' He shrugged.

'A little exercise, a little food, and then we'll come back here. You're getting to be too demanding, my girl.' He gave her a playful slap on her bottom. Too demanding. Now that was a joke, he thought. The one thing she had never been, in any way. That made it worse really. He tried to comfort himself with the thought of all that money she now had to make herself secure.

They decided on a quick swim before dinner, Tim reassuring Ursula that the water was safe even in the dark. And it wasn't that dark anyway. The moon lit the water with its churning surf and phosphorescent waves so that it almost seemed like day. They walked down the beach until they found a sheltered area beside a groyne. The rocks were black and glistened wetly, causing Ursula to shiver at the thought of what might be lurking beside them. She swam in the quieter surf but Tim disappeared out beyond the breakers, his shoulders lifting him clear in a strong crawl. After a few minutes he reappeared and the two of them continued walking down the beach. Their bathing suits dried in the warm night air and they stopped to pull on shorts and tops and to slip thongs on their feet. Then they crossed the road and bought fish and chips from the shop on the corner. They asked for flake but Tim said later that it was shark. It was always shark.

And then they went back to the motel.

'Not much of a honeymoon sort of place, is it?' Tim said. The room was basic: a bed, a chair, a chest of drawers and a tiny bathroom. Ursula smiled and slipped her arm through his, rubbing her hand across his back.

'Well, this isn't a honeymoon. I don't know about you, but all I need is a bed. And I don't really even need that . . . ' He turned and pulled her in tightly, kissing the skin behind her ear, the tip of her jawline, the hollow of her temples. She was so

449

lovely and as young looking as the day he had first seen her. They had made love so many times before but this time seemed particularly important to them both. It was the only time they had ever gone away together. The only time they hadn't had to worry about somebody else and what they would think. Ursula slipped her hand under Tim's shirt, her palm cold against his skin. She felt him shiver.

'Happy?' he asked again. She smiled.

'As long as I can have you to myself like this, I'll always be happy.' She felt him pull her in tightly, squeezing the breath from her as though he were frightened of losing her. He hesitated, opening his mouth to speak several times before he found the words.

'Maybe that won't be possible so much any more. If I get the deputy leadership, and everyone seems to think I will, I won't dare be seen with you. You know what the press are like. They'd spot you immediately, and any strange trips I kept making to Perth would be asking for it. I don't know that they haven't got an idea of something already but they won't make anything of it unless I flaunt it under their noses. I can't tell you what a scandal about a mistress and illegitimate child would do to me, or to the party. If the party's going to have a chance at all in the next election, I have to keep a clear profile. Besides, with Rhea being the young society matron in Perth and Tom just starting at Christchurch, I'd hate to put them through all that scandal.' He felt her shudder against him. 'Ursula, listen to me – you and the children are everything precious to me in the world but I just can't be with you. I'm so sorry, love, but it's just got to be like this. That's why I wanted to have this time with you,' he said softly into her hair, trying to ease the blow.

She tried not to feel the numbing shock, tried to brush it off. He'd said things like this before and always come back. It was just another non-event. But the tremble couldn't be kept from her mouth and he kissed her fiercely, as though he would never let her go.

He waited, eventually, for her to say something but she turned away from him, slipping from his grasp and going to stand in front of the chest of drawers. The silence continued, impossibly long and impossibly fraught with emotion that

450

neither felt strong enough to wade into. Ursula looked down at the wood, and tried to make her mind work. Tim combed blunt fingers through short hair and rested his inner arm across nose and forehead; a habit of frustration. Ursula still didn't turn around. He spoke then, in an even tone, wanting her to understand.

'You know I can't leave Joanna. It would jeopardize the next elections. I don't particularly care whether I get the deputy leadership or not. I've almost got to the point where I'm fed up with it all anyway, the way it keeps us apart. But I can't let a scandal wreck the party's chances.'

There was a long pause while each gauged the other.

'I guess maybe I was hoping I meant enough to you. But there's always been an excuse, hasn't there? First the baby, then the by-elections, now the deputy leaderships and party elections. You'll be trying for party leader next, I suppose. Anthony's the same age as you. What if he gets it instead? He'll be around a long time.'

'I'm thinking of leaving the Country Party after the elections. I've been talking with Bill McMahon. He thinks there's a place for me in the Liberal Party if the leadership goes to Anthony. Joanna's family want to back me.' He sat on the bed, chin supported by his fist.

'I see.' She gave a shaky laugh. 'Well, just watch your back, won't you? I'm not sure good ole Bill's my idea of a mentor. He's not made it himself yet but when he does, he won't want any young Caesars behind him. Have you thought of that?'

'Look, I'm not a fool, Ursula. It'll mean a much longer wait than I ever expected, that's all. But what hope have I got in the Country Party if Anthony does get the leadership? I don't intend to be the bridesmaid for the rest of my career.'

'No, and neither do I.' There was total silence.

'What's that supposed to mean?'

'Ohh, Tim! We're not young anymore. I don't feel young. Can't you understand our lives are slipping away? You left me once before and I could just about deal with that because I still had Rhea. Well, now Rhea's married and Tom's at school and I need you. I can't deal with this constant tug-of-war between me and your precious politics.'

451

He came up behind her, put his arms around her, pulled her in against him. She leaned back on him.

'I need you too, love. But we've got time yet. You're only thirty-eight and,' he slid his hand down her hip, 'you're not showing it at all.' Once, just a few months ago, she would have shivered at his touch – and given in. Now she heard him in silence, willing her body to feign indifference. 'Anyway, love, we haven't lost all those years. We shared most of the important parts together.'

'Most of the important parts? Tim, if you added up the days you've spent with me over the last six or seven years, they wouldn't come to a single year – just a few months. And that's how important we are together. I've had enough. I can't wait forever. I won't! All I've ever wanted was someone to love me like . . . someone with whom I always came first, no matter what. Because that's how I love. And I want the same back. I told you, I could take it before because I had the children and they always love me that way too. But not now, not with Rhea married and with her own life, and Tom off at boarding school. I deserve something better than just sitting around the next half century hoping you'll turn up once a year. If you want your shot at party leader, waiting out the years respectably with someone you don't love and who doesn't love you, then I can't say anything, can I? I've offered everything I have and it isn't enough. But I won't be there for you anymore, Tim. I'm the one who'll walk away this time.'

Tim stepped back, releasing her. 'Is that it then? Give up everything I believe in, my whole career. And do what? Just sit around the property all day? Ursula, I love you but I won't stand for that sort of pressure, you know that. It has to be the right moment, when I know politics doesn't mean anything to me anymore, or I'll just be hankering after it all the time and unfairly blaming you for making me give it all up.' He softened his tone. 'Please try and understand.'

'Understand what? You once said you'd be glad to come and live with me on the property. How has that changed? Are you so involved with all the pomp and ceremony of being a politician, you can't see what matters in life anymore? I can't stand waiting any longer. Why must it always be on your terms? Why never mine? I need something for myself.' She hesitated.

'I think we better call this holiday off. You'd better go, Tim. You know the way back – that's something you've always known.' She picked something up from the chest of drawers, holding it clenched in her fist. 'Here, you better have these too.' And then she tossed the necklace and ring on the bed.

He stood awkwardly, his shoulders tightly together. He waited for her to turn around but she didn't. She just stood in front of the dresser, her fingertips pressed onto its surface. There had been no rage, no fury in her voice; more an inconsolable sadness. He didn't really think she had meant this to happen. But now it had been said, was there no going back? It made his throat ache with pain of loss. He ignored the jewellery and bent to pick up his things, bundling them haphazardly into his case.

'All right. I guess it really is goodbye then. I'm . . . so sorry. I'll always love you. There'll never be anyone else, you know that.'

She turned then and he saw her face was quite smooth and blank, only a few creases around the mouth and a certain weariness in her eyes betraying her. She lifted her hand and touched her hair, pushing back the imaginary strand.

'Yes, I know. There won't be for me either.' Then she turned back and stared out through the half-closed blinds.

Will waited up by the bore-head. It was almost dusk, the shadows riding long over the ground and the mosquitoes droning around his head. He swatted them away listlessly. He hoped his dad didn't decide to check the pump out. Stoney had said he'd keep him away, keep them all away, but it was still a risk. He hoped Rhea had a good reason for all this.

When she arrived, he almost didn't hear her as she stepped quietly out from behind the tanks. She wore flat tennis shoes with a light, cotton shift and moved as silently as he had himself. Sound carried a long way on still evenings like this.

She touched his arm. 'I'm sorry I'm late. It was hard to get away. I had to say I was coming up to the property to check on Tom.'

'Who to? Your husband. Doesn't he trust you enough to go out on your own with telling him where you are all the time?'

'He'd be worried if I didn't turn up for dinner, or later. This

453

way he knows where I am and won't think anything more about it. I've put Tom to bed now and Kim'll keep an eye on him.' She hunched thin shoulders against the night air. Will looked at her.

'You sound like you've got something in mind. Any particular reason you asked me here? It's a long way to come for an evening's chat.' He was surprised by her restlessness. Normally she was contained in her movements; tonight she was pacing, wrapping her arms around herself and then letting them drop free. She stopped and looked at him and he thought then how much he loved that face, even with its unhappy expression, its shadowed eyes. He forced himself to look away.

'I want . . . I want you to leave your wife and, and we'll go away somewhere, I don't know where, it doesn't even matter. Just somewhere, together.' Her voice was abrupt, even gruff. She came to stand beside him and he smelled her body fragrance, felt her warmth as she gripped his shirt between her fingers. 'Please, Will, I can't take this anymore! Please!' She leaned against him and he couldn't help but hold her, her face buried against his chest. He stroked her hair.

'I can't.' He sounded almost conversational in tone. Rhea caught at the pain in her throat that tried to rip itself free in a cry of anguish.

'You can! Will, it doesn't matter what people think. We were always supposed to be together anyway. I'm not giving you up to someone who just met you a few months ago, someone you don't even love!' Her desperation made her face gaunt in the last light. Will looked up at the sky, at the streaks of dark cloud trailing across the evening blue. Then he closed his eyes, holding Rhea tightly against him.

'Sue's pregnant.' He felt Rhea lurch in his arms, wrenching herself free.

'No! No! She can't be! No!' She shrieked the words into the night air, hearing them echo off into the stillness. Will caught her to him, shaking her until she slumped against him.

'Ssh, Rhea, shh! Someone'll hear you.' They waited in the silence that followed for any hint that Rhea's screams had been heard. Nothing. Eventually Will turned to the girl who leaned so heavily in his arms. 'I'm so sorry, Rhea. I can't do anything about it. She only told me a month or so ago. If only you'd

454

come to me sooner, we could've still gone away. But I can't now. You must see that. I can't walk out on a wife and baby.' He kissed her then, all their years of longing going into that embrace. Then Rhea laughed.

'This is unbelievable. I can't take it in. It's Mother's mistake all over again. Oh Will! I don't care about your wife or her child. I want you!' She was crying and later, neither of them was sure how it happened. It began with them kissing, and then became something more passionate, more intense, dying down to laughter, gentle murmurs and when it was over, they both lay together on the ground, fiercely entwined in each other's bodies. Will lay partly on top of Rhea, protecting her from the openness around them. He kissed her breasts gently.

'I suppose this was bound to happen sooner or later.' He sounded contented and even happy. Rhea shifted her head languidly.

'Yes.' She strummed a finger down his back. 'We were always supposed to be together. We are the same sorts, we just never admitted it. We should just never have waited so long.' She brushed her lips over his forehead, through his hair, her arms holding him tightly across her.

'What happens now?' Will looked up at her, at the still expression in her eyes.

'Nothing, I suppose. You say you won't leave Sue. I guess that's all there is to that. But I want to see you from time to time too. I can't not see you for another two years, Will.'

'No. I can't do that either.' They lay quietly together, while the night clouded over the rest of the sky and the cicadas sang.

Chapter Twenty Eight

Rhea greeted Ursula's return with the news that she was going to have a baby. Everyone was ecstatic at the news except Rhea herself. She was oddly silent and uncomfortable when it was mentioned, blushing when well-meaning jokes were directed at her and altogether acting as though it were something to be ashamed of.

Ursula was worried but Charlie laughed and said she was just young and needed time to get used to it all. Hadn't Ursula been embarrassed to mention her state in the first few months? She remembered then, with amusement, the annoyance she had felt when Christopher had been so awkward with her. So long ago now. Twenty years! And now she was about to become a grandmother. That was a horrible thought, she decided. She didn't want to be called 'granny'. Rhea set her mind at rest by reminding her that all Australian grandmothers were called 'nan'. Ursula smiled painfully and kissed her, wishing Tim was about to be made a grandfather so he could know how it felt; know how old and undesirable she suddenly felt. Not that that mattered anymore. That part of her life was over; he had made that very clear. She had sensed his detachment for some time, wondering whether he felt coming to see her and Tom was becoming tiresome, a duty rather than a pleasure. He had a young, beautiful wife and son; what need did he have of her? A woman of thirty-eight who was about to become a grandmother. Josh was still only nine or so and it would be years before he had to suffer the same awakening to

456

age; feel the same fear that someone he loved didn't desire him anymore. Maybe he never would.

She stood up, a little stiff from the long flight home and walked slowly into the kitchen. She hadn't mentioned the break with Tim to anyone; not even Rhea. Especially not Rhea. It looked as though she had problems of her own. Ursula stood by the countertop, glancing across at her daughter while pretending to organize the napkins and plates for lunch. Rhea was buttering bread for sandwiches and Charles was cooking steaks outside on the brick-built barbecue they'd added to the house. Ursula watched him through the window, expertly turning the steaks while standing up-wind from the smoke. He looked contented and as happy as any married man had a right to be. She turned back and looked at her daughter.

Rhea seemed different to the girl who had laughed and teased her way through school and university. Now she seemed heavy, as though she had aged ten years. Not in weight. The pregnancy was only a month old and Rhea looked as tall and slim as ever. But marriage had faded the blush from her cheeks, the sparkle from her eyes. Ursula watched as Rhea impatiently pushed the pile of bread out of her way. It knocked the glasses that were stacked ready to be taken outside. Rhea didn't notice. They teetered, rocking on the countertop with a drumming sound before two of them tipped over in a tinkle of broken glass. Rhea stared at the pieces for a moment, her face quite blank, then she slammed down her knife and tried to pick up the glass. Shards of glass had embedded themselves in the bread. She let it drop back onto the countertop again, her mouth wincing up so that she looked like a child whose security has just been taken away, her top lip folding over her lower one. There were tears of mascara making their way down her cheeks but Ursula didn't hear a sound coming from her daughter. The emotion was the more disturbing for its silent control than for its tears. Ursula left the window and pulled Rhea into her arms. She rocked her gently backward and forward, as she had done when Rhea was a baby.

'Oh Rhea! Darling, what is it. Shh, don't cry now, I'm here.' For a moment Rhea clung to her mother and then she pulled away. Ursula held her hand tightly. 'Can you tell me about it, darling? Is it the baby? Or are you and Charles having problems?' She felt Rhea stiffen and pull her hand away.

'No! Charles and I are fine. He's so good, so kind! It's just . . . I didn't want a baby so soon. I don't feel like I'm old enough yet to cope with all that. I mean, that's it, isn't it? There's no way out after that . . . And everyone's being so gross about it. Making jokes, winking. It's sick! A baby's a private thing, produced by a private act. I don't want my sex-life being a topic of discussion for most of Perth! I just want them to leave me alone!' She turned back to the countertop, picked up a brown paper bag and threw the bread and glass into it. Her hair fell around her face so that Ursula couldn't see her expression.

'Does Will know?'

'No! . . . Oh God, no! I couldn't tell him. And he won't know, will he? Not from me and not from you either.' She looked at her mother fiercely. Ursula held up her hands.

'Seen him at all since the wedding?' Ursula had always known when Rhea was lying. Now she felt the hesitation, the swift thoughts flying through her daughter's mind like the shadows of clouds on a field in high wind; barely seen but noticed.

'No. He hasn't been back. Look, I'll have to make more sandwiches. There's too much glass lying around to risk these. Can you get more glasses from the cupboard and then carry them outside before I break any more?' Rhea tried to laugh while she wiped her face with the back of her hand. She sniffed once and finished throwing the last pieces of bread and glass away. Then she washed her hands and started buttering again.

Ursula didn't press the issue. She collected the glasses and carried them carefully outside to the table by the pool. It was a new house, built at the back of an older house, the original block of land subdivided into four quarter acre lots. Most of Peppermint Grove would be like this one day, Ursula thought. It was a shame but property was getting so expensive in Perth, particularly in this area between the river and the sea. The garden was doing very well in spite of the heat. But then, they'd planted Buffalo grass instead of the finer Queensland Blue. It was more sensible and grew more easily, she thought. Maybe it wasn't going to ever look like an English garden with stripes of turf and roses, but it would be beautiful in its own way.

Several kookaburras were lined up on the fence, shaking their wings and knocking their beaks against the post. One of them suddenly swooped down low over the limpid green of the pool, splashed into the water, recovered and flew back to his seat on the fence. Then he shook his feathers again and began his cry, rising to a crescendo. Ursula barely heard him, so used to the early morning chorus that she could block the sound from her mind. The kookaburras were pests: noisy, impertinent, and constantly having to be rescued from drowning in the pool when they misjudged their dives. Ursula had no time for them.

'Here we are, one well-done, one medium, and one rare. Where's Rhea?' Charles laid the steaks down on a platter in the middle of the table, brushing flies away automatically while he placed the net cover over them. Ursula gestured with her head.

'Buttering bread inside still. She won't be a minute. I'm sorry Tim couldn't make it after all, but he had to check there'd been no change in the format for the conference tomorrow in Melbourne.' Ursula could see Charles was startled but too polite to bring the matter up for discussion. She smiled, her normal good-humour over such a reaction becoming strained now. She wished she could say:

'Charles, I know you'd never let anyone know this. Not even your family. But Tim and his wife only stay together for appearances sake. He's the incumbent for the seat in his area when the next by-election comes up and he'll be trying for deputy leadership in the next couple of months but he really only loves me.' And Charles would nod and think that makes sense, Australians being such puritans about what they expect from their public figures. But she didn't say any of that because it wasn't true anymore. Tim didn't love her and he had gone back to his wife for good. Charles, however didn't notice Ursula's abstraction. He looked up instead to see Rhea coming out of the house carrying a large tray of sandwiches, a jug of lemonade and two bottles of Swan beer.

'Here, let me take that, Rhea. You mustn't carry such heavy things all on your own.' Rhea handed over the tray and smiled

459

tightly at her mother. Ursula smiled back. 'Right! We're all set. Rhea, my love, you sit here and, Ursula, you sit opposite me. There! Now, how about a toast? To Ursula's new-found wealth and to Rhea's and my new baby! May they both bring happiness!'

Chapter Twenty Nine

Tim closed the door on the last of the guests, arching his back to ease the ache and strain of the last few hours. So, he had done it. He was Deputy Leader of the Country Party. The thought left him with little joy. He smiled automatically at his wife as she carried out a tray of glasses.

'Leave it 'till the morning, Joanna. Your daily comes in tomorrow, doesn't she?' It was past two in the morning and he was tired. She paused to look at him.

'Yes, but I'd rather tidy up now. Put things back in their place, tidy up a few loose threads.' She smiled back and Tim felt himself grow cold. There was a look on her face he had never seen before. She put the tray down.

'I haven't really had a chance to congratulate you before.' She put her arms around his neck and leaned in to kiss him, her mouth pouting a bright red and her nails like red talons around him. They hadn't exchanged more than a friendly kiss on the cheek in years and he felt an overwhelming urge to back away, to thrust her out of his arms, like some harpy who smelt of rotting flesh. God, what had he done? What was it all worth? The smiles, the slaps on the back, the handshakes. For what? Ursula and Tom, both given up for what? Joanna saw the expression in his eyes and drew away.

She picked up the tray again. 'Now that you're safely tied to the position you're supposed to have been filling for so many years,' she smiled sweetly, 'as my husband, I mean, I think there's probably something you should know. I haven't wanted

461

to tell you this until the deputy leadership was safely in the bag, but now you really should know. You've left it too late to go back to your precious Ursula and your son by her. A plain MP might have been forgiven for a divorce as long as it was done discreetly. A second in command, never. Dad said you'd be stuck after this.' She smiled again. Tim looked impatient.

'You know damn well I'm not going anywhere and never was. I told you that when I came back from my trip. It's all over between Ursula and me. So what's all this in aid of?'

'Oh, just because I've been waiting a long time to tell you that when I sent that telegram about being pregnant . . . I'm afraid I lied just a little. Josh isn't your son.' She said it with amusement as though she expected him to be devastated. When he looked at her coldly instead, her mouth formed itself into the pout it wore habitually.

'Why tell me now, after all these years?'

'Because I want you to know now that you'll never have what you want. A happy family life with dear, good little Ursula and your charming little son, Tom. You've put me through a lot, Tim. I was in love with you, at one point. And then you started cooling off, and you were always so damned careful when you made love to me that I knew I'd never get you that way. So,' she took a deep breath and smiled that brilliant, politician's wife smile that brought in so many votes. So unlike Ursula's, Tim thought. Ursula, with her rueful, twisting sort of smile that really meant something, not just a rearrangement of the lips. But he stopped the thought sharply, trying to concentrate on what his wife was saying. 'Are you listening to me, Tim? Because I think you'll want to hear this.' She saw she'd got his attention again. 'I slept with another man.' She saw the question forming in his mind and added, ' . . . no, you don't know him and it wouldn't matter if you did; it was all so long ago but he loved me a lot, something you never did – and then, when you went off to England, I knew I could call you back whenever I wanted. And I did.' She put the last glass on the tray. 'I never expected you to have been un-faithful too. Not good old Tim, Mr Perfection. But you had. I can't tell you how much that hurt. I've never really forgiven you for that, you know. For loving her and not me. Anyway, I wasn't about to let it all slip through my fingers, not when I'd worked so hard to get you.'

She laughed. 'God knows why I bothered. I'd've been better off sticking with Josh's real father. He's made quite something of himself too. You do see the irony, don't you? You could've had Ursula and Tom and your political career – all the important things in your life in one big happy package, if only you'd known Josh wasn't yours. I just wanted you to know that, for a fact. So it can keep you warm at night while you play at Mr Politician. Such a pity really.' She smiled and carried the tray from the room. Tim stared after her, the colour bleached from his face.

He sat alone in the dark for hours after Joanna had gone to bed. Separate beds, as always. He couldn't bear the thought of touching her after he had first gone to find Ursula. And that had never changed. He had only ever wanted Ursula. Right from the very first moment he had met her. And now that was over. Finished.

He picked up the phone beside his chair and looked at it, wondering if he dared call. But Ursula had said it was over, enough, never call again. Slowly he replaced the receiver and closed his eyes, trying to picture Ursula, walking towards him through the paddock. Or out of the surf as she had that last time together. But he couldn't. The image was blurred, distorted by time and distance and, maybe, loving her too much. He could always remember insignificant people, acquaintances, friends, but not the people he loved. And now Ursula's face wouldn't come to him at all. Nothing Joanna could say to him hurt as much as that. And that made him weep at last.

Ursula read the news about the deputy leadership in silence, occasionally shaking the paper to straighten it so she could see the picture more clearly. Tim stared back at her, a smiling Joanna by his side as they waved to their supporters. The picture blurred for a moment while Ursula blinked to clear her eyes of the annoying tears that slid past her lashes, no matter how hard she tried to suppress them. She dropped the paper and stood up, walking angrily over to stand and stare out at the back orchards. 'Damn him! Oh God, damn him!' She wiped her face with quick, firm movements and then returned to pick

463

up the paper again, examining the picture once more.

Tim looked good. There was no doubt about that. He wasn't pining away for her at all. He stood tall and erect and hand-some beside his wife, that generous mouth open in a surprised smile that had to be fake, she thought bitterly. He had known he would get the deputy leadership. And those honest, here-I-am-your-buddy eyes shining with sincerity as he told everyone how much good he was going to do for them. Ursula hit the paper with the flat of her hand, staring up into the verandah rafters to blink back any more tears. Then she looked at Joanna. Damn that woman! Joanna looked equally good. She was only just past thirty and her newly slim figure told of a serious diet in the last couple of months. Blonde hair was arranged in a becoming halo around an expertly made-up face that knew how to smile into the camera's eye. And her arm was linked through Tim's.

'Handsome couple, aren't they?' Kim said disparagingly from over Ursula's shoulder. Ursula jumped. She hadn't heard Kim's approach.

'Yes,' Ursula tried to laugh. 'Aren't they? Tim's been made deputy leader. Isn't that great?' But she couldn't look at Kim and stood up immediately, her back very straight. 'Oh, I didn't realize the time. I better go get the children.' And then she had to hurry into the house, leaving the paper flapping idly in the wind.

'Yeah, really great,' Kim said and threw the paper out.

In June Rhea came to stay with Ursula for a few days. She said she was tired of Perth and tired of the gossiping social scene. Ursula thought Rhea looked tired altogether. It was nearly her seventh month and she looked too slight to be carrying such a weight. Her normally clear skin and shining hair seemed muddied and she walked as though she barely had the strength to stand up. Ursula tucked her up by the fireplace with a blanket around her to stop the chill dampness seeping into her bones. It was raining, of course.

The rain started in April and ended around August. It was not like the Wet in Singapore but still a steady, drenching downpour that filled the creeks and the lagoon so that it spread out over the low-lying land like molten silver, turning the dust

464

to mud and the trees a slick black. It was cold too. Australian houses were built to keep cool in the summer, not to keep warm in the winter. Ursula had been thinking of installing a proper heating system now that she had money to spare. But it had turned cold before she had made a decision and now, this week, the winds were blowing in a frost at night. That was unusually early for the time of year and she had a feeling they were in for a bad winter.

'Tea, darling? I'm just about to make a pot.' Rhea nodded. She had become silent over the last few months, almost as though she were too tired to speak. Her thoughts were too painful and complicated to explain and she didn't have the energy to attempt it. So she nodded, or shrugged, or didn't react at all. Charles was worried. It was his idea, as much as hers, that Rhea come up and stay with her mother for a while. Maybe the country air would perk her up a little. He had teased her that she was always a rural at heart, despite her decision to live in Perth. And Rhea had turned large, pale eyes on him that were filled with such pain that Charles had been startled – and devastated. How could his wife be so sad? And why?

Ursula carried the tray in and set it down beside the fireplace on a low stool. Rhea didn't even look when Ursula put the cup on the table beside her. She just continued to stare into the flames, blinking from time to time, her face quite expressionless.

'I made your favourite biscuits, darling. Almond slices. Will you try one for me?' Ursula held out the plate and Rhea seemed to stir herself, making an effort to come back from wherever she had been. She smiled and took one of the slices, biting a tiny piece off and chewing for a long time. Finally, with a convulsive motion of her throat she managed to swallow it. Ursula looked at how thin her daughter had become, her arms nothing more than two delicate bones covered by skin.

'This can't go on, Rhea. You have to think of the baby even if you won't think about yourself. Look at you! Skin and bone! Please, Rhea, tell me what's wrong!' But Rhea just shook her head and stared at the fire.

'Is it Will? Do you still miss him so much? I . . . do know what you're going through, darling. I miss Tim more than

465

ever. But you just have to cope with that. There are other things in your life than just the man you love.' There was a long silence to the point where Ursula wondered whether Rhea had heard her, or if she had, whether she intended to answer.

'Yes. I'll always miss him. He was right, you know. He said I'd get sick of Perth and all its social snobberies. He said it wasn't such a great place and that I wasn't really suited to it. And you know,' she turned and looked at her mother with such a strange expression on her face that Ursula was chilled. 'You know, he was right all along. Isn't that a laugh? I thought I knew so much more than him. That I was the sophisticated, educated miss know-all and that he was just a country hick. God, how could I have been so wrong? And there's nothing I can do about it. I can't reverse things, can't change anything anymore. I thought maybe I could before I knew about the baby. But I can't now, can I? He won't leave his wife – I hear she had a son a couple of months ago – and I can't leave Charles. I'm stuck!'

Once she started talking she didn't seem able to stop. Ursula felt herself wither inside at the words and the pain behind them. She would have done anything to take that pain away but she couldn't. It had to be endured.

'Does Will know how you feel? You've seen him since your wedding, haven't you?' There was another long silence.

'Yes. Yes I've seen him twice and . . . and we've talked. I had to see him in secret because Charles doesn't like him and Will's wife goes berserk when she hears my name. Sneaking about behind people's backs, without their permission. Permission! Who the hell are they to tell me I can't see Will. He's mine! And I'm his!'

'We, went away together one weekend. I told Charles I was coming up here and didn't want to talk to him for a few days. I was close to leaving him then, and he knew it, so he said all right. And Will . . . I don't know how he got away. I didn't ask. I didn't care. We just had to have some time together. We went down to Mandurah, stayed in a cottage belonging to someone he knows. Oh Mother! If you only knew how much I love him . . . I thought perhaps he would say he'd leave his wife. I knew even then she was pregnant but I just hoped I could win him back.' She broke off, her voice dropping back to a whisper. 'But he doesn't know about my baby and until now I couldn't bear him to. It just seemed too awful, too . . . embarrassing, for him to think . . . He's bound to think that, isn't he? I mean, Oh God! Why did I say I was leaving the property that time to go see Jennie? None of this would've happened. I'd be married to him by now and we'd be so happy about . . . I wrote to him. I asked him to come here. You don't mind, do you? I had to see him and Charles would have a fit if he knew. It's only going to be a short visit.'

'He's coming here, now? Today?'

'Yes. He should be here by evening, he said. I'm sorry, Mother. I should've asked you first but I just couldn't until I'd explained things. And I couldn't do that over the phone. You see?'

Ursula sighed and looked at her daughter, wondering whether there was something genetic in this wilful mismanaging of their lives. She nodded.

'Yes, I see. It's all right, Rhea. I'll stand by you no matter what you decide to do. I don't want to see Charles hurt – he's too good to deserve that. But I do understand what you're going through. Who better?' She laughed without amusement. 'And I'll always be there for you, no matter what. You always helped me to get through the rough bits. And I'll always help you. Don't worry, sweetheart. Things have a way of working out for the best.'

'You really believe that? You really think everything that's happened to you in the past was for the best? Your father and family being killed, your tutor – Billy? – was that for the best? And Tim, getting married like that after he'd begged you to come to Australia and now him just ditching you and Tom for all that fame and glory. You wouldn't say that's for the best, would you?' She was silent for a few minutes, waiting for her mother to reply. When she didn't, Rhea continued, her voice rising again. 'And Daddy? That must have been for the best, of course!' Rhea had wrapped her arms around herself, around the belly that protruded beneath her breasts so that she almost had to lean flat to drink her tea.

'I wouldn't have had you if I hadn't married your father. I wouldn't have met Tim if I hadn't lived in the wilds of Essex like that and he is very special to me, no matter what you might think. And Tom is the product of that meeting and I'd never regret that. You'll see, darling. Time goes on no matter what you do and things that seemed so impossible at one time become easier to bear. You'll see.' She closed her eyes, hoping Rhea wouldn't notice the lies buried in her half-truths. Tim, who hadn't called even once after she told him she wouldn't wait. He probably never would again. Simon who had tried to blackmail them. And the pain that was still there for Billy and her family. No, that hadn't been for the best and it never got any easier. No, it wasn't for the best.

'But I don't want to see! I can't live with Charles for the rest of my life in that fishbowl, waiting for someone to mention that Will's had another son or that he's bought another company. You know he's doing all that now with his father-in-law? Quite the entrepreneur all of a sudden is our rustic Will. And she's got it all – him, and his baby, and his new desire to make it big and make a name for himself in WA. He wouldn't do it for me. But for someone who doesn't care, who's happy to be a bush-bunny for the rest of her life, he'll do it. It's not fair! I just have to sit back and be the perfect, young Mrs Peel with her family name to live up to and her perfectly charming husband whom everyone loves so much! And it's too late to do anything about it but I can't go on with this stupid lie. It's not worth it! I want to come home, Mother. I want to come back to live with you here.' Ursula recognized the cry of both a child who can't have what she wants and a woman who knows she will never have it and is in despair.

Rhea was working herself into hysterics and Ursula helped her up, out of her chair, and led her through to her bedroom. It would be better if she slept for a while, Ursula thought. She hushed her daughter's wild cries, trying hard not to cry herself, and tucked the blankets in around her. She was glad Tom wasn't here to see this. He wouldn't understand. At least with him at school things seemed more manageable; and she didn't see Tim's face in his every time he turned around. She left Rhea sleeping and went back into the kitchen, wondering whether it would be best if Rhea came back home to live. The two of them living here together again, sharing everything to do with the new baby and with Tom home on holidays. It was a wonderful thought. Or was she just being selfish, wanting

Rhea to fill the empty place Tim had left in her life? The thought nagged at her and she looked impatiently at her watch. When was Will coming.

It was the flat bang of the screen-door that first told Ursula she wasn't alone. She called through to the sitting room:

'Will? Will is that you?' But there was no answer. Ursula wiped her hands on a tea-towel, closed the oven door on her last batch of almond slices, and walked through into the other room.

Simon was standing by the window, looking out at the rain. He was wet and looked much older than his years; older and a little seedier. His moustache wasn't as neatly clipped as before, his hair was longer and plastered wetly to his skull, his cheek-bones were more prominent, the hollows under them shadowed unhealthily in a pale face. He turned when Ursula came in, the late afternoon sun, obscured behind dark clouds, casting a faint shadow on the boards. Ursula froze.

'Well, if it isn't my beautiful and loving wife come to greet me. Hallo, Ursula, it's been quite a while, hasn't it?' He walked forward with the same easy grace that he had always had, a little arrogance in the tilt to the head, a lot of anger in the pale eyes. Ursula felt like someone had opened the darkest hole inside her and let out all her fears and dreads at once. She felt engulfed. He stood in front of her and smiled. She could smell the whisky on his breath.

'My, you must be doing quite well for yourself, my dear. This is a nice slice of land to own, isn't it? And such good fortune about your mining shares. It was so thoughtful to let Lettice know how rich we are now. If I hadn't seen your letter on her desk I might never have known. Oh, and how's our daughter Rhea? She must be quite a young lady now? Is she here? And your bastard son? Now, I'd really like to see him.' He looked around and Ursula felt a strong desire to run to Rhea's bedroom and bar the door. Instead she smiled back.

'No, they're not. But it's kind of you to ask about them after all this time. Tom's away at school and Rhea's happily married to a very nice young man and she doesn't ever want to see you again. Nor do I. Get out!'

Simon laughed. 'No, I don't think so. I've decided I'm

469

rather partial to Australia after all. And as we're still married, I'd say I'm a wealthy man now, wouldn't you?' He lifted a hand to stroke her cheek. Ursula flinched.

'Oh no you don't, Simon! I'm not just some little nobody here, waiting on your whims. I've made a place for myself here. I'm well-known, respected, and I have very powerful friends. You're not going to get away with this, any more than you got away with that blackmailing stunt some time back. So why don't you just go back to your flash friends in England and beg them not to put you in jail for debt? Or maybe Julia can help you? After all, you serviced her long enough, didn't you? But then, I heard she'd decided to find herself another stud who's a little younger and less of a social embarrassment?'

She didn't see his hand raised against her, only the sudden whiteness of his eyes and the tight, pursed-in mouth under his moustache. Then the blow hit her, knocking her down against the doorway. He hit her again and then she managed to stand up and run for the back door. If she could call for help, call for the Winbys, for Stoney. She'd never seen such rage before. Oh God! He caught her on the verandah, swinging her around viciously and clawing his fingers around her throat.

'You-are-my-wife!' He shook her with each word. 'Do-you-understand?' Ursula felt a pounding in her temples and a searing, rushing noise in her ears. She clawed at his face but nothing seemed to happen. Her vision began to fade into a tunnel of sparking light surrounded by black and red, her hands frantically pulling at his fingers, hitting his chest. Then, suddenly, she was free and left to drop to the floor, dusty and hard beneath her knees. She bent double, choking for breath, her head feeling as though it were swollen, her body wracked with shakes. Somewhere around her she could hear moaning and shuffling, and then a cry. She looked up just as Simon, bleeding heavily from a cut on his head, knocked Rhea away from where she was clinging to his arm. Rhea hovered, almost regaining her balance, and then fell heavily down the verandah stairs onto the ground. She didn't move.

'Rhea!' Ursula screamed, the same high-pitched scream of terror and fear that she had once screamed for Billy. Simon slipped to one knee, trying to clear the blood from his eyes, clutching the wound. Then he rolled over and lay still. Ursula

470

ignored him. She pulled herself up by the verandah railing and made her way, as quickly as she could manage with her still blurred vision and weak legs, down to Rhea. It wasn't a very long drop. No more than five feet. She would be all right. She'd often fallen down the stairs as a child and cried about a grazed knee or cut head. But she wasn't a child anymore. And for a heavily pregnant woman it could be fatal.

'Rhea? Rhea, darling? Can you hear me?' She gently brushed the hair back from Rhea's face, terrified to move her. Rhea's eyes were shut, pale lashes on an even paler face. The rain fell steadily onto her upturned face. And then Ursula saw the blood coming through her skirt.

'Oh God, no! Please God.' She climbed to her feet, clumsy and old suddenly, and ran for the Winbys, her breath pumping out in short gasps of terror.

'Mr Winby! Mr Winby! Come quickly. Call the doctor. Mr Winby!' The Winbys were startled by her call and slow to react. She told them again, and again, to come with her, to call the doctor, while they stood gaping at her swollen and bruised throat and her mud-spattered clothes.

Finally Mrs Winby seemed to understand and pushed her husband at Ursula, telling him to go help. She returned inside to try and raise the nearest doctor. He lived in Gidgeeeganup but he might be anywhere for a hundred miles around or so. She would do her best. Ursula pulled Mr Winby back along towards the house and when he saw Rhea lying in the mud he began to run, a shuffling sideways movement that covered the ground more quickly than Ursula would have imagined.

He picked Rhea up and carried her up and into the house, laying her on the bed gently. She was still unconscious but groaning. Ursula hurried to the bathroom and picked up a couple of towels. Rhea was haemorrhaging badly now; the blood a dark, clotted red against the white of the bedspread. Ursula tried to stop it with the towels and by raising Rhea's legs but she didn't know what else to do. Where did you tie a tourniquet? And what about the baby? Would it still live? She paced back and forth beside the bed, stopping to feel Rhea's pulse and notice the waxy whiteness of her face. Oh God, why didn't the doctor come?

It was nearly dark outside now and the rain was still falling

471

heavily. Kim and Stoney had joined Mr Winby in the sitting room, each pacing awkwardly or sitting tense on the edge of their chairs. Ursula remembered with a start that Simon had been lying on the verandah with a cut on his head. Had Rhea done that? She hurried out to the back verandah to see how Simon was. He was gone. A shovel that she had been using in the garden and had leaned up against the back door was now lying on the verandah near the stairs, its blade covered in blood. But Simon couldn't be dead or anywhere near it. She looked around briefly before going back to Rhea.

'Mother? Mother?' Rhea's eyes were open and terrified. She clutched at her mother's hand.

'I'm here, darling. It's all right. We're getting the doctor for you. Just lie back and be quiet.'

'Mother? Is Will here yet? I want you to tell him. He doesn't know. No-one knows but me. You'll tell him for me won't you? He should know.'

'Tell him what, darling? He's going to see you're pregnant. I don't have to tell him that. And he'll be here very soon. Don't you worry, darling. Everything's going to be fine.'

'No, no! He doesn't know! You've got to tell him. Don't let Daddy know. I don't want, I don't . . . ' Rhea's voice trailed off and she shut her eyes again. Ursula sat beside her holding her hand.

Mrs Winby arrived a few minutes later with the news that the doctor was unavailable. He was out on another call and they didn't know when they could reach him. Ursula cursed and sopped up more blood with the towel.

'We'll have to drive her down to Perth then. Mr Winby, you get the Holden ready. Put blank . . . ' A loud groan from Rhea told Ursula the worst. The baby was coming. They couldn't move her now.

'Never mind the car. Mrs Winby, get on the radio and try and raise a hospital in Perth or anyone who might be able to help. We've got to stop this bleeding.' She broke off as the front door slammed. There was a commotion from out in the sitting room, voices raised in fear and anger. And then the door opened.

'What the hell's goin' on here? Mum? Why . . . Rhea! Jesus Christ!' Will walked in on the group gathered around the blood-stained bed. They started as though caught at some guilty act. Then Ursula said.

'Will! Thank God you're here. Rhea fell down the stairs and she's haemorrhaging. The doctor's out on a call. And now the baby's coming! What do we do?'

'Baby! What baby? Rhea's pregnant?' Will seemed as dazed as his parents. Ursula wanted to hit him. After a few moments of staring at the pale girl, he said, 'What about the Clunys? Mrs Cluny was an RN. She'll know what to do. Mum? You call her. Tell her if she can't get over here, I'll come get her. Ask her what to do in the meantime.' He moved further up the bed to stand beside Rhea. She opened her eyes when he took her hand in his and knelt against the bed. There was fear in both their faces but more than that, there was a deep understanding. Ursula felt she was intruding by just being there.

'I'll get some more towels. Mr Winby, could you get some lemonade, or maybe hot tea. I think everyone could do with that.' Ursula pushed everyone out of the room, leaving Will and Rhea alone.

'Aw Jesus, Rhea. Why didn't you tell me? I'd've, oh God, I dunno. Just hang on now love. We'll get you fixed up.' He lay his cheek against hers. She sobbed in dry jerks. And then she screamed. He held her hands tightly through the second set of contractions, helping her with her breathing, trying to remain calm. When it was over, she lay limply looking at him.

'I couldn't. I didn't want you thinking it was Charles's.'

'It's mine?' For a moment, he looked distrait. It was his fault she was in pain like this. But Rhea smiled up at him, her love easing some of that fear.

'Yes. That very first time – up by the bore-head. Oh God, I love you, Will. I wish we were married and, and . . . ' She ended in another convulsive gasp, her mouth opening to cry out at the pain tearing her in two.

'Hang on to me, Rhea. Just dig your nails in if it helps. We'll find Mrs Cluny for you, don't worry and she'll know what to do. Shhh, sweetheart, it'll be all right.' Will mumbled anything he could think of to soothe the girl who screamed and writhed on the bed in front of him. He wiped her hair away from her forehead, the sweat soaking her hair and clothes. Rhea relaxed and lay limply exhausted, her cheek against his hand.

The door opened and Will's mother entered.

'Will, Mrs Cluny says she'll come but you'll have to go get her in the landrover. The roads are just about under water and her car won't make it. Dad'll go with you in case you get stuck in mud somewhere. I'm still trying to get hold of someone in Perth,' she said. Ursula entered behind her and went to wipe Rhea's face with a wet flannel. Will hesitated, unsure whether to leave Rhea or not but she smiled up at him, urging him to go with her eyes. He leant down and kissed her mouth.

'I'll be back in about half an hour. Don't worry, Rhea. I won't let anything happen to you.' And then he was gone, his footsteps retreating at almost a run.

'Try and drink this, Rhea, will you? You must take a lot of liquids to replace the blood you're losing, Mrs Cluny says. That's it, good girl.' Ursula raised Rhea's head and trickled some lemonade down her lips. Rhea made a feeble effort to swallow, most of the liquid soaking the pillow instead. Ursula mopped it with a towel and sat beside her daughter, holding her hand tightly and stroking her hair.

'I hope it's a daughter, don't you, Rhea? It'd be nice to have some more girls around here. If it's a girl, what would you like to name her?' She sought to distract Rhea's thoughts, to dampen the fear she saw etched in the face below her.

'I don't . . . know, really. Maybe,' Rhea paused, trying to sort out her muddled mind. 'Maybe, Candida? I've always liked that . . . uuh!' But her words ended in a grunt of pain that became rapidly more highpitched as the contractions came again. Ursula held her hand tightly, looking at the clock, wishing Will would arrive.

As the minutes ticked away, it seemed as though Rhea's life force was ebbing with them. Her face grew white, her lips waxy and her eyes sinking into her head. The convulsions barely moved her, just shuddering the pain through her body without moving the child any further towards birth. And the blood spread out around her body like fire on snow.

Finally Ursula knew there was no hope. Rhea was looking at her, the eyes barely focused but still staring up as though sure her mother could help, even now. And then there was nothing in those eyes and her hand slid from Ursula's onto the counter-pane.

'Rhea? Rhea darling? Please . . . please . . . ' But Ursula knew she was dead. She bowed her head over her daughter, her mind quite blank. From somewhere she could hear a commotion, feel people pushing her back from the bed but she wasn't sure who. She felt arms around her, leading her out of the room and somewhere, quite close by, she heard Will's cry of grief as he found Rhea.

'There's still a chance for the baby,' Mrs Winby was saying and Ursula looked at her, shocked to see the tears streaking down the old woman's face. And she was old. Aged by years in the space of an hour. Ursula nodded.

'Yes, try and save the baby.' But she didn't care that much. It was only Rhea that had mattered. And Rhea was dead.

Perth, July 1966

They christened the baby girl Candida Margaret Peel at St Luke's in Mosman Park. Jennie was one godmother, Tim the godfather. Charles still seemed almost unaware he had a daughter. He went through the motions, said the appropriate words, but he was still grieving for his wife of little more than a year. Ursula felt as though part of her had died too and if it hadn't been for the tiny, defenceless baby she had taken from her daughter, she almost felt she could have followed Rhea into the grave they had dug for her on the property. Rhea had always said she would hate to be buried at Karakatta Cemetery with rows and rows of endless slabs. So now she was buried on a small mound overlooking the lagoon. Ursula had promised her she would be buried there too, to keep her company.

Will hadn't come to the funeral or to the christening. Ursula felt his agony as keenly as her own. There was nothing she could do to lessen it. She knew that through bitter experience. Only time would heal the wound. Such a hackneyed expression that made the sufferer want to lash out that anyone could be so insensitive as to use it. But, as with most hackneyed phrases, it was true. Mostly, it was true.

Tim came, first and foremost for the funeral, for Rhea. He looked grey with sorrow and pain, made all the worse for the reporters who hovered around the outer edge of the property and tried to take photographs of his grief. He had been unable

475

to do more than hold her hand to support her through the ceremony.

Ursula took the baby home to the Peel's house with her and Charles and Will stayed alone with their ghosts.

Tim followed Ursula back to the house, intending to try and mend the rift between them. The Peels smiled politely, uneasily, and closed the door behind them, leaving them alone. But before Tim could find the words he had been searching for all day, Ursula told him, instead, that she intended to return to Singapore. It struck Tim as a bizarre thing to be doing, anger rising in his gut with a fierce conviction that she shouldn't go. She mustn't! It was all wrong. He hated the idea. He couldn't remember the last time he had felt so strongly opposed to anything. She wouldn't listen.

'It'll be all right, I promise you, Tim. I just have to get away for a while. You know,' she half-smiled and turned away, 'go and "find myself"'. It's quite the fashionable thing to be doing nowadays. Besides, you know you really should be relieved. It's not a good time for you right now even being here. Why did you come, anyway?' There was a coldness, a deadness to the voice that belied her composure. She had been polite and kind and dignfied to everyone who had turned up at the funeral, accepting their condolences, murmuring her thanks. Tim thought she looked half-dead herself.

He ignored her question. 'But why Singapore? Why now, after Rhea's death? What're you gonna do – wallow in your grief? Everyone who's ever died in your life all mixed up in one big . . . ' He stopped, exasperated at not finding the words. 'I want to be with you through this, you know that, and you just keep shutting me out. Okay, yes, it's a problem with those bloody reporters. But, you're supposed to be a family friend and you're going through hell right now over Rhea. It's natural I should be with you. Please, don't turn away, Ursula. I want to help. Jesus!' He couldn't believe she could be so hard or so withdrawn. She was looking at him now with cold eyes and he wanted to pull her into his arms and hold her tightly and never let her go, never let anything or anyone hurt her again. He knew she wouldn't let him. She wouldn't even believe him.

'Help? What's that? Something you dispense with a smile

and brief shake of the head to flashing bulbs and cries of ''oh, isn't he wonderful?'' How can you help? Rhea's dead.' She wrapped her arms around herself as though that would warm her heart. Tim's pale face became white. 'When I needed you before Tim, you weren't there for me. Your career came first, as always. So why should I expect you here now?' She wondered how it was he could still look so hurt, so sincere, when she knew he didn't care at all. He was tired of it all, of everything that had been between them and had simply turned up at the funeral and christening out of a sense of duty. And so the Peels wouldn't be offended. They would think it odd otherwise, for him not to turn up when he was such a friend of the family. He certainly wasn't there for her. But even as she thought it, a part of her knew it wasn't true. He did care. Just not enough. 'I'm surprised you didn't bring Joanna while you were at it. Now that would've looked good in the newspapers. ''Loving, Caring Politician and Wife Hold Hands of Little Nobody While She Grieves Over Dead Daughter.'' Or maybe you thought it'd look good enough if you were here on your own and perhaps Joanna wouldn't have wanted to come, all things considered.' Her voice was harsh, lashing at Tim. 'Well your son, remember him? Tom? He needs a little help too right now. Maybe the reporters can catch you patting him on the head instead?'

'Ursula! For God's sake! Don't do this to yourself.' Tim took hold of her arms and shook them, his eyes searching hers for some sort of recognition. 'Please, darling. This is me. I loved Rhea just like I still love you and Tom. I'm not here for any other reason than that. Don't you see what you're doing to yourself with all this bitterness?' He knew she wasn't listening when she said harshly.

'Then why don't you go tell that reporter, who's been hovering outside the door for hours, exactly that. Or is that too much to ask?' He closed his eyes. Oh God, what he wouldn't give to do just that. Say to all the world, 'I don't care anymore about anything except this woman here, and this boy, my son.' But he couldn't.

'Ursula be reasonable. I can't right now. The elections are nearly here. Think what a scandal it would cause. A lot of people are depending on me right now. I can't let them down.

Please, just believe I love you and be patient a little longer.'

'Enough, Tim. Enough.' Ursula held up her hand. 'I've heard it all before and I really don't care one way or the other anymore. I've lost Rhea. That's all that matters. Now please go away.' And with that, she walked out of the room. And out of his life for good this time, Tim thought, his face losing its composure, all the pain there on view now that there was no-one to see. He looked around in a daze, stumbling for a moment against a chair. And then he breathed in deeply and became nothing more than a grim-faced man who had braced himself to deal with life accordingly. He said his farewells to the Peels and opened the front door to face the reporters outside.

It was the crying of the baby that finally penetrated Ursula's thoughts. She glanced at her watch. Nearly an hour. He'd been gone nearly an hour. She walked quickly into the next room and leaned over the crib. The baby continued to scream, dark hair plastered wetly across its skull. She picked it up and cradled it in her arms, pacing gently back and forth over the wooden boards, over bars of gold turning paler as the sun lost its strength, bleaching to grey.

Chapter Thirty

Ursula returned to the property with Didee in her carry-cot between Tom and herself. The car bounced awkwardly over the unsealed road and she winced when she hit a pothole. Tim had told her to get a new car, a four-wheel drive, but she didn't care about cars; they were just a means of getting from A to B. Why did she need a new one? Far better to macadamize the road. She was rich now; she could do what she wanted. She talked to Tom about her plans for the homestead, about how she was going to turn it into a real house with full central heating and ceiling fans and, maybe, just maybe a pool outside by the back pump. Now wouldn't that be nice? Tom obligingly said 'Great!' and 'Wow!' but didn't elaborate. He was missing Rhea too.

She looked at his face, set and determined, the way Tim's looked when he was in pain but wouldn't show it. There were still dark smudges under his eyes and he seemed to have lost his tan. Even his hair looked darker, as though the light had been dimmed inside. She stroked his head. She and Didee would have to make up for everything else.

Ursula drew up by the verandah and waved to Mrs Winby. She was hanging out the washing on the rotary hoist, twirling it expertly past as the next sheet was hung out. She put down the washing and came to open Tom's door, gathering him into her arms with a cry.

'Oh! I didn't think you'd be back for another day or two,

Mrs Paterson. Hallo Tom, my boy. Have you missed me?' She planted a smacking kiss on his cheek and laughed when he squirmed free. He ran off towards Kim and Stoney's house to see Percy. Mrs Winby then helped Ursula carry Didee and her luggage up to the house.

'You've been such a short time. Is anything wrong? I thought the christening would take a little while and that you'd probably stay on with the Peels for a few days after that.' The older woman was puffing under the weight of Didee's carry-cot. Ursula forced a smile.

'No. Nothing's wrong. I just thought I'd take a trip and get away for a while. Go back home – to Singapore. Tom's going to go and stay with a schoolfriend, Neil, at Mandurah while I'm away. At least until the school holidays are over, then he can go back to school with Neil. And the Peels will look after Didee.' She took the carry-cot from Mrs Winby and lifted Didee out. 'Isn't that right, sweetheart?' She held the baby against her cheek. Didee yawned.

'Oh well, so much for the greeting.' Ursula shrugged and Mrs Winby thought how dreadfully pale Ursula looked. All grey and shadowed the way she'd been since Rhea's death. It was tragic really the way life had been so hard on the poor woman. Then she remembered her own news.

'Will came by two days ago. To see his dad and me. He said he wanted to make up, to say he was sorry. I thought Dad was going to bust a gut trying not to show how much he cared.' Mrs Winby smiled, her own relief showing in the brightened eyes, the tautened skin. Ursula opened her mouth in surprise.

'Well thank God for that. How did he look? Is he getting over things?'

'Not Rhea. But he wants to see Didee now. That's a break-through. Said he's thinking of claiming her as his own but I told him that'd have to wait until he'd talked things through with you. I think that'd be the last straw for poor young Mr Peel. He's not coping at all well.'

'No, no, he's not. Oh, why does everything have to be so complicated all the time? Well, never mind, let's go have some tea shall we, Mrs Winby. Here, you hold Didee while I get the last suitcase in. Is Kim around?' Ursula sent Mrs Winby ahead of herself and looked around for Tom. She could see him in the corner near the chicken run, bent over something with Percy.

'Boys! Tea and biscuits if you get yourselves washed up in the next two minutes,' she shouted and wasn't particularly surprised when they waved and continued to peer down at the ground. She climbed the steps and went into the house.

There was a pile of mail waiting for her on the table near the front door. Mostly bills, a letter from Lettice that made Ursula wonder immediately if it were news about Hugh, a few more condolence notes that had taken time to arrive from far-off stations where Rhea's old schoolfriends now lived, and a scruffy looking letter with a stain on the outside. Nothing else.

She put off reading the mail until she had fed Didee and put her down for a nap. Mrs Winby had the tea ready by then and Ursula supervised the boys, both of whom were sharing a mysterious joke between them that meant they had to keep bursting out into loud laughter at strategic moments during tea. Ursula smiled and said nothing, glad to see the pinched look retreating from Tom's face and Percy's normal mischievous expression back in place. They were good for each other right now, she thought as she kissed them both and sent them off to play again. Mrs Winby sat back over her own tea and Ursula fished in her pocket for the letters.

The news from Lettice wasn't good. Hugh wouldn't last more than a few more weeks. Lettice hoped the end would come soon. It had been dragging out for so long now that Ursula almost couldn't feel anything except sadness. She knew Lettice must be feeling the same. She sighed, mentally resolving to write to Lettice tonight.

Finally she opened the soiled letter, wondering why its handwriting looked familiar. With a sudden jolt, she realized it was from Simon.

'Dearest wife,

Such a welcome you and my dear daughter laid on for me last time. I shall carry the scar from that meeting for the rest of my life. Perhaps it's easier all round, knowing our temperaments, if we communicate in future in writing. That way no-one will come to harm and you may, in fact, be glad to be rid of me so cheaply. For a mere fraction of what I am entitled to as your husband I am more than willing to divorce you and let us both

481

go our separate ways. As you said so forcefully before, neither you nor Rhea wish me to return to your lives and I feel it could be an embarrassment to have a long-dead husband suddenly revive so heartily. So, let's be frank. You give me just a mere quarter of what you made on the shares and I will sign all appropriate documents to free you for life. The money will just be enough to set me up in a new life somewhere far away from here and far away from you. Isn't that fair? Do write soon to the post box above and let me know what you think. Your even more disillusioned ex, S.'

Ursula looked at the letter in disbelief. He didn't know. He really had no idea about Rhea. She breathed in deeply, a heavy pain in her chest becoming tighter each time she drew breath. Then she turned and looked at Mrs Winby.

'I need Will. Can you get him for me?'

They met in the solicitor's office. At first, when Will suggested she pay Simon off, Ursula had been furious. But he had explained patiently that she would never be rid of Simon in any other way. This would be a legal contract, binding both parties. Simon would get his money; Ursula would get a divorce. There would be no more Simon in her life with the power to cause her harm, Will had said, and she had agreed.

Will hadn't wanted her to see Simon face-to-face. She had insisted. He had done all the preliminary contact by telephone, meeting Simon only once to ensure that they understood everything before they went to the lawyer. Will hadn't told her how that meeting had gone. But he had returned looking satisfied, even a little smug, as she had pointed out. He had smiled and told her not to worry.

But when Simon walked in, arrogant and a little dishevelled, his eyes pink-veined from too much drink, and his suit flashily off-the-peg, Ursula felt herself recoil in anger and fear. She looked away.

'Ah! Ursula, my dearest, looking perfect as always. Perfect for the occasion: the afternoon tea; the cocktail party; the prize-giving; the divorce! So kind of you to come.' He leaned over her, his breath smelling of spirits. Will caught his arm.

'Sit down, Mr Patterson. We are here to do business, not trade insults. I hope you remember what I told you before?'

Simon looked up at Will, his forehead creasing with anger. Then he sat down.

The solicitor looked uneasy, one leg crossed over the other, behind his desk. He passed across the papers to be signed.

'If you would care to read the contract, Mrs Paterson, you will find it exactly as Mr Winby specified in his instructions. I have a copy here for you, Mr Patterson. That way we can get on a little faster and settle this matter to everyone's satisfaction.'

There were a few minutes of protracted silence.

'Thank you, Mr Bryce. I think everything is in order.' Ursula signed the paper and passed it back to the solicitor. It was not her normal solicitor, Mr Waters, of course. Mr Bryce then handed it to Simon.

'Mr Patterson?'

'Not so fast. Where's the money? I'm not signing anything until I have the money.'

Mr Bryce looked pained. 'I have it right here. Now, if you wouldn't mind adding your signature beneath your wife's, I will pass the money across and we can all be on our way.'

Simon hesitated, wondering whether he was doing the right thing. But that Winby bastard had made it clear that this was the only time he would be offered any money. After that . . . Simon felt a bead of perspiration break out along his hairline. An accident, the fellow had said. That bastard! But there was nothing he could prove. And something in that young man's eyes had scared him. He knew when a threat was being made seriously, and the man looked like he would enjoy doing it – personally. Anyway, how could he go to the police? Here, this man's threatened to kill me because I'm trying to blackmail my wife! He wondered what the relationship was between Ursula and this Winby fellow. Bit young for her, wasn't he? The thought made Simon sick. He looked angrily across at her. The bitch! Then he signed.

Ursula bowed her head in relief while Simon picked up the envelope from the desk, slit it open, and counted the money inside. The solicitor examined his fingernails. Only Will watched Simon, his face carefully without expression.

'Right. That's it then. Congratulations, Ursula, on your divorce, whenever it comes through. I hope it brings you . . . everything you deserve.' Simon's lips twitched into the pretence of a smile. 'Give my love to Rhea, won't you. Tell her your sexual preferences have matured into the gutter and that she had better take note.' His voice was light.

Ursula's head snapped up. Her eyes regarded Simon with almost pleasure. 'You still don't know, do you, Simon?' She ignored Will's hand on her arm as she stood up to confront her husband. 'You really don't know.' The solicitor walked quickly to the door. He didn't want to be involved in a scene.

'What don't I know?' Simon was laughing, thinking he had struck a nerve.

'You don't know Rhea's dead.' She saw Simon's mouth sag, the shock in his eyes. 'And you killed her. That's something for you to live with, isn't it? Maybe it'll keep you warm at night.' Simon flinched. His face took on a bleached, death-mask appearance. Ursula saw him withering inside and her voice rose. 'You knocked her down the verandah stairs and she haemorrhaged to death, Simon!' She came closer. 'You killed your own daughter and then you walked away. May you rot in hell! And when you did so, you ruined not just my life, but Will's too. So remember that, late at night, if you're thinking of causing more trouble. Because I had to convince Will that you weren't worth killing. But he still might one day.' Will pulled her past Simon, past the solicitor holding the door open, his face appalled. They walked out into the fresh, afternoon air.

Ursula still hadn't called or heard anything from Tim. She hadn't wanted to involve him with Simon; not after the way they had parted last time, with her lashing out with wild accusations and him looking so cold, indifferent. No, she couldn't have turned to him for help. And he probably wouldn't have wanted to get involved anyway. He had his beautiful young wife and his successful career. What could she possibly offer him? Only her love, and he didn't want that anymore.

She laid a hand on Will's arm as he drove.

'Thank you, Will. I know that must have been hell for you. But I didn't have anyone else to turn to.' He looked at her with that almost sheepish expression he had as a young boy: pleased at the praise but not knowing how to accept it gracefully. She smiled back.

*　　*　　*

484

It hadn't been hard to arrange the trip to Singapore. The Peels would look after Didee while she was gone. And it was only for a few weeks. Just to get away for a while. That was all. They would take care of everything for her, the way they were taking care of everything for Charles. Someone had to.

When she left the air-conditioned arrival lounge of Changi airport, it was nearly noon. She walked to the taxi, into a wall of heat that tipped forward over her, engulfing, smothering; the heat of the tropics, the East. But it wasn't that so much as the smell: that almost forgotten mix of decay and spices, warm air laden with frangipani and nutmeg dust, cumin, rotting vegetables, and swamp water. She breathed it in deeply, feeling her dress gently cling against sweat-drenched skin. This was what had once been home. It smelt alien to her now.

They had tried to make her stay at one of the newer hotels along Orchard Road. But she had insisted on Raffles. Perhaps it was getting a little run-down, perhaps it wasn't in the right part of town anymore. But this was a pilgrimage – her own *haj*. She would stay where she pleased.

Her room overlooked the central courtyard with its traveller palms and limpid, heat-soaked pool. No-one was out in the gardens. It was too hot in the midday sun. And too cool and comfortable in the shade under the fans of the verandahs. Ursula sat and stirred the ice in her drink.

It was her choice. She knew that. But all the frantic urge of the last week to get away, to get here, seemed to have evaporated in the torpor of heat. Did she really want to push it, to go out to the kampong? It had seemed so clear before, the desire to see Fatimah, to bury her head against those huge breasts and let her grief heal where it had before. But now she was frightened, putting off the act with idle movements: unpacking, washing, changing her clothes, and now, sitting with her drink under the deep eaves of the verandah, she felt close to panic. It was no good. She shouldn't have come. There were too many ghosts here. She pressed the thin, iced glass against her lips, resisting the urge to bite down, to snap it off cleanly between her teeth. If she didn't go today, she never would. She needn't see the bungalow – just go straight through the Polo Club to the kampong behind. She would go to see the living, not the dead.

Abruptly she put the glass down and walked out, passing

through green-shadowed walls like subterranean caverns into the glare of the forecourt. A taxi eased forward to snapped fingers and a broken, piercing whistle. Ursula pressed a coin into the waiting palm.

'Thomson Road,' she said nervously. 'Polo Club. Quick quick, *can la?*' The boy handed her into the car, admiring the way this mem held herself; her tall, slim body swaying gracefully, the khaki skirt and linen blouse fresh and crisp. He wondered at the tense expression on the mem's face. Then he closed the door and the taxi drove off.

It was strange sitting back against the seat, watching a familiar, yet unfamiliar city flash by. So many new buildings. So many strange sights. But it held her close, pricking at her memories with painful jabs.

She passed by Newton Circus and her stomach muscles tightened. Not long now. Not far. But the city continued with them out into remembered jungle, arrogantly asserting itself against creeping green. Ursula breathed deeply. Maybe the kampong was gone? Maybe rows of little houses with wrought-iron fences lined the creek, maybe the big house . . . But she refused to think any further, clamping down on the panic and frowning into the sun.

The taxi turned left suddenly, swinging Ursula across the seat. She gripped the door handle. There. It was still there. The padang of the Polo Club, the black and white chick blinds drawn down over the verandah of the club house, the stables. All there still, drowsing quietly in the heat. She smiled and then grimaced to hide her tears.

The taxi driver stopped in front of the club house, depositing his strange passenger with her strange expressions with little curiosity. He was a Sikh and not much interested in the Europeans and their doings. He wanted to go to sleep in the shade somewhere. It was too hot.

Ursula paid him and stood back while the taxi turned and bumped off down the cement drive. She should have asked him to wait perhaps. But it didn't matter. She could find another taxi later. She looked around the yard and across to the stables. Nothing stirred.

Beyond the covered ring, the grass track was rutted and baked hard, mud cracked into scales. Ursula walked over it, knowing by instinct as much as memory that the villagers would be sleeping in the cool of their huts, avoiding the bite of the sun as though it might suck their life force from them. She crossed the plank bridge and hesitated. There were new huts, the roofs covered in corrugated iron, to the left of the creek. But Ibrahim's hut was still there, pale blue in the sun.

A young boy answered her knock, stepping back in wide-mouthed surprise to whisper into the gloom. There was a shuffle, rustles of dried palm fronds, and another face appeared; an older, sterner face with dark, unsmiling eyes.

'Yes?'

Ursula hesitated again, feeling suddenly alien and very white, like a jug of milk among cups of coffee. It was a silly thought and, as it flashed through her mind, she smiled. The face smiled too, uncertain at first but with increasing conviction.

'Ooosalah?'

She nodded, trying to summon words from a locked throat.

'Yahyah? Is it you?'

A howl of welcome rose from within the darkened hut and a large, grizzled woman rolled forward, her fat arms outstretched in a crooning song. Ursula slid into Fatimah's arms.

It took time to tell the years that lay between them and Fatimah could barely believe Ursula was a grandmother now. She held her little missy against her, trying to ease some of the pain she could feel inside the woman now, grieving with her for a daughter that was never known. And Ursula listened as often as she spoke: to the marriage of Yahyah to Hamila, their old playmate; to the death of Ibrahim and the choice of Yahyah as the new Lembaga; to the trials and sorrows of his first-born's death; to the joys of the present. The boy who had answered the door sat chewing his finger in anticipation throughout the tales. He was Yahyah's youngest. Ursula handed him her mirrored compact and his face split apart in a cry of joy. She smiled and told Yahyah that his son was a terrible little monkey. He laughed and smiled his appreciation. She had not forgotten their ways. The child was safe from a jealous God. He dipped his head.

Eventually, Fatimah walked with Ursula back along the

path. In the quickening dusk, the shadows spiked out sharp edges and the clatter of evening stables carried clearly in the air. Fatimah smiled a hidden, sleepy smile.

'You have been up to the big house?'

Ursula shook her head. 'No, I couldn't. Not yet.'

'You know there are new owners? They will show you around.' Fatimah's voice smiled too.

'No. I didn't know. Who? No, it doesn't matter. I can't go up there.' She shied from the thought.

'Come.' Fatimah held out her hand. 'Come, I will take you, little one. It is right you should go back there. Send your ghosts away by looking in their faces. Come, hold Fatimah's hand.' How many times had she said that to Ursula, the child?

Ursula stood for a moment, her hand clenched by her side. But there was something about Fatimah's smile that warmed through the chill fright she still felt. Could she go up there and confront her ghosts? Could she remember it all and still remain whole? Slowly her hand unclenched and she placed it within Fatimah's grasp. They passed in silence by stalls that had once housed Bintang and Jambang, and Ursula remembered sobbing in the still air of noon, cursing with a grief stronger than any man's fury. They climbed, still in silence, up the hillside and stood together by the mound of rough grass.

Ursula stopped. There it was. The mound – Billy's grave. She swallowed stiffly, pain lodging like a hard pellet in her side. Fatimah released her hand.

'I will speak with the owner,' she said as she moved away, swaying across the lawn to the house. Ursula didn't hear or see her go. Her thoughts were pressed sharply against her forehead, fighting to get out, pulsing with half-remembered terror.

'Billy? Oh God, Billy! How could I have ever left you? Billy.' She shut her eyes, breathing in tautly through her nose the smell of fear and death. 'Why did you have to die? You and Rhea. Tell me that, God! Tell me why?' The last sound tore from her throat in a cry of wild grief that shook the birds from the trees in clouds of alarm. Tears streaked unnoticed down her face while she stood silently communing with her dead; with Billy, with Rhea. The minutes passed and she turned away, unable to bear the memories.

In the final shade of twilight, a figure detached itself from the porch and moved towards her. The owner, Ursula thought numbly. She must not cry. She must not. She breathed deeply and looked up again. He was tall and walked with an un-hurried stride that caught her attention. Somehow the house and its gardens were subtly different now; they were owned by people who knew nothing of her and what had happened here. The thought stilled her soul. The figure was silhouetted blackly against the house lights, a dark figure that, in her grief, reminded her of someone she had used to know. She stood still, unsure, waiting for him to reach her. For a moment . . . but no, it was a stranger who stopped in front of her, smiling politely.

'Ursula Fraser? Is it really you?' the man said and Ursula peered at him in the half-light, wondering who he reminded her of. He was tall with greying, curled hair, a thin, serious face.

'Yes, uh, I'm sorry . . . do I know you?' She saw him smile, a tentative, almost hurt smile and suddenly she recognized him. Stephen Hendricks, Sally's cousin. It was his older brother, Rodney, who had flicked twine against her legs at Sally's wedding, and then let her taste champagne on their last Christmas together. Rodney who had died beside her father, fighting for his home. 'Stephen! I'm sorry. I had no idea you were still here in Singapore.'

'Yes, 'fraid so. Almost didn't recognize you myself, now you're grown up. Fatimah told me you'd arrived. Come on up to the house and have a drink. I'd like you to meet my wife.' He grinned with relief that she had recognized him and he didn't have to go into complicated explanations. He had always been a little weak, she thought. Rodney had had all the fire; Stephen just had the ability to stay out of trouble. At least he had lived.

'Yes, all right. I'd like that.' She followed him into the house, stopping to stare at the new furnishings, the way the house had been transformed. Stephen's wife, a quiet middle-aged woman called Victoria, or Vicky for short as she told Ursula, led them into the study. She seemed tentative about what to say to someone who had once lived in the house.

'Would you like a gin and tonic, or perhaps just some lime juice?' Ursula turned away at the mention of lime juice.

'Uh, just . . . anything really, except lime juice if you don't mind. Can't take that anymore.' She smiled stiffly, and faltered, about to sit down where there was now no chair. Stephen led her gently over to an elephant chair in the corner, by the open window. The night sounds blew in with the warm air. She braced herself, looking about what had once been Papa's study. It looked quite different now. As different as the two men were. Stephen's room was sparsely furnished: dark Indonesian furniture against whitewashed walls, no curtains, a simple straw mat over the tiled floor. There were no hunting photographs on the walls or cricket or rugby or polo shots. No animal heads. Just bare walls.

He noticed her looking at them.

'We haven't lived here very long. And I didn't feel like doing very much. There were so many memories but the Japanese left nothing but a shell when they left. I had to have every wall replastered, repainted.'

'But, did you buy this house? For your family?' She studied the carving on the desk opposite her.

'Sort've. I thought it would be nice to live here. It's so crowded around Tanglin now and I wanted my family to have room to grow up in. Like you did.' He placed the glass down on the table beside her and turned to look out the window. 'But I didn't buy this place. I lease it from the government, through a new scheme they brought in very recently. Before that it stood unoccupied for years and years. Since the war.' He sipped his drink. There was a long moment of silence.

'How many children do you have, Stephen?' She felt totally out of place as though she were an imposter trying to fill the role of a member of the family. Even her questions were stilted.

'Two. One boy and one girl. They're both away at boarding school in England. What about you? You got married and had children?'

'Yes, I married. After I got home to England,' she said. 'And I had two children – my daughter just died. That's why I came here. To get away for a while. My son's in school down in Australia.'

She drank the wine, feeling it chill her inside.

'Ah, I see. I'm terribly sorry. Was it an accident of some sort?' He breathed in deeply, the sound like a long sigh.

'She died in childbirth out on the property. You know, the one Sally's parents used to own. I inherited it and live there now. Rhea fell down some stairs and died before the doctor could get to her.'

'How dreadful. But that's what it's like in Australia once you get outside the cities. And your husband?'

'Um, he died years ago.' She didn't want to go into all this, to pretend grief over Simon and try and hide her real grief over Rhea. She took a sip of her drink instead. Stephen looked embarrassed and his wife smiled broadly as though that might make up for everything.

'Well, I am glad you had someone to look after you when you first left here. I checked once, some months after you had returned to England. They told me you had married.' He smiled. 'I wanted to be sure you were happy in England, you see. And we had so little after the War. We wouldn't have known what to offer you out here anyway.' He didn't look at her but went and sat himself at his desk. Ursula felt some of the pain inside her subside. She was glad she had come back, if only to know there was no going back. This wasn't her life anymore. No-one here was family, not in the sense she knew it back in Australia.

She finished her drink in near silence and stood up to leave. Stephen made some half-hearted protests about her staying for dinner or perhaps even for a few days but Ursula knew he didn't want her there. She reminded him of things he couldn't remember without pain. As he did her. She shook her head and left.

The following morning, Ursula sat on the terrace of Raffles eating breakfast. She wouldn't stay. Not in Singapore; there was no point. Tim had been right about her coming back here; trying to grieve for everyone in one collecting grave. Well, they were gone. Loved, mourned, but gone. She would take a real holiday instead, up in Penang where there was no-one she knew and no memories to tug at her painfully every time she turned around. And then she would return to the property. It would be so good to see Tom and Didee and . . . no, Tim wouldn't be there. She would have to learn to live without him.

Tim, when he was finally passed through a maze of secretaries

491

to Charles Peel, sounded different, Charles thought. As though he had finally come to a decision that he liked, not one that was forced on him by circumstances. Maybe he had finally woken up to how much Ursula meant to him? Charles hoped so.

'Tim! I hadn't expected to hear from you. Nothing wrong is there?'

'I don't know really, Charles. I called the property and Mrs Winby told me Ursula's left. Gone back to Singapore. She wouldn't tell me anything else. Said she didn't know but I think she was just being protective. I tried calling a few hotels in Singapore but no-one seemed to have Ursula listed. D'you know where she is?'

'Raffles, I think. Yes, that's right. Insisted on staying there.'

'But I tried there. Tried it first of all, in fact. She's not listed.' There was a blank pause while both men thought.

'Well, I don't know then, Tim. I'm sorry. We've got Didee at the moment and Tom's down with some school friend in Mandurah. If Ursula isn't there, well, I guess she'll get in touch. Any messages?'

Again there was a long pause. Tim sat at his desk, his knuckles white against his eyes, trying to still the pain.

'Ah, no. I guess not. Thanks, Charles. I'll talk to you soon.' He rung off before Charles heard the change in his voice. So, she was gone and all his agonizing for the last week, all his long talks with his advisers, were for nothing. She didn't want him and she had gone away.

He missed her terribly, he thought, listening in his mind to her voice with that high pitch that still sounded like a young girl. He suddenly had a vision of what she must have looked like before she went away, standing in the sitting room near her desk, wearing her jeans and boots, a big man's shirt billowing around her slight figure. He closed his eyes against the longing inside him, tears stinging like acid against his eyelids. It was only when he thought she was really gone for good that he knew how much she meant to him, she and Tom. He thought about Joanna and his life here behind a desk, constantly answering tedious questions as though the country's security depended on it. He thought about the offer he had turned down only the night before, to join the Liberal Party as soon as the next elections were safely over. And he remembered the tiredness, the washed-out nothing in particular feeling that had given him. Once he would have given everything for it. Now he knew he had given too much. God, he wanted it all to stop so he could get off, walk out the door, and back into Ursula's life. But it was too late.

He saw a flash out of the corner of his eye, an aide waving a sheet of paper. More signatures. He tried to listen, to pull himself together, as he sat up and glared at the aide.

'Sorry, sir, but we need this signed immediately in order to get enough copies out before the press conference at 3.00. It's the party's official line on trade with China.' The aide thought Mr Nowlton was looking very grim for someone who had just about everything a man could want: a successful political career; a personal fortune; a son who was supposed to be very bright; and he was married into a powerful political family. He wondered what it would be like to be that successful, everything just falling into place so easily that you never had to worry about money or your wife or what she was up to when you worked at night to bring in some extra cash. Then the aide was brought smartly back to attention by a typing error in the press sheet.

'Bring it back as soon as it's retyped. I'll sign it then.' Tim dismissed the aide and settled back down to the pile of papers that must be read before the 3.00 o'clock press call. He sighed.

There were no real surprises from the reporters who led a steady trade in political journalism. They all wanted to know the same things. Would America continue to pledge support to ANZUS if Australia were seen to be doing trade with Communist China? Would the wheat export quotas be enlarged if the contract with China were signed? What did the rural communities think about sending grain to little yellow men? Tim shifted irritably and tried to rephrase the questions and his answers so that they were less offensive to all sides. He slid a look at his watch.

'What d'yer think the Country Party should be doing to get ready for the next elections?' That was Rawlings, a small intense fellow who worked for *The Age*. Tim tried to parry the question.

'We'll be canvassing support for our party manifesto throughout the rural and urban areas, making sure the average man on the street or on the land truly understands the issues and is prepared to come out and vote on them. Preparation and perseverance. My own personal guidelines. We'll be try . . . ' He broke off when Rawlings suddenly shouted across him.

'Then if you're always so prepared, Mr Nowlton, perhaps you wouldn't mind telling us now, on the spot, about your relationship with a Mrs Ursula Paterson. I think the Australian public would like to know about that, and I'm sure we'll all be delighted to persevere in our interest on such a matter. Your comment, sir?' There was a sudden hush while Tim felt the air around him contract, tilting in with an awkward perception of his ruin. He stood perfectly still, looking at Rawlings, his face drained of colour. He didn't try to deny it, or to ask foolish, blustering questions. From the look in Rawlings' eyes, there was nothing to be gained from delaying tactics. Tim sighed and then smiled, a crooked, wry smile that defused some of the tension in the air.

'Ah, I see the subject has been well and truly changed. If you don't mind, gentlemen, I would prefer to give my,' he hesitated and looked at Rawlings, ' "comments" to just a handful of you who may then pass on the news to the rest. Rawlings, I expect you had better be present, John, you come too – I need someone who likes me,' there was a titter of laughter from the gathering 'and, Douglas Furber, you make up the third. Come to my office please. To the rest of you gentlemen, thank you for your patience and for coming today.' He turned then and walked off the podium amid a clamour of voices, pushing microphones, cameras, and notepads in his face. He retreated into an ante-room that led to his office, closing the door on them. They sounded like hounds baying for his blood.

The aide was standing beside him, eyes starting in his still immature face. Tim put a hand on his shoulder.

'Oh well, that's that then. Send those three along as soon as possible, will you? And hold all my other calls.' He then leaned against the desk, trying to summon the energy needed for the scandal that was about to rip his life apart.

When the door opened and the three reporters were shown in, Tim's face was composed and his hands steady. He knew it was all over now, sooner rather than later, and the thought was a relief. He had already made the decision to go before this hit him and, while he had hoped it could be done discreetly, he had suspected the press would find out about Ursula eventually. He would bluff it at first and if that failed, well, it would just have to be endured.

'Come on in, gentlemen. Take a seat. Would you like coffee?' When all three shook their heads, he sighed.

'Ah well, let's get on with it then, shall we? Just so you get the true version and not some half-cocked one. Rawlings, d'you mind my asking first how you came by your information?' He looked across at the man, feeling no real emnity towards him. Rawlings looked back.

'A tip-off, you might say, Mr Nowlton. Telephone call from someone in Perth who claims to be Mrs Paterson's ex-husband. He told me everything and I got someone in Perth to check things out. I take it you know this fellow?'

'Oh yes, I'm afraid so. He's tried to blackmail both of us before. Ursula left England because he'd taken to beating her up. But then, I'm getting ahead of myself. What about you two? Did you know anything about this?' When they looked irritated, he smiled. 'Sorry, I know I'm taking my time but I need to know exactly where I stand. John, had you any idea about all this?'

'Aw, yeah, Tim, course I did. Most of us knew a bit, and there were enough other rumours flying around from time to time to make a right scandal if we'd wanted to. But we figured it wasn't worth bringing it to light unless you made it to party leader. Then we'd probably've started the muck raking. 'Course, now, this ex-hubby's pointed it all out, we can't very well ignore it, can we?' He smiled a tired, rueful sort of smile that said friendship only counted for so much. A story was a story.

'I see. And what exactly has been brought to light? Ursula is an old family friend. I've known her for years. In fact, she comes from the same village in England as my grandmother did. When she decided to leave her husband – who, as you probably know by now, Rawlings, is not the most reliable character in the world – she turned to me since she didn't know anyone else who lived in Australia. And she had decided to put as much distance between herself and her husband as possible, both for her own sake and for the sake of her daughter. Simon

495

had begun beating Ursula up after drinking too much and Rhea had witnessed one such attack – and Ursula was pregnant with her second child. She didn't feel safe with her husband.

'I advised her to move down to her property in Western Australia. She inherited it from her step-mother and it just seemed the best place for her and her children. She stopped off briefly, for the day, to see me in Melbourne and then went on by ship to Perth. Over the last ten years or so I've tended to visit a few times a year to make sure everything is going well and to let people know she's not alone in the world without anyone to take care of her.

'In the last few years, Simon has tried to take advantage of that situation by sending blackmail threats to both of us, threatening to reveal all. He really seems to believe there is something going on between us. We both, separately, told Simon to go ahead. And we haven't heard from him since – until now. You probably all know I visited Perth just recently for a funeral. That was Ursula's daughter's funeral. And I don't think Ursula needs anything else being thrown at her right at the moment.' Tim spread his hands wide. 'Now, that is your story, gentlemen. Surely it's not going to warrant a full-page spread. It won't help you and it won't help me.'

'Is that your final word on the matter, sir?' Douglas Furber tapped a pencil against his notepad, his face surprisingly stern. Tim nodded.

'That's it, gentlemen. Any questions on your side?' He waited a moment and, when there was no response, continued. 'I'd appreciate it if you would print the correct version as soon as possible before the others out there start embroidering on already unsavoury speculation. I don't want my wife and son being hurt by this, nor Ursula and her family being embarrassed. And, as you know, the elections are far too close for this sort of wild story to be allowed to spread.' Tim stood up and shook hands with the three men in turn, thinking as he did so that Douglas continued to look uncompromisingly grim, no trace of the smile the other two wore crossing his lips. What did he know, Tim wondered?

The story, when it hit the papers, was worse than Tim had anticipated. Either his denial had had no effect or there was more known than he had suspected. Douglas had printed a scathing article, using heavy-handed irony to dismiss Tim's version without actually having to accuse Tim of lying. A cheap trick, Tim thought, and one he hadn't expected from Douglas. But maybe it could still all be smoothed over if no new information came to light. Tim threw down the last of the papers he had ordered brought to his office and cursed, yet again, that he hadn't made the decision to leave years earlier. Even a few months would have been enough. Now it was too late.

The Winbys and Kim and Stoney were about the only ones who could give the game away and he didn't think they would for an instant. They cared too much about Ursula and Tom. So, who else knew anything? As long as they kept the lid on things, the fuss would die down in a while. Maybe then he could quietly resign and go over to Ursula. If she would have him. That worried him dreadfully. Would she just turn around and say, 'you made your bed, now lie in it'? She would never believe he had been on the point of resigning anway. She'd think he was coming to her because he didn't have anywhere else to go.

And what about Joanna? Would she divorce him? And the boys – Josh would end up believing whatever his mother told him: all the bitterness, the half-truths, the distortions and the outright lies; he would never forgive Tim. And what if Tom got to hear and then wouldn't forgive either Tim or Ursula? Jesus! He wished he could get hold of Ursula to warn her. He tried ringing the Peels but there was no answer. He'd have to keep trying.

As events turned out, Tim was right to fear the worst. He regretted, with the knowledge of how much damage that missed opportunity had caused him, the chance to have been honest with the public. But, when he had talked it through with his advisers and suggested that he just resign, they had been adamant that that would amount to an admission of guilt and he owed it to the party not to panic. Reluctantly he had agreed and all the time it had been a farce. But how could he have known Joanna would have done what she did? Who would have thought such a thing possible?

There had been an emergency meeting, of course, of the few

497

really powerful figures in his party to discuss the scandal and its implications. Tim had told them everything, denied nothing, and they had believed in him, thought the situation could be retrieved. That was what made it worse. They had all spent days pondering over the possibilities of how to minimize the backlash, and all along Joanna was busy selling her story to the press – to Douglas Furber, now wasn't that a joke? – with as many embellishments as her bitter mind could produce. She hadn't considered Josh, or how her family would feel, or what harm she was doing to the party. All she wanted was revenge for what she saw as a ruined life. She blamed Tim for that. And now this was her chance.

Tim resigned immediately her story appeared, the gutter press screaming obscenely alliterative headlines from every street corner and every radio and television station carrying the news with sharpened ferocity. The anger he faced from his own party was appalling. And any thoughts of the Liberal Party supporting him were swiftly put paid to. McMahon didn't even return his calls. Tim's political career was well and truly over. As was his family life with Joanna.

She threw him out from the house in Marne Street, dramatically and with more than an eye out for the stage effect with the press, and denied him access to Josh. That had angered Tim more than anything else. Joanna hadn't considered her son's feelings when she was selling her story and now she was denying Tim access. He couldn't believe it. They had argued fiercely over it, Tim insisting he would fight to see Josh and Joanna retorting acidly that Josh wasn't even his son, so what was all the fuss about? What was the fuss about? Tim looked over at the boy, feeling the panic and fear inside the child's wounded eyes, knowing that this was something Josh would never forget.

'Because to me he is my son, Joanna. I brought him up and I love him. And if you think you can deny me access, you have another think coming. I'll drag you through every court in the land, reveal every sordid affair you ever had, and make your life hell. D'you understand me?' he had said calmly, evenly, the tone emphasizing the threat more than shouts or anger could have ever done. Joanna hit him then. A single sharp slap across the cheek, the marks outlined in pink on his skin. And he knew then he had won that battle, if no other. He kissed Josh goodbye, told him he'd come and see him soon, and left.

Josh was bewildered and hurt by the sharp words and tense scenes between his parents, unable to understand how this could be happening to his safe, happy world. His thinly-veined skin acquired a bluish tinge under eyes that flinched at the sound of his mother's voice and his shoulders hunched over to shut out the pain in his father's face as he kissed him goodbye. After the first twenty-four hours, Josh didn't look up anymore but stared aimlessly at the floor, scared dark eyes darting quick, furtive looks out the window at the sea of faces, the flashing bulbs, the mouths opening and shutting with questions, questions, questions, while the phone lay off the hook and his mother smoked cigarette after cigarette and stubbed them out with hard jabs in the ashtray. Josh missed his father terribly.

Tim delivered a brief public apology upon his resignation and then retreated to an unknown address. The press, unable to find out more, began to lose interest in the story. And Joanna filed for divorce.

Ursula arrived back from Penang, via Singapore, after the immediate press furore was over. She walked up to the Peels' front door with no inkling that anything had happened and was faced by a sudden whirlwind of sound with Bettina insisting they were all with her and would stand by her to the end, Mr Peel talking over and over about suing for defamation of character, and Jennie vigorously seconding anything her mother said. Charles came to the rescue.

'Don't worry, Ursula. You're yesterday's news already. There's a spy scandal between some Eastern Bloc delegate and a call girl. You and Tim are definitely old hat now,' he assured her, dragging her in from the doorstep as she still stood blankly staring at them all. Didee went by in the arms of Jennie's younger sister, with a tribe of Peel youngsters in tow but Ursula didn't even notice. She was too busy trying to understand what had happened. She had thought it would be nice to enjoy herself for a day or two at the Peels without worrying about feeding times and nappy changes and now, instead, they were telling her about some scandal and how they would always be there for her. What scandal? She and Tim?

Thank heavens Charles was there, a strained unhappy Charles who also barely noticed the baby daughter who had caused so much turmoil in his life. He hugged Ursula, shooed his family away, and told her Tim had called. He didn't notice the sudden flush on her cheeks as he led her into the sitting room overlooking the garden. It was quiet in there and he could close the door on the children's happy laughter and his parents' and sisters' loud affirmations of loyalty.

'What is all this about, Charles? Jennie and Bettina keep going on about some scandal but I don't know anything about it. I haven't picked up a newspaper in about three weeks, or listened to the radio. I've been on Penang,' she added to explain this strange state of affairs. Charles never missed the news.

'Oh,' he said and then absent-mindedly popped a boiled sweet in his mouth that one of the children had left on the table. 'Well, I'm afraid it's all come out. About you and Tim. I knew everything from Rhea anyway. I hope you don't mind? Tim rang, as I said, before any of the scandal broke. Must've been about the third or fourth day after you left for Singapore. Said he couldn't find you at any of the hotels and really wanted to talk to you. I told him where you were and when he said you weren't there any longer, well, I didn't know where to suggest he try. He didn't want to leave a message. Sounded very dispirited, as though, well, he'd been on the point of giving it all up and then you weren't anywhere to be found. Rang off very suddenly.' Charles gave her a knowing look. 'Then, about a week later, bang, out comes everything in the papers. His wife sold her story. Can you believe it? Tim just resigned and hasn't been heard from since.' He sat back in his chair and let Ursula digest this in silence.

'And Tom?'

'Out of the way, isn't he? At Mandurah? Mind you, I'd probably keep him home this term. Children can be malicious little devils sometimes. Take him back to the property and put it all behind you. And Didee. Take her too.' He looked at Ursula suddenly. She smiled her understanding. He wasn't over Rhea yet and couldn't cope with Didee. Ursula would have to be the strong one, because he didn't have any strength left. And over the next few hours as she gathered Didee's things together and refused to let herself dwell on events, refused to let herself begin to hope that Tim might eventually think of coming back to her, Ursula saw only too well what Charles meant.

It wasn't that he ignored Didee on purpose; merely that his thoughts were elsewhere and he seemed not to remember his baby daughter unless she was placed in his arms. Then he looked bewildered and frightened, handing the child back as quickly as possible. Jennie shook her head and the Peel family rallied around. Charles must be protected. Ursula must keep Didee a little longer.

That suited Ursula very well. The baby felt more her own than Rhea had at the same age. It was good to be older and less frightened of doing the wrong thing; she was enjoying this round of motherhood much more than the first, or even Tom's. She smiled at the thought, playing with Didee's little fingers. Rhea would understand. She hadn't wanted this baby anymore than Ursula had originally wanted her or Tom. Perhaps maternal love missed a generation in her family? At the baby stage anyway.

She drove away from the Peels, waving briefly as they stood grouped around the doorway, and headed out of town towards Mandurah. Didee slept peacefully on the seat beside her.

Mandurah

Tom lay flat on his stomach in the long grass. He kept as still as he could, holding his breath every time the bird circled overhead. He could see the nest further down the bluff where the bird was kept busy with her young, often returning four or five times a day with offerings of food. He hadn't seen the male egret for some time. Perhaps it was dead.

The wind ruffled his hair, blond like the sun-dried grass that waved gently about him and he turned lazily over onto his back, his eyes screwed up against the glare of the sun. He was just nine last April but already tall for his age with long, clean limbs turning brown with the wind and sun. He plucked a stalk of grass and chewed it absent-mindedly, trying to make some sort of sense of what had happened earlier. The earth beneath his body was warm and soft, and he felt drowsy with the release of tension, his body's stiffening bruises as yet not felt.

What had got into Neil and the other guys, he wondered. They had always liked him before, been best of mates. What had started them teasing like that? Saying things about his mother, about Tim. It hadn't just been in fun because everyone had begun to look tense and embarrassed when the guys had said that, and then Neil's dad had threatened to take a belt to them if they didn't stop it. Tom wondered why they would try and make up such stories. And if they weren't made up, then, did that mean they were true? Were Tim and his mother really lovers? Was Tim really his father? The thought, oddly enough, did not hurt him in the way he knew it ought to. But he couldn't let the guys get away with saying things like that. Even now the anger filled his mind, like something black and hot and without thought, so that he wanted to hit again and again into Neil's taunting face, smack that knowing grin off his mouth. He slammed his fist against the ground.

The tears that had fallen earlier with enough force to make his shirt damp and his face swollen and red had now subsided, although a sudden shake still went through him at odd moments; some distress within him he could not, as yet, understand. It was something to do with the way Ian had looked so pleased with the gossip he shared with his brother Neil. Tom spat out the last of his grass stalk and, shielding his eyes with his arm, looked up at the sky. It was a clear, washed blue that faded to almost white at the edges where it met the ground. The warm, golden wind filled his lungs and he sighed sharply. At first, it had been the unexplained atmosphere of tension and embarrassment that had puzzled him. And the way all the guys, but especially Neil, who had been his best friend until this morning, had stood off from him, making him the butt of their jokes, excluding him from their circle. And it wasn't just amongst the guys. It had been amongst all the family and their friends too. They all knew something that he didn't and they all made him feel apart, as though he were a creature to be examined and wondered about. His not knowing wasn't all that surprising; normally he was out of doors in good weather and bad and so missed any gossip. Neil could be relied upon to fill him in later if he could be bothered to ask. But not this time. His hard looks reassured him on that point. Tom didn't dare ask Neil's parents – they wouldn't tell him anyway, even though Neil's mum had tried to be kind to him, to comfort him after Neil and he had fought, rolling around in the dust, pummelling into each other. But he hadn't wanted that sort of comfort. He had wanted to know the truth. So he had run off to his favourite place on the bluff and thrown himself down amongst the grass where Neil couldn't find him.

Tom sighed again and levered himself up on one elbow to stare out over the bluff to the sea, shimmering and flat as far as the eye could see before merging with the sky. There was no horizon line. It was just a blur of hazy white. He could hear the gentle murmur of the waves as they lapped the beach below him and the keening wail of seagulls swooping down from their nests to dive into the water with graceless splashes and then reappear, shrieking defiance at the wind. He had been gone hours now, all day really. But he didn't want to go back to the house. Not yet. His eyes closed briefly, the long line of dark lashes sweeping the planes of his cheeks like black moths. A cloud scudded over the sun, plunging the promontory into shadow before flying swiftly out over the sea. The sudden drop in temperature made him shiver, the wind plucking at his wet shirt and sending eddies of air down his back. He straightened abruptly and stood up.

'To-om, To-om!' The familiar cry, broken in the middle in a singsong, reached him on the wind and he turned and squinted into the distance. Walking between the dunes, barely visible, was his mother. She waved and Tom slowly raised his arm to wave back. The wind caught at his sleeve, snapping it like a sail and he waited patiently for her to reach him. He hadn't expected her for a few more days yet. She must have heard about his fight with the guys, about their taunts, he thought resignedly, knowing he couldn't avoid this.

She was out of breath when she finally reached him, her hair flopping down untidily around her face as the wind plucked at it and her cheeks flushed with exertion. He studied her while she took deep, gasping breaths and he then knew that the rumours were true. She had that look on her face that said she would see this through, just like everything else, just like

503

Rhea's death. But there was embarrassment in her eyes, and, yes, maybe even fear.

'I couldn't find you,' she said evenly enough. He shrugged. 'I was up here. How was Singapore?'

'Fine, fine. I had a nice time. How about you?'

'Okay, I guess. What's going on?'

'We're leaving now. Going back to the property.' She smiled but he wouldn't respond, simply looking at her accusingly. After a moment she began again, hesitantly. 'I expect you've heard what people are saying – that, well Tim and I . . . ' But Ursula couldn't repeat what people were saying. It caught in her throat and made her eyes sparkle with unshed tears. Her cheeks were blotched with pink amidst pale white. Tom stood staring, trying to understand how it was that he could be leaving Mandurah before the alloted time was up.

'Don't Neil's parents want me to stay any longer?' he asked painfully.

'Of course they do, dear. But I thought you'd like to come and spend the last few days with me on the property. I could do with the company and you can see Percy before school starts.' Ursula stroked Tom's hair, staring silently across the dunes and sea, the lump in her throat too large to swallow. Tom cried quietly then, the wind whipping the tears across his cheeks to trickle into his ears and down his neck. After a few minutes, he suddenly said:

'Is that why you're here? Did they tell you to come and take me away because of all these rumours? Is Tim my Dad then? That's what Neil said. He said you and Tim had been, well . . . you know, for years and that Tim was my father and everyone had just found out and now Tim's resigned and his wife's leaving him. He hasn't been to see us in such a long time, I guess I knew something was wrong. Is all that true then?' His tone was belligerent, forcing an answer that he didn't want to hear. He picked up a stone and threw it at a post, hearing it hit the wood with a flat crack.

'I'm so sorry, darling. I had meant to tell you, when you were older and it would be more, understandable to you. I never wanted you to find out like this,' Ursula said, her hand hovering near her son but unable to actually touch, knowing he would flinch away. 'It's such a long story, Tom, I don't even

504

know where to begin – but Rhea knew all about it and accepted it. And you know how fair Rhea was. She wouldn't have loved Tim if she'd thought there was anything wrong about us being together, now would she?'

Tom glanced across at his mother, seeing the pain, wanting to help. But something inside him refused to open up. He shrugged. 'Maybe not. I dunno. She never had to cope with her schoolfriends taunting her and making rude . . . anyway, I guess there's nothing I can do about it now, is there?' He sounded bitter.

'Yes, of course there is. You can come back to the property and take classes there if you can't bear to go to school in Perth anymore. I can get you a tutor.'

'No! I like it where I am. And I'm not gonna go hide from everyone like I did something wrong. I didn't do anything wrong. You did! You and Tim!'

'That isn't true, Tom. And I won't have you say it. You don't even know the facts. I never thought you'd be the sort to judge people, especially people you love, without finding out the truth first.'

'And what is the truth?'

Ursula looked at her son, seeing Tim in every curve of the face, in the clear, grey eyes, in the firm mouth. She smiled awkwardly.

'All right. I'll tell you, if you really want to hear.'

'Yes, I do.' And so they sat together in the sand and Ursula told her son everything, holding nothing back, good or bad, letting him judge for himself this time. She wished she had done this before.

'And you say Tim was coming back to us just before all this news got out? He was really giving it all up for us?' The thought pleased Tom immensely. He had always assumed his father was some shadowy creature from England who had died before he was born and now, to find out that Tim was really his father and that he had been on the point of sacrificing his whole career to come back and be with Tom and his mother! Well! That was entirely different. Tom smiled.

'When's Tim coming then? Will it be soon?'

'Oh, that I don't know, darling. I hope it's soon but it'll depend on how bad this scandal becomes.' She looked away for

505

a moment and hoped she was doing the right thing. But Tom had to believe his father loved him and wanted to be with them. If Tim didn't, well, maybe that could be explained in some other way. Later. 'Are you really sure you want to go back to school this term?' When Tom nodded emphatically, his jaw very set, Ursula shrugged.

'All right, then how about if we all go back and spend some time on the property together. You and me and Didee. And then, in a while, Tim too.' They both smiled with satisfaction at the thought.

Ursula pulled the car over to the side of the road while Tom went to open the first gate. This was the point from which she and Rhea had first seen the property all those years ago. Now she looked at it and thought, this is beautiful and better still, this is home. My home, for me and my children and their children and no-one can ever take that away.

She drove up to the homestead, noting the way the garden had grown up around the front of the house in the last few weeks and how neatly the grass had been cut. She parked beside the steps and Tom climbed out eagerly, looking around to see if there were any changes, running to perch on the steps and look for Percy. There were golden chalice leaning over the verandah edge and she saw Tom squeeze a flower between his fingers, the liquid spurting out from inside the fleshy cup. It smelled of sweet rain and earth.

Tom whooped with delight. An answering whoop came from the Winbys' house and Ursula saw Percy slither under the railings and head towards the barn. Skiving off his homework again, she thought with amusement. Tom grinned at her and ran to join Percy.

Ursula, humming to herself now, lifted Didee out and leaned over to pick up her bag. Oh, it was good to be back! She left her bag by the stairs and carried Didee up and into the house, smelling the fresh wax on the boards, the clean breeze blowing through the windows. Kim must have been hard at work, Ursula thought with surprise. She put Didee down in her cot before turning to carry the rest of her bags into the house.

'Can I do that for you?' The voice came from behind her. She whirled around in surprise. Tim stood there, wearing old stained workpants and a flannel shirt, his voice as much as his face suggesting how unsure he was of his welcome. Ursula fought down the urge to throw herself headlong at him. She smiled coolly and nodded.

'Please.' Then she stopped and looked at him again. 'But before you do, just tell me one thing, Tim. When you called Charles to ask where I was. Before the scandal broke. What did you want to say?'

He swallowed and shrugged, trying to sound normal, as though his whole life didn't depend on his answer.

'You may not believe it, but . . . I wanted to ask if I could come home,' he said.

'Home? Here?' Ursula asked. When Tim nodded, she smiled with difficulty.

'For good, or just for a while? What about your career?'

'I'd already asked to resign. Just my luck they found out about us before I could tell you.'

'Then this is for good?' She had to be sure.

'For good.' He touched her cheek. 'If you'll have me?'

And then he smiled with relief because he knew, suddenly, she would.

'I'll call Tom. Let him know you're home,' Ursula said, and walked over to the window, feeling the fresh wind on her face.